PLANNING YOUR CAREER IN
ALTERNATIVE MEDICINE

A GUIDE TO DEGREE AND CERTIFICATE PROGRAMS IN ALTERNATIVE HEALTH CARE

DIANNE J. B. LYONS

Avery Publishing Group

Garden City Park, New York

All information in this book has been carefully researched, with data being reviewed and updated throughout the production process. Inclusion of a program in this book does not indicate endorsement on the part of the publisher or author. However, we feel that the information presented in this book should be available to the public. Because the information—locations, telephone numbers, courses, and fees—is subject to continual change, the publisher and author suggest that the reader contact the programs for the most up-to-date information.

Cover Design: William Gonzalez and Rudy Shur
In-House Editor: Jennifer L. Santo
Typesetter: Al Berotti
Printer: Paragon Press, Honesdale, PA

Avery Publishing Group
120 Old Broadway
Garden City Park, NY 11040
1-800-548-5757

Cataloging-in-Publication Data
Lyons, Dianne J. Boulerice, 1958-
      Planning your career in alternative medicine: a guide to degree and certificate programs in alternative healthcare / Dianne J.B. Lyons.—1st ed.
      p.cm.
      Includes bibliographical references and index.
      ISBN: 0-89529-802-3

      1. Alternative medicine—Vocational guidance. I. Title.

R733.L96 1997   610.69
                                                 QBI97-40925

Printed in the United States of America

10 9 8 7 6 5 4 3 2 1

Contents

Appendices

To Bub—
thank you for sharing
your life with me.

Acknowledgments

First and foremost, I want to thank the Lord for His inspiration and the opportunities He laid before me; I feel this book is a part of my mission here on Earth, and, like the little drummer boy in the song, I played my best for Him. A big hug goes out to Bob, Scott, and Kristina for their love and support; without the three of you, none of this would have been any fun. I also want to thank the many kind and helpful people staffing the schools and organizations listed in this book; your enthusiastic, supportive comments brightened many a bleak day. Debbie Blann from NCBTMB, Gary Peterson from APTA, and Zorka from Polarity Healing Arts of Santa Monica were among the most pleasant and helpful, but then nearly all of you were; alternative therapies seem to draw the kindest and gentlest of souls.

I would like to acknowledge the following practitioners who took part in the ranking of schools shown on page 38: Dr. Anthony Adesso, Phoenix, Arizona; Sheldon Altman, D.V.M., Burbank, California; Latifa Amdur, Hanalei, Hawaii; Bharata, Yoga and Inner Peace, Lake Worth, Florida; Robert Beloud, D.C., N.M.D., Clearlake, California; Su Bibik, Kalamazoo, Michigan; Jeri Bodemar, C.M.T., C.H.T., Watsonville, California; Prudence A. Broadwell, N.D., L.Ac., Fountain Valley, California; Michael Carlston, M.D., Santa Rosa, California; Dick Cassidy, C.A., M.A., Washington Crossing, Pennsylvania; Mitchell Chavez, B.S., C.N., Colton, California; Wimsey Cherrington, L.M.P., Seattle, Washington; Kay Clay Yoga, Inc.; Mary Alice Cooper, M.D., Albuquerque, New Mexico; Dr. Martin Dayton, Miami Beach, Florida; Peter Dubitsky, New Paltz, New York; Carolyn Dye, Shannon, Mississippi; Wayne Gender, Toronto, Ontario; Scott Gerson, M.D., New York, New York; Christopher Gibney, L.Ac., H.M.D., San Rafael, California; Jay L. Glaser, M.D., Lancaster, Massachusetts; Pam Green, D.C., Lakeland, Florida; Fred C. Hill, D.C., Blackfoot, Idaho; Dr. F.J. Huskey, Tulsa, Oklahoma; Eli Jacobe, L.Ac., Gloucester, Massachusetts; Charlene Curry, C.Ht., Whitmore Lake, Michigan; Brian A. Kleinberg, D.C., Concord, Ontario; Dr. J. Michael Lemus, Miami, Florida; Drs. Enrico Liva, Jacqueline Germain, and Keli Samuelson, Middletown, Connecticut; Norma McArthur, L.M.T., L.H.T, Sioux Falls, South Dakota; Ilan Migdali, Hollywood, California; Christine Miller, D.C., Ukiah, California; Suzanne C. Miller, Coopersburg, Pennsylvania; John S. Misiewicz, D.C., Sayreville, New Jersey; Jean Y. Mitchell, R.N., B.N., R.M.T., North Vancouver, British Columbia; Marlis Moldenhauer, Milwaukee, Wisconsin; Richard Moskowitz, M.D., Boston, Massachusetts; Tara Nelson, N.D., Mystic, Connecticut; Pathways to Health, Nesconset, New York; Zoe Elva Putnam, Denville, New Jersey; Elizabeth E. Rohack, Delray Beach, Florida; Melvin J. Rosenthal, D.C., New Castle, Delaware; Drs. Amy Rothenberg, Paul Herscu, and Paul Mittman, Enfield, Connecticut; Robert Rowen, M.D., Anchorage, Alaska; Judy Russell, Arvada, Colorado; William H. Sayer, D.C., Atlanta, Georgia; Gary Stiles, L.M.T., and Jan L. Stiles, R.N.C.S., D.I.Hom., Manchester, New Hampshire; Glenda Stroup, D.Ht., Richardson, Texas; Laurie Towers, Brooklyn, New York; Marijke van de Water, B.Sc., D.H.M.S., Nanaimo, British Columbia; Dr. W.A. Watkinson II, Newport, Rhode Island; Skye Weintraub, N.D., Eugene, Oregon; Dr. Shandor Weiss,

Acknowledgments

Ashland, Oregon; and Dr. Dennis Williams, Palm Springs, California.

Finally, I want to thank Rudy Shur for believing in this project and fine-tuning the execution; it really is a better book because of you, and together we'll touch many thousands of lives.

Preface

"I find the medicine worse than the malady."

—John Fletcher, 1579–1625

Over the course of my life, more often than not I have indeed found the medicine—allopathic medicine, that is—worse than the malady. As a child, a botched tonsillectomy left me with memories of terrifying, whirling sounds—an early part of the near-death experience, I'm told—not to mention another surgery six months later to finish the job. My adult medical experiences weren't much better—migraine medications that made me sicker than the migraine itself, and birth control pills that left me depressed.

What pushed me into alternative medicine, however, was my allergist. The doctor was concerned because I couldn't get past a particular vial in my immunotherapy; all her patients were supposed to go from vial one to vial three, and I couldn't get past vial two without massive welts. "But my dust mite allergies are controlled at this dose," I told her. "It doesn't matter," she said. "We need to push you up to the higher level." Five minutes after the shot, I had my first panic attack. Epinephrine stopped the reaction, but the "rain barrel" had already overflowed; from that point on, the bedroom carpet, grass, sulfites, dust mites, formaldehyde in stores, and almost anything else would cause extreme anxiety, shortness of breath, or swelling in my throat that made it nearly impossible to swallow. The turning point, though, was when the allergist declared that what I really needed was psychological help; I was producing these attacks myself, she said, from memories of the first one. At that point, I knew our association was over; as I left her office, my quest for health began.

Shortly after this, I read a newspaper article about Dr. Theron Randolph's clinic for the chemically sensitive. Dr. Randolph's pioneering work in clinical ecology, or environmental illness, seemed to be just what I was looking for. I went to the clinic, underwent weeks of testing, and found the correct doses of antigens for my specific allergies. I started a program of antigens, dietary changes, and vitamin and mineral supplements that had me feeling much better in a matter of weeks, and completely well in about a year.

Once I was well, I was so excited about what I had learned that I wanted to see what kinds of courses I could take in nutrition, herbology, and related alternative fields so that I might further help myself and others as well. I searched the library, *Books in Print,* anywhere I could think of, but I found no guide to educational programs in alternative medicine. Any writer, upon finding a gap, seeks immediately to fill it—and I'm doing just that with this book.

This is a book that is just as useful to serious students of alternative medicine—the would-be acupuncturists and naturopathic physicians—as it is to the individual who simply wants a better understanding of alternative therapies to treat family and friends. It is practical as a quick reference tool—for finding phone numbers, for example—and it is a good book to spend some time with, investi-

Preface

gating schools within commuting distance or correspondence courses in various fields of interest. In fact, I couldn't wait to be finished writing it so that I might have time to take some classes myself! Like most of you, I am a beginner, and very eager to learn; this book will help all of us to take more responsibility for our own health and to share our knowledge with others.

While I have tried hard to make this book as accurate and inclusive as possible, it does have its limitations (many of which are spelled out in the section, "How Schools Are Selected"). As fast as we try to get this printed, area codes are changing, schools are moving, and programs are being restructured. I did the best I could to capture the alternative health education movement at a moment in time, but some changes will have occurred by the time this book reaches the stores. But while tuition has probably gone up a few dollars and a program may have been added, this book serves as a reliable, quick, and painless way to compare programs, tuition, accreditations, and so on, without ever leaving your home.

This is the first edition of a book that I plan to update and revise on a regular basis, and your input is an important part of making the next edition better. I want to know what you think. If I overlooked a program that you attended and found beneficial, send me the address. If I missed a professional organization that has an informative newsletter, tell me about it. Likewise, if a school or program listed here was unsatisfactory to you, let me know that, too.

If you represent a school that should have been included (according to the criteria on page xvii) and wasn't, send a catalog and I may consider you for the next edition. Similarly, if you're a publisher who would like your books, catalogs, videos, or magazines mentioned next time, send them along for review.

I want this to be as complete and useful a guide as possible, and I sincerely welcome your input. Send inquiries, suggestions, catalogs, review copies, and other information to:

Dianne Lyons
c/o Avery Publishing Group
120 Old Broadway
Garden City Park, New York 11040

How to Use This Book

This guide is divided into two major sections. Part I contains short articles that briefly describe the philosophy of, and treatments used in, each field of study. Part II makes up the bulk of the book; it lists, alphabetically by state and within each state, schools that offer degree or certificate programs in various fields of alternative medicine. The key to finding the school you need is the Listing of Programs by Field, located on page 41.

THE LISTING OF PROGRAMS BY FIELD AND PROFILES OF SCHOOLS AND PROGRAMS

Many schools offer instruction in more than one subject area. Rather than listing schools by subjects offered—which would result in many duplications—we opted for the Listing of Programs by Field.

This section simplifies the task of finding programs of interest: just look under the desired field of study and you'll find an alphabetical, state-by-state listing of programs available. Scan the list for a state that you're interested in, check the name of the school, and locate its listing under that state in the Profiles of Schools and Programs. For example, to find schools of naturopathic medicine, look in the Listing of Programs by Field for "Naturopathy." The listing is reproduced below.

NATUROPATHY

AZ Southwest College of Naturopathic Medicine and Health Sciences
OR National College of Naturopathic Medicine
WA Bastyr University

CANADA

ON The Canadian College of Naturopathic Medicine

To read about Southwest College of Naturopathic Medicine and Health Sciences, find Arizona in the "Profiles" section, then scan the alphabetical list of schools until you locate Southwest College. There are several points to remember about the Listing of Programs by Field and the Profiles of Schools and Programs.

• The schools listed in this part of the book are all classroom-based programs; correspondence courses are listed on page 358.

• Entries are made under each specialty only for complete programs that result in a certificate, degree, or other credential relating to that specialty. Modalities that are taught as part of a larger specialty are not listed separately. For example, many schools of massage therapy offer instruction in polarity, reflexology, and aromatherapy, but they are listed only under Massage Therapy unless a separate, distinct certificate or program is also given in the subspecialty.

• Many of the terms used in the program descriptions are defined in the corresponding Part I chapter. For example, terms such as shiatsu, Rolfing, hydrotherapy, and Feldenkrais are defined in the Part I chapter on massage therapy.

• Canadian schools appear after the United States entries, alphabetized by province. Schools that offer instruction in many locations throughout the United States, Canada, and/or the world are listed in the section called "Multiple State Locations," which appears after the Canada section.

THE PRACTITIONER SURVEY

To make the comparison of schools at least a little easier, we surveyed a number of established practitioners from throughout the United States and Canada and asked them to name what they thought were the five best schools or training programs in their particular specialty. For more information on this survey, see page 38.

READING THE LISTINGS

The listings for the various schools and programs are fairly self-explanatory. Each listing contains the name, address(es), phone number, fax number, E-mail address, and/or Internet address where applicable. Following this information is a general introduction to the school, then, in sequence, as many of the following categories as apply: Accreditation, Program Description, Community and/or Continuing Education, Admission Requirements, Tuition and Fees, and Financial Assistance.

Each school or program was given at least one opportunity to read and correct its listing prior to publication. Most schools made changes, but some did not; some, despite urgings to the contrary, rewrote their entire listing. We tried to keep some consistency between listings and worked to fit all sorts of programs into one format.

Accreditation

Prospective students should acquaint themselves with the principal accrediting agencies in their selected area of study. If the big-name accreditations are missing in a listing, look carefully at what is included. Sometimes a school does not want to be locked in by the requirements of the accrediting agency; sometimes the program is just too short to meet the standards. Usually, a shorter program is still sufficient for licensing in that state, but it may not be in yours; check first. In general, if a school is accredited by one of the recognized agencies, the

less important approvals are omitted; if a school is not accredited, it may list a lengthy series of lesser certifications or approvals. Don't assume that a longer list is better; in many cases, the reverse is true.

Other details that may be, but are not always, included in this section are facts about licensing, eligibility for certification exams and for membership in professional organizations, and other related information.

Program Description

Every listing, no matter how small, contains this section. Included here is a brief description of what the school offers; the length of the program; and some additional requirements (such as having five polarity sessions or receiving two massages per semester). Be sure to get the catalog for a more complete description of the program and individual courses.

Community and/or Continuing Education

Included here are classes or programs that are open to the public for entry-level instruction and/or that offer continuing education to professionals, some of which may be taken for continuing education units (CEUs).

Admission Requirements

Every applicant should expect to submit a completed application form and high school and/or college transcripts. The requirements listed in this section are generally in addition to this. Students should, of course, consult with an admissions representative if any of the requirements presents a problem.

Tuition and Fees

Schools were asked to supply 1997 figures. Most of them did; some did not make corrections to their listings, so these figures may be out of date. As nothing changes more often than tuition and fees, all of these numbers should be viewed only as a general basis for comparison. Again, consult the school's current catalog and/or call the school directly for the most accurate figures.

Financial Assistance

Many schools will take VISA or MasterCard—a simple, though usually high-interest, way to finance your education. All of them will take cash or checks. This section lists other forms of financial assistance for which you may qualify. Some of these—like payment plans—are open to everyone; others, like veterans' benefits, are not. If you think you will need assistance in paying for your education, you should speak directly with a financial aid representative at the school you would like to attend. Don't let a lack of funds keep you from a career; most schools will work very hard to find a way for qualified students to attend.

MULTIPLE STATE LOCATIONS

This section lists schools that offer instruction in many locations throughout the United States, Canada, and/or the world. These schools are cross-referenced in the state-by-state listings based on their mailing addresses or the locations of their headquarters.

SELF-STUDY RESOURCES

This chapter provides a listing, arranged alphabetically by specialty, of periodicals, videos, correspondence courses, and other materials that offer basic instruction, serve as handy reference sources, offer a unique perspective, provide ongoing education, or otherwise serve to familiarize you with a field of study.

The temptation, particularly in a field so unregulated as alternative medicine, is to forgo the expensive, time-consuming, and inconvenient classroom education in favor of an easier home study course. Some of the programs that appeared suspect in the compilation of this book (i.e., anything offering Ph.D.s, N.D.s, or other advanced degrees through the mail) were not included in this guide. Even so, you still need to scrutinize those programs you consider. Think about this: would you rather be treated by a nutritionist who studied at an accredited and highly-regarded school, or one who received a "degree" through the mail? Correspon-

dence courses can be valuable for learning how to treat oneself or one's family with nutrients, but those who are preparing for a career should consider classroom training.

THE APPENDICES

Before spending thousands of dollars on a program, it's smart to learn as much as you can about both the field of study and the school. Naturally, you should call or write for a catalog, but other organizations can provide important additional information. This book contains three appendices that will tell you how to contact the organization you're looking for.

Appendix A: Accrediting Agencies lists the names and addresses of a number of agencies that accredit, approve, or recommend schools or programs within schools. It gives a very brief description of the accrediting agency and some of the criteria they use to accredit or approve schools. You may want to contact these agencies about a particular program you have in mind.

Appendix B: Professional Associations lists just a fraction of the hundreds of organizations that cater to the needs of practicing professionals, but that may also be open to students of that profession or interested individuals. These organizations usually offer a newsletter and/or magazine to their members, as well as discounts, referrals, and information about the field.

Appendix C: Licensing and Certification gives only a general description of the types of laws and licensing requirements that are currently in place for a number of fields of alternative medicine. Students are strongly urged to contact the appropriate boards or licensing agencies in the state and city in which they intend to practice prior to putting down a deposit on any educational program.

CONVENTIONAL MEDICAL SCHOOLS OFFERING COURSES IN ALTERNATIVE MEDICINE

As alternative (or "complementary") medicine becomes more accepted, more and more conventional medical schools are including alternative medicine in their curriculums. In most cases, these schools only offer one or two courses, but some, such as the University of Arizona's Program in Integrative Medicine (see page 60), offer more complete programs.

THE SCHOOL AND ORGANIZATION INDEX

An alternative way to use this book, if you know the name of the school but not the state it's in, is to go directly to the School and Organization Index for a page number. This is also useful when you don't know whether a given institution is a school, an accrediting or certifying agency, or a membership organization.

LET THE BUYER BEWARE

In collecting information for this book, I tried to include only schools that are accredited, approved, or in some way recognized by someone, but some fields of study are as yet so unregulated that this is simply impossible. You are ultimately responsible for investigating the quality of the program you choose. What's beneficial to one person may be worthless to another, and inclusion in this book is in no way to be construed as a personal recommendation.

Prospective students of alternative health care should be every bit as careful in their selection of a school or training program as they would be in choosing a conventional college—perhaps more so. While it may be a bit more difficult to find reputable schools in the field of alternative medicine than it is to find such schools in more regulated fields, it's not a situation where you have to cross your fingers and hope for the best; there are guideposts along the way. The following are a few steps to getting a good return on your educational investment.

• Do some reading and educate yourself in the area in which you plan to specialize. Get a feel for the principles and philosophy, the diagnostic and treatment methods, and the job opportunities.

• Go for treatment. There's no better way to find out what an acupuncturist, massage therapist, or naturopathic physician really does than to become a patient. Visit more than one practitioner for a broader view.

• Contact your local Board of Health or other agencies to determine the licensing requirements in your area. In some states, a specific number of hours of education are required to practice.

• Talk to practitioners in your area to see which schools they would recommend. Ask them about specific schools you have in mind.

• Send for catalogs from all the schools in which you have even a remote interest. Compare programs between schools in your immediate area, and if circumstances permit, consider a longer commute or a relocation; convenience should not necessarily be your first criterion.

• Look at accreditations. In general, a school must be fairly well established, offer a quality program, and tolerate a good deal of paperwork and on-site scrutiny to be approved by the major accrediting agencies. No fly-by-night outfit will even try to get accredited.

• Compare program lengths. A one-hundred-hour massage program will have you practicing sooner, but what will you really know? Be sure the training is sufficient to meet your future needs. That one-hundred-hour program won't get you licensed in very many states.

• Look at the course schedules. Some programs may be taken part-time and/or in the evenings; others are strictly full-time days.

• If finances are an issue, see what type of financial assistance the school offers. There is tremendous variation between schools in this area; one may offer scholarships, federal grants, and a variety of loans, while another may not have so much as a payment plan.

• Visit the school and get a feel for the place. Is it a warm, close-knit community or does it offer a cooler, more professional atmosphere? Do you feel comfortable there? Talk to the instructors and other students. If you can, talk to some recent graduates and ask how their training prepared them for a career.

Please keep in mind that while all the information contained within this guide was accurate at press time—and that every school or program was given the opportunity to correct or update their listing prior to publication—things change very quickly, particularly in the field of alternative health care. Schools outgrow their facilities, associations move, newsletters cease publication, and telephone numbers change. This book is a general guide to what's out there and a basis for comparison between schools and programs. However, *always* call or write the school for a current catalog and answers to specific questions.

How Schools Are Selected

A book this size could not possibly contain every school or program offered in every form of alternative health care. Though alternative health care may seem like an emerging field, there are many hundreds of schools of massage therapy alone; if all of these were listed in one volume, along with all the schools in other alternative fields, this would look less like a guide and more like a phone book, with room for little more than names and addresses.

And it's not just about space—it's about quality. Many schools were not included simply because I feel they don't offer sufficient training to produce a knowledgeable health care professional. It may be legal in some places to open a massage practice with two weeks' training, but would you want to be treated by that kind of practitioner?

The schools included in this book have been selected because they either represent the best training in their field, or because they offer a program that is unique in a way that is too valuable, for any of a number of reasons, to exclude merely because it lacks a particular accreditation or sufficient classroom hours.

The following are the criteria used to select the schools in various fields. Keep in mind that there is nothing hard and fast about these rules, but they served as general guidelines during the selection process.

Ayurveda

There are no accredited programs of instruction in Ayurveda in the United States; what instruction there is is minimal at best and not sufficient training for a career in the field. A few schools offer limited programs in Ayurveda that may be taken for enjoyment or enlightenment, or by practitioners licensed in another field who would like to apply some knowledge of Ayurvedic principles to their practice. The schools included here are whatever I could find in this very limited field.

Biofeedback

The makers of biofeedback instruments were the only ones offering a complete biofeedback educational program.

Chiropractic

All of the chiropractic schools included here are accredited by the Council on Chiropractic Education (CCE).

Herbology

Other than Chinese herbology taught as part of an Oriental medicine program, there is no accreditation in the field of herbal medicine. The programs in existence range from apprenticeships at family-run herb farms to extensive programs in Western, Chinese, and Ayurvedic herbology, and meet all kinds of different needs. I've included any school that offers an organized program leading to a certificate of some kind; those that offer individual courses not organized into a series or certificate program were not included. These programs appeared on lists put out by the American Herbalists' Guild and other organizations. It is up to you to assess what type of instruction will best meet your needs.

How Schools Are Selected

Homeopathy

The guidelines were not as rigid for homeopathy as for some of the other fields. The five programs accredited by the Council on Homeopathic Education (CHE) are, of course, included. Some other schools of homeopathy have only recently opened their doors and appear to offer a comprehensive educational program. But not all homeopathy students are M.D.s looking for advanced education; some merely want to learn how to treat themselves and their families. With that in mind, all of the homeopathic programs I could find, which by and large appeared on a list distributed by one of several homeopathic organizations, are included. Again, it is up to you to determine if the level of education will meet your needs.

Hypnotherapy

The schools listed here are included on a list distributed by the International Medical and Dental Hypnotherapy Association.

Massage and Bodywork

With well over 600 massage and bodywork schools in existence, I needed a way to pare these down while being sure to include the best of them. I started with those schools accredited or approved by the American Massage Therapy Association Commission on Massage Training Accreditation/Approval (AMTA/COMTAA), which is generally recognized as the most important agency for massage school accreditation. I added schools accredited by the International Massage and Somatic Therapies Accreditation Council (IMSTAC), a division of the Associated Bodywork and Massage Professionals (ABMP)—another recognized name in the field. I also tried to include many of the providers of continuing education courses that are approved by the National Certification Board for Therapeutic Massage and Bodywork (NCBTMB), but not all of them; some of these offer only a single course or are individuals, not schools as such.

Some massage and bodywork schools are included that do not meet any of these criteria. Most often, these are schools that offer at least a 300-hour program, so that graduates would be eligible to take the national certification exam. A few schools offer less than this, but in every case these schools offer something else that would have included them—for example, a polarity therapy or herbal medicine program—in addition to the massage program.

In the case of continuing education or programs in specialized fields of bodywork, such as Feldenkrais or Hellerwork, these programs are included regardless of hours because of the specialized nature of the course and the need that it meets.

Naturopathy

All four of the schools that are accredited by, or are candidates for accreditation with, the Council on Naturopathic Medical Education (CNME) are included.

Oriental Medicine/Acupuncture

All of the programs that are accredited by, or are candidates for accreditation with, the National Accreditation Commission for Schools and Colleges of Acupuncture and Oriental Medicine (NAC-SCAOM) are included.

Polarity Therapy

The American Polarity Therapy Association (APTA) accredits polarity therapy schools and training programs—and there are quite a few. In keeping with the reasoning applied to massage therapy, included here are those schools that are accredited by APTA and that provide training leading to APTA registration as a Registered Polarity Practitioner (R.P.P.), rather than those that offer only Associate Polarity Practitioner (A.P.P.) training. However, an A.P.P.-only school may be included if it offers a program in another field that would qualify it, such as a 500-hour massage program or a certificate in herbology.

Yoga

There is no agency that accredits schools of yoga. The schools included here are those that offer an organized program of teacher training, not just yoga classes.

Other

There are a handful of schools that don't seem to fit the above criteria, yet are included in this book. They may offer a hard-to-find program, such as iridology, or an independent degree program, in which students can major in virtually any aspect of holistic health. Most often, you can look through the listing and find the reason we included it in the list above. All of these courses seem to offer some value and return on investment, even if that value is only evident to a tiny percentage of the population.

HEY, WHY ISN'T IT HERE?

If your school is accredited by one of the agencies mentioned above and is not included in this book, it's most likely because of human oversight—either I overlooked you or you never returned any of the questionnaires I submitted. If your school meets some of the more vague criteria, (for example, a 500-hour professional massage program that's not accredited), send a catalog to my attention so that I may consider it for the next edition. But do bear in mind that I was looking for you and didn't find you; how many potential students were also unable to find you and opted for the more visible school instead? Many schools don't like to be harnessed by the restrictions of the accrediting agencies, but these are the schools that get noticed; if you're not accredited, you've certainly got to advertise.

Schools deliberately excluded are those that offer advanced degrees such as M.A., Ph.D., or N.D. through correspondence; those that only offer very short programs or single-day courses; those that offer only part of a recognized program (i.e., courses in polarity therapy that are not sufficient for R.P.P. or A.P.P. designation); those that offer training that is primarily of a spiritual nature; those that offer training that is of primary benefit to the individual, rather than training for a career in helping others; and those that offer only training in an area that I feel is not accepted by the alternative health community at large, and for which the career prospects are questionable.

Introduction

The term "alternative medicine" is something of a misnomer, but it is one of a handful of terms used in the United States to identify various forms of healing that lie outside of mainstream (allopathic) medicine. Here in the United States, those who graduate from established medical schools and subscribe to conventional healing methods, including the prescribing of controlled medications and the use of surgery for the treatment of disease—the people we refer to as doctors, physicians, or M.D.s—are the "norm." All other types of medicine are lumped under the terms "alternative" or "complementary."

What may seem odd to those just beginning to explore these alternative kinds of healing is that some of the philosophies and techniques dismissed by many physicians as quackery—including acupuncture, homeopathy, and herbal medicine—have been the standard way of treating illnesses in other parts of the world for thousands of years. One could argue that there is no older medicine than herbs; references to medicinal herbs abound in the Bible. Aromatherapy may have been embraced by at least one store in every mall, but it, too, has a long history—the Romans used scented oils in their baths, and Avicenna, a tenth-century Persian doctor, was the first to distill essential oils. Traditional Chinese medicine, including acupuncture, has been around for about 5,000 years. Homeopathy is an established practice in Great Britain today—Queen Elizabeth's medical staff includes a homeopathic physician—and may date back to 3,000 B.C. When compared to these time-honored traditions, our own allopathic medicine looks rather new and, some would argue, suspect.

Not even the most headstrong of alternative practitioners would deny that allopathic medicine has made important contributions to our national health and longevity. Even the most dedicated herbalist would welcome the sight of a skilled surgeon were his appendix to suddenly rupture. But the emergence of deadly, antibiotic-resistant germs, the lack of attention to disease prevention, and the many illnesses for which no cures have been found all point to a need for another kind of medicine. Alternative medicine seeks not to replace the allopathic tradition but to work alongside it, as partners in the healing process; hence, many now refer to "complementary" rather than "alternative" therapies.

A Chinese proverb nicely summarizes the relationship between alternative and allopathic medicine: "The superior doctor prevents sickness; the mediocre doctor attends to impending sickness; the inferior doctor treats actual sickness."[1] While allopathic medicine focuses on a malfunctioning heart or kidney, alternative approaches look at the whole person—his or her environment, diet, exercise and activities, stress level, and spiritual health. Most forms of alternative medicine focus on the reasons behind the illness; individualize treatment for each patient depending on other physical, mental, emotional, and/or spiritual considerations; and bolster the body that is trying to heal itself, rather than attacking the symptoms of that healing (for example, inflammation or fever). As one naturopathic physician says, "The first thing I tell people is, 'I will be your coach, not your doctor.' My role is to give patients the power of their own healing systems."[2]

Rather than replacing one healing system with another, it is the synthesis of these many fields that

Introduction

will bring American medicine into the twenty-first century. In the future, a trip to "the doctor" may mean seeing a physician, a naturopath, an herbalist, a homeopath, and/or an acupuncturist—all housed together in one office complex, consulting each other to determine the best course of treatment for the patient.

Actually, a few such holistic treatment centers already exist, but they are the exception, rather than the rule. Generally, finding a reputable acupuncturist or massage therapist is a hit-or-miss proposition. Licensing laws vary from state to state, even from county to county; in some states, the acupuncture we feel may help us isn't even legally obtainable. The alternative practitioners we do find are often booked so far in advance that it's impossible to run in for a simple sinus infection with the same short notice we give our M.D.

While the current situation is a bad one for patients, it's promising for the student who plans to enter the field. Opportunities are everywhere, as alternative medicine is experiencing tremendous growth and ever-increasing legitimacy. A survey conducted by *The New England Journal of Medicine* in 1993 reported that 34 percent of Americans consulted alternative healers that year, spending nearly $14 billion for their largely uninsured services.[3] Even the United States government is beginning to see the light, as evidenced by the creation of the Office of Alternative Medicine, largely in response to pressure from Congress over the growing costs of health care and the frustrating lack of progress being made in the fight against the likes of AIDS, arthritis, and cancer.

This new way of thinking about age-old remedies presents tremendous opportunities for prospective students of naturopathy, homeopathy, massage therapy, herbal medicine, acupuncture, and other alternative therapies. Interest and acceptance by the public is growing daily, licensing laws are continually being reworked, and training programs are becoming more standardized and sophisticated. It's an exciting time to get involved in alternative medicine. Let the healing begin.

PART ONE

Understanding the Fields of Alternative Medicine

This section defines some of the various fields of study that are available in alternative medicine. The historical background, general philosophy, and treatments used in each field are explained; in fields such as massage therapy that have several different methods of treatment, each method is also explained. Career opportunities in each field are discussed, as well as general licensing requirements. Keep in mind, however, that these are general descriptions; since you should familiarize yourself as much as possible with a field of study before committing to it, the Bibliography section on page 393 lists books that discuss each field in greater depth.

AROMATHERAPY

Stopping to sniff the lavender, putting a pot of pot-pourri by the door, or using scented bath oils gives many of us a psychological lift, even if we've never heard of aromatherapy and aren't aware of the physiology involved.

But aromatherapy goes way beyond flowers on the breakfast table. The inhalation or external application of essential oils—obtained by distilling or cold-pressing different parts of a plant—allows molecules to penetrate the tissues and create actual physiological changes within the body. In this way, aromatherapy has been found to have a healing effect on such diverse physical ailments as viral and bacterial infections, herpes simplex, shingles, arthritis, skin conditions, and muscular disorders—hence the use of essential oils in the practice of massage. Research conducted in 1973 showed that a blend of cloves, cinnamon, lavender, and melissa or lemon balm was as effective as prescription antibiotics in treating bronchial conditions—with none of the side effects.[1] Studies conducted in Munich, Germany, have demonstrated that essential oils of cloves, thyme, and cinnamon show anti-inflammatory effects in the treatment of arthritis.[2] And *The British Journal of Occupational Therapy* reported in 1992 that the potential uses of aromatherapy are vast, and include diminishing stress, relieving depression, promoting alertness, treating medical problems, and relieving pain.[3]

Aromatherapy is defined as the practice of using the naturally distilled essences, or essential oils, of plants to promote health and well-being.[4] These essential oils are extremely concentrated, with many pounds or even tons of plant material required to produce a small amount of oil. Though yield varies from plant to plant, on average the yield of essential oil from plant material is 1.5 percent; that is, 70 pounds of raw material produce just 1 pound of essential oil.[5]

Despite their name, essential oils are not greasy; they are volatile oils that readily evaporate given the chance, and are closer in consistency to water than to oil. Some of our most fragrant flowers, such as lilac, gardenia, and lily of the valley, produce no essential oils whatsoever. Others yield oils that smell little or nothing like the original flower, and some of the most important essential oils, such as black pepper, ginger, fennel, and thyme, seem more at home in our spice rack than in the bath water.

Surprisingly, fewer than 300 essential oils can be produced from the hundreds of thousands of plants on earth using today's extraction methods. Essential oils are distilled by a variety of methods, including steam distillation, cold-pressing, solvent extraction, and carbon dioxide extraction. While extraction methods may vary, it is most important to find reputable suppliers of pure essential oils, rather than synthetic, laboratory-born scents. While there is no absolute way to be sure, the label should at least read "essential oil" or "pure essential oil," rather than "perfume oil" or "infused oil." Other indicators of a quality product include price (you get what you pay for, at least some of the time) and opaque glass bottles.

Undiluted essential oils can be so potent when used alone that they may actually burn the skin. For this reason, a few drops of an essential oil are often mixed with a much larger quantity of a carrier oil. Almond, grapeseed, canola, sunflower, sesame, and hazelnut are frequently used carrier oils; rose hip, evening primrose, borage, and other oils may also be added in small amounts. Any carrier oil should be cold-pressed, unscented, and organically grown.

Aromatherapy can be practiced in a number of ways. Essential oils can be used to treat specific mental or physical disorders, just as herbs and conventional Western medicines are used; added to a beauty routine; or used in the kitchen in the form of aromatic honeys or hydrosols. Some practitioners use aromatherapy as part of another modality; though many link aromatherapy with massage and, less often, with chiropractic, the energetics of particular oils are also recognized in Ayurvedic approaches. As such, aromatherapy can be seen as a complement to virtually any form of alternative or allopathic health care.

A CAREER IN AROMATHERAPY

A handful of schools offer separate certificate programs in aromatherapy, either through classroom instruction or home study; many more schools combine a study of essential oils with instruction in herbology. A class in aromatherapy is often part of the curriculum, as either a required or an elective course, at many schools of massage therapy.

Most states require a license of some kind to practice massage, and, of course, all states require specific forms of medical training before permitting practitioners to diagnose and treat illnesses. Aside from these restrictions, aromatherapy falls in the essentially unregulated area shared by herbology and certain other modalities. That is, though aromatherapists can't legally diagnose and treat illnesses, they may teach others how to prepare blends, create aromatic bath oils, and use essential oils to treat themselves and their family members, and may produce and sell a variety of aromatic products.

There are as yet no legal standards for aromatherapy training or certification in the United States; however, the National Association for Holistic Aromatherapy is currently developing educational standards for aromatherapy certification that will provide guidelines for students and teachers.

AYURVEDA

Ayurveda is not only a healing science, but a philosophy and a religion as well, for it concerns itself with the whole journey of life, with love and truth, and with an open mind and heart; the word is Sanskrit for "science of life."[1] Ayurveda is indigenous to India, where it has been practiced for some 5,000 years. In contrast to Western allopathic medicine, Ayurveda teaches that each individual has the power to heal him- or herself.

Ayurveda teaches that man has four biological and spiritual instincts: religious, financial, procreative, and the instinct toward freedom. Good health is essential for the fulfillment of these instincts, and is the basis for happiness and growth. Consciousness is energy manifested into five basic principles or elements: Ether (space), Air, Fire, Water, and Earth. These five elements, the heart of Ayurvedic science, exist within each individual, as we are a microcosm of nature. For example, Ether exists in the mouth, respiratory tract, abdomen, and tissues; Air is in the movements of the lungs, stomach, and intestines, and in the larger movements of the muscles; Fire is present in our metabolism, in the digestive system, and in our intelligence; Water takes the form of digestive juices, mucous membranes, and plasma; and Earth is manifested in bones, cartilage, muscles, skin, and hair. The five senses of hearing, touch, vision, taste, and smell correspond to the five elements.

In Ayurveda, the human constitution manifests the five elements, combined in pairs, in one of three principles or humors known as doshas. The human constitution is determined at conception and is categorized as vata, pitta, or kapha. Within and between these types, there exist subtle variations depending on the predominance of one element over another. Ether and Air combine to produce vata; Fire and Water manifest as pitta; and Earth and Water produce kapha. Though one's constitution manifests a predominant dosha, all three doshas are present in every cell of the body.

Persons with a primarily vata constitution tend to be physically underdeveloped, with flat chests, thin frames, visible veins and tendons, and cold, rough, dry skin; either quite tall or quite short, with bent or turned-up noses, brittle nails, and cold hands and feet. Vata types are creative, active, and restless; talk and walk fast but tire easily; and tend to be nervous and fearful.

Those with a pitta constitution are of medium height, slender but not as flat-chested as vata types. The skin is soft and warm and not as wrinkled as that of vata persons; the nose is sharp; the hair is thin and may gray prematurely; and the body temperature is higher, with much perspiring. Pitta types are leaders, are generally very intelligent and ambitious, and tend toward anger and jealousy.

The kapha body is well-developed, often with excess weight, a broad chest, thick skin, and good muscle development. The skin of kapha people is fair and oily, and their hair is thick and wavy. They move and speak slowly, sleep soundly, and are generally happy, healthy, tolerant, and forgiving, though they may also be greedy and possessive.

The individual constitution comes with a corresponding susceptibility to disease. Vata types are prone to arthritis, lower back pain, paralysis, and gas; those with a pitta constitution suffer from skin disorders, gallbladder and liver disorders, ulcers, and gastritis; kapha types are more likely to suffer attacks of sinusitis, tonsillitis, bronchitis, and other types of lung congestion. Disease is caused by an imbalance of the humors, which may in turn be caused by repressed fear (excess vata), anger (pitta), or envy and greed (kapha). Food, lifestyle, and environment may also play a part in creating imbalance.

Ayurvedic diagnosis emphasizes day-to-day observation that detects an imbalance before any signs of disease are present. Observation of the pulse, tongue, face, eyes, nails, and lips yields important information regarding which organs are impaired and where toxins have accumulated.

Once there is an understanding of what has caused an illness, there are four main methods of treatment: cleansing and detoxifying, palliation, rejuvenation, and mental hygiene.[2] Cleansing and detoxification, or shodan, are used in cases where excess mucus, bile, or gas has accumulated. The pancha karma (five actions) of vomiting, purgatives or laxatives, enemas, the nasal administration of medication, and bloodletting are used to cleanse the body. Palliation, or shaman, uses herbs, fasting, yoga, breathing exercises, meditation, and exposure to sunlight to balance the doshas. Rejuvenation, or rasayana, uses herbs, mineral preparations, yoga, and breathing exercises to enhance the body's ability to function. Mental hygiene and spiritual healing, or satvajaya, uses sound therapy, meditation, crystals, and mental exercises to release stress and negative beliefs, and to direct energies through the body.

The three doshas exist in plants as they do in all forms of life. Their characteristics parallel those of the constitutional types: vata plants have rough, cracked bark and gnarled, spindly branches, and contain little sap; pitta plants are brightly colored and moderate in sap and strength; kapha plants are heavy, dense, and luxuriant, with abundant sap and leaves. In addition, herbs are classified according to which prana, or life force, they work on: prana (brain), vyana (heart), samana (small intestine), udana (throat), or apana (lower abdomen). Ayurveda also recognizes the energetic properties of herbs: taste, elements, heating or cooling effects, effect after digestion, and other properties.

A sound diet is essential to the maintenance of health. Foods should be selected in accordance with the constitution. For example, apples, melons, potatoes, tomatoes, ice cream, and beef aggravate vata; but brown rice, bananas, grapes, and oranges are beneficial. Spicy foods, peanut butter, tomatoes, and garlic aggravate pitta; pears, plums, oranges, green salads, and mushrooms inhibit it. Bananas, pineapples, melons, and dairy products increase kapha, while cranberries, basmati rice, chicken, and sprouts are beneficial for kapha types. General dietary recommendations include eating only when hungry and drinking only when thirsty; eating foods that work together and don't contradict one another's actions; chewing thoroughly; and eating only about two handfuls of food at one time. Fasting is sometimes recommended, but it should be done in accordance with the constitution. Supplementation of vitamins is normally not recommended.

A CAREER IN AYURVEDIC MEDICINE

There is currently no licensing of Ayurvedic physicians in the United States, nor are there any colleges offering the five years of training that is the educational standard in India, where some 108 colleges offer the degree.[3] A handful of schools offer a minimal degree of training in Ayurvedic principles. These courses may be taken by the public for their personal use, or by health care professionals who may want to incorporate principles of Ayurveda into their established practices. Since Ayurveda is based on the assumption that we each have the power to heal ourselves, and since the overall emphasis is on prevention rather than treatment, Ayurveda is a logical choice for those seeking complementary methods of self- and family care.

BIOFEEDBACK

The term biofeedback was coined in the late 1960s to describe a process used to develop control over certain biological responses. The process generally involves seeing and/or hearing an indicator of a biological state (for example, hearing a tone that indicates skin temperature) and learning to control the indicator, or feedback, by acquiring control over the physical response itself. Once the client can successfully control the indicator, the feedback is removed, leaving the client with control over the biological function whenever he or she feels the need to use it.

As odd as it may sound at first, we are in fact able to control a variety of physical states; in addition to skin temperature, subjects can learn to voluntarily influence brain waves, blood pressure, heart rate, and many other autonomic functions. The realization that we have such control has enabled individuals to make considerable progress in the self-treatment of a variety of ailments.

While the technology is relatively new, learning to control the autonomic functions is certainly not. Yogis in eighteenth-century colonial India astounded the British army physicians by exerting control over their breathing and heart rates, not to mention performing the bed-of-nails routine.[1] But it wasn't until the 1950s that Kamiya, Brown, and Green discovered that individuals could learn to control physiological processes when measuring instruments supplied them with information about these processes. It was Kamiya who first used EEG readings to teach subjects to produce alpha brain waves, which identify a very relaxed, waking state; he learned, too, that once subjects had learned how to produce the alpha state with biofeedback, they could do so when the machines were removed.

Later studies indicate that biofeedback, like hypnosis and guided imagery, works by altering the direction of blood flow, which is one of the most common factors in the resolution of mind-body problems. T.X. Barber and others have used this principle of redirected blood flow to control blushing, to

cure dermatitis, to aid coagulation in hemophiliacs, and even, in a well-publicized study, to increase breast size.[2]

Today, psychologists, physicians, and other health professionals use biofeedback to treat migraines and tension headaches, high and low blood pressure, anxiety, insomnia, Raynaud's disease (characterized by cold extremities), epilepsy, paralysis, stomach and intestinal disorders, and a host of other ailments.

A CAREER IN BIOFEEDBACK

The biofeedback training practitioner teaches the client how to use any of several types of biofeedback instruments available. Training programs certified by the Biofeedback Certification Institute of America (BCIA) typically include courses in introduction to biofeedback, preparing for clinical intervention, neuromuscular intervention, central nervous system interventions, autonomic nervous system interventions, biofeedback and distress, instrumentation, adjunctive techniques and cognitive interventions, and professional conduct.

Biofeedback practitioners are not required by law to be certified; in states that license psychologists, nurses, and other professionals, the state license is all that is required to practice biofeedback, and technicians may work under their employer's license. Practitioners who wish to be certified by BCIA must have a bachelor's degree or higher in a health care field, and must have completed a prescribed number of hours of biofeedback education and supervised clinical training.

CHIROPRACTIC

Of all the forms of alternative health care, chiropractic is perhaps the most mainstream. Many insurance companies pay for chiropractic care, and it's not hard to find someone you know who sees a chiropractor regularly. Chiropractic is no doubt so widely accepted because most Americans have some type of back trouble, and conventional medicine can do little to alleviate it. Allopathic physicians may recommend drugs or surgery, but those who have tried these methods will attest to their limited success and significant downsides. And yet, patients who were told their only option was surgery frequently find that chiropractic relieves their chronic pain and restores freedom of movement in just a few sessions. As with many other alternative approaches, it's not only the positive results but the enthusiastic recommendations of chiropractic patients that have done the most to promote the practice.

Chiropractic (the word comes from the Greek *chiro* and *praktikos,* meaning "done by hand") was first developed by Daniel David Palmer, a self-taught healer who was informally educated under Paul Caster, a "magnetic healer," in the late nineteenth century. Palmer used a drug-free approach that involved the laying on of hands, and came to believe that most illnesses result from spinal misalignment. He based this belief on his experience with cases such as that of a janitor whose hearing was restored when Palmer slipped the man's protruding vertebra back into place, and another patient who reported relief from a persistent and painful heart condition after Palmer adjusted the misaligned spine.

Over the years, Palmer refined his system; he later recognized that it was the pressure of misaligned vertebrae on the nerves of the spinal column—what he termed "subluxation"—that interfered with nerve transmission and created disease. Palmer opened the first school of chiropractic in Davenport, Iowa, in 1897. Though he was fined and jailed for six months for practicing medicine without a license, at the time of his death in 1913, Kansas had passed the first state law licensing chiropractic. Today, every state and Canadian province licenses chiropractors, and millions of Americans are treated by them every year.

Just as Palmer did, today's chiropractors perform adjustments or manipulations, in which they ease the spinal vertebrae back into their normal positions. While innovative devices have been developed to aid in this process, most adjustments are still done by hand, usually on a specially-designed table with separate sections that can move as the adjustment is being made. While the patient may hear some cracks or pops, the treatment is usually painless, though the patient may feel sore afterward. More interesting are the effects that sometimes show up after the third or fourth treatment— headaches, dizziness, digestive complaints, and a low-grade fever may accompany the muscle soreness and joint tenderness. These are called recovery symptoms, and are seen as an indication that the body is beginning to heal itself as it adapts to the new spinal alignment.

Today's chiropractor may use a number of other tools that Palmer had to do without. X-rays are a fairly standard part of the chiropractic exam, both for a determination of misalignment and to look for other pathologies, such as a fracture or growth. Activator instruments—small, pen-sized guns loaded with a powerful spring—may be used for applying thrust on a small area.

There are two schools of chiropractic practice. "Straight" chiropractic uses only the Palmer philosophy of adjustments—that is, locating and treating subluxations. "Mixed" chiropractic may involve nutritional counseling, heat, or hydrotherapy, as well as spinal adjustments.

While chiropractic may be an obvious choice for those with lower back or neck pain, it has also been successful in treating a host of seemingly unrelated problems. Although today's chiropractors have backed away from the idea that all disease is caused by spinal misalignment, according to Dr. Chester A. Wilk, disorders that have been successfully treated with chiropractic include arthritis, sciatica, bursitis, headache and migraine, nervous disorders and emotional problems, sinusitis, heart trouble, asthma, high blood pressure, respiratory conditions, and the common cold.[1] Anecdotal evidence points to the positive effects of chiropractic on patients with cancer and AIDS, not so much because chiropractic cures these diseases, but because it aids in the restoration of the immune function, helping the body to better protect itself.[2]

A CAREER IN CHIROPRACTIC

All fifty states plus the District of Columbia, the U.S. Virgin Islands, and Puerto Rico license chiropractors as health care providers. In general, students must have completed two years (in some states, four years) of a preprofessional, college-level education prior to attending a four-year (at least 4,200-hour) chiropractic college. For a graduate to be eligible for licensure, the chiropractic college must be accredited by the Council on Chiropractic Education (CCE) and/or approved by the state board; national exams and some state assessment are also required. Like other alternative health care fields, chiropractic is growing; between 1994 and 1995, the number of D.C. degrees bestowed by CCE-accredited institutions increased by 7 percent to nearly 2,900.[3]

Legally, chiropractors are permitted to do much more than align a spine. Like any doctor, a chiropractor will take a medical history and conduct a physical exam, and may order lab tests or X-rays in order to arrive at a diagnosis. Most chiropractors will also work with their patients to develop a plan for a healthier lifestyle through better nutrition, exercise, improved posture, and other changes.

ENERGETIC HEALING

Several schools offer certificate programs in what they call energetic healing or subtle energy therapies. These are hybrid programs that generally combine courses in color therapy, flower essence therapy, magnetic therapy, aromatherapy, hypnotherapy, the laying on of hands, meditation, sound healing, and other topics with a more mainstream base in massage, craniosacral therapy, polarity therapy, and/or reiki.

While licensing laws vary, in general, programs such as these are not in and of themselves a sufficient base on which to build a career. These courses can, however, be a valuable way to increase one's knowledge of lesser-known practices in alternative health care and can add another dimension of healing to an education or established practice in such fields as massage or polarity therapy.

ENVIRONMENTAL MEDICINE

In the 1940s, Theron G. Randolph, M.D., treated a woman named Sally who had been admitted to a mental hospital for psychosis. Dr. Randolph, convinced that food allergies could be contributing to her problem, put Sally in an allergen-free environment and started her on a water fast. By the fourth day, Sally had regained her sanity. Randolph reintroduced foods, one at a time, and found that beet sugar brought back her psychotic symptoms. Once the offending food was removed from her diet, Sally was no longer in need of hospitalization.[1]

In addition to food allergies, Randolph found that common environmental chemicals could also have profound effects on a patient's physical and emotional well-being. Every day, we encounter formaldehyde and toluene in our carpeting; artificial colorings, preservatives, and pesticides in our food; natural gas fumes and the toxic byproducts of their combustion from our stoves and furnaces; and petroleum from our cars. All of these things can be the direct cause, depending on our susceptibility, of migraines, eczema, arthritis, anxiety, depression, gastrointestinal problems, attention deficit disorder, bed-wetting, lupus, and any number of other problems.[2] According to Sherry Rogers, M.D., a Fellow of the American Academy of Environmental Medicine, the most common symptoms of chemical sensitivity are feeling dopey, dizzy, "spacey," and unable to concentrate[3]—which should give pause to every parent of a "learning-disabled" child.

Of course, not everyone is sensitive to environmental chemicals. Those who are, according to the American Academy of Environmental Medicine, can blame a combination of genetics, poor nutrition, infection, stress, and excessive chemical exposure.[4] Exposure to formaldehyde, which is in our walls, cabinets, furniture, and carpeting, can cause an individual to become sensitive to a variety of other chemicals that previously had no effect.[5] Most of us are not born sensitive to new carpeting, but we are worn down by years of chemical attacks on our bodies and one day, we fall apart. Many in the field speak of the "rain barrel effect," which is similar in concept to the straw that broke the camel's back. We begin with a fairly empty rain barrel. Over the years, our dust allergies develop; we get a pet and add dander allergies to the barrel. We eat too many colored and preserved snack foods, linger too long over the gas stove, and fill our barrel near to the brim. Then we get the new bedroom carpeting, and the barrel overflows. We suddenly develop breathing difficulties, panic attacks, scaly hands, or migraines—or all those and more. We can't understand why, all of a sudden, we're a physical wreck. But the rain barrel theory holds that it's not "all of a sudden" at all; we just overflowed our barrel's capacity.

Physicians trained in the treatment of environmental illness, or multiple chemical sensitivities (MCS), take an extensive medical history that helps both doctor and patient to see that it's not just the new carpeting—it's the accumulation of a lifetime of bad habits. The good news is that in many cases, the rain barrel can be effectively emptied, or at least decanted a little. Physicians accomplish this by identifying and treating the underlying allergies and sensitivities, and working to rebuild the immune system through diet, stress reduction, and other holistic means.

Environmental physicians may test for food and airborne allergies through blood tests, but some prefer the slower and, they believe, more accurate method of provocation/neutralization. In this form of testing, the patient is injected with a suspected allergen and waits a few minutes to see whether there is a reaction, either visible on the skin or felt by the patient as a change in mental state. The practitioner then finds a dose of the same substance that will turn off the reaction; this is the neutralizing dose. The patient is then able to self-administer the antigen on a regular basis for the control of symptoms.

Many practitioners and patients are reluctant to routinely inject possible carcinogens such as formaldehyde and natural gas. For these types of substances, education and avoidance are the key. Once a patient has identified the chemicals to which he or she is sensitive, they can be removed from the home. This is usually neither easy nor cheap; Dr. Randolph was responsible for the removal of many a natural gas furnace and yards of wall-to-wall carpeting.

A CAREER IN ENVIRONMENTAL MEDICINE

Environmental physicians are generally just that— M.D.s or D.O.s who were trained by fellow physicians and/or have taken advanced courses in the treatment of environmental illness. The American Academy of Environmental Medicine offers such a course to licensed physicians. However, a knowledge of the effects of food and chemical sensitivities can be beneficial in any area of alternative health care. Practitioners should always be aware that a patient's headache could be caused not by overworked muscles, a spine out of adjustment, or blocked chi, but by the carpeting in the waiting room.

GUIDED IMAGERY

Goose bumps from a ghost story, salivating while reading a recipe, sweating when an actor teeters on a ledge—we've all experienced the physical effects of an image that existed only in our imagination. To our brains, real and imagined experiences look exactly alike; hence, our worrying about problems can cause as many—or more—hives and ulcers as the actual problems themselves. This powerful mind-body connection can be harnessed to work in our favor in a technique known as guided imagery, where we can learn to visualize positive outcomes and experiences rather than imagining the worst.

Belleruth Naparstek, author of *Staying Well with Guided Imagery,* enumerates several operating principles of imagery. These can be summarized as follows: first, our bodies can't tell the difference between sensory images in the mind and reality; second, in a relaxed state, we are capable of rapid healing, learning, and change; and third, we feel better when we have a sense of mastery over what happens to us.[1]

Therapists trained in guided imagery use these principles in developing techniques to help their clients cope with, and sometimes defeat, chronic diseases such as multiple sclerosis, cancer, AIDS, or back pain. Cases have been reported in which patients have visualized their tumors under attack by "bullets of energy" or Star Wars-type weapons, and their tumors have, in fact, disappeared.[2]

In its simplest form, a guided imagery session may go something like this: the client is asked to get comfortable, take some deep breaths, release all tension, and enter into a relaxed, peaceful state. The client is then asked to remember a specific instance in which he or she felt totally at peace—a special place, a particular time or event, in which all was well with the world. Depending on the client's needs, he or she may be asked to use a physical gesture, or anchoring device, that will become linked in his or her mind with the relaxed response—something as simple as touching two fingers together. After several weeks of practice evoking the peaceful scene and then making the gesture, the client will be able to make the gesture and then *automatically* feel the relaxed response, even in a time of stress, such as when giving a speech or boarding an airplane.

A CAREER IN GUIDED IMAGERY

Workshops in helping others through guided imagery are generally open to professionals in the counseling field, including psychologists, certified counselors, social workers, and nurses. Many hospitals or health organizations offer self-help courses in guided imagery to patients or to the general public; several books and audio tapes are on the market that can teach an individual to use imagery to help solve specific problems.

HERBAL MEDICINE

Herbal medicine is a prime example of how what is considered alternative or unproven medicine in the United States is standard practice in most of the rest of the world. In 1985, the World Health Organization estimated that approximately 80 percent of the world's population relies primarily on herbs to meet their health care needs.[1] What Americans may find surprising is that it isn't only primitive cultures that rely on herbs; 30 to 40 percent of all medical doctors in Germany and France use herbs as their primary medicines.[2]

Despite its lack of acceptance in the United States, herbalism is by far the oldest form of medicine in the world, used by all cultures throughout every period of history. It remains an important part of traditional Chinese medicine, naturopathy, and Ayurvedic medicine. Indeed, plants are the source of many of the drugs sold by prescription in the United States; some 125 plant-derived drugs are in use here, and of these, three-fourths are used in similar ways in native cultures.[3] But despite the proliferation of news reports showing khaki-clad botanists roaming the rain forests in search of cancer cures, dozens of plants indigenous to North America are world-renowned for their healing powers. Not the least of these is the unassuming purple coneflower—better known in herbal circles as echinacea—which has been found to show anti-inflammatory, antiviral, antibacterial, and even anti-cancer properties.[4] Perhaps the answers to many of our health problems lie not in exotic jungle leaves, but in our own back yards.

Echinacea is just one of many substances derived from garden- (or roadside-) variety plants that can contribute to our collective wellness. The dandelions that our neighbors find so resistant to herbicides and uprooting are that hardy for a reason: this humble plant has been found to aid digestion, to improve liver conditions such as jaundice and hepatitis, and to act as a safe diuretic. It is also used by the Chinese to treat breast cancer. Peppermint has long been a treatment for indigestion and intestinal colic. And garlic has been in use for over 5,000 years in the treatment of a wide variety of conditions, including high blood pressure, diabetes, high cholesterol, and all sorts of infections. It is only we Americans who fail to fully recognize the herbal treasure trove under our feet; of the 232 monographs in the British Herbal Pharmacopoeia, seventy-three are about native North American plants that are exported to Britain for medicinal purposes.[5]

Though the vast majority of herbs are beneficial and well-tolerated, not all are harmless; some have the potential to be toxic when taken improperly. In 1994, a California woman died after trying to induce an abortion with pennyroyal; other herbs that have produced dangerous side effects include chaparral, comfrey (when taken internally), and ma huang, a stimulant sometimes used in weight-loss products.[6] Though extremely rare, stories of harmful side effects make headlines when they do occur, and are used as ammunition by those who would attempt to limit the public's access to herbs. However, the American Association of Poison Control Centers reported that in 1988 to 1989, pharmaceuticals caused a total of 809 deaths and 6,407 major nonfatal poisonings, while plants (most of which were houseplants, not herbs) caused two fatalities and fifty-three major poisonings.[7] Still, while herbs are considerably less toxic than what's in the medicine chest, it makes sense for anyone who wants to use medicinal herbs to become educated enough to do it safely and effectively.

HERBAL PREPARATIONS

Courses offered at any of the classroom or correspondence schools will instruct the student in identifying, gathering, and growing herbs; Western and Eastern theories of healing; materia medica (healing properties and actions of specific herbs and conditions for their use); and creating a number of types of herbal preparations.

While herbal products may be purchased in a variety of forms, the simplest and often most effective herbal preparations are easily prepared at home with only a knife, strainer, and mortar and pestle. The following is a list of these preparations.

- *Tinctures* are alcohol-based solutions of herbal extracts, and are among the more common formulations; they can be taken orally or used externally.

- *Infusions,* or teas, are made by pouring hot water or other liquid over fresh or powdered herbs, which are then allowed to steep for ten or twenty minutes. The infusion is then strained for drinking.

- *A decoction* is very similar to an infusion, but it is made from woody herbs that are not soluble in hot water; in this case, the herbs are simmered for up to twenty minutes and strained while hot.

- *A poultice* is a mashed or powdered herb applied directly to the skin to reduce inflammation or to draw out toxins.

- *Ointments* are prepared by boiling herbs together with a petroleum jelly-like substance; these can be applied to the skin for long periods of time, such as in the treatment of injuries.

- *Compresses* involve soaking sterile gauze in a solution of boiled herbs, applying the warm pad to the affected area, and replacing it when cool.

- *Salves* are prepared by adding boiled herbs to a mixture of vegetable oil and beeswax.

A CAREER IN HERBAL MEDICINE

Naturopaths and practitioners of traditional Chinese and Ayurvedic medicine all use herbs as part of their arsenal of treatment options, though in somewhat different ways. In Western herbology, herbs are used to treat particular symptoms, in much the same way as Western medicines are used. In Chinese and Ayurvedic medicine, herbs are used energetically; that is, particular herbs are either "warm" or "cold," and the herb used would depend on an assessment of the individual's overall condition and constitution. Whatever the approach, a license to practice naturopathy or traditional Chinese medicine would permit a practitioner to prescribe herbal preparations.

In the United States, Native American reservations are the only places where a nonmedically trained herbalist can legally diagnose and prescribe.[8] The role of the herbalist, then, is limited largely to teaching and/or manufacturing, wildcrafting (harvesting native wild herbs), and growing herbs. Michael Tierra, a naturopath, certified acupuncturist, and developer of the home study East West Herb Course, notes that a properly trained herbalist may incorporate a practice as an herbal consultant because "the system of holistic analysis based upon principles of Oriental diagnosis has nothing to do with the Western concepts of pathological disease, and so can be used as a basis of practice without infringing on the law."[9]

The National Commission for the Certification of Acupuncturists has recently instituted an examination process for certification of practitioners as Diplomates of Chinese Herbology. But outside of state and local licensing, there is no association that regulates or accredits education in herbal medicine in this country; it's strictly "let the buyer beware." Prospective students should examine the materials from a number of schools and compare the orientation (Western, Eastern, or both), depth of course offerings, reputation of instructors, and costs.

HOLISTIC HEALTH PRACTITIONER/HOLISTIC HEALTH EDUCATION/ HOLISTIC COUNSELING

Several schools offer programs, ranging from one month to as much as three years in length, in areas they call Holistic Health Practitioner, Holistic Health Education, or Holistic Counseling. These programs typically combine a base program of massage, counseling, or yoga with offerings from many other fields of alternative health care, including nutrition, herbs, stress management, dreamwork, hypnotherapy, traditional Chinese medicine, acupressure, polarity, and others.

Such programs generally provide extra hours of education beyond licensing requirements in, for example, massage therapy, thereby allowing the therapist to incorporate an added dimension of healing into his or her practice. The shorter programs, however, may not provide sufficient training for a career and should be taken in conjunction with other career training programs.

Those schools that offer a degree in counseling with specialization in holistic health enable counselors to incorporate knowledge of nutrition and eating disorders, diet and disease, and the physiology and psychology of stress into their practices. While requirements vary by state, programs that offer a master's degree in counseling are generally sufficient for licensing as a counselor.

HOLISTIC NURSING

As alternative medicine becomes increasingly mainstream, there is more and more of an overlap between conventional, allopathic medicine and various alternative fields. Many professional Registered Nurses are seeking additional training in such areas as massage as a means of providing even better patient care.

Holistic nursing programs provide continuing education for licensed health care professionals, covering topics such as AMMA therapy, stress management, nutrition, herbology, Oriental diagnosis, tai chi, and others.

HOMEOPATHY

Paracelsus said, "All things are poison, it is the dosage that makes a thing not poison."[1] This is as true in the various fields of alternative medicine, where treatments are generally viewed as wholesome and natural, as it is in the allopathic world of synthetic drugs with side effects that can be worse than the original affliction. Medicinal herbs may sometimes produce allergic or toxic reactions in some individuals, and certain vitamins and minerals can cause damage when taken in excess. But homeopathy uses remedies that not only *can* be toxic, but definitely *are* toxic, even in fairly small doses. Who wouldn't raise an eyebrow at the homeopath's remedies of petroleum, bee venom (*apis mellifica*), deadly nightshade (*belladonna*), mercury (*mercurius*), and snake venom (*lachesis*)?

The critical element in homeopathy, however, is the dose. Homeopathy is criticized in print and on talk shows because, as a finger-pointing host is sure to point out, homeopathic remedies are so dilute that not a single molecule of the original substance is present. But what the talk show host doesn't understand is that homeopathy is an energetic system, much like Chinese medicine or Ayurveda; homeopathic remedies work because of the energy pattern, not the material content, of the substance used in its preparation. When a substance is shaken (known as succussion) and repeatedly diluted until no trace of the original substance is left, the resulting remedy is actually more potent than the tincture from which it was made. Critics have argued that any successes attributed to homeopathy were more likely due to the placebo effect. This argument falls apart, however, when one looks at the numbers of successful homeopathic treatments on animals who were not, in all likelihood, staunch believers in the practice.

The practice of homeopathy was founded by the German physician Samuel Hahnemann in 1790 (the word is derived from the Greek *homoios,* meaning "similar," and *pathos,* meaning "suffering"). Hahnemann believed that the symptoms produced by an illness are the body's attempt to heal itself. Therefore, he reasoned, a remedy that could mimic the symptoms of a particular illness would strengthen the healing response—a principle referred to as "like cures like" or the Law of Similars. In this regard, homeopathy differs only in potency from immunizations and allergy shots.

Hahnemann developed two other primary principles. One, the Law of the Infinitesimal Dose, states that the more dilute the remedy, the greater its potency. The other involves looking at each patient and his or her illness on an individual basis; no two cases will be manifested in exactly the same way, so the remedy given to one patient may be completely different from that given to the next.

To determine the proper remedy, the practitioner would need to look beyond the obvious stuffy nose and sore throat to find the more peculiar symptoms—a red face, waking in the night, bloating, twitching, or anxiety, for example. He or she would then select the proper potency. Potencies are expressed in centesimal (c) and decimal (x) scales. Commonly available potencies usually range from 6c (the lowest potency commonly available) to 30c (the highest potency normally obtained over the counter). In general, lower potencies are used for physical pathologies, while the highest potencies are used with diseases that are mental or emotional in nature.

Homeopathic remedies are derived not only from the poisonous substances mentioned earlier, but from a variety of plants (in whole or part), animals, reptiles, insects, and minerals. Potencies in the lower ranges are available in health food stores and through numerous mail order companies. While a trained practitioner should be consulted for any serious illness, an individual can learn enough through courses or independent study to treat minor ailments in himself and in his family.

A CAREER IN HOMEOPATHY

In much of the world, homeopathy is not considered "alternative" at all; some 500 million people around the world receive homeopathic treatment, including Britain's royal family.[2] In Britain, homeopathic hospitals are part of the national health care system; in France, pharmacies are required to stock homeopathic remedies along with standard drugs. Even in the United States, an estimated 3,000 physicians and health care professionals practice homeopathy.[3]

In order to diagnose illnesses and prescribe homeopathic remedies in the United States, one must be a licensed medical doctor or osteopathic physician; in many states, naturopathic physicians may also diagnose and prescribe. Other health care practitioners may or may not be allowed to prescribe homeopathic remedies, depending on state laws. Interested individuals should contact the National Center for Homeopathy for further information. Homeopathy is currently unregulated in Canada.

Training courses in homeopathy in the United States are typically three years in length, meeting perhaps one weekend per month during this time, and requiring a significant amount of home study. A number of certification programs are available.

HYPNOTHERAPY

There's really nothing alternative about hypnotherapy; it's been approved by the American Medical Association as a valid medical treatment since 1958. It's also nothing new. Hypnotic trances have been in use nearly since the dawn of time; there are reports of hypnotic suggestion in the writings of ancient Egypt and Greece, and it is still observed in the ceremonies of primitive cultures. Franz Anton Mesmer, an eighteenth-century Austrian physician, is credited with the founding of modern hypnosis; he called it animal magnetism because he believed that the human body possessed a magnetic polarity. The term mesmerism, which is still used today, was derived from his name.

Despite its long history, the only hypnosis most of us have ever witnessed is the hokey parlor-trick form we see now and then on television. But hypnotherapy is actually quite effective in the treatment of a host of ailments, from migraines and ulcers to anxiety, phobias, and depression; over 15,000 doctors combine hypnosis with other forms of treatment.[1]

We have all experienced states of awareness that are very similar to the early stages of hypnosis. The feeling of drifting off, of being not quite asleep yet not awake, feels very much like the average hypnotic trance. In fact, the trance-like state in which we find ourselves when we drive past our exit ramp or get lost in a daydream at work is a common hypnotic experience that has been defined as "an altered state of consciousness, characterized by an inward focusing and temporary inattention to the ordinary environment."[2] Virtually everyone who is willing can be hypnotized; likewise, it is virtually impossible to hypnotize a subject against his or her will.[3] There is no difference in susceptibility to hypnosis between male and female or in correlation to body build, intelligence, or personality, though children and those with higher levels of anxiety are actually somewhat more susceptible than others.[4]

Inducing a trance is not complicated. The subject is usually asked to relax and to fix his or her gaze on an object; as the subject's eyes grow weary, the hypnotist suggests that they close. Subjects may also focus on a body part or on their breathing, a technique common to yoga, karate, and Lamaze.

There are several types or depths of trance. In a light trance, subjects feel calm and somewhat detached, muscles are relaxed, respiration slows, and the heart rate usually drops. In a medium trance, subjects may feel altered bodily perceptions (such as feeling smaller or larger, or floating in space), will lose their gag reflex, and may experience hallucinations. Surgery may be performed on people in a medium trance. In a deep trance, blood pressure may drop to very low levels and major surgery may be performed without pain.[5]

Hypnotherapy has been used to successfully treat a variety of disorders, including blindness, alcoholism, addictions, and phobias, and in such medical settings as anesthesiology, psychiatry, obstetrics, and dentistry.

A CAREER IN HYPNOTHERAPY

Just as nearly anyone can be hypnotized, just about anyone can learn to perform hypnosis. Several programs will teach just that in a weekend or less—but would you want to be hypnotized by someone with twelve hours' training? The minimum amount of education acceptable by such organizations as the International Medical and Dental Hypnotherapy Association is 120 hours of basic and advanced training in order to become a certified hypnotherapist, with thirty CEUs required each year for renewal of membership.

There is currently no state or federal licensing of hypnotherapists; anyone can legally offer hypnotherapy services to the public.

INTEGRATIVE MEDICINE

The goal of integrative medicine is to combine the best of both conventional and alternative ideas and practices in an effort to produce an environment in which the body can heal itself. Neither standard medical practices nor alternative approaches are accepted blindly; both are subjected to laboratory research and testing in clinical settings in an attempt to sort the effective from the useless.

Practitioners of integrative medicine are encouraged to practice a healthy lifestyle themselves. In addition, they work from the assumption that prevention is medicine's primary responsibility, as many illnesses are entirely preventable; that the body has the ability to heal itself and that the best kind of medicine is that which stimulates and encourages this natural healing; and that simple, cost-effective treatments should be tried before invasive and costly procedures.

The University of Arizona's Program in Integrative Medicine is currently the only one of its kind. Physicians (licensed M.D.s and D.O.s) trained in this two-year program will be educated in the use of botanical, nutritional, and energy medicine, as well as such modalities as homeopathy, acupuncture, guided imagery, osteopathic manipulation, and others.

IRIDOLOGY

Iridology had its beginnings, it is said, when a boy tried to capture an owl in his garden and inadvertently broke its leg in the struggle. As the boy looked into the owl's eye, he saw a black streak forming. After the owl's leg healed, the black line faded to white. That boy, Ignatz von Peczely, later became a physician and one of the fathers of iridology.[1]

In the practice of iridology, the eyes—or more specifically, the irises—provide the knowledgeable practitioner with a map through which he or she can determine the health or weakness of the various systems of the body. Iridology is not designed to diagnosis specific diseases (and in fact, practitioners are not legally able to do so without a medical license); rather, the iridologist can discern the location of inherent weaknesses and various stages of inflammation. This can be done by using several tools.

The primary tool of the iridologist is the iris chart. Around 1880, Dr. Peczely and Swedish minister Nils Liljequist, working independently, developed iris charts that showed a striking similarity to one another. Such charts have been refined by various practitioners over the years. The charts created by Dr. Bernard Jensen, a twentieth-century chiropractor, nutritionist, and iridologist, contain some 166 named areas (eighty-six in the left iris, eighty in the right) that correspond not only to the major organs like the liver, the kidneys, and the heart, but also to very specific regions, such as areas of the brain that control acquired mental speech, senses, and mental ability, the upper jaw, tonsils, scapula, or left foot.[2] These grids are superimposed over an enlarged photograph of the iris to help the iridologist identify areas more precisely than could be done with hand-held magnifiers.

What does the iridologist look for? Fiber quality, or constitution, is rated from one to ten, and is determined by the graininess or weave of the iris fibers; a fine weave or tight grain would be a one, a very loose weave or grainy fibers would be a ten. An individual's constitutional pattern is inborn and cannot be changed. Beyond this, an iridologist might look for specific wreaths (rings around the pupil) that correspond to the autonomic nervous system, the stomach, or nutrient absorption; open or closed lesions or healing lines in specific areas; a string of puffs near the perimeter of the iris (indicating lymphatic system congestion); a dark rim (indicting a problem with the elimination of toxins) or a rim that is milky-white (indicating high sodium and high cholesterol levels); and other lines, rings, or lesions that appear in particular colors or patterns.

Dr. Jensen believes that iridology can reveal a host of conditions. He contends that, along with showing the inherent strength or weakness of organs, glands, and tissues, the iris reveals the nutritional needs of the body; which organs are in greatest need of rebuilding; where inflammation is located; sluggishness or spastic conditions of the bowel; pressure on the heart; nerve force and depletion; hyper- or hypoactivity of the organs, glands, and tissues; lymphatic system congestion; poor nutrient assimilation; the need for rest; high or low sex drive; allergy to wheat; potential for senility; and much more.[3]

A CAREER IN IRIDOLOGY

The National Iridology Research Association (NIRA) offers a certification program covering eye anatomy and physiology, topography and mapping of the iris, and case studies, as well as certification testing. In order to maintain certification, a certified iridologist is required to complete two NIRA-approved continuing education classes each year. The organization also maintains a referral listing of NIRA-certified iridologists.

As an iridologist does not attempt to diagnose or prescribe, no license is required. Iridology is often combined with other holistic approaches to health care.

MASSAGE THERAPY AND BODYWORK

Hippocrates taught his students, "The physician must be acquainted with many things and assuredly with rubbing," and used massage as a treatment for ailments from sprains to constipation. The ancient Japanese healing art of shiatsu, Ayurvedic massage from India, the massage techniques of Chinese Taoist priests, even texts found in Egyptian tombs all testify to the healing power of touch.

Some of the greatest physicians in history advocated the use of massage. Celsus (25 B.C.–A.D. 50), Galen (A.D. 131–A.D. 200), and Avicenna (A.D. 980–A.D. 1037), authors of the most authoritative

medical texts of their times, all wrote about the techniques and indications for massage. But it wasn't until the 1850s that massage was introduced into the United States by New York physicians George and Charles Taylor, brothers who had studied massage in Sweden. Swedes opened the first massage therapy clinics in the United States just after the Civil War; Baron Nils Posse founded the Posse Institute in Boston and Hartwig Nissen opened the Swedish Health Institute in Washington, D.C., where several members of Congress and Presidents Benjamin Harrison and Ulysses S. Grant were clients.

By the early 1900s, massage was delegated to the nursing and physical therapy staff, and by the 1940s it had been all but abandoned by these health care workers as well. The resurgence of interest in massage in the 1970s occurred outside the medical establishment, in the gray area we call alternative health care.

Research conducted today is helping to bring massage therapy closer to the mainstream. Dr. Tiffany Field, director of the Touch Research Institute at the University of Miami, studied the effect of massage on premature babies and found that those who received massage gained 47 percent more weight and left the hospital six days earlier than those who did not.[1] Touching has also been found to reduce anxiety, high blood pressure, and a host of other ills—and it's not all in our heads. Research has shown that massage can increase levels of serotonin, a natural antidepressant, and encourages the release of endorphins—nature's painkillers. In a study of the effects of massage on cancer patients, subjects' perception of pain was reduced by 60 percent and anxiety by 24 percent; feelings of relaxation increased 58 percent, along with a measurable reduction in heart rate, blood pressure, and respiratory rate.[2]

Massage not only makes us feel better, it can make us smarter too. Another study by the Touch Research Institute found that subjects were able to complete math problems in half the time with half as many errors following a twenty-minute chair massage.[3] Studies like this have helped fuel the boom in on-site massage at the workplace, with employers often picking up the tab.

According to the American Massage Therapy Association, the United States is the only developed country in which massage is not part of the official health care system. In Germany and the former Soviet Union, for example, every major hospital has a massage therapy department; China, Japan, and India also recognize massage as an important part of health care. But our society is coming to recognize the need for touch, and the field of massage therapy is growing at an astronomical rate. More than a million Americans get a massage each year, and over a recent ten-year period, membership in the American Massage Therapy Association increased tenfold. *The New England Journal of Medicine* reports that massage is the third most frequently used form of alternative health care.[4]

WHAT IS MASSAGE THERAPY?

Massage therapy has been defined by the National Institutes of Health as "the scientific manipulation of the soft tissues of the body to normalize those tissues. It consists of a group of manual techniques that include applying fixed or moveable pressure, holding, and/or causing movement of or to the body, using primarily the hands but sometimes other areas such as forearms, elbows, or feet."[5] The emphasis, in this and virtually all other forms of alternative medicine, is on assisting the body in healing itself.

Swedish massage started it all in the United States, but there are now some eighty different types of hands-on therapy. A massage therapist may incorporate one or several of these techniques into a given treatment, and schools of massage usually offer instruction in a number of them.

Acupressure

Acupressure is essentially acupuncture without needles. Finger pressure is applied to specific points along meridians, the highways of energy flow (chi or qi) that run through bones, muscles, organs, and the bloodstream. It is thought that the even distribution of chi along these meridians results in strength and health; when chi is unbalanced, physical or emotional problems may result. Acupressure seeks to restore the balance of chi.

While most often used for relief of chronic pain, acupressure is also successful in treating hyperactivity, mood disorders, stress, asthma, and other physical or emotional problems. Individuals can learn to treat themselves with acupressure. In varying forms of acupressure, points are stimulated with heat, cold, electricity, ultrasound, or lasers. Burning herbs over the acupressure points is called moxibustion, a traditional Chinese method of stimulating the flow of chi.

Alexander Technique

F. Mathias Alexander, an Australian actor, suffered periodically from inexplicable voice loss; after nine years of study, he determined that the way he held his head contributed to the problem. He developed a philosophy founded on the principle that proper alignment of the spine was the key to good health, and that poor alignment was simply the result of habitual misuse of body motions. He taught students his techniques to free the neck, lengthen the spine, and reeducate patients though the use of massage and studied movements. Since exercises are developed for each individual, Alexander wrote no manual; techniques are passed down from teacher to teacher. The Alexander technique has been used to eliminate knee pain, tendinitis, chronic back pain, and a variety of other ills.

Applied Kinesiology

In the 1960s, a chiropractor named Dr. George Goodheart introduced applied kinesiology in response to the connections he'd noticed between muscle weakness and dysfunctioning organs; for example, a weakness in a pectoral muscle might indicate gastric disease. Applied kinesiologists see health as a triangle—the chemical side takes into account nutrition and the effects of drugs; the structural side considers the interrelationship of muscles, bones, joints, and organs; and the mental side includes attitudes and expectations.

Aromatherapy

Aromatherapy may be used alone or in combination with some form of massage (see page 5).

Craniosacral Therapy

Craniosacral therapists subtly manipulate bones in the face, head, and vertebral column, and the membranes beneath the skull in order to treat headache, TMJ-related jaw pain, ear infections, strokes, and other ailments. The therapist focuses on reducing tension and stress in the meningeal membrane and its fascial connections, allowing free movement by the cerebrospinal fluid and balancing energy fields.

Deep Muscle Therapy/Deep Tissue Massage

These therapies are corrective or therapeutic massages that use greater pressure to reach deeper layers of muscle, most often as a treatment for muscle spasms, scar tissue, or chronic patterns of muscular tension. In Pfrimmer deep muscle therapy, muscle fibers are worked back and forth in both directions. Cross-fiber friction works against the muscle grain to break up adhesions in the tendons and muscle fiber.

Do-In

Do-in (pronounced dough-in) is a macrobiotic exercise program that was introduced into the United States in 1968. Do-in exercises resemble yoga postures and are thought to stimulate the same energy meridians as acupuncture or shiatsu. Foot massage, abdominal massage, neck extensions, nose squeezes, eye exercises, and ear stretches are all part of the do-in practice.

Esalen Massage

Esalen is a hybrid style of massage taught at the Esalen Institute in California that uses the techniques of Swedish massage, Rolfing, deep tissue massage, and others in long flowing stokes. The goal is to promote relaxation and healing.

Feldenkrais Method

A series of exercises designed to release habitual patterns and introduce new ways of moving, the Feldenkrais method was developed by Moshe Feldenkrais in response to his own incapacitating injury. Feldenkrais used his knowledge of anatomy, physiology, physics, and the martial arts to produce a method of movement reeducation that can improve flexibility and coordination. As the client lies on a table, fully clothed, the practitioner guides the body in various movements and in essence reprograms the nervous system, resulting in more efficient body movement and relief of muscle tension.

Hydrotherapy

Usually used in conjunction with massage, hydrotherapy involves the use of water, heat, and ice in the form of hot and cold packs, saunas, whirlpools, and steam baths.

Infant Massage

Infant massage is common in many other countries, and is gaining a toehold in the United States and Europe, particularly in cases of drug-addicted babies. Massage is said to help the infants relax, move and react better, and bond more closely with their mothers.

Jin Shin Do

This system employs sequences of meridian point pressure that are designed specifically for a particular illness or ailment. A product of the 1980s, Jin Shin Do was derived in part from Jin Shin Jyutsu, which was developed in Japan in the early 1900s and brought to the United States in the 1960s. Though similar to acupuncture and other meridian-based techniques, these systems differ in their use of specific patterns of pressure on particular points, depending on the ailment, in order to energize or enervate qi.

Manual Lymph Drainage

Edema, inflammation, and other conditions related to poor lymph drainage can be treated with manual lymph drainage, a system of light, rhythmic strokes. In a study conducted in 1984, it was found to be more effective than diuretic drugs in controlling lymphedema after radical mastectomy.[6] Used by European hospitals and clinics for decades, manual lymph drainage may be helpful for chronic infections, excess scar tissue, poor circulation, edema caused by surgery or other trauma, chronic pain, or stress.

Myofascial Massage

This massage technique manipulates the connective tissue and fascia that surround the muscles for pain relief (as in the case of carpal tunnel syndrome) and structural integration (see page 22) of the entire body. Myofascial massage may incorporate light strokes or deep massage, depending on the muscle involved.

Myotherapy

Similar to neuromuscular therapy (NMT) and using trigger points (see page 23), the aim of myotherapy is to eliminate pain and reeducate the muscles into healthy, pain-free patterns of movement. Myotherapy involves the use of knuckles, fingers, and elbows to press on trigger points, and stretching and exercises to unlearn painful habits.

Neuromuscular Therapy (NMT)

A combination of myofascial, trigger point, and deep cross-fiber techniques, NMT is designed to relieve acute or chronic pain by balancing the muscular and neurological aspects of body alignment. Applied to individual muscles, it is used to increase blood flow, release trigger points (see page 23), release pressure on nerves, and relieve pain.

On-Site Massage

In on-site massage, the therapist uses a specially designed chair to give employees a fifteen- to twenty-minute head, shoulder, and arm massage at the workplace, without disrobing or oils.

Orthobionomy

Gentle movements and comfortable positions, in harmony with the body's own preferred posture, are used in orthobionomy to relieve muscle tension and discomfort. Clients learn, under the guidance of a practitioner and through home exercises, to realign and reeducate nerves and muscles for the reduction of pain.

Oriental Massage/Amma

Amma is the traditional Japanese massage, which is much more commonly taught in Japan than shiatsu. Prior to World War II, it was traditionally performed by the blind. Like shiatsu, amma focuses on energy meridians and points called tsubos (sueboes). The thumbs are normally used for pressure, kneading, tapping, and rubbing. Unlike Swedish massage, Japanese massage doesn't use oils and may be performed through clothing, and whereas the strokes of Swedish massage move toward the heart, Japanese massage stresses movements away from the heart.

Polarity Therapy

Developed by Randolph Stone, an American osteopath, naturopath, and chiropractor, polarity therapy attempts to release obstructed energy flow and thereby reduce pain. (See page 27.)

Pregnancy Massage

Massage during pregnancy can help relieve fluid retention, improve muscle tone, and relieve the sore back, neck, and muscles that are often part of pregnancy. Shiatsu and massage of the abdomen are avoided, and large pillows are used for comfort.

Qigong

Qigong exercises are somewhat similar to tai chi chuan, a nonaerobic, rhythmical series of exercises. Qigong differs in that the exercises do not flow from one to another and are done in shorter movement groups repeated a number of times. But it is the accompanying mental effort that is crucial; during the exercises, one must concentrate on moving qi along the meridian pathways, and in so doing, increase the amount of qi to aid in healing.

Reflexology

In reflexology, deep pressure is applied to particular spots (or reflex points) on the hands or feet believed to correspond to particular organs and glands. One can visit a reflexologist for manipulation of only the feet and hands, or opt for the technique as part of a full-body massage (see page 28).

Reiki

One of the biofield therapies (see Therapeutic Touch, below), reiki (Japanese for "universal life force") was developed in Japan during the 1800s, but first appeared some 2,500 years ago in the Buddhist scriptures, the sutras. It was introduced into the United States in 1936. Using rituals, symbols, and spirit guides, the practitioner channels spiritual energy to heal the client's spiritual body, which in turn will heal the physical body. There is no massaging involved; practitioners simply hold or place their hands on the afflicted part and other key points for several minutes. One doesn't need a special spiritual gift to heal with reiki; anyone can learn to be a healer of others or of himself.

Rolfing/Structural Integration

Developed by Ida P. Rolf, Ph.D., during more than fifty years of study, Rolfing and structural therapy are systems of body manipulation and reeducation. The goal of the therapy is structural integration; that is, the balance and alignment of the body along a vertical axis. Withheld emotions, illness, surgery, and other actions can result in compression and distortion of the body; a properly aligned body can function more gracefully and effectively. The gospel of Rolfing, according to Ida Rolf herself, is that "When the body gets working appropriately, the force of gravity can flow through. Then, spontaneously, the body heals itself."[7]

The Rolfer or structural therapist uses thumbs, knuckles, and elbows in a deep, sometimes painful massage to manipulate connective tissue and realign the body by altering the length and tone of these tissues. This method requires ten sessions to complete.

Shiatsu

Shiatsu, a Japanese method of activating the flow of chi, involves the firm and prolonged pressing of prescribed points that lie along meridians by the practitioner's fingers, thumbs, hands, elbows, feet, or knees in a rhythmic (often painful) pattern. This may be accompanied by stroking that resembles a traditional massage, and with rotating joints to increase range of motion. The client remains clothed and lies on a hard massage table, exercise mat, or floor. Benefits include increased mental alertness, deep relaxation, and relief from muscle soreness.

Sports Massage

Techniques of Swedish massage, perhaps combined with other modalities, are used to relax an athlete before an event and to help speed recovery afterwards. Sports massage focuses on the stresses, injuries, or sore muscles caused by exercise or vigorous athletic performances.

Swedish Massage

The grandfather of the massage movement in this country, Swedish massage is what most of us think of when we hear "massage." Used to promote relaxation, improve circulation and range of motion, and relieve muscle tension, it was developed about 150 years ago by Peter Ling of Sweden, who combined ancient Oriental techniques and principles with modern physiology.

The five basic techniques used in Swedish massage are effleurage (long, soothing strokes), petrissage (squeezing and kneading the muscles), tapotement (a repetitive striking or drumming), vibration (a trembling movement of the hands and fingertips), and friction (a circular movement around joints and tendons). Oil is a must for a smooth, flowing massage. The client is generally undressed but draped with sheets for both warmth and modesty; only the part of the body being worked on is exposed.

Therapeutic Touch

Therapeutic touch, SHEN therapy, healing science, healing touch, or the laying on of hands are all considered biofield therapies, a type of healing that dates back some 5,000 years. In these therapies, a practitioner places his or her hands directly on or just slightly above the client's (usually clothed) body and merges his or her biofield with that of the client to promote general well-being or to help heal a specific ailment. Both client and healer may detect subtle changes in temperature, tingles, pressure, or other sensations. Some practitioners attribute the healing power to an outside source—God, the cosmos, or a higher power; others believe that the manipulation of the biofield is itself the healing mechanism. Therapeutic touch is best used for stress-related illnesses, pain relief, and relaxation prior to dental or surgical procedures.

Trager Method

Trager psychophysical integration was developed by a Hawaiian physician and former boxing trainer, Milton Trager. This method of movement reeducation employs light rocking, bouncing, and shaking movements to loosen joints and release chronic tension, as well as interrupting deep-seated psychophysiological patterns that project into body tissues. Another part of the method taught to clients, Trager Mentastics are mentally-directed physical movements designed to enhance flexibility and a feeling of freedom. Improvement has been reported in patients suffering from multiple sclerosis, lung disease, cerebral palsy, TMJ, recovery from stroke, and a host of other ailments.[8]

Trigger Point Therapy

When compressed by tense muscles, particularly sensitive nerve bundles, known as trigger points, can send referred pain to areas of the body far removed from the source. Trigger point therapists use finger pressure to relax the spastic muscle and relieve pain.

A CAREER IN MASSAGE THERAPY

It has been estimated that there are approximately 50,000 massage therapists practicing in the United States.[9]

Many states have no education or training requirements whatsoever for massage therapists; those states and provinces that do license massage therapists have varying requirements, from 250 hours of education in Texas to 2,200 hours in some Canadian provinces. Prospective students should be sure to look into the state and local requirements where they plan to practice before choosing a training program.

The American Massage Therapy Association (AMTA) is the largest accrediting organization in the field of massage education. The AMTA Commission on Massage Training Accreditation/Approval (COMTAA) uses a minimum 500-hour, six-month curriculum as its standard for approval. Only about one-fourth of the massage schools in the United States are accredited or approved by AMTA/COMTAA.

In 1992, the National Certification Board for Therapeutic Massage and Bodywork (NCBTMB) introduced a massage therapy certification exam. Since that time, more than 13,000 body therapists have passed the exam,[10] and six states use this exam as their licensing exam. Graduates must have completed at least 300 hours of formal education in order to take the exam.

A massage therapist can work in a variety of settings: health clubs, spas and resorts, cruise ships, in medical offices with chiropractors or physical therapists, for an athletic team or department, or most commonly, as an entrepreneur. More than two-thirds of all massage therapists are self-employed.

NAPRAPATHY

Naprapathy is the evaluation of persons with connective tissue disorders through the use of case history and palpation or treatment using connective tissue manipulation, postural and nutritional counseling, and assistive devices utilizing the properties of heat, cold, light, water, radiant energy, electricity, sound, and air. The practice includes the prevention and treatment of contractures, lesions, laxity, rigidity, structural imbalance, muscular atrophy, and other disorders.

Naprapathy was founded in 1905 by Oakley Smith, a graduate of the Palmer School of Chiropractic who was educated by D.D. Palmer, the founder of chiropractic. Dr. Smith conducted extensive research into the bony subluxation theory that was the heart of Palmer's philosophy, and through human dissection, histologic specimens, clinical observation, and patient record keeping, he found no scientific support for Palmer's theory. Rather, he found that the scarring and shortening of the soft connective tissue was the cause of many structural joint problems. Smith named his manipulative science "naprapathy," developed his own treatment system, wrote several books, and opened his own school in 1908.

Licensing generally requires that the applicant have graduated from a two-year, college-level program and be a graduate from a curriculum in naprapathy.

NATUROPATHY

Naturopathy, or naturopathic medicine, is not based on the treatment of specific symptoms or diseases, but on achieving a state of optimal wellness in which the body can not only heal itself of any current afflictions but also prevent the occurrence of illness in the future. Though considered alternative in the United States, this approach, like most other forms of natural health care, is nothing new—Hippocrates, considered the first naturopathic doctor, looked for the causes of disease in the air, water, or food that the patient ingested.

Naturopathy took hold in Europe and the United States in the eighteenth and nineteenth centuries. The first school of naturopathic medicine in the United States, founded in New York by Dr. Benedict Lust, graduated its first class in 1902; by the 1920s, there were more than twenty naturopathic colleges

in the country. Naturopathy fell out of favor around the 1940s, when allopathic medicine managed to eliminate virtually all conflicting modalities. However, in recent years, naturopathic medicine has staged a comeback, and there are now four colleges in North America devoted to increasing the number of naturopaths.

There are six philosophies that distinguish naturopathy from other forms of medical practice[1]:

1. The healing power of nature; that is, the body's natural ability to establish, maintain, and restore health. It is the physician's duty to assist in this natural, orderly healing process by removing obstacles to health.

2. Identify and treat the cause. An M.D. may have neither the time nor the interest to speculate as to why your hands break out in a scaly rash each October; it's quicker to prescribe a steroidal cream. An N.D., however, seeks out the causes underlying that nagging rash; perhaps it's that dye-filled Halloween candy or your mother-in-law's annual visit that triggers the flare-up. When the cause is known, the treatment can be much more effective.

3. First, do no harm. Symptoms are an expression of the body's efforts at healing; the suppression of symptoms without removing the underlying cause is considered harmful.

4. Treat the entire person. Physical, emotional, spiritual, mental, genetic, environmental, and social factors all contribute to a person's state of wellness and should all be taken into account by the physician.

5. The physician as teacher. The role of the physician is to educate the patient by showing him or her the relationships between actions and illnesses, thereby making the patient responsible for his or her own healing. The physician needs to inspire hope and be a catalyst for change.

6. Prevention. The ultimate goal of the naturopathic physician is to prevent disease through education and promotion of a healthy lifestyle.

In practice, naturopathic medicine is not so much a separate modality, but a combination of many of the most widely used forms of alternative therapy. In this way, an N.D. is the general practitioner of complementary medicine—a one-stop shop for a host of natural alternatives. The following are some of the N.D.'s commonly-used natural healing techniques.

Clinical nutrition, or diet therapy, is at the core of naturopathic medicine; even allopathic doctors recognize that a diet high in fats and sugars contributes to such illnesses as heart disease, diabetes, colitis, and premenstrual syndrome (PMS), among others. Naturopathy takes nutrition a step further by treating a wider variety of ailments—including eczema, depression, asthma, arthritis, and acne—with dietary changes and nutritional supplements.

Herbal remedies are also an important part of the naturopath's treatment plan. N.D.s are skilled herbologists familiar with the medicinal uses of plants, and they are likely to use herbs for illnesses from the common cold to AIDS.

Homeopathic medicine is another of the N.D.'s tools. Homeopathy uses extremely dilute formulations of substances that, were they given to the patient in a larger dose, would produce the same symptoms as the disease itself—the principle of "like cures like." Hippocrates noticed this effect in his studies of the actions of toxic herbs, and Hahnemann based homeopathy on this concept.

Acupuncture is used to stimulate the immune system through the insertion of fine needles into prescribed points along meridians, or energy pathways, in the body. In the West, acupuncture points may be stimulated with the traditional needles or with lasers, massage, or electrical pulses.

Physical medicine may include the therapeutic manipulation of bones and tissues, as well as hydrotherapy, ultrasound, massage, and exercise.

Psychological medicine such as hypnotherapy, counseling, stress management, and biofeedback may also be used or recommended by a naturopathic physician. As mental states can do much to produce either health or illness, these tools can be important in achieving a balanced emotional, and therefore physical, state.

Minor surgery can be performed by N.D.s in their offices. Such surgical procedures may include

stitching a wound, lancing a boil, or removing a foreign object.

Naturopathic physicians can also rely on X-rays, ultrasound, and other forms of diagnostic testing, but they generally do not perform major surgery or prescribe synthetic drugs.

A CAREER IN NATUROPATHIC MEDICINE

There are currently only four naturopathic colleges in operation in the United States and Canada that are recognized by the Council on Naturopathic Medical Education (CNME), a nationally recognized accrediting agency. Admission is competitive, and students are generally required to have completed all or the better part of a bachelor's degree, with an emphasis on premedical sciences.

Eleven states and four provinces have laws that specifically license or register naturopathic physicians, and N.D.s practice in virtually all of the remaining states and provinces under various legal provisions. Those states that license naturopathic physicians require graduation from an approved resident college program of 4,200 hours or more, and many require graduates to take the Naturopathic Physicians Licensing Exam (NPLEX), a national licensing examination, and/or another licensing exam.

NUTRITION

There's nothing alternative about nutrition; we all were taught about the four basic food groups (children today learn the food pyramid) by the elementary school nurse or health teacher. Many of us watch our fat grams, calories, or sodium intake, depending on our own personal afflictions and dearly-held beliefs. Everyone, from the medical establishment to the vegan, agrees that a bad diet leads to illness, and a good diet can prevent illness.

What we don't agree on, of course, is what constitutes a "good diet." Therefore, before you embark on a career in nutrition, you must be aware of the many belief systems out there and align your-self with one of them.

Conventional approaches to nutrition include the aforementioned food pyramid school of thought—all foods are more or less good, but the foods near the bottom of the pyramid (grains, fruits, and veg-etables) should be eaten in greater quantities than the fats, oils, and sweets at the top. Conventional nutrition is most of what we read in mainstream magazines, see on television, and get in menu form from our doctors in a usually belated attempt to stave off heart disease or diabetes. It's what most nutritional counselors are trained in; it's what most bachelor's or master's degree programs teach. And it's not at all alternative. In fairness, though, the world of nutrition is changing; vegetar-ianism is taught and practiced by many conven-tionally educated registered dietitians.

Alternative approaches to nutrition include many very different schools of thought, some of which are in direct opposition to one another. Vegetarian-ism, which eliminates the consumption of meat products, is probably the most widely known and accepted; in fact, the primarily vegetarian diet is the most common on the planet.[1] It can take the form of the lacto-ovo-vegetarian diet, which includes eggs and milk products, or the vegan diet, which in-cludes no animal products of any kind. In either case, the diet consists primarily of fruits and veg-etables, grains, legumes, nuts, and seeds. Through its elimination of meat, a vegetarian diet will reduce an individual's consumption of saturated fat and protein (unless excessive eggs and dairy products are consumed in its place), and increase fiber, vit-amins, minerals, and other important nutrients, par-ticularly if organically grown foods are chosen.

While there is not as much concern today about the combining of foods in order to obtain all the amino acids required to build proteins, there is still some concern that a strict vegetarian diet may re-sult in deficiencies of particular vitamins and min-erals, most notably vitamin B_{12}, iron, and zinc; for this reason some practitioners suggest a multivita-min and mineral supplement to their vegetarian clients. However, the health rewards of a vegetari-an diet are great—lower blood pressure, lower weight, and a reduced risk of cancer, heart dis-ease, diseases of the digestive tract, and osteo-porosis[2]—and are usually even more pronounced in the vegan diet.

The macrobiotic diet was brought to the United States from Japan by George Ohsawa and ex-panded upon by Michio and Aveline Kushi, founders of the Kushi Institute. Ohsawa's beliefs, as presented in *Essential Ohsawa,* are based on the concept that good air, water, and sunshine are necessary for life, and therefore the most important foods; other necessary foods such as whole grains, vegetables, beans, sea vegetables, and fish are products of these three basic foods.[3] Furthermore, the proper foods are those that are traditionally eaten, grown locally and in season, and that pro-vide a good balance of yin and yang. Whole grains provide the basis for each meal, and comprise 50 to 60 percent of the diet. Well-cooked vegetables and sea vegetables make up 20 to 25 percent of the diet; fresh fish is used in even smaller amounts, and dairy products, fruits, and nuts are used as pleasure foods. Drinks are to be used in the small-est quantity and only as dictated by thirst. Chewing should be thorough; each mouthful should be chewed at least fifty times, up to one hundred or 150 times. The macrobiotic diet contains adequate protein and nutrients, is low in fat and sugar, and would likely do much to improve the health of the average American.

Vitamin therapy is another approach to nutrition that is not exactly embraced by the American Med-ical Association, but is slowly winning converts. While many physicians still tell patients they don't need supplements if they eat a healthy diet, most Americans simply won't eat a healthy diet. Defi-ciencies can and do develop in both children and adults because of poor eating habits, dependence on processed and fast foods, overworked soils, and poor absorption; simply cooking some foods diminishes or depletes essential nutrients. Physi-cians, naturopathic and otherwise, can order tests to determine a patient's vitamin and mineral levels and correct the identified deficiencies; or, patients can educate themselves regarding the symptoms of deficiency (i.e., irregular heart rhythm as a symp-tom of magnesium deficiency[4], Meniere's Syn-drome as a symptom of a deficiency of the B vitamins[5]) and order tests only for the suspected deficiencies. Some physicians prefer to have their patients take the full range of vitamins, minerals, amino acids, and fatty acids instead of testing for individual deficiencies, which can be quite expensive. Consuming large quantities of particular nutrients in supplement form can, however, lead to an unbalanced, unhealthy nutritional state in which, for example, too much molybdenum causes a loss of copper, or too much manganese interferes with iron utilization.[6] For this reason, individuals should not take large quantities of individual supplements willy-nilly, but in a balanced fashion under the advice of a physician or other trained health care professional.

A CAREER IN NUTRITION

In contrast to conventional nutrition, there are very, very few schools that teach these alternative approaches. Many practitioners are licensed health care professionals who are self-taught in some aspect of nutrition or who have taken a course here or there; some may get a degree in conventional nutrition and swerve left after graduation, counseling clients in macrobiotics; and some learn the value of vitamin therapy in schools of naturopathy or the joys of macrobiotic cooking at a summer intensive.

The programs listed in this book offer several ways of beginning a career in alternative nutrition. Applicants should first be aware of the laws in their particular state regarding nutritional counseling and find a program that will meet their specific needs.

POLARITY THERAPY

Polarity therapy is an energetic approach to healing that recognizes that energy flows through and around the body in bipolar currents, and that blockage or imbalance of this energy flow results in disease. The approach was developed in the mid-twentieth century by Dr. Randolph Stone, a chiropractor, naturopath, and osteopathic physician who believed, "Energy is the real substance behind the appearance of matter and forms."[1] Stone combined insights common to Eastern energy-based healing practices, such as Ayurveda and Chinese medicine, with his extensive knowledge of Western medicine and structural manipulation to create a system of polarity-based bodywork.

Polarity theory holds that the head is the source of a positive pole and the feet of a negative pole; the right side of the body is positive and the left side is negative; the joints are neutral, permitting a crossover of energy currents.[2] The pulsation between the two poles provides the basis for life; this is Stone's Polarity Principle.[3] Stone also borrowed the Ayurvedic concept of the Five Elements—ether, air, fire, water, and earth—that correlate to five of the seven chakras, or energy centers, that occur throughout the body. Energy enters through the forehead via the third eye, flows through the chakras, and is then directed by the nervous system to the various muscles and organs.

The polarity therapist uses hands-on bodywork that ranges from a feather-light touch, to rocking and vibrating motions, to deep pressure that may leave the client sore. When energy is blocked, it may manifest as pain or tenderness; the practitioner places his or her left hand on the painful area and the right hand opposite it on the front, back, or side of the body. The rebalancing usually takes about an hour or more. During the treatment, the client is clothed and lies on a massage table.

Stone taught that each person must take responsibility for his or her own health, and that wellness can be achieved through some simple steps. For that reason, the polarity practitioner counsels the client in regard to diet, emphasizing vegetarianism as a means of promoting internal cleansing and well-being; exercise, using self-help energy techniques known as polarity yoga; and self-awareness, so that a client might become aware of sources of tension.

Because polarity therapy rebalances the flow of energy so that the body may better heal itself, it can be of value in the treatment of almost any ailment. The deeply relaxed state it produces can be of particular value in the treatment of migraines, cramps, digestive disorders, and stress-related problems.

A CAREER IN POLARITY THERAPY

The American Polarity Therapy Association (APTA) accredits schools and training programs based on their Standards for Practice. A practitioner must complete 155 hours of accredited training for certification as an Associate Polarity Practitioner (A.P.P.), and 615 hours of training for certification as a Registered Polarity Practitioner (R.P.P.).

Today there are over 600 APTA-certified polarity practitioners. Though in many cases an A.P.P. will work under an R.P.P., both may work independently. Licensing of polarity practitioners falls into a gray area of sorts: in some states, polarity is considered a form of massage and is subject to the same licensing requirements; in other states, it is essentially unregulated. Prospective students should consult with local regulatory agencies before signing up for any educational program, to be certain it will meet their career objectives.

REFLEXOLOGY

Far more than a foot massage, reflexology involves the application of pressure to areas of the feet and hands, called reflex areas, that are believed to correspond to specific organs, glands, and other parts of the body in an effort to relieve tension, improve blood flow, reduce pain, and unblock nerve impulses. The principles of reflexology are similar to acupuncture and acupressure in that the stimulation of specific points leads to an improvement in functioning in some distant area of the body.

Reflexology is the most popular form of alternative health care in Denmark, according to Dwight Byers, President of the International Institute of Reflexology.[1] While still relatively unknown here, the practice is catching on. Reflexology was first brought to the United States by William Fitzgerald, M.D., a laryngologist from Connecticut, who based

the system on European zone therapy. Fitzgerald found he could induce numbness and relieve symptoms in various parts of the body by applying pressure to specific points on the hands and mouth. Physiotherapist Eunice Ingham expanded the system, creating maps of the reflex areas of the feet and developing techniques for stimulating them.

Some reflexologists believe that because of their position, the feet are the most likely site for accumulated toxins; as blood pools in the feet and is pushed back up the leg, these toxins, most often uric acid crystals, are deposited in the feet. Reflexologists break up these crystals so that they may be recirculated and cleansed from the body.[2]

Others see reflexology more as an energetic healing system. Reflex zones are akin to meridians, with life energy or qi flowing through them; a blockage of this energy results in illness. By reducing tension and breaking up deposits, a reflexologist can restore the flow of energy and rebalance the body.

In a typical foot reflexology session, the client either sits on a chair or lies on a massage table, fully clothed except for his or her socks and shoes. The reflexologist, using powder, lotion, or nothing at all, will stroke the foot with his or her thumbs and fingers for up to an hour. Hand reflexology may also be performed.

Research has demonstrated the effectiveness of such stimulation of the hands and feet. Bill Flocco, founder of the American Academy of Reflexology, found a 62 percent reduction in symptoms of premenstrual syndrome (PMS) in those receiving reflexology treatment.[3] Other problems that are relieved by reflexology include anxiety, hypertension, or painful conditions anywhere in the body.[4]

A CAREER IN REFLEXOLOGY

Reflexology is practiced worldwide by over 25,000 certified practitioners; while some practice reflexology alone, it is also commonly used in conjunction with massage therapy, chiropractic, podiatry, and other alternative and conventional modalities. Many, if not most, massage schools include at least minimal instruction in reflexology in their curriculum, while a few schools devote their entire curriculum to the practice.

There is no national licensure for reflexologists, though practitioners may choose to be certified by the American Reflexology Certification Board (ARCB). In order to take the certification exam, applicants must have completed at least one hundred hours of education and submit thirty documentations, along with other requirements.

TRADITIONAL CHINESE MEDICINE

Traditional Chinese medicine (TCM) has been in use for over 3,000 years and is still used by one-fourth of the earth's population.[1] Its emphasis is on prevention—correcting disharmonies and imbalances before they manifest themselves in the form of disease. As the legendary Yellow Emperor of China told doctors, treating a patient when disease had already taken hold is "like digging a well only when one feels thirsty. Is it not already too late?"[2] In traditional Chinese medicine, patients are partners in healing; educating the patient regarding diet, exercise, and relaxation is essential to the cure.

In TCM, the human body is seen as a microcosm of the natural world. The air, sea, and land of the earth correspond to the energy and fluids of the body. Just as the earth can be parched and dry, so can our skin; as rivers can swell and become bloated, so too can our feet or abdomen—hence the references to inner dampness, dryness, heat, or cold. Health is affected by both the internal and external climates, so to remain healthy, we must strive for the three harmonies: harmony with nature (being in tune with the seasons), internal harmony (among the five main organs), and mental and physical harmony (avoiding emotional and physical extremes).[3]

One concept essential to the understanding of traditional Chinese medicine is that of yin and yang. Every event or entity has both a yin and a yang aspect. Yin refers to more permanent states, such as solidity, concreteness, and completion; yang refers to the active component and to more transitional states such as being, moving, changing, and developing.[4] In TCM, yin and yang refer to opposing physical conditions of the body: yin refers to the tissue of an organ, yang to its activity.

Qi, or chi, is a critical concept that is completely absent from Western medicine. Qi is the life force that flows throughout the body along certain prescribed pathways, or meridians, on the skin and through the internal organs. A blockage in the flow of qi can result in illness.

The Five Phase Theory, another important concept in Chinese medicine, holds that each organ either aids or detracts from the functioning of another organ. Ten organs are assigned to the five elements of fire, earth, metal, water, and wood, and, as each element acts on another in particular ways on the earth, so too does each organ act on another organ in predictable ways. For example, water quenches fire, so the kidneys (a water organ) control the heart (a fire organ). Organs are also divided into yin and yang groupings. Yin organs are the more solid, substantive organs such as the heart, liver, lungs, spleen, and kidneys; yang organs are hollow areas through which materials pass, such as the small and large intestines, stomach, bladder, and gallbladder.

When a TCM practitioner examines a patient, he or she is likely to inspect the tongue, complexion, demeanor, and body language; take an extensive medical history and ask the patient about diet and lifestyle; listen to the sound of the voice; smell the patient's body, breath, and any excretions; and take the pulse at the wrists, abdomen, and meridians. The practitioner is looking for excesses of heat, cold, wind, dampness, and dryness, and deficiencies of blood, moisture, and qi. Herbs and acupuncture are the primary means of resolving imbalances and replenishing blood, moisture, and qi.

Western TCM doctors typically use no more than 200 different herbs, though some 50,000 are held at the Institute of Materia Medica in Beijing.[5] Herbs are classified according to the Four Natures (cold, cool, warm, and hot); the Five Flavors (bitter, sweet, pungent, sour, and salty); and the Four Directions (rising, sinking, floating, or descending), as well as by the organs and meridians affected.[6] Every herb is also either yin or yang; yin herbs act internally with a downward motion, yang herbs rise upward and outward and act on the upper body, limbs, and skin. The actions of an herb are also affected by where it is grown and in what proportions it is used. Herbal remedies are used to treat a variety of symptoms, to regulate qi, to warm or cool, to expel dampness, and to otherwise regulate the internal environment.

Acupuncture, often thought to be synonymous with traditional Chinese medicine, originated some 5,000 years ago in China. It is an essentially painless procedure in which fine needles are inserted into several (usually just ten or twelve) of over 1,000 possible acupoints along the meridian system, helping to unblock the flow of qi, relieve pain, and restore health. Research conducted in the 1960s and 1970s has shown that radioactive isotopes and electrical currents did indeed flow along pathways that corresponded to the ancient Chinese meridians, and that 25 percent of acupuncture points lie along these proven meridians.[7] According to the World Health Organization, acupuncture has been successfully used to treat 104 conditions ranging from the common cold and tennis elbow to ulcers and paralysis.[8] It is particularly successful in pain relief and the treatment of addictions; this is no doubt due to the fact that acupuncture has been found to stimulate the release of endorphins, our body's natural painkillers. Proving that its success is not due to the placebo effect, veterinary acupuncture has been successful in relieving arthritic pain in 84 percent of animals.[9]

Acupuncture points are also used in other related therapies. Moxibustion, in which herbs are combusted on the skin above an acupoint, is often used in conjunction with acupuncture; the combination of these two techniques is referred to as acu-moxa-therapy. Laser acupuncture (which focuses a laser beam on acupoints), auriculotherapy (ear acupuncture that involves many more than the four classic acupoints of the ear), and acupressure or shiatsu (the application of pressure from a fingertip, pencil, or other blunt instrument to the acupoints) are other derivative therapies that have enjoyed varying de-

grees of success, but whose results are not thought to be as reliable as those of acupuncture itself.

A CAREER IN TRADITIONAL CHINESE MEDICINE

Traditional Chinese medicine has become fairly well established in the United States. Twenty-six states and the District of Columbia currently offer licensure for acupuncturists, and since 1984, over 4,700 acupuncture practitioners have been certified by the National Commission for the Certification of Acupuncturists (NCCA).

While the instruction itself is challenging, finding a school of acupuncture and Oriental medicine is not at all difficult. The National Accreditation Commission for Schools and Colleges of Acupuncture and Oriental Medicine (NACSCAOM) has accredited twenty-one schools in the United States; an additional twelve programs are candidates for accreditation. A master's degree program can generally be completed in three or four years of full-time study; applicants usually must have completed two years of college prior to enrollment.

VEDIC PSYCHOLOGY

The study of psychology at Maharishi International University, founded by Maharishi Mahesh Yogi, is based on a deep understanding of consciousness through both direct experience of the inner field of pure consciousness—through daily practice of transcendental meditation—and knowledge of the theoretical model of the Maharishi's Vedic psychology, which explores the full range of consciousness based on India's Vedic tradition. Students are taught to identify the deepest level of their own intelligence as the cosmic psyche, the fundamental intelligence underlying all of nature, and to recognize how it functions in their own psyche. Vocational psychology, psychophysiology, developmental psychology, and other fields are taught in terms of the Maharishi's theories.

Maharishi International University offers bachelor's- through doctorate-level programs in Vedic psychology; the faculty and students are currently developing a Vedic approach to counseling.

VETERINARY MASSAGE

Veterinary massage is just what it sounds like: the application of therapeutic massage to animals, most commonly horses, dogs, and cats. Like its counterpart in the human population, veterinary massage has been shown to aid recovery from injury and increase performance and endurance. While cat and dog massage is typically performed by owners on their own pets, equine sports massage (ESM) has far greater career potential.

According to the Tufts University School of Veterinary Medicine, the most likely cause of a horse's poor performance is a musculoskeletal problem. By increasing circulation and relieving stress and muscular tension, equine sports massage can improve performance and reduce the likelihood of injury for racehorses, barrel racers, jumpers, or just about any horse.

In an article in *Practical Horseman,* Equissage originator Mary Schreiber gives a brief description of her equine sports massage technique.[1] Schreiber explains that the only tools required are your fingers, thumbs, and palms; the backs of your hands; and your elbows and fists, which at times will require the pressure of your full body weight. The therapist palpates the entire horse, one side at a time, gently at first to warm up the area and then applying more pressure to find the knotted muscles. These spots are marked with liniment for further work that may include percussion, compression, cross-fiber friction, and other strokes. Massage not only makes the animal more relaxed and cooperative, but can also create a special bond between a horse and its owner.

A CAREER IN EQUINE SPORTS MASSAGE

While equine sports massage is a relatively new field, the demand for ESM therapists is growing. As individuals seek out alternative therapies for themselves, they are increasingly interested in the same type of care for their animals.

Training programs in ESM are few in number. Programs run two weeks or less and, while no additional training in massage is required, it is usually recommended that those seeking a full-time career in ESM attend a professional massage therapy school either before or after ESM training in order to bring maximum knowledge of technique and theory to their work. Experience with horses is generally required.

A national ESM survey taken in 1995 by Equissage, operators of a training program in Virginia, indicates that of those who had taken the training with the intention of starting an income-producing business, about 84 percent were successful in starting either a full- or part-time business; about 16 percent were unsuccessful due to lack of persistent effort or perceived lack of acceptance of ESM in that area.[2] The same survey indicated that the mid-Atlantic region was the most receptive to equine sports massage.

Currently, no state recognizes certification in equine sports massage. As with any other career in alternative health care, prospective students should check with their own city and county for any applicable local regulations.

YOGA

Not long ago, many of us viewed yoga as a hippie, counterculture nonexercise, perhaps okay for those with lots of time to contemplate their navels but certainly not anything we could squeeze into our own frenetic schedules. Over the past couple of decades we've progressed from jogging to aerobics to power walking to in-line skating, and though our thighs may be a little firmer, we're still as rushed and uptight as ever. It's no surprise, then, that a quiet revolution is taking hold in the fitness world, as more and more of us are turning to yoga to quiet our minds and relax our muscles—not to mention help us get in touch with our spiritual selves.

It's been estimated that between three and five million Americans now practice some form of yoga.[1] Yoga's increasing popularity is evident in the increased circulation of *Yoga Journal,* up some 60 percent between 1988 and 1993.[2] And while yoga exercises won't get your heart rate into your target zone, burn many calories, or get rid of the thirty pounds around your middle, the health benefits are very real. Not only have studies found that yoga can produce general health benefits, such as increased circulation, stronger immune systems, and reduced stress, but large percentages of individuals who have used yoga as a treatment for specific medical conditions have also reported positive effects. In a survey of 3,000 individuals conducted by the Yoga Biomedical Trust in the early 1980s, 98 percent of respondents with back pain claimed the practice of yoga was beneficial for them; the reported success rate was 94 percent for anxiety, 90 percent for arthritis, 84 percent for hypertension, 94 percent for heart disease, 90 percent for duodenal ulcers, 80 percent for diabetes, 90 percent for cancer, and 100 percent for alcoholism.[3]

Classical yoga follows an eightfold path that combines postures, breathing, and meditation to produce harmony between the mind, body, and spirit. Purification is also an important aspect of yoga, and takes the form of a vegetarian diet and cleansing and detoxification routines.

Most people are familiar with yoga in the form of hatha yoga postures, or asanas ("ease" in Sanskrit). Meditative asanas align the head and spine, promote blood flow, and aid relaxation. Therapeutic asanas, such as the shoulder stand and cobra positions, are used today to benefit back or joint pain and other specific medical conditions, though originally they served as another way to produce a meditative state. Either type of asana requires little movement but a great deal of mental discipline, allowing an openness that permits the free flow of prana, or life energy.

Pranayama is the regulation of the breath, and hence, of the prana that flows throughout the body. A calm mind will produce regular, rhythmic breathing, and, as we are all aware in times of fright or flight, an anxious mind produces irregular, agitated breathing. The goal of pranayama is a smooth, deep breath from the diaphragm rather than the shallow chest breathing in which so many of us unconsciously engage. Pranayama, like the asanas, serve as preparation for meditation.

Meditation makes up four of the eight limbs of yoga. Meditation has been embraced for thousands of years as a path to spiritual enlightenment, and for the past decade or two as an effective means of treating stress-related illnesses. In fact, in 1984 the National Institutes of Health recommended meditation—rather than medication—as the first line of treatment for mild hypertension.[4]

Meditation is often thought to be a state of not thinking, but that description is not entirely accurate. Meditation is more the training of the mind to concentrate only on the breath or a particular sound or phrase; as other thoughts enter our consciousness—about breakfast, the ache in our knees, or how long this is taking—they are briefly noticed and released, and we resume our concentration on the breath or phrase. Nobody said it was easy: Buddhists say the untrained mind is like a drunken monkey stung by a bee, and once aware, we find it remarkable how much clamor goes on in there day after day. After much daily practice, meditation can calm the mind and put us in touch with our higher selves.

The spiritual culmination of a long, disciplined meditation practice is samadhi, or spiritual realization. At this stage we enter a fourth state of consciousness, neither awake nor asleep nor dreaming.

There are a number of different schools of yoga, including Ashtanga, Iyengar, Sivananda, Kundalini, Kriya, and others, and each has a different emphasis.

A CAREER IN YOGA

Becoming a yoga instructor or yoga therapist involves much more personal dedication than some of the other fields of alternative health care. The prospective yoga instructor must not only attend a training program but must, on a daily basis, practice what he or she preaches. To be admitted to most teacher training programs, the student must have been practicing yoga—meaning asanas, pranayama, and meditation—daily for six months to a year or more; must abstain from drugs, alcohol, and tobacco; and must be committed to a vegetarian diet. Even after completing the teacher training course, which may take as little as a few weeks or as long as three years, the teacher is never finished learning; he or she must continue, even while teaching, to study under another and to continue his or her daily practice. In this sense, becoming a yoga teacher is more of a commitment to a lifestyle than just a career choice, and takes an extreme measure of dedication and perseverance.

PART TWO

The Schools & Programs of Alternative Medicine

The following section lists, alphabetically by state and within each state, schools that offer degree or certificate programs in various fields of alternative medicine. Classroom-based programs in the United States are listed first, followed by programs in Canada and a section called Multiple State Locations. These are schools that offer instruction in many different locations throughout the United States, Canada, and/or the world. The key to finding the school or program you need is the Listing of Programs by Field, located on page 41; just look under the desired field of study and you'll find an alphabetical, state-by-state listing of available programs. Scan the list for a state that you're interested in, check the name of the school, and locate its listing under that state in this section.

Following the state-by-state listing is the Self-Study Resources chapter. This chapter is arranged alphabetically by specialty and lists correspondence courses, periodicals, videos, and other materials that offer basic instruction, serve as handy reference sources, offer a unique perspective, provide ongoing education, or otherwise serve to familiarize you with a field of study. There is also a section on courses in alternative medicine that are now available at conventional medical schools.

CHOOSING A SCHOOL
OR PROGRAM

Prospective students of alternative health care should be every bit as careful in their selection of a school or training program as they would be in choosing a conventional college—perhaps more so. While it may be a bit more difficult to find reputable schools in the field of alternative medicine than it is to find such schools in more regulated fields, it's not a situation where you have to cross your fingers and hope for the best; there are guideposts along the way. Here are a few steps to getting a good return on your educational investment.

• Do some reading and educate yourself in the area in which you plan to specialize. Get a feel for the principles and philosophy, the diagnostic and treatment methods, and the job opportunities.

• Go for treatment. There's no better way to find out what an acupuncturist, massage therapist, or naturopathic physician really does than to become a patient. Visit more than one practitioner for a broader view.

• Contact your local Board of Health or other agencies to determine the licensing requirements in your area. In some states, a specific number of hours of education are required to practice.

• Talk to practitioners in your area to see which schools they would recommend. Ask them about specific schools you have in mind.

• Send for catalogs for all the schools in which you have even a remote interest. Compare programs between schools in your immediate area, and if circumstances permit, consider a longer commute or a relocation; convenience should not necessarily be your first criterion.

• Look at accreditations. In general, a school must be fairly well established, offer a quality program, and tolerate a good deal of paperwork and on-site scrutiny to be approved by the major accrediting agencies. No fly-by-night outfit will even try to get accredited. However, don't rule out a school just because it lacks major accreditation. Often, a school does not want to be locked in by the requirements of the accrediting agency, or the program is too short to meet the agency's standards, but still sufficient for licensing in that state.

• Compare program lengths. A one-hundred-hour massage program will have you practicing sooner, but what will you really know? Be sure the training is sufficient to meet your future needs. That one-hundred-hour program won't get you licensed in very many states.

• Look at the course schedules. Some programs may be taken part-time and/or evenings; others are strictly full-time days.

• If finances are an issue, see what the school offers for financial assistance. There is tremendous variation between schools in this area; one may offer scholarships, federal grants, and a variety of loans, while another may not have so much as a payment plan.

• Visit the school and get a feel for the place. Is it a warm, close-knit community or does it offer a cooler, more professional atmosphere? Do you feel comfortable there? Talk to the instructors and other students. If you can, get the names of recent graduates and ask how their training prepared them for a career.

THE TOP
SCHOOLS AND PROGRAMS

THE PRACTITIONER SURVEY

In order to give you a little additional guidance in selecting from the numerous schools offering instruction in any given specialty (and also to ensure that I didn't miss any of the really good ones), I conducted an informal survey of over one hundred licensed practitioners whose names were chosen at random from *The Alternative Medicine Yellow Pages*[1] and other sources. In this very brief survey, practitioners were asked to list what they considered to be the top five (or fewer) schools or programs in the United States and Canada in their area(s) of expertise. The results are tabulated below.

This survey does have its flaws. A practitioner who, unknown to me, teaches at or owns a particular institution will of course recommend it highly. Likewise, unless the school he or she attended was truly awful, a practitioner is likely to list his or her alma mater among the top. Even with these biases, however, the survey has merit—certain schools do appear again and again. While this is no surprise in a field such as naturopathy, where there are only four schools to choose from, it's more meaningful in a field like massage therapy, where the choices are far more numerous. It's also significant that practitioners from California to Maine were recommending many of the same schools.

The categories of hypnotherapy, herbal medicine, and Ayurveda were eliminated after the survey was conducted because, in the cases of hypnotherapy and herbal medicine, most of the programs recommended were too minor even to be included in the book; in the case of Ayurveda, there is no training available in the United States or Canada that would fully prepare one to become an Ayurvedic physician. Be assured that many fine, reputable schools are not on this list. Do not worry if a school that interests you is not listed—remember, this was an extremely small survey. Please do not hesitate to attend a school that you've investigated and found highly desirable simply because it doesn't appear here.

INTERPRETING THE RESULTS

The schools are listed below in the order of how many votes they received; a school listed first within a category received the most votes, and so on. Schools that were mentioned on a practitioner survey but do not appear in this book because they don't meet my criteria were not included in the survey results. In those instances in which schools and/or programs tied, they share the same numerical position in the listings.

CHIROPRACTIC

1. Palmer College of Chiropractic, IA
2. National College of Chiropractic, IL
3. Parker Chiropractic College, TX
   Western States Chiropractic College, OR
4. Canadian Memorial Chiropractic College, ON

5. New York Chiropractic College, NY
6. Life Chiropractic College, GA
   Los Angeles College of Chiropractic, CA
   Sherman College of Straight Chiropractic, SC
7. Palmer College of Chiropractic West, CA
   Logan College of Chiropractic, MO
8. Cleveland Chiropractic College, MO
9. Texas Chiropractic College, TX
10. Northwestern College of Chiropractic, MN

HOMEOPATHY

1. Hahnemann College of Homeopathy, CA
2. International Foundation for Homeopathy, WA
3. Bastyr University, WA
4. New England School of Homeopathy, MA
   Pacific Academy of Homeopathic Medicine, CA
5. Homeopathic College of Canada, ON
   National College of Naturopathic Medicine, OR
6. National Center for Homeopathy, VA
7. The British Institute of Homeopathy (correspondence), CA
8. Canadian Academy of Homeopathy, ON
   Atlantic Academy of Classical Homeopathy, NY

MASSAGE AND BODYWORK

1. The Trager Institute, CA
2. International Alliance of Healthcare Educators, FL
3. Lehigh Valley Healing Arts Academy, PA

4. Brian Utting School of Massage, WA
5. Boulder School of Massage Therapy, CO
   Swedish Institute School of Massage Therapy and Allied Health Sciences, NY
6. Alexandar School of Natural Therapeutics, WA
7. Colorado School of Healing Arts, CO
8. Acupressure Institute, CA
   Bancroft School of Massage Therapy, MA
   Integrative Therapy School, CA
   Jin Shin Jyutsu, AZ
   Kalamazoo Center for the Healing Arts, MI
   Kripalu Center for Yoga and Health, MA
   The Massage Institute of Memphis, TN
   Massage Therapy Institute of Colorado, CO
   The New Center for Wholistic Health Education and Research, NY
   Self-Health, Inc., School of Medical Massage, OH
   Seminar Network International School of Massage and Allied Therapies, FL
   Twin Lakes College of the Healing Arts, CA
9. International School of Shiatsu, PA
   Pacific College of Oriental Medicine, CA
   Harold J. Reilly School of Massotherapy, VA
10. Brenneke School of Massage, WA
11. Polarity Wellness, NY

NATUROPATHY

1. Bastyr University, WA
2. National College of Naturopathic Medicine, OR
3. Southwest College of Naturopathic Medicine and Health Sciences, AZ
4. The Canadian College of Naturopathic Medicine, ON

TRADITIONAL CHINESE MEDICINE/ACUPUNCTURE

1. New England School of Acupuncture, MA
2. Northwest Institute of Acupuncture and Oriental Medicine, WA

   Pacific College of Oriental Medicine, CA
3. Emperor's College of Traditional Oriental Medicine, CA
4. Oregon College of Oriental Medicine, OR
5. Tri-State Institute of Traditional Chinese Acupuncture, NY
6. Traditional Acupuncture Institute, MD
7. Five Branches Institute, CA

   Samra University of Oriental Medicine, CA
8. Academy of Chinese Culture and Health Sciences, CA
9. International Institute of Chinese Medicine, NM

   South Baylo University, CA

   Yo San University, CA
10. Pacific Institute of Oriental Medicine, NY
11. American College of Traditional Chinese Medicine, CA

YOGA

1. Sivananda Ashrams, PQ
2. Satchidananda Ashram—Yogaville, VA
3. B.K.S. Iyengar Yoga Institute of Los Angeles, CA
4. Himalayan International Institute of Yoga Science and Philosophy, PA

   Kripalu Center for Yoga and Health, MA

LISTING OF PROGRAMS BY FIELD

This section will help you find the programs that interest you; look under the desired field of study and you'll see an alphabetical, state-by-state listing of available programs. Scan the list for a state that you're interested in, check the name of the school, and locate its listing under that state in the Profiles of Schools and Programs. Schools in the United States are listed first, followed by Canadian schools and schools that offer instruction in more than one location (Multiple State Locations). The schools in this listing are all classroom-based programs; correspondence courses are listed on page 358.

ACUPRESSURE

CALIFORNIA

Academy of Chinese Culture and Health Sciences
Acupressure Institute
Desert Resorts School of Somatherapy
Emperor's College of Traditional Oriental Medicine
Heartwood Institute
Integrative Therapy School
Jin Shin Do Foundation for Bodymind Acupressure
Mueller College of Holistic Studies
Royal University of America
Taoist Sanctuary of San Diego

MASSACHUSETTS

New England Institute for Integrative Acupressure

MULTIPLE STATE LOCATIONS

DoveStar Institute

ACUPUNCTURE

(*See also* ORIENTAL MEDICINE)

ARIZONA

Southwest College of Naturopathic Medicine and Health Sciences

FLORIDA

Worsley Institute of Classical Acupuncture

MARYLAND

Traditional Acupuncture Institute

MASSACHUSETTS

New England School of Acupuncture

MINNESOTA

Minnesota Institute of Acupuncture
　and Herbal Studies

NEW YORK

The New Center for Wholistic Health Education
　and Research

Tri-State Institute of Traditional Chinese
　Acupuncture

TEXAS

Academy of Oriental Medicine

WASHINGTON

Bastyr University

Northwest Institute of Acupuncture
　and Oriental Medicine

WISCONSIN

Midwest Center for the Study of Oriental Medicine

CANADA

ONTARIO

Shiatsu School of Canada

MULTIPLE STATE LOCATIONS

American Academy of Medical Acupuncture

Pacific College of Oriental Medicine/
　Pacific Institute of Oriental Medicine

AROMATHERAPY

COLORADO

Artemis Institute of Natural Therapies

CONNECTICUT

Connecticut Institute for Herbal Studies

FLORIDA

The Atlantic Institute of Aromatherapy

NEW JERSEY

Morris Institute of Natural Therapeutics

NEW YORK

New York Open Center

MULTIPLE STATE LOCATIONS

The Michael Scholes School for Aromatic Studies

AYURVEDA

CALIFORNIA

Mount Madonna Center

COLORADO

Rocky Mountain Institute of Yoga and Ayurveda

IOWA

Maharishi International University

NEW MEXICO

The Ayurvedic Institute

NEW YORK

Ayurveda Holistic Center

WASHINGTON

Sri Chinmoy Institute of Ayurvedic Sciences

BIOFEEDBACK

MULTIPLE STATE LOCATIONS

Stens Corporation

CHIROPRACTIC

CALIFORNIA

Cleveland Chiropractic College of Los Angeles
Life Chiropractic College West
Los Angeles College of Chiropractic
Palmer College of Chiropractic West

CONNECTICUT

University of Bridgeport College of Chiropractic

GEORGIA

Life College School of Chiropractic

ILLINOIS

National College of Chiropractic

IOWA

Palmer College of Chiropractic

MINNESOTA

Northwestern College of Chiropractic

MISSOURI

Cleveland Chiropractic College

MONTANA

Logan College of Chiropractic

NEW YORK

New York Chiropractic College

OREGON

Western States Chiropractic College

SOUTH CAROLINA

Sherman College of Straight Chiropractic

TEXAS

Parker College of Chiropractic
Texas Chiropractic College

CANADA

ONTARIO

Canadian Memorial Chiropractic College

CHIROPRACTIC ACUPUNCTURE

COLORADO

Colorado School of Healing Arts

CHIROPRACTIC ASSISTANT/ PARAPROFESSIONAL

CALIFORNIA

Los Angeles College of Chiropractic

GEORGIA

Life College School of Chiropractic

ILLINOIS

National College of Chiropractic

MINNESOTA

Northwestern College of Chiropractic

PENNSYLVANIA

Pennsylvania Institute of Massage Therapy

TEXAS

Parker College of Chiropractic

COLONIC IRRIGATION THERAPY

FLORIDA

Florida School of Massage
Seminar Network International

ENERGETIC HEALING

CALIFORNIA

Diamond Light School of Massage
  and Healing Arts

MICHIGAN

Health Enrichment Center

MISSOURI

Massage Therapy Training Institute L.L.C.

ENVIRONMENTAL MEDICINE

MULTIPLE STATE LOCATIONS

American Academy of Environmental Medicine

FLOWER ESSENCE PRACTITIONER

CALIFORNIA

Flower Essence Society

GUIDED IMAGERY

CALIFORNIA

Academy for Guided Imagery

HERBOLOGY

CALIFORNIA

The California School of Herbal Studies

Dry Creek Herb Farm and Learning Center
East West School of Herbalism

COLORADO

Artemis Institute of Natural Therapies
Rocky Mountain Center for Botanical Studies

CONNECTICUT

Connecticut Institute for Herbal Studies

ILLINOIS

Northern Prairie Center for Education
    and Healing Arts

MAINE

Avena Botanicals

MASSACHUSETTS

Blazing Star Herbal School
Ellen Evert Hopman
New England School of Acupuncture

MONTANA

Rocky Mountain Herbal Institute

NEW MEXICO

The National College of Phytotherapy
The New Mexico Herb Center

NEW YORK

Green Terrestrial
The New Center for Wholistic Health Education
    and Research
New York Open Center
Susun S. Weed/Wise Woman Center
Tri-State Institute of Traditional Chinese
    Acupuncture

OREGON

The American Herbal Institute

UTAH

School of Natural Healing

VERMONT

Sage Mountain Herbal Retreat Center

WASHINGTON

Bastyr University
Northwest Institute of Acupuncture
    and Oriental Medicine

WISCONSIN

Wisconsin Institute of Chinese Herbology
Wisconsin Institute of Natural Wellness

CANADA

BRITISH COLUMBIA

Coastal Mountain College of Healing Arts
Dominion Herbal College

HOLISTIC HEALTH PRACTITIONER/ EDUCATION/COUNSELING

CALIFORNIA

California Institute of Integral Studies
Desert Resorts School of Somatherapy
Heartwood Institute
International Professional School of Bodywork
John F. Kennedy University Graduate School
    for Holistic Studies
Mueller College of Holistic Studies
Pacific College of Oriental Medicine
School of Healing Arts

MASSACHUSETTS

Kripalu Center for Yoga and Health

OHIO

Ohio Academy of Holistic Health

MULTIPLE STATE LOCATIONS

DoveStar Institute

CANADA

BRITISH COLUMBIA

Coastal Mountain College of Healing Arts

HOLISTIC NURSING

NEW YORK

The New Center for Wholistic Health Education and Research

HOMEOPATHY

CALIFORNIA

Hahnemann College of Homeopathy
Pacific Academy of Homeopathic Medicine
Santa Barbara Center for Homeopathic Arts

COLORADO

Colorado Institute for Classical Homeopathy

MAINE

Northwestern School of Homeopathy

NEW JERSEY

Five Elements Center

NEW YORK

Atlantic Academy of Classical Homeopathy
Teleosis School of Homeopathy

VERMONT

National Center for Homeopathy

WASHINGTON

Bastyr University
International Foundation for Homeopathy

CANADA

BRITISH COLUMBIA

Vancouver Homeopathic Academy

ONTARIO

Homeopathic College of Canada

MULTIPLE STATE LOCATIONS

Canadian Academy of Homeopathy
National Institute of Classical Homeopathy
New England School of Homeopathy

HYPNOTHERAPY

ARIZONA

Wesland Institute, Inc.

CALIFORNIA

Alchemy Institute of Healing Arts

Alive and Well! Institute of Conscious BodyWork
Diamond Light School of Massage and Healing Arts
Heartwood Institute
Hypnosis Motivation Institute
School of Healing Arts
Twin Lakes College of the Healing Arts
Valley Hypnosis Center

ILLINOIS

Midwest Training Institute of Hypnosis

MICHIGAN

Infinity Institute International, Inc.

NEW JERSEY

East West Institute for Wholistic Studies

OHIO

Ohio Academy of Holistic Health

VERMONT

Eastern Institute of Hypnotherapy

WASHINGTON

Institute for Therapeutic Learning

MULTIPLE STATE LOCATIONS

DoveStar Institute
The Wellness Institute

INDEPENDENT STUDY DEGREE PROGRAMS

MASSACHUSETTS

Lesley College

VERMONT

Vermont College of Norwich University

INTEGRATIVE MEDICINE

ARIZONA

Program in Integrative Medicine/University
of Arizona

IRIDOLOGY

MULTIPLE STATE LOCATIONS

National Iridology Research Association

MASSAGE THERAPY

(*See also* MASSAGE/BODYWORK SPECIALTIES;
QIGONG; REFLEXOLOGY; REIKI; SHIATSU)

ARIZONA

Arizona School of Integrative Studies
Desert Institute of the Healing Arts
Phoenix Therapeutic Massage College
RainStar School of Therapeutic Massage

ARKANSAS

White River School of Massage

CALIFORNIA

Alive and Well! Institute of Conscious BodyWork

American Institute of Massage Therapy
Body Therapy Center
California Institute of Massage and Spa Services
Central California School of Body Therapy
Desert Resorts School of Somatherapy
Diamond Light School of Massage and Healing Arts
Emperor's College of Traditional Oriental Medicine
Esalen Institute
Heartwood Institute
Integrative Therapy School
International Professional School of Bodywork
Monterey Institute of Touch
Mueller College of Holistic Studies
National Holistic Institute
Pacific College of Oriental Medicine
Phillips School of Massage
reSource
School of Healing Arts
School of Shiatsu and Massage
    at Harbin Hot Springs
Twin Lakes College of the Healing Arts

COLORADO

Academy of Natural Therapy
Boulder School of Massage Therapy
Colorado Institute of Massage Therapy
Colorado School of Healing Arts
Crestone Healing Arts Center
Massage Therapy Institute of Colorado

CONNECTICUT

Connecticut Center for Massage Therapy

DISTRICT OF COLUMBIA

Potomac Massage Training Institute

FLORIDA

Core Institute
Educating Hands School of Massage

Florida Institute of Massage Therapy
    and Esthetics
Florida School of Massage
Humanities Center Institute of Allied Health
    School of Massage
Sarasota School of Massage Therapy
Seminar Network International
Southeastern School of Neuromuscular
    and Massage Therapy, Inc.
Suncoast School

GEORGIA

Academy of Somatic Healing Arts
Atlanta School of Massage
Lake Lanier School of Massage

HAWAII

Hawaiian Islands School of Body Therapies
Honolulu School of Massage

IDAHO

Idaho Institute of Wholistic Studies

ILLINOIS

Chicago School of Massage Therapy
LifePath School of Massage Therapy
Northern Prairie Center for Education
    and Healing Arts
Redfern Training Systems School of Massage
Wellness and Massage Training Institute

INDIANA

Alexandria School of Scientific Therapeutics
Lewis School and Clinic of Massage Therapy

IOWA

Carlson College of Massage Therapy

LOUISIANA

Blue Cliff School of Therapeutic Massage

MAINE

Downeast School of Massage

MARYLAND

Baltimore School of Massage

MASSACHUSETTS

Bancroft School of Massage Therapy
Massage Institute of New England
Muscular Therapy Institute
Polarity Realization Institute
Stillpoint Center School of Massage

MICHIGAN

Kalamazoo Center for the Healing Arts
Lansing Community College
Michigan Institute of Myomassology

MINNESOTA

Northern Lights School of Massage Therapy

MISSOURI

Massage Therapy Training Institute L.L.C.

NEW HAMPSHIRE

North Eastern Institute of Whole Health

NEW JERSEY

Health Choices Center for the Healing Arts
Morris Institute of Natural Therapeutics
Somerset School of Massage Therapy

NEW MEXICO

Crystal Mountain Apprenticeship in the
    Healing Arts
The Medicine Wheel
New Mexico Academy of Healing Arts
New Mexico School of Natural Therapeutics
The Scherer Institute of Natural Healing
Taos School of Massage

NEW YORK

Finger Lakes School of Massage
The New Center for Wholistic Health Education
    and Research
Swedish Institute School of Massage Therapy
    and Allied Health Sciences

NORTH CAROLINA

Body Therapy Institute
Carolina School of Massage Therapy

OHIO

Central Ohio School of Massage
Self-Health, Inc., School of Medical Massage

OKLAHOMA

Oklahoma School of Natural Healing
Praxis College of Health Arts and Sciences

OREGON

Ashland Massage Institute
Cascade Institute of Massage
    and Body Therapies
East-West College of the Healing Arts

PENNSYLVANIA

Career Training Academy
East-West Therapeutic Massage
Lehigh Valley Healing Arts Academy
Mt. Nittany School of Massage
Pennsylvania Institute of Massage Therapy
Pennsylvania School of Muscle Therapy

SOUTH CAROLINA

Pinewood School of Massage Therapy

TENNESSEE

Cumberland Institute for Wellness Education
The Massage Institute of Memphis

Middle Tennessee Institute of Therapeutic Massage
Tennessee Institute of Healing Arts

TEXAS

Academy of Oriental Medicine
Austin School of Massage Therapy
Hands-On Therapy School of Massage
The Institute of Natural Healing Sciences, Inc.
The Lauterstein-Conway Massage School
Phoenix School of Holistic Health
The Winters School, Inc.

UTAH

Myotherapy College of Utah
Utah College of Massage Therapy

VERMONT

The Vermont School of Professional Massage

VIRGINIA

Fuller School of Massage Therapy
Harold J. Reilly School of Massotherapy
Richmond Academy of Massage
Virginia School of Massage

WASHINGTON

Alexandar School of Natural Therapeutics
Brenneke School of Massage
Brian Utting School of Massage
Seattle Massage School
Spectrum Center School of Massage
Tri-City School of Massage

WEST VIRGINIA

Mountain State School of Massage

WISCONSIN

Blue Sky Educational Foundation
Lakeside School of Natural Therapeutics
Wisconsin Institute of Natural Wellness

CANADA

ALBERTA

Massage Therapy Training Institute

ONTARIO

Canadian College of Massage and Hydrotherapy
Kikkawa College
Sutherland-Chan School and Teaching Clinic

QUEBEC

Le Centre Psycho-Corporel

MULTIPLE STATE LOCATIONS

Asten Center of Natural Therapeutics
DoveStar Institute
Health Enrichment Center
New Hampshire Institute for Therapeutic Arts

MASSAGE/BODYWORK SPECIALTIES AND ADVANCED TRAINING

(*See also* MASSAGE THERAPY; QIGONG;
REFLEXOLOGY; REIKI; SHIATSU)

ARIZONA

Bonnie Prudden School for Physical Fitness
and Myotherapy

CALIFORNIA

The Institute for Health Improvement
International Professional School of Bodywork
Reese Movement Institute, Inc.

COLORADO

The Rolf Institute of Structural Integration

FLORIDA

Center for Life Energy
Florida Institute of Psychophysical Integration

MASSACHUSETTS

Kripalu Center for Yoga and Health

NEVADA

Aston-Patterning

NEW YORK

Omega Institute
The Rubenfeld Center

WASHINGTON

Soma Institute

CANADA

ONTARIO

Feldenkrais Institute of Somatic Education

MULTIPLE STATE LOCATIONS

BioSomatics
Day-Break Geriatric Massage Project
Dr. Vodder School—North America
Feldenkrais Resources
Hellerwork International
Institute for Awareness in Motion
International Alliance of Health Care Educators
Jin Shin Jyutsu, Inc.
Myofascial Release Treatment Centers
   and Seminars
Ohashi Institute
The School for Body-Mind Centering
School for Self-Healing
The Trager Institute
Wyrick Institute for European Manual
   Lymph Drainage

NAPRAPATHY

ILLINOIS

Chicago National College of Naprapathy

NATUROPATHY

ARIZONA

Southwest College of Naturopathic Medicine
   and Health Sciences

OREGON

National College of Naturopathic Medicine

WASHINGTON

Bastyr University

CANADA

ONTARIO

The Canadian College of Naturopathic Medicine

NUTRITION

CALIFORNIA

Los Angeles East West Center for
   Macrobiotic Studies

School of Healing Arts
Vega Institute

MASSACHUSETTS

Kushi Institute

NEW YORK

Gulliver's Living and Learning Center
Institute for Food and Health
The Natural Gourmet Cookery School/
   The Natural Gourmet

WASHINGTON

Bastyr University

CANADA

ONTARIO

Canadian School of Natural Nutrition
East West Centre

ORIENTAL MEDICINE

CALIFORNIA

Academy of Chinese Culture and Health Sciences
American College of Traditional Chinese Medicine
Emperor's College of Traditional Oriental Medicine
Five Branches Institute
Meiji College of Oriental Medicine
Royal University of America
Samra University of Oriental Medicine
Santa Barbara College of Oriental Medicine
South Baylo University
Yo San University

COLORADO

Colorado School of Traditional Chinese Medicine

FLORIDA

Atlantic Institute of Oriental Medicine
Florida Institute of Traditional Chinese Medicine

HAWAII

Tai Hsuan Foundation College of Acupuncture
   and Herbal Medicine
Traditional Chinese Medical College of Hawaii

MARYLAND

Maryland Institute of Traditional Chinese Medicine

MINNESOTA

Minnesota Institute of Acupuncture
   and Herbal Studies

NEW MEXICO

International Institute of Chinese Medicine
Southwest Acupuncture College

NEW YORK

The New Center for Wholistic Health Education
   and Research

OREGON

Oregon College of Oriental Medicine

TEXAS

Academy of Oriental Medicine
American College of Acupuncture
   and Oriental Medicine
Texas Institute of Traditional Chinese Medicine

WASHINGTON

Bastyr University

MULTIPLE STATE LOCATIONS

Pacific College of Oriental Medicine
Pacific Institute of Oriental Medicine

PERSONAL TRAINER/ WELLNESS CONSULTANT

MISSOURI

Massage Therapy Training Institute L.L.C.

POLARITY THERAPY

CALIFORNIA

Heartwood Institute
Polarity Healing Arts of Santa Monica
Polarity Therapy Center of Marin

COLORADO

Polarity Center of Colorado

FLORIDA

Center for Life Energy
Florida School of Massage

MAINE

Polarity Institute

NEW MEXICO

New Mexico Academy of Healing Arts
Wellness Institute

NEW YORK

The Linden Tree Center for Wholistic Health
New York Open Center
Polarity Wellness Network of New York
Reese Williams, L.Ac., R.P.P.

NORTH CAROLINA

Body Therapy Institute

VIRGINIA

The Polarity Center

CANADA

ONTARIO

Reaching Your Potential

MULTIPLE STATE LOCATIONS

Health Training Group
Polarity Realization Institute

QIGONG

MULTIPLE STATE LOCATIONS

East West Academy of Healing Arts/
 Qigong Institute

REFLEXOLOGY

COLORADO

Colorado School of Healing Arts

FLORIDA

Florida School of Massage

ILLINOIS

Redfern Training Systems School of Massage

NEW YORK

New York Open Center

OHIO

Ohio Academy of Holistic Health

MULTIPLE STATE LOCATIONS

International Institute of Reflexology

REIKI

CALIFORNIA

Diamond Light School of Massage
  and Healing Arts

MICHIGAN

The Center for Reiki Training

NEW YORK

The Linden Tree Center for Wholistic Health

TENNESSEE

Reiki Plus Institute

MULTIPLE STATE LOCATIONS

DoveStar Institute

SHIATSU

(*See also* MASSAGE THERAPY,
MASSAGE/BODYWORK SPECIALTIES)

ARIZONA

Desert Institute of the Healing Arts

CALIFORNIA

Acupressure Institute
Body Therapy Center
Santa Barbara College of Oriental Medicine
School of Shiatsu and Massage at
  Harbin Hot Springs
Shiatsu Massage School of California

HAWAII

Aisen Shiatsu School

MICHIGAN

Health Enrichment Center

NEW JERSEY

Associates for Creative Wellness School
  of Asian Healing Arts
Morris Institute of Natural Therapeutics

NEW YORK

Swedish Institute School of Massage Therapy
  and Allied Health Sciences

PENNSYLVANIA

Career Training Academy
East-West Therapeutic Massage
Pennsylvania Institute of Massage Therapy

CANADA

ONTARIO

Shiatsu Academy of Tokyo
Shiatsu School of Canada

TUI NA

(*See* Acupressure)

VEDIC PSYCHOLOGY

IOWA

Maharishi International University

VETERINARY ACUPRESSURE

FLORIDA

Equine Sports Massage Program

VETERINARY ACUPUNCTURE

MULTIPLE STATE LOCATIONS

International Veterinary Acupuncture Society

VETERINARY MASSAGE/ BODYWORK

FLORIDA

Equine Sports Massage Program
Seminar Network International

OHIO

Optissage, Inc.

VIRGINIA

Equissage

MULTIPLE STATE LOCATIONS

DoveStar Institute

YOGA TEACHER TRAINING/ YOGA THERAPY

CALIFORNIA

B.K.S. Iyengar Yoga Institute of Los Angeles
Mount Madonna Center
Yoga College of India

COLORADO

Day-Star Method of Yoga
Rocky Mountain Institute of Yoga and Ayurveda
Shambhava School of Yoga

FLORIDA

Yogi Hari and Leela Mata Ashram

MARYLAND

The Yoga Center

MASSACHUSETTS

American Yoga College
Kripalu Center for Yoga and Health

NEW JERSEY

Associates for Creative Wellness School
of Asian Healing Arts

NEW YORK

Omega Institute

PENNSYLVANIA

Himalayan International Institute of Yoga Science
and Philosophy

VIRGINIA

Satchidananda Ashram—Yogaville

WASHINGTON

The Center for Yoga of Seattle
Yoga Centers
Yoga Northwest

CANADA

BRITISH COLUMBIA

Yasodhara Ashram

MULTIPLE STATE LOCATIONS

3HO International Kundalini Yoga
Teachers Association
American Yoga Association
DoveStar Institute
Integrative Yoga Therapy
Maui School of Yoga Therapy
Phoenix Rising Yoga Therapy
Sinvananda Ashram Yoga Camp

PROFILES OF SCHOOLS AND PROGRAMS

ARIZONA

Arizona School of Integrative Studies

753 North Main Street
Cottonwood, Arizona 86326
Phone: (520) 639-3455

The Arizona School of Integrative Studies (ASIS) was founded in January 1996 by Jamie and Joseph Rongo and Nancy Matthews, all formerly of the Florida School of Massage.

Accreditation

While the school is too new to be accredited by the American Massage Therapy Association, which requires that a school be in operation for two years prior to applying for approval, the curriculum was designed to meet the requirements for AMTA approval. ASIS graduates are qualified to take the national certification exam, and ASIS is approved by the National Certification Board for Therapeutic Massage and Bodywork (NCBTMB) as a continuing education provider.

Program Description

The 650-hour Massage and Hydrotherapy Training Program consists of 312 hours of massage modalities, 208 hours of conjunctive course studies, and 130 additional hours. Massage modalities include Swedish Massage, Connective Tissue Massage, Reflexology, Neuromuscular Therapy, Shiatsu, Integration, Polarity Therapy, Sports Massage, Connective Tissue Therapy, Awareness and Integrative Massage, and Review. Conjunctive course studies include Anatomy and Physiology, Kinesiology and Palpation, Hydrotherapy, Nutrition, Herbology, Homeopathy, Communication Skills, Life Skills (CPR and HIV), Business and Arizona Law, and Review. Additional hours are required in orientation, massage journals, and community outreach. Classes are held five days per week.

Continuing Education

Continuing education workshops for massage and bodywork professionals include Present Centered Awareness Therapy, Connective Tissue Therapy, Aromatic Impressions: The Art and Science of Aromatherapy, Soft Tissue Injuries for Runners, Orthobionomy, Advanced Sports Massage, Process Oriented Polarity Therapy, Structural Integration, and others.

Admission Requirements

Applicants must be at least 18 years of age (this requirement may be waived through a personal interview), have a high school diploma or equivalent, submit a self-recommendation, and interview with an admissions representative.

Tuition and Fees

Application fee, $50; student packet, $30; tuition, $5,000; optional massage table, $300 to $600; books (approximate), $175; oils and linens are additional.

Financial Assistance

Payment plans may be arranged if needed.

Bonnie Prudden School for Physical Fitness and Myotherapy

7800 East Speedway
Tucson, Arizona 85710
Phone: (520) 529-3979 / (800) 221-4634
Fax: (520) 722-6311

Bonnie Prudden established the first institute for physical fitness in the country in 1945 after realizing how little exercise the public schools provided. Prudden tested the fitness levels of students in Europe, Central America, and the United States and reported her results to President Eisenhower; this report was responsible for the President's Council on Youth Fitness and the resurgence of interest in physical fitness in America. In 1979, Prudden founded the School for Physical Fitness and Myotherapy. Bonnie Prudden Myotherapy uses finger, knuckle, and elbow pressure on trigger points to relax muscle spasms, improve circulation, and relieve pain; this is followed by specific corrective exercise.

Accreditation

The Bonnie Prudden School is licensed by the Arizona State Board for Private Postsecondary Education as a private vocational school, and is approved by the Washington State Board of Massage. Graduates are qualified to take the national certification exam.

Program Description

The 1,300-hour, thirty-three-week Myotherapy and Exercise Therapy Course offers instruction in Bonnie Prudden Myotherapy. Three trimesters cover Myotherapy, Anatomy, Kinesiology, Clinical Application, Sports and Injuries Myotherapy, Exercise Therapy (including Exer-Gym, Physically Challenged, Older People, Pre-Sport, Aqua-Therapy, Exercise Choreography, and Exercise Psychology), Anatomy/Physiology, Communications, Introduction to Myotherapy and Exercise (philosophy and history of Bonnie Prudden), Life Drawing and Sculpture, Modern Dance, Business, Animal Myotherapy, Analysis of Human Movement, and Other Voices/Other Rooms (an introduction to chiroprac-

tic, biofeedback, homeopathy, meditation, and other complementary techniques). Students are required to receive one professional myotherapy treatment per trimester.

Introductory weekend workshops in myotherapy are offered five times each year to health professionals, coaches, athletes, health club personnel, and those considering attending the full-time program. The workshop explains the concepts of myotherapy, Kraus-Weber testing to locate muscle weakness, "quick fix" myotherapy, corrective exercises, and use of the bodo and crook (self-help tools).

Admission Requirements

Applicants must be at least 18 years of age, have a high school diploma or equivalent, and be physically able to perform myotherapy and exercise therapy.

Tuition and Fees

Application fee, $35; tuition, $12,500; books, video- and audiotapes (approximate), $540; uniforms (approximate), $425; three professional myotherapy treatments (approximate), $90; and board exams for certification (optional), $150. Introductory weekend workshops are $190 ($175 for early registrants).

Financial Assistance

A payment plan is available.

Desert Institute of the Healing Arts

639 North Sixth Avenue
Tucson, Arizona 85705
Phone: (520) 882-0899 / (800) 733-8098

The Desert Institute of the Healing Arts was founded in 1982 by Margaret Avery-Moon, and is located in Tucson's historic West University neighborhood.

Accreditation

The Desert Institute's massage therapy program is approved by the American Massage Therapy Association Commission on Massage Training Accreditation/Approval (AMTA/COMTAA). The school is a member of the AOBTA Council of Schools and Programs, and is accredited by the Accrediting Commission of Career Schools and Colleges of Technology (ACCSCT).

Program Description

The Desert Institute offers certificate programs in Massage Therapy and Zen Shiatsu.

The 1,000-hour Massage Therapy Certificate Program consists of courses in Massage Theory and Practice (including hydrotherapy), Anatomy and Physiology, Communication Skills, Business and Professionalism, and Benefits of Massage Therapy, plus electives in Massage Practicums (including addictions recovery, massage and HIV/AIDS, physically challenged, prenatal massage, senior massage, and sports massage), Professional Development (including movement integration, stretching and joint mobilization, tai chi chuan, and yoga), Classroom Lab/Clinic (including Anatomiken and palpatory integration), Beginning Shiatsu, On-Site Chair Massage, and others. CPR/First Aid certification is required and must be arranged by the student. Students are expected to receive two professional massages per trimester.

The 600-hour Zen Shiatsu Certificate Program includes Western Anatomy and Physiology, Zen Shiatsu Technique, Qi Dance, Foundations of Eastern Medicine, Communications, Business and Professionalism, Shiatsu Clinic, Practicum, and Survey of Bodywork Modalities. CPR/First Aid certification is required and must be arranged by the student. Students are expected to receive two professional shiatsu treatments per trimester. Please note that this program is scheduled to become a 650-hour program beginning in the Fall 1997 term.

Admission Requirements

Applicants must be at least 21 years of age (exceptions will be made with parental consent), have a high school diploma or equivalent, interview with an admissions representative, and agree to adhere to codes of conduct and ethics. Anyone who has been convicted of a felony may not be eligible for city licensing, which is a requirement for the massage therapy practicums (check with the City of Tucson prior to applying).

Tuition and Fees

Application fee, $25. Fees for the Massage Therapy Program are as follows: tuition, $8,700; books and supplies, $700; City Student Trainee License fee, $25; massage table (average cost), $600; AMTA student membership (optional), $168; CPR/First Aid, up to $35; and six professional massages (two per trimester), $150 to $250. Fees for the Zen Shiatsu Program are as follows: tuition, $5,220; books and supplies, $350; futon, $50 to $100; AOBTA student membership (optional), $40; and six professional shiatsu treatments, $150 to $250.

Financial Assistance

Federal grants and loans are available.

Jin Shin Jyutsu, Inc.

(*See* Multiple State Locations, page 307)

Phoenix Therapeutic Massage College

2720 East Thomas Road, Suite C-140/B-170
Phoenix, Arizona 85016
Phone: (602) 955-2677
Fax: (602) 468-0564

Founded in 1981 by Robert and Gean Schneider, Phoenix Therapeutic Massage College (PTMC) is centrally located in metropolitan Phoenix.

Accreditation

PTMC is accredited by the Accrediting Council for Continuing Education and Training (ACCET). The Professional Certification Program for Therapeutic Massage is approved by the American Massage Therapy Association Commission on Massage Training Accreditation/Approval (AMTA/COMTAA).

Program Description

The 1,110-hour Professional Certification Program for Therapeutic Massage is divided into two parts. The core curriculum consists of 735 hours of basic education in therapeutic massage, including Anatomy, Physiology, Massage, Health Care, Career Development, and Externship. The advanced program consists of 375 credit hours earned in a variety of specialty classes, including Advanced Joint Mobilization Techniques, Deep Tissue Massage, Myofascial Release Technique, Kinesiology, Human Disease (Pathology), Psychology for the L.M.T., Lymphatic/Immune System Massage, Pregnancy Massage, Advanced Sports Massage, and Geriatric Massage.

Classes are held days and evenings.

Admission Requirements

Applicants must be at least 18 years of age; have a high school diploma or equivalent with a minimum G.P.A. of 2.0; be physically, mentally, and emotionally capable of performing massage therapy; and interview with an admissions representative. Students must have a cumulative G.P.A. of 2.0 in the core program in order to enroll in the advanced program.

Tuition and Fees

Tuition for the core program is $6,200. Tuition for the advanced program is $3,000. Other fees include the following: application fee, $100; books and supplies, $275; massage table, $425; college uniform, $175; three professional massages, $135; reference books and tapes, $175; oil and astringents, $45; licenses, $25 to $150; and malpractice insurance, $120 per year.

Financial Assistance

Federal grants and loans and payment plans are available.

Program in Integrative Medicine

University of Arizona
P.O. Box 245153
Tucson, Arizona 85724-5153
Fax: (520) 626-2757
Internet: www.ahsc.arizona.edu/integrative_
  medicine/qanda.html

The Program in Integrative Medicine at the University of Arizona College of Medicine was founded by Dr. Andrew Weil, M.D., the author of numerous best-selling books (including *Spontaneous Healing* and *Natural Health, Natural Medicine*) and an internationally recognized expert on holistic medicine. The activities of the program are currently in the planning and fundraising phase of development.

Program Description

The program will offer two curricula: a two-year fellowship program for physicians, and a variety of professional development and continuing medical education activities. Core subjects will include Philosophy of Science, History of Medicine, Healing-Oriented Medicine, Mind/Body Medicine, Spirituality and Medicine, Nutritional Medicine, Botanical Medicine, and Energy Medicine, featuring such modalities as Interactive Guided Imagery, medical acupuncture, basic homeopathy, and osteopathic manipulative therapy.

The two-year fellowship program will train leaders in the new discipline of integrative medicine. Initially, the program will be limited to a maximum of four fellows per year. Contact the university for additional information.

The professional education activities will include short courses (beginning in January 1996 with a quarterly mini-conference series and integrative medicine grand rounds), a week-long course in integrative medicine, week-long courses focused on the concerns of particular subspecialties, and a botanical medicine course.

In addition, a two- to three-year course of study is being developed that will be provided to physicians and nurses via "distance learning." Participants will come to Tucson several times a year for study; practicum and study during the interim will take place via the Internet and study groups.

Admission Requirements

The fellowship is open only to M.D.s and D.O.s who have completed residencies in primary care specialties. The professional development and continuing education activities are designed for physicians and other health care providers.

Tuition and Fees

As programs are still being developed, no tuition information is available at this time.

RainStar School of Therapeutic Massage

4130 North Goldwater Boulevard, Suite 119
Scottsdale, Arizona 85251
Phone: (602) 423-0375 /
   (888) RAINSTAR (toll-free)

The RainStar School of Therapeutic Massage was founded in 1988 by Jody Russell. The school was previously known as the New Life Therapy Center and A Touch of Health.

Accreditation

The RainStar School of Therapeutic Massage is accredited by the International Massage and Somatic Therapies Accreditation Council (IMSTAC), a division of Associated Bodywork and Massage Professionals (ABMP).

Program Description

RainStar offers several levels of massage therapy training: the Basics Program (200 hours), the Advanced Program (300 hours), the Graduate Program (the Basics plus Advanced Programs for a total of 500 hours), and the Master's Program (the Graduate Program plus an additional 500 hours, for a total of 1,000 hours).

   The eight-week Basics Program includes Anatomy, Physiology, and Kinesiology 101; Health Awareness 102; Massage 103 (consisting of fifty hours instruction and lab, seventy-six hours clinical practicum, and two hours evaluation massage); and Opportunities in Business 104. The three-month Advanced Program includes Anatomy, Physiology, and Kinesiology 201; Health Awareness 202; Massage 203 (consisting of 142 hours selected coursework, forty hours internship/externship, and twelve hours special events); Opportunities in Business 204; and Apprenticeship and Research 205. In the Masters Program, students take

Anatomy 301, Health Awareness 302, Opportunities in Business 304, and 380 hours of specialized course work (seminars), plus fifty hours of Externship or Internship in Massage 303. Day and evening classes begin each month.

Community and Continuing Education

A wide variety of continuing, introductory, and advanced certifications are offered on a regular basis and are open to the public. Topics include acupressure, aromatherapy, Ayurveda, geriatric massage, Chinese herbs, essential elements of nutrition, iridology, reiki, sports massage, and many more.

Admission Requirements

Applicants must be at least 18 years of age and have a high school diploma or equivalent.

Tuition and Fees

Tuition is as follows: Basics Program, $1,495; Advanced Program, $1,995; Graduate Program, $3,295; Master's Program, $2,895; all three programs combined, $5,895. Books, manuals, oil, lotion, and linens are additional.

Financial Assistance

A payment plan is available.

Southwest College of Naturopathic Medicine and Health Sciences

6535 East Osborn Road, Suite 703
Scottsdale, Arizona 85251
Phone: (602) 990-7424
Fax: (602) 990-0337

Southwest College of Naturopathic Medicine and Health Sciences was established in January 1992. The student body is diverse, with an average age of 34.

Accreditation

Southwest College has approval to operate from the State of Arizona Naturopathic Physicians Board of Medical Examiners. The college was approved as a candidate for accreditation in 1994 by the

Council on Naturopathic Medical Education (CNME). While candidacy is not accreditation, it does indicate that the college has demonstrated the potential to achieve accreditation within five years. In April 1995, the college was granted a Regular License from the Arizona State Board of Private Postsecondary Education to offer the Doctor of Naturopathic Medicine degree. In October 1996, the college was granted a Regular Vocational Program License to offer the Certificate in Acupuncture program.

Program Description

The four-year graduate program leading to the Doctor of Naturopathic Medicine degree may be completed in either twelve or sixteen quarters by a full-time, year-round student. Students are prepared to take the licensing examinations necessary to practice as naturopathic physicians.

Courses offered in the basic sciences include Anatomy with Lab, Biochemistry, Embryology, Histology, Medical Genetics, Medical Microbiology, Physiology, and Pathology. Diagnostic courses include Physical Diagnosis, Clinical Diagnosis, Laboratory Diagnosis, and Diagnostic Imaging. Other related courses include Public Health and Environmental Medicine, Psychology and Counseling, and Research.

Clinical courses include Naturopathic Manipulative Therapies, Hydrotherapy, Orthopedic and Sports Medicine, Acupuncture and Oriental Medicine, Emergency Medicine, Minor Surgery, Pharmacology and Pharmacognosy, Botanical Medicine, Homeopathic Medicine, Nutritional Medicine, History and Philosophy of Naturopathic Medicine, Naturopathic Standards of Care, Medical Ethics, Jurisprudence, Business Practices, and Clinical Practice.

The Clinical Competency Program (clinical training) takes place at the Southwest Naturopathic Medical Center. This program (Posts, Assistant Intern, Primary Intern, and Senior Intern) allows students the opportunity to build clinical skills.

The Professional Master's-Level Program in Acupuncture is a three-year, 2,232-hour program designed using national standards. Successful completion enables students to take the National Commission for the Certification of Acupuncturists (NCCA) national board exams. Courses offered include Anatomy and Physiology, Biochemistry, Living Anatomy, Western Psychology, Research Methodologies, Physical Diagnosis, Western Pathology, Fundamentals of Oriental Medicine, Basic Acupuncture Techniques, Western Nutrition, Point Location and Pathology, Traditional Chinese Medicine (TCM) Diagnosis, Ethics/Practice Management, Auricular Acupuncture, Pharmacology, Clinic Observation, TCM Therapeutics, Clinic Internship, Meridian and Points, Chinese Prepared Medicines, Qigong (TCM meditation), Tui Na (TCM massage), TCM Gynecology, and Master's Project.

In their eighth quarter, students enter the Clinic Internship Program at the medical center. Students are required to take the Clean Needle Techniques Course (CNT) of the Council of Colleges of Acupuncture and Oriental Medicine (CCAOM) prior to entering the clinic to ensure their knowledge of clean needle techniques for the safety of the patients. A maximum of eight credits of clinical training may be earned by taking part in an optional externship trip to China.

Admission Requirements

Applicants must submit three letters of recommendation; those with complete files are invited to the campus for a series of interviews. The college follows the "rolling admissions" model. In addition, each program has specific requirements.

For the N.D. program, applicants, beginning with September 1997 entry, are required to have a bachelor's degree with a G.P.A. of 2.5 or greater. Specific course requirements include English (six semester hours, at least three of which must be English composition), psychology (six semester hours), humanities (six semester hours), general chemistry (eight semester hours), organic chemistry with lab (four semester hours), general biology (eight semester hours), anatomy and physiology with lab (four semester hours), botany (four semester hours), and medical terminology (one to three semester hours). The student must have a G.P.A. of 3.0 or greater in prerequisite courses.

For the acupuncture program, applicants must have completed ninety semester hours, of which at least thirty semester hours are in upper-division courses, toward a bachelor's degree. A G.P.A. of 2.5 or greater is required. Specific course requirements include English composition (three semester hours), psychology (six semester hours), general biology (eight semester hours), general chemistry (eight semester hours), organic chemistry (four semester hours), and medical terminology (one to three semester hours). The student must have a G.P.A. of 3.0 or greater in prerequisite courses.

Tuition and Fees

The application fee is $65. For the N.D. program, tuition is $3,815 per quarter for students in the twelve-quarter program. Tuition for students in the sixteen-quarter program is $3,052 per quarter for quarters one through ten, and $3,815 per quarter for quarters eleven through sixteen. Tuition for the acupuncture program is $3,000 per quarter.

Financial Assistance

For the N.D. program, subsidized and unsubsidized Stafford Loans are available, up to a maximum of $18,500 for each three-quarter period. No federal financial aid is available for the acupuncture program at this time.

Wesland Institute, Inc.

3367 North Country Club Road
Tucson, Arizona 85716
Phone: (520) 881-1530

The Wesland Institute, Inc., was established in 1988. The Hypnotherapy Certification Program is also available in a home-study format (see page 376).

Accreditation

Wesland Institute, Inc., is licensed by the Arizona State Board for Private Postsecondary Education, and is endorsed by the International Medical and Dental Hypnotherapy Association and the American Hypnotherapy Association.

Program Description

The Hypnotherapy Program consists of one hun-

dred hours of in-class instruction and 130 hours in an externship program. Topics covered include Introduction, Glossary of Terms, Historical Overview, Overview of Current Psychotherapies, Basic Physiology, Patterns of Programming, Laws of Suggestion, Experiential Suggestibility Tests, Types of Suggestibility, Preinduction Interview, Traditional Inductions, Deepening Techniques, Visualizations, NLP Theories and Techniques, Smoking Cessation, Weight Control, Analytical Hypnotherapy, Age Regression, Past Life Regression, Phobias, Anesthesiology, Ericksonian Hypnosis, Hypnotherapy and Children, Marketing, and Law. The supervised externship allows the student to work with clients in a simulated office or clinical situation.

Classes may be completed in four weeks in the accelerated, Tuesday-through-Friday program, or in twelve weeks of Saturday classes.

Continuing Education

Continuing education classes are held periodically throughout the year.

Admission Requirements

Applicants must be at least 18 years of age and have a high school diploma or equivalent.

Tuition and Fees

Tuition is $1,200, including a $100 preregistration fee.

Financial Assistance

Payment plans are available.

ARKANSAS

White River School of Massage

48 Colt Square, Suite B
Fayetteville, Arkansas 72703
Phone: (501) 521-2550

1405 North Pierce, Suite 209
Little Rock, Arkansas 72207
Phone: (501) 663-1900

The White River School of Massage was founded in 1991 and offers instruction in both Fayetteville and Little Rock.

Accreditation

The program at White River School of Massage has been approved by the Arkansas State Board of Massage Therapy. Graduates are eligible for licensing in the state of Arkansas and are qualified to take the national certification exam.

Program Description

The 500-hour Professional Massage Training Program includes Anatomy and Physiology, Swedish Massage, Sports Massage, Myofascial Therapy, Polarity Therapy, Shiatsu, Craniosacral Therapy, Reflexology, Hydrotherapy/Helio-Electro Therapies, Hygiene/First Aid/CPR, Business Management and Marketing, Body Mechanics/Self-Care, Clinical Practice, and Assessment Skills. Optional electives are also offered in such areas as herbology, aromatherapy, yoga, and others at additional cost.

Students may take weekday, weekend, or summer intensive courses in Fayetteville, and weekday or weekend classes in Little Rock.

Admission Requirements

Applicants must be at least 18 years of age, have a high school diploma or equivalent, and interview with an admissions representative.

Tuition and Fees

Tuition is $3,200. Other fees are as follows: registration fee, $100; books and supplies, $160 in Fayetteville, $90 in Little Rock; massage table, $350 to $600; oils and linens additional; Arkansas State licensing exam (Arkansas residents), $130; and national certification exam (optional), $160.

Financial Assistance

Several types of financial assistance are offered, including payment plans, a 5 percent prepayment discount, veterans' benefits, and some state assistance.

CALIFORNIA

Academy for Guided Imagery

P.O. Box 2070
Mill Valley, California 94942
Phone: (415) 389-9324 / (800) 726-2070
Fax: (415) 389-9342

The Academy for Guided Imagery was founded in 1989 by Martin Rossman, M.D., and David E. Bresler, Ph.D. (See page 364 for the Interactive Guided Imagery self-paced study program.)

Accreditation

The academy has been approved for continuing education credits by the American Psychological Association, the National Association of Social Workers, the California Board of Registered Nursing, and the California Alcoholism and Drug Counselors Education Program.

Program Description

The 150-hour Certification Program is offered to professional health care providers over a period of twelve to twenty-four months. The course includes thirteen hours of Interactive Guided Imagery, fifty-two hours of Advanced Tools for Success home study courses (including the Role of the Imagery Guide; Advanced Work with the Inner Advisor; Resistance and Parts Work; Parts, Polarities, and Conflict Resolution; Imagery with Children; Adult Survivors of Childhood Trauma; Physical Illness; and Death, Dying, Loss, and Transformation), fifty-two hours of "live" hands-on work at two preceptorships, and thirty-three hours of independent study.

Admission Requirements

The applicant must be a licensed health care professional, usually in a counseling field.

Tuition and Fees

Tuition for the entire program is $2,995.

Financial Assistance

A monthly payment plan is available.

Academy of Chinese Culture and Health Sciences

1601 Clay Street
Oakland, California 94612
Phone: (510) 763-7787
Fax: (510) 834-8646

The Academy of Chinese Culture and Health Sciences was founded in 1982 by Dr. Wei Tsuei, an accomplished practitioner of traditional Chinese medicine, tai chi chuan, and tai chi meditation, as well as a sixth-generation qigong master. Over 90 percent of academy graduates pass the state's acupuncture licensing exam each year.

Accreditation

The academy's Master of Science in Traditional Chinese Medicine degree program is accredited by the National Accreditation Commission for Schools and Colleges of Acupuncture and Oriental Medicine (NACSCAOM). Graduates are eligible to take the acupuncture licensure examination given by the California State Acupuncture Committee, and are eligible for licensure in other states. The academy is approved by the California Acupuncture Committee as a continuing education provider for licensed acupuncturists, and by the California Board of Registered Nursing as a provider of continuing education for registered nurses.

Program Description

The academy offers a four-year Master of Science in Traditional Chinese Medicine program that may be completed in three calendar years of full-time study. The curriculum is divided into two portions: the preprofessional courses of the first two calendar years and the graduate courses of the final calendar year. The preprofessional courses are considered equivalent to the latter two upper-division years of a baccalaureate program. Comprehensive exams are given at the end of the first and second years to determine a student's eligibility for the next level of study.

The 2,572½-hour program (3,532½ California licensure clock hours include 960 clock hours of prerequisites) includes course work in Theoretical Foundations of TCM, Acupuncture Sciences, Tai Chi, Theory of Chinese Medicine, History of Medicine, Combined Western and Chinese Nutrition, Herbology, Tui Na—Acupressure Technique, Medical Chinese, Ethics/Practice Management, Western Pharmacology, Differential Diagnosis, Western Pathology, Western Physical and Lab Diagnosis, Research Methodology, Classics: Nei Jing, Classics: Jin Kui, Western Medical Science, TCM External Medicine, Classics: Shang Han Lun and Wen Bing, TCM Traumatology and Orthopedic, TCM Pediatrics, TCM Gynecology, Clinic, Research, and others, including electives in Advanced Tai Chi Chuan, Comparative Medical Sciences, Chinese Herbal Dietetics, TCM Psychology, and more.

The academy also offers a separate Tui Na Acupressure Certificate Program; the curriculum consists of Foundations of Traditional Chinese Medicine I and II, Acupuncture I, Tui Na Acupressure, and Medical Ethics/Practice Management. Students who enroll in the Master of Science program will usually fulfill the requirements for the Tui Na Acupressure Certificate by the end of their first year.

Continuing Education

The academy offers a special graduate-level program for California licensed acupuncturists who wish to earn a master's-level degree. The Master of Science in Traditional Chinese Medicine—Special Program for Licensed Acupuncturists consists of a minimum of forty-two graduate trimester units from the third-year graduate curriculum, as well as special electives that vary from term to term, and a number of clinic hours. Past electives have included Spinal Orthopedics, Pediatrics, and Geriatrics.

Admission Requirements

Applicants must have completed at least sixty semester units of general education at any accredited college or university and attained a G.P.A. of at least 2.3 (C+) in all prerequisite work and a 2.0 (C) in any individual course. Prerequisites include course work in communications, mathematics, humanities, social sciences, and Western medical sciences, including psychology, biology, chemistry, physics, anatomy, physiology, Western medical terminology, and others (see the catalog for specific requirements). Applicants must also submit an essay and résumé, three personal references, and interview with admissions personnel. No applicant will be admitted who has been dismissed from any school for legal, ethical, or moral reasons.

Prerequisites for the Tui Na Acupressure Certificate Program include human anatomy and physiology.

Tuition and Fees

Application fee, $50; registration fee, $50; graduation fee, $150; comprehensive exams, $75 to $100 each; tuition for Didactic Course Instruction, $126/unit; Clinic Instruction, $9/hour; and books and supplies, $600. Total estimated fees for the Master of Science program: tuition, $25,875; and books and fees, $1,300. Total estimated fees for the Special Program for Licensed Acupuncturists: tuition, $6,800 to $8,000; and books and fees, $500.

Financial Assistance

Payment plans are available.

Acupressure Institute

1533 Shattuck Avenue
Berkeley, California 94709
Phone: (510) 845-1059 /
(800) 442-2232 (outside California)

Since it was founded in 1976, the Acupressure Institute has offered training at both the basic and advanced levels. Institute founder and author Michael Reed Gach, Ph.D., has practiced acupressure for over twenty years and is trained in point location, Zen shiatsu, and Jin Shin acupressure. In addition to programs at the Berkeley location, the institute offers yearly intensive training in Atlanta, Minneapolis, and Baltimore. The institute also has a mail order catalog featuring healing books, charts, cassette tapes, and instructional videos (see page 359).

Accreditation

The Acupressure Institute is an approved provider of continuing education credits for registered nurses, physical therapists, and acupuncturists and has been granted institutional approval by the California State Council for Private Postsecondary and Vocational Education. Upon completion of the Basic Acupressure and Shiatsu Training Program, students may practice acupressure and massage in California, and may legally charge a fee for sessions.

Program Description

The 150-hour Basic Acupressure and Shiatsu Training Program leads to certification as an acupressure or shiatsu technician. Students study over seventy-five acupressure points and ten styles of acupressure, as well as the twelve organ meridians. Classes include Fundamentals of Acupressure; Basic, Intermediate, and Advanced Acupressure; Anatomy and Physiology; Business Practice and Ethics; Supervised Sessions; Documented Practice; and three electives chosen from Reflexology and Acupressure, Touch for Health, Zen Shiatsu, Barefoot Shiatsu, Tui Na: Chinese Massage, Acu-Yoga Self-Help Techniques, and Acupressure Oil Massage. The program may be completed in six months to one year of part-time study, or in one-month intensives. Classes may be taken individually without enrollment in the certificate program.

The 200-hour Advanced Training Acupressure Specialization Programs allow students to further their skills and knowledge of acupressure in such areas as women's health, advanced shiatsu, sports acupressure, emotional balancing, arthritis and pain relief, traditional Oriental therapy, and acupressure stress management. Programs may be completed in eighteen months to two years of part-time study, or in one-month intensives.

The 850-hour Acupressure Therapy Program is designed for those who wish to practice as professional acupressure therapists, and may fulfill requirements in other states for massage therapy. Students may complete the program within one year of full-time study, or two to four years of part-time study. Course work includes 350 hours of advanced training classes, plus Anatomy and Physiology, Self-Development (including tai chi, qigong, or another internal healing art), Apprenticeship Training Classes, Documented Practice, Advanced Practice, and Teacher Training and/or Project.

Some of the classes offered as part of the Advanced Training and Acupressure Therapy Programs include Acupressure First Aid, On-Site Acupressure, Arthritis Relief: Self-Help, Table Shiatsu, Advanced Five Elements, Intuitive Acupressure and Self-Awareness, Pulse and Tongue Assessment, Traditional Oriental Theory, Sports Applications, Body Psychology, Counseling Skills, the Chakras, Emotional Balancing Using the Meridians, Major Medical Disorders, Western Herbology, Chinese Herbal Patent Remedies, Acu-Yoga Teacher Training, and others. Students in the four-day Acu-Yoga Teacher Training Class receive a diploma upon completion.

Admission Requirements

Applicants must be at least 18 years of age and in good health. Applicants to the Acupressure Therapy Program must have taken courses in anatomy/physiology and business practice and ethics.

Tuition and Fees

Tuition for the 150-hour Basic Acupressure and Shiatsu Training Program is $1,025; there is a registration fee of $75. Tuition for the 200-hour Advanced Training Acupressure Specialization Program is $1,350; there is a registration fee of $75. Tuition for the 850-hour Acupressure Therapy Program is $5,200, plus a $100 registration fee. Books average $75 per program.

Financial Assistance

A payment plan and full payment discount is available. Work-trade is available to a limited number of students; request an application for work-trade.

Alchemy Institute of Healing Arts

2310 Warwick Drive
Santa Rosa, California 95405
Phone: (707) 579-4984 / (800) 950-4984
E-mail: quigley@sonic.net

The Alchemy Institute of Healing Arts was founded in 1986 as the Alchemical Hypnotherapy Institute, for the purpose of preparing students to work as hypnotherapists. Alchemical hypnotherapy is a therapeutic process that assists clients in accessing and using their inner guides—autonomous beings that live within the subconscious mind—to change their lives. This type of hypnotherapy includes techniques from many schools of hypnotherapy and psychology, including gestalt, regression therapy, neurolinguistic programming (NLP), and others. The institute was founded by David Quigley, a state-approved hypnosis trainer since 1983 and a member of the advisory board of the American Council of Hypnotist Examiners (ACHE).

Accreditation

All courses offered by the Alchemy Institute of Healing Arts are approved by ACHE. The school is authorized by the California Board of Registered Nursing to provide continuing education credits for nurses, and is approved by the California State Council for Private Postsecondary and Vocational Education.

Program Description

AIHA offers three levels of hypnosis certification, each building on the one before.

The 150-hour Master Hypnotist Training Program qualifies the student for certification as a Master Hypnotist. Students will make contact with their inner child and inner mate, and will learn techniques applied to smoking, weight loss, addictions, and phobias, along with instruction in establishing a professional practice. Completion of certification requires four evaluated alchemical sessions as a client; completion of two professional sessions with an assistant or an alchemical hypnotherapist concurrent with the training program; and two (for resident students) or three (for weekend students) hypnotherapy practice sessions with a fellow student.

The Certified Hypnotherapist Training (200 hours total) builds upon the basic training with an additional fifty hours of study, and leads to certification as a Certified Hypnotherapist.

The Alchemical Hypnotherapist Training (350 hours total) leads to certification as an Alchemical Hypnotherapist. Students must complete the basic training and receive the Alchemical Hypnosis certification; complete one hundred hours of further instruction at any AIHA-approved school (400-level courses); complete ninety hours of assisting at a basic alchemical training; and receive five documented alchemical sessions.

Core courses offered in the three programs include Introduction to Hypnotherapy and Post-Hypnotic Suggestion, Emotional Clearing Work, Past Life Regression and Inner Guides, Conference Room Therapy, Specific Regimens, and Establishing a Professional Practice. Advanced electives include Pain and Disease Control, Advanced Alchemical Techniques, Touch Skills for the Hypnotherapist, NLP for the Alchemist, Ericksonian Hypnosis, Weight Management, Clearing the Trauma of Sexual Abuse, Wilderness Intensive, and others.

Instruction is offered in both residential and weekend formats.

Continuing Education

The eighty-five-hour Alchemical Package for Hypnotherapists is offered to those who have completed at least one hundred hours of hypnosis study.

Admission Requirements

The Master Hypnotist, Certified Hypnotherapist, and Alchemical Hypnotherapist Certification Programs were designed to accommodate the entry-level student. Applicants must complete an application form, be fluent in the English language, pass the Wonderlic Basic Skills Test (a standardized test of basic math and verbal skills), and interview with an admissions representative.

Tuition and Fees

Costs for the Master Hypnotist Certification (150 hours) are as follows: registration fee, $75; tuition, $1,800 to $2,160 (depending on payment plan); books, $75; two alchemical sessions, $150; ACHE membership, $125; AIHA membership, $100; and practicums, $15 to $120. Costs for the Certified Hypnotist Certification (200 hours) are the same as for Master Hypnotist Certification, plus an additional $660 to $720 in electives. Costs for the Alchemical Hypnotherapist Certification are the same as for Certified Hypnotist Certification, plus an additional $660 to $720 in electives, $75 for an apprenticeship program, and $350 for additional alchemical sessions. Facility and residence fees for residential intensives vary with the program and type of accommodation, and range from $144 for commuter fee without lunch to $1,495 for private room.

Financial Assistance

A payment plan, scholarships, and loans are available.

Alive and Well! Institute of Conscious BodyWork

100 Shaw Drive
San Anselmo, California 94960
Phone: (415) 258-0402

Alive and Well! was founded in 1987 by Jocelyn Olivier, whose creation of Conscious BodyWork was influenced by her studies in neuromuscular reeducation, educational and applied kinesiology, American Indian and Hawaiian shamanism, and tui na. The school is located thirty minutes north of San Francisco.

Accreditation

The certification programs at Alive and Well! meet the minimum educational requirements for the state of California. Nursing CEUs are available. Applicants should check with the city in which they intend to work to be sure these courses meet local educational requirements.

Program Description

Alive and Well! offers state-approved certification courses for Certified Massage Technicians, Advanced BodyWorkers, Conscious BodyWorkers, and Master Hypnotists in Hypno Dharma Facilitation, which uses both Eastern and Western approaches in working with the subconscious patterns of the mind.

The 140-hour Certified Massage Technician Program takes nine weeks to three months to complete. The curriculum consists of Anatomy, Conscious BodyWork Level I, Principles of Polarity or Conscious BodyWork Level II, Conscious Breathwork, Counseling for Bodyworkers of Massage Ergonomics, Establishing a Business, Kinesiology, Nutritional Physiology, Reflexology, and Supervised Clinical Practice. A summer intensive allows completion of this program in just three weeks.

The 300-hour Advanced Bodyworker Course builds on the 140-hour C.M.T. Program with additional courses in Advanced Anatomy, Conscious BodyWork Level II or Principles of Polarity, Deep Tissue I: Soft Tissue Mobilization, Heart of the Matter: Bodywork with Abuse Survivors, Advanced Kinesiology, Lymphatic and Visceral Massage, and Supervised Clinical Practice.

The 570-hour Conscious BodyWorker Program requires, in addition to the 140-hour C.M.T. Training (or equivalent) and 160-hour Advanced Bodyworker Training, courses in Brain Function Facilitation, Building Your Practice, Qigong, Conscious BodyWork Level III, Emotional/Energetic Tune-Ups, On-Site Massage, Self-Care for Bodyworkers, Touch for Health, thirty-four hours of electives, and sixty-six hours of supervised clinical practice.

A 1,000-hour Master BodyWorker Program includes the Certified Massage Practitioner and Advanced BodyWorker Training, plus an additional 700 hours of instruction in such areas as Acupressure: Five Element, Biomechanics, Brain Function Facilitation, Building Your Practice, Chi Gung, Counseling Skills, Craniosacral, Emotional/Energetic Tune-Ups, Exercise Physiology, Movement Education, Neuromuscular Reprogramming, On-Site Massage, Personal Nutrition, Principles of Polarity, Sacred Touch, Self-Care for BodyWorkers, Somatic Process and Integration, Sports Injury and Chronic Pain, Touch for Health, Transformational Kinesiology, Trigger Points and Pain Release, electives, and clinic. An optional study group is provided for the national certification test, and may be taken as one of the electives.

The 150-hour Professional Hypnotherapy Certification Program leads to certification as a Master Hypnotist approved by the State of California, and optional certification with the American Council of Hypnotist Examiners. This program explores a basic theoretical understanding of hypnotherapy and the unconscious mind, Eastern and Western methods, methods of past life regression, more than twenty ways to induce deep relaxation, and more. An additional 100 hours of training leads to Clinical Hypnotherapist certification.

Community and Continuing Education

Free introductory evenings provide a discussion and demonstration of the programs offered at the school; other free lectures open to the public focus on such topics as qigong, releasing chronic pain, Feldenkrais and massage, somatic technique, aromatherapy and practical applications, clearing phobias and fears, shiatsu, and more.

A sixty-hour professional development course in Conscious BodyWork Neuromuscular Reprogramming is offered to bodyworkers. This technique uses postural analysis, muscle testing, body reading, and rehabilitation exercises to accelerate recovery from injuries, recondition coordination patterns, and optimize athletic performance.

Admission Requirements

The State of California requires that students enrolling in the 140-hour Certified Massage Technician Program take an Ability to Benefit test (a test of basic math and verbal skills).

Tuition and Fees

Tuition is as follows: Certified Massage Technician, $1,295; Advanced BodyWorker, $2,700; Conscious BodyWorker, $5,300; Master BodyWorker, $10,900; Professional Hypnotherapy Certification, $2,000; and Conscious BodyWork Neuromuscular Reprogramming, $995.

Tuition does not include books and supplies.

Financial Assistance

Payment plans, prepayment discounts, work-study, and veterans' benefits are available.

American Academy
of Medical Acupuncture

(*See* Multiple State Locations, page 295)

American College
of Traditional Chinese Medicine

455 Arkansas Street
San Francisco, California 94107
Phone: (415) 282-7600
Fax: (415) 282-0856

The American College of Traditional Chinese Medicine was founded in 1980 as a not-for-profit corporation. In 1981, the college opened its Community Clinic, which provides low-cost health care to an average of 800 patients per month. The clinic operates a program for HIV-positive patients funded by the Ryan White Comprehensive AIDS Resources Emergency Act.

Accreditation

The Master of Science degree program in traditional Chinese medicine is accredited by the National Accreditation Commission for Schools and Colleges of Acupuncture and Oriental Medicine (NACSCAOM).

Program Description

The four-year Master of Science in Traditional Chinese Medicine degree program may be completed in three calendar years.

First-year courses include History of Healing Symposium, Fundamental Theory of TCM, Point Location and Indications, Meridian Structure and Point Systems, Medical Chinese, Tai Chi, Differential Diagnosis, the Pharmacopoeia, Medical Terminology, Qigong, Pathophysiology, Clinical Practicum, Supervised Observation, Clinical Procedures, and others.

Second-year courses include Intermedical Communications, Advanced Diagnosis and Treatment Principles, Meridian Structure and Point Systems, Herbal Prescriptions, Clinic: Close Supervision, Chinese Physio-massage and Therapy, Advanced Acupuncture, Nutrition and the Treatment of Disease, Pathophysiology: Shang Han Lun, Clinic: Partial Supervision, and others.

Third-year courses include Professional Issues and Bioethics, Survey of Biomedical Pharmacology, Pathophysiology: Wen Bing, Grand Clinical Rounds, Classical Prescriptions, Introduction to Clinical Research Methodology, Proseminars, Internship, and others.

The curriculum requirements of either the eleventh or twelfth quarters may be met through the study abroad program.

Classes are held both days and evenings.

Admission Requirements

Applicants should have a bachelor's degree or equivalent and have completed the preprofessional general education requirements, which consist of specific courses in language communication (thirteen quarter credits), comparative studies (six quarter credits), reasoning (six quarter credits), and general science (twenty-two quarter credits). Students who have deficiencies in these requirements will be considered on an individual basis and may be admitted provisionally. In addition, applicants must submit two letters of recommendation (one from a health care practitioner), a health certificate, and a statement of purpose.

Tuition and Fees

There is an application fee of $50 for full-time students and $100 for part-time students; tuition is $102 per credit; graduation fee is $75; and books and supplies are additional.

Financial Assistance

A payment plan is available.

American Institute
of Massage Therapy, Inc.

2156 Newport Boulevard
Costa Mesa, California 92627-1710
Phone: (714) 642-0735
Fax: (714) 642-1729

Dr. Myk Hungerford, AIMT's founder, served as the National Director of Education for the American Massage Therapy Association from 1981 to 1984. He began giving individual instruction in 1983, and in 1989 the school constructed a 2,000-square-foot building.

Accreditation

The AIMT program is approved by the American Massage Therapy Association Commission on Massage Training Accreditation/Approval (AMTA/COMTAA). AIMT is approved and recognized by the International Myomassethics Federation (IMF), the Alberta (Canada) Massage Therapy Association, International Sports Massage Federation, and is approved for continuing education by the California Board of Registered Nursing.

Program Description

The forty-eight-week, 1,009-hour Scientific Swedish Massage and Sports Massage Program includes 507 classroom clock hours, 102 apprentice classroom clock hours, and 400 clinical internship hours, plus supervised hours working at sporting events and taking field trips.

The program consists of both massage therapy and sports massage components, taught simultaneously. The massage therapy program is based on Swedish massage and includes Anatomy and Physiology, Pathology, Nutrition (including herbology), Hydrotherapy, Specialized Modalities (which may include acupressure, Chinese/Russian techniques, reflexology, remedial exercise, and lymphatic drainage, and are subject to change), Psychology and Philosophy, and Supplementary Basic Courses (including Hygiene, CPR, First Aid, Medical Ethics, Clinical Practice, and Didactic Studies of other manipulative therapies). The sports massage component emphasizes Sports Kinesiology, Functional Muscle Testing, Counterstrain, PNF Stretches, Sports Pathology and Psychology, and Immediate Injury Care. Pre-event massage, post-event massage, training and conditioning, and restoration/rehabilitation are also covered. Graduates receive a certification/diploma as both a massage therapist and sports massage specialist.

Admission Requirements

Applicants must be a high school graduate or equivalent, pass the entrance exam, and submit two letters of recommendation.

Tuition and Fees

Tuition is $5,100; other fees are as follows: application/registration fee, $60; books (approximate), $95; massage table, $200 to $800; AMTA membership (optional), $178; and International Sports Massage Congress (optional), $150.

Financial Assistance

Monthly and trimester payment plans are available.

B.K.S. Iyengar Yoga Institute of Los Angeles

8233 West 3rd Street
Los Angeles, California 90048
Phone: (213) 653-0357

The B.K.S. Iyengar Yoga Institute of Los Angeles was founded in 1984 by the B.K.S. Iyengar Yoga Association of Southern California; Gloria Goldberg is the training program coordinator. The institute is located in the West Hollywood/Beverly Hills area. This program is also offered in the San Diego area, where the group format meets monthly.

Program Description

A three-year comprehensive Iyengar Yoga Training Program is offered for teachers and serious students. The program is created with direct and continuous input from B.K.S. Iyengar. The curriculum covers Fundamental Asanas and Pranayama, Yoga Philosophy, Anatomy and Physiology of Yoga Poses, Teaching Asanas and Pranayama, Basic Adjustments, and Therapeutics (Special Issues). The program includes weekly classes, weekend workshops, a three-day residential intensive, practice and principles, and more.

Admission Requirements

Applicants should have practiced Iyengar yoga for at least two years with a certified Iyengar yoga teacher. Students with less than two years' experience who feel ready for this program should contact the program coordinator at (619) 444-7948.

Tuition and Fees

Tuition for entire three-year program is $4,800; there is a $25 application fee, and books are approximately $150.

Financial Assistance

Payment plans and some scholarships are available.

Body Therapy Center

368 California Avenue
Palo Alto, California 94306
Phone: (415) 328-9400
Fax: (415) 328-9478
E-mail: btcbdywrk1@aol.com

The Body Therapy Center was founded in 1983 by Maria Torregrosa and Lucia Miracchi. Ms. Torregrosa is a nationally certified massage therapist whose background includes Hatha yoga, Touch for Health, shiatsu, and Swedish/Esalen massage. Ms. Miracchi has been involved in the healing arts for over twenty years; she is nationally certified in therapeutic massage and bodywork and has an extensive background in body therapy, continuum movement, breathwork, tai chi, yoga, and meditation.

Accreditation

All certificate programs have been approved by the California Board of Registered Nursing for CEU contact hours for nurses. The Fundamentals of Massage Program fulfills the State of California's minimum requirement for massage therapy; however, many cities require additional training for licensing. Prospective applicants are urged to know the educational requirements of the city in which they plan to work. State approval is pending for the Fluid Body Program.

Program Description

The 145-hour Fundamentals of Massage Program meets nine hours per week for approximately three months. Classes include Anatomy, Physiology, When to Refer, History, Client/Therapist Relationship, Business Issues, Movement Awareness, Bodyreading, Demonstration and Practice, Practicum, and Introduction to Other Forms of Bodywork. In addition, students must complete and document 10 one-hour, full-body massages; have one outside session; pass a one-hour written final exam; and complete required reading.

For optimum employment opportunities, it is recommended that students combine various Body Therapy Center programs into a 500-hour certificate. These additional programs include Therapeutic Massage Practitioner (Advanced Level), Fundamentals of Shiatsu, Intermediate Shiatsu, Clinical Deep Tissue Massage, and The Fluid Body: Explorations of Touch and Movement.

The 175-hour Advanced Massage Program meets two evenings per week, plus six Saturdays, for a total of four months, and is open to those who have completed any one-hundred-hour state-approved training in Swedish/Esalen massage. Topics include Anatomy, Demonstration and Practice, Movement Awareness, Communication Skills, Tutorial and Final, and Practicum Sessions.

The 155-hour Clinical Deep Tissue Massage Program meets six hours per week and at least one Saturday per month, and is open to graduates of Fundamentals of Massage or equivalent. The class is divided into Demonstration and Practice; Theory, Anatomy, and Physiology; Practicum; and Final and Tutorial. Areas covered include anatomy, physiology, and kinesiology; different theories and techniques; body mechanics and self-care; looking and thinking strategically; soft tissue injuries; contraindications; bodywork philosophy; and myomassethics.

The 145-hour Fundamentals of Shiatsu Program meets two evenings per week, plus six Saturdays, for three months. Classes include Demonstration and Practice, Awareness and Touch, Practicum, Anatomy and Physiology, Theory, Meridian Location, and Final and Tutorial.

The 136-hour Intermediate Shiatsu Program meets two evenings per week and five Saturdays for four months, and is open to graduates of the

Fundamentals of Shiatsu Program or equivalent. Topics include Demonstration and Practice, Theory, Practicum, Meridian Location, Clinical Application of Theory/Meridians, Clinic, and Final and Tutorial.

The 120-hour program, The Fluid Body: Explorations of Touch and Movement, takes a symposium format; students may choose five elective twenty-four-hour classes taught by leaders in their fields. Topics include Movement and Manipulation, Touch: The Mother Sense, Massage and Shiatsu, The Hakomi Approach: An Introduction to Hakomi Therapy Method for Bodyworkers, The Alchemy of Anatomy and Movement, and Dissolving Body Armor.

Continuing Education

In addition to the programs listed above, the Body Therapy Center offers a variety of classes for professional continuing education. Such courses have included Body Logic, Bodywork with Abuse Survivors, Qigong: Cultivating One's Energy for Health and Bodywork, Introduction to the Five Element Theory, Hara Assessment, Hawaiian Huna and Lomi Lomi Massage Workshop, Taxes for Bodyworkers, The Trager Approach: An Introductory Workshop, Muscle Sculpting, Reiki I, Therapeutic Touch: Level I, and many others.

Community classes open to those with little or no massage experience include Aromatherapy Workshop; Back, Neck, and Shoulders Massage; Basic Shiatsu; Introduction to Biofeedback; Foot Reflexology; Infant Massage; and others.

Admission Requirements

Applicants must be 18 years of age or older and interview with an admissions representative.

Tuition and Fees

Tuition for the Fundamentals of Massage Course is $1,095; other fees include materials, $30; required outside session, $60; books (approximate), $45; and oil, $15. Students are encouraged to purchase a massage table by week three.

Tuition for the Advanced Massage Course is $1,275; other fees include two required outside sessions, $120; two recommended sessions, $120;

books (approximate), $73; and oil, $15.

Tuition for the Clinical Deep Tissue Massage Course is $1,100; other fees include four required outside sessions, $240; books (approximate), $234; and oil, $15.

Tuition for the Fundamentals of Shiatsu Course is $1,125; other fees include one required outside session, $60; and books (approximate), $98.

Tuition for the Intermediate Shiatsu Course is $1,125; other fees include four required outside sessions, $240; and books (approximate), $45.

Tuition for The Fluid Body is $1,125; other fees include books (approximate), $118; oil, $15; and outside sessions, $240.

There is a $75 registration fee for all courses.

Financial Assistance

Payment plans are available.

California Institute of Integral Studies

9 Peter Yorke Way
San Francisco, California 94109
Phone: (415) 674-5500

The California Institute of Integral Studies was founded in 1968 by Haridas Chaudhuri, and was originally known as the California Institute of Asian Studies. The institute emphasizes comparative and cross-cultural studies in philosophy, religion, psychology, counseling, cultural anthropology, organizational and business studies, health studies, learning theory, and the arts.

Accreditation

The institute is accredited by the Western Association of Schools and Colleges.

Program Description

The institute offers a large number of academic programs, most of which are postgraduate master's degree or Ph.D.-level programs dealing with various aspects of psychology, philosophy, religion, and/or business.

A twenty-seven-unit Certificate in Integral Health Studies may be taken with focus areas that may include women's health, human and global ecology, Asian healing, Western complementary therapies, indigenous healing, somatic health, expressive arts, and others. Required courses include Introduction to Integral Health, Foundations of Western Healing Traditions, Foundations of Asian Healing Traditions, and Nutrition as a Living Philosophy. The program may be completed in nine to twelve months.

A seventy-six-unit master's degree program in integral health education prepares graduates to pass the national certifying examination for health educators and includes coursework in health education, core integral health studies, health education practicum (fieldwork), electives, and thesis preparation and writing. Required courses include Introduction to Integral Health, Foundations of Western Healing Traditions, Foundations of Asian Healing Traditions, Psychoneuroimmunology: Bridging Body-Mind-Spirit, Fundamentals of Health Education, Health Informatics, Contemporary Health Problems, Wellness, Program Planning, Group Facilitation, Epidemiology for Health Professionals, Research Methods, Grant Writing, Health Communication Skills, Ethics, Community Health Advocacy, Integrative Seminar/Thesis Preparation, and Thesis Writing/Project.

Admission Requirements

The Certificate in Integral Health Studies is open to all health professionals and graduates or students of healing arts programs. The master's degree program in integral health education requires a bachelor's degree (preferably in the health sciences), two letters of recommendation, and a writing sample.

Tuition and Fees

Tuition for both programs is $330 per unit. There is a registration fee of $82 per quarter.

Financial Assistance

Payment plans and federal loans are available to eligible students.

California Institute of Massage and Spa Services

139 East Napa Street
P.O. Box 673
Sonoma, California 95476
Phone: (707) 939-8964

The California Institute of Massage and Spa Services was founded in 1992. The two faculty members have more than thirty years' combined experience in massage.

Accreditation

The California Institute of Massage and Spa Services was licensed in 1992 by the California State Council for Private Postsecondary and Vocational Education. Some California cities require a minimum number of hours of training prior to granting a business license; in the city of Sonoma and unincorporated Sonoma County, only compliance with zoning laws is required.

Program Description

The 165-hour Massage Technician Program includes 120 hours of in-class instruction and forty-five hours of outside practice. The curriculum includes Anatomy and Physiology; Body Mechanics and Stretching; Swedish Massage; Reflexology; Massage Theory and History; Shake, Rock, and Roll: Gentle Joint Mobilization; Business and Ethics; and Introduction to Aromatherapy.

The one-hundred-hour Advanced Massage I Program covers Kinesiology, Energy Balancing, Trigger Point Therapy, Seated Massage, and Prenatal and Side-Lying Massage.

Advanced Massage II offers 135 hours of electives in Shiatsu, Spa Massage, Geriatric Massage, Therapeutic Touch, Lymphatic Massage, Deep Tissue Massage, and practice-building skills.

The one-hundred-hour Spa Services Program covers holistic body treatments offered in spas and home health care. Topics covered include Hydrotherapy; Body Scrubs; Aromatherapy; Seaweed Wraps; Mud Wraps; Paraffin Baths; Hand, Foot, and Face Treatments; Ayurvedic Treatment; and Setting Up the Spa Environment.

These four courses may be taken in sequence for a 500-hour Massage Therapist Certification. Massage Technician and Advanced Massage Courses may be taken weekdays or weekends. Spa Services may be taken as weekday classes or as intensives.

Admission Requirements

The Massage Technician Program is open to interested individuals over 18 years of age (those younger than 18 may be accepted with permission of a parent or guardian and the admissions staff). The Advanced Massage and Spa Services Programs are open to those who have taken the 150-hour Massage Technician Program or its equivalent.

Tuition and Fees

There is a $75 registration fee for all courses. Tuition for the Massage Technician Program is $965, plus $45 for books and materials; tuition for Advanced Massage I is $715, plus $45 for books and materials; tuition for Advanced Massage II is $1,135, plus $75 for books and materials; and tuition for the Spa Services Program is $725, plus $95 for books and materials. Room and board for intensives are additional.

Financial Assistance

A payment plan is available.

The California School of Herbal Studies

P.O. Box 39
Forestville, California 95436
Phone: (707) 887-7457

Founded in 1978, CSHS is America's oldest school for herbalists. The school is located on eighty acres in Sonoma County, about an hour and a half north of San Francisco and a half-hour from the Pacific coast. The facility includes a working garden of medicinal and native plants.

Accreditation

CSHS is accredited to give continuing education credits to nurses, and credits earned here are generally transferable to institutions such as naturopathic colleges.

Program Description

The nine-month, 480-hour Foundations and Therapeutic Herbalism Program includes two separate, semester-long programs: Foundations of Herbalism (240 hours) and Therapeutic Herbalism (240 hours). The two semesters may be taken separately, although the Therapeutic Herbalism Program requires previous herbal or therapeutic experience.

The 240-hour Foundations of Herbalism curriculum includes Materia Medica: Anatomy, Physiology, and Body Systems; Introduction to Herbal Actions; Medicine Making and Lab; Botany and Field Identification; Introduction to Global Healing Traditions; Aromatherapy; Herb Cultivation; Harvesting Techniques; Principles of Ethical Wildcrafting; Basics of Therapeutics; Principles of Bioregionalism; Nutrition and Healing Foods; Herbal Information Gathering; Herbal First Aid; Natural Cosmetics and Crafts; Green Politics; Bach Flower Essences; History and Mythology; the Business of Herbalism; Student Projects; and Medicine Show.

The 240-hour Therapeutic Herbalism curriculum includes System and Actions Model of Western Herbalism; Western Constitutional Herbalism; Materia Medica; Herbal Dispensatory; Phytochemistry; Phytopharmacology; Case Studies; Therapeutic Aromatherapy; Botany and Field Identification; Herb Cultivation; Informed Consent Issues; Interview Techniques; Student Projects; and Student Case Studies.

Classes meet Tuesday through Thursday in the daytime; students spend additional time outside class in medicine making, special projects, and overnight identification and wildcrafting trips.

Students in the second-year apprenticeship program continue their studies by working with CSHS staff in running the Student Wellness Center, sharing responsibility for the garden, and working with first-year students.

A six-month, sixty-hour weekend course, Body

Systems and Herbal Wellness, meets one weekend per month and explores physiology, materia medica, and therapeutics.

A two-week, fifty-hour course, Therapeutic Intensive, is a compressed version of the Body Systems and Herbal Wellness course held in the daytime, Monday through Friday.

Another six-month, sixty-hour weekend course, the Technology of Independence, bases its curriculum on plants within a half-day's drive of San Francisco. The curriculum includes Plant Identification, Field Trips, Medicine Making, and Materia Medica.

A six-week, twelve-hour introductory course, Evening Herbalism in San Francisco, meets on Thursday evenings and offers a curriculum in Gaia, Herbs, and Transformation; Herbal Medicine Making; How Herbs Work; Green Cross Herbal First Aid; Introduction to Aromatherapy; and Kitchen Medicinals.

One-day workshops are held spring through fall in Herbal Medicine Making, Therapeutic Applications of Essential Oils, Food as Medicine, Herbal Ways for Women, Plant Energetics, and Herbs for Winter Health. Spring and summer herb walks include Plants of Pomo Canyon, Berkeley Botanical Gardens, Springtime in Emerald Valley, and Summer at Shell Beach.

Admission Requirements

Students must complete an application questionnaire.

Tuition and Fees

There is a $15 application fee. Tuition for the Foundation and Therapeutic Herbalism Program is $2,600 per semester or $4,995 for the entire program, plus $300 to $500 for books and materials. Tuition for Body Systems and Herbal Wellness, Therapeutic Intensive, and Technology of Independence is $475; register with a friend for $425 each. There is a $15 lab fee for Technology of Independence. Tuition for Evening Herbalism in San Francisco is $120 (or $100 each for two people); individual classes are $30 each. The one-day workshops are $35 per class, or $30 per class for two people. Herb Walks are $15 each or all four for $45.

Financial Assistance

A limited number of work-study positions are available.

Central California School of Body Therapy

Administration:
448 Woodland Drive

Classroom Facility:
2030 10th Street
Los Osos, California 93402
Phone: (805) 528-7519

The Central California School of Body Therapy was established in 1991, and is located eight miles west of San Luis Obispo.

Accreditation

The 550-hour Massage Therapist Program is accredited by the American Massage Therapy Association Commission on Massage Training Accreditation/Approval (AMTA/COMTAA).

Program Description

The curriculum for the 550-hour Massage Therapist Program consists of Circulatory Massage, Lymphatic Massage, Deep Tissue Therapies, Anatomy/Physiology for Massage Professionals, Natural Therapeutics, Joint Structure and Function, Acupressure/Shiatsu, Reiki, Reflexology, Sports Massage, Health in the 90s, Business Management, and supervised practice.

The 200-hour Massage Practitioner Course concentrates on circulatory massage, and is transferable into the Massage Therapist Program.

Continuing Education

Instruction is available in craniosacral rhythms, seated massage, sports massage, Aston fitness, and other topics.

Admission Requirements

Prospective students must submit an application, scores from a standardized test of basic math and verbal skills, and a personal interview. Reading and writing at the eleventh-grade level is required.

Tuition and Fees

Tuition for the Massage Therapist Program is $4,300; other fees include: massage table, $200 to $550; and books, $400. Tuition for the Massage Practitioner Course is $725; other fees include: massage table, $200 to $550; and books, $50. There is a $75 registration fee for both courses.

Cleveland Chiropractic College of Los Angeles

590 North Vermont Avenue
Los Angeles, California 90004-2196
Phone: (213) 660-6166 / (800) 466-CCLA
Fax: (213) 660-5387

Dr. C.S. Cleveland Sr., Dr. Ruth R. Cleveland, and Dr. Perl B. Griffin founded Cleveland Chiropractic College of Kansas City in 1922. In the 1940s, the Board of Trustees acquired Ratledge Chiropractic College in Southern California. Ratledge was rechartered as Cleveland Chiropractic College of Los Angeles in 1950, and in 1992, the college joined with its sister school, Cleveland Chiropractic College of Kansas City, to form a multi-campus system. Though unified in governance and administrative function, each college operates independently with academic and instructional autonomy.

Accreditation

Cleveland Chiropractic College of Los Angeles is accredited by the Council on Chiropractic Education (CCE).

Program Description

The 4,865-hour Doctor of Chiropractic degree program may be completed in forty months. The program consists of courses taken from each of several departments: the Department of Basic Sciences (Anatomy, Physiology, Pathology, Microbiology, Chemistry, and Public Health courses); the Department of Diagnostic Sciences (including Di-

agnosis, X-Ray Interpretation, X-Ray Procedure, and Public Health); the Department of Chiropractic Sciences (Chiropractic Orientation, Philosophy, Technique, Physiotherapy, Clinic Management, and Practice Management courses); Research; and Clinical Internship.

Continuing Education

The Office of Continuing Education presents relicensing seminars in various subject areas that have included clinical nutrition, sports injury technique, X-ray, neurology, workers' compensation, infectious diseases including AIDS, and others.

Admission Requirements

Applicants must have completed at least sixty semester units of prechiropractic courses at a regionally accredited college with a cumulative G.P.A. of 2.5 or higher. Students with a cumulative G.P.A. of 2.25 to 2.49 may be considered for admission on the strength of other factors. Candidates having a bachelor's degree are preferred. Specific numbers of prerequisite semester units are required in biological science, general chemistry, organic chemistry, general physics, general psychology, social science/humanities, and English/communications. Applicants must also submit two letters of recommendation; ideally, one should be from a chiropractor or other health care professional.

Tuition and Fees

Application fee, $50; tuition, $4,985 per trimester (part-time tuition, $166 per contact hour); malpractice insurance, $20 per trimester; and books and supplies (approximate), $300 per trimester.

Financial Assistance

Payment plans, federal and non-federal scholarships, grants, loans, and work-study programs are available.

Day-Break Geriatric Massage Project

(See Multiple State Locations, page 299)

Desert Resorts School of Somatherapy

13090 Palm Drive
Desert Hot Springs, California 92240
Phone: (619) 329-1175

The Desert Resorts School of Somatherapy was founded in 1991 by Ramona Moody French, who has more than 3,000 hours of training in massage, manual lymph drainage, and related techniques, and was an instructor at Mueller College in San Diego for eight years.

Program Description

The one-hundred-hour Massage Technician Program provides an introduction to massage. In many areas, this course may not be sufficient training for licensing, and students are advised to research the requirements in their communities. The curriculum consists of classes in Systems of the Body, History and Theory, Business and Ethics, and Massage Instruction.

The one-hundred-hour Acupressure Therapist Program teaches the student to give a full-body acupressure massage. This course is designed as continuing education for massage professionals, or as an exposure to Eastern philosophy for nonprofessionals. Acupressure I and II are the two 50-hour courses.

The 250-hour Massage Therapist Program is open to graduates of the Massage Technician Program. Prior to completing the Massage Therapist Program, students must also complete the Acupressure Therapist Program and fifty hours of clinic practice. The curriculum consists of Advanced Massage Techniques I and II (including aromatherapy, spa services, and sports massage), Anatomy and Physiology, Kinesiology, and Communication Skills and Ethics.

Prior to completing the 250-hour Holistic Health Practitioner Course, students must also complete the Massage Therapist Program, as well as 300 hours of practice including massage clinic, massage seminars, sports events, and a volunteer project. The curriculum includes classes in Advanced Anatomy, Nutrition, Polarity, Deep Tissue Massage, and Holistic Theory.

The 160-hour Comprehensive Decongestive Therapy Course provides instruction in performing manual lymph drainage. The curriculum includes Anatomy and Physiology, Pathology, Indications and Contraindications, Additional Techniques, Bandaging/Exercises, Practice, review, and testing.

Admission Requirements

Applicants must be at least 18 years of age, in good health with no communicable disease, and United States residents. Applicants must also interview with an admissions representative.

Tuition and Fees

Tuition for the Massage Technician Program is $695; supplies are $55. Tuition for the Acupressure Therapist Program is $800; books and supplies are $50. Tuition for the Massage Therapist Program is $1,385; books and supplies are approximately $100. Tuition for the Holistic Health Practitioner Course is $1,440; books and supplies are approximately $50. Tuition for the Comprehensive Decongestive Therapy Course is $1,995; supplies are approximately $100.

Diamond Light School of Massage and Healing Arts

45 San Clemente Drive
Corte Madera, California 94925
Phone: (415) 454-6651

Mailing Address:
P.O. Box 5443
Mill Valley, CA 94942

Diamond Light School of Massage and Healing Arts was founded in 1987 by Vajra Matusow, who has been practicing and teaching bodywork and healing for over twenty-four years.

Accreditation

Diamond Light is accredited by the California State Council for Private Postsecondary and Vocational Education.

Program Description

The 150-hour Massage Certification Course consists of one hundred hours of training and fifty hours of practice. Courses include Swedish/Esalen Massage; Foot Reflexology; Business, Hygiene, and Ethics; Massage Theory and History; Lymphatic Massage; Anatomy and Physiology; Survey of Massage Technique; and Supervised Practicum.

The fifty-six-hour Deep Bodywork Certification Program offers instruction in techniques developed to address core patterns underlying chronic, functional, and structural problems of the musculoskeletal system. Courses include Theory of Deep Bodywork, Demonstration and Practice of Deep Bodywork Technique, and Anatomy.

A one-hundred-hour Advanced Bodywork Practitioner Course offers instruction in Anatomy, Deep Tissue Massage, Meditation, Advanced Healing Techniques, and Supervised Practicum.

A 200-hour Hypnotherapy Course offers instruction in Advanced Hypnotic Induction Methods, Advanced Verbal Skills Development, Intuitive Abilities Development, Advanced Past Life Regression Therapies, Dealing with Bizarre Hypnotic Phenomena, Treatment Strategies for Complex Cases, and Business and Ethical Issues.

A one-hundred-hour, individually-structured Energetic Healing Course focuses on such topics as Energy and Chakra Work, Laying On of Hands, Working with the Elements, Meditation and Healing Practices from Various Traditions, Sound Healing, Reiki Certification, and Subtle Sense Perception.

Other programs include Reiki Levels I and II Certification, offered over a two-day weekend, and a one-day seminar in Hypnotherapy for Bodyworkers.

Classes are held evenings and weekends at 45 San Clemente Drive in Corte Madera and at 100 Sacramento Avenue in San Anselmo.

Admission Requirements

Applicants must be at least 16 years of age or have parental permission; there is no minimum education requirement.

Tuition and Fees

Tuition is as follows: Massage Certification, $1,145; Deep Bodywork, $595; Advanced Bodywork, $4,500; Hypnotherapy, $1,450; Energetic Healing, $1,200 to $1,800 depending on courses chosen; Reiki Levels I and II, $195; and Hypnotherapy for Bodyworkers, $80.

Financial Assistance

A discount is given for early payment; payment plans and work-study are also available.

Dry Creek Herb Farm and Learning Center

13935 Dry Creek Road
Auburn, California 95602
Phone: (916) 878-2441
Fax: (916) 878-6772

Dry Creek Herb Farm and Learning Center was founded in 1989 by Shatoiya de la Tour. In addition to internships, apprenticeships, and classes, the center offers garden tours and sells organically grown herbs (fresh, dried, or as live plants) and other bulk herbs and teas by mail order.

Accreditation

Nursing continuing education units are available for advanced, intern, and apprenticeship programs, and some classes.

Program Description

The nine-month Earth-Centered Apprenticeship Program meets one weekend per month or one Thursday per week. The course combines Rosemary Gladstar's correspondence course, *The Science and Art of Herbology,* with extensive hands-on herbal instruction, usage, and much more. Topics covered include Herbal Philosophies; Herb Walks and Plant Identification; Harvesting Roots; Healing Through the Seasons; Spiritual Attunement with the Plants; Tea and Tincture Formulation; Herb Actions and Body Systems; Making Tinctures, Liniments, Salves, Poultices, Compresses, and Capsules; Herbal First Aid; Essential Oils, Infused Oils, and Aromatherapy; Herb Gardening; Wildcrafting; Herb Crafts and Cosmetics; Trends in Herbalism, Legal Herbalism, and Herbal Careers; and much more.

A four-month, 545-hour internship program is also offered. Rosemary Gladstar's *The Science and Art of Herbology* and David Hoffman's *Therapeutic Herbalism* serve as the written texts. This program honors the folk and scientific approaches to Western herbalism, while also exploring Chinese and Ayurvedic traditions.

Individual classes and workshops are held evenings and weekends throughout the year on a wide variety of topics that have included Planning Your Herb Garden, Herbal Brewing, Spring Foods and Tonic Remedies, the Healing Mind, High Blood Pressure Workshop, Living Healthier with Diabetes, Basic Herb Usage, Medicinal Herb Garden Tour, Feng Shui, and more.

A Spring Herbal Intensive offers instruction in the tradition of herbs through lectures and hands-on participation.

Advanced and progressive study programs are offered annually. Each provides an opportunity to study with a variety of teachers from around the country.

Tuition and Fees

Tuition for the Earth-Centered Apprenticeship Program is $1,350; books and materials are approximately $200. Tuition for the Internship Program is $3,800; books and materials are $200 to $400. Classes and workshops are $15 to $75. The Spring Herbal Intensive is $350. Advanced programs are $600 to $1,150.

East West Academy of Healing Arts/Qigong Institute

(*See* Multiple State Locations, page 302)

East West School of Herbalism

Box 712
Santa Cruz, California 95061
Phone: (800) 717-5010

The East West School of Herbalism was founded by Michael Tierra, C.A., N.D., who maintains an herb and acupuncture clinic in Santa Cruz, teaches, writes, and creates a line of herbal products.

Accreditation

The East West School of Herbalism is approved by the California Board of Registered Nursing to provide continuing education credits for 400 contact hours.

Program Description

The East West School's primary method of instruction is through three correspondence courses in herbalism (see page 366). However, a week-long seminar is offered each year in the mountains outside Santa Cruz. Topics covered in the past include the Five Stagnations: The Mother of All Diseases; Treating Skin Diseases with Herbs; Biomagnet Healing; Treatment of Stress, Anxiety, and Insomnia with Herbs; Herb Walks; Preparations; Pulse and Tongue Diagnosis; and Planetary Formulas. Mornings begin with pranayama, yoga, qigong, tai chi, or meditation.

Admission Requirements

There are no minimum age or educational requirements.

Tuition and Fees

Tuition is $550, or $450 with early registration; room and board are $285, or camping with meals is $225.

Emperor's College of Traditional Oriental Medicine

1807-B Wilshire Boulevard
Santa Monica, California 90403
Phone: (310) 453-8300
Fax: (310) 829-3838

The Emperor's College of Traditional Oriental Medicine was founded in 1983 by Dr. Bong Dal Kim.

Accreditation

The Master of Traditional Oriental Medicine (MTOM) Program is accredited by the National Accreditation Commission for Schools and Colleges of Acupuncture and Oriental Medicine (NAC-SCAOM); licensing eligibility is approved by the Acupuncture Committee of the California Medical Board. Graduates are qualified to take the California Acupuncture Licensing Examination, as well as the national certification examinations in acupuncture and Chinese herbology administered by the National Commission for the Certification of Acupuncturists (NCCA).

Program Description

The 2,500-hour Master of Traditional Oriental Medicine (MTOM) Program is a three- or four-year course of study (1,700 academic hours, 800 clinic hours) that includes courses such as Introduction to Oriental Medicine, Introduction to Meridians, Introduction to Herbology, Tai Chi, Chemistry, Anatomy/Physiology, Zang-Fu Syndromes, Herb Pharmacopoeia, Biochemistry, Oriental Diagnosis, Acupuncture Anatomy, Physics, East/West Medical History, Western Medical Terminology, Acupuncture Techniques, Acupressure, Pathology, General Psychology, Basic Nutrition, Therapeutic Massage, Herb Formulas, Clinical Nutrition, Clinical Point Selection, Medical Qigong, Microsystems, Herb Pharmacy, CPR, Chinese Internal Medicine, Shang Han Wen Bing, Principles of Treatment, Secondary Vessels, Western Pharmacology, Ethics/Jurisprudence, Chinese Nutrition, Clinical Diagnosis by Lab Data, Introduction to Medical Imaging, and more.

English is the primary language spoken within the college, but classes are offered in English and Korean. Students may elect to complete 320 hours of internship at a medical university hospital training program in the People's Republic of China.

Community and Continuing Education

The Extension Program offers an array of courses that may be taken for educational enrichment or may be transferred for full credit into the MTOM program.

A one-hundred-hour Certificate in Basic Acupressure/ Massage may be completed in one quarter. Courses include Therapeutic Massage, Shiatsu (Acupressure), and Reflexology.

A 300-hour Acupressure/Massage Technician Certificate includes instruction in Therapeutic Massage, Shiatsu (Acupressure), Reflexology, Tui Na, Physical Training and Body Sculpting, Overview of Oriental Medicine for Acupressurists and Massage Practitioners, Anatomy/Physiology, and Acupressure/Massage Therapy Internship. Students are required to obtain a valid Red Cross CPR/First Aid certificate.

A 640-hour Acupressure/Massage Therapist Certificate consists of the 300-hour program plus Sports Massage, Aromatherapy, Color and Sound Therapy, Treatment Principles of Acupressure and Massage Therapy, and more, including electives chosen from among Tai Chi, Medical Qigong, Chinese Nutrition, General Psychology, Clinical Psychology, Basic Nutrition, and Clinical Nutrition.

Graduates may continue their studies at Hei Long Jiang TCM College in Harbin, China; the Certificate Program requires a two-month internship. Students here speak the Mandarin dialect.

Graduates may undergo a one-and-a-half-year internship leading to the Bachelor of Science degree in medicine, which allows them to practice acupuncture and Oriental medicine in several East Asian countries, and may also qualify them to take the Foreign Equivalency Examination in Western Medicine in the United States.

Admission Requirements

Applicants for admission to the MTOM degree program must have completed sixty semester units of undergraduate course work from an accredited college, submit two letters of recommendation, and interview with an admissions representative.

Applicants to the certificate programs must be at least 18 years old, have a high school diploma or equivalent, and submit two letters of reference.

Tuition and Fees

Tuition for academic courses is $90 per unit; for clinical courses, $7 per hour. Other fees include: application fee, $50; registration fee, $60; graduation fee, $150; and books, herb samples, and clinic supplies (approximate), $1,200. The approximate total tuition and clinical internship cost is $21,400.

Financial Assistance

Federal student aid and direct loans are available.

Esalen Institute

Highway 1
Big Sur, California 93920-9616
Phone: (408) 644-8476 (catalogs) /
   (408) 667-3000 (information)
Fax: (408) 667-2724 (reservations only)

The Esalen Institute was founded in 1962 as an educational center devoted to exploring unrealized human capacities through East/West philosophies and didactic/experiential workshops. Visitors may stay overnight or longer. Esalen is located on twenty-seven spectacular acres of Big Sur coastline.

Accreditation

A number of workshops may be taken for continuing education credit by nurses and psychologists, and are approved by the California Board of Registered Nursing and the California Psychological Association. Two-day workshops offer ten hours of CEU credit; five-day workshops offer thirty hours of CEU credit for nurses, and twenty-six hours for psychologists.

Program Description

The twenty-eight-day Massage Practitioner Certification Program is a professional training program that, coupled with thirty documented massage sessions, leads to a California state-approved Certificate of Completion. The training includes Anatomy, Movement, Meditation, Gestalt Awareness, Ethics and Business Practices, and Self-Care.

Continuing Education

Workshops that provide continuing education credit for nurses are offered throughout the year. Some topics include Adventures in Bodywork, the Subtle Art of Meditation, Psychoneuroimmunology and Its Implications, Weekend Massage Intensive, Sports Massage: Keeping the Player Playing, Hanna Somatics: Mastery of Muscles and Emotions, Religious and Spiritual Problems: A Paradigm Shift in Mental Health, Gestalt Practice, Polarity Massage Intensive, Zero Balancing Open Forum, Five-Day Massage Intensive, Birth Experience: A Pathway to Life, the Heart of the Shaman, Caring for the Dying: What Really Works?, Practical Herbology: An Esalen Garden Workshop, and many others.

Workshops that offer continuing education credit for psychologists have not been outlined at this writing.

Tuition and Fees

Tuition for the Massage Practitioner Certification Program is $3,325 with standard accommodations, or $2,350 with bunk bed room, if available. Tuition for continuing education programs is $1,110 for seven days, $740 for five days, and $380 per weekend with standard accommodations; tuition with bunk bed room, if available, is $845, $550, and $300, respectively. Lower rates are available for sleeping bag space and those with their own accommodations. All rates include meals.

Financial Assistance

Work-study is available, and a discount is offered for senior citizens.

Feldenkrais Resources

(*See* Multiple State Locations, page 302)

Five Branches Institute

200 Seventh Avenue, Suite 115
Santa Cruz, California 95062
Phone: (408) 476-9424
Fax: (408) 476-8928

Five Branches Institute was founded in 1984 and is located one block from Twin Lakes Beach on Monterey Bay. The institute is named for the five branches of traditional Chinese medicine: energetics, dietary medicine, acupuncture, herbology, and bone medicine.

Accreditation

The master's degree program offered at Five Branches Institute is accredited by the National Accreditation Commission for Schools and Colleges of Acupuncture and Oriental Medicine (NAC-SCAOM), and fulfills the requirements for students wishing to take the California State Licensing Exam and the National Commission for the Certification of Acupuncturists (NCCA) Exam.

Program Description

The 2,704-hour, four-year master's degree in traditional Chinese medicine includes courses from six departments: Traditional Chinese Medical Theory, Acupuncture, Chinese Herbology, Auxiliary Studies, Modern Sciences, and Clinical Training.

First-year courses include Theory, Acupuncture, Philosophy/History, Qigong, Medical Terminology, Medical Model, Herbology, Pathophysiology, and Clinical Theater.

Second-year courses include continuing studies in Theory, Acupuncture, Herbology, Pathophysiology, and Clinical Theater, as well as Bodywork, Dietetics, Clinical Sciences, and Clinical Rounds.

Third-year courses continue to build on Theory, Acupuncture, Herbology, and Bodywork, and also include Ethics/Business Management, Pharmacology, electives, Clinical Rounds, and Supervised Practice.

In the fourth year, students take TCM seminars, electives, Medical Research, Psychology, Clinical Rounds, and Supervised Practice.

Electives include such classes as TCM Patent Herbal Medicines, Herb Stocking, Women's Medicine, Children's Medicine, Structural Medicine, TCM Treatment of HIV/AIDS, Tai Chi Chuan, Chinese Language, TCM Treatment of Alcohol and Drug Addiction, and others.

Continuing Education

Postgraduate studies at various TCM colleges in China are offered to graduates and other licensed acupuncturists. The one- to four-month program allows each student, working closely with a personal translator, to design an individualized curriculum that may include qigong, tai chi, and clinical rounds with experienced specialists. Phone Dr. Joanna Zhao for specific information at (408) 476-8211.

Admission Requirements

Applicants must have completed at least sixty semester units of general education from a nationally accredited college, including college-level courses in human anatomy and physiology, physics, chemistry, and biology. In addition, applicants must submit a statement of purpose and three letters of personal reference, and interview with an admissions representative.

Tuition and Fees

Tuition for academic units is $140 per semester unit; for clinical units, $280 per semester unit. The estimated total for the four-year program, including tuition, fees, and books, is $25,460.

Financial Assistance

Payment plans are available, as well as a Founder's Scholarship (35 percent tuition waiver).

Flower Essence Society

P.O. Box 459
Nevada City, California 95959
Phone: (916) 265-0258 / (800) 548-0075
Fax: (916) 265-6467
E-mail: fes@nccn.net

The Flower Essence Society is a division of Earth-Spirit, Inc., a nonprofit educational and research organization dedicated to the development of flower essence therapy (see page 349 for membership and page 364 for catalog information). The society has been offering its Practitioner Intensive for over fourteen years.

Program Description

Introductory weekends offer a comprehensive overview of flower essence theory and practice, including flower essence selection techniques and the study of live plant specimens.

The Practitioner Intensive is a week-long program open to those who have completed the weekend program or its equivalent. The program presents extensive profiles of major flower remedies, including typical combinations, case studies, and remedies for special populations; counseling; selection techniques; key "meta-levels" of in-depth flower essence therapy; essence combining; and distinctions between flower essences and other remedies such as homeopathic or psychiatric drugs. Features include plant observation, artistic sessions, and a field trip with optional overnight camping to the Sierra Nevada mountains to prepare a flower essence. Practitioner certification is available to those who complete all the assignments and submit three in-depth case studies and a related paper within seven months after the program.

Tuition and Fees

The cost for introductory weekends is $170 to $220 ($153 to $198 for Flower Essence Society members). The Practitioner Intensive costs $780 ($702 for FES members); camping and lunches are additional.

Hahnemann College of Homeopathy

828 San Pablo Avenue
Albany, California 94706
Phone: (510) 524-3117

The Hahnemann College of Homeopathy began its educational program in 1986. The college is located in a modern medical facility, along with the Hahnemann Medical Clinic and Hahnemann Pharmacy.

Accreditation

The Hahnemann College of Homeopathy has been accredited by the California State Council for Private Postsecondary and Vocational Education, and by the Council on Homeopathic Education (CHE) as an advanced-level postgraduate course.

Program Description

The 864-hour Comprehensive Professional Course in Classical Homeopathy is open to all licensed health care practitioners. The course meets in four-

day sessions nine times per year for four years. A new course begins every two years, usually in January. The curriculum includes History, Philosophy, and Theory; Materia Medica: Comparative Materia Medica; Case Analysis; Case Taking and Management; and additional topics. In addition to classes, students are responsible for ten to twenty hours per week of home study, and are required to analyze and treat twenty-four chronic cases. Each student is assigned to a preceptor in the community who assists with case analysis.

Admission Requirements

Admission is open to licensed health care professionals—M.D., D.O., D.C., N.D., D.D.S., P.A., N.P., L.Ac., D.P.M., or D.V.M.—from accredited, residential schools. Applicants must submit a copy of their medical license. Prior background in homeopathy is not required.

Tuition and Fees

Tuition is $15,000. There is an application fee of $50, and books are approximately $500; students must also have a video camera for making videotapes for review and critique.

Heartwood Institute

220 Harmony Lane
Garberville, California 95542
Phone: (707) 923-5002 (admissions) /
    (707) 923-5000 (reception)
Fax: (707) 923-5010

Heartwood Institute, founded in 1978, is located on 240 remote acres in the mountains of California's North Coast. Students live on campus in simple rooms and enjoy freshly prepared, organic, and largely vegetarian meals in a log lodge surrounded by forests and meadows.

Accreditation

Heartwood Institute's Massage Therapist and Advanced Massage Therapist Programs are approved by the American Massage Therapy Association Commission on Massage Training Accreditation/Approval (AMTA/COMTAA), the Oregon Board of Massage Technicians, and the Washington State Board of Massage. The Polarity Therapy Training is accredited by the American Polarity Therapy Association (APTA). The institute is approved by the California Board of Registered Nursing as a provider of continuing education credits.

Program Description

Heartwood offers two AMTA/COMTAA approved massage therapy programs: a 570-hour Massage Therapist Program and a 750-hour Advanced Massage Therapist Program. Both programs emphasize five major types of healing: Swedish massage, Neo-Reichian massage, deep tissue massage, polarity therapy, and Zen shiatsu acupressure and Oriental healing arts. Students in both programs must also complete the AIDS education class.

The curriculum for the 570-hour Massage Therapist Program includes Massage Theory and Technique, Integrative Massage, Deep Tissue Massage, Musculoskeletal Anatomy, Introduction to Body Systems, Body Systems 2, Kinesiology, Pathology, Successful Business Practices, Therapeutic and Professional Skills, Clinical Practicum in Massage Therapy, Tai Chi or Yoga, Exercise Therapy, Hydrotherapy, Standard First Aid, and CPR.

The 750-hour Advanced Massage Therapist Program includes all the classes taught in the 570-hour program, plus Polarity Therapy or Zen Shiatsu Acupressure, and other classes that may include Seated Massage, Fragile Care Massage, and Body/Mind Integration.

Students who complete the Polarity Therapy Massage Practitioner Training offered in the 750-hour program and receive five professional sessions may join APTA as an Associate Polarity Practitioner; they may then become Registered Polarity Practitioners by completing the Polarity Internship, Polarity Diet, Craniosacral Therapy, and Counseling for Bodyworkers intensives, and receiving five professional sessions.

Heartwood also offers a 750-hour Somatic Therapist Program that synthesizes therapeutic methods such as bodywork, breathwork, and hypnotherapy. Students completing this program are eligible to take the certification exam administered by the National Certification Board for Therapeutic Massage and Bodywork (NCBTMB). Graduates earn a diploma and a hypnotist certificate. The curriculum includes Neo-Reichian Massage, Polarity Therapy, Zen Shiatsu Acupressure, Shiatsu Practicum, Musculoskeletal Anatomy, Successful Business Practices, Clinical Practicum in Somatic Therapy, Breath and Transformation, Breathwork II, Conscious Communication Skills, Body/Mind Integration, Integrating Hypnotherapy with Bodywork, Hypnotic Approaches to Bodywork, Therapeutic Applications of Hypnotherapy, and Tai Chi or Yoga. Students must also complete the AIDS education class.

The twelve-month, 1,000-hour Holistic Health Practitioner Program offers a broad-spectrum approach to health and wellness. The curriculum includes course work offered in the 750-hour Advanced Massage Therapist Program, combined with 250 additional hours in courses such as Body/Mind Integration, Integrating Hypnotherapy with Bodywork, Hypnotic Approaches to Bodywork, Breath and Transformation, or a combination of intensives that include energy work, Oriental techniques, neuromuscular therapy, sports massage, structural bodywork, and others.

Continuing Education

Heartwood Institute offers intensive trainings throughout the year that may be taken as continuing and advanced education by massage practitioners and other professionals, as entry-level trainings, or for personal growth and spiritual development. Such intensives include Neuromuscular Therapy, Craniosacral Therapy, Zen Shiatsu Acupressure, Lymphatic and Visceral Massage, TMJ Dysfunction, and more.

A certificate may be earned in Jin Shin Do Bodymind Acupressure that meets the requirements for practicing in parts of California and most of the United States, as well as those of Module I of the Jin Shin Do Foundation.

The Alchemical Hypnotherapy Institute at Heartwood offers a 200-hour program in alchemical hypnotherapy that qualifies graduates for hypnotherapist certification. This program explores such topics as Hypnotic Communication, Rescuing the Inner

Child, Inner Guide Work, Past Life Explorations, Conference Room Therapy, Establishing a Professional Practice, Client Assessment, Techniques for Working with Survivors of Sexual Abuse, and others.

Admission Requirements

Applicants must have a high school diploma or equivalent, be drug- and chemical dependency-free, supply two personal references, and be interviewed by admissions personnel.

Tuition and Fees

Tuition for the Massage Therapist Program is $4,845; for the Advanced Massage Therapist Program, $6,375; for the Somatic Therapist Program, $6,375; and for the Holistic Health Practitioner Program, $8,500. For the Alchemical Hypnotherapy Level I Program (100 hours), tuition is $1,200 and materials are $50; for Level II (fifty hours), tuition is $600 and materials are $25; for Level III (fifty hours), tuition is $600 and materials are $20.

Room and board is $2,050 per quarter double occupancy, $3,175 per quarter single occupancy, $1,835 per quarter camping space (available summer and fall quarters); other fees include: cleaning deposit, $200 (refundable); health fee, $35 (health intake conference); Standard First Aid/CPR class, $38; and malpractice insurance, $20; books, transportation, and massage table are additional.

Financial Assistance

Payment plans and veteran's benefits are available.

Hellerwork International

(*See* Multiple State Locations, page 304)

Hypnosis Motivation Institute

18607 Ventura Boulevard, Suite 310
Tarzana, California 91356
Phone: (818) 758-2745 /
    (818) 344-4464, ext. 745

The Hypnosis Motivation Institute, founded in 1967 by Dr. John G. Kappas, has over fifty therapists on its staff and serves several hundred clients per week. In addition to its resident program, HMI Extension School offers a Foundations in Hypnotherapy course on video (see page 375).

Accreditation

HMI is the only college of hypnotherapy nationally accredited by the Accrediting Council for Continuing Education and Training (ACCET). HMI is approved by the California Board of Registered Nursing as a provider of continuing education units, and by the Board of Behavioral Science Examiners for the hypnosis training of licensed marriage and family therapists. There is currently no state or federal license available for hypnotherapists; anyone can legally offer hypnotherapy services to the public.

Program Description

The 720-hour Hypnotherapy Program consists of Hypnosis 101 (which covers such topics as History of Hypnosis, Theory of Mind, Environmental Hypnosis and Hypersuggestibility, Various Hypnotic Inductions, Deepening Techniques, Postsuggestion to Re-Hypnosis, Three Stages of Somnambulism, Self-Hypnosis, Group Hypnosis, and more); Clinical Hypnosis 201 (which covers Hypnotic Modalities, Neurolinguistic Programming, Ericksonian Hypnosis, Hypnotic Regressions, Dream Therapy, Hypnotic Extinction of Fears and Phobias, Kappasinian Hypnosis, Medical Model of Hypnosis, Child Hypnosis, Hypnodiagnostic Tools, Hypnodrama, and Practice Law and Ethics); Hypnotherapy 301 (covering Physical and Emotional Sexuality, Systems Approach, Clinical Case Presentation, Low Blood Sugar Symptoms, Eating Disorders, Substance Abuse, Residency Orientation, Advertising and Promotion, First Consultation, Advanced Child Hypnosis, Adult Children of Dysfunctional Families, Crisis Intervention, Defense Mechanisms, Mental Bank, Sexual Dysfunction, General Self-Improvement, Habit Control, and Counseling and Interviewing); Handwriting Analysis; Clinical Applications 401; and Clinical Internship 501.

Admission Requirements

Applicants must be at least 18 years of age; have a high school diploma or equivalent or pass the Wonderlic Basic Skills Test (a standardized test of basic math and verbal skills); and interview with an admissions representative. The Taylor-Johnson Temperament Analysis Profile will also be administered to every applicant and results must fall within a range deemed acceptable by HMI.

Tuition and Fees

Tuition for the entire program is $6,270.

Financial Assistance

Payment plans and federal financial aid are available. Clinical Internship 501 students may earn money working in the clinic.

The Institute for Health Improvement

6076 Claremont Avenue
Oakland, California 94618
Phone: (510) 428-0937
Internet: http://www.breema.com

The Institute for Health Improvement was founded in 1980 by Manocher Movlai in order to introduce Breema bodywork to the West. Breema is an ancient Kurdish bodywork system that emphasizes nonjudgmental treatment and practitioner's comfort; treatments, performed comfortably clothed on a padded floor, release tension and create vibrant health, mental clarity, and emotional balance for both practitioner and recipient. Director Jon Schreiber, D.C., has been practicing and teaching Breema bodywork for over fifteen years, and directs the Advanced Arts Breema Chiropractic Clinic, where Breema bodywork is the primary healing modality.

Accreditation

The Institute for Health Improvement is a vocational school licensed by the California State Council for Private Postsecondary and Vocational Education.

Program Description

The institute offers a 165-hour Practitioner Certificate in Breema bodywork. The requirements for certification include Breema bodywork classes and workshops, supervised practicum sessions, Practitioner Colloquium, Anatomy and Physiology, Nutrition and Cleansing Workshop, Self-Breema classes, and fifteen hours of electives. Students may choose from weekly classes, weekend workshops, and longer intensive programs in order to accrue the required number of Breema bodywork hours. The program requires at least six months to complete. Graduates are prepared to establish a private Breema bodywork practice.

Admission Requirements

Students applying for the Certificate Program must have a sincere interest in Breema and the ability to do basic sequences comfortably.

Tuition and Fees

Total tuition varies with the courses chosen. Five-week modules cost $140 for one module, $230 for two modules, and $315 for three modules. A seventeen-day Breema Intensive is offered for $550. Weekend workshop packages are offered for $250.

Financial Assistance

Early registration and multiple class discounts, and some work exchange positions are available.

Integrative Therapy School

3000 T Street, Suite 104
Sacramento, California 95816
Phone: (916) 739-8848

The Integrative Therapy School (ITS) was founded in 1982 by Patricia Lahey, James Peal, and John Sibbet, and is housed in a two-story building in downtown Sacramento.

Accreditation

The Massage Therapist Program is approved by the American Massage Therapy Association Commission on Massage Training Accreditation/Approval (AMTA/COMTAA). The school is approved by the California Board of Registered Nursing as a continuing education provider.

Program Description

Graduates of the 130-hour Massage Practitioner Course are eligible to work as massage practitioners or technicians in most California cities and/or counties requiring 130 or fewer hours. This course constitutes Level I of the Massage Therapist Course. Classes include Swedish Massage, Basic Anatomy, Introduction to Deep Tissue Work, Legal Issues and Ethics, Introduction to Energy Systems, and Reflexology and Zone Work. Classes are offered days or evenings.

The 500-hour Massage Therapist Course is taught in two levels. Level I is the same as the 130-hour Massage Practitioner Course. Level II consists of classes in Deep Bodywork, Muscle Monitoring, Tai Chi, Sports Massage and Hydrotherapy, Beginning Acupressure, Anatomy and Physiology, Beginning Shiatsu, Building a Successful Bodywork Practice, Communication Skills, Massage and Medical Considerations, Nutrition, Polarity Therapy, and Mind Over Movement (Somatics). Classes may be taken days or evenings.

The 150-hour Advanced Acupressure Course is designed for students with previous training in massage/bodywork and anatomy. Courses include Beginning and Advanced Acupressure, Beginning and Advanced Shiatsu, Practical First Aid, Advanced Chinese Five Elements, Working with Acute and Chronic Illness, Assessment and Practical Application, and Interactive Processing. Classes are held on weekends every three to four weeks.

Admission Requirements

Applicants must be at least 18 years of age, interview with an admissions representative, and may be asked to pass a standardized entrance exam. Applicants for the Advanced Acupressure Course must have completed at least one hundred hours of massage training.

Tuition and Fees

Costs for the Massage Practitioner Program are as follows: tuition, $988; books, $48; materials, $31; insurance, $15; and optional massage table, $500 to $1,000. Costs for the Massage Therapist Program are: tuition, $3,800; books (approximate), $375; materials, $110; supplies, $100; and insurance, $30. Costs for the Advanced Acupressure Course are: tuition, $775; books, $100; materials, $31; and insurance, $15. There is a $75 registration fee for all courses.

Financial Assistance

A payment plan is available.

Integrative Yoga Therapy

(*See* Multiple State Locations, page 305)

International Professional School of Bodywork (IPSB)

1366 Hornblend Street
San Diego, California 92109
Phone: (619) 272-4142 / (800) 748-6497
Fax: (619) 4772
E-mail: beingipsb@aol.com

Founded in 1977, IPSB has earned a reputation as an innovative school on the leading edge of contemporary bodywork and massage. Dr. Edward W. Maupin, president of IPSB and licensed clinical psychologist, has practiced the Rolf method of structural integration since 1968 and worked at the Esalen Institute with Ida Rolf, Fritz Perls, Mary Whitehouse, and others.

Accreditation

IPSB is approved by the California State Council for Private Postsecondary and Vocational Education (CPPVE) as a vocational school, and has been granted temporary approval by that organization as a degree-granting school in order to enable the council to conduct a quality inspection of the institution. In addition, the school is accredited by the American Massage Therapy Association Commission on Massage Training Accreditation/Approval (AMTA/COMTAA), is a member of the AOBTA

Council of Schools and Programs, and is approved by the California Board of Registered Nursing for continuing education credits.

Program Description

The 150-hour (fifteen-credit-unit) Essentials of Massage and Bodywork Certificate Program covers theory and practice of circulatory massage (including Swedish and Esalen massage), deep tissue work, passive joint movement, and muscle sculpting, along with tai chi and the IPSB movement form. Classes include Anatomy, Physiology, and Hygiene; Massage Techniques; Somatic Psychology; Support and Maintenance Systems; Ethics, Business, and Legal Issues; Practice Session; and a Portfolio.

The 180-hour (eighteen-credit-unit) Contemporary Methods of Massage and Bodywork Certificate Program offers instruction in six specialized areas of advanced bodywork to those who have completed the Essentials. Courses include Circulatory Massage Applications, Deep Tissue Sculpting, Oriental Theories and Healing Massage, Somatic Assimilation, Somatic Psychology, and Passive Joint Movement.

Additional certificate programs are offered in specialized internships that range from ninety to 250 hours (nine to twenty-five credit units). These include Relational Somatics, Sensory Repatterning, Somato-Emotional Integration, Structural Integration, Sports Massage, Neuromuscular Therapy, Circulatory Massage Therapeutics, Tui Na Massage, Jin Shin Acutouch, Thailand Medical Massage, Seitai Shiatsu, and Teacher Training.

The Associate of Occupational Studies degree is a diploma program of 104 credit units (approximately 1,200 hours) with a major course of study in massage and bodywork. It includes the Essentials and Contemporary Methods of Massage and Bodywork Programs above, along with studies in Anatomy, Physiology, Massage Electives (which may include Alexander Technique, Feldenkrais Awareness Through Movement, Sports Massage, Foot Reflexology, Tui Na Massage, Lymphatic Massage, Jin Shin Acutouch, Thailand Massage, and others), electives in Kinesiology, Creating a Professional Practice, Neuromuscular Therapy, Principles of Structural Integration (Rolfing), Clinical Applications, Supervised Practice, and other courses, plus one internship in a specialized form of advanced techniques of massage and bodywork.

The Associate of Arts degree is a diploma program of 132½ credit units (approximately 1,470 hours) with a major course of study in massage and bodywork that may be taken in Clinical Methods, Integrative Somatic Methods, Oriental Methods, or Individualized Methods. All of the courses listed in the Associate of Occupational Studies Program above are included in this program, plus four internships in a specialized form of advanced techniques of massage and bodywork.

The Bachelor of Arts degree in humanities is a diploma program of 224 credit units (approximately 2,400 hours) with its major course of study in massage and bodywork. It includes one of the four Associate of Arts degrees or their equivalents plus additional classes in humanities. Courses include Learning Seminars, Language and Communication, Biology, Nutrition, History, Mathematics and Numbers, Music Appreciation, Physics, Psychology, Great Books, Anthropology/Sociology, Self-Directed Learning, Other Humanities, and a Portfolio of Learning.

The Master of Arts degree in somatics is a diploma program of fifty credit units (approximately 650 hours) that has a prerequisite of the IPSB bachelor's degree or its equivalent. The major course of study is in massage and bodywork. The master's degree includes Learning Seminars, Advanced Specializations, Self-Directed Specialization, Self-Directed Comprehensive Studies, Self-Directed Studies, Seminars in Advanced Specializations, Portfolio of Logs and Learning, and a thesis, project, or dissertation.

Classes are held both days and evenings. Full-time, all-day intensive programs are available to those who wish to minimize the time required for training. All students are required to complete First Aid/CPR training.

Admission Requirements

Applicants must be at least 18 years of age, have a high school diploma or equivalent, be free of any diseases or disabilities that would limit physical exertion, have the ability to apply techniques or breathing, and show no evidence of mental instability. Applicants who do not have a high school diploma or equivalent may enroll in certificate programs or individual classes, and may be eligible to continue after taking an approved test to demonstrate their ability to benefit from the program.

Tuition and Fees

Tuition costs are as follows: for the Essentials of Massage and Bodywork Program, $900; for the Contemporary Methods of Massage and Bodywork Program, $1,080; for the Associate of Occupational Studies Program, $8,128; for the Associate of Arts in Clinical Methods, Integrative Somatic Methods, Oriental Methods, or Individualized Methods Programs, $10,775; for the Bachelor of Arts degree, $20,840; and for the Master of Arts degree, $6,000. Other fees include an application fee of $100 and a supply fee of $50 per quarter; books are additional.

Financial Assistance

Payment plans, limited work-study, veterans' benefits, and Vocational Rehabilitation are available. Residents of some Canadian provinces may finance their training through Canadian Government Student Loans.

Jin Shin Do Foundation for Bodymind Acupressure

Mailing Address:
P.O. Box 1097
Felton, California 95018

Facility:
366 California Avenue, Suite 16
Palo Alto, California 94306
Phone: (415) 328-1811
Fax: (408) 338-3666

Jin Shin Do acupressure combines deep finger pressure on acupoints with simple body focusing techniques to release physical and emotional tension and produce a pleasurable trance state. A typical session lasts one to one-and-a-half hours and may be effective in relieving headaches, back and shoulder pain, sinus pain, allergies, and other conditions.

Accreditation

The Jin Shin Do Foundation is a member of the AOBTA Council of Schools and Programs and is approved by the National Certification Board for Therapeutic Massage and Bodywork (NCBTMB) as a continuing education provider.

Program Description

Jin Shin Do Introductory, Module I, and Module II classes are taught by authorized JSD teachers located throughout the country and around the world. Students may contact the foundation for a directory of authorized JSD teachers and registered JSD acupressurists.

Classes offered by registered JSD acupressurists and authorized JSD teachers include short introductory classes such as Five-Step JSD Neck-Shoulder Release (three hours), Fundamentals of Self-Acupressure (twelve to sixteen hours), and JSD Acupressure Facial (six hours).

Module I consists of 150 hours of theory and technique necessary for effective practice of Jin Shin Do, including locating over 200 acupoints, identifying the eight strange flows or extraordinary meridians, the twelve organ meridians, pressure technique, Five Phases theory, and more. Module I is divided into Basic, Intermediate, and Advanced JSD, and Bodymind Processing Skills.

Module II consists of one hundred hours of modality technique and practice, including an indepth study of strange flows, organ meridians, zang-fu, causes of imbalance, precise point location and angle of pressure, point combining, and more.

Module III consists of seventy hours of clinical experience, either as an internship at a bodywork school or as an externship with supervision from an authorized JSD teacher, acupuncturist, or other health professional.

An Intensive Teacher Training Program with Iona Marsaa Teeguarden is offered periodically, and includes in-depth training and practice teaching.

Requirements for registered Jin Shin Do acupressurists include Modules I and II, plus Module III or 125 logged experience hours, along with ten private sessions, practical examination, and compliance with local licensing requirements, if any. To become a certified practitioner with AOBTA requires completion of Module III plus an additional seventy hours of study (of JSD or any recognized Oriental modality), one hundred hours of anatomy and physiology, and an eight-hour CPR class.

To become authorized to teach the Jin Shin Do Basic class, practitioners must have taken Module I and Module II, be a registered JSD acupressurist, take the Intensive Teacher Training Program, log a total of 300 experience hours, take a practical exam, and assist two classes; to teach the Intermediate class, practitioners must have a total of 600 experience hours, have taught four Basic JSD classes, assist with two Intermediate classes, and take a practical exam; to teach the Advanced class requires a special project and practical exam with Iona.

When authorized JSD teachers have been actively practicing for five years and teaching for two, they may be accepted as candidates for AOBTA certified instructor in the style of Jin Shin Do. The certifying process includes an interview with three certified instructors.

Admission Requirements

Classes are open to anyone who has met the prerequisites (i.e., has taken the preceding classes with an authorized JSD teacher).

Tuition and Fees

Fees for classes vary according to the area and class setting. Fees for Modules I and II generally range from $8 to $12 per class hour.

Financial Assistance

Payment plans and work-study may be available from individual instructors.

John F. Kennedy University Graduate School for Holistic Studies

360 Camino Pablo
Orinda, California 94563
Phone: (510) 254-0105
Fax: (510) 254-3322

John F. Kennedy University was founded in 1964 as one of the first universities in the United States dedicated solely to adult education, and has since expanded to meet the full range of student needs. Today, undergraduate and graduate programs in liberal arts, management, psychology, holistic studies, and law enroll approximately 1,800 students, 80 percent of whom are in the graduate program.

Accreditation

John F. Kennedy University is accredited by the Western Association of Schools and Colleges.

Program Description

The Graduate School for Holistic Studies offers Master of Arts (M.A.) degrees in arts and consciousness, with specializations in expressive arts, individual/theoretical, and studio; counseling psychology, with specializations in transpersonal and holistic health; holistic health education; interdisciplinary consciousness studies; and transpersonal psychology.

The M.A. in counseling psychology with holistic health specialization meets the educational requirements for California Marriage, Family, and Child Counselor licensure. Courses offered in the holistic health specialization include Principles of Holistic Health, Psychology of Nutrition and Eating Disorders, Diet in Health and Disease, and Physiology and Psychology of Stress.

Admission Requirements

Students entering the Master of Arts in holistic health education program are required to demonstrate their ability to write a coherent essay by taking the Kennedy English Proficiency Essay Test. All students in the holistic health specialization are required to complete at least nine months, or thirty-six hours, of individual psychotherapy with a licensed counselor.

Graduate applicants who have not completed their Bachelor of Arts degree may enroll in the school's articulated studies option, which allows up to eighteen to twenty-four graduate level units to apply to both a B.A. and M.A. degree concurrently.

Tuition and Fees

Graduate tuition is $237 per unit; books are additional. There is a $50 application fee.

Financial Assistance

Federal grants and loans, California State Graduate Fellowships and California grants, university scholarships, and payment plans are available.

Life Chiropractic College West

2005 Via Barrett
San Lorenzo, California 94580-1368
Phone: (510) 276-9013 / (800) 788-4476
Fax: (510) 276-4893 (admissions)

Life West was originally incorporated as Pacific States Chiropractic College in 1976, and reorganized as Life Chiropractic College West in 1981.

Accreditation

Life Chiropractic College West is accredited by the Council on Chiropractic Education (CCE).

Program Description

The 4,862-hour Doctor of Chiropractic (D.C.) curriculum consists of twelve quarters of full-time study. A fourteen-quarter option is also available, for students who wish to take a slightly reduced load.

Freshman classes (quarters one through three) include Systemic and Histologic Anatomy; Skeletal Anatomy; Peripheral Neuroanatomy; Cell Physiology; Palpation; Chiropractic Philosophy and Principles; Spinal Anatomy; Terminology; Embryology; Regional Anatomy; Systemic Physiology; Biochemistry; General Pathology; Exam Procedures; Introduction to Research Methodology; Central Neuroanatomy; Neuromuscular Physiopathology; Microbiology; Diversified Technique; and Seminars.

Sophomore classes (quarters four through six) include Regional Anatomy; Neuromuscular Physiopathology; Pathology of Infectious Diseases; Chiropractic Philosophy and Principles; Pathology of Metabolic Diseases; Biomechanics of the Spine; Endocrinology; Nutrition; Public Health; Pathology Lab; Bone and Joint Pathodiagnosis; Emergency Care; Exam: Heart, Lungs, and Abdomen; Neurologic Exam; Spinal Orthopedic Exam; Physics of Diagnostic Radiology; Chiropractic Clinical Research Methodology; Scientific Basis of Chiropractic and the Subluxation Complex; Diversified Technique; Reproductive Pathology; Seminars; and others.

Junior classes (quarters seven through nine) include Exam: Eyes, Ears, Nose, and Throat; Case History and Introduction to Diagnosis; Correlative Chiropractic Exam; Integrated Drop Table; Radiology; Physiotherapy; Neurodiagnosis; Chiropractic Philosophy and Principles; Radiographic Positioning; Clinical Laboratory Diagnosis; Clinic; Extremity Adjusting; Practice Skills; Seminars; and others.

Senior classes (quarters ten through twelve) include Neuromusculoskeletal Diagnosis and Management; Obstetrics and Gynecology; Geriatrics; Psychiatry; Clinic; Pediatrics; Toxicology; Differential Diagnosis; Ethics and Jurisprudence; Public Health; Office Procedures/Management; Practice Skills; and others.

Students must also complete at least one technique elective prior to graduation.

Continuing Education

The postgraduate curriculum includes certification and diplomate programs of the Council on Applied Chiropractic Sciences of the International Chiropractors Association. Programs include a 360-hour Diplomate in Applied Chiropractic Sciences Program (DACS) offered by the Council on Applied Chiropractic Sciences; a one-hundred-hour Council on Applied Chiropractic Sciences Certification Program in Whiplash, Spinal Trauma, and Soft Tissue Injury: Diagnosis, Treatment, and Rehabilitation; and a 120-hour Chiropractic Extremity Specialist Certification Program. Twelve-hour license renewal courses include Whiplash and Spinal Trauma, Motor Vehicle Collision Injuries, Management of Pediatric Patients, Headaches: Diagnosis and Management, and others.

Admission Requirements

Applicants must have completed at least sixty college-level semester credits with a G.P.A. of at least 2.25, including at least six semester credits each in biology, physics, organic chemistry, inorganic chemistry, and English; three semester credits in psychology; and fifteen semester credits in social sciences and/or humanities. All science prerequisite courses must have been passed with a grade of C or better. Applicants must submit two letters of recommendation (at least one from a chiropractor) and answers to essay questions, and must interview with a faculty member.

Tuition and Fees

Tuition is $3,850 per quarter. Other fees include a graduation fee of $100 and an application fee of $45; books and equipment are additional.

Financial Assistance

Forms of financial assistance include federal grants, loans, and work-study; state grants; scholarships; Chiroloan; additional loan programs; institutional work-study; veterans' benefits; and aid from the Bureau of Indian Affairs.

Los Angeles College of Chiropractic

16200 Amber Valley Drive
P.O. Box 1166
Whittier, California 90609-1166
Phone: (310) 947-8755 / (800) 221-5222

The Los Angeles College of Chiropractic was founded by Dr. Charles Cale and his wife Linnie in 1911; the first classes of their nine-month program were held in their home. The college moved several times before arriving at its present site in 1981. The ADVANTAGE program was added to the curriculum in 1990.

Accreditation

The Doctor of Chiropractic degree program at the Los Angeles College of Chiropractic is accredited by the Council on Chiropractic Education (CCE) and the Accrediting Commission for Senior Colleges and Universities of the Western Association of Schools and Colleges (WASC).

Program Description

The 4,860-hour Doctor of Chiropractic degree pro-

gram is based on the ADVANTAGE program of chiropractic education. This program is an innovative approach that aims at acquiring competencies, rather than learning subjects, and begins skill development on day one. The program integrates patient care with the basic sciences, and increases lab and hands-on experiences. The twenty chiropractic competencies that drive the ADVANTAGE program are History Taking, Physical Examination, Neuromusculoskeletal Exam, Radiological Exam, Clinical Lab Exam, Special Studies, Diagnosis and Clinical Impression, Referral/Collaborative Care, Treatment Plan, Spinal Adjusting, Extra Spinal Adjusting, Non-Adjustive Physical Procedures, Psychosocial Exam, Emergency Care, Case Follow-Up and Review, Record Keeping, Nutritional Consulting, Practice Management, Research, and Professional Responsibilities.

As students progress through the ADVANTAGE curriculum, they will be involved with four divisions: Basic Sciences (including the departments of Anatomy, Physiology, Biochemistry and Nutrition, and Pathology/Microbiology); Clinical Sciences (including the departments of Principles and Practice, Chiropractic Procedures, Diagnosis, and Radiology); Clinical Internship; and Research.

Continuing Education

The college offers postgraduate educational programs leading to professional certification and/or eligibility to take a board examination in a specialty area, as well as continuing education programs for paraprofessionals. Postgraduate courses include Chiropractic Neurology, Chiropractic Orthopedics, Chiropractic Rehabilitation, and Sports and Recreational Injuries: Prevention, Evaluation, and Treatment. Residency programs are offered in clinical sciences and radiology. A series of postgraduate seminars for license renewal credit is offered throughout the state.

A Chiropractic Assistant Course is conducted twice a year and includes training in both front and back office procedures. The curriculum includes Front Office Management, Insurance, Nutrition, History and Chiropractic Principles, Interpersonal Skills, Anatomy and Physiology, Physical Therapy, X-Ray Fundamentals, Basics of Massage, CPR and Vital Signs, and Legal Aspects of Chiropractic. Classes meet for thirteen Saturdays.

Admission Requirements

Applicants must have completed at least eighty semester units leading to a baccalaureate degree; prechiropractic credits must have been earned at an accredited institution. Not less than six semester units each must have been taken in biological sciences, general chemistry, organic chemistry, and general physics; other prerequisites include English and/or communication skills, psychology, social sciences, or humanities. Applicants should have attained a cumulative G.P.A. of 2.5 or better. Additionally, applicants must submit three letters of recommendation (at least one should be from a Doctor of Chiropractic or other health care professional) and interview with an admissions representative.

Graduation requirements for the Chiropractic Assistant Course include proof of high school education, typing skills of at least 30 w.p.m., and a Red Cross CPR certificate.

Tuition and Fees

Tuition for the Doctor of Chiropractic degree program is $5,207 per trimester. Other fees include an application fee of $50; an associated student body fee of $30 per trimester; books (approximate), $600 per trimester; and equipment (approximate), $1,200.

Tuition for the Chiropractic Assistant Course is $525; either the Front Office or Back Office modules may be taken individually for $290 each. There is a $30 registration fee.

Financial Assistance

Payment plans, federal and private scholarships, grants, loans, and work-study are available.

Los Angeles East West Center for Macrobiotic Studies

11215 Hannum Avenue
Culver City, California 90230
Phone: (310) 398-2228

The Los Angeles East West Center for Macrobiotic Studies was founded in 1973 by Cecile Tovah Levin, who has been a student and teacher of the macrobiotic way of life since 1960. She studied macrobiotic cooking in Japan for six years under Mme. Lima Ohsawa; she has also studied such health disciplines as shiatsu, do-in, qigong, and meditation. Ms. Levin is a well-known author and speaker. The center plans to publish the periodical *Gateways* (see page 383).

Program Description

A series of courses is offered that provides an in-depth study of macrobiotics for both beginning and advanced students, and for those who simply want to improve their own health and that of their families. Certificates will be given to students who complete all the courses.

Fundamentals of Macrobiotic Cooking is a one-year series of seasonal cooking courses designed to guide beginners making the transition to macrobiotic cooking. Topics covered include Fundamentals of Nutrition, Cooking with the Seasons, Cutting Techniques, Cooking for Regeneration, Cooking for One, and Family Cooking. Students are urged to simultaneously attend the Macrobiotic Life Seminars.

The Macrobiotic Life Seminars are a series of day-long participatory seminars. They include Intermediate Macrobiotic Cooking Class, Luncheon, Special Foods Processing Workshops, Home Remedies and Healing Workshops, and Way of Life Studies.

The Macrobiotic Study Intensive offers a one-year, in-depth exploration of life, healing, and personal development according to macrobiotic principles. Topics covered in fireside discussions include the nature of disease and health, the mechanism and function of universal order, how to improve mental clarity, developing judgment and consciousness, and more. The course is appropriate for students at all levels of macrobiotic practice.

The Classic Macrobiotic Cuisine Gourmet Cooking Courses and Gourmet Dinners help students to elevate their macrobiotic cooking repertoire to a level of elegance and sophistication. The course is an extension of the Macrobiotic Life Seminars.

Admission Requirements

There are no minimum age or educational requirements.

Tuition and Fees

Tuition for the Fundamentals of Macrobiotic Cooking Course is $500 per eleven-week course or $60 per individual class. Tuition for the Macrobiotic Life Seminars is $450 per six-week course or $80 per seminar. Tuition for the Macrobiotic Study Intensive is $245 per ten-week course or $25 per individual class. The cost of the Classic Macrobiotic Cuisine Gourmet Cooking Course/Dinners is $65 for the workshop and dinners, or $25 for the dinners only.

Financial Assistance

Payment may be made in two installments or on a per-class basis.

Meiji College of Oriental Medicine

1426 Fillmore Street, Suite 301
San Francisco, California 94115
Phone: (415) 771-1019
Fax: (415) 771-1036

Meiji College of Oriental Medicine (MCOM) was founded in 1990. MCOM integrates Western clinical sciences with acupuncture and herbology, and emphasizes the contributions of the Japanese tradition to Oriental medicine.

Accreditation

The curriculum at MCOM meets both the didactic and clinical requirements of the California Acupuncture Committee. Graduates are qualified to take the California State Licensing Exam and the National Commission for the Certification of Acupuncturists (NCCA) exam. MCOM has also been granted institutional approval from the California State Council for Private Postsecondary and Vocational Education. The program is a candidate for accreditation with the National Accreditation Commission for Schools and Colleges of Acupuncture and Oriental Medicine (NACSCAOM).

Program Description

MCOM offers a full-time, 2,455-hour program leading to the Master of Science degree in Oriental medicine. The curriculum consists of 1,415 lecture hours and 1,040 clinical practice hours. The three-year course of study is equivalent to four academic years. A part-time program is also available.

The first-year curriculum includes Anatomy, Physiology, Pathology, History of Healing and Medical Terminology, Nutrition and Vitamins, Traditional Chinese Medicine Theory, Meridian Points, Theory of Meridians, Acupuncture Technique, Acupuncture Hygiene, Moxibustion and Cupping, Oriental Herbology, Oriental Herbology and Dispensary, Herbal Prescription, Acupressure and Massage, Qigong and Tai Chi, and Clinic Observation.

The second-year curriculum includes Western Clinical Science, Pharmacology, Clinical Psychology, Practice Management and Ethics, Four Classic Texts, TCM Diagnosis, Oriental Clinical Medicine, Acupuncture Treatment Points, Electrical Acupuncture, Extraordinary Meridians and Points, Auricular and Scalp Acupuncture, Extra Points and Hand and Foot Acupuncture, Pathways and Crossing Points, Herbal Prescription, Research Methodology, and the Guided Practice phase of the clinical internship program.

The third year includes over 700 hours of clinical internship, a research project, and courses in Oriental Clinical Medicine, CPR, and First Aid.

Admission Requirements

Applicants must hold a bachelor's degree from an accredited postsecondary institution with a cumulative G.P.A. of 2.5 or higher; submit two letters of recommendation, an essay, a résumé, and a health certificate; and interview with an admissions representative.

Tuition and Fees

Tuition is $7,000 per year ($21,000 total). There is an application fee of $50 and a graduation fee of $50; books, supplies, and other fees are additional.

Financial Assistance

In-house loans and Nellie Mae's EXCEL Education Loan Program are available.

The Michael Scholes School for Aromatic Studies

(*See* Multiple State Locations, page 309)

Monterey Institute of Touch

27820 Dorris Drive
Carmel, California 93923
Phone: (408) 624-1006
E-mail: mit@redshift.com

The Monterey Institute of Touch (MIT) was founded in 1983 by John Sanderson, a certified massage therapist; today it is headed by Birgit Ball Eisner and her daughter, Barbara Ball, both certified Rolfers.

Accreditation

There are no licensing requirements for the City and County of Monterey other than a normal business license. Some courses are approved by the California Board of Registered Nursing for continuing education units. Course approval is granted by the California State Council for Private Postsecondary and Vocational Education.

Program Description

The 200-hour Massage Practitioner Program includes courses in Therapeutic Massage Techniques, Anatomy, Physiology, Polarity, Shiatsu, Self-Care and Movement Awareness, Reflexology, Sports Massage, Intuitive Massage, Business Practice and Ethics, and Supervised Internship Sessions. Students are required to have completed MIT's fourteen-hour Introduction to Massage class prior to enrollment. Beginning in 1997, MIT will also offer a certification program meeting every other weekend for twenty weeks.

The 500-hour Massage Therapist Program is open to students who have completed the 200-hour Massage Practitioner Program and may be completed in a minimum of twelve months. The program follows AMTA guidelines and includes one hundred hours of Intermediate Massage (Anatomy, Massage, Clinical Massage, and Movement), one hundred hours of Advanced Massage (Anatomy,

Body Handling, Massage, Hand/Wrist and Forearm Care, and CPR/Emergency Medical Practice), and one hundred hours of specialization in areas such as sports massage, craniosacral therapy, prenatal massage, and Swedish massage.

Continuing Education

A variety of courses are offered, to both professional massage practitioners and the general public. Offerings typically include Chair Massage, Prenatal Massage, Soft Tissue Release, Aromatherapy, Lymphatic and Visceral Massage, Range of Motion/Body Handling, Movement Awareness, Trigger Point, and others.

Admission Requirements

Applicants must be at least 18 years of age; have a high school diploma or equivalent; be physically capable of performing and receiving massage; interview with an admissions representative; complete MIT's Introduction to Massage class; and submit a short autobiography, two letters of recommendation, and a photograph.

Tuition and Fees

There is an application/registration fee of $75. The Introduction to Massage course costs $85. Tuition for the 200-hour program is $925, plus a final fee of $40; books are approximately $60. Tuition for the 500-hour program is approximately $3,000 to $5,000, depending on the electives chosen.

Financial Assistance

Payment plans are available.

Mount Madonna Center

445 Summit Road
Watsonville, California 95076
Phone: (408) 847-0406
Fax: (408) 847-2683
E-mail: programs@mountmadonna.org
Internet: infopoint.com/orgs/mmc

The Mount Madonna Center, founded in 1978, is a community dedicated to the daily living of spiritual ideals through the practice of yoga. The mountain-top facility is surrounded by redwood groves and serves vegetarian meals.

Accreditation

Many workshops offered at the center may be taken by nurses for continuing education credit.

Program Description

The Mount Madonna Center offers a variety of workshops, many focusing on yoga, but also including psychology, personal growth, spiritual pathways, and related topics. The three-part Phoenix Rising Yoga Therapy Certification Training Program offers a blend of the ancient wisdom of yoga with contemporary approaches to body/mind therapy. The course consists of two 4-day sections that may be taken back-to-back, followed by a six-month home study course in which students are assigned mentors to guide their studies and help refine their technique.

The Ashtanga Yoga Teacher Training Intensive runs twenty to twenty-five days (those without experience in Ashtanga, or eight-limbed, yoga are required to attend the entire twenty-five days). Training focuses on methods of body/mind purification, asana, pranayama, mudra (energy raising techniques), and meditation, and provides opportunities for student teaching.

A five-week class is offered in Ayurveda, Ancient Health Science of India. The course focuses on Functional Assessment of Doshic Subtypes; Clinical Evaluation of Thirteen Main Srotamsi (body energy channels); the Ancient Art of Balancing Your Agni (metabolic fire); First Aid Management of Common Elements According to Ayurveda; and Etiology, Symptomatology, and Management of Psychological Disorders, as well as Ayurveda in daily life, diet and sex in relation to constitution, and more.

Admission Requirements

There are no minimum age or educational requirements.

Tuition and Fees

Tuition for a typical weekend program is $130 plus meals and lodging.

Costs for the Phoenix Rising Yoga Therapy Certification Training Program are as follows: fees for Levels I and II combined range from $1,243 for commuters to $1,684 for a single room, including meals. Fees for Level I only are $605 commuting to $801 single; fees for Level II only are $635 commuting to $831 single.

The Ashtanga Yoga Teacher Training Intensive costs $565 to $615, plus a meals/lodging fee of $17 (commuting) to $69 (single room) per day.

Tuition for the Ayurveda, Ancient Health Science of India Program is $1,895 for the full program, $395 for a week, and $130 for a weekend, plus a meals/lodging fee of $17 (commuting) to $69 (single room) per day.

Financial Assistance

Work-study is available.

Mueller College of Holistic Studies

4607 Park Boulevard
San Diego, California 92116-1243
Phone: (619) 291-9811 / (800) 245-1976

Mueller College was founded in 1976; it was the first school in California and the fourteenth in the United States to receive curriculum approval from the American Massage Therapy Association (AMTA). Mueller has been active in influencing the regulation of massage and body therapies in San Diego.

Accreditation

The 512-hour Massage Therapist Course is approved by the American Massage Therapy Association Commission on Massage Training Accreditation/Approval (AMTA/COMTAA). The Acupressurist Course is approved by the American Oriental Bodywork Therapy Association (AOBTA). The school is approved by the California Board of Registered Nursing and by the National Certification Board for Therapeutic Massage and Bodywork (NCBTMB) as a continuing education provider.

Program Description

The "Mueller Method" Massage Technician Course is a one-hundred-hour, hands-on program in massage fundamentals, covering Introduction to the Body Systems, History and Theory, Business and Ethics, and Demonstration and Practice. This course is a prerequisite for all the other courses. It may be completed in a ten-day accelerated training or in ongoing Tuesday and Thursday classes.

The 512-hour Massage Therapist Course prepares a student for private practice through a curriculum that includes Advanced Massage Techniques (Passive, which consists of manual lymph drainage, myofascial release, craniosacral techniques, and other noninvasive styles, and Active, which incorporates sports massage, deep tissue work, and other Swedish techniques), Acupressure, Essentials for Body Therapists (including Cells/Nutrition, Business and Ethics, and Pathology), Body Systems (comprised of Anatomy, Physiology, and Kinesiology), and Clinical Applications.

The 626-hour Acupressurist Course curriculum includes Acupressure I and II (covering the theories of traditional Chinese medicine, the meridian systems of the body, yin and yang, qi, qigong breathing, shiatsu massage, zone therapy with reflexology, and more), Intermediate Acupressure (with instruction in types of qi, point selection concepts, chi nei tsang and micro-circuits, and syndromes and traditional functions), Advanced Acupressure (a comparison of Eastern and Western techniques), Western Studies (anatomy and physiology, kinesiology, and business), and Clinical Applications.

The 1,000-hour Holistic Health Practitioner Course combines either massage therapist or acupressurist training with additional instruction to prepare a student to care for clients in a nonmedical health care setting. The additional instruction differs somewhat depending on the core training, but includes Advanced Applications, Workshops, Community Event, Peer Review, Teaching Assistant, and Professional Bodywork.

Admission Requirements

Applicants must be at least 18 years of age and in good health. A qualifying process is required for each course of study and must be completed at the school.

Tuition and Fees

There is a registration fee of $75 for all courses. Tuition for the Massage Technician Course is $695, plus $100 for supplies. Tuition for the Massage Therapist Course is $3,600, plus approximately $290 for supplies. Tuition for the Acupressurist Course is $4,625, plus approximately $235 for supplies. Tuition for the Holistic Health Practitioner Course is $1,080 (in addition to Massage Therapist or Acupressurist Courses), plus $62 for supplies.

Financial Assistance

Payment plans, veterans' benefits, and California Vocational Rehabilitation are available. Ongoing Massage Technician students can receive a $75 tuition reduction if they enroll at least twenty-one days before start date; coupon must be presented.

National Holistic Institute

5900 Hollis Street, Suite J
Emeryville, California 94608-2008
Phone: (510) 547-6442

The National Holistic Institute was founded in 1979 by Carol Carpenter, who began her career as a massage therapist in 1976. Since its founding, NHI has graduated over 4,500 students.

Accreditation

NHI is accredited by the Accrediting Council for Continuing Education and Training (ACCET). The Massage Therapy Program is approved by the American Massage Therapy Association Commission on Massage Training Accreditation/Approval (AMTA/COMTAA).

Program Description

The Massage Therapist and Health Educator Program consists of thirty-six quarter-credit hours, and takes approximately ten months to complete (one year for the evening/weekend program). The curriculum consists of Massage Theory and Practice (including Swedish massage, acupressure/shiatsu, seated massage, foot reflexology, deep tissue massage, hydrotherapy, stress management, and more), Anatomy, Physiology, Kinesiology and Pathology, Practice Management, Student Clinic, and Externship/Community Service. A new weekend class meets for twelve hours per week and takes seventeen months to complete.

Admission Requirements

Prospective students must have a high school diploma or equivalent or successfully complete an entrance exam, and be interviewed on campus or by phone.

Tuition and Fees

Tuition is $6,050. Other costs include books and supplies, $294; massage table, face rest, and case, $526; and registration fee, $75.

Financial Assistance

Federal grants, loans, and work-study are available.

Pacific Academy of Homeopathic Medicine

2054 University Avenue #305
Berkeley, California 94704
Phone: (510) 548-2275
Fax: (510) 548-2179

The Pacific Academy of Homeopathic Medicine (PAHM) was founded in 1985 as a nonprofit educational organization.

Accreditation

PAHM is in consultation with the Council for Homeopathic Certification and the European Council for Classical Homeopathy/International Council for Classical Homeopathy to ensure that its curriculum meets the highest standards. PAHM is also a member of the North American Council for Classical Homeopathy, which cooperatively develops and standardizes curricula.

The laws of California state that only licensed health professionals may diagnose and prescribe, and graduation from PAHM will not enable the student to practice legally. A professional homeopath must therefore become licensed as a certified acupuncturist, chiropractor, medical doctor, osteopath, or naturopath (licensed in some states) in order to diagnose and prescribe.

Program Description

PAHM offers its Foundations in Classical Homeopathy Course with two options.

The one-year program covers basic homeopathic principles, first aid, and acute self-limiting conditions. It is appropriate for those who wish to study the basics of homeopathy for home treatment, as well as for those who are preparing for in-depth study. Topics covered include Philosophy and Principles of Practice, Acute Therapeutics, Keynote Materia Medica, and Materia Medica of Polycrests, followed by a proficiency exam. Additional requirements for nonmedically licensed students include Anatomy and Physiology, First Aid and CPR, and Physical Exam and Acute Disease Differential.

The three-year professional program includes the one-year program described above, along with two additional years of homeopathic study, plus additional requirements for nonmedically licensed students. Year Two includes Principles of Practice, Therapeutics, Materia Medica, Second-Year Research Paper, and a proficiency exam; nonmedically licensed students are also required to take the first year of Pathology for Alternative Practitioners. Year Three includes Principles of Practice, Therapeutics, Advanced Materia Medica, Third-Year Research Paper, and a proficiency exam; nonmedically licensed students are also required to take Pathology.

Classes are held one weekend per month from October through August. Students are required to complete twenty-five to forty hours of home study monthly in preparation for each weekend.

Admission Requirements

Admission is open to both medically licensed and nonmedically licensed students. Questions regarding academic qualifications should be directed to the admissions committee.

Tuition and Fees

Tuition is $3,400 per year. Other costs include an application fee of $25; Pathology for Alternative Practitioners, $445; Physical Exam and Acute Disease Differential, $300; and books (approximate), $350 in Year One, $200 in Year Two, and $250 in Year Three.

Financial Assistance

Payment plans are available.

Pacific College of Oriental Medicine

(*See* Multiple State Locations, page 313)

Palmer College of Chiropractic West

90 East Tasman Drive
San Jose, California 95134
Phone: (408) 944-6000 / (800) 44-CHIRO /
   (800) 442-4476

The Palmer Chiropractic University System includes both Palmer College of Chiropractic West and Palmer College of Chiropractic (Davenport, Iowa). Palmer College of Chiropractic West (PCCW) was established in 1980, and is housed in a 96,000-square-foot, two-story campus in the Silicon Valley.

Accreditation

PCCW is accredited by the Council on Chiropractic Education (CCE).

Program Description

Palmer West's Doctor of Chiropractic degree program consists of a minimum of 4,800 hours of lecture, laboratory, and clinical education over thirteen quarters. The program may be completed in as little as three-and-one-quarter calendar years of continuous residency. Courses are organized into nine disciplines: Anatomy, Physiology, Chemistry/Physics, Microbiology/Pathology, Assessment, Specialties, Philosophy and Principles, Chiroprac-

tic Procedures, and Chiropractic Practice and Elective. A unique feature of the curriculum is the Practice Development Quarter (PDQ), the thirteenth quarter of study, which assists students in making the transition from students to doctors through field training in the office of a practicing doctor.

Continuing Education

Palmer West offers seminars, symposia, and conferences for Doctors of Chiropractic seeking additional education to meet relicensure requirements.

Admission Requirements

Applicants must have completed at least sixty semester units of college or university credit leading to an associate or bachelor's degree, including a specific number of units of biology, general chemistry, organic chemistry, physics, English composition and/or communications, humanities and/or social sciences, and psychology, and must have earned a minimum G.P.A. of 2.25. Additionally, applicants must submit two letters of recommendation and an essay, and be interviewed by an admissions representative.

Tuition and Fees

There is an application fee of $50 and a registration fee of $15 per quarter. Tuition is $3,820 per quarter; books and materials are approximately $250 per quarter.

Financial Assistance

Federal and private grants, loans, scholarships, and work-study are available.

Phillips School of Massage

101 Broad Street
P.O. Box 1999
Nevada City, California 95959
Phone/Fax: (916) 265-4645

Judy Phillips founded the Phillips School of Massage in 1983. The school, located in the foothills of the Sierras, takes a holistic view of treatment, with emphasis on balancing the body structure and energy flow of both therapist and client.

Accreditation

The State of California does not certify massage therapists directly, but rather licenses the schools of massage and authorizes them to issue a certificate of completion. Phillips School of Massage has been licensed by the California State Board of Education since 1983. Licensing requirements vary from city to city; prospective applicants should check with their local licensing offices prior to enrolling. The school is also licensed by the California Board of Registered Nursing.

Program Description

The 200-hour Massage Therapy Training Program may be completed in six weeks of daytime classes or eight to nine months of evening classes. Included in the instruction are elements of acupressure, Swedish and lymphatic massage, shiatsu, reflexology, polarity, orthobionomy, and energy balancing, as well as self-awareness, anatomy and physiology, and how to start a business.

The 500-hour Massage Therapy Certificate Course includes the 200-hour program above, as well as 200 hours of Student Assistantship, thirty hours of Creative Anatomy, thirty hours of Advanced Intensive, forty hours of continuing education seminars, and 10 one-hour practice sessions.

Continuing Education

Many continuing education seminars are open to both professional and nonprofessional bodyworkers; these include Acupressure, Jin Shin Do, Rosen Therapy Acupressure for Emotional Healing, Watsu, Craniosacral Therapy, Orthobionomy, Reflexology, Energy Kinesiology, Transformational Breath, Massage for Couples, Women's Self-Defense, Drumming, and others.

Classes open only to certified massage therapists include Taikyo Zen Table Shiatsu, Sports Massage, and Heart of Massage Intensive.

Admissions Requirements

Applicants must be in good health.

Tuition and Fees

Tuition for the Massage Therapy Training is $1,200. Tuition for the Massage Therapy Certificate is $1,945 to $2,150, depending on the selected payment plan and continuing education classes.

Financial Assistance

Payment plans, prepayment discounts, and limited work scholarships are available.

Polarity Healing Arts of Santa Monica

1131 California Avenue, Suite 302
Santa Monica, California 90403
Phone: (310) 393-7329

Polarity Healing Arts of Santa Monica (PHASM) was founded in 1986 by Gary B. Strauss, R.P.P. and past board member of the American Polarity Therapy Association. Classes are held at the Institute of Psycho-Structural Balancing in Los Angeles.

Accreditation

The A.P.P. (Associate Polarity Practitioner) and R.P.P. (Registered Polarity Practitioner) training programs are accredited by the American Polarity Therapy Association (APTA).

Program Description

The 179-hour A.P.P. Certification Course consists of five courses, each seventeen to forty-two hours in length: Polarity I and II (which cover basic principles of energy flow, the polarity general session, an exploration of polarity energetics and the expression of life energy through the Five Elements, bodywork sessions for balancing each element, and polarity exercises), Communication, Evaluation, and Study Group (which constitutes professional clinical development in the polarity healing arts). Students must also receive five and give thirty sessions. Courses may also be taken individually.

The seventy-two-hour Craniosacral Unwinding Program offers specialty training for bodyworkers and other health care professionals in using palpation skills to get into harmony, resonance, and rapport with the fluid nature of the body. Four courses (Cranial I through IV) cover an introduction to the craniosacral rhythm, concepts, and motion; developing palpation skills; and physical and energetic techniques for working with the connective tissue system of the body, focusing extensively on the cranium. Courses may be taken individually.

The R.P.P. Program is currently being restructured; the new program will be in place in 1997. This program will add approximately 500 to 550 hours to the A.P.P. training above and will take twelve to eighteen months to complete. Classes will include Cranial I through IV, Intermediate IA, IB, and II (covering the autonomic nervous system, organ systems, and integration), Spinal/Structural Balancing, Advanced Communication, Nutrition, Business and Professional Ethics, Cleanse Group, Fire Into Water, Advanced Supervision, Polarity Exercise, Advanced Study Group, Internship, and elective classes taught by visiting instructors. Classes may also be taken individually.

Admission Requirements

There are no specific admission requirements for the A.P.P. Program. R.P.P. applicants must have completed an A.P.P. program.

Tuition and Fees

Tuition for the entire A.P.P. Course is $1,748; individual courses range from $214 to $504. Tuition for the entire Craniosacral Unwinding Program is $864; individual courses range from $192 to $288. Tuition for the R.P.P. Course is approximately $6,000 to $7,000.

Financial Assistance

Payment plans and discounts are available.

The Polarity Therapy Center of Marin

P.O. Box 23
Tomales, California 94971
Phone: (707) 878-2278

The Polarity Therapy Center of Marin was founded in 1991 by Hanna Hammerli, a Registered Polarity Practitioner (R.P.P.) and certified polarity instructor with over sixteen years of experience as a bodyworker. Trainings are held in a rural, scenic area on a small organic farm.

Accreditation

Trainings are accredited by the American Polarity Therapy Association (APTA).

Program Description

The 155-hour A.P.P. Training consists of five 3-day intensives that offer instruction in methods of physical, mental, and spiritual healing through polarity therapy, polarity yoga, polarity reflexology, the five-pointed star, structural balance, client communication, nutritional counseling, and business management. Intensives may also be taken separately.

The 615-hour R.P.P. Training, which consists of the A.P.P. Training above and an additional 460-hour segment, is taught in one- or two-week segments for a total of nine weeks over a two-year period. One week is devoted to Ether; one-and-a-half weeks each are devoted to Air, Fire, Water, and Earth; one week for orthodox Anatomy and Physiology; and one week for review and exams.

Both levels of training may be taken through private instruction that follows the format and content of the intensives but allows greater flexibility for individual needs and abilities.

Community and Continuing Education

Introductory evenings are scheduled periodically to provide a short introduction to basic energy theory and the basics of polarity therapy. Other courses open to the public include Discover Polarity Therapy Day, Body Fun Polarity Yoga Class, and Inner Bonding Healing Circle.

Admission Requirements

The A.P.P. Training is open to everyone. The R.P.P. Training is open to those who have completed a 155-hour A.P.P. course and are certified through APTA as an A.P.P.

Tuition and Fees

The A.P.P. Training costs $1,650 total for five intensives. These intensives are $325 to $350 each if taken separately. Private instruction is $75 per two-hour class (minimum forty classes for entire program). The R.P.P. Training costs $500 per week for nine weeks, six days per week. Private instruction is $500 per week for nine weeks, four days per week.

Financial Assistance

Limited work-study is available.

Reese Movement Institute, Inc.

Feldenkrais Southern California
160 Chesterfield Drive, Suite 8
Cardiff-by-the-Sea, California 92007
Phone: (619) 436-9087 / (800) 500-9087
Fax: (619) 436-9141
E-mail: rmiinc@aol.com

Beginning in January 1997, the Reese Movement Institute will begin a new Feldenkrais Professional Training Program in San Diego. Previous trainings have been held in Los Angeles, West Virginia, Italy, and Germany. The institute's directors are Mark Reese, Ph.D., and Donna Ray-Reese, M.F.C.C. Mark Reese is one of the world's foremost authorities on the Feldenkrais method and graduated from the first United States Feldenkrais training program in 1977.

Accreditation

The Reese Movement Institute San Diego Feldenkrais Professional Training Program is fully accredited by the Feldenkrais Guild. The institute is in the process of receiving recognition as a private postsecondary educational institution from the state of California.

Program Description

The four-year Feldenkrais Professional Training Program spans 168 teaching days and meets during January, May, and August of each year. After satisfactory learning of Awareness Through Movement, Functional Integration, and Feldenkrais Theory, graduates are awarded certificates as Guild Certified Feldenkrais Practitioners or Guild Certified Feldenkrais Teachers. Those who do not wish to become certified practitioners but wish to study for their own personal growth may also participate; in this case it is not necessary to satisfy the same graduation requirements.

Admission Requirements

There are no specific educational prerequisites. Applicants must submit three letters of recommendation.

Tuition and Fees

There is a $50 application fee. Tuition is $3,600 per year.

Financial Assistance

Payment plans are available.

reSource

Box 5398
Berkeley, California 94705
Phone: (510) 433-7917
Fax: (510) 841-3258

reSource was founded in 1982 by Gail Stewart, the current director.

Accreditation

reSource is approved by the California State Council for Private Postsecondary Vocational Education.

Program Description

The 200-hour Massage Practitioner Program covers the Fundamentals of Massage and Bodywork, Anatomy, Physiology, and Professional Development in core classes; electives include Massage Review, Body Reading, and Bodymind Survey.

The 500-hour Bodywork Practitioner Program offers continuing education for massage and bodywork practitioners interested in upgrading their certification to 500 hours. The core professional support and practice group is open to massage and bodywork practitioners in their first two years of professional practice. Credit toward certification may be earned by taking electives at reSource or other state-approved schools.

The 1,000-hour Advanced Bodywork Practitioner Program is a program of continuing support, supervision, and practice for massage and bodywork practitioners with at least two years of professional experience. Classes are selected from a list of required and elective subjects that include the Trager approach, Rosen method, deep tissue, bodyreading, and others.

Admission Requirements

Those applying to the Massage Practitioner Program must be at least 18 years of age and be able to read, write, and speak English. All applicants must interview with an admissions representative.

Tuition and Fees

Tuition for core classes in the Massage Practitioner Course is $850; electives are $350, on a "pay-as-you-go" basis. Tuition for other programs varies with the courses selected.

Royal University of America

The School of Oriental Medicine
   and Acupuncture
1125 West 6th Street
Los Angeles, California 90017
Phone: (213) 482-6646 / (213) 482-6647 /
   (800) 303-1800
Fax: (213) 482-6649

Royal University of America was founded in 1976 with an initial enrollment of eleven students; today the school occupies a 23,552-square-foot facility, maintains an Oriental Medical Health Center for students' clinical education, and has more than 200 students enrolled. The school is located in downtown Los Angeles.

Accreditation

The Master of Oriental Medicine program is accredited by the National Accreditation Commission for Schools and Colleges of Acupuncture and Oriental Medicine (NACSCAOM).

Program Description

The university's entire academic program is given (in separate classes) in English, Korean, and Mandarin Chinese.

The four-year Master of Oriental Medicine program may be accelerated by attending four quarters per year. The program includes instruction in Oriental medical theory, acupuncture, herbology, physical therapy and exercises, Western sciences, Western medicine, clinic instruction, basic science, Western pharmacognosy, management and ethics, and electives.

First-year courses include History of Oriental Medicine, Botany: Introduction to Herbology, Principles of Biology, Fundamentals of Chemistry, Principles of Nutrition, General Pathology in Oriental Medicine, Tai Chi Chuan, Qigong, Meridian Theory, Fundamentals of Physics, Psychology and Human Behavior, Nutrition in Oriental Medicine, Basic Diagnosis of Oriental Medicine, Anatomy and Physiology, Western Medical Terminology, Acupuncture Anatomy, Herbs, Survey of Clinical Medicine, Western Medical Test and Lab, First Aid/CPR, Differential Diagnosis: Exogenous, Practice Observation, and others.

Second-year courses include Differential Diagnosis: Endogenous, Acupuncture Techniques, General Pathology in Western Medicine, Pathophysiologic Diagnostics in Western Medicine, Pharmacology, and others.

Third-year courses include Internal Medicine, Herbs, Tui Na, Diagnosis and Evaluation, Acupuncture Therapeutics, Medical Ethics, and others.

Fourth-year courses include Internal Medicine: Gynecology, Management, Case Seminar, Internal Medicine: Pediatrics, Diagnosis and Evaluation, Supervised Practice, and others.

Royal University also offers a 200-hour certificate program in acupressure (tui na: Chinese massotherapy) that consists of 140 hours of instruction in tui na (acupressure) and sixty hours of anatomy and physiology. Units earned in this program may be applied toward the Master of Science program.

Continuing Education

In addition to the tui na certificate (above), the university offers continuing education seminars for licensed acupuncturists, alumni, and students.

Admission Requirements

Applicants must have completed two years of college (sixty semester units) with an overall G.P.A. of 2.0 or higher, and submit two letters of recommendation. Requirements for admission to certificate programs are determined by the faculty for each program.

Tuition and Fees

Tuition for academic courses is $90 per quarter unit; for clinical internship, $75 per quarter unit. There is a $100 application fee.

Financial Assistance

Payment plans, federal and private grants, loans, scholarships, and work-study are available.

Samra University of Oriental Medicine

600 St. Paul Avenue
Los Angeles, California 90017-2014
Phone: (213) 482-8448
Fax: (213) 482-9020
E-mail: president@samra.edu
Internet: www.samra.edu

Samra University derives its name from the acronym of its parent, the Sino-American Medical Rehabilitation Association, chartered in 1969. While earlier training had been limited to health professionals, the Los Angeles branch of the University of Health Sciences began to admit students from the general population in 1979. Also in 1979, the university became the first acupuncture school in California to be approved by the State Medical Board.

Accreditation

The Master of Science in Oriental Medicine degree program is accredited by the National Accreditation Commission for Schools and Colleges of Acupuncture and Oriental Medicine (NACSCAOM). Graduates are qualified to take the California Acupuncture Licensing Examinations.

Program Description

The entire academic program of Samra University is given, in separate classes, in English, Korean, and Mandarin Chinese. The Master of Science in Oriental Medicine degree program includes 800 hours of clinical training, as well as 1,700 hours of didactic courses that cover specific requirements from the departments of Basic Studies and General Sciences, Herbology, Theory and Practice of Oriental Medicine, Practice Management, Western Clinical Sciences, and electives. Full-time students attend a total of twelve quarters; part-time students may spread their studies over eighteen quarters.

Continuing Education

Samra University offers a three-month advanced internship in cooperation with the Zhejiang College of Traditional Chinese Medicine in Hangzhou, China. This program is designed to meet the needs of American students who have completed their formal training.

Admission Requirements

Applicants must have earned grades of C or better in at least sixty semester units in general education and/or technical courses from an accredited college or university, and must demonstrate an ability to read and write English, Mandarin Chinese, or Korean at the college entrance level. In addition, applicants may be required to submit letters of recommendation, a résumé, or other materials as requested by the admissions office.

Tuition and Fees

Tuition for academic courses is $90 per unit; for clinic courses, $120 per unit. Other costs include: application fee, $75; general fee, $15 per quarter; student identification card, $5 per year; malpractice insurance for observers and interns, $45 per quarter; and herb samples, $90. Books and supplies are additional.

Financial Assistance

Payment plans and federal financial aid are available.

Santa Barbara Center for Homeopathic Arts

(formerly Ananda Zaren Seminars)

Applications and Payments:
Ananda Zaren
28 East Canon Perdido Street
Santa Barbara, California 93101

Inquiries:
Marsha Abel
3432 North Tenaya Way
Las Vegas, Nevada 89129
Phone: (702) 658-3464

Ananda Zaren has studied homeopathy since 1977, has taught seminars internationally for the past eight years, and is the author of two materia medica texts.

Program Description

The Santa Barbara Center for Homeopathic Arts offers two courses in homeopathy. The Basic Course is a comprehensive two-year program leading to fundamental knowledge of the repertory, theory and history, case taking, case analysis, prescribing and follow-up, analysis of chronic cases, and materia medica. This course is designed for beginners and meets every other month for two years.

An advanced two-year course, Clinical Supervision, gives the practicing homeopath an opportunity to deepen the skills of case taking, case analysis, and long-term case management. This course meets for five 3-day weekends per year for two years.

Admission Requirements

The Basic Course is open to students at all levels of knowledge and experience, including, but not limited to, chiropractors, medical doctors, osteopaths, dentists, veterinarians, nurses, and others.

Those applying for admission to the Clinical Supervision Course must interview with an admissions representative, should have a working knowledge of classical constitutional homeopathy, and be actively involved in practice.

Tuition and Fees

Tuition for the Basic Course is $2,500 per year; books are additional. Tuition for the Clinical Supervision Course is $2,500 per year.

Financial Assistance

Tuition for the Basic Course may be paid in two installments per year.

Santa Barbara College of Oriental Medicine

1919 State Street, Suite 204
Santa Barbara, California 93101
Phone: (805) 898-1180
Fax: (805) 682-1864

The Santa Barbara College of Oriental Medicine, founded in 1986, grew out of the Santa Barbara branch of the California Acupuncture College, which was established in 1981. Classes are held at the Anacapa School, a private high school in the heart of Santa Barbara, about ninety miles north of Los Angeles.

Accreditation

The Master of Acupuncture and Oriental Medicine degree program is accredited by the National Accreditation Commission for Schools and Colleges of Acupuncture and Oriental Medicine (NACSCAOM) and meets the requirements of the California Acupuncture Committee. Graduates of this program are qualified to take the California State Licensing Exam.

Program Description

The 2,368-hour Master of Acupuncture and Oriental Medicine degree program may be completed in as little as three calendar years. Required courses include Acupuncture Science: Theories, Acupuncture Science: Techniques, Western Medical Science, Eastern Medical Heritage, Herbology: Chinese Herbal Medicine, Practice Management, Clinical Practice, and Master's Degree Preparation.

A 288-hour Shiatsu Practitioner Program offers

in-depth training in Shiatsu, Therapeutic and Sports Massage, and Moxibustion, as well as an Introduction to Foot Reflexology, Trigger Point Therapy, Aromatherapy, Energy Work, Draping Techniques, and Business and Ethics. This program offers sufficient hours for the student to be licensed in the city and county of Santa Barbara as a massage technician.

Admission Requirements

Applicants must have completed at least sixty semester units of postsecondary education with a minimum cumulative G.P.A. of 2.0; specific numbers of courses are required in the humanities, social sciences, natural sciences, and basics. In addition, applicants must submit two letters of recommendation and interview with an admissions representative.

Tuition and Fees

Tuition for the Master of Acupuncture and Oriental Medicine Program is $130 per trimester unit. Other costs include application fee, $50; registration, $25; intern malpractice insurance per trimester (approximate), $117; and books and supplies, approximately $300 per year. Total estimated expense for the three-year program is $21,000. Tuition for the Shiatsu Practitioner Program is $1,300 ($850 for those with a massage license, and $700 for graduates of SBSM). There is a $50 application fee.

Financial Assistance

Payment plans and federal loans are available.

School for Self-Healing

(*See* Multiple State Locations, page 318)

School of Healing Arts

1001 Garnet Avenue #200
San Diego, California 92109
Phone: (619) 581-9429

The School of Healing Arts was founded in 1984 as the Institute of Health Sciences. In 1990, Seymour Koblin took over the school and turned it into a nonprofit organization.

Accreditation

The School of Healing Arts offers state-certified vocational training. The school is approved by the National Certification Board for Therapeutic Massage and Bodywork (NCBTMB) as a continuing education provider; by the California Board of Registered Nursing; and by the American Board of Hypnotherapy. The school has not sought approval by the American Massage Therapy Association (AMTA). The Massage Technician, Zen Touch Technician, Clinical Massage Therapist, and Holistic Health Practitioner Programs meet or exceed San Diego licensing requirements.

Program Description

The 110-hour Massage Technician Course may be taken over fourteen days or eight to eleven weeks. The curriculum includes Anatomy and Physiology, Massage Techniques: Parasympathetic, Massage Techniques: Zen Touch, Introduction to Advanced Techniques, and Ethics and Licensing. This program is also offered in a Spanish-speaking section.

The 120-hour Zen Touch Technician Program may be completed in three to four months. It includes instruction in Zen Touch, Traditional Home Remedies, Oriental Health Assessment, and Destiny Studies.

A 300-hour Nutritional Counselor Program may be completed in six to nine months. Courses include Basic Nutrition, Comparative Nutrition, Herbology, Oriental Health Assessment, Food Preparation, Communication for Counselors, Anatomy and Physiology, Nutritional Studies, Body Chemistry Balancing, Traditional Home Remedies, Electives, Business Practices, First Aid and CPR, and Nutritional Counselor Internship.

Hypnosis and Mind-Body Therapy is a 200-hour program that may be completed in six to nine months. Courses include Introduction to Mind/Body Healing, Hypnosis Strategies and Structures, Working with Clients and Hypnosis Techniques, and Hypnosis Internship.

The 500-hour Clinical Massage Therapist Program takes six to twelve months to complete.

Course work begins with the 110-hour Massage Technician Program, then adds additional classes in Anatomy and Physiology, Hydrotherapy, Basic or Comparative Nutrition, Movement Therapy, Oriental Health Assessment, Counseling, First Aid and CPR, Business Practices, and Massage Methods and Body Therapy electives. The Zen Touch Practitioner/Instructor Certification may be included in this program for an additional $600.

The 1,000-hour Holistic Health Practitioner Program takes one to two years to complete. This is the most versatile program, as it may include any of the modalities and/or certifications offered at the school. A typical program includes courses in Anatomy and Physiology, Massage Technician, Hydrotherapy, Basic or Comparative Nutrition, Movement Therapy, Oriental Health Assessment, Counseling, First Aid and CPR, Business Practices, and Massage Methods and Body Therapy electives. Hypnotherapy certification may be included in the program for an additional $205.

Community and Continuing Education

One-day and longer individual courses are offered throughout the year in many areas of holistic health. Classes include Destiny and Intuition Studies, Holistic Care for Pets, Self-Care for the Holistic Practitioner, Soul Retrieval Workshop, Watsu, Yoga, Herbs and Foods, Tui Na Massage, Ayurveda: Introduction to Principles, Learn to Meditate, Iridology: What the Eye Reveals, and many others.

Tuition and Fees

Tuition for each course is as follows: Massage Technician, $600; Zen Touch Technician, $650; Nutritional Counselor, $1,750; Hypnosis and Mind/Body Therapy, $1,385; Clinical Massage Therapist, $2,600; and Holistic Health Practitioner, $5,200. Any course may be taken on an individual basis at the rate of $6.50 per hour.

Financial Assistance

Payment plans are available. C.M.P. and H.H.P. students may work in the student clinic after 110 hours of massage technician training; a San Diego work permit is required.

School of Shiatsu and Massage at Harbin Hot Springs

P.O. Box 889
Middletown, California 95461
Phone: (707) 987-3801
Fax: (707) 987-9638
E-mail: info@waba.edu

The School of Shiatsu and Massage at Harbin Hot Springs is owned by the Worldwide Aquatic Bodywork Association. Watsu, or water shiatsu, was developed here by the school's director, Harold Dull, and has been used as a tool for rehabilitation by the physical therapy community.

Program Description

California state law requires a minimum of one hundred hours' training in order to obtain a massage practitioner's certificate (some counties require more; inquire with your local authorities before enrolling). The School of Shiatsu and Massage offers a one-hundred-hour Practitioner Course that provides a foundation for additional independent fifty- and one-hundred-hour modules. Each one hundred hours leads to a separate certificate. After completing 500 hours, students receive a Therapist Certificate; after 1,000 hours, an Advanced Body Therapist Certificate.

Massage 100, an eleven-day, one-hundred-hour intensive, provides training for certification in California. Students learn a comprehensive massage that includes Swedish, deep tissue, shiatsu, rebalancing, and Esalen techniques, along with an introduction to Watsu. Introduction to Massage, together with Therapeutic Massage, also provides training for certification in California.

Other entry-level bodywork intensives open to beginners include Watsu, Introduction to Massage, Shiatsu, Tantsu, Rebalancing, Acupressure, Sensitive Gestalt Massage, NLP, Pain Relief, and Communication as a Healing Art.

Intensives that require previous bodywork intensives or experience include Therapeutic Massage, Lymphatic Massage, Deep Tissue, Integrative Massage, Living Anatomy, Watsu Body Wave, Waterdance, Sports Massage, Diving into the Self, and others.

Admission Requirements

Applicants should have the physical ability and emotional maturity to perform bodywork.

Tuition and Fees

Students pay for each class as they take it. Total tuition and fees for programs are as follows: Weeklong fifty-hour intensive, $600; Practitioner Course, $1,200; Therapist Course, $5,200; and Advanced Body Therapy Course, $10,400. Prices include lodging in the form of indoor camping.

Shiatsu Massage School of California

2309 Main Street
Santa Monica, California 90405
Phone: (310) 396-4877 / (310) 396-2130
Fax: (310) 396-4502

In 1976, Dr. DoAnn T. Kaneko, a licensed acupuncturist and Doctor of Oriental Medicine, established shiatsu-amma workshops for foreigners in Tokyo; later, Dr. Kaneko developed the Shiatsu Massage School of California (SMSC), which began offering its 500-hour curriculum in 1986. SMSC teaches both traditional amma massage and contemporary, scientific shiatsu therapy. (See page 379 for available videos.)

Accreditation

SMSC is approved by the California State Council for Private Postsecondary and Vocational Education. Its programs are approved by the California Board of Nursing for continuing education units.

Program Description

SMSC offers three diploma courses in shiatsu-amma that may be taken successively for a total of 500 hours.

The Program A Diploma Course is a 150-hour, six-month Shiatsu-Amma Practitioner Program covering Shiatsu/Amma Practice, Anatomy/Physiology, Traditional Chinese Medicine Theory, Shiatsu/Amma Theory, Do-In (a self-healing art), CPR/First Aid, Ethics/Legal/Business Issues, Pain and Orthopedic Evaluation, and Clinical Study.

The Program B Diploma Course is a 150-hour, six-month Shiatsu-Amma Therapist Course that may be taken concurrently with or after the completion of Program A. Program B includes Shiatsu/Amma Practice, Anatomy/Physiology, Clinical Study, Shiatsu/Amma Theory, and Traditional Chinese Medicine Theory.

The Program C Diploma Course is a 200-hour, seven-month Shiatsu/Amma Specialist Course that may be taken after the completion of Programs A and B. Program C includes Shiatsu/Amma Theory, Shiatsu/Amma Practice, Traditional Chinese Medicine Theory, Anatomy/Physiology, Clinical Study, and twenty-four additional hours in healing arts workshops and electives.

SMSC also offers a 104-hour, three-month Certificate Course that includes all of the courses in Program A, with the exception of Pain and Orthopedic Evaluation and Clinical Study. This course is also given on weekends over two months.

Community and Continuing Education

Shiatsu/amma weekend workshops and a Summer Shiatsu Short Course are open to high school graduates. Healing Arts weekend workshops may be taken by nurses for continuing education credit and include such topics as Jin Shin Do Acupressure, Touch for Health, Tui Na Chinese Massage, Basic Sports Massage, Basics in Nutritional Metabolism, and others.

Admission Requirements

Certificate Course or Program A Diploma Course applicants must have a high school diploma (Program B and C prerequisites are listed above). All new students must attend a Sunday orientation program or make special arrangements to meet with the director.

Tuition and Fees

Tuition for the Program A Diploma Course is $1,225; for the Program B Diploma Course, $1,175; for the Program C Diploma Course, $1,550; and for the Certificate Course, $830. There is a $50 registration fee for all courses. Fees for weekend workshops vary.

Financial Assistance

A discount is given for payment in full by the first day of class.

South Baylo University

Main Campus:
1126 North Brookhurst Street
Anaheim, California 92801-1701
Phone: (714) 533-1495
Fax: (714) 533-6040

Los Angeles Campus:
2727 West 6th Street
Los Angeles, California 90057-3139
Phone: (213) 738-0712
Fax: (213) 480-1332

South Baylo University was founded in 1977 as the Academy of Political Economy and Management for the purpose of redirecting the deterioration of the values of modern society. The academy was authorized to grant academic degrees in 1978, and moved to Anaheim in 1994.

Accreditation

The master's degree program in acupuncture and Oriental medicine is accredited by the National Accreditation Commission for Schools and Colleges of Acupuncture and Oriental Medicine (NACSCAOM). Graduates may take the California State Acupuncture Licensing Examination.

Program Description

The master's degree program in acupuncture and Oriental medicine consists of 190 units in didactic courses and 840 hours of internship. Required courses include Biology, Inorganic/Organic Chemistry, Physics, Psychology, Medical Terminology, Anatomy/Physiology, History of Medicine, Oriental Medicine Principles, Herbal Principles, Herbology, Acupuncture, Oriental Medicine Diagnosis, Pharmacology, Pathology, Nutrition and Therapeutic Diet, Herbal Prescription, Acupressure/Breath Exercise, Herbal Practice, Oriental Medicine Principle, Oriental Medicine Internal Medicine, Western Diagnosis, Practice Management, Clinical Medicine, Clinical Sciences, Clinical Training, Acupuncture Theory/Therapy, Oriental Medicine Infectious Diseases, Research Methodology, Direct Research, and more. Classes are conducted in English, Chinese, and Korean.

Admission Requirements

Applicants must have completed at least sixty semester units at an accredited institution and be proficient in the English language (students wishing to take instruction in Chinese or Korean will not need to show English proficiency). An oral or written examination may be given to applicants whose qualifications are questionable.

Tuition and Fees

Tuition is $85 per unit. Other fees include: application fee, $100; internship fee, $5 per hour; malpractice insurance for intern, $50 per quarter; and evaluation for graduation, $150.

Financial Assistance

Federal grants, loans, work-study, and state grants are available.

Stens Corporation

(*See* Multiple State Locations, page 318)

Taoist Sanctuary of San Diego

4229 Park Boulevard
San Diego, California 92103
Phone: (619) 692-1155
Fax: (619) 692-0428
E-mail: taosanct@cts.com

Tui na is an ancient Chinese system of healing bodywork that uses soft tissue manipulation, structural alignment, and traditional Chinese medical theory. Director Bill Helm has taught tui na since 1978 and is also Dean of Allied Arts at Pacific College of Oriental Medicine.

Accreditation

The Taoist Sanctuary is approved by the California Acupuncture Committee for its tui na courses, and by the California Board of Registered Nursing to offer continuing education units.

Program Description

The fifty-hour Level 1 Tui Na Intensive Certificate Program includes Oscillating Hand Techniques, Pressure Hand Techniques, Passive Joint Movement, and Traditional Chinese Medical Theory, which includes Eight Principles of Differentiation, Theory of Trauma/Blood Stasis-Qi Stagnation, Painful Obstruction Syndrome, Theory and Uses of Herbal Preparations, Major Acupoints, Channel Palpation, Qigong, and more.

The fifty-hour Level 2 Tui Na Intensive Certificate Program includes Qigong, Traditional Chinese Medical Theory (including Zang Fu Theory, Organ Syndromes, Tongue Assessment, Pulse Assessment, and Palpation Assessment), and Tui Na Treatment Protocols for the Digestive, Respiratory, and Reproductive Systems.

Two-day workshops are offered throughout the year in Upper Extremity, Lower Extremity, Tonification Dispersion Treatments, and Spine Treatments.

Admission Requirements

The workshops and certificate programs are designed for nurses, massage therapists, and other health professionals.

Tuition and Fees

Tuition for Levels 1 and 2 is $500 each. Books, linens, and optional massage table are additional. Tuition for the two-day workshops is $175.

The Trager Institute

(*See* Multiple State Locations, page 320)

Twin Lakes College of the Healing Arts

1210 Brommer Street
Santa Cruz, California 95062
Phone: (408) 476-2152

Twin Lakes College of the Healing Arts, founded in 1982, is located in the Live Oak region of Santa Cruz. The current director, Becky Williams, studied polarity therapy with Dr. Pierre Pannetier, and has been teaching in the health field since 1977.

Accreditation

All the courses at Twin Lakes College are approved for continuing education units for nurses. The 200-hour Massage Practitioner Certificate Program exceeds the minimum requirements for the California State Council for Private Postsecondary and Vocational Education to practice massage in the state of California.

Program Description

Massage certificate programs include the 200-hour Massage Practitioner, 300-hour Massage Practitioner and Natural Health Educator, and 500-hour Massage Therapist and Natural Health Counselor Programs. These programs are designed as a progression of increased levels of training.

The 200-hour, beginning-level Massage Practitioner Certificate Program focuses on technical skills and professional growth, and serves as a foundation for Levels II and III. The program consists of Massage (including integrative Swedish massage, polarity therapy, energy balancing, acupressure, and shiatsu), Introduction to Anatomy and Physiology for Bodyworkers, Counseling and Communication Skills for Bodyworkers, Business Practices, Internship/Practice Sessions, and the Massage-A-Thon event.

The 300-hour, intermediate-level Massage Practitioner and Natural Health Educator Certificate Program is open to those who have completed the Massage Practitioner Certificate Program. Courses include Anatomy II and III, Advanced Professional Studies (including business planning and practices, self-care, and prevention of burn-out), and CPR/First Aid.

The 500-hour, advanced-level Professional Massage Therapist and Natural Health Counselor Certificate Program is open to those who have completed the Massage Practitioner and Natural Health Educator Program. In this program, students may independently design a program in one or more specific areas of bodywork (150 hours) and electives (forty hours) over one to three quarters of enrollment. Courses offered include Subtle Body/Energywork; Prenatal, Infant, and Baby Massage; Deep Tissue Massage and Structural Balancing; Sports Massage; Ayurvedic Massage and the Facial; and others.

Massage classes are held days, evenings, and weekends; students may attend full-or part-time.

The one-hundred-hour Hypnosis Practitioner Certificate Program includes self-hypnosis training; using direct hypnotic suggestion with clients to reduce anxiety, manage pain, and more; active listening; case management; client education; ethical issues; therapeutic polarity; metaphor; storytelling; parts work; and process hypnosis.

The 200-hour Professional Hypnotherapist Certificate includes the Level I training, along with Transpersonal and Spiritual Perspectives in Hypnosis (which draws upon Eastern, Western, and shamanic traditions) and Advanced Studies in Business and Career Development (focusing on professional studies and exploring practice issues).

Admission Requirements

Applicants must have a high school diploma or the equivalent and interview with an admissions representative.

Tuition and Fees

There is a $50 application fee. Tuition for the 200-hour Massage Program is $1,198 (books, materials, and linens are additional); for the Intermediate Massage Program, $2,095; for the Advanced Massage Program, $4,000; for the one-hundred-hour Hypnosis Program, $1,300; and for the 200-hour Hypnotherapist Program, $2,500 (this includes the one-hundred-hour program).

Financial Assistance

Early bird discounts and student referral incentives are offered.

Valley Hypnosis Center

3763 Arlington Avenue, Suite 102
Riverside, California 92506
Phone: (909) 781-0282

The Valley Hypnosis Center, founded in 1982 by Sally Cernie, Ph.D., has a spiritual focus that allows hypnotherapists to reach clients beyond the physical realm.

Accreditation

The Valley Hypnosis Center is approved by the California State Council for Private Postsecondary and Vocational Education, and by the California Board of Registered Nursing and the Academy of General Dentistry as a provider of continuing education units.

Program Description

Principles of Hypnosis 101.1 is designed for students with no prior hypnosis experience. Topics covered include Preinduction Techniques, Reflexive Exercises for Suggestibility, Awakening Procedures, Post-Hypnotic Suggestion, Automatic Writing, Pain Alleviation, Memory and Concentration, Self-Confidence Building, Obesity and Weight Control, and Age Regression. The course is given in two formats: three hours per week for sixteen weeks, or one 3-day weekend intensive.

Principles of Hypnosis 101.2 is a fast-paced, intensive training in the art and science of hypnotism, from history to modern uses. Students will learn how to hypnotize themselves and others.

Hypnotherapy 201.2 is an accelerated course in psychology and advanced hypnotic techniques for those who have completed Principles of Hypnosis 101.1 or 102.2. Subjects include Psychosexual Development, Defense Mechanisms, Psychopathology, Insight vs. Supportive Treatment, Transference and Counter Transference, Behavior Modification Techniques, Biofeedback and Autogenic Training, and Interviewing and Communication Skills. The course consists of seventy-two hours of training: twelve weeks of classroom work for three hours per week, and thirty-six hours of clinical work under the supervision of a trained health care professional.

Clinical Applications of Hypnotherapy 301.3 is an advanced form of hypnotherapy connecting us with our spiritual roots. The fifty-four-hour course is divided into three 16-hour weekend intensives: Emotional Clearing and Inner Child Work, Inner Guides and Past Life Regression, and Conference Room Therapy.

Tuition and Fees

Tuition is as follows: for Principles of Hypnosis 101.1, $625; for Principles of Hypnosis 101.2, $495; for Hypnotherapy 201.2, $625; and for Clinical Applications of Hypnotherapy, $625.

Financial Assistance

Weekly payments may be arranged per agreement between the student and the director.

Vega Institute

1511 Robinson Street
Oroville, California 95965
Phone: (916) 533-4777 /
    (800) 818-VEGA (registration or class
    information)

The Vega Institute, founded in 1974 by Herman and Cornellia Aihara, is the world's oldest macrobiotic residential school, teaching concepts in macrobiotic nutrition, healing, cooking, and outlook that are unavailable elsewhere. The center is in the midst of residential neighborhoods in old Oroville.

Program Description

The three-week Cooking Teachers' Training Foundations Program prepares students to teach macrobiotic cooking classes. Topics covered include Developing the Spirit of a Macrobiotic Cooking Teacher, Macrobiotic Nutrition and Food Products, Macrobiotic Cooking Techniques, Design Macrobiotic Cooking Courses, Balance Between Service and Business, and Student-Teacher Practice Demonstration.

The four-week Counselor Training Foundations I Program prepares students to become macrobiotic counselors. Topics covered include Personal De-velopment, How to Begin Macrobiotic Counseling, Food Selection and Preparation Theory, Herman Aihara's Acid/Alkaline Theory, Macrobiotic Recommendations, Yin/Yang Principle in Diet and Healing, Natural Healing From Head to Toe, How to Read the Body, Practice Sessions and Constructive Critique, and final exam.

Macrobiotic Counselor Training II offers continued development of macrobiotic counseling skills. The four-week program consists of one week discussing the macrobiotic needs of individuals with major health concerns; two weeks attending the Cancer and Healing Program, during which students assist with private and group consultation sessions; a fourth week of exploration into the counseling process; and completion of projects and special assignments.

Macrobiotic Counselor Training III is a three-month apprenticeship. Students assist the experienced counselors, do their own practice sessions and projects, and help in the day-to-day operations of the Vega Study Center.

Reading the Body: A Holistic Diagnosis Intensive is a one-week course in macrobiotic visual diagnosis techniques. This course is part of the four-week Counselor Training Foundations Program, but may also be taken separately. Topics include determining strengths and weaknesses of a person's constitution, seeing how the external reflects the internal, the relationship between facial features and specific internal organs, and more.

Community Education

A wide variety of additional courses and programs are offered to the public, including two-week Cancer and Healing, Macrobiotic Lifestyle Essential, and Arthritis: Living Without It programs; a one-week Natural Healing From Head to Toe intensive; and programs in cooking, internal cleansing, diabetes and hypoglycemia, qigong healing, meditation, and more.

Admission Requirements

Counselor Training Foundations I or its equivalent is a prerequisite for the Macrobiotic Counselor Training II, and Macrobiotic Counselor Training II is a prerequisite for Macrobiotic Counselor Training III.

Tuition and Fees

Tuition is as follows: for Cooking Teachers' Training, $1,980; for Counselor Training, $2,100; for Macrobiotic Counselor II, $2,100; for Macrobiotic Counselor III, $500; and for Reading the Body, $645. Tuition includes meals and all class fees. Accommodations are additional and range from $95 to $425 per week, depending on the type of housing and number of occupants.

Financial Assistance

Discounts are available for couples or for early registration.

Wyrick Institute for European Manual Lymph Drainage

(See Multiple State Locations, page 321)

Yo San University

1314 Second Street
Santa Monica, California 90401-1103
Phone: (310) 917-2202
Fax: (310) 917-2267

Founded by Taoist Master Hua-Ching Ni in 1989, Yo San University is a Taoist school dedicated to the principles of harmony and balance. The university is housed in a two-story building between Palisades Park and the Third Street Promenade.

Accreditation

YSU's Master of Acupuncture and Traditional Chinese Medicine Program is accredited by the National Accreditation Commission for Schools and Colleges of Acupuncture and Oriental Medicine (NACSCAOM). YSU has been approved by the California Acupuncture Committee to have graduates take the California State Licensing Examination. Graduates may also take the National Commission for the Certification of Acupuncturists (NCCA) exam. YSU is approved by the California State Acupuncture Committee as a provider of continuing education certification for licensure renewal for licensed acupuncturists.

Program Description

The four-year Master of Acupuncture and Traditional Chinese Medicine Program enables full-time students to graduate in four years, spending the last year as a practice intern in the teaching clinic, a full-service, low-cost facility open to the public, which includes a complete herbal pharmacy. The program may also be taken on a part-time basis.

Courses in the first year typically include General Biology, Western Medical Terminology, Fundamentals of Taoism, Principles and Theories of TCM, Herbal Pharmacopoeia, Qigong/Eight Treasures, Introduction to Chinese Herbology, Fundamentals of Natural Healing, Human Anatomy and Physiology, General Chemistry, Fundamentals of the Health Practitioner, Biochemistry, and others.

Topics covered in the second year include Acupuncture Anatomy and Therapeutics, Herbal Prescriptions, TCM Diagnosis, Western Nutrition, Pathophysiology, Chinese Nutrition, Chinese Medical Terminology, Introduction to Botany, Practice Management, Psychology and Counseling, and a continuation of topics begun the first year.

Courses introduced in the third year include TCM Internal Medicine, Western Clinical Medicine, Acupuncture Techniques, General Physics, Tui Na/Acupressure, Tai Chi Chuan, Western Pharmacology, TCM Gynecology and Pediatrics, Biomedical Understanding of Acupuncture, Shang Han/Wen Bing, Auricular/Scalp Acupuncture, Survey of Health Professions, Laws and Ethics, Introduction to TCM and Acupuncture Classics, Medical History, and Observation Internship, followed by a preclinical examination.

The fourth year consists of Practice Internship and Tai Chi Chuan, followed by the graduation examination.

Community and Continuing Education

Laypersons, professionals, and students at other schools may enroll as special students and take some courses for enrichment without enrolling in the Master's Degree Program. Introductory courses are offered to the public in such topics as Introduction to TCM, Introduction to Herbology, and Qigong. In addition, public workshops and seminars are scheduled on a periodic basis.

Advanced seminars and workshops are offered for the refinement of skills of the licensed acupuncturist.

Admission Requirements

Applicants must have completed at least two years (sixty semester units or ninety quarter units) at an accredited undergraduate institution. Applicants must submit two letters of recommendation, interview with an admissions representative, and submit a personal essay. The essay and academic training must demonstrate the applicant's desire to become a healer and the ability to successfully complete the medical curriculum.

Tuition and Fees

Tuition for the Master's Program is $135 per unit; tuition for the Qi Development Program is $67.50 per unit. Other fees include the following: application fee, $50; new student registration, $100; continuing student registration, $25; student association fee, $10 per trimester; clinic hours, $5 per hour; herb pharmacy lab fee, $25 per fourteen hours; clinic malpractice insurance, $90 per trimester enrolled; and graduation fee, $100. The total estimated tuition is $24,997 ($2,160 per trimester); books and clinic supplies are approximately $800 per year.

Financial Assistance

Partial scholarships, federal loans, and work-study are available.

Yoga College of India

8800 Wilshire Boulevard, 2nd Floor
Beverly Hills, California 90211
Phone: (310) 854-5800
Fax: (310) 854-6200

The Yoga College of India was founded over twenty years ago by Bikram Choudhury; its Teacher Training Program began in 1994.

Program Description

The intensive three-month Accelerated Yoga Teacher Training Program requires over 500 hours of study. The course includes Yoga Philosophy, Theory and Practice of Bikram's Hatha Yoga System (eighty-four poses), Allopathic Physical Systems (taught by guest doctors), Yogic Physical Systems (energy fields, energy flow, and energy regeneration), Integration of Medical and Yogic Systems, Yoga Therapy (the application of asanas to diseases and disorders), and Marketing (promotion, setting up a yoga studio, and administration). Classes are held all day Monday through Friday, and Saturday morning, with an optional Sunday morning class.

Tuition and Fees

Tuition is $3,500; room and board is available for not more than $1,000.

COLORADO

Academy of Natural Therapy

P.O. Box 237
123 Elm Avenue
Eaton, Colorado 80615
Phone: (970) 454-2224
Fax: (303) 454-3147

The Academy of Natural Therapy was founded in 1989 by Dorothy Mongan. Classes are limited to ten students, with two to four classes per year.

Accreditation

The Academy of Natural Therapy is approved and regulated by the Division of Private Occupational Schools, State of Colorado Department of Higher Education.

Program Description

The 1,100-hour, twelve-month Massage Therapy Program includes classes in History of Massage, Interpersonal Communication, Pathology for Massage Practitioners, Reflexology, Anatomy and

Physiology, Swedish Massage, Counseling Techniques, Infant Massage, CPR, Kinesiology, Neuromuscular Reeducation, Shiatsu, Clinical Practice, Career Development and Professional Ethics, Field Experience, Nutrition, Hydrotherapy, Sports Massage, Yoga, and Tai Chi. The program may also be taken on a part-time basis.

Admission Requirements

Applicants must be at least 18 years of age, have a high school diploma or equivalent, be physically able to perform massage, have a physical exam and submit a medical history, and provide three letters of reference. A college background in the sciences is encouraged but not required.

Tuition and Fees

Tuition is $5,000; this includes books, supplies, and liability insurance.

Financial Assistance

Payment plans and scholarships are available.

Artemis Institute of Natural Therapies

P.O. Box 1824
Boulder, Colorado 80306
Phone: (303) 443-9289

The Artemis Institute of Natural Therapies was founded in 1990 by Peter Holmes, a medical herbalist and licensed acupuncturist. The institute was named for the Greek goddess Artemis, Lady of the Wild Things and protector of plant life.

Program Description

The institute offers an annual five-day Herbal Medicine Intensive, two-day seminars in clinical aromatherapy, and part-time professional programs in aromatherapy and herbal medicine.

The five-day, thirty-five-hour Herbal Medicine Intensive includes classroom training in the holistic and energetic principles of herbal medicine; constitutional typing according to the four elements; herbal formulas for common ailments; herb and weed walks in and around Boulder; hands-on experience preparing herbal extracts; and slide shows and videos covering various aspects of herbal medicine.

A two-day seminar in clinical aromatherapy is offered to both students and health professionals, and covers clinical aromatherapy for health care, massage, emotional balancing, and first aid. Topics include the hands-on formulation of essential oils, concepts of quality, scent psychology, types of applications, and more.

The 125-hour Professional Certification Program in Clinical Aromatherapy includes the basics of self-help and symptom relief, in-depth clinical skills, theory, and hands-on direction. The program is suitable for both the beginner and the health professional wishing to add aromatherapy to his or her practice. CEU credits for nurses and acupuncturists are pending.

A 400-hour Professional Certification Program in Herbal Medicine meets three days per month for sixteen months. This program is designed for the serious student of botanical medicine and covers natural medicine, herbology, pathology, diagnostics, and therapeutics in a holistic integration of traditional herbal energetics and science. Students learn skills in health maintenance and disease prevention, plant identification and collection, herb extract making and formulating, treatment of simple and complex conditions, and how to conduct a health evaluation.

Admission Requirements

Applicants must interview with an admissions representative.

Tuition and Fees

Tuition for the Herbal Medicine Intensive is $375; an optional certification test costs $20. The Clinical Aromatherapy Seminar costs $165. Tuition for the Professional Certification Program in Clinical Aromatherapy is $1,050 for the entire program or $165 per weekend. Tuition for the Professional Program in Herbal Medicine is $2,500.

Financial Assistance

Payment plans are available by special arrangement.

BioSomatics

(*See* Multiple State Locations, page 298)

Boulder School of Massage Therapy

3285 30th Street
Boulder, Colorado 80301
Phone: (303) 443-5131 / (800) 442-5131
Fax: (303) 541-9068

Boulder School of Massage Therapy was founded in 1975, initiated its Community Service/Internship Program in 1978, and opened its student clinic in 1986. The clinic now provides over 6,000 massages per year to the Boulder community.

Accreditation

BSMT is accredited by the Accrediting Commission of Career Schools/Colleges of Technology (ACC-SCT), and the massage therapy curriculum is approved by American Massage Therapy Association Commission on Massage Training Accreditation/ Approval (AMTA/COMTAA). All continuing education classes are recognized by AMTA for continuing education credit.

Program Description

The 1,000-hour Diploma Program in Massage Therapy includes 905 in-class hours (students select forty-five hours in electives), seventy-five hours in the student clinic giving thirty-nine sessions to clients, and twenty hours of internship activities. Classes include Zen Shiatsu, Anatomy/Physiology, Client Communication Skills, Movement, Nutrition, Swedish Therapeutic Massage, Anatomiken, Structural Kinesiology, Professional Ethics, Movement II, Normalization of Soft Tissue, Clinical Kinesiology, Pathophysiology, Career Development, Integrated Healing Techniques, Special Populations Symposium, and Field Placement. Electives include Shiatsu I and II, Sports Massage, Infant and Prenatal Massage, Introduction to Polarity Therapy, Yoga, Foot Reflexology, Herbology, Advanced Anatomiken, Normalization of Soft Tissue, and Orthopedic Massage.

Classes are offered on both a day and evening schedule.

Community and Continuing Education

Community education classes and workshops are offered throughout the year. These carry no credit toward the diploma program. Classes include Basic Massage, Massage Therapy Sampler Weekend, Foot Reflexology, Barefoot Shiatsu, Zen Shiatsu, Healing Touch for the Elderly and Chronically Ill, and others.

Continuing education workshops and courses (which also carry no credit toward the diploma program) offer advanced and specialized training for professional massage therapists and other allied health professionals. Courses include On-Site Chair Massage Technique, TMJ Syndrome, Repetitive Motion Syndrome, Deformities of the Spine, Table Shiatsu, the St. John Neuromuscular Therapy Pain Relief Institute, Deep Massage: The Core, Hospital-Based Massage Therapy, Dr. Vodder's Manual Lymph Drainage, Carpal Tunnel Massage Treatment, Bodywork for the Childbearing Years, Progressive Stretching, and Whiplash Assessment/Treatments.

Admission Requirements

Applicants to the diploma program must be at least 21 years of age (exceptions may be made on an individual basis); have a high school diploma or the equivalent; submit two letters of recommendation, four essay questions, up-to-date immunization records, and a health history form; complete a financial plan; have received at least two professional massages; and interview with a faculty team leader.

Tuition and Fees

Tuition for the diploma program is $7,350. Other costs include: application fee, $60; lab fees, $310; books and supplies, approximately $620; massage table, approximately $500; required professional massages, $320; and graduation fee, $35. Community education courses range from $25 to $188. Continuing education courses range from $60 to $575.

Financial Assistance

Financial aid is available to those who qualify.

Colorado Institute for Classical Homeopathy

Mailing Address:
2299 Pearl Street, #212
Boulder, Colorado 80302
Phone: (303) 440-3717

Classroom:
1441 York Street, #306
Denver, Colorado 80206
Phone: (303) 329-6345
E-mail: bseideneck@aol.com

The Colorado Institute for Classical Homeopathy was founded in 1991 and graduated its first class in 1993. It is in the process of becoming a nonprofit organization.

Accreditation

The institute is approved and regulated by the Division of Private Occupational Schools, State of Colorado Department of Higher Education.

Program Description

The institute offers a two-year, 430-hour program in classical homeopathy. The second year of study prepares students to take the examination for national certification in classical homeopathy given by the Council for Homeopathic Certification.

The curriculum includes 400 hours of instruction in such courses as History and Philosophy, Study of the Repertories, Materia Medica, Principles of Homeopathic Practice, Case Taking, Case Analysis, Process Supervision, Supervision of Study, Philosophy, Homeopathic Practice Methodology, Human Sciences, Clinical Experience and Training, and Practice Management. An additional thirty hours of seminar experience with leading instructors of homeopathy is required. Classes are held evenings and weekends.

Admission Requirements

Applicants should be over 21 years of age, have taken (or be taking concurrently) college-level anatomy, physiology, pathology, and first aid/CPR, and have a personal interview.

Tuition and Fees

Tuition is $2,500 per year, or $5,000 for the entire program; other costs include: registration fee, $25; books, $150 to $250 per year; and thirty hours of seminar experience, $400 to $500.

Financial Assistance

A payment plan is available.

Colorado Institute of Massage Therapy

2601 East St. Vrain
Colorado Springs, Colorado 80909
Phone: (719) 634-7347

Colorado Institute of Massage Therapy (CIMT) was founded in 1985 by Mrs. Togi Kinnaman, a nationally recognized workshop leader on trigger point release therapy. CIMT is currently affiliated with the Penrose-St. Francis Health Care System and is working to develop one of the first hospital-based massage therapy certification programs in the United States.

Accreditation

CIMT's Massage Therapy Program is approved by the American Massage Therapy Association Commission on Massage Training Accreditation/Approval (AMTA/COMTAA).

Program Description

The 1,150-hour Massage Therapy Program prepares students for careers as licensed massage therapists specializing in neuromuscular therapy (CIMT method). Courses include Massage Ethics, History, Equipment, Hygiene, Business Practices, Wholistic Health and Bodywork Concepts, Theories and Methods of Healing, Muscle Tension Release, Massage Theory and Movements in

Swedish Massage, Deep Tissue Massage, Foot Reflexology, Anatomy and Physiology, Structural Kinesiology, Pathology, Applied Massage: Athletic and Sports Massage, Elderly, Arthritic, Bedridden, Intuitive Massage, Applied Massage for Common Physical Complaints, Psychological Aspects of Massage and Support Group Discussion, Related Therapies: Hydrotherapy, Exercise/Stretching, Muscle Testing, Nutrition, Motion Pressure Point Therapy, Foot Reflexology, Definitions and Discussion of Various Bodywork Disciplines in the Health Care Field Today, Self-Care Practices, and Clinical Practice of Swedish and Neuromuscular Therapy, Deep Tissue Massage (CIMT System), and Foot Reflexology.

Students prepare for private practice by performing one hundred full-body massages, forty-eight massage appointments in the student clinic, thirty chair massages, ten foot reflexology charted sessions, thirteen trigger point therapy charted sessions, six preceptor evaluation massages (outside class), three instructor evaluation massages, and record keeping on each massage, as well as receiving twenty massages. In addition, twelve hours each are spent outside the classroom in marketing, sports massage, and research.

Community and Continuing Education

Introduction to Massage Therapy workshops are offered monthly for prospective students at no charge.

A series of courses in neuromuscular therapy (NMT) are offered through the International Academy of NMT of St. Petersburg, Florida. Independent workshops are offered in Spinal Muscles, Upper Extremity, Lower Extremity, and Cranium/Core Muscles. Classes may be taken in any order.

Admission Requirements

Applicants must be at least 21 years old (but may be younger with permission of the admissions committee) and have a high school diploma or equivalent.

Tuition and Fees

The program cost, including application, registration, tuition, clinic, and other expenses is $5,900. Other costs include: massage table, $60 to $500;

oils, $25 to $50; linens, $30 to $50; student clinic uniform, $50 to $100; and graduation dinner, $15 to $25. NMT workshops cost $275 per weekend (review $215), plus an extra $25 if registered less than three weeks prior to the event.

Financial Assistance

Payment plans are available.

Colorado School of Healing Arts

7655 West Mississippi, Suite 100
Lakewood, Colorado 80226
Phone: (303) 986-2320

The Colorado School of Healing Arts has been owned and operated by Health Care Associates, Inc., since 1986. The school serves students from the Denver/Boulder metropolitan areas as well as the front range mountain communities.

Accreditation

CSHA is approved by the International Massage and Somatic Therapies Accreditation Council (IM-STAC), a division of Associated Bodywork and Massage Professionals (ABMP); by the Division of Private Occupational Schools, State of Colorado Department of Higher Education; and by the State of Washington Department of Health.

Program Description

The 670-hour Certified Massage Therapist Program may be completed in as little as twelve months; fifteen- and eighteen-month programs are also available. Courses include Massage Levels I, II, and III; Anatomy; Physiology; Body-Centered Therapy; Healing Touch; Applied Kinesiology; Diet and Nutrition; Business; Sports Massage I; and Clinical Massage. A current CPR card is required upon graduation.

A C.M.T. program for nurses is designed to train R.N.s and L.P.N.s as massage therapists. Students must transfer in 330 hours of previous educational and occupational experience and complete the 670-hour Certified Massage Therapist Program to receive 1,000-hour certification.

The 1,000-hour C.M.T. Program offers an additional 330 hours of advanced instruction beyond the 670-hour program. Students may select 330 hours from advanced training programs and electives such as Trauma Touch Therapy, Sports Massage, the AnchorPoint System, Reflexology, Chiropractic Acupuncture Levels I and II (open to chiropractors only), Teaching Assistant, Internship, Palpation of Anatomy, Natural Alternatives to Chronic Disease, Herbology, Prenatal Massage, Aromatherapy, Seated Massage, Introduction to Polarity, and others.

Community and Continuing Education

Introduction to Massage Therapy is an optional introductory survey class for those considering a career in massage therapy. The $50 fee may be applied toward the full program tuition upon enrollment.

Advanced training certificate programs in reflexology, sports massage, AnchorPoint, chiropractic acupuncture, and Trauma Touch Therapy may also be taken independently of the 1,000-hour program.

The 230-hour Reflexology Certificate Program prepares students to become professional reflexology practitioners. The curriculum includes Reflexology I and II, Anatomy, Physiology, and Business; thirty hours of documented sessions with thirty different clients are also required. There is no prerequisite.

The one-hundred-hour Sports Massage Certificate Program trains therapists to provide sports massage at athletic events, including pre-, inter/intra-, and post-event sessions. In addition to three levels of sports massage course work, students are required to provide sports massage at five events. Massage Level I, Anatomy, and Physiology are prerequisites to this course.

The one-hundred-hour AnchorPoint Certificate Program provides the massage therapist with the tools of systemized acupuncture point application, proper breathing, energetic flows, and biomechanics in order to make their work more effective. Instruction is provided in three segments over the course of one year. Massage Levels I and II are prerequisites to this course.

Chiropractic Acupuncture Certificate Programs are offered at two levels (Level I is 128 hours and Level II is 112 hours); Level I is in accordance with the Colorado state acupuncture requirements of one hundred classroom hours with a minimum of twenty-five managed patients. These programs are open only to chiropractors.

Trauma Touch Therapy Certificate Programs are offered at Levels I and II; each is fifty hours in length. These programs are designed for health care professionals who are incorporating consciously-applied touch into their work with individuals who have experienced trauma or abuse. For Level I, students must have completed 500 hours in massage therapy training or be a psychotherapist or chiropractor; Level I is the prerequisite for Level II.

Courses are also offered in such areas as CPR/First Aid for bodyworkers, infant massage, reflexology, insurance billing, and many others.

Admission Requirements

Applicants to the C.M.T. programs must be at least 18 years of age, emotionally stable, and physically able to perform and receive massage; interview with an admissions representative; and submit three personal references.

Tuition and Fees

There is a $50 application fee for all courses.

Tuition for the 670-hour Certified Massage Therapist Program is $600. Other costs include: books, approximately $300; two professional massages, approximately $100; uniform, $25; massage table, approximately $400; and linens and supplies, approximately $200.

Tuition for the 1,000-hour C.M.T. Program varies with courses selected.

Tuition for the Introduction to Massage Therapy class is $50.

Tuition for the Reflexology Certificate Program is $1,540, plus $160 for books; tuition for the Sports Massage Certificate Program is $745, plus $30 for books; tuition for the AnchorPoint Certificate Program is $745, plus $85 for books; tuition for the Chiropractic Acupuncture Program, Levels I and II, is $1,700; tuition for the Trauma Touch Therapy I Program is $495, plus $45 for books; and tuition for the Trauma Touch Therapy II Program is $295, plus $15 for books.

Financial Assistance

Payment plans are available.

Colorado School of Traditional Chinese Medicine

1441 York Street, Suite 202
Denver, Colorado 80206
Phone: (303) 329-6355

The Colorado School of Traditional Chinese Medicine was founded in 1990 by Dr. George Kitchie, O.M.D., Dipl.Ac., Dipl.CH., L.Ac.(N.M.), Ph.D.; Dr. Mark Manton, N.D., Dipl.Ac.; and Dr. Cheng Shi, C.M.D., Dipl.Ac. The school offers a faculty of both Chinese and Western instructors, providing a well-rounded experience representing several modalities of diagnosis and treatment.

Accreditation

The curriculum at CSTCM has been designed to prepare students for the National Commission for the Certification of Acupuncturists (NCCA) exam and follows the guidelines set by NCCA and the Council of Colleges of Acupuncture and Oriental Medicine (CCAOM).

Program Description

CSTCM offers a three-year, 1,800-hour program in traditional Chinese medicine, and is currently working on changing to a four-year program. Students may enroll in a part-time program.

Year One includes Basic Theory of TCM, Acupuncture Meridian and Point Theory and Practicum, Chinese Herbal Medicine, Acumoxa Technique, TCM Diagnosis, TCM Differentiation, Clinical Diagnosis, and Clinical Observation.

In Year Two, the curriculum covers such topics as Acupuncture Treatment of Disease, Chinese Herbal Medicine Prescriptionology, Clinical Diagnosis Forum, Clinical Acupuncture Internship, Chinese Herbal Patent Medicine, Advanced Acupuncture Techniques, Allopathic Pathology and Physical Diagnosis, Professional Ethics and Human Services, Clinical Observation, and Student Acupuncture Clinic.

Year Three covers Advanced Student Acupuncture Clinic, Chinese Herbal Medicine Clinical Internship, TCM Internal Medicine, Clinical Diagnosis Forum, and Business Management.

Specialty electives include Aesthetic Acupuncture, Basic Chinese Language, Feng Shui: The Chinese Art of Placement, Integrating Oriental and Western Medicine, Qigong, Tai Chi Chuan, TCM and Dermatology, TCM and Nutrition, TCM and Tui Na, Tibetan Medicine, Wen Bing Lun/Shang Han Lun, and others.

Students must also complete training in First Aid/CPR prior to graduation.

Admission Requirements

Applicants must be at least 21 years of age and have completed an A.A., B.A., or B.S. degree (these requirements may be waived based on life experiences). Applicants without A.A. equivalency will be required to complete such equivalency prior to graduation. Ninety hours of anatomy and physiology must be completed prior to enrollment in the second year of study. In addition, applicants must submit a letter of intent, interview with an admissions representative, and read *The Web That Has No Weaver: Understanding Chinese Medicine,* by Ted Kaptchuk, prior to beginning classes.

Tuition and Fees

Tuition is $5,300 per academic year ($15,900 for the three-year program). Other costs include: application fee, $25; books, approximately $400 for the three-year program; training supplies, $300; student liability insurance, $160 per year; and elective workshops, $50 to $200 each.

Financial Assistance

A payment plan is available.

Crestone Healing Arts Center

P.O. Box 156
Crestone, Colorado 81131
Phone: (719) 256-4036

At Crestone Healing Arts Center, owned and operated by Dan Retuta, massage is seen as a spiritual as well as a technical discipline. The school is an experiment in community, as students live, study, and train together in a retreat-style environment.

Accreditation

In Colorado, licensing requirements for massage therapists are determined by individual cities and counties; it is the student's responsibility to determine whether the program offered meets the requirements for licensing for the city in which he or she plans to practice.

Program Description

A twelve-week, 520-hour Massage Therapy Certification Program divides instruction into massage and support courses. Massage courses comprise 279 hours and include Acupressure, Reflexology, Shiatsu, Swedish-Esalen Massage, Integrated Massage, and electives. Support courses take up the remaining 241 hours and include Group Dynamics and Open Forum, Movement and Qi Development, Herbology for Massage Therapists, Business Practice, Basic Oriental Healing Philosophy, CPR/First Aid, Community Massage Practicum, and Anatomy and Physiology.

Admission Requirements

Applicants must be at least 18 years of age, have a high school diploma or equivalent, have received at least one professional massage, and interview with an admissions representative. Students must also be ready to engage in all aspects of CHAC programs.

Tuition and Fees

A catalog costs $4; this may be applied toward the application and interview fee. There is a $40 application fee. Tuition is $3,500. Other costs include: in-residence housing, $800; books, $100 to $170; CPR training, text, and certification, $38; herbology training, texts, and materials, $140 to $180; supplies and materials, $50 to $150; and student liability insurance, $45.

Financial Assistance

Payment plans are available.

Day-Star Method of Yoga

2565 South Meade Street
Denver, Colorado 80219
Phone: (303) 934-6309

Susan Flanders, director and instructor of Day-Star Yoga, has been training classical yoga teachers for over fifteen years.

Program Description

The one-hundred-hour Hatha Yoga Teacher's Course is a purely classical system. The thirteen-class program meets one Sunday per month and includes Yogic Thought, Basic Principles of Classic Hatha Yoga, Asana, Breath, Teaching Techniques, Body-Mind, Five Ways of Bending, Working with the Body, Body Work, Student Teaching, Lesson Plans, Stress, Relaxation, Meditation, Special Populations, Business, Advertising, and more. Students are required to read and report on six books, take seven quizzes, teach eight student teaching sessions, submit a final exam, attend a full semester of standard yoga classes (as a student teacher), teach a mini-class to a group of friends, and make a relaxation tape.

Tuition and Fees

Tuition is $900; books are additional.

Financial Assistance

A payment plan is available.

International Veterinary Acupuncture Society

(*See* Multiple State Locations, page 307)

Massage Therapy Institute of Colorado

1441 York Street, Suite 301
Denver, Colorado 80206-2127
Phone: (303) 329-6345

The Massage Therapy Institute of Colorado (MTIC) was founded in 1986 by Mark H. Manton, N.D., D.H.H., Dipl.Ac., C.M.T. MTIC has developed a unique style of clinically effective massage techniques that integrate information from several massage and healing disciplines. MTIC shares space with the Colorado School of Traditional Chinese Medicine and the Colorado Institute of Classical Homeopathy.

Accreditation

MTIC is approved and regulated by the Division of Private Occupational Schools, State of Colorado Department of Higher Education.

Program Description

A 1,051-hour program is offered in Western clinical massage that emphasizes the use of Swedish massage, deep tissue massage, neuromuscular therapy, reflexology, and allied massage methods such as myofascial techniques and abdominal organ manipulation. Courses include General Anatomy and Pathology, Anatomy Project Lab, Kinesiology I and II, General Pathology, Allied Modalities—Hydro- and Heliotherapy, Business Management, Basic Student Massage Clinic, Advanced Student Massage Clinic, Swedish Massage, Deep Tissue, Neuromuscular Therapy, Reflexology, Myofascial Therapy, and one hundred hours of electives that include Shiatsu, Neuromuscular Therapy, Sports Massage, Craniosacral Therapy, Myofascial Therapy, Soft Tissue Manipulation, Therapeutic Touch, Polarity Therapy, and Energy Work. In addition, in Practicum I—Giving, students perform 350 program hours of massage; in Practicum II—Receiving, students receive one hundred hours of massage; in Practicum III—Private Evaluations, which is scheduled quarterly, students' progress in hand skills and massage techniques is assessed. Students must also complete a CPR certification course in order to be certified as massage therapists. Day and evening programs are available.

Continuing Education

Second-year advanced training is offered in myofascial therapy and remedial massotherapy.

Admission Requirements

Applicants must be at least 21 years of age and preferably have completed an A.A., B.S., or B.A. degree. Age and degree requirements may be waived providing the applicant has equivalent life experiences and demonstrates a desire and aptitude for massage therapy training.

Tuition and Fees

Tuition is $4,900. Other costs include: application fee, $25; books, $175; prepared literature, $35; student liability insurance, $95 per year; table and accessories, $450 to $750; elective seminars, $700 to $1,200; four to six optional massages, $140 to $200; and Banya session (hydrotherapy session at Izba Spa), $65.

Financial Assistance

A payment plan is available.

Polarity Center of Colorado

2410 Jasper Court
Boulder, Colorado 80304
Phone: (303) 443-9847 / (303) 499-4675
Fax: (303) 415-1839
E-mail: chittyj@aol.com

The Polarity Center of Colorado (PCC) was founded in 1991. PCC emphasizes the importance of craniosacral therapy and its integration within polarity, and includes craniosacral training in both its A.P.P. and R.P.P. programs.

Program Description

PCC offers Polarity Level I and Level II training, based on APTA's educational requirements for Associate Polarity Practitioner (A.P.P.) and Registered Polarity Practitioner (R.P.P.), respectively.

The 120-hour Level I Associate Polarity Practitioner Training includes eighteen days of training covering such topics as Cranial I and II, Polarity Theory and Practice, Verbal and Theory (practitioner skills to verbally guide and support the client), Nervous Systems, Five Elements, Bodyreading, and Integration. For APTA certification, students must also give 30 one-hour polarity sessions, receive five sessions from R.P.P.s, and complete ten hours of anatomy and physiology.

The 500-hour Level II Registered Polarity Practitioner Training meets once a month, with additional scheduled events, over a two-year period.

Tuition and Fees

For the A.P.P. Training, Cranial I and II cost $295 per three-day weekend; remaining weekends cost $195 per two-day weekend. For the R.P.P. Training, Cranial III and IV cost $295 per three-day weekend; all others cost $195 per two-day weekend.

Financial Assistance

The Polarity Center of Colorado is a State of Colorado approved school for occupational education aid.

Rocky Mountain Center for Botanical Studies

P.O. Box 19254
Boulder, Colorado 80308-2254
Phone: (303) 442-6861

The Rocky Mountain Center for Botanical Studies was founded in 1992 by herbalist Feather Jones.

Accreditation

RMCBS is approved and regulated by the Division of Private Occupational Schools, State of Colorado Department of Higher Education.

Program Description

The 736-hour Professional Training for Western Herbalism Program meets three days per week for four 10-week quarters (one year). Courses include Introduction to Herbalism, Botany, Materia Medica: Organ Systems and Herbal Therapeutics, Herbal Pharmacy, Nutrition, Anatomy and Physiology, Earth-Centered Herbalism: The Talking Leaves, Physical Assessment, Botanical Cosmetics, Forest Ecology and Introduction to Permaculture, Herb Walks and Ethical Wild Harvesting Techniques, Organic Gardening, Pathology, Ethnobotany, Pharmacognosy, Wild Foods: Gathering and Preparation, Clinical Seminar, Student Case Studies Review, Standard Practice Medicine, Business Management, and Business Ethics and Practice Issues.

The 229-hour Essence of Herbalism evening certification program meets two evenings per week, plus two Saturdays per month, for seven months. Courses include Introduction to Herbalism, First Aid, Botanical Cosmetics/Aromatherapy, Earth-Centered Herbalism, Botany, Materia Medica: Organ Systems and Therapeutics, Nutrition, Physiology, Herb Walks and Ethical Wild Harvesting Techniques, Pharmacy, and Wild Foods: Gathering and Preparation. The curriculum also includes a four-day camping trip to northern New Mexico.

Community and Continuing Education

Non-certificate courses covering a variety of topics are offered to the public, and noted guest lecturers from around the country hold workshops throughout the year.

Students who have completed at least 500 hours of herbal education may enroll in the 224-hour Clinical Herbalism Program. The curriculum includes Interview Skills, Advanced Organ Systems Review, When to Refer Out, Herb Walks and Wildcrafting, Field Trips, Herbal Pharmacy, Clinical Nutrition, Pathology, Herb/Drug Interactions, Clinical Case Studies, Eastern/Western Diagnostics, Earth-Centered Herbalism, Toxicology, and Biochemistry.

Admission Requirements

Applicants will be accepted with different educational backgrounds. A high school diploma or equivalent is recommended and an interview is required.

Tuition and Fees

There is a $15 application fee for all courses.

Tuition for the Professional Training for Western Herbalism Program is $4,500; books are approximately $200, and activities, supplies, and tools are approximately $400. Tuition for the Essence of Herbalism evening certification program is $1,500; books and supplies are additional. Tuition for the Clinical Herbalism Program is $3,200; books and supplies are additional.

Financial Assistance

Payment plans are available.

Rocky Mountain Institute of Yoga and Ayurveda

P.O. Box 1091
Boulder, Colorado 80306-1091
Phone: (303) 443-6923

The Rocky Mountain Institute of Yoga and Ayurveda (RMIYA) was founded in 1990 by five instructors; by 1996, the faculty had expanded to a core of seven, with nine guest faculty members. Because each teacher arranges his or her own class space, classes are offered in Allenspark, Boulder, Denver, and Longmont.

Program Description

The Certification Program in Yoga Therapy and Ayurveda requires twenty-five to thirty-five credits, depending on prior yoga asana experience; it is recommended that students take or have taken at least one course in biochemistry, anatomy, or physiology. Courses include Pranayama and Meditation Levels I and II, Introduction to Ayurvedic Medicine, Intermediate Ayurveda: Assessment and Treatment, Medicine for Holistic Health Practitioners, Women's Health Care Through Ayurveda, Asana as Therapy, Ayurvedic Massage, Ayurvedic Diet/Ayurvedic Cooking, Karma Yoga: The Yoga of Action and Service, Yoga Psychology and Ayurvedic Psychiatry, Diagnostic Skills in Ayurveda, Pancha Karma: The Cleansing Practices of Yoga and Ayurveda, Ayurveda/Yoga Therapy Internship, and others.

The Practice and Teaching of Yoga Certification Program requires twenty credits. Courses include Yoga Philosophy and the Yoga Sutras; Pranayama and Meditation Levels I through III; Mantra, Ritual, and the Devotional Practices of Yoga; Asana and Ayurveda; Shat Karma and Pancha Karma; Asana as Therapy; Karma Yoga and the Bhagavad Gita; Yoga Psychology; Internship/Student Teaching; Asana for Teachers; and others. In addition, a total of ninety to 150 hours of asana practice time must be accumulated, distributed in the three asana lineages of Classical, Structural/Iyengar, and Ashtanga Vinyasa. Previous asana training may be credited toward this requirement. Students with extensive asana background may complete the program in three semesters.

Tuition and Fees

Tuition is charged on a per-class basis, ranging from $75 to $325 per class; average early registration tuition is approximately $8 per hour.

Financial Assistance

A discount is given for early registration; work exchanges are available.

The Rolf Institute of Structural Integration

205 Canyon Boulevard
Boulder, Colorado 80302
Phone: (303) 449-5903
Fax: (303) 449-5978

The Rolf Institute was founded by Ida P. Rolf, Ph.D., who examined many systems, including osteopathy, yoga, and chiropractic, in her search for an understanding of structural order. She developed a sequence of work called structural integration that releases the body from lifelong patterns of tension and balances the body, leading to improved appearance and relief from neck, back, and other mobility problems.

Accreditation

The Rolf Institute is the sole certifying body for Rolfers. Graduates of the training programs may refer to themselves as Certified Rolfers and Rolfing Movement Teachers, and may offer this work to the public.

Program Description

In order to become Certified Rolfers, students must complete a series of steps.

1. Experience a ten-session Rolfing series and eight Rolfing Movement Integration sessions (a list of area teachers may be obtained from the institute).

2. Unit One: Foundations of Bodywork (FOB). This five-week course explores skillful touch, therapeutic relationship, anatomy, kinesiology, and physiology as they relate to Rolfing. Those with training in massage or bodywork may skip this step.

3. Complete the admissions packet and take the entrance exam.

4. Principles of Rolfing. This five-day course presents the principles of Rolfing and Rolfing Movement Integration.

5. Unit Two: Embodiment of Rolfing and Rolfing Movement. This six-week course includes the study of fascial anatomy, recognizing simple structural patterns, integrating functional and structural approaches to Rolfing, and gaining a working knowledge of Rolfing principles. Students give and receive a series of ten Rolfing sessions and three Rolfing Movement sessions.

6. Interim Period. Students are assigned a written paper.

7. Unit Three: Clinical Application of Rolfing Theory. In this eight-week course, students take three clients through the ten series of Rolfing and study fascial anatomy, efficient body use, and business skills and ethics. At this point, the student becomes a Certified Rolfer.

8. Rolfing Movement Certification. This four-week course permits students to deepen their understanding of Rolfing Movement. At this point, the student is a Certified Rolfing Movement Teacher.

Rolfing training is also available in Brazil, Europe, and Australia.

Community and Continuing Education

Once graduates are certified as Rolfers, they must attend a minimum of eighteen days of approved continuing education over a period of three to seven years in preparation for Advanced Rolfing Training. Such continuing education workshops include instruction in specific manipulative techniques, craniosacral therapy, visceral manipulation, and other subjects.

After a minimum of three years in Rolfing practice and eighteen approved continuing education credits, practitioners must complete a 216-hour, six-week Advanced Rolfing Certification Course. This course must be completed within seven years of Rolfing Certification in order to maintain membership in the institute.

Admission Requirements

Applicants must have experienced the benefits of Rolfing; demonstrate an understanding of anatomy, kinesiology, and physiology; have experience with touch in hands-on application; have experience with the therapeutic relationship; and be of sound moral character. Before beginning Unit Two, applicants must have received ten sessions of Rolfing from a Certified Rolfer; have received eight Rolfing Movement Integration sessions from a Rolfing Movement Teacher; submit letters of recommendation from a Rolfer and Rolfing Movement Teacher; have a B.A. or B.S. degree or comparable life experience; successfully complete the Rolf Institute equivalency exam; have documented experience of training and practice of touch; have fieldwork experience evaluated by a Rolfer; complete the application packet; and successfully complete Principles of Rolfing.

Tuition and Fees

There is a $75 application fee. The equivalency exam for those not taking FOB is $225; books are $250 to $500. Tuition for Unit One is $2,200; for Principles of Rolfing, $700; for Unit Two, $4,200; for Unit Three, $4,900, and for Rolfing Movement Certification, $2,700.

School of Natural Medicine

P.O. Box 7369
Boulder, Colorado 80306-7369
Phone: (303) 443-4882
Fax: (303) 443-8276

The School of Natural Medicine (SNM) was founded in Cambridge, England, in 1977 as the British School of Iridology and Holistic Healing. The school moved to Boulder in 1988.

Program Description

A variety of classes and workshops focusing on iridology and naturopathy are held throughout the year. The Summer School offers three consecutive weeks of instruction consisting of Transcendence: Elements of Life Experiential Transformation; Iridology and Foundation of Natural Medicine; Advanced Iridology; Wildcrafting and Advanced Herbology and Naturopathy; and Natural Physician Clinical Training.

The school also offers home study programs; see page 358.

Admission Requirements

SNM courses are designed for orthodox and alternative practitioners who desire a foundation in holistic natural medicine, or those seeking to learn how to live a healthy life.

Tuition and Fees

Summer school costs $600 per six-day week. Workshops cost $85.

Shambhava School of Yoga

2875 County Road #67
Boulder, Colorado 80303
Phone: (303) 494-3051

Susan Fontaine, director of Hatha yoga with the Shambhava School of Yoga, has been a close student of Swami Shambhavananada's since 1975.

Program Description

The six-month Hatha Yoga Teacher Training Program is designed to bring a meditative focus to the practice of yoga, transforming the student into the teacher. Classes meet Sundays, Wednesdays, and one additional day per week. Session One emphasizes classical yoga postures and using the elements of yoga to release our inner energy and open within. Principles of anatomy are also taught, and a meditative practice will be established. Session Two develops an understanding of the principles of vinyasa, counterpose, and modification, emphasizing the development of the student as teacher. Students are exposed to various styles and levels of teaching, including, for those interested, advanced teachings of Kundalini yoga. Students also continue meditation classes. Requirements for the certificate include instructor evaluation, completion of a six- to eight-week yoga course outline, participation in a minimum of 180 course hours, and two weekend yoga retreats at Shoshoni Retreat.

Tuition and Fees

Tuition is $1,650 ($825 per session) or $1,800 ($300 per month); this includes all classes and two weekend retreats with dorm accommodations at Shoshoni Retreat; books and materials are additional. Residential accommodations are available.

CONNECTICUT

Connecticut Center for Massage Therapy

Main School Address:
75 Kitts Lane
Newington, Connecticut 06111-3954
Phone: (860) 667-1886

Branch Address:
25 Sylvan Road South
Westport, Connecticut 06880
Phone: (203) 221-7325

The Connecticut Center for Massage Therapy (CCMT) began with small workshop trainings in the Hartford area in 1978. In 1980, the school was incorporated as a teaching center; in 1982, its programs were approved by the American Massage Therapy Association (AMTA); and in 1992, CCMT opened its Westport branch.

Accreditation

CCMT is accredited by the Accrediting Commission of Career Schools and Colleges of Technology (ACCSCT) and by the American Massage Therapy Association Commission on Massage Training Accreditation/Approval (AMTA/COMTAA).

Program Description

The 600-hour Massage Therapist Program, offered in Newington only, includes Acupressure, Anatomy and Physiology, Business Practices, Clinic/Internship, Energetic Foundations, Kinesiology, Massage Therapy, Palpation Lab, Pathology, Professional Foundations, and Standard First Aid/CPR.

Graduates of the 635-hour New York Massage Therapist Program, offered in both Newington and Westport, are eligible to take the New York massage licensing exam. The core of the program is the same as the 600-hour program, with the substitution of Neurology, Jin Shin Do, Integrating Acupressure, and Acupressure Theory courses in place of the Student Clinic/Internship.

Classes are held mornings, afternoons, and evenings.

Community and Continuing Education

A two-day Touch of Massage workshop is offered throughout the year as an introduction to the school and to massage techniques.

The Advanced Studies Program provides continuing education to practicing massage therapists, bodyworkers, and other health care practitioners. Offerings include one-day and weekend workshops and certification programs in specific techniques.

Admission Requirements

Applicants must be 18 years of age or older, have a high school diploma or equivalent, be proficient in the English language, be physically capable of performing massage techniques, and interview with the admissions director. Prospective students must also show evidence of receiving at least one professional massage within one year prior to application.

Tuition and Fees

There is a $25 application fee and a $150 registration fee. Tuition for the Massage Therapist Program is $8,750, and $8,950 for the New York Massage Therapist Program; books are $400 to $700; and an optional massage table costs $400 to $700 and up.

The Touch of Massage workshop costs $75 per person.

Financial Assistance

Federal grants and loans and payment plans are available.

Connecticut Institute for Herbal Studies

87 Market Square
Newington, Connecticut 06111
Phone: (860) 666-5064

The Connecticut Institute for Herbal Studies (CIHS) was founded in 1992 by director Laura Mignosa, a certified Chinese herbologist and vice president of the Connecticut Herbal Association. Ms. Mignosa has studied for many years with Arthur Shattuck, Lic.Ac., O.M.D., a noted author, national lecturer, and master herbalist, who serves as program advisor at CIHS and director of the Wisconsin Institute for Chinese Herbology.

Accreditation

Most courses are eligible for continuing educational units granted by the National Commission for the Certification of Acupuncturists (NCCA) and the Massachusetts Committee on Acupuncture.

Program Description

A five-month course in traditional Chinese herbology meets one weekend per month and offers instruction in individual herbs, guiding formulas, and diagnostic paradigms used in Chinese medicine. Topics covered include herbs and formulas used for specific organs, shang han lun, wen bing theory, and yin and yang tonics.

A five-month course in Western herbology is also offered. Classes meet one weekend per month and include all organ systems, herb identification, weed walks, and safety of herbs and contraindications, with special attention to formulas for children, women, and the elderly. Students will create their own herbal medicine cabinets.

A five-month Chinese Herbology and Theory Program meets one weekend per month and is accepted by the National Accreditation Commission for Schools and Colleges of Acupuncture and Oriental Medicine (NACSCAOM) for credits toward national certification. Students must have completed a course in Oriental medical theory prior to enrollment. The program teaches the fundamentals of Chinese medicine and the therapeutic use of over one hundred herbs, and includes herb identification, tastes, formulas, usages, contraindications, preparations, and how and where to purchase herbs.

An Accelerated TCM Theory Course may be taken as a prerequisite for Chinese Herbology and Theory (above). This six-week course meets one evening per week and covers such topics as yin/yang, eight principal and five element theories, physiology, pathology, boundaries and ethics, and more.

A two-weekend Aromatherapy Certificate Program teaches lay persons and practitioners the history, uses, and benefits of aromatherapy, and includes hands-on training.

A Bach Flower Essence Certificate Program is offered to those with a beginning understanding of essences. The program consists of an intermediate class, covering essences in depth, and certification, with further teaching of the essences and experiential study in a clinical setting.

Community and Continuing Education

Evening and weekend community and continuing education courses are offered in a wide variety of topics, including Vegetarian Cooking, Feng Shui, Chinese Herbs and Common Ailments, Jin Shin Do, Qigong, Pulse Diagnosis, Backyard Herbs, and Evening Weed Walks.

Admission Requirements

Applicants must be at least 18 years of age, have a high school diploma or equivalent, and interview with an admissions representative.

Tuition and Fees

Tuition for the Traditional Chinese Herbology Course is $1,250. Tuition for the Western Herbology Course is $595. Tuition for the community and continuing education courses varies with the length of the course, from $19 for some evening seminars to $189 for weekend seminars. Tuition for the Chinese Herbology and Theory Course is $875; for the Accelerated TCM Theory Course, $259; for the Aromatherapy Certificate Program, $159; and for the Bach Flower Essence Certificate Program, $895.

Financial Assistance

Payment plans may be arranged on an individual basis.

University of Bridgeport College of Chiropractic

Bridgeport, Connecticut 06601
Phone: (203) 576-4279 / (888) UB-CHIRO
    (toll-free—admissions office only)
Internet: http://bridgeport.edu/ubpage/chiro/
    ubcc.html

Founded in 1990, the University of Bridgeport's College of Chiropractic is the only chiropractic college in New England and the first university-based chiropractic college in North America. The University of Bridgeport was founded in 1927, and its urban campus comprises ninety-one buildings.

Accreditation

The University of Bridgeport College of Chiropractic is accredited by the Council on Chiropractic Education (CCE) to award the Doctor of Chiropractic (D.C.) degree.

Program Description

The 5,118-hour Doctor of Chiropractic degree program is a four-year course of study that includes a clinical internship. The program is divided into Basic Sciences (1,422 hours) including Anatomy, Physiology, Biochemistry, Neuroscience, Pathology, and Microbiology and Public Health; Clinical Sciences (2,550 hours), including Principles and Practice, Radiology, Research, Physiologic Therapeutics, Differential Diagnosis, Chiropractic Skills and Technique, Diagnosis, Nutrition, Emergency Procedures, and Business Procedures; and Clinical Services (1,140 hours of supervised patient care).

The College of Chiropractic and the Nutrition Institute offer a joint program for those who wish to pursue a Master of Science degree in human nutrition while working toward the D.C. degree. Chiropractic students will enter the master's program at an advanced level, completing seventeen semester hours of required nutrition courses (including Vitamin and Mineral Metabolism, Nutritional Therapeutics, Developmental Nutrition, Research in Nutrition, and Biostatistics) and three semester hours from an elective.

The University of Bridgeport also offers three prechiropractic programs: Bachelor's degree programs consisting of a four-year bachelor's degree prior to entering Chiropractic College, or three years of prechiropractic study with credit earned in Chiropractic College for a bachelor's degree in biology or elective studies with a specialization in prechiropractic; the Basic Program (ninety credits), in which students can meet all requirements for Chiropractic College in three years of prechiropractic study; and the Accelerated Science Program, designed for students who already have a bachelor's degree, in which students complete all science prerequisites in two semesters. The university also offers a seven-year combined B.S./D.C. degree program.

Admission Requirements

Applicants for the doctoral program must have completed at least three years (ninety semester hours) of study toward a baccalaureate degree from an accredited, degree-granting institution with a cumulative G.P.A. of 2.25 or greater; a baccalaureate degree is recommended. Specific courses in communication/language skills, psychology, humanities, general chemistry, organic chemistry, general physics, and general biology, zoology, or anatomy and physiology are required. Applicants must also submit three letters of recommendation.

Tuition and Fees

Tuition is $5,450 per semester; books and supplies are additional. Other fees include: application fee, $75; registration fee, $25 per semester; general university fee, $170 per semester; and campus ID and security fee, $80 per semester. Chiropractic students may reside in on-campus residence halls for an additional $1,740 to $2,625 per semester.

Financial Assistance

Federal loans, work-study, and scholarships are available.

DISTRICT OF COLUMBIA

Potomac Massage Training Institute

4000 Albemarle Street N.W., 5th Floor
Washington, D.C. 20016
Phone: (202) 686-7046

The Potomac Massage Training Institute was founded in 1976 by Kevin Andreae, and moved to its present location in 1993.

Accreditation

The curriculum of the Professional Training Program is approved by the American Massage Therapy Association Commission on Massage Training Accreditation/Approval (AMTA/COMTAA), and graduates of the institute are eligible to take the national certification exam administered by the National Certification Board for Therapeutic Massage and Bodywork (NCBTMB).

Program Description

The Professional Massage Training Program consists of a minimum of 500 in-class hours, field work, and clinic, plus completion of at least two practice massages outside of class per week. Semester I: Foundation covers the majority of the eleven body systems, giving a full-body Swedish massage, and participation in nursing home projects. Semester II: Specialization focuses on the musculoskeletal system and kinesiology, with specialization in deep tissue work for the shoulder and pelvic girdles and extremities, and field work in the student clinic. In Semester III: Integration, students continue to develop their deep tissue and Swedish techniques; work on communication, business, and professional skills; and continue to participate in the student clinic. Students are required to complete a minimum of forty-two hours of electives before graduation; these include introductions to various massage and bodywork techniques and modalities, and may meet on weekends or evenings. Students are also required to take CPR/First Aid classes. Outside professional sessions are required each semester. Students attend morning or evening classes.

Continuing Education

A number of continuing education programs are offered to massage and bodywork professionals. These include Sports Massage, Neuromuscular Training (NMT), Myofascial Release, Craniosacral Therapy, Massage with Survivors of Abuse, Tui Na (Chinese Massage), Bodywork for the Childbearing Year, and Alexander Technique.

Admission Requirements

Applicants must be at least 18 years of age; have a high school diploma, GED, or college transcript; demonstrate literacy in English; submit a written statement, two personal references, and a medical/health history form; have received at least one documented massage from a PMTI graduate or AMTA member; have a flexible schedule that allows some weekend, daytime, and evening commitments; be able to devote fifteen to twenty hours per week to classes and study time; and have the necessary financial resources.

Tuition and Fees

Tuition is $4,950, including registration fee and deposit. Other costs include: books, approximately $150; polo shirt, approximately $25; CPR/First Aid, $15 to $50; outside professional sessions, $30 to $60 each; optional massage table, $400 to $500; and sheets and oil, approximately $100.

Financial Assistance

Payment plans are available. Outside sources of support have included the Virginia Commission for the Visually Handicapped; the District of Columbia, Virginia, and Maryland Departments of Rehabilitation Services; and Georgetown University Personnel Support.

FLORIDA

American Yoga Association

(*See* Multiple State Locations, page 296)

The Atlantic Institute of Aromatherapy

16018 Saddlestring Drive
Tampa, Florida 33618
Phone/Fax: (813) 265-2222

The Atlantic Institute of Aromatherapy was founded in 1989 by Sylla Sheppard-Hanger, a licensed massage therapist, cosmetologist, and esthetician who twice served on the Board of Directors for the American Aromatherapy Association.

Accreditation

Some classes and correspondence courses provide state-certified continuing education units for licensed massage therapists. There are no current regulations in the United States regarding the practice of aromatherapy, and certificates awarded by the school in no way imply a license to treat, prescribe, or diagnose.

Program Description

Introduction to Aromatherapy is a one-day overview covering topics such as essential oil properties, effect on body and mind, safety data, and practical applications. The course includes a set of essential oils, and provides six CEUs for L.M.T.s.

Basics of Blending is a one-day class that explores the blending of essential oils into effective synergies, essential oil chemistry, and techniques of perfuming. All supplies are included.

Aromatherapy Part I: Basic is a two-day introductory course covering essential oil production, qualities and chemistry, and psychological, cosmetological, and medical applications including massage, skin care, and hair care. All supplies are included.

Aromatherapy Part II: Advanced may be taken over two or three days. The course includes a complete study of twenty-five medicinal, chemotype, and exotic essential oils and their therapeutic application, along with the study of botanical families and olfaction research. This course provides eighteen hours of CEUs for L.M.T.s.

The certification program consists of Aromatherapy Parts I and II, taken through classroom or home study, and a written exam. A certificate is awarded upon successful completion.

A five-day Intensive Aromatherapy Retreat in the Florida Keys consists of instruction in the history of aromatherapy; identifying quality of essential oils; basic chemistry and constituent properties; production processes; a review of fifty oils; applications in skin care, hair care, and massage; holistic healing; practical uses and applications with case histories; study of perfume; and much more. All materials are provided. This course provides thirty hours of CEUs for L.M.T.s.

Correspondence courses are also offered; see page 360.

Tuition and Fees

The Introduction to Aromatherapy course costs $150; Basics of Blending costs $150; Aromatherapy Part I costs $275; Aromatherapy Part II costs $375; and the five-day Intensive Aromatherapy Retreat costs $600.

Atlantic Institute of Oriental Medicine

1057 S.E. 17th Street
Fort Lauderdale, Florida 33316-2116
Phone: (954) 463-3888 / (954) 522-6405

The Atlantic Institute of Oriental Medicine (ATOM), a not-for-profit school, was founded in 1994 by Johanna Chu Yen, M.D., C.A., Michael C.J. Carey, M.A., M.P.H., and Betty Z. Shannon, B.A. The school has clinical training centers at other locations in Fort Lauderdale and Lauderdale Lakes.

Accreditation

ATOM is in the process of seeking accreditation at this time. The Traditional Chinese Medicine Program prepares students to take not only the Florida licensure examination but also the national certification exams given by the National Commission for the Certification of Acupuncturists (NCCA) in acupuncture and herbology.

Program Description

The three-year, 2,745-hour Traditional Chinese Medicine Program consists of twenty-eight courses divided into four groups: Acupuncture and Related Topics, Biomedical Clinical Sciences and Related Topics, Clinical Practicum, and Herbal Therapy and Related Topics.

Year One classes include History of Eastern Medicine, Theory of Chinese Medicine, Acupuncture Channels and Points I and II, Acupuncture Anatomy, Public Health and Preventive Medicine, Western Physiology, Western Anatomy, Western Pathology, History of Western Medicine, and Clinical Practicum I (Acupuncture).

Classes in Year Two include Acupuncture Channels and Points III and IV, Practice of Chinese Medicine, Clinical Diagnosis and Treatment, State Acupuncture Law and Rules, Therapeutic Exercise, Manual Therapies, Medical Terminology, Clinical Practicum II (Acupuncture), and Introduction to Chinese Herbology.

Year Three classes include Pediatric and Gynecological Acupuncture, Thesis, Select Topics in Linguistics, Basic Knowledge of Diagnosis of Imaging and Lab Testing, Medical Ethics and Office Management, Clinical Practicum III (Acupuncture and Herbology), Oriental Herbal Studies, Herbal Formulas and Herbal Therapy, and Introduction to Homeopathy. Students are also required to attend each of the two annual seminars conducted by the institute. Clinical training takes the form of Observing (first 240 hours), Assisting (next 360 hours), and Interning (final 417 hours).

Admission Requirements

Applicants must be at least 18 years of age; be competent in speaking, reading, and writing English and in understanding spoken English; have completed at least two years' accredited baccalaureate education (sixty or more semester credits); and visit the institute and interview with the director of education. Applicants must also submit a physician's statement of health, one to three letters of recommendation, and an essay.

Tuition and Fees

There is a $100 registration fee. Tuition is $15,000 for the entire three-year program; uniforms, books, supplies, and special materials are approximately $1,825 to $2,000 for the three-year period.

Financial Assistance

Payment plans are available.

Center for Life Energy

505 South Orange Avenue
Sarasota, Florida 34236
Phone: (941) 953-2242 / (800) 296-3242
  (out-of-state)
Fax: (941) 365-6758

The Center for Life Energy was founded in 1988. Program director Philip Aberman, a Registered Polarity Practitioner and licensed massage therapist, has worked with energy healing since 1975.

Accreditation

The Center for Life Energy is accredited by the American Polarity Therapy Association (APTA) and approved by the State of Florida as a continuing education provider for Florida licensed massage therapists.

Program Description

The 175-hour Polarity Therapy Certification Program is offered as a series of three intensive classroom modules, grounded and integrated through outside practice, clinical supervision, and personal polarity process. Level 1 is a six-day, fifty-hour intensive that establishes a foundation of theory and hands-on work for five element balancing, vitality balancing, polarity reflexology, introduction to craniosacral, stretching postures, and food energetics. Level 2 is a second six-day, fifty-hour intensive deepening the work of Level 1 by addressing the interrelation of emotional balance, stress and trauma, structural balancing, additional craniosacral work, and healing with sound. Level 3 is a five-day, forty-hour intensive that completes workshop requirements and clinical practicum for those who wish to apply for APTA certification as Associate Polarity Practitioners.

A nine-day Craniosacral Certification Program develops the skills to do hands-on work with the craniosacral system. Students learn the twelve-step foundation protocol for evaluating and clearing the craniosacral system; advanced techniques for addressing commonly encountered craniosacral problems; craniosacral unwinding techniques to unravel strain patterns; cranio-mandibular work; and structural-energetic work to align structure with core energies. Breath, movement, sound, and meditation are used to clear the craniosacral pathways and activate consciousness. Complete certification consists of three 3-day seminars: Craniosacral Foundation, Craniosacral Unwinding, and Craniosacral Completion.

Other seminars offered include Healing with Sound and Music, and Drum Class.

Admission Requirements

There are no specific age or educational requirements.

Tuition and Fees

Tuition for the Polarity Therapy Certification Program is as follows: Level 1, $550; Level 2, $550; and Level 3, $450.

Tuition for the Craniosacral Certification Program varies with course location; estimated tuition for each three-day seminar is $225 to $275.

Financial Assistance

A 10 percent discount is given for early registration; other financial aid is offered on an individual basis.

CORE Institute

223 West Carolina Street
Tallahassee, Florida 32301
Phone: (904) 222-8673
Fax: (904) 561-6160

The CORE Institute was founded in 1990 by George and Patricia Kousaleos and has graduated more than 450 professional massage therapists. The CORE Institute is owned by GEO Touch, Inc.

Accreditation

The CORE Institute's Professional Massage Therapy Training Program is accredited by the American Massage Therapy Association Commission on Massage Training Accreditation/Approval (AMTA/COMTAA), and the school is approved by the Florida Board of Massage.

Program Description

The 500-hour Professional Massage Therapy Training Program includes instruction in Therapeutic Massage (including an introduction to CORE myofascial therapy, neuromuscular therapy, medical massage, and sports massage), Human Physiology, Human Anatomy, Hydrotherapy, Florida Law, Allied Modalities (including such topics as sports massage, polarity, traditional Oriental medicine and acupuncture, shiatsu, neuromuscular therapy, seated massage, Trager approach, wellness, communication skills, community outreach, practical business skills, continuity techniques, and trigger point therapy), and HIV Education. All students are required to participate in at least thirteen-and-a-half hours of community service, and may participate in the student clinic on a voluntary basis. CPR/First Aid certification is required for graduation. Day and evening programs are available.

Continuing Education

CORE Institute offers certification training and continuing education in CORE bodywork, sports massage, medical massage, neuromuscular therapy, TMJ therapy, and seated massage.

Admission Requirements

Applicants must be at least 20 years of age, have a high school diploma or equivalent, submit a biographical essay and two letters of reference, interview with an admissions representative, and submit a physician's letter stating past medical history.

Tuition and Fees

There is a $75 registration fee. Tuition is $4,500. Books and supplies are approximately $250; an optional massage table may be purchased through the school at a discount.

Financial Assistance

Payment plans, work-study, book scholarships, and veterans' benefits are available.

Educating Hands School of Massage

261 Southwest 8th Street
Miami, Florida 33130
Phone: (305) 285-6991 / (800) 999-6991
Fax: (305) 857-0298

The Educating Hands School of Massage was founded in 1983 by Iris Burman. It is located in downtown Miami, six blocks from Biscayne Bay.

Accreditation

The Educating Hands curriculum is approved by the American Massage Therapy Association Commission on Massage Training Accreditation/Approval (AMTA/COMTAA). In addition, the school is authorized by the Immigration and Naturalization Service for student visas.

Program Description

The Therapeutic Massage Training Program (624 total class hours) includes courses in Human Anatomy and Physiology, Kinesiology and Palpation, Therapeutic Massage, Student Clinic, Theory and Practice of Hydrotherapy and Heliotherapy, Introduction to Allied Modalities (including thirty-five hours of advanced hydrotherapy), Florida State Law, Business Principles and Development, and HIV-AIDS. Massage classes have one teacher to a maximum of twenty students; in some lecture classes, two classes may be combined (forty students). Student clinic hours will have one instructor to a maximum of ten students.

Community and Continuing Education

For those who are seeking an introductory course in massage therapy, Educating Hands offers Massage For Fun, a workshop for nonprofessionals in full-body massage.

Licensed professionals in Florida are required to accumulate continuing education credits for biannual license renewal. Many of the continuing education programs have been approved by the Board of Massage for CEU credit. Typical courses include Connective Tissue Massage, On-Site Massage Technique, Infant Massage, NMT, Polarity Therapy, Shiatsu, and Sports Massage.

Admission Requirements

Applicants must be a high school graduate or equivalent, 18 years of age or older, and interview with the director of admissions or an associate.

Tuition and Fees

Tuition for the Therapeutic Massage Training Program is $3,900. Other costs include: registration fee, $100; books, approximately $290; and student supplies, $100; other supplies are additional.

Financial Assistance

Payment plans and veterans' benefits are available; an extended finance plan is offered through an independent company. If payment is made in full, student supplies will be provided at no charge.

Equine Sports Massage Program

14735 S.W. 71 Avenue Road
Ocala, Florida 34473
Phone: (904) 347-3747

The Equine Sports Massage program was founded by Don Doran, a graduate of the Florida School of Massage and a licensed massage therapist certified in sports massage. He has been working full-time in the field of equine massage since the late 1980s.

Program Description

The one-hundred-hour Equine Sports Massage Professional Program takes twelve days to complete. The curriculum includes Equine Anatomy, Equine Physiology, Equine Kinesiology, Equine Acupressure, Hands-On Application of ESM, Contraindications, Therapeutic Massage Techniques, Neuromuscular Therapy, Stretching, Motion Evaluation, Pre- and Post-Event Massage, Alternative Healing Methods, Building a Business, and more.

The school also offers a six-day Equine Acupressure Program (Equi-Pressure). The course offers instruction in pre- and post-event Equi-Pressure massage, Equi-Points that maintain and improve stamina and health, the fourteen major energy channels (meridians), evaluation of potential problem areas, and using Equi-Pressure in combination with magnetic therapy.

Forty-hour Advanced Anatomy courses are open to graduates of the one-hundred-hour course or equivalent.

Admission Requirements

A desire to learn and to assist horses is the only requirement. While it is not necessary to be a licensed massage therapist, it is recommended that those contemplating a full-time career in equine massage enroll at an accredited massage school either before or after training in equine massage. Applicants must submit two personal references and a biographical essay; a knowledge of horsemanship is required.

Tuition and Fees

The cost of the Equine Sports Massage Program is

$1,295. The cost of the Equi-Pressure Program is $695.

Florida Institute of Massage Therapy and Esthetics

Ft. Lauderdale Campus:
2001 West Sample Road, Suite 100
Pompano Beach, Florida 33064
Phone: (954) 975-6400 / (800) 541-9299
Fax: (954) 975-9633

Miami Campus:
7925 N.W. 12th Street, Suite 201
Miami, Florida 33126
Phone: (305) 597-9599 / (800) 599-9599
Fax: (305) 597-9110

Reese Campus:
425 Geneva Drive
Oviedo, Florida 32765
Phone: (407) 365-9283 / (800) 393-7337
Fax: (407) 365-7597

The Florida Institute was founded in 1986 by Neal R. Heller, president, as a private vocational-technical school. The Florida Institute is owned and governed by Natural Health Trends Corporation.

Accreditation

The Florida Institute is nationally accredited by the Accrediting Commission of Career Schools and Colleges of Technology (ACCSCT). The 624-hour Therapeutic Massage Training Program is accredited by the American Massage Therapy Association Commission on Massage Training Accreditation/Approval (AMTA/COMTAA). The institute is approved as a provider of continuing education units by the Florida State Board of Massage and the National Certification Board for Therapeutic Massage and Bodywork (NCBTMB).

Program Description

The Florida Institute offers seven different programs of study of massage therapy, skin care/esthetics, electrolysis, or a combination thereof for unlicensed individuals, and one advanced clinical training program in massage. Included here are only those programs that include or are a supplement to a therapeutic massage program.

The curriculum for the 624-hour Therapeutic Massage Training Program consists of Human Anatomy and Physiology, Therapeutic Massage, Theory and Practice of Hydrotherapy, Introduction to Allied Modalities (such as shiatsu, reflexology, sports massage, neuromuscular therapy, Trager, Rolfing, craniosacral technique, and others), Florida State Law Business Principles and Development, and HIV-AIDS.

The 900-hour Advanced Therapeutic Massage Training Program supplements the initial 624 hours of training with additional courses in Pathology, Kinesiology, Athletic Injuries, Medical Documentation, Medical Terminology, Advanced Practical Training, and Professional Practices.

The 900-hour Therapeutic Massage and Esthetics Training Program supplements the initial 624 hours of therapeutic massage training with additional courses in Hair Removal, Applied Clinical Training, Understanding the Skin and Its Functions/Anatomy and Physiology, Make-Up Artistry, Electricity, Sterilization and Sanitation, Bacteriology, Mask and Spa Therapy, and Ethical Business Practice and Marketing.

The 1,200-hour Advanced Therapeutic Massage Training and Skin Care/Esthetics Program supplements the initial 624 hours of therapeutic massage training with additional courses in Pathology, Kinesiology, Athletic Injuries, Medical Documentation, Medical Terminology, Advanced Practical Training, Professional Practices, Hair Removal, Applied Clinical Training, Understanding the Skin and Its Functions/Anatomy and Physiology, Make-Up Artistry, Electricity, Sterilization and Sanitation, Bacteriology, Mask and Spa Therapy, and Ethical Business Practice and Marketing.

Continuing Education

Seminars and workshops are held throughout the year, covering such topics as infant massage, aromatherapy, seated massage, neuromuscular therapy, acupressure, reflexology, craniosacral technique, and others.

Admission Requirements

Applicants must be at least 18 years of age; have a high school diploma or equivalent or demonstrate an ability to benefit from the course; and provide a statement of health from a licensed physician.

Tuition and Fees

The Therapeutic Massage Program costs $4,500 plus fees. The Advanced Therapeutic Massage Program costs $6,200 plus fees. The Therapeutic Massage and Esthetics Program costs $6,100 plus fees. The Advanced Therapeutic Massage and Skin Care Esthetics Program costs $7,600 plus fees.

Financial Assistance

Federal grants, loans, and work-study are available to those who qualify.

Florida Institute of Psychophysical Integration

5837 Mariner Drive
Tampa, Florida 33609
Phone: (813) 286-2273

The Florida Institute of Psychophysical Integration was founded in 1976 by Joy K. Johnson, Ph.D., a practitioner of gestalt therapy and humanistic psychology who is also trained in craniosacral therapy and certified as an International Trainer of Postural Integration.

Program Description

The institute offers a 150-hour, fifteen-day residential tutorial program in the field of deep tissue therapy known as postural integration. The training has a maximum of four students, and may be individually tutored and scheduled by mutual agreement.

The curriculum includes Theory of Postural Integration, Manipulation, Techniques for the Practitioner, Psychological Testing, Movement, Professional Ethics and Responsibilities, and Setting Up a Postural Integration Practice. Training consists of Phase I: Independent Study, Phase II: Residential Intensive, and Phase III: Work/Study Mastery.

Admission Requirements

Prerequisites are flexible but include completion of ten standard sessions of postural integration or its equivalent; minimum age of 25; a college degree, preferably with a counseling background, and a license to touch; massage experience and knowledge; and knowledge of the muscle system.

Tuition and Fees

Tuition for the entire program is $3,100.

Financial Assistance

Financing is available.

Florida Institute of Traditional Chinese Medicine

5335 66th Street North
St. Petersburg, Florida 33709
Phone: (813) 546-6565
Fax: (813) 547-0703

The Florida Institute of Traditional Chinese Medicine (FITCM) was founded in 1986 by Su Liang Ku, who was trained as an apprentice to his grandfather and received formal education in acupuncture and TCM in Hong Kong and China. Professor Ku has served as chairperson of the Florida State Board of Acupuncture, as president of the American Association of Acupuncture and Oriental Medicine (AAAOM), and on the Board of Examiners of the National Commission for the Certification of Acupuncturists (NCCA).

Accreditation

FITCM is licensed by the Florida State Board of Independent Postsecondary Vocational, Technical, Trade, and Business Schools, Florida Department of Education, and has been accredited by the Accrediting Council for Continuing Education and Training (ACCET) since 1988. FITCM is currently a candidate for accreditation with the National Accreditation Commission for School and Colleges of Acupuncture and Oriental Medicine (NACSCAOM). Graduates of the TCM program are eligible to apply for various state licensing exams and the NCCA exam. Graduates become licensed acupuncturists upon passing the Florida State Licensure Examination.

Program Description

FITCM offers a three-year, 2,882-hour program in traditional Chinese medicine; 800 of these hours are attained through clinical intern/externship training. The program closely parallels the training programs in China and encompasses a broad spectrum of TCM theories. Upon graduation, students receive a diploma in TCM.

The six-semester curriculum covers Fundamentals of TCM; Acupuncture Theories; Tui Na (Chinese massage); TCM Materia Medica; Traditional Chinese Medicinal Formulas; Anatomy, Physiology, Pathology, Physical Exam; Bian Zheng (Differentiation of Syndrome); Disease and Treatment; Seminars; Semester Exams; and Clinical Training (Internship/Externship).

Admission Requirements

Applicants must be at least 18 years of age; have completed at least two years of college or postsecondary education (sixty semester credit hours) at an accredited institution; submit two letters of recommendation; submit a statement of health from a TCM or Western physician; have a keen interest in and basic understanding of TCM; and interview with the school director.

Tuition and Fees

Tuition is $7,000 per year. Other costs include: application fee, $25; registration fee, $75; books, approximately $1,100 for the three-year program; and miscellaneous supplies, approximately $400.

Financial Assistance

Federal grants and loans and payment plans are available.

Florida School of Massage

6421 S.W. 13th Street
Gainesville, Florida 32608
Phone: (904) 378-7891

The Florida School of Massage first enrolled students in 1973. In 1979, the American Institute of Natural Health and the Florida School of Massage merged their programs of massage therapy and allied holistic health training.

Accreditation

The Therapeutic Massage and Hydrotherapy Program is approved by the American Massage Therapy Association Commission on Massage Training Accreditation/Approval (AMTA/COMTAA). The school is licensed by the Florida State Board of Independent Postsecondary, Vocational, Technical, Trade, and Business Schools.

Program Description

The 750-hour Therapeutic Massage and Hydrotherapy Program prepares participants to take licensing boards before the Florida State Department of Professional Regulation. The program consists of Massage Therapy (which includes Swedish massage, reflexology, neuromuscular therapy, sports massage, polarity, connective tissue massage, and more), as well as Clinic Internship, Hydrotherapy, Human Anatomy and Physiology, Awareness and Communication Skills, Stress Awareness and Movement, Massage Law and Business Practice, CPR and First Aid, Living with AIDS, Directed Independent Study Project (optional), and Introduction to Practical Shiatsu (required for New York licensure)

Continuing Education

The Colonic Irrigation Therapy Certification Program offers instruction in the cleansing of the intestinal tract. Upon completion of this program, students who have also been trained in massage will be eligible to apply for licensing before the State Department of Professional Regulation. The State of Florida requires one hundred hours; a fifty-hour program is available for students from out of state. This course is scheduled as interest demands.

A 112-hour Polarity Therapy Certification Program leads to certification through the Florida Institute of Natural Health. Instruction includes theory, demonstration, supervised practice, and group process.

A 200-hour Sports Massage Program includes Sports Massage Theory and Application, Supervised Field Event Experience, and Supervised Practicum and Independent Study. Topics covered include hydrotherapy protocol, injury evaluation and treatment, strength training and conditioning, and more.

The Structural Bodywork and Awareness Program is a three-phase, 500-hour program leading to certification in structural integration. Course work includes Theory of Structural Integration and Structural Models, Techniques and Procedures of Structural Integration, Advanced Anatomy and Physiology, Clinical Internship, and Psycho-Physical Awareness and Therapy.

A 200- to 500-hour Teacher's Assistant Program exposes therapists to the theory and techniques necessary to become instructors through observation and experience as classroom assistants. Course work includes Instructional Principles and Procedures and Personal and Video Feedback on Participant Presentations.

A 260-hour Therapeutic Hand and Foot Reflexology Program prepares practitioners to offer skilled hand and foot nondiagnostic reflexology sessions within the context of a client-directed holistic health program. Instruction includes Reflexology Theory and Application (which includes history, principles, Oriental and Western allopathic theories, techniques, hydrotherapy, ethics, HIV-AIDS education, and more), as well as Anatomy and Physiology, Supervised Clinical Internship, and Externship.

Admission Requirements

Prospective applicants must be 19 years of age (this may be waived through a personal interview) and submit written biographical data; an interview with the school administrator may be required. Prerequisite for the Teacher's Assistant Program is completion of the basic massage licensing program, plus Phase I of the Structural Bodywork and Awareness Program.

Tuition and Fees

There is a $100 application fee for all courses.

Tuition for the Therapeutic Massage and Hydrotherapy Licensing Program is $4,500. Other costs include: massage table, $400 to $600; books, approximately $250; and New York State required shiatsu class, $450.

Tuition for the Polarity Therapy Certification Program is $1,275; books cost $75 to $300 (optional).

Tuition for the Sports Massage Program is $1,500; books cost $75 to $100.

Tuition for the Structural Bodywork and Awareness program is $3,650.

Tuition for the Teacher's Assistant Program is $2,150, including Structural Bodywork and Awareness Program Phase I; books are $75 to $100.

Tuition for the Therapeutic Hand and Foot Reflexology Program is $1,500; books are $75 to $100 (optional); and an optional massage table costs $400 to $600.

Financial Assistance

Payment plans, veterans' benefits, and vocational rehabilitation are available, as well as aid from the Bureau of Blind Services.

The Humanities Center

Institute of Applied Health School of Massage
4045 Park Boulevard
Pinellas Park, Florida 34665
Phone: (813) 541-5200

The Humanities Center was founded in 1981 and was purchased by its current owner, Sherry Fears, in 1983. In 1990, the school moved to its current location just minutes from Tampa.

Accreditation

The Humanities Center's massage curriculum is approved by the American Massage Therapy Association Commission on Massage Training Accreditation/Approval (AMTA/COMTAA). The school is accredited by the Accrediting Commission of Career Schools and Colleges of Technology (ACC-SCT), approved by the Florida Board of Massage as an approved-curriculum school and as a provider for continuing education units, and is recognized as an eligible institution by the Department of Education for the granting of state and federal financial aid.

Program Description

The 625-hour Therapeutic Applications of Massage Program includes Theory and Practice of Massage (which includes Swedish massage, relaxation massage, neuromuscular therapy, and more), Business Practices, Internship, Visiting Professor and Additional Techniques, Massage Law, Hydrotherapy, HIV/AIDS Education, and Anatomy and Physiology. Day and evening programs are available.

Continuing Education

Various continuing education seminars are offered in such areas as lower body sports therapy and cervical dysfunction.

Admission Requirements

Applicants must be at least 20 years old, have a high school diploma or equivalent, be physically able to learn and receive massage, interview with an admissions representative, and observe classes for at least two hours.

Tuition and Fees

There is a $75 registration fee. Tuition is $5,820; this includes books, supplies, lotion, five school polo shirts, and more. Linens are additional.

Financial Assistance

Payment plans, federal grants, and loans are available.

International Alliance of Health Care Educators

(*See* Multiple State Locations, page 305)

International Institute of Reflexology

(*See* Multiple State Locations, page 306)

Sarasota School of Massage Therapy

1970 Main Street
Sarasota, Florida 34236
Phone: (941) 957-0577
Fax: (941) 957-1049

The Sarasota School of Massage Therapy was founded in 1979, and purchased in 1991 by Michael and Mary Rosen-Pyros. Michael, a chiropractic physician, is the director of the school.

Accreditation

The school is accredited by the Council on Occupational Education (Atlanta, Georgia). The Massage Therapy Program is approved by the American Massage Therapy Association Commission on Massage Training Accreditation/Approval (AMTA/COMTAA).

Program Description

The 540-hour Massage Therapy Program may be taken on either a full-time (twenty-five weeks, days or evenings) or part-time (fifty weeks, evenings) basis. The curriculum includes Anatomy and Physiology, Hydrotherapy, Florida Massage Law, Massage Theory/Practice, Allied Modalities (such as myology and neuromuscular therapy, first aid and CPR, and Massage Cornucopia, which includes a variety of bodywork specialties), AIDS, Oriental Bodywork, Business of Massage, and Student Clinic. Almost every class will include movement and relaxation in such forms as yoga, Feldenkrais, tai chi chuan, calisthenics, visualization, and meditation.

Admission Requirements

Applicants must be at least 18 years of age, have a high school diploma or equivalent, schedule a pre-enrollment interview, and submit a signed enrollment agreement.

Tuition and Fees

Tuition is $3,300. Other costs include: application fee, $75; books, $160; First Aid/CPR, $20; optional massage table, approximately $450; and state board exam, $330.

Financial Assistance

An interest-free monthly payment plan and veterans' benefits are available.

Seminar Network International, Inc.

d/b/a SNI School of Massage and
  Allied Therapies
518 North Federal Highway
Lake Worth, Florida 33460
Phone: (561) 582-5349 / (800) 882-0903
Fax: (561) 582-0807

Seminar Network International began in 1985 to provide continuing education for massage professionals. In 1987, the organization acquired the School of Massage Therapy and began to offer training at both the beginning and advanced levels.

Accreditation

SNI School of Massage and Allied Therapies is accredited by the Accrediting Council for Continuing Education and Training (ACCET). The Massage Therapy Program is approved by the American Massage Therapy Association Commission on Massage Training Accreditation/Approval (AMTA/ COMTAA) and designed to exceed the 500-hour educational requirement set forth by the Florida State Board of Massage. The Colon Therapy Program also exceeds the board's present requirements.

Program Description

The 600-hour Massage Therapy Program includes Human Anatomy and Physiology, Massage Theory and Practice, Hydrotherapy, Allied Modalities (including introductions to such fields as reflexology, shiatsu, sports massage, nutrition, polarity, infant massage, and others), Statutes/Rules and History of Massage, Practice Building and Business Practice, Basic Psychology, and HIV/AIDS.

The one-hundred-hour Colon Therapy Program is designed for licensed massage therapists, massage therapy students, or students planning to practice in a state with no licensing requirements. The curriculum includes Human Anatomy and Physiology, Practicum (during which the student administers a minimum of twenty colonic treatments and an additional twenty-five hours of either receiving or administering treatments), and Equipment and Sterilization Techniques.

Continuing Education

One-hundred-hour Advanced Training Workshops are offered to professional massage therapists in the areas of NISA (Neuromuscular Integration and Structural Alignment), aromatherapy, traditional medical massage of Thailand, sports massage, clinical sports massage, colon hydrotherapy, craniosacral therapy, equine therapies, and shiatsu. As part of these advanced trainings, students receive a total of twenty hours in Advanced Anatomy and Physiology, Advanced Maniken (nerves and vessels), Advanced Marketing, and Advanced Case Management.

Admission Requirements

Applicants must be at least 18 years of age; have a high school diploma or GED, or demonstrate an ability to benefit by achieving a passing score on the PAR Test (a test of basic skills); complete a personal health inventory; submit a physician's statement; and interview with an admissions representative.

Tuition and Fees

There is a $100 registration fee that is applied toward tuition or returned if the student is not accepted. Tuition for the Massage Therapy Program is $5,000; books and fees are $210. Tuition for the Colon Therapy Program is $1,200.

Financial Assistance

Federal grants and loans are available to qualified applicants; payment plans are also available.

Southeastern School of Neuromuscular and Massage Therapy, Inc.

9088 Golfside Drive
Jacksonville, Florida 32256
Phone: (904) 448-9499 /
  (800) 287-8966 toll-free
Fax: (904) 448-9270

The Southeastern School of Neuromuscular and Massage Therapy was founded in 1992. President and director Kyle C. Wright, L.M.T., founded the Wright Center of Neuromuscular Therapy and was named Massage Therapist of the Year by the Florida State Massage Therapist Association, North Florida Chapter, in 1992.

Accreditation

The school is licensed by the Florida State Board of Independent Postsecondary Vocational, Technical, Trade, and Business Schools, Florida Department of Education. The curriculum is approved by the Florida Department of Business and Professional Regulation Board of Massage.

Program Description

The Master Program curriculum of over 500 hours includes Anatomy and Physiology I and II, Swedish Massage, Neuromuscular Therapy, Advanced Neuromuscular Therapy, Segmental Structural Bodywork, Theory and Practice of Hydrotherapy, Practice Parameters: Statutes/Rules/Ethics, Allied Modalities (ninety-seven hours that may include sports massage, craniosacral therapy, myofascial release, Oriental philosophy and technique, flexibility, dynamic structural learning, neurolinguistic programming, health and hygiene, business practices and development, CPR, and First Aid), HIV/AIDS, and a practical internship in which students perform and document a minimum of fifty full-body sessions. Day and evening classes are available.

A second massage program of 500 hours is a somewhat scaled-down version of the master program, with fewer hours of neuromuscular therapy.

Admission Requirements

Applicants must be at least 18 years of age, have a high school diploma or equivalent, be of good moral character and appearance, submit three personal references (including one from a licensed health professional), and interview with one of the directors.

Tuition and Fees

Tuition is $5,300 for the Master Program and $4,100 for the Massage Program. A $100 applica-

tion fee is included in these costs. Books and supplies are $200.

Financial Assistance

Payment plans, student loans, and veterans' benefits are available.

Suncoast School

4910 Cypress Street
Tampa, Florida 33607
Phone: (813) 287-1099 / (813) 287-1050

The Suncoast School was founded in 1982 as a private vocational-technical school to provide professional training in massage therapy for state licensure.

Accreditation

The Massage Therapy Program is approved by the American Massage Therapy Association Commission on Massage Training Accreditation/Approval (AMTA/COMTAA). Suncoast School is approved by the Florida State Board of Massage and the Florida State Board of Nursing as a provider of continuing education units.

Program Description

The 500-hour Basic Massage and Hydrotherapy Program includes Massage Therapy Theory and Practice, Anatomy and Physiology, Hydrotherapy, Florida Massage Law, HIV/AIDS, and Allied Modalities (including Introduction to Instrumentation, Helping Relationship, Exercise Physiology, Musculoskeletal Pathology, Health Care Practice Building, CPR, and three classes required of New York State license candidates: Myology, Oriental Modalities—Acupressure, and First Aid).

The 600-hour Basic Massage and Hydrotherapy Program includes the 500-hour program with specialization in either Oriental modalities (acupressure), basic sports massage, or Coremassage.

Day and evening classes are available.

Continuing Education

A 300-hour, twelve-week CORE Bodywork Practitioner Program instructs students in the theory and practice of CORE bodywork and neurosomatic integration, a ten-session connective tissue approach to muscular reeducation. Topics include CORE bodywork theory, CORE bodywork clinical practice, anatomy and physiology, business practices and professional standards, exercise physiology, allied health professions, and Coremassage.

SEED (The Southeast Institute for Education and Development) regularly sponsors workshops, seminars, and lectures at the school by experts in the field of massage and natural health care for the benefit of both students and the community at a cost of $60 to $550 each.

Admission Requirements

Prospective students must be at least 18 years of age, have a high school diploma or equivalent, and interview with school administrators.

Tuition and Fees

There is a $75 registration fee for all courses.

Tuition for the 500-hour Basic Massage and Hydrotherapy Program is $4,200; books are approximately $300.

Tuition for the 600-hour Basic Massage and Hydrotherapy Program is $4,900; books are approximately $300.

Tuition for the CORE Bodywork Practitioner Program is $5,000.

Financial Assistance

Federal grants and loans and veterans' benefits are available.

Worsley Institute of Classical Acupuncture

Tao House
Suite 324
6175 N.W. 153rd Street
Miami Lakes, Florida 33014-2435
Phone: (305) 823-7270 / (800) 823-7270
Fax: (305) 823-6603
E-mail: 103104.3251@Compuserve.com

The Worsley Institute was founded in the United States in 1988, but the study of five-element acupuncture has been taught in Professor J.R. Worsley's school in England since 1944.

Accreditation

The Worsley Institute is a candidate for accreditation by the National Accreditation Commission for Schools and Colleges of Acupuncture and Oriental Medicine (NACSCAOM). The program meets eligibility conditions given by the National Commission for the Certification of Acupuncturists (NCCA) and the State of Florida.

Program Description

The 2,239-hour, twenty-seven-month Classical Acupuncture Program is divided into three academic years: Year One emphasizes basic laws and skills; Year Two is applying those skills to people; and Year Three consists of practical clinical application. The curriculum includes History of Acupuncture, Basic Acupuncture Theory, Point Location, Diagnostic Skills, Treatment Planning, Treatment Techniques, Specialized Treatment Patterns, Emergency First Aid and Special Symptom Situations, Equipment and Safety, Ethics and Human Service Skills, and Practice Management; other requirements include Pathology, Western Human Sciences, Anatomy and Physiology, and Biomedical Clinical Sciences. Preclinic consists of pulse taking, point location practice, and written and practical exams; Clinic includes observation, clinical introduction, and supervised clinical experience.

Admission Requirements

Applicants must have completed two years of general education at the baccalaureate level, interview with a clinical supervisor, and submit two letters of reference.

Tuition and Fees

There is a $150 registration fee. Tuition for the three-year program is $19,500; books are approximately $300, and supplies and equipment are approximately $100.

Financial Assistance

Payment plans are available.

Yogi Hari and Leela Mata Ashram

2216 N.W. 8th Terrace
Ft. Lauderdale, Florida 33311
Phone/Fax: (954) 563-4946

The Yoga Teachers Training Course at Yogi Hari's ashram was founded in 1989. Sri Yogi Hari and Leela Mata have been disciples of Swami Vishnudevananda since 1975.

Program Description

The two-week residential Yoga Teachers Training Course is personally conducted by Yogi Hari and Leela Mata. The intensive program permits total immersion in the practice of yoga. The curriculum includes Asanas, Pranayama, Meditation, Vedanta Philosophy, Karma and Reincarnation, Raja Yoga (mysteries of the mind), Jnana Yoga (inquiry into the nature of self), Bhakti Yoga (the path of devotion), Nada Yoga (study of sound vibration), Karma Yoga, Bhagavad Gita, Proper Diet, and Yoga Kriyas (cleansing techniques). Two buffet-style vegetarian meals are served daily. Full participation in all activities is required; no meat, fish, eggs, alcohol, tobacco, or narcotics are allowed.

Continuing Education

Continued training is offered through an Advanced Teachers Training Course and Sadhana Week programs.

Admission Requirements

Interest in yoga and self-unfoldment is the only prerequisite. A basic knowledge of asanas and philosophy is helpful, but beginners are welcome.

Tuition and Fees

The Yoga Teachers Training Course costs $1,500, including tuition, accommodations, meals, and course materials.

GEORGIA

Academy of Somatic Healing Arts

1924 Cliff Valley Way
Atlanta, Georgia 30329
Phone: (404) 315-0394
Fax: (404) 633-1270

Jim Gabriel's seriously injured elbows led him to seek help from Paul St. John, developer of neuromuscular therapy (NMT). Gabriel's positive response to treatment led him to attend massage therapy school and learn NMT himself. In 1982, he opened the Neuromuscular Center of Atlanta, and in 1991, the Academy of Somatic Healing Arts.

Accreditation

ASHA graduates are eligible to take the Florida Board of Massage exam. The school is authorized by the Nonpublic Postsecondary Education Commission of the State of Georgia and approved for State of Florida CEU credits. ASHA has consciously chosen not to seek accreditation from the various trade associations.

Program Description

The 660-hour Massage Therapy Program includes Anatomy and Physiology, Maniken: Building Human Anatomy, Somatic Nutrition: From a Holistic Perspective, Swedish Massage, Clinical Sports Massage, Hygiene/HIV/AIDS Awareness Training, Hydrotherapy and Associated Therapeutic Modalities, Neuromuscular Therapy (NMT), Clinical Practicum and Community Events, and Business Alignment and Management. An optional twenty-hour survey class offers eight introductory lectures/classes to be selected by the student from topics that include Rolfing, shiatsu, polarity, geriatric massage, lymphatic massage, reflexology, aromatherapy, herbal preparations for the body, Alexander technique, and others. Classes are offered in a day, evening, or weekend format.

Continuing Education

Seminars are offered in such topics as brainwave biofeedback, craniosacral foundations and integration, visceral reflex massage, seated massage experience, and others.

Admission Requirements

Applicants must be at least 18 years of age, have a high school diploma or equivalent, be of sound moral character, submit two letters of recommendation, interview with an admissions representative, and submit a physician's report and a massage therapist's verification report.

Tuition and Fees

Tuition is $5,600. Other costs include: application fee, $75; linens, approximately $50; massage table, $460 to $600; books and Maniken model, approximately $300; clinical vest and white clothing for class, approximately $125; four professional massages, $160; and Red Cross CPR/First Aid certification, $49.

Financial Assistance

An interest-free payment plan and veterans' benefits are available.

Atlanta School of Massage

2300 Peachford Road, Suite 3200
Atlanta, Georgia 30338
Phone: (770) 454-7167

The Atlanta School of Massage was established in 1980 and moved to the Dunwoody area of North Atlanta in 1986. The school now graduates over 200 massage therapists a year.

Accreditation

The school is accredited by the Accrediting Commission of Career Schools and Colleges of Technology (ACCSCT). The massage therapy curriculum is approved by the American Massage Therapy Association Commission on Massage Training Accreditation/Approval (AMTA/COMTAA).

Program Description

The 620-hour Integrated Massage and Deep Tissue Therapy Program includes Introduction to Massage Therapy (including ethics and massage, massage history, massage law, massage theory, and more), Human Sciences (including anatomy and physiology, illness care, AIDS awareness, CPR, and others), Massage and Supervised Practice (including assessment skills, body mechanics, community events, coaching sessions, deep tissue massage, energetic studies, introductions to shiatsu, cross fiber, and sports massage, trigger point, Swedish, and more), Mind/Body (including altered states of consciousness and massage, communication skills, focusing, intuition, emotions and massage, and more), Hydrotherapy, Professional Preparation (including clinical practice, designing sessions, student clinic, and more), and required student activities.

The 620-hour Clinical Sports Massage Program includes Introduction to Massage (including ethics and massage, massage history, massage law, and more), Human Sciences (including AIDS awareness, anatomy and physiology, CPR, first aid, kinesiology, rheumatic conditions/chronic pain, principles of exercise and conditioning, and more), Massage Techniques and Supervised Practice (including coaching sessions, community events, cross fiber, energetic techniques, lymphatic massage, massage tools, myofascial skills, positional release, shiatsu, sports massage, stretching, Swedish, trigger point, and more), Mind/Body, Hydrotherapy, Professional Preparation, and required student activities.

The 620-hour Wellness Massage and Spa Therapies Program includes Introduction to Massage (including ethics and massage, massage history, massage law, massage theory, and more), Human Sciences (including anatomy and physiology, illness care, AIDS awareness, CPR, and others), massage and supervised practice (including body mechanics, energetic techniques, integrated wellness massage, introduction to shiatsu and acupressure, Swedish massage, on-site massage, and more), Mind/Body (including altered states of consciousness and massage, focusing, self-care for the massage therapist, and more), Spa Therapies Introduction (including hydrotherapy, spa theory and history, spa treatments, and more), Professional Preparation (including student clinic and more), and required student activities.

Each student must also receive two professional massages from two different therapists.

One-evening introductory classes are scheduled monthly to explain the school's program and to demonstrate massage techniques.

Admission Requirements

Applicants must be at least 18 years of age, have a high school diploma or equivalent, submit two letters of recommendation from licensed massage therapists or health professionals, submit a physician's examination report, and interview with an admissions representative. Applicants must have received at least one massage from a certified massage therapist.

Tuition and Fees

Tuition is $6,875. Other costs include: application fee, $25; books, $300 to $350; massage table, approximately $600; CPR certification, approximately $25; linens, lotion, and supplies, approximately $100; school shirt, $25; and three professional massages, one to be received prior to beginning the program, approximately $120.

Financial Assistance

Payment plans, federal grants, and loans are available.

Lake Lanier School of Massage

400 Brenau Avenue
Gainesville, Georgia 30501
Phone: (770) 287-0377
Fax: (770) 536-7350

The Lake Lanier School of Massage was founded in 1993 and is co-owned by Sadie M. McElroy, L.M.T., and Sandra K. Easterbrooks, L.M.T. It is, at present, the only massage school in northeast Georgia. The school is located in downtown Gainesville; Stress Breakers massage clinic occupies the first floor of the building, and the school is on the second floor.

Accreditation

The Lake Lanier School of Massage is accredited by the International Massage and Somatic Therapies Accreditation Council (IMSTAC), a division of Associated Bodywork and Massage Professionals (ABMP); authorized by the State of Georgia Nonpublic Postsecondary Education Commission; and approved by the Florida State Board of Massage. The school is approved for continuing education by the Florida State Board of Massage, and by the National Certification Board for Therapeutic Massage and Bodywork (NCBTMB) as a continuing education provider under Category A. Graduates of the 550-hour course who pass the national certification exam are eligible to apply for a Florida state license and for continuing education credits for Florida licensure and national certification.

Program Description

The 550-hour Massage Therapy Program consists of Anatomy and Physiology, Massage Theory, Massage Practice (which includes Swedish Massage, Neuromuscular/Trigger Point Therapy, On-Site Seated Massage, Student Clinic/Community Events, and Applied Kinesiology), Hydrotherapy, AIDS Awareness, History of Massage, Law, Rules and Regulations, and modalities that include Aromatherapy, Nutrition and Prevention, Business Marketing, Stress Management, Applied Kinesiology, Pathology, Introduction to Russian (a massage system using heat, friction, and specific massage techniques), Craniosacral, CPR, and Assault Prevention. Classes are held days or evenings, with some Fridays and Saturdays required for the student clinic.

Continuing Education

Continuing education courses include Reflexology, Introduction to Shiatsu, Introduction to Infant Massage, Sports Massage One-Hundred-Hour Certification Program, and Touch for Health I, II, and III (kinesiology).

Admission Requirements

Applicants must be at least 16 years of age, have a high school diploma or equivalent, be in good physical health and of good moral character, and be sincerely committed to providing quality care. Applicants must submit a physician's statement, two personal references, and a short essay, and interview with an admissions representative.

Tuition and Fees

Tuition is $4,900; books cost approximately $200. Linens and massage table for home practice are additional.

Financial Assistance

Payment plans are available.

Life College

School of Chiropractic
1269 Barclay Circle
Marietta, Georgia 30060
Phone: (770) 424-0554 (Admissions: X231) /
　(800) 543-3202
Fax: (770) 428-9886

Life College was founded in 1974 by Dr. Sid E. Williams and opened in 1975 with twenty-two students; enrollment now exceeds 4,200, making Life College the world's largest chiropractic college.

Accreditation

Life College is accredited by the Commission on Colleges of the Southern Association of Colleges and Schools. The School of Chiropractic is accredited by the Council on Chiropractic Education (CCE).

Program Description

The fourteen-quarter Doctor of Chiropractic (D.C.) degree program is provided by six major organizational components: Division of Chiropractic Sciences (analysis, chiropractic philosophy, clinic proficiency, and technique); Division of Clinical Sciences (diagnosis, radiology, practice and profes-

sional relations, psychology, and public health); Division of Diagnostic Imaging and Alignment; Division of Basic Sciences (anatomy, chemistry, microbiology/pathology, and physiology); the Sid E. Williams Research Center; and the Division of Patient Care Facilities.

Life College offers a multilevel approach to chiropractic education. Basic and clinical sciences are taught concurrently with chiropractic techniques, and students are taught hands-on techniques beginning in the third quarter. Students are permitted to give chiropractic care to patients during their third academic year.

Students' schedules are "blocked" (that is, they consist of a required sequence of courses) to a greater or lesser degree throughout the fourteen quarters of study, although a minimum of eighteen credit hours of electives may be selected beginning with the tenth quarter.

The four-quarter Chiropractic Technician (C.T.) Program covers Chiropractic Philosophy, Chiropractic History, Terminology, Nutrition, Introduction to X-Ray/Physics, Anatomy/Physiology, Introduction to Clinic, Computer Literacy, CPR/Basic Life Support, Emergency Procedures, X-Ray Positioning, Clinic/Field Interning, Patient Management/Office Protocol, Public Relations/Speech, Public Health, Physical Diagnosis, Radiographic Practicum, Office Skills, Chiropractic Instrumentation, Laboratory Diagnosis, Computerized Office Management, and more.

Admission Requirements

Doctor of Chiropractic program applicants must have earned a cumulative G.P.A. of 2.25 on a 4.0 scale and must have completed at least sixty semester hours (ninety quarter hours) of prechiropractic, college-level courses, including six semester hours of English, three semester hours of psychology, fifteen semester hours of humanities/social studies, six semester hours of organic chemistry, six semester hours of inorganic chemistry, six semester hours of physics, and six semester hours of biological sciences, in either animal or human biology. Each science course must have a lab and must be passed with a grade of C or better. Applicants must have not been convicted of a felony.

Chiropractic Technician applicants must be at least 17 years of age, have a high school diploma or equivalent, and submit two letters of recommendation.

Tuition and Fees

Tuition for the D.C. program is $3,000 per quarter. Other costs include: application fee, $50; books and supplies, approximately $352 per quarter; graduation fee $75; and other fees, approximately $332 per quarter.

Tuition for the C.T. program is $600 per quarter. Other costs include: application fee, $25; books and supplies, approximately $190 per quarter; and other fees, approximately $137 per quarter.

Financial Assistance

Available financial assistance includes federal grants, loans, and work-study; Georgia Tuition Equalization Grants and State Student Incentive Grants; scholarships; and additional loans, including Health Education Assistance Loans, Life College International Student Loans, Life College Emergency Loans, TERI, and PEP Loans.

HAWAII

Aisen Shiatsu School

Interstate Building
1314 South King Street, Suite 601
Honolulu, Hawaii 96814
Phone: (808) 596-7354
Fax: (808) 593-8282

The Aisen Shiatsu School was founded in 1977 by Fumihiko Indei, a graduate of and former instructor at the Japan Shiatsu College in Tokyo.

Accreditation

The Aisen Shiatsu School is licensed by the Hawaii State Department of Education.

Program Description

The 200-hour Shiatsu Therapy Program is designed to produce skilled shiatsu therapists. The curriculum includes eighty hours of anatomy and physiology and 120 hours of theory and practice of shiatsu therapy (therapeutic muscle and nerve shiatsu). Classes are held in the evening.

Admission Requirements

Applicants must have a high school diploma or equivalent, good moral character, and temperate habits; submit a health certificate and three letters of reference; and interview with an admissions representative.

Tuition and Fees

There is a $200 registration fee; tuition is $4,600, including lab fees and books.

Hawaiian Islands School of Body Therapies

78-6239 Alii Drive
P.O. Box 390188
Kailua-Kona, Hawaii 96739
Phone: (808) 322-0048

Lynn Wind, former clinical director of the Canadian College of Massage and Hydrotherapy, founded the Hawaiian Islands School of Body Therapies (HIS) in 1988. The school offers a uniquely challenging and transformative program; the Knight-Wind Method of Restorative Treatment Therapy integrates medical treatment massage with holistic therapies to nurture each student's intuitive abilities.

Accreditation

The State of Hawaii requires 570 hours of training for licensing as a massage therapist. The program offered by HIS is approved by the Hawaiian State Department of Education and fulfills the requirements to take the Hawaii State Board of Massage licensing exam. The school is also approved by the Florida State Board of Massage, as well as by most states with licensing requirements, as a CEU provider.

Program Description

The Knight-Wind Method of Restorative Therapies is a compilation of various bodywork disciplines taught primarily from a series of therapeutic massage manuals written by Lynn Wind, including *Principles of Assessment and Treatment, Therapeutic Massage, Treatment Techniques for Massage Therapy Volumes I, II, and III,* and *Illustrated Guide to Treatment Techniques.*

Level I may be taken alone for 165 hours of training. The 645-hour Professional Massage Therapy Program consists of Levels I through III, three 13-week semesters. An extended program—Levels I through IV—offers 1,000 hours (one additional semester) of instruction.

Level I (the first semester) consists of Theory and Practice of Massage (one hundred hours), Introduction to Anatomy (fifty hours), and Principles of Assessment and Treatment (fifteen hours). Levels II through IV (second through fourth semesters) consist of three intensive areas of study (shoulder/thorax/upper extremities; cervical/cranium/TMJ; and low back/pelvis/lower extremities), each in excess of 128 hours. Also included are Anatomy/Physiology/Pathology, Kinesiology, Clinical Integration, Practical Integration, and Business. Other modalities taught during the course of the program include lomi lomi, hydrotherapy, reflexology, polarity, neuromuscular techniques, aromatherapy, shiatsu, body-mind integration, geriatric massage, lymphatic drainage, brain gym (education kinesiology), subtle body therapies, soft touch, myofascial release, craniosacral, and sports massage. Students must have completed a Hawaiian Heart Association CPR course prior to graduation. Classes are held weekday mornings and evenings.

Each October, students are part of the world's largest massage team at the annual Ironman Triathlon.

Admission Requirements

Applicants must be at least 18 years of age, have a high school diploma or equivalent, interview with an admissions representative, provide documentation of good health and TB clearance, submit two letters of recommendation, be physically able to perform massage therapy, and be able to finance their education.

Tuition and Fees

There is a $50 application fee that is credited toward tuition upon acceptance.

Tuition for Level I (165 hours) is $1,650; books and supplies are approximately $550.

Tuition for Levels I to III (645 hours) is $5,483; books and supplies are approximately $950.

Tuition for Levels I to IV (1,000 hours) is $7,538; books and supplies are approximately $1,050.

Financial Assistance

A payment plan is available.

Honolulu School of Massage

1123 11th Avenue #102
Honolulu, Hawaii 96816
Phone: (808) 733-0000

The Honolulu School of Massage began in 1981 with a one-hundred-hour basic massage therapy training and a 420-hour clinical internship program to fulfill state of Hawaii licensing requirements. In 1984, the curriculum expanded, and it was approved by the American Massage Therapy Association (AMTA) in 1986.

Accreditation

Honolulu School of Massage's Massage Therapy Training Program is approved by the AMTA Commission on Massage Training Accreditation/Approval (COMTAA) and exceeds the educational requirements for licensure in Hawaii. Graduates of the AMTA Professional Training Program are eligible to take the national certification exam administered by the National Certification Board for Therapeutic Massage and Bodywork (NCBTMB).

Program Description

The one-year, 630-hour AMTA Professional Training Program consists of two sections: a 180-hour Basic Massage Therapy Training (which fulfills the minimum academic portion of state of Hawaii licensing requirements) and a 450-hour Professional Massage Therapy Training Program.

The Basic Training consists of eighty hours of anatomy, physiology, and kinesiology, and one hundred hours of theory, demonstration, and practice of massage, including history, basic principles and application of Swedish massage strokes, contraindications, personal hygiene, and client assessment. Completion takes four months in the extended format and eight weeks in the full-time format.

The Professional Training consists of 350 hours of classroom study and one hundred hours of supervised student clinic and community service. Topics covered include Foot Reflexology, Pregnancy Massage, Senior Citizen Massage, Hydrotherapy, Professionalism, Lomi Lomi, Shiatsu, Sports Massage, Assessment and Therapeutic Applications, Session Planning, Ethical Issues and the Professional Massage Therapist, HIV and Massage, Craniosacral Technique, Myology, Neuroanatomy, Deep Tissue Massage, Kinesiology, Pathology, CPR/First Aid, and state exam review. Completion takes approximately four to nine months.

Continuing Education

Individual courses listed under Professional Massage Therapy Training may be taken by students who wish to continue their education after licensing. .

Admission Requirements

Applicants must be at least 18 years of age or have the consent of a parent or guardian; have a high school diploma or equivalent; have fluent English language skills; have TB clearance and no diseases or disabilities that would limit physical exertion; and interview with an admissions representative.

Tuition and Fees

For all courses, there is a $25 application fee and a $100 registration fee; supplies are approximately $100.

Tuition for the Basic Massage Therapy Program (180 hours) is $1,950. Tuition for the Professional Massage Therapy Program (450 hours) is $4,600, or $2,300 per semester. Total tuition for the AMTA Professional Massage Therapy Program (630 hours) is $6,550. Tuition includes books, lubricant, taxes, and deposits.

Financial Assistance

Payment plans are available.

Maui School of Yoga Therapy

(See Multiple State Locations, page 308)

Tai Hsuan Foundation College of Acupuncture and Herbal Medicine

Mailing Address:
P.O. Box 11130
Honolulu, Hawaii 96828

Street Address:
2600 South King Street, #206
Honolulu, Hawaii 96782
Phone: (808) 947-4788 / (800) 942-4788
Fax: (808) 947-1152
E-mail: 71532,2642@compuserve.com

Tai Hsuan Foundation College was founded in 1970. Since its first class graduated in 1976, the Master of Acupuncture and Oriental Medicine degree program has a 100 percent first attempt pass rate for both the Hawaii State licensing exam and the certification exam of the National Commission for the Certification of Acupuncturists (NCCA).

Accreditation

The Master of Acupuncture and Oriental Medicine program is accredited by the National Accreditation Commission for Schools and Colleges of Acupuncture and Oriental Medicine (NACSCAOM).

Program Description

The 2,625-hour Master of Acupuncture and Oriental Medicine Program consists of 1,725 hours of Acupuncture Medical (traditional Chinese medicine, Taoist medicine and treatment, and needle technique) and Clinical Sciences, 540 hours of Herbal Medicine (materia medica, herbs, and herbal formulas) and Clinical Sciences, and 360 hours of Biomedical Sciences (anatomy/physiology, terminology, pathology, disease processes, pharmacology, and lab test/physical exam/clinical process).

Admission Requirements

Applicants must have completed a minimum of two years of college education or professional training from an accredited institution, and should have a professional attitude and flexibility in personal relations as evidenced by professional experience, education, life experiences, and letters of recommendation. Applicants must submit a brief essay and professional experience history, two letters of recommendation, and tuberculin skin test or chest X-ray results no more than three months old.

Tuition and Fees

Tuition is $6,600 per year, or $3,450 per semester. Other costs include: application fee, $50; herbal lab fee, $40 per semester; uniform, $30; and graduation fee, $100.

Financial Assistance

Federal loans and veterans' benefits are available.

Traditional Chinese Medical College of Hawaii

Waimea Office Center/Mamalahoa Highway
P.O. Box 2288
Kamuela, Hawaii 96743
Phone/Fax: (808) 885-9226

The Traditional Chinese Medical College of Hawaii, founded in 1986 by Angela Longo, Ph.D., was the first such college on the Big Island of Hawaii. Dr. Longo apprenticed under Dr. Lam Kong, a two-term chairman of the California Board of Acupuncture.

Accreditation

The college's Professional Diploma of Oriental Medicine Program is a candidate for accreditation with the National Accreditation Commission for Schools and Colleges of Acupuncture and Oriental Medicine (NACSCAOM). Graduates of the three-year program are qualified to take the Hawaii State Licensing Exam administered by the National Commission for Certification of Acupuncturists (NCCA). Over 90 percent of graduates have passed this exam.

Program Description

The 2,466-hour, three-year program leads to a Diploma in Oriental Medicine. The school year is divided into three 15-week trimesters. Courses include Origins of Acupuncture and Fundamental Theory of Oriental Medicine; Comparison of Western and Oriental Medical Models; Traditional Meridian and Point Study; Meridian Theory; Clinical Acupuncture and Moxibustion Procedures; Auriculotherapy; Traditional Diagnosis and Pathology; Chinese Pharmacology; Nutrition and Its Relation to the Disease State; Western Medical Terminology and Lab Analysis; Acupressure Techniques; CPR and Basic Emergency Procedures; Human Anatomy and Physiology; Qigong and Preventive Medicine; Tai Chi; Ethics and Human Services Skills; Chinese Medical Communication Skills; Case Presentations; Neurophysiology and Brain Gym; Clinic Management; Clinical Observation; Clinical Patient Care; Practice Management; and Supervised Clinical Practice.

Admission Requirements

Applicants must be at least 21 years of age; have completed two years (sixty semester credits) of postsecondary education at an accredited college or university; be proficient in English; submit a résumé, an essay, and two letters of recommendation; and interview with an admissions representative.

Tuition and Fees

Tuition is $2,175 per trimester; this includes both classroom and clinical instruction. Other costs include: application fee, $50; new student registration fee, $25; required seminars, $1,080 total; books (annual average), $200 to $300; supplies, $50; needles and moxa (annual average), $50; and annual malpractice insurance, $323.

Financial Assistance

A discount is offered for tuition prepayment; a payment plan and work-study are available.

IDAHO

Idaho Institute of Wholistic Studies

1412 West Washington Street
Boise, Idaho 83702
Phone: (208) 345-2704
Fax: (208) 367-9242

The Idaho Institute of Wholistic Studies (IIWS) was founded in 1993 by Brandie Redinger, C.M.T., Karen VanDeGrift, C.M.T., and Barbera Bashan, L.M.T.

Program Description

The 350-hour Massage Practitioner Program may be completed in nine months of full-time study. The curriculum includes Anatomy, Physiology, Body Work I and II (which includes Swedish, polarity, reflexology, yoga, muscular release, and supervised clinic), Body Work III: Shiatsu, CPR, Chinese Anatomy and Physiology, Emotional Armoring and Trauma, Movement, Professionalism and Ethics, Self-Healing and Communication, Sports Medicine, and Whole Foods and Health.

Advanced Certified Body Therapist Programs include courses in Dimensional Integrity, Healing Body/Mind, and Traditional Chinese Medicine.

The Dimensional Integrity Course adds 200 hours toward the 550 hours required for advanced certification as a body therapist. The curriculum includes Overview of Bodywork; Neuromuscular Facilitation; Dimensional Breathwork; Tension Assessment: Seeing the Body in Stillness; Tension Assessment: Seeing the Body in Motion; Introduction to Structural Anatomy; Defense and Fixation: Emotional Armor and Physical Structure; and Tissue, Touch, and Dimension.

The Healing Body/Mind Course also adds 200 hours toward the 550 hours required for advanced certification as a body therapist. The curriculum includes Rebirthing, Touching the Trauma of Sexual Abuse, Introduction to Abuse and Recovery, Transference Issues, Interviewing and Screening Clients, Co-Treatment, Treatment from the Victim's Perspective, Post-Traumatic Stress Disorder, Trust and Power Issues, Disassociation, Emotional Healing, Body Image vs. Body Reality, Offender Profile, Assessing Trauma, Keeping Your Balance, Survivor's Spirituality, and Emotional Release Techniques.

IIWS coordinates a 795-hour AMMA Therapy Course with Wellspring, an educational institute dedicated to traditional Eastern medicine. AMMA Therapy integrates bodywork with manipulation of energy channels, diet, herbal and vitamin supplements, detoxification, application of external herbal preparations, and exercise. Completion of this course earns advanced certification as a body therapist and meets qualifications for membership in the American Oriental Bodywork Therapist Association (AOBTA). The curriculum includes Oriental Anatomy and Physiology, AMMA Technique, Applied Technique, Clinic, Food in Treatment of Disharmony, and Oriental Clinical Assessment. Other requirements include sixty hours of tai chi chuan and/or qigong and six private sessions with a senior AMMA therapist; the student must also give a senior therapist one treatment.

Admission Requirements

Applicants must be at least 18 years of age and have a high school diploma. Applicants must also be able to lift fifty pounds, to stand one to two hours at a time, and must see, hear, speak, and move well enough to meet the demands of the work.

Tuition and Fees

There is a $75 registration fee for all courses. Tuition for the 350-hour Massage Practitioner Program is $3,500. Tuition for the 550-hour Massage Therapist Program is $5,500. Students transferring in with at least 350 credit hours and taking only the 200 credit hours of the advanced program pay $2,000. Tuition for the 795-hour Wellspring AMMA Program is $5,000.

Financial Assistance

A payment plan, Vocational Rehabilitation, and Job Service aid are available.

ILLINOIS

Chicago National College of Naprapathy

3330 North Milwaukee Avenue
Chicago, Illinois 60641
Phone: (312) 282-2686

Naprapathic practice is the evaluation of persons with connective tissue disorders through the use of naprapathic case history and palpation or treatment using connective tissue manipulation, postural counseling, nutritional counseling, heat, cold, light, water, radiant energy, electricity, sound, and air. The practice includes the treatment of contractures, lesions, laxity, rigidity, structural imbalance, muscular atrophy, and other disorders. The first chartered school of naprapathy, the Oakley Smith School of Naprapathy, was founded in 1908 in Chicago; it became the Chicago College of Naprapathy. Another school, the National College of Naprapathy, was founded in Chicago in 1949. The two schools merged in 1971 to become the Chicago National College of Naprapathy.

Accreditation

The Chicago National College of Naprapathy is accredited by the Council of Colleges of the American Naprapathic Association and recognized by the Illinois State Board of Higher Education to grant the degree Doctor of Naprapathy (D.N.). Graduates are eligible to take the examination for licensure in the State of Illinois.

Program Description

The four-academic-year (three-calendar-year) Doctor of Naprapathy Program consists of sixty-six credit hours in the basic sciences and sixty-four credit hours in the naprapathic sciences, for a total of 130 credit hours of academic work. An additional sixty credit hours are spent gaining clinical experience. Courses in the basic sciences include Anatomy I, II, and III; Applied Biomechanics; Biochemistry I and II; Embryology/Genetics; Exercise Physiology/Biomechanics; Histology; Inorganic Chemistry; Kinesiology; Laboratory Interpretation and Symptomatology; Microbiology and Public Health; Neuroscience I and II; Organic Chemistry; Physiology I, II, and III; Pathology I and II; and Science of Nutrition and Diet I and II. The naprapathic science curriculum covers naprapathic theory and practice; evaluating connective tissue disorders and how they effect neurological control of the connective tissues; how to apply naprapathic therapeutic techniques; the educational, ethical, legal, and psychological issues involved in clinical practice; and courses in therapeutic exercise, biomechanics, and nutrition. The clinical experience phase is supervised by clinic faculty. Courses in this phase include Accessory Technique; Accessory Techniques/Adjunctive Therapies; Clinical Nutrition Approach to Wellness; Clinical Orthopedic and Neurological Evaluation; Clinical Practice; Clinical Preparation; Ethics and Jurisprudence; Gross Anatomical Examination; Integrational Clinic Seminars; Naprapathic Charting and Clinical Evaluation I, II, and III; Naprapathic History and Philosophy; Naprapathic Technique I and II; Naprapathic Therapeutics; Physiological Therapeutics; Principles of Rehabilitation; Principles of Massage; Spinal Anatomy; Sports and Exercise Injury Assessment; Treatment and Rehabilitation; Therapeutic Exercise; and Clinic Review.

Admission Requirements

Degree-seeking candidates must have completed two years of college (sixty semester hours), including a minimum of twenty-four semester hours of general education with a G.P.A. of 2.0 on a 4.0 scale; complete the Naprapathic Aptitude Exam and interview administered at the college; and submit two letters of reference. Students-at-large—those undecided about pursuing the degree—need only submit the application form and fees and interview with an admissions counselor.

Tuition and Fees

Tuition is $115 per credit hour. For degree candidates, there is a matriculation fee of $50. For students-at-large, there is a matriculation fee of $30 and an application fee equal to the cost of one class, which is refunded if the student does not enroll. All students pay a registration fee of $25 and a student activity fee of $50 per year.

The Chicago School of Massage Therapy

2918 North Lincoln Avenue
Chicago, Illinois 60657-4109
Phone: (312) 477-9444
Fax: (312) 477-7256

The Chicago School of Massage Therapy was founded in 1981 by James Hackett and Robert King; in 1993 the school graduated its one thousandth massage therapist. CSMT is extensively involved in community service—the school has provided assistance at each Chicago Marathon since 1984, and in 1994 it received an Outstanding Community Peacemaker award for community outreach from the Chicago Peace Museum.

Accreditation

The Chicago School of Massage Therapy received program approval from the American Massage Therapy Association (AMTA) in 1981 and achieved AMTA Commission on Massage Training Accreditation/Approval (COMTAA) accreditation in 1994. CSMT is approved as a vocational school by the Illinois State Board of Education, and is approved by the National Certification Board for Therapeutic Massage and Bodywork (NCBTMB) as a continuing education provider. At this time, there is no licensing requirement in the state of Illinois to practice massage therapy.

Program Description

The 650-hour Massage Certification Program is offered in either a twelve-month day and evening program or a fourteen-month, one-day-per-week program. Courses include Massage Theory and Technique (covering therapeutic massage, biomechanics and self-care, palpation skills, body mobilization techniques, hydrotherapy/cryotherapy, muscle energy techniques/stretching, principles of exercise, sports injuries, and more), Anatomy and Physiology, Stress Management, Professional Development, Muscle Therapy, Business Intensive, Introduction to Bodywork Approaches (including myofascial therapy, Oriental medicine, acupressure, shiatsu, and energy approaches), Business Practices, Student Internship Program, Directed Independent Study, Maniken or Cadaver Study, CPR/First Aid, and three elective intensives. The remaining thirty hours are completed at various agencies in the Chicago area, providing massage therapy for special populations including the elderly, homeless, hospice patients, and others.

Community and Continuing Education

CSMT provides ongoing continuing education programs and advanced certifications for massage therapy and bodywork professionals. Programs include Infant Massage Instructor Certification, Advanced Certification Program in Sports and Soft Tissue Injuries, Manual Lymph Drainage, Myofascial Massage Therapy, Cadaver Anatomy Study, Therapeutic Stretching and Strengthening for Massage Therapists, and others.

Introductory classes are open to prospective students and to the public. These include Massage I, which meets one night per week for ten weeks and focuses on Swedish massage, basic anatomy and physiology, massage theory, and sensitivity and awareness; Massage Basics, which may be taken one night per week for five weeks or as a weekend intensive, and covers basic Swedish massage theory and individual body sequences; and the Massage Mini-Course, which meets three consecutive Saturdays, and offers practical techniques to share with friends and family.

Admission Requirements

Applicants must be at least 18 years of age; have a high school diploma or equivalent; have received at least one professional massage; have prior introductory-level training or instruction in massage therapy; be in good health and physically able to perform massage; and interview with an admissions representative.

Tuition and Fees

Tuition ranges from $6,400 to $6,700, depending on the payment plan. This includes a $100 registration fee, books, CPR/First Aid training, professional liability insurance, and some materials and supplies; massage oil, linens, and massage table are additional.

The Massage I course costs $250; the Massage Basics course costs $140; and the Massage Mini-Course costs $85.

Financial Assistance

Payment plans are available.

LifePath School of Massage Therapy

7820 North University, Suite 110
Peoria, Illinois 61614
Phone: (309) 693-7284 / (309) 693-PATH
E-mail: rwasher@cencom.net

The LifePath School of Massage Therapy was founded in 1991. The school emphasizes the integration of various modalities in order to therapeutically affect body, mind, and spirit.

Accreditation

The school is accredited by the International Massage and Somatic Therapies Accreditation Council (IMSTAC), a division of the Associated Bodywork and Massage Professionals (ABMP), and is approved by the Illinois State Board of Education as a private vocational school.

Program Description

The nine-month, 660-hour Massage Therapy Program includes Fundamental Massage Techniques, Anatomy and Physiology, Kinesiology, Nutrition, Reflexology, Psychology for the Bodyworker, Wellness Concepts, Massage Technique Variations, Massage Technique Applications, Deep Muscle

Therapy, Sports Massage, Joint Mobilization and Stretching, Hydrotherapy, Polarity Therapy, Business Ethics and Professional Practice, Neuromuscular Principles in Deep Tissue Bodywork, and Clinical Experience in Massage Therapy. Classes meet two evenings and one Saturday per week, with one weekend intensive per month.

Admission Requirements

Applicants must be at least 18 years of age; have a high school diploma or equivalent; be proficient in the English language; be in good health and free of communicable disease; submit two letters of recommendation and a biographical sketch; and interview with an admissions representative.

Tuition and Fees

Tuition is $6,105. Other costs include: application fee, $75; materials and liability insurance, $250; and books and massage table, $600 to $800.

Financial Assistance

Tuition may be paid in two payments.

National College of Chiropractic

200 East Roosevelt Road
Lombard, Illinois 60148
Phone: (708) 629-2000 / (800) 826-NATL
Internet: www.national.chiropractic.edu

The National College of Chiropractic (NCC) was established in 1906 in Davenport, Iowa, as the National School of Chiropractic. After years of growth and several moves, the school moved to its current facility in Lombard—the first such facility ever constructed for the exclusive use of chiropractic educators.

Accreditation

NCC is accredited by the Council on Chiropractic Education (CCE), the Commission on Institutions of Higher Education of the North Central Association of Colleges and Schools, and by registration by the State Education Department of the State of New York.

Program Description

The curriculum for the 4,819-hour, ten-trimester Doctor of Chiropractic degree program is divided into four major areas: Basic Sciences (including the Departments of Anatomy; Pathology, Microbiology, and Public Health; and Physiology and Biochemistry), Clinical Sciences (including the Departments of Chiropractic Practice and Diagnosis), Research, and Internship. NCC initiated a change in curriculum beginning in May 1996; the educational process has been modified to a more innovative, problem-based learning methodology in which the curriculum is much more integrated from the basic sciences through the clinic internship, with clinical competencies driving student assessment.

NCC also offers a Bachelor of Science degree in human biology that consists of sixty-nine trimester hours of credit (sixty credits are required for admission). Required courses include Human Embryology; Gross Anatomy; Human Genetics; Human Histology; Human Neuroanatomy; Biochemistry; Cells and Body Fluids; Circulation and Respiration; Digestion, Metabolism, and Endocrines; Neurophysiology; Fundamentals of Pathology; and Clinical Microbiology.

A 120-hour Chiropractic Assistant Certification Program provides general training for chiropractic office personnel. Courses include History and Principles of Chiropractic; History Taking; Terminology; Basic Anatomy and Physiology; Spinal Anatomy and Function; Physical Examination; Office Procedures; Insurance Procedures; Emergency Procedures and CPR; Physiological Therapeutics; Exercise, Rehabilitation, and Massage; X-Ray Technology and Safety; and X-Ray Positioning.

Continuing Education

The National-Lincoln School of Postgraduate Education offers a number of postgraduate study opportunities. Specialty seminars are offered in such areas as AIDS/HIV, Clinical Management of Infants and Children, Adjusting Technique, Electromyography, Hospital Protocol, and others. Diplomate programs are offered in Orthopedics, Diagnostic Imaging, Neurology, Sports Physician, Nutrition, Diagnosis, and Internal Disorders. Clinical residency programs are available in Orthopedics, Clinical Practice, Clinical Research, Family Practice, and Diagnostic Imaging. Certificate programs are offered in Chiropractic Assistant (above), Clinical Thermography, Cox Distraction Technique, Electrodiagnosis, Physiological Therapeutics, Meridian Therapy/Acupuncture, Sports Physician, Industrial Consulting, and Addictionology.

Admission Requirements

Applicants for the Doctor of Chiropractic degree program must have completed a minimum of seventy-five semester hours (ninety credit hours for those entering in September 1997, and a baccalaureate degree or equivalent for those entering in September 1999) of credit earned in an accredited college or university with a cumulative G.P.A. of no less than 2.5 on a 4.0 scale. A specific number of hours are required for prerequisite courses in general or inorganic chemistry, organic chemistry, physics, the biological sciences, English, humanities and social sciences (including psychology), and others. Applicants must also submit two letters of recommendation, with one preferably from a chiropractic physician.

Applicants for the Bachelor of Science in Human Biology Program must have completed at least sixty semester credit hours at an approved junior or community college, college, or university, with specific requirements in general or inorganic chemistry, organic chemistry, physics, the biological sciences, English, humanities and social sciences (including psychology), and others. Applicants must have a cumulative G.P.A. of no less than 2.25.

Tuition and Fees

There is a $55 application fee. Tuition is $197 per credit hour. Books cost $250 to $350 per trimester; lab fees are additional.

Financial Assistance

A payment plan, federal and private scholarships, grants, loans, and work-study programs are available.

Northern Prairie Center for Education and Healing Arts

130 North Fair Street
Sycamore, Illinois 60178
Phone: (815) 899-3382
Fax: (815) 899-3381

The Northern Prairie Center for Education and Healing Arts (a.k.a. the Northern Prairie School of Therapeutic Massage and Bodywork, Inc.) was founded in 1993. Director/administrator Jeannette Vaupel, R.N., B.S.N., C.M.T., has been practicing therapeutic massage since 1986; assistant administrator Margaret Zonca has been pursuing herbal studies for over twelve years.

Accreditation

Accreditation is being pursued.

Program Description

The 550-hour Therapeutic Massage and Bodywork Program consists of 400 hours of in-class instruction, fifty hours of self-study (anatomy coloring book), and one hundred practice hours. The curriculum includes Anatomy and Physiology, Anatomy Coloring Book, Fundamental Bodywork Techniques, Guided Imagery, Aromatherapy, Therapeutic Touch, Herbal Remedies, Body Mechanics: Parts I and II, Reflexology, Assessment of Problems and Pathology, Optimal Health Practices, Stretching and Myofascial Release, Complementary Therapies, Psychology for Bodyworkers, Lymphatic Massage, Shiatsu, Physical Therapy Modalities, Touch For Health, Special Considerations, Nutrition, and Business Practices.

The nine-month, 155-hour Therapeutic Herbalism Program consists of Herbalism: Gaia in Action, Selection Criteria, Classification of Medicinal Plants, Formulation and Preparation of Herbal Medicines, Digestive System, Cardiovascular System, Respiratory System, Nervous System, Urinary and Reproductive Systems, Musculoskeletal System and Skin, Immunity, Holism and Phytotherapy, Phytotherapy and Children, Phytotherapy and the Elderly, Actions, Aromatherapy, Flower Essences, Materia Medica, Assessment Modalities, Business

Practices, and final exam. Labs are held throughout the program to provide hands-on experience with teas, packs, poultices, salves, tinctures, and other forms of treatment.

Admission Requirements

Applicants must be at least 18 years of age; have a high school diploma or equivalent; be proficient in the English language; be in good general health and submit results of TB skin test; and interview with an admissions representative. Therapeutic Massage and Bodywork applicants must be physically able to perform movements and techniques inherent to massage therapy practice.

Tuition and Fees

There is a $25 application fee and a $75 registration fee for all courses.

Total tuition for the Therapeutic Massage and Bodywork Program is $6,600. Other costs include: books, materials, and liability insurance, approximately $500; massage table, approximately $625; and graduation fee, $45. The approximate total cost is $7,845.

Tuition for the Therapeutic Herbalism Program is $1,860; books are $225 and additional optional materials are approximately $200.

Financial Assistance

Payment plans are available.

Redfern Training Systems School of Massage

9 South 531 Wilmette Avenue
Darien, Illinois 60561
Phone: (708) 960-5636

The Redfern Training Systems (RTS) School of Massage was founded in 1992 by Rhonda A. Wolski, a certified massage therapist since 1986, who has additional certifications in sports massage, reflexology, and day spa treatments.

Accreditation

RTS was approved in 1992 by the Illinois State Board of Education and the Associated Bodywork and Massage Professionals (ABMP), indicating that its course materials meet or exceed the requirements for membership at the professional level.

Program Description

The 690-hour Massage Certification Class meets one day per week for thirty weeks, and includes instruction in the following subject areas: Massage Techniques (including Swedish, French, reflexology, sports, cranial, and positional release), Theory and History of Massage, Anatomy and Physiology, Benefits and Contraindications, Self-Awareness and the Body-Mind Connection, and practical experience.

A twenty-four-hour Basic Reflexology Class meets one day per week for eight weeks, and includes instruction in the history and basis of reflexology, energy, and the body zones.

An eight-hour class is offered in Day Spa Treatments that includes several different body treatments and wraps.

Community and Continuing Education

An eight-hour Introduction to Massage course introduces the student to basic massage techniques and is intended for personal use only; this class does not qualify the student to work with the public.

A twenty-four-hour Sports Massage Course is open to certified massage therapists, and meets once a week for eight weeks. Classes are divided into theory and practical sessions, and involve working with the athlete before, during, and after training and competition; theory and history; and preventive, curative, and emergency treatments.

Admission Requirements

Applicants for the Introduction to Massage, Massage Certification, Basic Reflexology, and Day Spa Treatment classes must be at least 18 years of age and have previous exposure to bodywork. Sports Massage applicants must be at least 18 years of age and certified in massage therapy. Applicants are interviewed prior to enrollment.

Tuition and Fees

Tuition for the Massage Certification Course is $3,330, including books and supplies. Other fees

include an enrollment fee of $200 and a student insurance fee of $100.

Tuition for the Basic Reflexology Course is $300, plus a $100 enrollment fee.

Tuition for the Day Spa Treatments Course is $100, plus a $50 enrollment fee.

Tuition for the Sports Massage Course is $300, plus a $100 enrollment fee.

Tuition for the Introduction to Massage Course is $100, plus a $50 enrollment fee.

Financial Assistance

Payment plans are available.

Wellness and Massage Training Institute

618 Executive Drive
Willowbrook, Illinois 60521
Phone: (630) 325-3773

The Wellness and Massage Training Institute (WMTI) enrolled its first students in 1989. The Student Massage Clinic, which provides massage sessions to the public at a nominal fee, opened in June 1991. In 1994, the institute expanded to occupy nearly 7,000 square feet.

Accreditation

The Massage Therapy Training Program is accredited by the American Massage Therapy Association Commission on Massage Training Accreditation/Approval (AMTA/COMTAA), and approved by the National Certification Board for Therapeutic Massage and Bodywork (NCBTMB) as a continuing education provider under Category A.

Program Description

The 700-hour Massage Therapy Training Program requires study in Introduction to Massage Therapy, Fundamental Massage Techniques, Basic Anatomy and Physiology, Kinesiology, Wellness Concepts, Anatomy and Physiology for Bodyworkers, Massage Technique Variations, Professional Practice, Clinical Experience in Massage Therapy, and Integrative Studies in Massage Therapy, plus 117 hours of electives selected from subjects that include Seated Massage Techniques, Basic Sports Massage Techniques, Positional Release and Massage, Active Assisted Stretching, Esalen-Style Massage, Principles of Structural Massage, Clinical Symposia, Advanced Sports Massage Techniques, Pressure Sensitivity Techniques, Practitioner Series, Reflexology, Touch for Health, Orthobionomy, Jin Shin Do, Shiatsu, Bodywork and the Adult Child, Bodywork and Survivors of Sex Abuse, Introduction to Nutrition, Communication Skills, Boundary Issues for Massage Therapists, Tai Chi, Creating Success Through Productive Thinking, Stress Management, and Ethical Considerations in Massage and Bodywork.

Students are also required to complete basic CPR and First Aid through the American Red Cross or American Heart Association, and to receive four professional massages during their training.

Students may attend either full- or part-time. Independent students are those who enroll in individual subjects on a space-available basis; they may later petition to enroll in the diploma program.

Continuing Education

A variety of courses are offered in the continuing education program, including Orthobionomy, Jin Shin Do Acupressure, Aromatherapy, Marketing On-Site Massage, Reflexology, Infant and Toddler Massage, and others.

Admission Requirements

Applicants must be at least 18 years of age; have a high school diploma or equivalent; be in general good health and free of communicable disease; and have received at least one professional massage prior to the start of classes.

Tuition and Fees

Tuition for required subjects is $4,535; tuition for electives is $120 to $420 per course. Books, depending on electives, range from $337 to $472; materials cost $155; a massage table costs $300 to $800; the cost of CPR/First Aid varies; and professional massages cost $80 to $100.

Financial Assistance

Payment plans are available.

INDIANA

Alexandria School of Scientific Therapeutics

P.O. Box 287
809 South Harrison Street
Alexandria, Indiana 46001
Phone: (317) 724-7745 / (800) 622-8756

The Alexandria School of Scientific Therapeutics was founded in 1982 by Herbert and Ruthann Hobbs. Ruthann Hobbs is a graduate of three AMTA-approved schools, and is a registered reflexologist, certified iridologist, and certified instructor for the Pfrimmer Technique Deep Muscle Therapist Association.

Accreditation

The Massage Therapy Program is approved by the American Massage Therapy Association Commission on Massage Training Accreditation/Approval (AMTA/COMTAA), and licensed and accredited by the State of Indiana.

Program Description

The forty-one-week, 656-hour Massage Therapy Program includes Anatomy, Physiology, Theory and Practice of Massage, Hydrotherapy, Nutrition, Health and Hygiene, Business Practices, Client Assessment, Polarity Techniques, Muscle Balancing Techniques, Postural Release Techniques, Iridology, Structural Alignment Techniques, Color Therapy, Acupressure, Shiatsu, Craniopathy, Infant Massage, Geriatric Massage, Sports Massage, and Manual Lymph Drainage. Students are also required to take EMR (Emergency Medical Response) training either at the school or elsewhere. Weekday and weekend classes are available.

Continuing Education

An eighty-hour postgraduate course in Pfrimmer Deep Muscle Therapy is offered to those with at least 500 hours of anatomy, physiology, hygiene, ethics, and other requirements, and who are willing to abide by the standards imposed by the Therese C. Pfrimmer School and the International Association.

Admission Requirements

Applicants must be at least 18 years of age, have a high school diploma or equivalent, submit two letters of recommendation, interview with an admissions representative, and be in good health.

Tuition and Fees

There is a $100 registration fee. Tuition is $4,603, including books; uniform is additional.

Tuition for the course in Pfrimmer Deep Muscle Therapy is $2,800. Other costs include: application fee, $25; registration fee, $100; and manual, $100.

Financial Assistance

Payment plans are available.

Health Enrichment Center

(See Multiple State Locations, page 303)

Lewis School and Clinic of Massage Therapy

3400 Michigan Street
Hobart, Indiana 46342
Phone/Fax: (219) 962-9640

The Lewis School and Clinic of Massage Therapy was founded in 1984 by Rose Marie Lewis, a registered massage therapist who has served on the board of directors of the Indiana Chapter of AMTA.

Accreditation

The Massage Therapy Program is approved by the American Massage Therapy Association Commission on Massage Training Accreditation/Approval (AMTA/COMTAA).

Program Description

The 550-hour Massage Therapy Program includes Anatomy and Physiology, Craniosacral Concepts, Massage Theory and Hands-On Experience (in-

cluding a variety of Swedish techniques), Sports Massage, Reflexology, CPR, Hydrotherapy, and Business Ethics and Practices. Classes are held on weekends.

Admission Requirements

Applicants must be at least 18 years of age; have a high school diploma or equivalent; submit three character references, one of which must be from a health care professional; interview with an admissions representative; provide a current photograph; and reveal a sincere interest in the natural health therapies field.

Tuition and Fees

Tuition is $5,000, including books, oils, and linens. There is a $100 registration fee.

Financial Assistance

An interest-free payment plan and veterans' benefits are available.

Midwest Training Institute of Hypnosis

2121 Engle Road, Suite 3A
Fort Wayne, Indiana 46809
Phone: (219) 747-6774

The Midwest Training Institute of Hypnosis was founded in 1990 by Gisella Zukausky, who holds a doctorate in clinical hypnotherapy and a B.A. in psychology.

Accreditation

Upon completion of Class 1, students are eligible for certification with the International Medical and Dental Hypnotherapy Association, the American Institute of Hypnotherapy, the Hypnotherapy Association of Indiana, and most other hypnotherapy associations. Concordia Lutheran College in Fort Wayne and St. John's University in Louisiana give credits for the institute's courses; all others must be consulted individually.

Program Description

The institute offers a series of classes in hypnotherapy.

Class 1: Hypnosis/Hypnotherapy/Regression Therapy consists of six days of instruction and forty hours of lab and homework, for a total of 150 hours. The course covers different depths of hypnosis; motivating clients to stop smoking, control weight, and control other problem behaviors; applying hypnosis to therapy; and more. A correspondence course covering the same material may be taken by those unable to attend classes. For those interested, an internship program for Class 1 meets two evenings a month for a total of fifty hours.

The twenty-hour Class 2: Analytical Hypnotherapy offers hands-on training in a technique in which clients are asked a series of yes-and-no questions and asked to respond with finger signals. This type of therapy leads to events locked into the subconscious. For those interested, an advanced internship program totaling fifty hours is offered after completion of this class.

The sixty-five-hour Class 3: Hypno-Anesthesia, Glove Anesthesia, Pain Control, and Improved Health with Imagery covers how to use hypnosis as anesthesia for operations, painless childbirth, and dental work.

Class 4: Past Life Therapy and Sub-Personality Release includes thirty hours of instruction in using a client's description of past life events, whether real or fantasy, to resolve problems and release sub-personalities.

Classes 2, 3, and 4 meet for one weekend each.

Admission Requirements

Applicants must be at least 18 years of age and have a high school diploma or equivalent.

Tuition and Fees

Tuition for Class 1, taken at the school or by correspondence, is $689; the internship is $3 per evening.

Tuition for Class 2 is $165; the internship is $3 per evening.

Tuition for Class 3 is $285. Tuition for Class 4 is $165.

Financial Assistance

Full or partial scholarships are given on an individual basis.

IOWA

Carlson College of Massage Therapy

11809 Country Road X28
Anamosa, Iowa 52205
Phone: (319) 462-3402

Carlson College of Massage Therapy was founded in 1985. It recently relocated twenty miles north of Cedar Rapids to a tranquil countryside setting.

Accreditation

The Massage Therapy Program at Carlson College is approved by the American Massage Therapy Association Commission on Massage Training Accreditation/Approval (AMTA/COMTAA).

Program Description

The 625-hour, five-and-a-half-month Massage Therapy Program consists of Anatomy/Physiology and Massage Theory, Techniques, and Practices (founded on intermediate and advanced Swedish technique), in addition to instruction in therapeutic touch, polarity, stretches, deep and connective tissue massage, reflexology, sports massage, hydrotherapy, musculoskeletal pathology, aromatherapy, shiatsu, myofascial work, herbology, tai chi/body movement, guided imagery, on-site chair massage, CPR, first aid, professional ethics, business practices, and an internship (outreach and clinic). This program meets during the day, and also includes AMTA meetings and information, videotapes on various subjects, and guest lectures and demonstrations.

Admission Requirements

Applicants must have a high school diploma or equivalent, be of high moral character, and be in good health.

Tuition and Fees

Tuition is $4,000. There is a $25 application fee; books, malpractice insurance, linens, uniforms, and massage table are additional.

Maharishi International University

1000 North Fourth Street
Fairfield, Iowa 52557
Phone: (515) 472-7000 /
  (515) 472-1110 (admissions office)

Maharishi International University (MIU) was founded in 1971 by Maharishi Mahesh Yogi. Students come from ninety countries to study at MIU, known for its excellence in holistic education. The 262-acre campus has over 1.2 million square feet of teaching, research, recreational, and living space.

Accreditation

MIU is accredited at the doctoral level by the North Central Association of Colleges and Schools, the oldest and largest accrediting organization in the United States.

Program Description

MIU offers doctorate, master's, bachelor's, certificate, and technical training programs in both the more usual disciplines, such as Computer Science, Business, Chemistry, Literature, Mathematics, and Electronics, and alternative fields including Maharishi's Vedic Psychology, the Science of Creative Intelligence, Maharishi Ayur-Veda, Maharishi Gandharva Veda Music, and Maharishi Ayur-Veda Technician.

The bachelor's degree program in Maharishi Ayur-Veda includes courses in Fundamental Skills; Vedic Physiology; Maharishi Ayur-Veda: Solutions to Problems in World Health; The Science of Perfect Health; Basic Principles and Balance and Imbalance; Advanced Practicum; and Experience in Research Methods.

The Bachelor of Arts and Bachelor of Science programs in Maharishi's Vedic Psychology include such courses as Maharishi's Vedic Psychology; Research Methods; Testing and Measurement; Developmental Psychology; Levels of Mind: Theory and Research; Collective Consciousness; Psychophysiology; Foundations of Applied Psychology; Statistics; Computer Applications for Psychology; and Seminar in Consciousness.

The Master of Science and Doctor of Philosophy programs in Maharishi's Vedic Psychology include advanced courses such as Maharishi Ayur-Veda I and II; Theory and Research in Collective Consciousness; Seminar in Consciousness: Source References in Vedic Psychology; Advanced Topics in Social Processes and Collective Consciousness; and much more.

Bachelor's, master's, and doctorate degrees are offered in the Science of Creative Intelligence. Courses in this department include SCI and Higher States of Consciousness; Sanskrit; Applications of Maharishi's Vedic Science and Technology; Scientific Research on Maharishi's Transcendental Meditation Technique and TM-Sidhi Program; the Unified Field of Natural Law as the Source of All Streams of Knowledge; Bhagavad Gita; Readings in Vedic Literature; and more.

Admission Requirements

Undergraduate applicants must be at least 18 years of age and have a high school diploma or equivalent. All applicants must provide transcripts, two letters of recommendation, and standardized test scores.

Tuition and Fees

Undergraduate costs per year are as follows: application fee, $25; tuition and fees, $13,976; double room, $1,440 (single room, $2,512); board, $2,288; and books and supplies, $500.

Graduate costs per year are as follows: application fee, $40; tuition and fees, $14,984; single room, $2,512 (double room, $1,440); board, $2,288; and books and supplies, $500.

Financial Assistance

Federal grants and loans, state grants, university scholarships, and work-study are available.

Palmer College of Chiropractic

1000 Brady Street
Davenport, Iowa 52803-5287
Phone: (319) 326-9600 / (800) 722-3648

Palmer College of Chiropractic's founder, D.D. Palmer, performed the first modern chiropractic adjustment in 1895 and held the first classes of the Palmer School and Cure in 1897. The college boasts the profession's largest chiropractic outpatient clinic system, a leading chiropractic research facility, and the most extensive chiropractic library. Today, one of every three chiropractors in the world is a Palmer graduate.

Accreditation

Palmer College of Chiropractic is accredited by the Council of Chiropractic Education and the North Central Association of Schools and Colleges.

Program Description

The 4,620-hour Doctor of Chiropractic (D.C.) degree program may be completed in as little as three-and-one-third consecutive years. Courses are offered in the departments of Anatomy, Chiropractic Protocol, Clinic, Diagnosis, Pathology, Philosophy, Physiology and Biochemistry, Radiology, Research, Special Programs/Electives, and Technique.

Students may also complete a Bachelor of Science degree in general science in addition to the Doctor of Chiropractic degree; this degree must be awarded concurrently with the D.C. degree.

Continuing Education

Advanced studies include the Clinical Teaching Residents Program, which prepares graduate doctors of chiropractic to be clinical faculty members. Graduate doctors of chiropractic may also participate in a residency program with the Department of Radiology to qualify for the diplomate exam of the American Chiropractic Board of Radiology.

Admission Requirements

Applicants for admission to the D.C. program must have completed at least sixty semester hours leading to a baccalaureate degree in a college or university program with a minimum G.P.A. of 2.75. Applicants whose G.P.A. falls between 2.25 and 2.74 may be considered after an on-campus interview. Candidates must meet specific course and credit requirements in the sciences, social sciences, and humanities. In addition, applicants must submit letters of recommendation and a personal essay, and interview with an admissions representative.

Tuition and Fees

Tuition is $4,635 per trimester full-time, or $200 per credit hour for less than twenty-three hours. Other costs include: application fee, $50; activities fee, $100; and liability insurance, $195. Books and equipment costs vary by trimester from approximately $50 to $500. Additional fees for students obtaining a Bachelor of Science degree in conjunction with the Doctor of Chiropractic degree include: application fee, $100; graduation and record fee, $100; and transcript evaluation fee, $50.

Financial Assistance

Scholarships, awards, and federal financial aid are available.

KANSAS

International College of Applied Kinesiology

(*See* Professional Associations and Membership Organizations, page 346)

LOUISIANA

Blue Cliff School of Therapeutic Massage

1919 Veterans Boulevard, Suite 310
Kenner, Louisiana 70062
Phone: (504) 471-0294

The Blue Cliff School of Therapeutic Massage was founded in 1987 by Vernon Smith, Ph.D., a sociologist, shiatsu practitioner, and nationally certified massage therapist. The school has an extensive history of community service and, through outreach programs, has brought massage therapy to the elderly and those living with chronic pain. The Blue Cliff Sports Massage Team participates in local athletic events, including the Mardi Gras Marathon.

Accreditation

The 600-hour Massage Therapist Diploma Program and the 740-hour Advanced Practitioner Diploma Program are accredited by the American Massage Therapy Association Commission on Massage Training Accreditation/Approval (AMTA/COMTAA), and both exceed the training required to take the Louisiana State Licensure Exam. For students who plan to practice out of state, the Florida State Massage Board has approved the Blue Cliff curriculum.

Program Description

The 600-hour Massage Therapist Program is offered on a day, night, or weekend schedule and includes courses in Anatomy and Physiology, Basic Shiatsu, Craniosacral Therapy, Deep Tissue Massage, Hydrotherapy, Laws and Legislation, CPR/First Aid/HIV, Marketing, Neuromuscular Therapy, Pathophysiology, Professionalism, Reflexology, Sports Kinesiology, Sports Massage, Sports Shiatsu, Subtle Body Energetics, Swedish Massage, Tai Chi, Therapeutic Communication, and Supervised Clinical Practice. Each student is also required to contribute a minimum of ten hours of community service to the outreach program of his or her choice, and to have one professional massage prior to graduation.

The 740-hour Advanced Practitioner Program offers 140 hours of training in addition to the 600-hour Massage Therapist Program on a day or weekend schedule. The additional training is based on the Five Transformations model of traditional Chinese medicine, and includes such courses as Body Systems Balancing, Intermediate Shiatsu, and Supervised Clinical Practice.

Community and Continuing Education

One-day introductory Eastern and Western style technique classes are offered to the public. A variety of continuing education workshops are offered to the massage community; many of these satisfy state and national CEU requirements.

Admission Requirements

Applicants must be at least 18 years of age, have a high school diploma or the equivalent, be physically capable of performing massage, and interview with an admissions representative.

Tuition and Fees

Tuition for the Massage Therapist Program is $4,400. Tuition for the Advanced Practitioner Program is $5,400.

The following fees apply to both courses: application fee, $50; liability insurance, $15; books and materials, $335; and one professional massage, $40 to $60. Linens, oils, and optional massage table are additional.

The one-day Eastern and Western Massage Techniques workshop costs $65.

Financial Assistance

Payment plans are available.

MAINE

Avena Botanicals

219 Mill Street
Rockport, Maine 04856
Phone: (207) 594-0694
Fax: (207) 594-2975
E-mail: avena@midcoast.com

Avena Botanicals was founded by Deb Soule, who has been organically growing, wildcrafting, and using medicinal herbs for over twenty years. She is the author of *The Roots of Healing: A Woman's Book of Herbs.*

Accreditation

The one-day workshop, Celebrating Wellness with Herbs and Naturopathic Medicine, may be taken for CEU credit by nurses and doctors.

Program Description

The six-month Herbal Course for Women is a foundation course taught by Deb Soule and guests. The course covers using herbs in our daily lives; digging spring roots for root tinctures, syrups, and teas; liver tonic herbs; identifying wild medicinal herbs; creating small woodland gardens of endangered herbs; flower meditation; making and using flower essences; herbal healing for women's health concerns, such as premenstrual syndrome, menopause, and breast health; herbal and homeopathic first aid; herbs for winter health; and more. Classes are held one day per month.

One- to three-day herbal workshops are held spring through fall on such topics as Herbal Care for Women and Children, Growing and Using Medicinal Herbs, Conservation Through Ecological Plant Restoration, and others.

Admission Requirements

Applicants must be at least 16 years of age.

Tuition and Fees

Tuition for the Herbal Course for Women is $385 to $450; this includes all materials. The cost of the one-day courses ranges from $40 to $50.

Financial Assistance

A payment plan is available.

Downeast School of Massage

P.O. Box 24
99 Moose Meadow Lane
Waldoboro, Maine 04572
Phone: (207) 832-5531

The Downeast School of Massage was established in 1981; in 1993, the school moved to a new three-story facility on ninety rural acres overlooking Moose Meadow Pond.

Accreditation

The program at DSM is approved by the American Massage Therapy Association Commission on Massage Training Accreditation/Approval (AMTA/COMTAA).

Program Description

The Massage Therapy Program may be completed in ten months full-time or two years part-time. Three concentrations are available: Swedish and Sports Massage (608 hours), Swedish and Shiatsu (689 hours), or Swedish and Body/Mind (600 hours). The required core curriculum for all three programs includes Introduction, Anatomy, Physiology, Kinesiology, Swedish Massage, Pregnancy Massage, Reflexology, Video Mechanics, Movement Analysis, Tai Chi, Ethics, Business Practice, Trauma Survival, Art of Practice Design, Nutrition, First Aid, CPR, Hydrotherapy, Chronic Pain, Maniken Muscles, Neuromuscular Therapy, Pathology, and Integrating Business. For the Sports Massage Program, additional classes include Shiatsu (Introduction), Sports Massage, Clinic, and Neuro Clinic; for the Shiatsu Program, students also take 150 hours of Shiatsu as well as the Neuro Clinic; and for the Body/Mind Program, additional courses include Shiatsu (Introduction), Polarity, Energy Field Healing, Clinic, Psychological Aspects of Massage, and Neuro Clinic. Students may take any of the electives listed under **Continuing Education,** below, in addition to their individual program, for additional cost.

Continuing Education

Electives and special guest workshops are open to students, graduates, and professional massage therapists. Electives and workshops include Shiatsu, Polarity, Sports Massage, Energy Field Healing, Herbology, Integrating Business, Psychological Aspects of Massage, The Art of Practice Design, Maniken Muscles, Working with Incest and Trauma Survivors for the Massage Therapist, New England Conference (AMTA), Advanced Techniques of Massage Therapy Clinical Applications—Robert King, and special guest workshops.

Admission Requirements

Applicants must have a high school diploma or equivalent, be of good physical and mental health and high moral character, interview with the admissions director, and submit two character references.

Tuition and Fees

Tuition for the Swedish and Sports Massage or Swedish and Body/Mind Programs is $5,075. Tuition for the Swedish and Shiatsu Program is $5,875. Other costs include: application fee, $25; registration, $100; books, $350; office supplies, $25; massage table, approximately $700 to $800; lotion and oils, $150; linens, $50; instruments, $40 to $100; AMTA student membership, $158; and lab fee, $50.

Financial Assistance

Payment plans are available.

New Hampshire Institute for Therapeutic Arts

(*See* Multiple State Locations, page 312)

Polarity Realization Institute

(*See* Multiple State Locations, page 316)

MARYLAND

Baltimore School of Massage

6401 Dogwood Road
Baltimore, Maryland 21207
Phone: (410) 944-8855

The Baltimore School of Massage (BSM) was founded in 1981 by Jerry Toporovsky, past chairman of the American Massage Therapy Association (AMTA) Council of Schools and chairman of the Zero Balancing Association.

Accreditation

The 500-hour massage training program has been approved by the American Massage Therapy Association Commission on Massage Training Accreditation/Approval (AMTA/COMTAA). BSM is approved by the National Certification Board for Therapeutic Massage and Bodywork (NCBTMB) as a continuing education provider, and by the Maryland Higher Education Commission.

Program Description

The one-hundred-hour Basic Program, an avocational course in relaxation massage, provides instruction in Swedish massage, seated massage, polarity and energy work techniques, anatomy, and physiology.

The 500-hour Professional Massage Training Program is a career-oriented course of study that is approved by AMTA/COMTAA. The program consists of three terms of massage instruction, covering Swedish massage, polarity work and energy concepts, seated massage, body mechanics, facial massage, anatomy and physiology, deep tissue work, massage for pregnant women, communication skills, and business practices. The program also includes a series of elective trainings and CPR certification.

Admission Requirements

Applicants must be at least 18 years of age, have a high school diploma or equivalent, be physically capable of performing massage manipulations, interview with a school representative, and complete a biographical sketch.

Tuition and Fees

Tuition for the Basic Program is $650. There is a $50 application fee, and a $40 fee for textbooks and supplies.

Tuition for the Professional Program is $4,650. There is a $100 application fee, and a $135 fee for books and supplies. Students must supply their own linens and oil for supervised practice.

Financial Assistance

Payment plans are available.

Maryland Institute of Traditional Chinese Medicine

4641 Montgomery Avenue, Suite 415
Bethesda, Maryland 20814
Phone: (301) 718-7373 / (301) 907-8986 /
  (800) 892-1209
Fax: (301) 718-0735

The Maryland Institute of Traditional Chinese Medicine (MITCM) was founded in 1987 and held its first classes in 1992. In 1996, MITCM moved to another site that accommodates larger enrollment and an increasingly active clinic.

Accreditation

The master's degree-level acupuncture program is a candidate for accreditation with the National Accreditation Commission for Schools and Colleges of Acupuncture and Oriental Medicine (NACSCAOM).

Program Description

The three-year, 1,800-hour master's degree-level program in traditional Chinese medicine consists of 900 hours of academic instruction and 900 hours of clinical training. Graduation from this program qualifies students to be licensed as professional acupuncturists in Maryland and other states, and also satisfies requirements for application to take the NCCA exam.

Course work includes History and Theory of TCM, Channel Theory, Clinical Anatomy and Pathophysiology, Clean Needle Technique, Research Project Planning, Diagnostic Theory of TCM, Acupuncture Points, Introduction to Clinical Western Medicine, Acupuncture Techniques, Acupuncture Treatment, Western Medicine Diagnostic Methods, Chinese Tui Na, Advanced Therapeutics, Clinical Observation, Clinical Treatment of Patients, and Business Management.

Community Education

A ten-class tai chi course is offered to the public as well as to currently enrolled students.

Admission Requirements

Applicants must have completed at least sixty semester hours of undergraduate study (including six college credits of anatomy and physiology) from an accredited college or university, and must interview with one or more members of the admissions committee.

Tuition and Fees

Tuition is $6,000 per year, or $18,000 total; books cost approximately $300, and acupuncture needles cost approximately $200.

For medical doctors and those not required to take the Western medicine curriculum, tuition is $5,000 per year for the first two years and $6,000 for the third year, or $16,000 total.

The tai chi course costs $50.

Financial Assistance

Payment plans are available.

Traditional Acupuncture Institute

American City Building
10227 Wincopin Circle, Suite 100
Columbia, Maryland 21044-3422
Phone: (301) 596-6006 / (410) 997-4888
Fax: (410) 964-3544

The concept for the Traditional Acupuncture Institute was formed in 1973 by a group of American acupuncturists completing their clinical residence in England. By 1980, the curriculum was developed and in 1985, the institute was accredited by National Accreditation Commission for Schools and Colleges of Acupuncture and Oriental Medicine (NACSCAOM).

Accreditation

The Master of Acupuncture Program is accredited by NACSCAOM and conforms to licensing requirements of most states, including Maryland and California. Those seeking licensing in California must meet specific course requirements, including the Chinese herbs class.

Program Description

The Master of Acupuncture degree program may be taken in either a twenty-nine-month or forty-month track. The curriculum consists of three levels of study.

Level I courses include a ten-day SOPHIA (School of Philosophy and Healing in Action) Theory Intensive that introduces basic laws, language, and diagnostic skills of traditional acupuncture; Clinical Observation and Diagnosis; Embodying Qigong; Acupuncture Theory/Elements; Basic Acupuncture Anatomy; Touching the Energy; Zero Balancing; Partnership with Nature; Mentor Groups; and more.

Level II courses focus on the development of diagnostic skills and include Introduction to Traditional Diagnosis: The Patient Examination and Physical Diagnosis; Introduction to Treatment Planning; Principles of Treatment; Introduction to Classical Chinese Medical Literature; Tai Chi/Breathing/Meditation; Spirit of the Points; Acupuncture Anatomy Lecture and Lab; Acupuncture Theory; Zang Fu; Patterns of Disharmony; History of Chinese Medicine and Philosophy; Diagnostic Interaction; Introduction to Western Medicine: Clinical Science and Pathology; Professional Project: Research/Communication; Treatment of Addiction and Community Health; and others.

Level III courses focus on clinical work and begin with a four-day student retreat. Courses continue to build on the foundations of Acupuncture Anatomy, Theory, and Diagnosis, and also include Distinct Traditions; Business, Ethics, and Legal Issues; Treatment Planning and Case Presentation; Patterns of Disharmony Lab; Being Practitioner: Observation; Mentor Groups; Professional Project: Research/Communication; and others.

Community and Continuing Education

The ten-day SOPHIA Theory Intensive, two-day Five Element Approach to Redefining Health workshop, evening Introduction to Traditional Acupuncture, and other programs are open to the public as a community service.

Admission Requirements

Applicants must have a bachelor's degree from an accredited institution with a minimum G.P.A. of C, at least fifteen semester credits in the biosciences, and fifteen semester credits in the social sciences. In addition, applicants must have at least 200 hours of clinical work experience in a Western medical setting such as a hospital, mental health facility, hospice, doctor's office, or similar situation; up to seventy-five hours may be completed through body work (such as massage therapy, acupressure, polarity, and reiki). Applicants must also have completed or plan to complete a CPR course from the Red Cross or American Heart Association. Also, applicants must submit three letters of recommendation and a letter from a practitioner documenting that they have received Five-Element treatment; and interview with two faculty members, graduates, or administrators.

Tuition and Fees

There is a $65 application fee. A tuition deposit of $800 is required; the tuition balance is $24,750. Books and materials cost approximately $500.

Financial Assistance

A payment plan and federal loans are available.

The Yoga Center

8950 Route 108, Suite 114
Columbia, Maryland 21045
Phone: (410) 720-4340

The Yoga Center was founded in 1992. Director Bob Glickstein is a certified Iyengar yoga teacher and holistic body worker who has taught yoga for twenty years.

Program Description

A six-month Teacher Training Course for Level I classes trains participants in the instruction and modification of asanas for Level I Hatha yoga classes based on the Iyengar method. Instruction includes effectively communicating step-by-step instruction for each Level I asana, recognizing and making adjustments for common problems, using props effectively, teaching relaxation and restorative poses, and identifying body types according to structural alignment. Topics include Opening and Standing Poses, Standing Poses, Seated Poses, Forward Bends, Twists, Hip Openers, Arm Work, Simple Backbends, Restorative Poses, Savasana and Philosophy, and review and evaluation. Participants meet one weekend per month for six months, and assist during Level I yoga classes once a month.

Admission Requirements

To participate in the Teacher Training Course and receive maximum benefit, applicants must have a regular daily practice, have completed a Level I class and be enrolled in at least a Level II class, and be committed to studying and developing the skills necessary to teach a Level I class.

Tuition and Fees

Total tuition is $995.

MASSACHUSETTS

American Yoga College

1689 Beacon Street
Brookline, Massachusetts 02146
Phone: (617) 277-8366 / (800) 440-8366

The American Yoga College (AYC) was built upon the foundation of the California Institute for Yoga Teacher Education (IYTE), an affiliate of the California Institute for Asian Studies, founded in 1974. The American Yoga College embraces the principles of unity, truth, and wisdom from all traditions and lineages of yoga. American Yoga College courses are available through a network of affiliates in Massachusetts, Washington, D.C., and Arizona.

Program Description

The programs at AYC are designed for those wishing to train as yoga teachers, yoga teachers seek-

ing continuing education, or yoga students who wish to deepen their practice.

The 400-hour diploma program consists of a 335-hour core curriculum that covers such topics as Comparative Systems of Yoga, Asana: Teaching and Application, Relaxation and Stress Management, Science of Breath and Pranayama, Overview of Yoga Philosophy, Introduction to Ayurveda, Yoga Therapy, Science of Sound and Mantra, Sanskrit Terminology, How to Begin Teaching, and others, along with sixty-five hours of electives that may be chosen from such offerings as Aromatherapy, Herbology, Vedic Astrology, Diet and Nutrition, Buddhist Meditation Forms, Overview of Eastern Religions, Bhagavad Gita, Yoga Research, Yoga for Common Ailments, Yoga for Seniors, Kinesiology and Yoga, and more.

Admission Requirements

The program is open to all students regardless of previous training.

Tuition and Fees

Classes are $10 per hour.

Financial Assistance

Work-study may be available.

Bancroft School of Massage Therapy

50 Franklin Street, Suite 370
Worcester, Massachusetts 01608
Phone: (508) 757-7923
Fax: (508) 791-5930

Henry LaFleur established the Bancroft School of Massage Therapy in 1950. In 1985, the school became the first massage therapy school to be licensed by the Commonwealth of Massachusetts' Department of Education.

Accreditation

Bancroft is accredited by the Accrediting Commission of Career Schools and Colleges of Technology (ACCSCT). The Certificate Program in Massage Therapy is approved by the American Massage

Therapy Association Commission on Massage Training Accreditation/Approval (AMTA/COMTAA), and by the Florida Massage Board. By taking the additional Florida Statutes and Laws course, graduates may seek licensure in Florida.

Program Description

The 752½-hour Certificate Program in Massage Therapy includes classes in Massage Techniques and Theory, Movement and Palpation, Reflexology, Anatomy and Physiology, Sports Massage, Oriental Massage Applications, Internship Program, Clinical Massage Applications, Hydrotherapy, Health (CPR/First Aid), Business Practices/Life Skills, and Seated/On-Site Massage. Classes meet two days or three evenings per week.

Continuing Education

Additional courses that are not part of the certificate program are available for students who wish to further their education. These include Myology, Neurology, Oriental Massage Applications II, and Florida Statutes and Laws.

Admission Requirements

Applicants must be at least 20 years of age (exceptions may be made for those 18 to 20), have a high school diploma or equivalent, submit personal references and a medical history form, have received a professional massage, and interview with the director of the school.

Tuition and Fees

Tuition for the entire program is $9,450, although some courses may also be taken individually. Other costs include: application fee, $50; books and anatomy equipment, $325; uniform, $48; portable massage table, $600; and supplies, $225.

Financial Assistance

A payment plan and federal loans are available.

Blazing Star Herbal School

P.O. Box 6
Shelburne Falls, Massachusetts 01370
Phone: (413) 625-6875

Gail Ulrich, founder and director of the Blazing Star Herbal School, has been an herbalist for over twenty years and has organized the New England Annual Women's Herbal Conference for the past nine years. The school is located on twenty-six wooded acres.

Program Description

The Weekday Apprenticeship Program for beginner and intermediate students meets one day per week for ten months. Instruction is given in Herbal Preparation, Herb Gardening, Ethical Wildcrafting, Herbs for Children, Flower Essences, Study of the Organ Systems, Developing Diagnostic Skills, Chronic Ailments, Herbal First Aid, Natural Cosmetics and Skin Care, Plant Culture and Cultivation, Herbal Business Practices, and more.

The Weekend Apprenticeship Program in Therapeutic Herbalism meets one weekend per month for seven months and is designed for those who are traveling some distance to attend. Course work includes Integration of Traditional and Western Medicine, Classification of Medicinal Plants, Formulation and Preparation of Herbal Medicines, Botanical Terminology, Plant Pharmacology, Sources of Herbal Information, Body Systems and Therapeutics, Herbal Actions, Materia Medica, and Selection Criteria.

A five-day Apprenticeship Intensive is offered to beginning and intermediate students. The course includes Herb Walks and Identification, History of Western Herbalism, Herb Gardening, Herbal Pharmacy, Herbal Preparation, Wildcrafting, Kitchen Cosmetics, Wild Foods Cooking, Herbal First Aid, and Flower Essences.

A variety of one-day and longer workshops are offered throughout New England. These include Herbal First Aid, Planning and Planting Your Herb Garden, Edible and Medicinal Uses of Wild Plants, and many others.

Admission Requirements

There are no minimum age or educational requirements.

Tuition and Fees

The Weekday Apprenticeship program costs

$1,400. The Weekend Apprenticeship Program in Therapeutic Herbalism costs $975, including text. The five-day Apprenticeship Intensive costs $350, including camping. Fees for all programs include written materials.

Financial Assistance

A payment plan is available.

DoveStar Institute

(*See* Multiple State Locations, page 299)

Ellen Evert Hopman

P.O. Box 219
Amherst, Massachusetts 01004
Phone: (413) 323-4494
E-mail: saille333@aol.com

Ellen Evert Hopman, M.Ed., is a psychotherapist, master herbalist, lay homeopath, and vice president of Keltria, the International Druid Fellowship. She has written several books, and has been teaching classes in herbal healing since 1983. Classes are held in Amherst, though Ms. Hopman also travels to conduct workshops.

Program Description

Ms. Hopman offers a four-month Introduction to Herbal Healing and Self-Care Program that meets one night per week. The course includes an introduction to Chinese Five Element theory and basic diagnostics, the art of formula making, Bach and FES flower essences, herbal therapeutics, and preparation of tinctures, salves, infusions, decoctions, poultices, and more. Classes include 400 pages of printed material, slides, case-taking techniques, and hands-on herbalism.

Tuition and Fees

Tuition is $15 per class, and $75 per weekend; cost of the entire program is approximately $325. There is a $25 photocopying fee.

Kripalu Center for Yoga and Health

Box 793
Lenox, Massachusetts 01240
Phone: (413) 448-3152 / (800) 741-7353
Fax: (413) 448-3196

The Kripalu Yoga Ashram was founded by Yogi Amrit Desai in Sumneytown, Pennsylvania in 1972, and moved its center of operation to Shadowbrook, a nineteenth-century, hundred-room mansion in Lenox, Massachusetts, in 1983. Kripalu takes its name from yoga master Swami Kripalvananda; it is founded on the belief that the whole world is one family and that the divine dwells within everyone.

Accreditation

Kripalu is recognized by NBCC as a provider of continuing education credits for national certified counselors.

Program Description

Kripalu offers a wide variety of seminars and workshops in such areas as yoga, self-discovery, spiritual attunement, health and well-being, and bodywork. Introductory workshops include Kripalu Yoga for Beginners; Yoga for a Better Back; Transformation Through Transition; Time-Out for Parents: Retreat, Relief, and Support; Painting from the Source; Opening to Expanded States of Awareness; Raw Juice Fasting; Feel Good Acupressure Workshop; and many others.

Certificate programs include Kripalu Yoga Teacher Training Basic Certification, Phoenix Rising Yoga Therapy Certification Program, Holistic Health Teacher Training, and the Kripalu Bodywork Training month-long certification program.

The month-long Kripalu Yoga Teacher Training Basic Certification includes learning how to teach postures with clarity and to lead students into a heightened sense of body awareness. Topics covered include warm-ups, basic postures and their benefits and contraindications, and anatomy and physiology as applied to yoga, pranayama, relaxation, meditation, and yogic philosophy. It is recommended that students practice yoga regularly for at least six months prior to attending the program.

Phoenix Rising yoga therapy uses classic yoga postures and nondirective dialogue, guided imagery, and visualization to help clients. The certification program consists of three levels of training: Level 1 and Level 2 are each five-day programs; Level 3, required for certification, is a six-month home study course in which students are assigned mentors.

The month-long Holistic Health Teacher Training Program prepares the participant to teach a wide range of workshops in wellness and stress management, including communication and self-expression; body awareness through yoga and movement; relaxation; meditation; learning to play; transforming attitudes about work; conscious eating; and creating a supportive environment and lifestyle.

The 150-hour, month-long Kripalu Bodywork Training Certification Program offers an in-depth experience of Kripalu's unique approach to bodywork. Students learn how to experience and direct their core energy; give full, individualized bodywork sessions with a variety of strokes; practice yoga asanas as a foundation for bodywork; and take the steps to become a licensed bodyworker. The program was designed to benefit beginning and experienced bodywork practitioners, yoga teachers, holistic health practitioners, and others in health-related fields.

Admission Requirements

All programs are open to guests 16 years of age and older. Special programs are available to children and youths.

Tuition and Fees

All programs include room and board; prices vary with the type of accommodation chosen.

Kripalu Yoga Teacher Training costs $2,268 to $4,900. Phoenix Rising Yoga Therapy Certification Levels 1 or 2 cost $695 to $1,155; Levels 1 and 2 combined cost $1,395 to $2,313. Holistic Health Teacher Training costs $2,184 to $4,816. Kripalu Bodywork Training costs $2,184 to $4,816.

Financial Assistance

Partial scholarships are available.

Kushi Institute

P.O. Box 7
Becket, Massachusetts 01223-0007
Phone: (413) 623-5741
Fax: (413) 623-8827
E-mail: kushi@macrobiotics.org

The Kushi Institute was founded in 1979 by Michio and Aveline Kushi. In 1994, the institute and the University of Minnesota were the recipients of a grant from the National Institutes of Health (NIH) for research on the macrobiotic approach to cancer therapy. Mr. Kushi is also the founder of the One Peaceful World Society (see page 355) and the author of several dozen books. The institute sells a variety of books, tapes, and other products (see page 380).

Program Description

The Dynamics of Macrobiotics Program is designed to develop skills in macrobiotic principles and practices, and is offered in a series of 3 one-month progressive levels. Each level is a comprehensive course of study encompassing all of the following subjects: the Art of Macrobiotic Cooking, the Keys to Health Care, the Order of the Universe, the Practice of Shiatsu and Qi-Energy, the Principles of Diagnosis, Traditional Food Processing, and Family Health Forum. The program is also offered in a weekend format in various cities throughout the United States and Canada; call the institute for locations.

The Macrobiotic School of Counseling is a forty-two-week intensive program for developing macrobiotic counseling skills. Topics covered include the macrobiotic perspective on health and illness, macrobiotic diagnosis, macrobiotic recommendations, case histories, and observing consultations. The program is arranged in three-week blocks.

A five-day Teachers' Seminar conducted by Michio and Aveline Kushi is offered to all macrobiotic teachers who have been practicing for at least one year. The seminar includes presentations by selected teachers, discussions, and classes with Michio Kushi.

The Macrobiotic Educators Association (MEA) is

a membership organization of teachers and counselors. Successfully passing a testing program, offered twice yearly at the Kushi Institute, is a prerequisite to becoming a member; for more information contact Bob Ross at the institute or see page 342.

Community Education

The institute offers a variety of introductory weekend and week-long programs, such as the Essentials of Macrobiotic Cooking, Naturally Gourmet, the Way to Health, the Macrobiotic Wellness Weekend, Women's Health, Feng Shui, Losing Weight Naturally, and others.

Tuition and Fees

There is a $100 application fee for week-long programs, a $300 fee for month-long programs; and a $50 fee for weekend programs. Meals cost $6 for breakfast and $12 for lunch, dinner, or Sunday brunch.

Tuition for the Dynamics of Macrobiotics Program is $2,900 per level. Tuition for the Macrobiotic School of Counseling Program is $5,625 per semester. Tuition for the Teachers' Seminar is $275, and accommodation is $175. Tuition for the MEA Counselor Testing or Cooking Testing is $300, plus $275 for accommodations.

Financial Assistance

A discount is given for prepayment of the Dynamics of Macrobiotics Program.

Lesley College

Graduate School
Independent Study Degree Program
29 Everett Street
Cambridge, Massachusetts 02138-2790
Phone: (617) 349-8300
Fax: (617) 349-8313

Lesley College was founded in 1909 and is comprised of four schools: the School of Undergraduate Studies, the Graduate School of Arts and Sciences, the School of Management, and the School of Education.

Accreditation

Lesley College is accredited by the New England Association of Schools and Colleges, Inc.

Program Description

While Lesley does not offer courses in the field of alternative health care per se, their Independent Study Program is designed for graduate students whose field of study is nontraditional or interdisciplinary, or for those who cannot attend course-based, on- or off-campus programs. Students develop their own unique study plan as part of the application process; this plan is to include goals, learning, documentation methods, and ideas for a final project. Learning methods may include tutorials, directed reading, course work at Lesley College or elsewhere, fieldwork, or apprenticeships. Students carry out their graduate studies over a period of one to three years with advisement from a team of three faculty members. Upon completion of the approved study plan, the student is awarded a Master of Arts (M.A.) in independent study, a Master of Education (M.Ed.) in independent study, or a Certificate of Advanced Graduate Study (C.A.G.S.) in independent study.

Admission Requirements

Students applying to the M.A. and M.Ed. programs are expected to have an undergraduate degree; students applying to the C.A.G.S. program must hold a master's degree and have professional experience in their fields. Applicants must develop a study plan and complete the application process.

Tuition and Fees

Tuition is $395 per credit; there is a $45 application fee, and books and supplies are additional.

Financial Assistance

Discounts are given to alumni and senior citizens; payment plans, federal loans, and TERI Professional Education Plan loans are available.

Massage Institute of New England

439 Cambridge Street
Cambridge, Massachusetts 02141
Phone: (617) 547-6554

The Massage Institute of New England (MINE) was established in 1982, achieved AMTA approval in 1983, and moved to its present location in 1988. Community outreach includes work with AIDS hospice programs and the Boston Marathon.

Accreditation

MINE's Massage Therapy Program is approved by the American Massage Therapy Association Commission on Massage Training Accreditation/Approval (AMTA/COMTAA).

Program Description

The 1,000-plus-hour Professional Massage Therapy Program includes Introduction to Swedish Massage (admissions requirement); Swedish Massage Theory and Technique; Anatomy and Lab; Massage and Movement; Movement Class; Physiology; Massage and Awareness (including zero balancing, aura balancing, and craniosacral therapy); Business, Marketing, and Placement; Clinical Modalities (including hydrotherapy, cryotherapy, thermotherapy, theory of phototherapy, and electrotherapy); Pathology; Putting It All Together; Clinical Practicum and Meetings; and electives (offerings include Sports Massage, Shiatsu, Reflexology, Polarity, Facial Massage, Acupressure, Crystals and Bodywork, AIDS Education, Career Development, Edgar Cayce Remedies, Nutrition, the Art of Meditation, and others).

Day and evening classes are available; part-time registration is available on a space-available basis.

A one-day Introduction to Swedish Massage workshop is offered throughout the year for those considering a career in massage therapy, or those who would like to learn basic techniques for use on family or friends.

Continuing Education

Graduates and other qualified students are eligible to take continuing education courses including the Sports Massage Certificate Program: Beginning Sports Massage, Intermediate Sports Massage; the Orthopedic Series: Advanced Injury and Rehabilitation; Zero Balancing; or any of the electives currently offered.

Admission Requirements

Prospective students must have a high school diploma or equivalent; be physically, emotionally, and academically qualified to practice massage therapy; attend one or more open houses; interview with a school representative; and attend the Introduction to Swedish Massage workshop (persons with prior training may apply for exemption).

Tuition and Fees

Tuition is $8,500, including electives and lab fees. There is a $50 application fee, and books, massage table, supplies, CPR course, and eight professional massages are additional.

The Introduction to Swedish Massage course costs $45, or $85 for two.

Financial Assistance

Payment plans are available.

Muscular Therapy Institute

122 Rindge Avenue
Cambridge, Massachusetts 02140
Phone: (617) 576-1300
Fax: (617) 864-8283

The Muscular Therapy Institute was founded in 1974 by Dr. Ben E. Benjamin, who developed muscular therapy from a synthesis of approaches. The Benjamin System of muscular therapy is a unique combination of treatment, education, and exercise designed to promote health and reduce muscle tension.

Accreditation

The program at the Muscular Therapy Institute is approved by the American Massage Therapy Association Commission on Massage Training Accreditation/Approval (AMTA/COMTAA) and accredited by the Accrediting Council for Continuing Education and Training (ACCET). In Massachusetts, the regulation of the practice of massage is under the jurisdiction of the health department of each city or town; students are encouraged to investigate the laws of the city in which they intend to practice prior to enrolling.

Program Description

The 51.9-credit-hour Intensive Professional Training in Muscular Therapy Program may be completed in either a three-semester/fifteen-month format meeting two days per week, or a four-semester/twenty-month format meeting one-and-a-half days per week. One classroom day in the first semester will be held at a retreat center. Courses include Skills and Dynamics of Therapeutic Relationships, Anatomy, Physiology, Clinical Considerations and Pathology, Muscular Therapy Technique, Sports Massage, Alternative Approaches to Holistic Therapy, Practice Development, Professional Development, the Foundations of Professional Development, and Individual Faculty Coaching Sessions.

Students interested in applying are required to attend an introductory workshop, held about once a month on a Saturday. These workshops include classes in Muscular Therapy Technique, Alignment in Movement, Tension Analysis, Communication Skills, and the opportunity for a private interview with an admissions representative.

Career Nights are free evenings at which prospective students may learn more about the school and about massage as a career.

Admission Requirements

Applicants must be at least 18 years of age, have a high school diploma or equivalent, be in good health and free of communicable diseases, and attend the introductory workshop. In addition, applicants are interviewed and evaluated for their aptitude for working with their hands, working with people in a professional fashion, and for motivation and self-directedness.

Tuition and Fees

The introductory workshop costs $25 to $45, and there is a $100 acceptance fee. Tuition is $12,500. Other costs include: insurance, $30 to $40; Off-Site Intensive, $238; books, approximately $380; massage table, $499; Maniken, $100 to $250; and uniform, $20; linens are additional.

Financial Assistance

Federal and private loans are available, and tuition credit is offered for previous training in massage.

National Institute of Classical Homeopathy

(*See* Multiple State Locations, page 310)

New England Institute for Integrative Acupressure

12 Fruit Street
Northampton, Massachusetts 01060
Phone: (413) 268-0338 / (800) 556-3442
Fax: (413) 268-0339

The New England Institute for Integrative Acupressure no longer offers a certification program in integrative acupressure. Instead, the institute is developing a number of acupressure-related continuing education programs that will be open to nurses, physical therapists, and other health care professionals. These courses are expected to begin as early as Fall 1997. Interested students should contact the institute for specific information.

New England School of Acupuncture

30 Common Street
Watertown, Massachusetts 02172
Phone: (617) 926-1788

The New England School of Acupuncture, founded in 1975 by master acupuncturist James Tin Yau So, is the oldest acupuncture school in the United States. Over 600 practitioners have graduated from the school.

Accreditation

NESA's master's degree and master's-level diploma programs are accredited by the National Accreditation Commission for Schools and Colleges of Acupuncture and Oriental Medicine (NACSCAOM).

Program Description

NESA offers both a master's degree program and a master's-level diploma program. The programs are identical, except the master's degree program requires additional pre- or corequisites in Western basic sciences (see **Admission Requirements,** below).

The three-year master's degree and master's-level diploma programs include 2,092½ hours of required courses, or 2,850 hours, including optional courses.

The first-year curriculum includes Traditional Chinese Medical Theory, Point Location, Materials and Methods of TCM, Cultural Foundations of TCM, Practical Anatomy and Structural Analysis, Counseling Skills and Professional Ethics, Diagnostic Skills of TCM, Biomedical Terminology and Professional Referral, Chinese Language and Medical Terminology, Clinical Assistantship, Clinical Skills of TCM, Studies in Palpatory Diagnosis and Treatment, Introduction to Herbal Medicine, Qigong, Research Design and Evaluation, and others.

Second-year courses include TCM Etiology and Pathology of Disease, Actions and Effects of Points and Channels, Biomedical Pathophysiology, Western Pharmacology, Micro Systems of Acupuncture Treatment, CPR and Standard First Aid, Substance Abuse and Detoxification, and others.

Third-year courses include Clinical Internship, Clinical Seminar, Tui Na, Western Nutrition and Concepts of Biochemistry, Eastern Nutrition, Practice Management, and continuation of topics from prior years.

In general, core courses are held evenings or Saturdays during the first two years; during the third year, classes may be held during the day or on weekends.

A 480-hour, twenty-seven-month Traditional Chinese Herbal Medicine Program may be taken concurrently with the acupuncture program beginning with the third semester. Courses include Introduction to Herbal Medicine, Pharmacopoeia, Formula, Internal Medicine, Assistantship, and Clinical Internship.

Admission Requirements

Applicants must have a bachelor's degree from an accredited institution, or be certified in a medical profession requiring at least the equivalent training. Applicants are expected to have completed course work in general biology (three credits), anatomy and physiology (six credits), and general psychology (three credits). Additional pre- or corequisites for the master's degree program include three-credit courses in each of the following: general chemistry, organic chemistry, biochemistry, general physics, microbiology, and precalculus. All applicants must submit a statement of purpose and three letters of recommendation; an interview is required in most cases.

Tuition and Fees

Tuition is $7,950 for full-time students and $240 per credit for part-time students. Other costs include: malpractice insurance (for clinical interns only), approximately $450 per year; and books and supplies, approximately $1,200 total for three years.

Tuition for the Traditional Chinese Herbal Medicine Program is $775 per semester.

Financial Assistance

A payment plan and federal loans are available.

New England School of Homeopathy

(*See* Multiple State Locations, page 311)

Phoenix Rising Yoga Therapy

(*See* Multiple State Locations, page 315)

Polarity Institute

17 Spring Street
Watertown, Massachusetts 02172
Phone: (617) 924-9150

The Polarity Institute was founded in 1990 by director Douglas Janssen, R.P.P., M.F.A., a polarity and craniosacral practitioner and teacher since 1981. Janssen served on the Board of Directors of the American Polarity Therapy Association from 1989 to 1992.

Accreditation

Both the Level 1 and Level 2 Programs are approved and registered by the American Polarity Therapy Association (APTA). The Polarity Institute is licensed by the Department of Education of the Commonwealth of Massachusetts.

Program Description

The Polarity Institute offers both Level 1 (A.P.P.) and Level 2 (R.P.P.) Certification Programs.

The Level 1 Registered Polarity Practitioner Training, Part 1 (also A.P.P.) consists of 170 hours of instruction divided into five classes: Theory and Practice of Polarity (seventy-four hours), Energetic Nutrition and Exercises (twelve hours), Introduction to Anatomy and Physiology (twelve hours), Energetic Evaluation and Integration and Building Your Polarity Practice (eleven hours), and Basic Communications and Clinical Supervision (fifty-one hours). To graduate, students must successfully complete all classes; give thirty documented one-hour polarity sessions; receive 10 one-hour polarity sessions from three Registered Polarity Practitioners; pass three out of four competency examinations; comply with all rules and regulations of the school; have valid CPR/First Aid certification; have all tuition and fees paid in full; and select an approved R.P.P. to serve as a postgraduate supervisor for private practice for a period of one year after graduation.

The Level 2 Registered Polarity Practitioner Training, Part 2 consists of 530 hours in addition to Level 1. Classes include Integrating Theory and Practice of Polarity (thirty-five hours); Polarity Body Systems and Structural Alignment (102 hours); Orthodox Anatomy and Physiology (one hundred hours); Energetic Theory and Evaluation Skills (twenty-eight hours); Polarity Communication and Facilitation Skills (thirty hours); Energetic Nutrition and Exercises (forty hours); Practice Management, Promotion, Ethics, and Law (thirty-five hours); Clinical Supervision and Internship (115 hours); and Energetic Components of Personality (twenty-five hours). To graduate, students must successfully complete all classes; give seventy documented one-hour polarity sessions; receive 20 one-hour polarity sessions from three Registered Polarity Practitioners; pass three out of four competency evaluations; comply with all rules and regulations of the school; have valid CPR/First Aid certification; have all tuition and fees paid in full; and select an approved R.P.P. to serve as a postgraduate supervisor for private practice for a period of one year after graduation.

Admission Requirements

Level 1 applicants must be at least 18 years of age; have a high school diploma or equivalent; agree to not use drugs, alcohol, or cigarettes during the training weekends; provide a list of all medications and dosages at time of application and throughout the program; and if under the care of a physician, psychiatrist, or counselor at the time of application, a letter from that health care provider stating the applicant's ability to participate in the program. Applicants must also submit two letters of recommendation, a photograph, and answers to essay questions. Level 2 applicants must also have completed the Level 1 training (or the equivalent from another school).

Tuition and Fees

Tuition for Level 1 is $1,350. Other costs include: application fee, $50; student liability insurance, $40; ten sessions received, approximately $400; and books and handouts, approximately $40 to $165.

Tuition for Level 2 is $4,840. Other costs include: application fee, $50; student liability insurance, $50; twenty sessions received, approximately $800; and books and handouts, approximately $185.

Financial Assistance

Work-study positions are available.

Polarity Realization Institute

(*See* Multiple State Locations, page 316)

The School for Body-Mind Centering

(*See* Multiple State Locations, page 317)

Stillpoint Center School of Massage

P.O. Box 15
60 Main Street
Hatfield, Massachusetts 01039
Phone: (413) 247-9322
Fax: (413) 247-9474

Founded in 1981, the Stillpoint Center School of Massage is located in Hatfield, a picturesque rural community in the heart of the Pioneer Valley of Western Massachusetts.

Accreditation

Stillpoint's Massage Therapy Certification Program is approved by the American Massage Therapy Association Commission on Massage Training Accreditation/Approval (AMTA/COMTAA), licensed by the Massachusetts Department of Education, and is currently pursuing national accreditation through the Accrediting Commission of Career Schools and Colleges of Technology (ACCSCT).

Program Description

The 916-hour Massage Therapy Certification Program is guided by three interrelated principles: Holism, Massage with Awareness, and Compassionate Action. The curriculum includes courses in Anatomy, Physiology, Myology, Swedish Massage, Professional Development, Pathology, Kinesiology, Hydrotherapy, Sports Massage and Professional Worklife, either a shiatsu or polarity therapy elective, on-site massage clinics, and a clinical practicum that places students in hospitals and nursing homes.

Optional courses include Advanced Hydrotherapy (thirty-eight hours) for New Hampshire state licensing, and Advanced Shiatsu and Neurology for New York State licensing.

Full-time day and part-time day and evening programs are offered.

Community and Continuing Education

Workshops are offered on a variety of topics including basic massage, craniosacral therapy, reflexology, equine massage, Thai yoga massage, and others.

Admission Requirements

Applicants must be at least 21 years of age (mature individuals between 18 and 21 may be considered) and have a high school diploma or equivalent.

Tuition and Fees

Tuition is $7,800; optional New York and New Hampshire licensing courses are additional. There is a $65 application fee, and books, supplies, and massage table are approximately $1,400.

Continuing education courses cost $45 to $400.

Financial Assistance

A payment plan is available, as well as Nellie Mae EXCEL Family Education Loans; call (800) 634-9308.

MICHIGAN

The Center for Reiki Training

29209 Northwestern Highway #592
Southfield, Michigan 48034
Phone: (810) 948-8112
Fax: (810) 948-9534

Certification Office:
3509 West Dogwood Circle
LaGrange, Kentucky 40031-9310

The Center for Reiki Training was founded in 1988 by William L. Radd.

Program Description

The Teacher Certification Program is an advanced course for Reiki Masters who wish to teach the programs offered by the Center for Reiki Training and to become Center Certified Teachers.

The program is self-paced; at least one year is suggested for completion. Requirements include sending a letter of intent to the certification office; trusting the reiki energy to provide the perfect healing result; actively working on one's own healing; working to fully express the reiki principles and the center's philosophy and purpose; agreeing to teach the minimum subjects required for each class and using the center manuals; taking Reiki I and II, ART, and Reiki III from a Center Certified Teacher twice; practicing reiki for one year or more before enrolling in the program; providing proof of doing fifty or more complete reiki treatments; passing a written test; writing a paper on the reiki subject of your choice; co-teaching a Reiki I and II class with another Center Certified Teacher; and paying an annual membership fee of $100 to the center.

Reiki I and II are taught together during a weekend intensive. Topics covered include reiki hand positions and giving a complete reiki treatment, the Reiki II symbols and how to use them, using reiki for specific conditions, and distant healing, scanning, and beaming.

Advanced Reiki Training (ART) is a one-day intensive that includes the Usui Master attunement, the Usui Master symbol, reiki meditation, advanced techniques to achieve goals, using reiki to protect yourself and others, using crystals and stones with reiki, reiki psychic surgery, guided meditation, and more.

Reiki III/Master is a two-day intensive that includes the complete Reiki III Usui/Tibetan Master attunement, instruction in giving all attunements, the healing attunement, two Tibetan symbols, advanced reiki meditation, and the values and spiritual orientation of a Reiki Master.

A three-day, weekend Karuna Reiki Class is offered to those who have completed Reiki Master Training. Reiki, guided meditation, NLP, past life regression, and other techniques are used to heal blocks to developing a thriving reiki practice. Connections are strengthened to guides, angels, ascended masters, and higher self. The class is complete with two levels, two attunements, three master symbols, and nine treatment symbols. Those completing the course will be able to teach all four levels of Karuna Reiki (two practitioner levels and two master levels).

Tuition and Fees

The Reiki I and II courses cost $300. The Advanced Reiki Training (ART) course costs $200. The Reiki III/Master course costs $600.

The Karuna Reiki course costs $800. Prices may vary with the instructor.

Health Enrichment Center

(*See* Multiple State Locations, page 303)

Infinity Institute International, Inc.

4110 Edgeland, Suite 800
Royal Oak, Michigan 48073-2285
Phone: (810) 549-5594

Anne Harriman Spencer, Ph.D., founded both the Infinity Institute International (in 1980) and the International Medical and Dental Hypnotherapy Association (in 1987), a referral service for certified hypnotherapists to health care providers and the general public.

Accreditation

There is no formal licensing for hypnotherapists at this time. Infinity Institute International has been granted course approval by the State of Michigan Board of Higher Education, and graduates are eligible to apply for certification with the International Medical and Dental Hypnotherapy Association.

Program Description

Courses are offered in Basic Hypnosis, Advanced Hypnosis, and Hypnoanalysis. Courses are given on two weekends and include directed independent study as well as classroom instruction.

The forty-hour Basic Hypnosis Course covers the History of Hypnosis, Suggestibility Testing, Group Participation and Practice, Principles of Suggestion, Relaxation/Stress Management, Induction Methods, Guided Mental Imagery, Group Hypnosis, Weight Loss, Stop Smoking, Self-Hypnosis, Setting Up a Practice, and more.

The forty-hour Advanced Hypnosis Course includes Advanced Methods, Rapid Inductions, Age Regression, Hypnotherapy, Dreams and Meaning, Visual Hallucination, Medical/Dental Hypnosis, Group Participation and Practice, Waking Hypnosis, Hickman Method, Amnesia and Surgery, Somnambulism, Post-Hypnotic Suggestion, and more.

In the forty-hour Hypnoanalysis Course, topics covered include Fundamentals of Hypnoanalysis, Basic Communication Type, Initial Comprehensive Intake, Word Association and Dream Analysis in Hypnosis, Spiritual Cleansing/Healing, Techniques for Release of Negative Energy, Regression Therapy, and more.

Admission Requirements

Applicants must be at least 18 years of age and have a high school diploma.

Tuition and Fees

Tuition for the Basic Hypnosis Program is $570; for the Advanced Hypnosis Program, $570; and for the Hypnoanalysis Program, $570.

Financial Assistance

Limited scholarships are available and a discount is given for prepayment.

Kalamazoo Center for the Healing Arts

3715 West Main Street, Number 3
Kalamazoo, Michigan 49006-2842
Phone: (616) 373-1000
E-mail: kchands@aol.com

Kalamazoo Center for the Healing Arts (KCHA) was founded in 1986; the school's program was started and state-licensed in 1993. KCHA is also a health care center offering private bodywork sessions, a store, and a variety of other services and classes.

Accreditation

In 1996, KCHA was accredited by the International Massage and Somatic Therapies Accreditation Council (IMSTAC), a division of the Associated Bodywork and Massage Professionals (ABMP).

Program Description

The 120-hour Basic Massage Program covers Anatomy (including names, locations, and functions of organs; the digestive, circulatory, lymphatic, skeletal, and nervous systems; and muscles); Range of Motion; Introduction to Acupressure; and Specific Techniques for Hips, Pelvic Region, Shoulders, Legs, Head, Arms, and Diaphragm Release.

The Professional Training Program provides an additional 400 hours of training in Integrated Bodywork Therapies (including myofascial release, craniosacral therapy, polarity, and related concepts), Acupressure, Advanced Anatomy, The Business of Being a Bodyworker, and one hundred hours of practicum (forty lab hours, thirty on-site hours, and thirty hours of seminars).

Admission Requirements

Basic Massage Program applicants must be at least 18 years of age or have the consent of the director of services, and complete a student contract. Professional Training Program applicants must have completed the Basic Massage Program, obtain the consent of the director of services, and complete the student contract.

Tuition and Fees

There is a $25 application fee for both courses.

Tuition for the Basic Massage Program is $1,100; pillow, towel, colored markers, and book are additional.

Tuition for the Professional Training Program is

$3,140; transportation to on-site and/or field trip locations, books, lab fee, and massage table are additional.

Financial Assistance

Payment plans are available for the Professional Training Program only.

Lansing Community College

400-600 North Washington Square
P.O. Box 40010
Lansing, Michigan 48901-7210
Phone: (517) 483-1410 (Human, Health,
and Public Service) /
(517) 483-1200 (admissions)
E-mail: mc1431@lois.lansing.cc.mi.us

Lansing Community College (LCC), founded in 1957, is one of the largest community colleges in the country, and offers over 150 degree and certificate programs, including a certificate program in massage therapy.

Accreditation

LCC is accredited by the North Central Association of Schools and Colleges.

Program Description

The Massage Therapy Certificate of Completion Program consists of twenty-five credits of required courses and two credits of limited choice requirements. Required courses include Introductory Anatomy and Physiology, Massage Therapy: Beginning, Massage Therapy: Intermediate, Independent Study Massage Practicum (consisting of one hundred hours of massage work, reading, and a report), Human Structural Dynamics for Massage Therapy, Touch for Health, Polarity Therapy I, Business Applications for Massage Therapists, Clinical Approaches to Therapeutic Massage, Sports Massage Techniques, Healthy Lifestyles, and Stress Management. Students must complete two credits chosen from Polarity Therapy II, Nutrition: Critical Issues, Self-Awareness: Key to Wellness, and the Consumer and Health Issues.

Admission Requirements

Applicants must be at least 18 years of age and have a high school diploma. Those who are under 18, enrolled in high school, and working to fulfill high school requirements may be admitted under the Dual Enrollment or Special Admission Programs.

Tuition and Fees

Tuition per credit hour is $43 for residents, $72 for nonresidents, and $101 for out-of-state or international students. There is a $10 application fee, and a registration fee of $20 per semester.

Financial Assistance

Financial assistance is available in the forms of scholarships, grants, loans, employment, and special situation funds.

Michigan Institute of Myomassology

School of Therapeutic Bodywork
25711 Southfield Road, Suite 101
Southfield, Michigan 46075-1881
Phone: (810) 443-1669
Fax: (810) 443-8906

The Michigan Institute of Myomassology was founded in 1993 by Thomas H. King, a practicing Yogi since 1966 and a Hatha yoga instructor since 1969. King was one of the founders and directors of the Myomassethics Center, which formerly operated at the same location as the Michigan Institute of Myomassology.

Accreditation

The Michigan Institute of Myomassology is certified by the International Myomassethics Federation (IMF).

Program Description

The forty-one-week, 500-hour Myomassology Program covers such topics as Scientific and Therapeutic Myomassology, Anatomy, Craniology, Resistive Movements, Strain/Counter Strain, Reflexology, Energy Balancing, Deep Tissue Massage, Compression, Face Massage, Paraffin Therapy,

Hydrotherapy, Modified Massage, Business Procedures, Sanitary Practice, and Massage Ethics. A total of 168 hours of electives may be chosen in such areas as Sports Massage, Shiatsu, Polarity, Touch for Health, One Brain, Physical Therapy Techniques, Prenatal and Infant Massage, Myofascial Release, Herbs, Nutrition, Iridology, Labor Massage, CPR, Aromatherapy, Therapeutic Touch, Colon Health, Neurolinguistic Programming, Alexander Technique, and others. Additional requirements include a research thesis, journal/summary, clinical experience, anatomy coloring book, and special credit earned through volunteer work and attending related events. Classes meet one day per week for four hours.

Admission Requirements

Generally, applicants must be at least 17 years of age and have a high school diploma or equivalent; however, some exceptions may be made. It is helpful, though not required, for the student to have a basic understanding of human anatomy and physiology.

Tuition and Fees

A deposit of $300 is due with the application; the total tuition cost is $2,500 to $2,630, including teaching manual, handouts, and oils. Books, supplies, and massage table are additional.

Financial Assistance

Tuition is payable in two-week intervals.

MINNESOTA

Minnesota Institute of Acupuncture and Herbal Studies

1821 University Avenue, 278-S
St. Paul, Minnesota 55104
Phone: (612) 603-0994
E-mail: miahs@millcomm.com

The Minnesota Institute of Acupuncture and Herbal Studies was founded in 1990.

Accreditation

MIAHS has been granted candidate status with the National Accreditation Commission for Schools and Colleges of Acupuncture and Oriental Medicine (NACSCAOM).

Program Description

The 2,400-hour Oriental Medical Program may be completed in four years. The program requires a minimum of 1,588 classroom hours, 606 clinical hours, and 150 hours of observation, and provides comprehensive education and training in Traditional Oriental Medical Concepts (physiology, pathology, diagnostics, energetics, and treatment principles); Acupuncture Principles and Skills; Tui Na; Traditional Chinese Herbalism; Western Medical Concepts; Chinese Culture and Philosophical Foundations of Oriental Medicine; Related Chinese Studies (tai chi chuan, qigong, and introductory language skills); Holistic Skills (counseling, nutrition, communication skills, bodywork, touch, and subtle energy therapies); and Chemical Dependency Treatment Through Acupuncture.

The 1,800-hour Professional Acupuncture Program is similar to the Oriental Medicine Program but does not include herbal studies. The program may be completed in three years plus one quarter; clinical requirements are 510 hours of supervised practice and 150 hours of observation.

Admission Requirements

Applicants to either program must have completed at least two years of college-level education at an accredited school, submit two letters of recommendation and a personal essay, and interview with an admissions representative.

Tuition and Fees

Tuition is $9.75 per contact hour. Other costs include: application fee, $40; registration fee, $10 per course; and books, approximately $200 to $300 per year; tuition, books, and other fees can be estimated at about $6,000 for the first year for full-time students. Total costs vary from year to year based on the number of hours for which a student registers.

Financial Assistance

State of Minnesota loans and work-study are available. Students who do not hold a bachelor's degree may be eligible for state grants based on financial need.

Northern Lights School of Massage Therapy

1313 S.E. Fifth Street, Suite 202
Minneapolis, Minnesota 55414
Phone: (612) 379-3822

Northern Lights School of Massage Therapy was founded in 1985.

Accreditation

The Northern Lights curriculum is approved by the American Massage Therapy Association Commission on Massage Training Accreditation/Approval (AMTA/COMTAA).

Program Description

The Massage Therapy Training Program consists of 600 hours taught in twelve months, plus fifty-five hours out of class. Courses include Orientation, Massage Therapy Techniques, Anatomy and Physiology, Clinical Applications of Massage Therapy and Pathology, Business and Practice Management, Communication and Client Management, First Aid/CPR, Out-of-Class Practice, and Professional Massage. Students are asked to receive one professional massage therapy treatment per term.

Community Education

A two-day weekend Basic Massage Therapy Techniques Workshop provides an introduction to massage for interested laypersons or potential students.

Admission Requirements

Students must be at least 18 years of age, have a high school diploma or equivalent, submit three let-

ters of recommendation and a physical examination form, be physically able to perform the manipulations of massage therapy, and interview with a director or instructor.

Tuition and Fees

Tuition is $4,500. Other costs include: application fee, $50; linen service, $105; books, $250 to $325; massage table, $400 to $700; professional massage treatments, $90 to $120; and AMTA student membership, $158 to $188.

The Basic Massage Therapy Techniques Workshop costs $105.

Financial Assistance

Payment plans are available.

Northwestern College of Chiropractic

2501 West 84th Street
Minneapolis, Minnesota 55431
Phone: (612) 888-4777
Fax: (612) 888-6713
E-mail: admit@nwchiro.edu

Northwestern College of Chiropractic was founded in 1941. It was among the first colleges to adopt the seven-year academic program, several years before it was required by the Council on Chiropractic Education (CCE). The twenty-five-acre campus was purchased in 1983.

Accreditation

Northwestern is accredited by the Commission on Accreditation of the Council on Chiropractic Education (CCE), and by the Commission on Institutions of Higher Education of the North Central Association of Colleges and Schools. Graduates with a Doctor of Chiropractic (D.C.) degree are eligible for examination before licensing boards in fifty states and all foreign countries; some states or countries may impose requirements in addition to a D.C. degree.

Program Description

The Doctor of Chiropractic (D.C.) curriculum consists of five academic years of chiropractic college instruction; each academic year is composed of two 15-week trimesters (Northwestern offers three trimesters: fall, winter, and summer). A twelve-month public clinic internship and preceptorship constitutes the last three trimesters.

The required curriculum for the D.C. degree consists of 4,380 contact hours of study, exclusive of electives. A Bachelor of Science degree in human biology is granted to candidates who have completed the equivalent of 133½ trimester credits by fulfilling specific requirements; see the catalog for more information.

The first year includes courses in Biochemistry, Gross Anatomy, Embryology, Histology, Skeletal Radiology, Professional Issues, Universal Precautions, Principles and Philosophy, Introduction to Chiropractic, Spine and Pelvis, Physiology, Peripheral Nervous System, and Chiropractic Methods.

The second year covers Physiology, Biology, Central Nervous System, Pathology, Skeletal Radiology, Physical Diagnosis, Critical Thinking, Chiropractic Methods, Neuromusculoskeletal, Principles and Philosophy, Microbiology, CNS-Neurodiagnosis, and Critical Appraisal of Scientific Literature.

The third year includes courses in Skeletal Radiology, EENT, Clinical Laboratory Interpretation, Infectious Disease, Community Health, Chiropractic Methods, Physiological Therapeutics, Clinical Nutrition, Neuromusculoskeletal, Patient Interviewing, Introduction to Clinical Chiropractic, Radiation Physics and Safety, Radiology of the Abdomen and Chest, Respiratory System, Cardiovascular System, Gastrointestinal System, Genitourinary System, Clinic Internship, and Principles and Philosophy.

The fourth year covers Radiographic Technology and Positioning, Gynecology, Endocrinology, Dermatology, Obstetrics, Emergency Procedures, Pharmacology and Toxicology, Mental Health, Chiropractic Methods, Physiological Therapeutics, Clinical Nutrition, Clinic Internship, Pediatrics, Geriatrics, Clinical Case Studies, and Northwestern Clinical Practice.

The final year consists of Clinic Internship, Clinical Case Studies, Practice Management, and Legal Aspects of Chiropractic Practice.

A two-year Associate in Applied Science degree program for the chiropractic paraprofessional is a cooperative program developed by the college and Normandale Community College. Classes are offered each term on both campuses. Chiropractic-related courses include Introduction to Chiropractic, Patient Relations, Professionalism and Boundaries, Patient Education, Employment Issues, Clinic Safety and Quality Controls, Chiropractic Office Procedures I and II, Computer Applications in Chiropractic, Human Physiology, Physical Examination Procedures, Introduction to Insurance, Advanced Topics in Insurance, Legal Issues, Advanced Computer Skills, Office Accounting, Outcomes Assessment in the Clinic, Public Relations/Marketing for a Clinic, Laboratory Examination Procedures, Nutritional Counseling, Physiotherapy Modalities, Radiation and Radiation Safety, X-Ray Technology, X-Ray Positioning for Chiropractic, and Massage I and II.

Continuing Education

The postgraduate department sponsors more than 150 continuing education seminars each academic year, including topics in radiology, orthopedics, neurology, sports injuries, family practice, rehabilitation, and occupational health. These courses may also fulfill relicensure requirements set by the State Board of Chiropractic Examiners.

Admission Requirements

Applicants for the Doctor of Chiropractic degree must have completed at least two academic years (sixty semester hours) of college credit acceptable toward a bachelor's degree. Prechiropractic courses must be completed at a regionally accredited institution. Specific course requirements include biology and/or zoology with lab (six semester hours), general or inorganic chemistry with lab (six semester hours), organic chemistry with lab (six semester hours), physics with lab (six semester hours), psychology (three semester hours), English or communication skills (six semester hours), humanities or social sciences (fifteen semester hours), and electives (twelve semester hours). All of these courses must have been passed with a grade of C or better. Applicants must have earned a cumulative G.P.A. of at least 2.5 and a science G.P.A. of at least 2.0. Applicants must also possess the strength, coordination, manual dexterity, and visual, hearing, and tactile senses (compensated if necessary) to perform all required aspects of diagnosis and treatment, and must submit three character references or letters of recommendation.

Applicants to the Associate in Applied Science Program must have a high school diploma or GED and submit immunization records and an essay.

Tuition and Fees

Tuition for the Doctor of Chiropractic Program is $4,800 per semester. Other costs include: application fee, $50; lab fee, $50 per lab; elective courses, $200 per credit hour; activity fee, $35 per trimester; health service fee, $10 per trimester (trimesters one through seven); graduation fee, $135; split schedule/part time schedule fee, $300; B.S. degree diploma and registration fee, $200; and books and supplies, approximately $3,600 for the four-year period.

Tuition for the Associate of Applied Science Degree Program is $125 per credit; there is a student activity fee of $20 per term.

Financial Assistance

Available financial assistance includes federal grants, loans, and work-study; state grants; Chiroloans; Worldwide Grants; scholarships; and private loans.

Northwestern School of Homeopathy

10700 Old County Road #15, Suite 350
Plymouth, Minnesota 55441
Phone: (612) 794-6445
Fax: (612) 593-0097
E-mail: remedy@mnn.net

The Northwestern Academy of Homeopathy was founded in 1994. The school's four core faculty members have years of clinical practice and teaching experience; they are all registered with the North American Society of Homeopaths (NASH).

Accreditation

Schools of homeopathy must have been in existence for three years in order to be accredited by the Council on Homeopathic Education (CHE). The academy has applied for accreditation and expects to receive it at the end of 1997.

Program Description

The Northwestern Academy of Homeopathy provides a three-year, 1,152-hour course of professional training designed to meet the guidelines of the International Council of Homeopathy.

The curriculum in Year One provides a basic foundation in homeopathic philosophy, an introduction to the repertory, case taking, case analysis, materia medica or major homeopathic remedies, and lectures on homeopathic treatment for basic acute conditions. Year Two continues with advanced training in materia medica, plus case management, computer software, and treatment of acute conditions, and begins clinical training with video and observation of live cases. Year Three is largely clinical, with students taking their own cases by the end of the year.

Admission Requirements

The course is open to all dedicated students with a variety of backgrounds. For those who are already licensed health care practitioners, there are no other prerequisites. Others will need to take one semester of the following college level courses in order to complete the class: anatomy, physiology, psychology, microbiology, medical terminology, biology, and chemistry. A first aid course such as the Red Cross EMT training is also required. Certain prerequisites may be waived based on occupational training.

Tuition and Fees

Tuition is $4,600 per year.

Financial Assistance

Payment plans are available.

MISSOURI

Cleveland Chiropractic College

Kansas City Campus
6401 Rockhill Road
Kansas City, Missouri 64131-1181
Phone: (816) 333-8230 / (800) 467-CCKC

Cleveland Chiropractic College of Kansas City was founded in 1922 by Dr. C.S. Cleveland Sr., Dr. Ruth R. Cleveland, and Dr. Perl B. Griffin. In 1992, the college joined with its sister school, Cleveland Chiropractic College of Los Angeles (see page 77), to form a multi-campus system. Though unified in governance and administrative function, each college operates independently with academic and instructional autonomy.

Accreditation

Cleveland Chiropractic College is accredited by the Council on Chiropractic Education (CCE) and the North Central Association of Colleges and Schools.

Program Description

The 4,400-clock-hour, twelve-trimester (forty-eight month) Doctor of Chiropractic (D.C.) degree may be completed in as little as nine trimesters (thirty-six months). The core program is divided among the Departments of Anatomy; Physiology and Chemistry; Pathology, Microbiology, and Public Health; Diagnosis; Radiology; Principles and Practice; Physiotherapy; and Clinic.

Students may earn a bachelor's degree in human biology independently of the Doctor of Chiropractic degree or as they work toward completion of the D.C. degree.

The Preprofessional Health Science Program offers required prerequisite courses that meet requirements for both the bachelor's and Doctor of Chiropractic degrees. Courses are offered in eight-week modules and include General Chemistry I and II, Organic Chemistry I and II, General Physics I and II, Anatomy and Physiology, and General Biology.

Continuing Education

The Postgraduate and Related Professional Education Program provides the practicing Doctor of Chiropractic with continuing education in areas of special interest.

Admission Requirements

Applicants for the Doctor of Chiropractic degree program must have completed at least two academic years (sixty semester hours) of undergraduate work leading to a baccalaureate degree at an accredited college or university, and must have earned a minimum G.P.A. of 2.5; students may be considered for acceptance with a minimum G.P.A. of 2.25 or better if other factors are strong. Specific hours of course work in such subjects as biology, inorganic chemistry, organic chemistry, physics, English composition/communication, psychology, and humanities/social sciences are also required. Applicants must submit two letters of recommendation (one from a health care professional).

Applicants for the bachelor's degree in human biology must first complete sixty credit hours from an accredited postsecondary institution, including six hours each in biology, inorganic chemistry, organic chemistry, and physics. (These courses may be taken on campus in the Preprofessional Health Science Program.)

Tuition and Fees

Tuition is $156 per weekly clock hour (for example, tuition for the first trimester on the twelve-trimester program is $3,588; for the first trimester on the nine-trimester program, $4,836). Other costs include: application fee, $50; student activity fee, $67 per trimester; and books and supplies, $280 to $350 per trimester. Dormitory rooms for single students are available at University of Missouri-Kansas City.

Financial Assistance

Federal and private scholarships, grants, loans, and work-study are available.

Logan College of Chiropractic

1851 Schoettler Road
P.O. Box 1065
Chesterfield, Missouri 63006-1065
Phone: (314) 227-2100 / (800) 782-3344 /
(800) 533-9210 (admissions)
Fax: (314) 207-2424
E-mail: logonadm@logan.edu

Logan College of Chiropractic, named for founder
Hugh B. Logan, D.C., enrolled its first class in
1935. In 1973, the college moved to its current
wooded hilltop location.

Accreditation

Logan College is accredited by the Commission on
Accreditation of the Council on Chiropractic Education (CCE) and the Commission of Institutions of
Higher Education of the North Central Association
of Colleges and Schools.

Program Description

The 5,340-hour, ten-trimester Doctor of Chiropractic degree program includes courses from the Departments of Chiropractic; Anatomy; Biology, Physiology, and Chemistry; Pathology and Microbiology;
Diagnosis: Physical, Clinical, and Laboratory; Diagnostic Imaging; Health Center Education; and
Research.

The Chiropractic Paraprofessional Program
consists of 214 classroom hours that include six
modules: Anatomy and Physiology, Basic X-Ray
Proficiency, Clinical Training, General Office Procedures, Laboratory Procedures, and Physiological
Therapeutics.

Students who have earned at least sixty semester units from an accredited college or university
may earn a Bachelor of Science degree in human
biology by completing all course work through the
fourth trimester of the Doctor of Chiropractic degree curriculum.

Continuing Education

Postdoctoral educational programs include Resi-
dency Programs in Chiropractic Diagnostic Imaging (three years) and Chiropractic Family Practice
(two years); Diplomate Programs in Chiropractic
Neurology (DACNB), Chiropractic Orthopedics
(DABCO), and Sports Injuries and Physical Fitness
(DABCSP); and Certification Programs in Acupunc-
ture/Acupressure/Meridian Therapy, Certified Chiropractic Sports Physician (CCSP), Chiropractic
Utilization Review/Quality Assessment Consultant,
Impairment Rating, Manipulation Under Anesthesia
(MUA), Physiologic Therapeutics, and Skeletal Radiology. Other continuing education seminars are
also offered to Doctors of Chiropractic.

Admission Requirements

Applicants must have completed sixty semester
hours leading to a bachelor's degree at an accredited college or university with a cumulative G.P.A.
of 2.25 or better; specific hours in language and/or
communications, psychology, social sciences or
humanities, biological science, general and organic chemistry, and physics are required. Applicants
must submit a recommendation from a licensed
Doctor of Chiropractic, three references, and a personal essay, and interview with an admissions representative.

Tuition and Fees

Tuition for the D.C. and B.S. degree programs is
$4,375 per trimester. There is a $35 application fee
for the D.C. program, a $15 application fee for the
B.S. program, and an activity fee of $25 per tri-
mester. Books cost approximately $600 per year.

Financial Assistance

Scholarships; loans; and federal grants, loans, and
work-study are available.

Massage Therapy Training Institute L.L.C.

9140 Ward Parkway, Suite 100
Kansas City, Missouri 64114
Phone: (816) 523-9140

The Massage Therapy Training Institute (MTTI)
was founded in 1988 and is Missouri's first and

Kansas City's only massage school certified to operate by the Missouri Coordinating Board for Higher Education.

Accreditation

MTTI is the only massage school in Missouri or Kansas accredited by the International Massage and Somatic Therapies Accreditation Council (IMSTAC), a division of the Associated Bodywork and Massage Professional (ABMP). Graduates of the 500-hour program are eligible to take the national certification exam administered by the National Certification Board for Therapeutic Massage and Bodywork (NCBTMB). MTTI is approved by NCBTMB as a continuing education provider.

Licensing requirements in Missouri and Kansas vary by city; each prospective student should check with the city where he or she intends to practice for specific requirements. There are no licensing requirements for personal trainers or energy therapy practitioners.

Program Description

The 500-hour Massage Therapy Practitioner Program includes courses in Basic Swedish Massage, Anatomy and Physiology, Sports Massage, Reflexology, Shiatsu or Chinese Meridian Therapy, Creating a Successful Practice, Creating Clarity in Bodywork: Defining Sexuality and Ethical Issues, Advanced Massage, Therapeutic Touch, Myofascial Release Massage, CPR/First Aid, Power of Touch, Introduction to Vibrational Healing, Pathophysiology, Tai Chi, and approximately one hundred hours of electives. On average, students complete the program in eighteen months by attending classes two evenings per week and one weekend per month; a more accelerated or extended pace is possible.

The 300-hour Personal Trainer/Wellness Consultant Program combines counseling skills with competency in fitness training, nutritional consulting, stress management facilitation, environmental awareness, and lifestyle assessment skills. Courses include Personal Trainer Training and Wellness Consultant I and II.

A 200-hour Energy Therapy Program includes Introduction to Vibrational Healing, Vibrational Healing I and II, Craniosacral Balancing, Therapeutic Touch, Flower Essence Therapy, Color Therapy, Polarity Therapy, Music and Healing, Creating Clarity in Bodywork: Defining Sexuality and Ethical Issues, and Creating a Successful Practice.

All courses may be taken individually, providing the student meets the prerequisites for the course.

Continuing Education

Many MTTI courses are eligible for continuing education credit for massage therapists, nurses, licensed counselors, and other health professionals.

Admission Requirements

Applicants must be at least 18 years of age; have a high school diploma or equivalent; and be physically, mentally, and emotionally capable of performing the work. Applicants must submit two letters of recommendation and interview with an admissions representative.

Tuition and Fees

Tuition for the Massage Therapy Practitioner Program is $5,500; books cost approximately $300.

Tuition for the Personal Trainer/Wellness Consultant Program is $3,000; books are approximately $150.

Tuition for the Energy Therapy Program is $2,200; books are approximately $80.

Other costs include: application fee, $50; massage table, $400 to $600; oil and linens are additional.

Financial Assistance

Payment plans are available and a discount is given for early payment.

MONTANA

Asten Center of Natural Therapeutics

(*See* Multiple State Locations, page 297)

Rocky Mountain Herbal Institute

P.O. Box 579
Hot Springs, Montana 59845
Phone: (406) 741-3811

Rocky Mountain Herbal Institute (RMHI) was founded in 1987 by Roger W. Wicke, Ph.D., a graduate of the American College of Traditional Chinese Medicine. The school began as the Colorado Herbal Institute and moved to Montana in 1991. Thirty-four graduates have completed the one-year training program; the majority of these were licensed health professionals.

Program Description

The one-year Chinese Herbal Sciences Training Program qualifies the student to develop herbal formulas tailored to individual needs. The program is offered to professionals and serious students unable to relocate for full-time study, and consists of three 6-day residential intensives in Hot Springs, each preceded by reading and homework assignments completed through correspondence. Study and homework time is estimated at fifteen to twenty hours per week. Topics covered include Traditional Chinese Health Assessment Methods (tongue inspection, pulse palpation, abdominal palpation, and body characteristics); TCM Herbal Pharmacopoeia; Tailoring Herbal Formulas to Individual Circumstances; Ordering Herbs and Inspecting Quality; Establishing a Practice; Legal and Ethical Issues; Alternative Perspectives in Epidemiology; Overcoming Environmental Pollution; Electromagnetic Fields and Human Health; Food Sensitivities and Intolerance; and much more.

Community and Continuing Education

Courses for nonprofessionals are occasionally offered on such topics as family health, environmental health, immunity and epidemics, herbal principles, and diet.

Courses in Advanced TCM Herbal Training are open to all herbalists with basic training in TCM assessment, materia medica, and herbal formulation. Each year, RMHI sponsors courses in various specialties of TCM that may include problems of the immune system, endocrine system, gastrointestinal tract, menopause, and others.

Admission Requirements

Admission requirements include high-level literacy, common sense, the ability to think and reason clearly, and prior training in anatomy and physiology. A sample homework assignment and textbook order is sent once the application is accepted; final admission to the program is contingent upon receiving a grade of 70 percent or above on the homework assignment.

Tuition and Fees

Tuition for the Chinese Herbal Sciences Training Program is $3,050. Other costs include an admission fee of $90; books, herb kits, and materials are approximately $600. Intensives meals and lodging are additional.

Tuition for the Advanced TCM Herbal Training Program is $445 per six-day seminar.

Financial Assistance

A payment plan is available.

NEVADA

Aston-Patterning

P.O. Box 3568
Incline Village, Nevada 89450
Phone: (702) 831-8228
Fax: (702) 831-8955

Aston-Patterning is an educational system developed by Judith Aston based on more than thirty years of teaching experience. The process includes a combination of bodywork, movement coaching, ergonomics, and fitness training. Although the work can be helpful to those in acute and chronic pain and those wishing to improve their body's posture, efficiency, and effectiveness, it is also useful for athletic performance and personal growth.

Accreditation

Certification as an Aston-Patterning practitioner is dependent on completion of the Level III clinical evaluation, signing the licensing agreement, and paying an annual licensing fee. Practitioners may then use the Aston-Patterning trademarks and logos and be included in the directory of practitioners. Applicants should check with their home state to determine specific licensing requirements.

Program Description

To become a certified Aston-Patterning practitioner, a student must complete approximately fifteen weeks of training (eighty-four days) over a period of one-and-a-half to two years. Training includes movement education (neurokinetics), soft tissue work (myokinetics), advanced massage, and ergonomics. The courses meet in three-week segments, followed by blocks of time for the application of skills in work situations.

Prior to beginning the certification program, students must complete Aston Therapeutics I (four days), Aston Therapeutics II (four days), Aston Therapeutics: Bodyworks I (four days), and Aston Therapeutics: Bodyworks II (four days).

Continuing Education

Continuing education of three days every three years is encouraged following certification. Continuing education courses are offered in Aston Fitness, Arthro-Kinetics, Facial Toning, and small group tutorials for specialized interests.

Admission Requirements

Applicants must be at least 21 years of age; submit a letter of endorsement from an Aston-Patterning practitioner and a statement of purpose; have completed Aston Therapeutics I, Aston Therapeutics II, Aston Therapeutics: Bodyworks I, and Aston Therapeutics: Bodyworks II; have a bachelor's degree or academic training in education, health care, or a related field or demonstrated career success; have knowledge of anatomy and physiology equal to one semester of college work; have a diploma from an accredited school of massage, a comparable license as a health professional, a business license, or have completed the Aston Massage Technician Program previously offered at Alive and Well! in California. Students are encouraged to have six private Aston-Patterning sessions with certified practitioners.

Tuition and Fees

Course fees may be determined by multiplying the number of days in a class by the current daily rate (approximately $110 per day). There is a $25 application fee, and Level III Certification Evaluation is $350.

Financial Assistance

Payment plans and discounts for advance payment are available.

NEW HAMPSHIRE

DoveStar Institute

(*See* Multiple State Locations, page 299)

New Hampshire Institute for Therapeutic Arts

(*See* Multiple State Locations, page 312)

North Eastern Institute of Whole Health

22 Bridge Street
Manchester, New Hampshire 03101
Phone: (603) 623-5018
Fax: (603) 641-5928

The North Eastern Institute of Whole Health was founded in 1993 by Gabrielle Grigore, M.D., N.D., D.O.M., L.M.T., and shiatsu master.

Accreditation

The institute and its curriculum are approved by the International Organization of American Association of Bodyworkers and Massage Practitioners, and the State of New Hampshire Department of Education.

Program Description

The 750-hour Massage Therapy Program consists of Anatomy and Physiology, Hydrotherapy, CPR/First Aid, Health Service: Management, Ethics and Professionalism, Chair Massage, Health and Hygiene for Bodyworkers, Introduction to Craniosacral Therapy, Eastern Traditional Medicine and Its Philosophies, Introduction to Touch Therapies, Massage Practicum, Neuromuscular Technique, Reflexology, Shiatsu, Sports Massage, and Swedish Massage, plus electives in Acupressure, Advanced Neuromuscular Massage, Aromatherapy, Craniosacral Therapy Level I, Equine Massage, Esalen Massage, Feng Shui, Geriatric Massage, Hawaiian Lomi Lomi Massage, Hypnotic Techniques for Bodyworkers, Lymphatic Drainage Massage, Marketing for Results, Pregnancy Massage, Polarity Therapy, Russian Massage, and Trigger Point Therapy. Morning or evening programs are available.

Admission Requirements

Applicants must be at least 18 years of age, have a high school diploma or equivalent by the end of the program, and submit a physician's note of good health and a completed Whole Health Medical Form.

Tuition and Fees

Tuition is $5,100. Other costs include: application fee, $50; texts, $112; other books and materials, $150; body wrap, $25 to $30; school T-shirt, $15; and diploma fee, $20, subject to change.

Financial Assistance

Payment plans, veterans' benefits, and Vocational Rehabilitation are available.

NEW JERSEY

Associates for Creative Wellness

School of Asian Healing Arts
1930 East Marlton Pike, N-72
Cherry Hill, New Jersey 08003
Phone: (609) 424-7501

The Associates for Creative Wellness/School of Asian Healing Arts was founded in 1986 by Ruth Dalphin, the current director of the school, and Judah Roseman.

Accreditation

The Associates for Creative Wellness/School of Asian Healing Arts is a member of the American Oriental Bodywork Therapy Association (AOBTA) Council of Schools and Programs, and is approved by the State of New Jersey Department of Education as a private vocational school.

Program Description

The school offers day or evening Shiatsu Certification Programs from 150 to 500-plus hours. Each semester includes seventy to seventy-five hours of instruction. A Basic Level (150-hour) Certificate in shiatsu is awarded after completion of Levels IA and IB, one hundred treatment reports, and receiving three treatments from a certified instructor or practitioner.

Level IA includes Meridian Theory, Fourteen Major Meridians, Chinese Anatomy and Physiology, the Four Examinations, Qi, Yin/Yang, Shiatsu in Relation to Other Healing Arts, Basic Full-Body Treatment, Use of Yu/Shu Points, Shiatsu Self-Care, Energetics of Food/Lifestyle, and Introduction to Western Anatomy and Physiology.

Level IB covers Principles of Assessment (Hara and Pulses), Law of Five Elements, Special Points, Ampaku, Traditional and Masunaga Bo Points, Side Shiatsu, Special Stretches, Keeping Records, Balancing Yin and Yang in Diet, Whole Foods, and more.

Level IIA instruction includes Element Points, Eight Principles, Six Evils, Assessment, Home Remedies, Transitional Cooking, Application of Assessment Skills, Psychological/Emotional Bodywork, and more.

In Level IIB, students are exposed to Source/Luo Points, Review of Zang Fu Functions, Detailed Study of Pathologies with Signs and Symptoms, Assessment and Treatment Plan, Case Studies, and more.

Level IIIA includes Review of One Hundred Major Points, Five Elements: Pathologies and Personal Relationships, Muscle Channels, Extraordinary Vessels, and a continuation of Level IIB shiatsu work.

Level IIIB consists of seventy hours of Clinic, in which students give full shiatsu treatments under supervision.

For Level III certification, in addition to class requirements, students must also complete two semesters of Western anatomy and physiology and CPR training, and receive ten shiatsu treatments.

A 200-hour Yoga Teacher Training Course includes fifty hours of yoga classes, taken over one to two years; fifty hours (one semester) of anatomy and physiology; and one hundred hours of postures, history, and philosophy (in four 25-hour segments).

Additional classes and workshops are offered in a variety of subjects including meditation, Thai massage, yoga, tai chi, do-in, acupressure, and others.

Admission Requirements

No experience is necessary for introductory workshops. For Yoga Teacher Training, applicants must be in good physical and mental condition; prior completion of at least one 6-session series of yoga classes is recommended.

Tuition and Fees

There is a $50 registration fee; books and supplies average $50 per semester.

Tuition for the Shiatsu Certification Programs is as follows: Level IA, $750; Level IB, $750; Level IIA, $700; Level IIB, $700; Level IIIA, $700; and Level IIIB, $665.

The anatomy and physiology course costs $750 ($375 per semester).

The Yoga Teacher Training Course costs $2,000; books, mats, and optional equipment are additional.

Financial Assistance

A payment plan is available.

East West Institute for Wholistic Studies

Light Lines Wholistic Center
4 Leigh Street
Clinton, New Jersey 08809
Phone: (908) 735-7403
Fax: (908) 735-4949

The East West Institute for Wholistic Studies was founded in 1995. The Integrated Hypnotherapy Course is the first of its kind, based on the twenty-five years' experience of Light Lines and East West Institute co-owner Carol Gill in helping others overcoming self-sabotage on the road to mental, physical, and spiritual health.

Accreditation

Students completing the Integrated Hypnotherapy Course are eligible for certification through the International Association of Counselors and Therapists as a certified hypnotherapist. The Bodywork and Massage Course has been approved for certification through the Associated Bodywork and Massage Professionals (ABMP).

Program Description

The six-month Integrated Hypnotherapy Course teaches a wholistic, co-creative healing process. The curriculum consists of separate courses in Hypnotherapy, Kinesiology, Energy Anatomy, and Synthesis.

The one-hundred-hour Bodywork and Massage Course is comprised of the general theory and comparison of Eastern and Western approaches to bodywork. Shiatsu: Eastern Method covers such topics as Meridians, Do-In, Tonification and Sedation Techniques, Governing and Conception Vessels, Five Element Theory, Tui Na, and more. Massage: Western Method covers Strokes and Patterns, Oils and Draping, Foot Massage, Anatomy and Physiology, Full-Body Massage, Polarity, Lymphatic Massage, Code of Ethics and Conduct, Business Practices, and more. Classes are held evenings and weekends.

Admission Requirements

Applicants must interview with an instructor.

Tuition and Fees

Tuition for the Bodywork and Massage Course is $1,400.

Total tuition for the Integrated Hypnotherapy Course is $970 (each class is paid separately).

Financial Assistance

A payment plan is available.

Five Elements Center

115 Route 46 West
Building D, Suite 49
Mountain Lakes, New Jersey 07046
Phone: (201) 402-8510

Jane Cicchetti, a registered member of the North American Society of Homeopaths and founder and president of the Five Elements Center, has been practicing homeopathy since 1981, and has also had extensive training in Five Elements Chinese medicine.

Program Description

Five Elements Center offers a three-year course in Essentials of Constitutional Homeopathy. Classes meet eight weekends (110 hours) per year. The first year includes an in-depth study of twenty-eight polycrest remedies; topics include How to Study Materia Medica, Introduction to Organon, History of Vitalist Medicine, Structure of Repertory, Case Taking, Theory of Miasms, Remedy Antidotes, Obstacles to Cure, and more. Second-year topics include an in-depth study of twenty-eight lesser-known

polycrest remedies, as well as Acute Illness During Chronic Treatment, Case Analysis, Analysis and Use of Nosodes, Vaccinations, Diet and Detoxification, Selection of Potency (Advanced), Practice Management/Licensing, and more. In the third year, students learn many small and rarely-used remedies, as well as Small Plant Remedies, Herbology and Mother Tinctures, Analysis of Difficult Cases, Homeopathy and Computer Technology, Student Cases, Failed Cases, and more. Students are expected to complete classes in anatomy, physiology, and pathology before a certificate of course completion will be given.

Prior to enrolling in the three-year course, students must complete the Homeopathy Workshop or equivalent. This is an introductory course available as a weekend course or on audiocassettes for home study. It includes acute treatment for first aid, flu, colds, and headaches, as well as basic principles.

Admission Requirements

The prerequisite for the first year is the Homeopathy Workshop or equivalent, as determined by the instructor. For the second year, students must have completed the first-year program or a minimum of 140 hours of study in classical homeopathy. Third-year applicants must have completed the second year or a minimum of 250 hours of study in classical homeopathy.

Tuition and Fees

Tuition for the three-year homeopathy course is $1,600 (or $1,490 for early registration); books are additional.

The Homeopathy Workshop weekend course costs $195; the home study course costs $89.

Financial Assistance

A payment plan is available.

Health Choices Center for the Healing Arts

170 Township Line Road, Building B
Belle Mead, New Jersey 08502
Phone: (908) 359-3995

Health Choices was founded by Kristina Shaw in 1977; in 1991, Renate Novak became the new owner and director.

Accreditation

Health Choices is approved as a private vocational school by the state of New Jersey. Continuing education workshops are approved by the National Certification Board for Therapeutic Massage and Bodywork (NCBTMB).

Program Description

Health Choices offers a 580-hour, one-year Holistic Massage Practitioner Training. Courses include Swedish Massage, Shiatsu, Polarity, Deep Tissue, Anatomy and Physiology, Clinical Application, Field Work, Self-Development, Business Skills, Associated Studies, electives, and student clinic. Other associated studies include yoga, DansKinetics, relaxation and breathing skills, and guest lectures in nutrition, chiropractic, and other topics. Classes are held days or evenings.

Continuing Education

Continuing education workshops offered to those who have completed basic massage training include Sports Massage, the Totally Effortless Massage, and On-Site Massage. Courses with no prerequisites include Feng Shui Workshop, Crystal Healing Workshop, and Newborn Massage. Advanced training in shiatsu, aromatherapy, reflexology, reiki, and polarity is offered to those with prior training in that specialty.

Admission Requirements

Applicants must attend one of the school's free introductory evenings; it is recommended that they receive a full-body massage from one of the graduates.

Tuition and Fees

Tuition is $5,650; there is a $25 application fee, and books cost approximately $250.

Financial Assistance

A payment plan is available.

Morris Institute of Natural Therapeutics

The Mareen Building
3108 Route 10 West
Denville, New Jersey 07834
Phone: (201) 989-8939
Fax: (201) 989-5554

The Morris Institute of Natural Therapeutics (MINT) was founded in 1963 and offers certification and continuing education in a wide variety of holistic health modalities.

Accreditation

The MINT School of Massage is approved by the Associated Bodywork and Massage Professionals (ABMP) and graduates are eligible for membership. Hands-on courses, workshops, and seminars meet American Massage Therapy Association (AMTA) and Associated Bodywork and Massage Professionals (ABMP) continuing education requirements.

Program Description

The 520-hour Therapeutic Massage Course consists of a fifteen-week Basic Massage Program and ten weeks of massage-related anatomy and physiology. The Basic Massage Program covers Principles of Massage, Terminology, Practical Techniques, Complete Body Massage and Body Movements, Indications/Contraindications, Preparation/Draping, Sanitation/Attire/Oils, Professional Ethics, Legislation/Insurance, and How to Become Established. The massage-related anatomy and physiology course includes an Introduction to Spatial Relationships and Systems of the Body, including cells, skeletal, muscular, circulatory, glandular, reproductive, respiratory, digestive, excretory, nervous, and endocrine systems. Classes are held days and evenings.

A six-day (three-weekend) Certificate Program in Aromatherapy offers a complete study of the therapeutic and cosmetic applications of twenty-five essential oils. The curriculum covers Introduction to Osmology, Aromatics in History, Aromatherapy Today, Essential Oils: Natural vs. Synthetic,

Applications, Materia Medica, Blending, Carriers, Cosmetic Applications of Essential Oils, Student Formulation and Blending, Chemistry of Essential Oils, Chemotypes, Toxicity and Safe Use of Essential Oils, Botanical Families, and more.

A 500-hour Shiatsu Program is currently being developed to meet American Oriental Bodywork Therapy Association (AOBTA) standards, and will be available in 1997.

Continuing Education

A two-day workshop in applied kinesiology and muscle balancing enables the student to put the body in balance to improve posture and increase energy, use muscle-balancing techniques, and test for allergies. Topics include Chinese Concepts of Medicine, Cross Crawl Exercise, Pain Relief, Visual Inhibition, Auricular Exercise, Balancing with Food, Forty-Two Major Muscle Testing, Surrogate Testing, Emotional Stress Release, Massage Reflexes, Holding Points, Meridians and Meridian Massage, Alarm Points, Muscle Origin/Insertion Technique, Pulse Testing, and Body Balancing.

A three-day workshop in reflexology covers such topics as Theory and Origin, Thumb and Finger Movements, Location of Reflex Points, Basic Anatomy, Breathing and Relaxation, Practice of Complete Pressure Massage, Work with Oil, Special Health Problems, and more.

A two-day workshop in sports massage covers specialized techniques, such as Neuromuscular Therapy, Neuroproprioceptive Therapy, Pre- and Post-Event Sports Massage (including Theory of Sports Massage, Proper Pre- and Post-Event Strokes, Muscle Problems, and Preventing and Improving Sports Injuries), and more.

A two-day shiatsu workshop covers Theory and Practice, Yin/Yang Meridians, Points of the Meridians, Adjunctive Techniques (including moxa, cupping, infant massage, seated shiatsu, and more), Emergency/Quick Fix Shiatsu Techniques (for headaches, fainting, hiccoughs, insomnia, relaxation, and others), and more.

Additional seminars are offered in Touch for Health, RejuvenEssence facial massage, neuromuscular therapy (NMT), craniosacral therapy, lymph drainage therapy, and other areas.

Admission Requirements

Applicants must be at least 18 years of age and have a high school diploma or equivalent. Other prerequisites vary depending on the program chosen.

Tuition and Fees

Tuition for the Therapeutic Massage Course is $2,895; for the Aromatherapy Course, $595; for the Applied Kinesiology Course, $325; for the Reflexology Course, $325; for the Sports Massage Course, $325; and for the Shiatsu Workshop, $325. Tuition for the 500-hour Shiatsu Program is not yet available.

Somerset School of Massage Therapy

Tall Pine Center
7 Cedar Grove Lane
Somerset, New Jersey 08873
Phone: (908) 356-0787
E-mail: ssmt@massagecareer.com

Approved by the New Jersey Department of Education in 1991, Somerset School of Massage Therapy is located less than an hour from New York City. The school's Sports Massage Team has worked with Olympic competitors, university athletic departments, and international cycling teams.

Accreditation

The 564-hour program at Somerset School is accredited by AMTA/COMTAA, approved by the Florida Board of Massage and the Iowa Massage Therapy Board, and was the first school in the United States to offer certification in neuromuscular therapy as part of its regular curriculum.

Program Description

Graduates of the 564-hour program are awarded a Diploma in Therapeutic Massage, including certification in neuromuscular therapy. Required courses include Anatomy and Physiology, Neuromuscular Anatomy, Therapeutic Massage and Related Modalities, Myofascial and Deep Tissue Techniques, Reflexology, Sports Massage, Prenatal Massage, Neuromuscular Therapy, Student Clinic, Business Management and Professional Ethics, CPR/First Aid, Hydrotherapy, HIV/AIDS Awareness, and Tai Chi.

Students may complete the program in twelve months on either a morning or evening schedule, or in six months in the accelerated program, which meets three full days per week plus some evenings or weekends.

Continuing Education

Elective courses are open to both practicing massage therapists and enrolled students. These include Beyond the Routine (required for Florida licensing), Myofascial Massage Therapy—An Advanced Certification Training Program, and Shiatsu.

Admission Requirements

Applicants must be 18 years of age or older, have a high school diploma or equivalent, be of sound mind and body, and interview with an admissions representative.

Tuition and Fees

Tuition is $4,790. Other costs include: application fee, $25; registration fee, $100; books, approximately $280; recommended massage table, $400 to $600; and linens, $25 to $50.

Financial Assistance

Payment plans and veterans' benefits are available.

NEW MEXICO

The Ayurvedic Institute

11311 Menaul N.E.
Albuquerque, New Mexico 87112
Phone: (505) 291-9698

The Ayurvedic Institute was founded in 1984 in Santa Fe, New Mexico. Dr. Vasant Lad, president, and Dr. Robert Svoboda, both well-known authors in the field of Ayurveda, are board and faculty members. The institute offers educational programs in Ayurvedic studies both on-site and through correspondence (see page 362).

Accreditation

The institute does not currently have any recognized accreditation, nor does it offer any degree programs; students receive a certificate upon completion of the course. At this time it is not possible to obtain a license to practice Ayurveda in the United States. The training offered by the Ayurvedic Institute is not sufficient for a practitioner to solely use Ayurveda when consulting with a client; in India, six years of study are required to become an Ayurvedic physician. However, health care professionals may incorporate their Ayurvedic knowledge into the work they are already licensed to perform.

Program Description

The First-Year Ayurvedic Studies Program consists of three trimesters. The first trimester explores such topics as Sankhya Philosophy and Shad Darshan (six philosophies of life), Gunas (universal attributes), Vata (the air principle), Pitta Dosha (the fire principle), Kapha Dosha (the earth principle), and Srotas and Dhatus (bodily systems and tissues). Topics covered in the second trimester include the Ayurvedic Concept of Health, Digestion and Assimilation, Trividha Pariksha (methods of acquiring information), Ashtavidha Pariksha (eightfold examination), Marmas (Ayurvedic energy points), and others. Third-trimester topics include Rugna Patrakam (client assessment form), Chikitsa (managing disorders utilizing various methods), Sapta Shamanam (seven palliative measures), General Management of Doshas, and others. Classes are held three evenings per week, with some Saturday sessions.

Serious, dedicated students may be accepted for additional studies as Dr. Lad's personal students.

Weekend seminars and intensives are offered throughout the year on such topics as Ayurvedic Herbology, Ayurveda and Immunology, Spiritual Healing, Introduction to Vedic Palmistry, Ayurvedic Cooking, and others.

Admission Requirements

Applicants to the First-Year Ayurvedic Studies Program must have a high school diploma or equivalent. Some understanding of Ayurveda, anatomy and physiology, Sanskrit, and other vedic traditions will greatly enhance comprehension of the program material.

Applicants to the Additional Studies Program with Dr. Lad must have a thorough understanding of the material in the Ayurvedic Studies Program, a good understanding of anatomy and physiology, and the ability to read Sanskrit in the Devanagari script and pronounce a sutra. Applicants will be given an oral entrance exam.

Tuition and Fees

Tuition for the Ayurvedic Studies Program is $1,600 for the first trimester, $1,400 for the second trimester, and $1,000 for the third trimester. There is a $200 registration fee.

Morning consultations with Dr. Lad in the Additional Studies Program cost $100 per week; there is a $200 registration fee.

Tuition for seminars and intensives ranges from $150 to $275, plus a $25 registration fee.

Financial Assistance

A limited number of work-study positions are available.

Crystal Mountain Apprenticeship in the Healing Arts

118 Dartmouth S.E.
Albuquerque, New Mexico 87106-2218
Phone: (505) 268-4411 /
   (800) 967-5678 (toll-free)
Fax: (505) 268-4007

Crystal Mountain first opened its massage therapy clinic in 1980 and began offering classes through the University of New Mexico's continuing education program in 1982. In 1988, the classes expanded into a 200-hour massage therapy program; with the passage of the New Mexico Massage Therapy Act in 1992, the program was expanded to its current 700 hours.

Accreditation

Crystal Mountain is registered with the New Mexico State Board of Massage and is a member of the Associated Bodywork and Massage Professionals (ABMP). New Mexico uses the national certification exam administered by the National Certification Board for Therapeutic Massage and Bodywork (NCBTMB) as its state licensing exam; Crystal Mountain graduates are eligible to take this exam.

Program Description

Crystal Mountain's 700-hour Massage Therapy Licensure Program includes Therapeutic Massage; Anatomy, Physiology, Pathology, and Kinesiology; Sports Massage and Therapeutic Exercise; Shiatsu; Esalen Massage; Polarity Therapy; Reflexology; Polar Reflexology; Chair/Seated Massage; Introduction to Neuromuscular Therapy (NMT); Deep Tissue Massage; Postural Analysis; Craniosacral Therapy; Body Centered Healing; Movement Reeducation; Pregnancy Massage; Hydrotherapy; Business Skills; Ethics; Herbology; Nutrition; CPR/First Aid; Clinical Internship Forum; and Internship Program. Programs are offered both days and evenings.

Admission Requirements

Applicants must be at least 18 years of age and have a high school diploma or equivalent. The academy looks for motivated students.

Tuition and Fees

Tuition is $4,000, including books, manual, and a minimum of five private training sessions.

Financial Assistance

Payment plans and work-study are available.

International Institute of Chinese Medicine

P.O. Box 4991
Santa Fe, New Mexico 87502
Phone: (505) 473-5233 / (800) 377-4561
Fax: (505) 473-9279

The International Institute of Chinese Medicine was founded in 1984 by Dr. Michael Zeng, who brought his extensive knowledge of acupuncture and traditional Chinese medicine from the People's Republic of China. Both he and his wife, Dr. Nancy Zeng, have thirty-four years of experience as acupuncturists, herbalists, and Oriental and Western doctors.

Accreditation

The Master of Oriental Medicine Degree Program is accredited by the National Accreditation Commission for Schools and Colleges of Acupuncture and Oriental Medicine (NACSCAOM). IICM is approved by the New Mexico State Board of Acupuncture and by the Medical Board of California Acupuncture Committee.

Program Description

The 2,400-hour, eight-semester Master of Oriental Medicine Degree Program includes 915 hours spent in observation, hands-on experience, and actual treatment. Graduates of the program are qualified to take licensing examinations in New Mexico, California, and other states, and the diplomate exam of the National Commission for the Certification of Acupuncturists (NCCA). New Mexico legislation awards the title "Doctor of Oriental Medicine" (D.O.M.) upon completion of this program and passage of the New Mexico licensing exam.

First-year courses include Traditional Chinese Medicine, Five Element Theory and Application, Theory of Meridians, Chinese Medicine Etiology and Pathology, Meridian and Acupoint Energetics, Acupuncture Practicum, Human Anatomy, Surface Anatomy, Western Approaches to Illness and Medical Terminology, Tai Chi Chuan, Human Physiology, Chinese Herbology, Acupuncture and Moxibustion Therapy, and others.

Second-year classes include Chinese Medicine Di-

agnosis, Chinese Patent Medicine, Treatment of Disease, Clinical Diagnosis by Lab Data, Qigong, CPR, Chinese Medicine Prescriptionology, and others.

Third-year classes include Chinese Acupressure and Tui Na Techniques, Chinese Medicine Diet and Food Therapy, Nutrition and Vitamins, General Psychology, Advanced Student Clinic, Ethics and Human Service Skills, Basic Chemistry, Organic and Biochemistry, and others.

Fourth-year courses include Chinese Medicine Internship, Advanced Student Clinic, Western Pharmacology, Clinical Aspects of Western Medicine, General Physics, and others.

Classes are usually held three days per week. An evening/weekend schedule is available at the Albuquerque campus.

Continuing Education

A forty-credit Continuing Education Certificate Program is open to licensed acupuncturists, graduates of Master of Acupuncture or Oriental Medicine degree programs, current students of IICM's degree program, and other qualified healing arts practitioners. Courses in Chinese herbology and Chinese medicine prescriptionology are prerequisites. These courses will eventually develop into the academic "Doctor of Oriental Medicine" (D.O.M.) degree program, which is currently awaiting approval by NACSCAOM on a national basis.

Students in the Continuing Education Certificate Program must complete forty credits. Courses offered include Advanced Student Clinic, Extraordinary Acupuncture Points, Chinese Internal Medicine, Chinese Medicine Longevity, Chinese Medicine Gynecology, Chinese Sports Medicine, Animal Acupuncture, Chinese Medicine Surgery, Laser Acupuncture, Basic Chinese Language, Chinese Medicine Ophthalmology, Herb Cultivation and Preparation, and others.

Admission Requirements

Applicants to the Master of Oriental Medicine Degree Program must have completed sixty credit hours of general education at the college level from an accredited institution, supply official transcripts, complete an autobiographical sketch, submit two letters of recommendation and a letter from a licensed health care practitioner regarding the applicant's physical condition, and interview with an admissions representative.

Tuition and Fees

Tuition is $145 per credit for fourteen credits or more, or $160 per credit for thirteen credits or less. Other costs include: application fee, $50; registration fee, $30 per semester; graduation fee, $150; student activity fee, $20 per semester; clinic fee, $20 per semester; and books and supplies, approximately $300 per semester.

Financial Assistance

A payment plan, work-study, and federal loans are available.

The Medicine Wheel— A School of Holistic Therapies

1243 West Apache
Farmington, New Mexico 87401
Phone: (505) 327-1914
Fax: (505) 327-2234

The Medicine Wheel is the educational branch of Wholistic Innerworks Foundation, Inc., a nonprofit corporation founded by Susan Barnes, H.H.P., L.M.T. Wholistic Innerworks began offering classes in 1991 and a complete certification program in 1992.

Accreditation

The Medicine Wheel is registered with the State of New Mexico Board of Massage Therapy #MTTP 8 for the 650-hour program and the 1,200-hour Associate of Occupational Studies degree. The Medicine Wheel is accredited by the International Massage and Somatic Therapies Accreditation Council (IMSTAC), a division of Associated Bodywork and Massage Professionals (ABMP). The school is approved by the National Certification Board for Therapeutic Massage and Bodywork (NCBTMB) as a continuing education provider.

Program Description

The educational programs at The Medicine Wheel allow students to choose the modalities that interest them, as well as the length of time to complete the program. Classes are offered primarily evenings and weekends; daytime classes are occasionally offered.

The 650-hour Licensed Massage Therapist Curriculum consists of required classes in Anatomy and Physiology, Business Practicum, Client Relationship and Stress Management, Ethical Issues, First Aid and CPR, Hydrotherapy, Legal Guidelines, and Mind-Body Connection. Students must also select a minimum of 300 hours of classes from Chinese Massage, Craniosacral, Deep Tissue Massage, Infant Massage, Lymphatic Massage, Neuromuscular Therapy, On-Site Massage, PNF and Counterstrain, Polarity, Prenatal Massage, Reflexology, Russian Conditioning Massage, Shiatsu, Sports Massage, Sports Injury Massage, Supervised Clinical Experience, Swedish Massage and Body Mechanics, and TMJ Workshop. In addition, students select a maximum of 150 hours of electives. This program may be completed in a minimum of nine months, up to a maximum of eighteen months.

The 1,200-hour Associate of Occupational Studies Program is open to those who have completed the 650-hour program. Required classes are Advanced Anatomy and Physiology, Clinical Research, Counseling Skills for the Massage Therapist, and Report Writing and Fundamentals of Assessment for Professionals. Electives include Aromatherapy, Bach Flower Remedies, Body Reading, Chakras, Color and Crystal Healing, Diet and Nutrition, Herbology, Home Remedies, Muscle Biofeedback, Neurolinguistic Programming, Reiki, Tai Chi, Therapeutic Touch, Traditional Chinese Medical Theory, and Yoga for Specifics. This program must be completed in the fifteen months following completion of the 650-hour program.

Community and Continuing Education

Most electives and several massage classes are open to the public; these may also be taken for continuing education by health care professionals.

Admission Requirements

Applicants must be at least 18 years of age, have a high school diploma or equivalent, and be emotionally stable and physically able to perform massage manipulations taught in the program.

Tuition and Fees

Tuition for the 650-hour program is $4,875; liability insurance is $75, books are approximately $200, and oil and supplies are $80.

Tuition for the 1,200-hour program is $9,000; liability insurance is $150, books are approximately $300, and oil and supplies are $100.

Other expenses for either program include: application fee, $50; three required professional massages, $105; and portable massage table, approximately $780.

Tuition for elective courses taken by non-enrolled students is $12 per hour if received two weeks before scheduled class; $15 is added to the total after that time.

Financial Assistance

A payment plan and veterans' benefits are available.

The National College of Phytotherapy

120 Aliso S.E.
Albuquerque, New Mexico 87108
Phone: (505) 265-0795

The National College of Phytotherapy was founded in 1996 by Tieraona Low Dog, M.D., and Amanda McQuade Crawford, who have been practicing herbalists for approximately fifteen years.

Accreditation

The college is pursuing accreditation.

Program Description

The college offers a three-year residency program leading to a Bachelor of Science degree in phytotherapy (herbal medicine). Classes emphasize American and Western plants, phytotherapy, health sciences, pharmacy, and field work, plus 650 hours of clinical and counseling experience. Classes meet two evenings per week, plus weekends.

The first year covers such topics as Philosophy of Healing, Botany, Materia Medica, Herbal Tradition and Culture of New Mexico, Biochemistry, Ecology and Ethics of Harvesting, Herbal Pharmacy, Cellular Physiology, Histology, Anatomy and Physiology, Pharmacology/Pharmacokinetics, and Western Energetics. In the second year, the curriculum includes Introduction to Pathophysiology, Therapeutic Ethics, Nutrition, Computer Skills, Stress Management, Pharmacognosy, Local Herbs and Field Identification, Introduction to the Client, The Physical Exam, Diagnostic Tests, Drugs and Herbal Medicine, Integrated Phytotherapy, Behavioral Medicine, Medical Microbiology, Field Work and Botany, and Applied Materia Medica. Third-year courses include Clinical Practicum, Business Skills for the Phytotherapist, Practice Management, Introduction to Western Drugs, Herbal Pediatrics, Herbal Geriatrics, Traditional Chinese Medicine, TCM Materia Medica, Ayurvedic Medicine, Ayurvedic Materia Medica, CPR, and more.

Admission Requirements

Applicants must be at least 21 years of age, fluent in English, and have a high school diploma or equivalent. One or more college-level classes in life sciences are recommended.

Tuition and Fees

Tuition is $1,950 per semester. There is a $30 application fee; books cost approximately $500 per year, and diagnostic tools for the third year cost $300. Field trip costs, lab, and library charges are additional.

Financial Assistance

Payment plans are available.

New Mexico Academy of Healing Arts

501 Franklin Avenue
P.O. Box 932
Santa Fe, New Mexico 87504-0932
Phone: (505) 982-6271
Fax: (505) 988-2621

Founded in 1979, the New Mexico Academy of Healing Arts is located in a residential area twenty minutes' walking distance from the plaza area of downtown Santa Fe.

Accreditation

The academy's Massage Therapy Certification Programs are approved by the American Massage Therapy Association Commission on Massage Training Accreditation/Approval (AMTA/COMTAA) and the New Mexico Board of Massage Therapy. The polarity certification programs are accredited by the American Polarity Therapy Association (APTA).

Program Description

Schedules for the 1,000- and 1,200-hour daytime Massage Programs may include, in the first semester, Community Meeting, Anatomy, Physiology, Anatomy with Manikens, Massage, Yoga and Meditation, Feldenkrais, Communication Skills and Ethics, Professional Development, and Student Intern Clinic. The second semester may include Community Meeting, Anatomy, Physiology, Polarity, First Aid, CPR, Yoga and Meditation, Professional Development, Medical Massage, Pathology, Hydrotherapy, Student Intern Clinic, Orthobionomy, and Aromatherapy. The 1,200-hour program includes an additional summer semester that offers a survey of Swedish massage.

The 650-hour day or evening programs are designed for very directed students who want a solid foundation in massage therapy in the shortest possible time. Instruction includes Massage, Anatomy, Physiology, Feldenkrais, Communication Skills and Ethics, Clinical Exposure, Professional Development, and Polarity.

The six-week, 155-hour Associate Polarity Practitioner (A.P.P.) Program provides an overview of polarity theory and bodywork techniques. Graduates are eligible to apply to APTA for an A.P.P. certificate.

The six-month, 650-hour Registered Polarity Practitioner (R.P.P.) Program provides an immersion in polarity theory, bodywork, nutrition, and counseling. The curriculum includes Polarity Stretching Postures; Business Management, Promotion, Professional Ethics, and Law; Communica-

tion and Facilitation: Didactic Study and Guided Personal Exposure; Anatomy and Physiology; Polarity Theory and Principles; Energetic Nutrition; Polarity Bodywork; Evaluation and Integration Skills; electives; and clinical supervision, consisting of 102 hours of giving treatments, sixty-one hours of feedback, and fifteen hours of receiving treatments. Graduates are eligible to apply for membership in APTA as a Registered Polarity Practitioner.

Continuing Education

A variety of introductory courses and weekend workshops are offered for continuing education credit. These include Massage Sampler, Polarity Sampler, Introduction to Hydrotherapy, Aromatherapy, Ayurvedic Massage, Traditional Amma Shiatsu, Sports Massage, Craniosacral Therapy (four levels of training), Thai Medical Massage, Nuat-Tui, Soft Tissue Injuries, and Massage Teacher's Training.

Admission Requirements

Applicants must be at least 18 years of age, have a high school diploma or equivalent, and interview with an admissions representative. It is recommended that prospective students view the academy's *Healing Touch* video and observe classes.

Tuition and Fees

There is a $35 application fee and a $50 financial aid processing fee. Massage students must have access to massage tables before the sixth week of the semester.

Tuition for the 1,200-hour Massage Program is $7,000; books and supplies cost $475 to $650; professional massages cost $250 to $350; and lab fees and optional supplies cost $125 to $500.

Tuition for the 1,000-hour Massage Program is $6,500; books and supplies cost $450 to $625; professional massages cost $200 to $300; and lab fees and optional supplies cost $125 to $500.

Tuition for the 650-hour Massage Program is $4,600; books and supplies cost $375 to $625; professional massages cost $100 to $350; and lab fees and optional supplies cost $100 to $550.

Tuition for the Associate Polarity Practitioner (A.P.P.) Program is $1,395. Tuition for the Registered Polarity Practitioner (R.P.P.) Program is $5,000; books and supplies cost $300 to $400; professional bodywork costs $750 to $1,050; and lab fees and optional supplies cost $200 to $500.

Financial Assistance

"Pay as you study" and partial deferred payment plans are available.

The New Mexico Herb Center

120 Aliso S.E.
Albuquerque, New Mexico 87108
Phone: (505) 265-0795
Fax: (505) 232-3522

Founded in 1991 by Tieraona Low Dog, M.D. and clinical herbalist, the New Mexico Herb Center is a not-for-profit educational facility and herbal clinic located in the Nob Hill area of Albuquerque. Programs are offered both in the classroom and by correspondence (see page 368). Located at the same address and under the same directorship is the National College of Phytotherapy (see page 200).

Program Description

The Foundations of Herbalism Program is an introductory course meeting one weekend per month for nine months. Topics include Introduction to Herbalism: Philosophy and History, Introduction to Herbal Preparation, Anatomy and Physiology (of the respiratory system, digestive system, women's health, and immune system), Materia Medica, Healing and Ritual, Herbal Pediatrics, Herbs for Elders, Gaia: Lectures/Discussion, Herbal Protocols for Men's Health, Herb Walks, and more.

The Clinical Practicum is an intensive, advanced training program for herbalists with a working knowledge of herbal therapeutics and an understanding of physiology. Herbalists see clients in the NMHC clinic under the supervision of a physician, prepare plant medicines in the apothecary, and discuss cases several times a month at Round Tables. Prior to working in the clinic, students have a four-week intensive of preparatory classes that include Applied Materia Medica, Herbal Pharmacology, Herbal Pharmacy and Formulations, Understand-

ing Herbal Constituents, Interactions of Western Drugs and Earth Medicine, Toxicology, Introduction to Clinical Skills, Introduction to the Client, the Physical Examination, Taking a Health History, and Accessing Medline and the Net.

Tuition and Fees

Tuition for the Foundations of Herbalism Course is $995, including all herbal preparations and handouts.

Tuition for the Clinical Practicum is $1,500, plus a $15 application fee.

Financial Assistance

Payment plans are available.

New Mexico School of Natural Therapeutics

117 Richmond N.E.
Albuquerque, New Mexico 87106
Phone: (505) 268-6870

The New Mexico School of Natural Therapeutics was founded by David Tinkle in 1974 under the name of the New Mexico School of Therapeutic Massage, and moved to its present location in 1986. The school emphasizes an integration of many different systems of healing, including Bach flower remedies, homeopathy, herbology, and others, and offers more polarity therapy than any other basic massage course in the country.

Accreditation

The NMSNT curriculum is approved by the American Massage Therapy Association Commission on Massage Training Accreditation/Approval (AMTA/ COMTAA), and by the New Mexico Board of Massage Therapy.

Program Description

The 750-hour massage therapy curriculum consists of Massage Techniques: Theory and Practice (including Swedish, sports massage, deep tissue, Swedish gymnastics, neuromuscular therapy, tai chi/table posture, pregnancy and infant massage, and postural analysis), Polarity Therapy (including body/mind counseling skills and reflexology),

Anatomy and Physiology, Internship/Clinical Practice, Shiatsu, Herbology (including traditional Chinese medicine diagnostics and mountain herb walk), Business Procedures and Professional Ethics, Flower Remedies/Homeopathy, Philosophy of Nature Cure, Hydrotherapy, Nutrition, AIDS Education, and First Aid, CPR, and Hygiene. A six-month day program and a one-year evening program are offered.

Continuing Education

An ongoing continuing education program includes such courses as Craniosacral Therapy, Colonic Irrigation, Advanced Polarity, Myofascial Release, Thai Massage, Chair Massage, and others. A thirty-hour Sports Massage Course is offered annually that fulfills AMTA sports massage certification requirements.

Admission Requirements

Applicants must be at least 18 years of age and have a high school diploma or equivalent. Applicants must submit an application form, including a personal statement and a completed health evaluation form, show evidence of financial readiness, interview with an admissions representative, and provide character references. It is recommended that students complete an anatomy and physiology course prior to beginning the program; NMSNT offers a preparatory class each May and November. Prospective students should submit applications at least two months prior to the program starting date.

Tuition and Fees

Tuition is $4,800. An application and supply fee of $500 includes books, linens, and oil. Optional expenses include a portable massage table, $400 to $600; Bach flower kit, $200; anatomical and treatment charts, $100; and products and remedies from the dispensary, approximately $40 per month.

Financial Assistance

Tuition may be paid in two installments. Students receive 100 percent of all donations for treatments given at student clinics; students may earn back approximately 15 percent of their tuition in four weeks of clinical internship practice.

The Scherer Institute of Natural Healing

1443 South St. Francis Drive
Santa Fe, New Mexico 87505
Phone: (505) 982-8398 /
(505) 751-3143 (In Taos)
Fax: (505) 982-1825

The institute first enrolled students in 1979, and in 1984 became a nonprofit 501-c-3 educational organization. Dr. Jay Scherer, the founder, was introduced to natural healing by his mother, Katherine Scherer, an herbalist and horticulturist, and later pursued studies in naturopathy, botanical medicine, philosophy, and divinity.

Accreditation

The institute is a registered school with the State of New Mexico Board of Massage Therapy. It is approved as a continuing education provider by the National Certification Board for Therapeutic Massage and Bodywork (NCBTMB).

Program Description

The 670-hour, six-month Massage Therapy Training Program includes the Healing Quality of Touch and Professional Development; Nurturing and Therapeutic Massage, in which students learn to give a complete Swedish massage; Connective Tissue Bodywork; Human Anatomy, Physiology, and Pathology; the Principles of Natural Therapeutics Using Herbal Medicine and Hydrotherapy; Shiatsu; Touch for Health, developed from a subfield of applied kinesiology; Naturopathic Principles and Techniques; Health Psychology; Spirit, Money, and Business; and Movement. Students complete a minimum of 120 out-of-class hours of practicum and internship.

An evening and weekend 670-hour, twelve-month Massage Therapy Training Program is available at the Taos location. Students wishing to meet New York State shiatsu licensing requirements must take an additional elective and tutorials offered in the evening.

A maximum of thirty students go through the entire program together.

Continuing Education

Additional courses for both beginning and advanced students are offered throughout the year. These include Life Impressions Bodywork, Shiatsu, Trigger Point Therapy, Infant Massage Instructor Training, Massage for the Child-Bearing Year, Basic Herbology and Herb Walks, Hakomi for Bodyworkers, and Orthobionomy. Courses open to licensed massage therapists include Introduction to Reunion Therapy, Deep Tissue-Specific Ailment Work, Whole Body Nutrition, Trigger Point Intensive, and Exploring Boundaries.

Admission Requirements

Applicants must be 18 years of age and have a high school diploma or equivalent. Students are screened for health, character, financial preparation, stability, and sincerity.

Tuition and Fees

Tuition for the Massage Therapy Training Program is $4,650. Other costs include: application fee, $50; books, $260; massage table, $500; linens, $50; and massage oil, $30.

Continuing education courses cost $160 to $350 each.

Financial Assistance

Payment plans and some scholarships and work-study are available.

Southwest Acupuncture College

325 Paseo de Peralta, Suite 500
Santa Fe, New Mexico 87501
Phone: (505) 988-3538
Fax: (505) 988-5438

Southwest Acupuncture College was founded in 1980, and an Albuquerque branch was opened in 1993. The college prides itself on its reputation as an "ivy league" college of Oriental medicine. A new branch opens in Denver in Fall 1997.

Accreditation

The college's Professional Master's Degree Program is accredited by the National Accreditation Commission for Schools and Colleges of Acupuncture and Oriental Medicine (NACSCAOM) and approved by the New Mexico Board of Acupuncture and Oriental Medicine. The school is also a member of the Council of Colleges of Acupuncture and Oriental Medicine (CCAOM).

Program Description

The college is a classical school of Oriental medicine and offers a professional program leading to a Master of Science degree in Oriental medicine. The 2,500-hour program is the equivalent of four academic years, and may be taken on a full-time, part-time, or accelerated basis (with completion in three calendar years). The daytime program is offered at the Santa Fe campus; the evening program, in Albuquerque.

The master's degree program consists of training in the five branches of traditional Oriental medicine: acupuncture, herbal medicine, physical therapy, nutrition, and exercise/breathing therapy, with the greatest number of hours devoted to acupuncture and herbal medicine. Courses include Botany, Chinese Medical Theory, Chinese Nutrition, Point Energetics, Point Location, Clinical Observation, Oriental Physical Therapy, Personal Energetics/Tai Chi or Qigong, Techniques of Acupuncture and Moxibustion, Introduction to Diagnosis, Chinese Herbal Materia Medica, Human Anatomy and Physiology, CPR, Tui Na, Needle Technique Practicum, Chinese Herbal Patent Medicines, Chinese Medical Theory/Zang Fu, Western Pathology and Diagnosis, Clinical Herbal Prescribing, and more. Over one-third of the program is spent in the college clinic.

Admission Requirements

Applicants must be 20 years of age or older, have completed at least two years of general education at the college level, and submit two letters of recommendation and a letter from a licensed health care professional regarding the applicant's physical condition. A personal interview is highly recommended.

Tuition and Fees

There is an application fee of $50 to $150 and a registration fee of $25 per semester/trimester. Total tuition is $26,300; books cost $500 to $600 per year; acupuncture supplies cost $200 to $300 per year; there is a clinic fee of $25 per semester/trimester and a student activity fee of $20 per semester/trimester.

Financial Assistance

Federal loans, scholarships, and a payment plan are available.

Taos School of Massage

P.O. Box 208
Arroyo Seco, New Mexico 87514
Phone: (505) 776-2024

The Taos School of Massage was founded in 1994 by J. Frederick Ritchie, whose focus is on working with people in a transformational bodymind context. Ritchie is trained in aikido and Feldenkrais, has done graduate work in family therapy, and has trained with Lar Short in bodymind clearing.

Accreditation

The 650-hour Massage Therapy Course is registered with the New Mexico Board of Massage Therapy; graduates are eligible to take the New Mexico State licensing exam.

Program Description

The 650-hour Massage Therapy Course consists of Therapeutic Massage (interviewing clients, contraindications, basic massage, Swedish massage, draping, corrective exercises, and reflexology), Advanced Sports Massage, Anatomy and Physiology, Hydrotherapy, Business Skills, Professional Ethics, CPR Certification/First Aid, Iridology, Aromatherapy, and Shiatsu, for a total of 450 hours. The remaining 200 hours consist of bodymind clearing, a system of transformational deep tissue massage, applied kinesiology, and body-centered facilitation skills, as well as meditation.

Admission Requirements

Applicants must be at least 18 years of age, have a high school diploma, and interview with an admissions representative.

Tuition and Fees

Tuition is $4,400; a summer intensive from mid-July through August costs $350 per week.

Financial Assistance

Students may deposit $2,200 and pay the balance in installments.

3HO International Kundalini Yoga Teachers Association

(*See* Multiple State Locations, page 319)

Wellness Institute

P.O. Box 2843
Taos, New Mexico 87571
Phone: (505) 758-8900

The Wellness Institute was founded in 1990 by Roger Gilchrist, M.A., R.P.P., who has been teaching polarity therapy since 1982. The programs at the institute focus on polarity therapy as well as craniosacral therapy and energy medicine.

Accreditation

The Polarity Therapy Professional Certification Training is accredited by the American Polarity Therapy Association (APTA), and all courses are based on the APTA Standards for Practice.

Program Description

The Wellness Institute offers Polarity Therapy Professional Certification Training and Advanced Training in Polarity Therapy in a modular continuing education program, as well as five-day introductory courses.

The three-week intensive Polarity Therapy Professional Certification Training is designed to serve the needs of both experienced professionals and newcomers to the healing arts. Topics include Theory and Research on the Human Energy System, Emotional Qualities Inherent in Specific Areas of the Body, Practical Interventions for Opening the Breath and Relaxing the Body, Craniosacral Balancing, Anatomical Adjustment Through Energy Balancing, Supervision of Clinical Work, and more. Upon completion, students are eligible to apply to APTA for Associate Polarity Practitioner (A.P.P.) status.

Community and Continuing Education

The modular program of Advanced Training in Polarity Therapy offers continuing education to Registered Polarity Practitioners (R.P.P.s). Modules include Craniosacral Therapy and the Energetic Body, Counseling Skills for Bodyworkers, Process-Oriented Bodywork, Deepening Polarity Therapy, the Healing Process, and Higher Love.

A five-day Introduction to Polarity Therapy seminar gives nurses, counselors, massage therapists and others in the healing arts an understanding of the five elements theory as well as hands-on skills in polarity therapy.

Tuition and Fees

Tuition for the Polarity Therapy Professional Certification Training is $1,500. Tuition for Advanced Training modules is $395 per module. Tuition for the Introduction to Polarity Therapy course is $395. Books, any private sessions, and lodging are additional.

Financial Assistance

Payment plans are available.

NEW YORK

Atlantic Academy of Classical Homeopathy

John F. McCourt, Secretary
399 Sixth Avenue, #3D
Brooklyn, New York 11215
Phone: (718) 518-4593

The Atlantic Academy of Classical Homeopathy (AACH) was founded in 1989. AACH offers a multifaceted approach to homeopathic study that includes introductory seminars, on- and off-campus programs, and advanced seminars. Classes are held in Manhattan.

Program Description

The 500-hour, on-campus program culminates in a Certificate in Homeopathy (CHom.). The program consists of a one-year foundation module and two years of advanced studies, plus advanced seminars that may be taken at the student's own pace. The Foundation Year may be taken on its own as a complete course in acute homeopathic therapeutics; more advanced students may enter at the second level.

The Foundation Year is a 140-hour first course in classical homeopathy covering such topics as History, Basic Philosophy, Principles of Health and Disease, Homeopathic First Aid, Acute Care, Introduction to Materia Medica and Repertory, and Introductory Case Taking and Case Analysis.

Advanced Studies: Materia Medica and Clinical Case Studies is open to anyone with 140 hours of prior instruction in homeopathy. Topics covered include In-Depth Analysis of Chronic Disease and Comparative Materia Medica, Clinical Analysis and Management of Complex Cases, and Applications of Homeopathy to Various Pathological States.

Classes meet one weekend per month for ten months, for a total of 140 credit hours per year. Students must take additional hours of study through optional AACH advanced seminars or at affiliated homeopathic schools in order to complete the 500 hours. Anyone may attend individual weekends without matriculating.

Students unable to attend classes in New York City may study with any AACH-approved instructor throughout the world through the Off-Campus Program. Students may progress and accumulate 500 hours at their own rate. The 500 hours of classroom study must include prescribed hours of instruction in Homeopathic Theory and Practice, Materia Medica, Repertory, Chronic Case Taking and Analysis, Therapeutics: Chronic, Therapeutics: Acute, Therapeutics: First Aid, Medical History,

Complementary Therapies, Counseling, Pharmacy, and Legal and Social Issues.

Admission Requirements

Either previous to or concurrent with classroom studies, students must complete college-level anatomy/physiology and pathology, CPR, and Red Cross First Aid.

Tuition and Fees

Annual tuition is $1,875, including a $100 application fee. The Advanced Class qualifying exam costs $50; there is a $150 fee for written exams; a $100 fee for research paper/cases reading; and a $250 fee for oral exams.

Ayurveda Holistic Center

82A Bayville Avenue
Bayville, New York 11709
Phone/Fax: (516) 628-8200

The Ayurveda Holistic Center was founded in 1988 by Swami Sada Shiva Tirtha; certification courses began in 1991. The center offers instruction both on-site and via correspondence.

Program Description

The one-year Certification Diploma Program consists of two semesters. Semester One covers Ayurvedic theory, including structure of the body, analyzing the client's cause of illness, health suggestions, introduction to Vedic spiritual counseling, and setting up an Ayurvedic business. Semester Two includes spiritual study (4 five-hour classes and 20 two-hour classes) and internship (6 one-on-one consultations and six pancha karma sessions). Classes meet one evening per week and five Sundays.

Admission Requirements

Prior to beginning either the on-site or correspondence program, students must receive an Ayurvedic consultation and follow the suggestions for some months; read four texts; and interview (in person, by phone, or by mail) with a center representative.

Tuition and Fees

Tuition is $2,000 for both semesters, including registration, books, and workbook.

Financial Assistance

A payment plan is available; a $100 discount is given for full payment in advance, and a $50 discount for half payment in advance.

Finger Lakes School of Massage

1251 Trumansburg Road
Ithaca, New York 14850
Phone: (607) 272-9024

The Finger Lakes School of Massage was founded in 1993 by Andrea Butje, who originally ran it as a branch of the Florida School of Massage. In December 1995, Andrea Butje and Cindy Black purchased the school from the Florida Institute of Natural Health, and are now co-owners and codirectors. The school is located in a historic stone building overlooking Cayuga Lake.

Accreditation

The Therapeutic Massage Licensing Program is approved by the New York State Board of Education. Graduates may take the New York or Florida state licensing exams or the national exam administered by the National Certification Board for Therapeutic Massage and Bodywork (NCBTMB).

Program Description

The 850-hour Therapeutic Massage Licensing Program may be completed in five-and-a-half months of full-time study, or as a part-time weekend program. The curriculum consists of Massage Therapy (including techniques of Swedish massage, neuromuscular therapy, sports massage, energy palpation, shiatsu, and connective tissue massage), Allied Modalities (including New York State massage law and business practices, pregnancy massage, infant massage, elderly massage, and others), Oriental Theory and Introduction to Practical Shiatsu, Massage Practicum: Clinic Internship, Hygiene and Hydrotherapy, Human Anatomy and

Physiology and Kinesiology, CPR and First Aid, and a directed independent study project.

Community and Continuing Education

Weekend continuing education workshops and advanced trainings are offered throughout the year. Introductory courses open to those with little or no experience include Introduction to Massage, Reflexology, and Polarity. Classes open to practicing massage therapists include Advanced Shiatsu, Polarity, Pregnancy Massage, Present Centered Awareness, and Reflexology.

Admission Requirements

Applicants must be at least 19 years of age (this requirement may be waived with a personal interview), have a high school diploma or equivalent, submit a biographical essay and two letters of reference from health care professionals, interview with an admissions representative, and have received massage. A tour of the school or attendance at an introductory workshop may, at the discretion of the staff, be substituted for the personal interview.

Tuition and Fees

Tuition is $6,300 to $6,500. Other costs include: application fee, $50; books, approximately $300; supplies, approximately $150; and optional massage table, $400 to $600.

Financial Assistance

Veterans' benefits are available, as well as aid through Vocational Education Services for Individuals with Disabilities (VESID) and the Job Training Program Administration (JTPA).

Green Terrestrial

Pam Montgomery
P.O. Box 266
Milton, New York 12547
Phone/Fax: (914) 795-5238
E-mail: greenpam@aol.com

Pam Montgomery has been teaching herbal apprenticeship programs since 1989. The facilities at Green Terrestrial are rustic and classes are largely outdoors.

Program Description

Green Terrestrial's Apprenticeship Program meets either two Tuesdays (for men and women) or one weekend (for women only) per month, April through October. The program combines classroom instruction with hands-on experience and includes Plant Identification; Wildcrafting; Co-Creative Partnership with Nature; Organic Herb Cultivation; Herbal Preparations/Formulations; Herbal First Aid Kit and Medicine Chest; Herbs for Women, Chronic Disease, the Immune System, Winter Discomforts, and Children; Wild Food Foraging and Cooking; Wise Woman Tradition of Healing; Creating an Herb Business; Herbal Networking; Flower Essences; and more.

An Advanced Intensive is offered to committed students who have already completed a basic course of study. The course combines classroom information exchange, field study, guest teachers, and home study, and meets for three 3-day periods in May, August, and October. Topics covered include Basic Anatomy, Women's Health and Hands-On Self-Help, Herbs and Systems of the Body, Diagnosis, Contraindications, Case Studies, Flower Erotica, Endangered Species, Plant Signatures, and Field Trip—Identification.

Admission Requirements

There are no age or educational requirements.

Tuition and Fees

Tuition for the Apprenticeship Program is $725 for Tuesdays, including materials, supplies, and lunch; and $950 for weekends, including materials, supplies, meals, and camping or indoor accommodations. Tuition for the Advanced Intensive is $675, including materials, food, and lodging.

Financial Assistance

Arrangements may be made on an individual basis.

Gulliver's Living and Learning Center

120 West 41st Street
New York, New York 10036
Phone: (212) 730-5433
Fax: (212) 730-5346

Gulliver's Living and Learning Center was founded in 1993. Faculty members include medical doctors, dietitians, macrobiotic chefs, authors, holistic health practitioners, and others.

Accreditation

There are currently no government standards for the licensing of macrobiotic teachers and counselors. Gulliver's is in the process of applying for government accreditation or affiliation with a degree-granting college. Graduates will be accepted into the Macrobiotic Educators Association (MEA) (see page 342) and receive a certificate of completion.

Program Description

The Modern Macrobiotics Professional Training Program, a one-year program with graduate studies, covers areas such as Macrobiotic Philosophy of Living, Cooking for Health and Spiritual Growth, Natural Healing, Visual Diagnosis and Health Assessment, and Massage. The setting at Gulliver's allows students to practice cooking, teaching, and counseling under the guidance of experienced instructors, thus honing their skills before beginning a professional practice. Small family groups provide support, sharing meals, massage, and personal experiences while creating a community environment. New students are assigned a mentor who will be their personal coach, speaking with them regularly and supervising their progress.

The course begins once a year in October; classes meet one weekend per month. The program permits students to enroll in most other classes at the center at no additional charge. Free orientations are scheduled on a regular basis.

Admission Requirements

Applicants must be able-bodied and emotionally stable to meet both the physical and mental demands of the program; there are no minimum age or educational requirements.

Tuition and Fees

Tuition is $1,750 when paid in full prior to class; otherwise, tuition is $1,950 payable in installments—$100 at registration and $250 per weekend until paid in full. Tuition includes instruction, handouts, course activities, a personalized binder, and several textbooks.

Financial Assistance

A payment plan, described above, is available. Any additional family member enrolling in this program is eligible for a 25 percent tuition reduction.

The Linden Tree Center for Wholistic Health

30 Manchester Road
Poughkeepsie, New York 12603
Phone: (914) 471-8000

The Linden Tree Center, founded in 1991 by Regina and Gary Siegel, was designed to provide wholistic care and educational experiences in such areas as herbs, nutrition, personal development, and alternative health practices.

Accreditation

The Polarity Therapy Training Professional Certification Program is certified by the American Polarity Therapy Association (APTA).

Program Description

In addition to seminars in such diverse areas as Yoga, Insight Meditation, Lyme Disease Support Group, Rebirthing, Creating Your Own Tarot Games, Natural Approaches to Menopause, and the Language of Astrology, the Linden Tree Center offers certificate programs in reiki and polarity therapy.

Reiki I and II are one-day programs limited to six students each. Reiki I is an introduction to reiki that teaches the students to channel healing energy for themselves or loved ones for the relief of stress and disease and for personal growth. In Reiki II, students receive one attunement and three symbols used for increasing the flow of energy, accessing the subconscious mind, and distance healing.

The 155-hour Polarity Therapy Training Professional Certification Program offers Level I training in polarity therapy; graduates are eligible to apply for national certification as an A.P.P. (Associate Polarity Practitioner). The course is divided into four independent courses that altogether take about a year to complete: Roots, a twenty-hour foundation course that teaches basic skills; Elements, a thirty-hour course in which students learn how Earth, Water, Fire, and Air manifest in the body through the chakras and in other ways; Systems, a thirty-hour course that offers an understanding of the nervous system and its functions from an energy perspective; and Wholes, a final thirty-hour course that explores the human body as a series of energetic systems and provides clinical practitioners training and more refined skills. Roots and Wholes are weekend intensives; Elements and Systems each consist of three 10-hour weekends.

Tuition and Fees

Reiki I costs from $100 to $150 on a sliding scale. Reiki II costs from $225 to $300 on a sliding scale.

Tuition for the polarity therapy courses is as follows: Roots, $300; Elements, $300; Systems, $300; and Wholes, $400.

Lodging is available for Roots and Wholes for an additional $25 to $35 per person.

The Natural Gourmet Cookery School/ The Natural Gourmet Institute for Food and Health

48 West 21st Street, Second Floor
New York, New York 10010
Phone: (212) 645-5170

The Natural Gourmet Cookery School was founded in 1977 by Annemarie Colbin, author of the best-selling books *Food and Healing, The Natural Gourmet,* and *The Book of Whole Meals.* The Chef's Training Program was instituted in 1985 and the school now trains approximately 144 students annually.

Accreditation

The school is licensed by the State of New York as a proprietary school and is in the process of applying for accreditation.

Program Description

The 600-hour Chef's Training Program (CTP), the only one of its kind in the world, trains students in the skills of health-supportive cooking in preparation for careers in natural foods establishments as well as private cooking and catering. The curriculum is divided into four segments: Tools, Techniques, Applications, and Improvisation. Instruction is given (through lectures, demonstrations, and hands-on cooking classes) in Equipment and Sanitation, Knives and Knife Skills, Ingredients, Food Science and Cooking Techniques, Cost Control and Pricing, Nutrition, Food and Health, Special Diet Cookery, Baking and Dessert Techniques, International Cookery, Creative Cooking and Meal Preparation, Opportunities in the Food Business, Business Skills, and more. Students must complete sixty hours of skills practice outside of regular classroom hours, including serving the Friday Night Dinner, stewarding practice, and auditing cooking classes for the public. In addition, students must complete an externship of ninety-five hours of work in an outside food establishment. The program is offered on a full- or part-time basis.

Community Education

A wide variety of classes are offered to the public in such areas as Basics of Healthy Cooking, Vegetarian Cooking Techniques, Gluten-Free Baking, Cooking With Herbs, Basics of Ayurveda, Food and Hypertension, PMS: A Dietary Approach, and many others. A two-week Basic Intensive offers an introduction and eighteen 3-hour cooking classes (two per day) in health-supportive cooking.

Admission Requirements

Applicants must have a high school diploma or equivalent, submit two letters of recommendation, and answer essay questions.

Tuition and Fees

Tuition is $9,400, including books, materials, and placement assistance; uniforms and equipment cost approximately $370, and there is a $100 application fee.

Tuition for individual classes varies from $60 to $220, depending on the length of the course.

Tuition for the Basic Intensive is $1,190.

Financial Assistance

Payment plans and long-term financing are available.

The New Center for Wholistic Health Education and Research

6801 Jericho Turnpike
Syosset, New York 11791-4413
Phone: (516) 364-0808
Fax: (516) 364-0989

The New Center for Wholistic Health Education and Research is a nonprofit institution founded in 1981 by Robert and Tina Sohn. The New Center provides education and training in acupuncture, Oriental medicine, Oriental herbal medicine, massage therapy, AMMA therapy, and wholistic nursing in a 43,000-square-foot facility on the North Shore of Long Island.

Accreditation

All New Center programs are accredited by the Accrediting Council for Continuing Education and Training (ACCET). The Acupuncture and Oriental Medicine Programs are seeking accreditation from the National Accreditation Commission for Schools and Colleges of Acupuncture and Oriental Medicine (NACSCAOM). The Massage Therapy Program is accredited by American Massage Therapy Association Commission on Massage Training Accreditation/Approval (AMTA/COMTAA) and has been submitted for approval to the American Oriental Bodywork Therapy Association (AOBTA) Council of Schools and Programs.

Program Description

The 1,230-hour Massage Therapy Program may be completed in sixteen months of full-time study or twenty-four months of part-time study. Courses include Anatomy and Physiology, Myology, AMMA Therapy Basic Technique, European Technique, Oriental Anatomy and Physiology, Ethics and Professional Development, Tai Chi Chuan, Massage Therapy Clinic, Neurology, Pathology, AMMA Therapy Applied Technique, European Applied Technique, Oriental Clinic Assessment, Kinesiology, Public Health, and others. Prior to treating patients at the New Center Clinic, students must pass a written entrance examination.

The 3,255-hour Oriental Medicine Program may be completed in four years of full-time study or six years of part-time study, resulting in a Diploma in Oriental Medicine. Year One includes Palpatory Anatomy, Myology, Introduction to TCM Philosophy and Wholistic Health, Oriental Physiology, Anatomy of Energy, Basic AMMA Therapy, Tai Chi Chuan, Biochemistry, TCM Pathogenesis, Points Location Lab, Western Pharmacology, Diagnostic Methods, Eastern Nutrition, Acupuncture Techniques, Introduction to Herbal Medicine, and more. Year Two includes Syndrome Analysis and Differential Diagnosis, Oriental Medicine Clinical Observation and Pharmacy, Herbal Pharmacopoeia, Treatment Principles, Internal Medicine, Western Nutrition, Oriental Medicine Clinical Assistantship, AMMA Therapy Clinic, and others. In Year Three, the curriculum covers Neurology, Patent Herbs, Oriental Medicine Clinic, Tai Chi Chuan/Qigong, Western Pathology, Western Medical Diagnosis, Current Oriental Medicine Research Data and Methodology, and more. Year Four includes Western Medical Treatment Principles, Clinical Analysis and Case Histories, Oriental Medicine Clinic, Kampo—Japanese Herbology, Classics: Shang Han Lun and Wen Bing, and more. First Aid and CPR certification must be obtained prior to the third year. Prior to treating patients, students must pass a written clinic entrance examination.

The 2,700-hour Acupuncture Program may be completed in three years of full-time study or five years of part-time study, resulting in a Diploma in Acupuncture. The first year of study is identical to that of the Oriental Medicine Program above. Year Two includes such courses as Western Physiology,

Neurology, Syndrome Analysis and Differential Diagnosis, Points Location Lab, AMMA Therapy Applied Technique, Acupuncture Clinical Observation, Western Medical Diagnosis, Treatment Principles, Acupuncture Techniques and Clinical Observation, Western Nutrition, Western Pathology, Internal Medicine, Acupuncture Clinical Assistantship, Ethics and Professional Development, and others. Year Three includes Western Medical Treatment Principles, Clinical Analysis and Case Histories, Acupuncture Clinic, Current Oriental Medicine Research Data and Methodology, Tai Chi Chuan/ Qigong, and others. First Aid and CPR certification must be obtained prior to the third year. Prior to treating patients, students must pass a written clinic entrance examination.

The 2,700-hour Oriental Herbal Medicine Program may be completed in three years of full-time study or five years of part-time study, resulting in a Diploma in Oriental Herbal Medicine. Year One includes Palpatory Anatomy, Western Physiology, Biochemistry, Introduction to TCM Philosophy and Wholistic Health, Oriental Physiology, Introduction to Herbal Medicine, Tai Chi Chuan, Neurology, Western Nutrition, TCM Pathogenesis, Herbal Pharmacopoeia, Herbal Pharmacy, Western Pharmacology, Western Pathology, Diagnostic Methods, Eastern Nutrition, Patent Herbs, Ethics and Professional Development, and more. Year Two includes Syndrome Analysis and Differential Diagnosis, Western Medical Diagnosis, Treatment Principles, a continuation of the herbal courses, Herbal Clinical Observation, Western Medical Treatment Principles, Internal Medicine, Kampo—Japanese Herbology, Classics: Shang Han Lun and Wen Bing, Herbal Clinic Assistantship, and more. Year Three includes Clinical Analysis and Case Histories, Herbal Clinic, Tai Chi Chuan/Qigong, Current Oriental Medicine Research Data and Methodology, and more. First Aid and CPR certification must be obtained prior to the third year.

Continuing Education

A 906-hour Advanced AMMA Therapy Program is offered to graduates of the Massage Therapy Program who have also completed sixty college credits and hold a license or New York State Limited Permit. The sixteen-month course consists of four 15-week trimesters, resulting in a Diploma in AMMA Therapy. Courses include TCM Pathogenesis, Advanced AMMA Therapy Technique, Patient Management/Case History Review, Advanced AMMA Therapy Clinic and Clinical Observation, Tai Chi Chuan, Western Medical Diagnosis, Diagnostic Methods, Western Pharmacology, Syndrome Analysis and Differential Diagnosis, Western Medical Treatment Principles, Introduction to Herbal Medicine, and more.

A 652-hour Wholistic Nursing Program with AMMA Therapy offers instruction to registered professional nurses who seek serious training in wholistic health care. Classes meet one weekend per month for thirty months. The curriculum includes Oriental Anatomy and Physiology, Conceptual and Theoretical Frameworks for Wholistic Nursing Practice, Basic AMMA Therapy, Stress Management, Tai Chi Chuan, Oriental Clinical Assessment, Nutrition, Introduction to Herbology, Oriental Diagnosis, Applied and Advanced AMMA Therapy, Professional Development, and Clinical Practice, which consists of seventy-five hours of observation, seventy-five hours of hands-on wholistic nursing, and twenty-two hours of documentation, in addition to regularly scheduled weekend classes.

Professional continuing education workshops in other areas of complementary health care are offered to health care professionals throughout the year.

Admission Requirements

All applicants must submit proof of a physical examination that demonstrates satisfactory health; be a United States citizen or an alien lawfully admitted for permanent residence; and be able-bodied and emotionally stable.

Applicants to the Massage Therapy Program must be at least 18 years of age and have a high school diploma or equivalent; submit three letters of recommendation, one of which must be from a New York State licensed health care professional; submit a short essay; and interview with an admissions representative.

Applicants to the Oriental Medicine, Acupuncture, and Oriental Herbal Medicine Programs must be at least 18 years of age and have completed at least sixty semester hours of study in an accredited college or university, at least nine semester hours of which are in the biosciences (this prerequisite may be completed concurrently with the program); submit three letters of recommendation, one of which must be from a New York State licensed health care professional; submit a brief essay; and interview with an admissions representative.

Tuition and Fees

Tuition for the Massage Therapy Program is $11,685. Other costs include: application fee, $50; registration fee, $100; books, $400 to $650; massage oils and uniforms, approximately $300; required massage table, $350 to $450; clinic liability insurance, $50; and clinic entrance exam, $50.

Tuition for the Oriental Medicine Program is $30,923 ($9.50 per clock hour). Other costs include: application fee, $85; registration fee, $100 per year; and books and supplies, approximately $2,000 per year.

Tuition for the Acupuncture and Oriental Herbal Medicine Programs is $25,650 ($9.50 per clock hour). Other costs include: application fee, $85; registration fee, $100 per year; and books and supplies, approximately $2,000 per year.

Tuition for the AMMA Therapy Program is $8,607 ($9.50 per clock hour). Other costs include: application fee, $65; one-time registration fee, $100; and books and supplies, approximately $400.

Tuition for the Wholistic Nursing with AMMA Therapy Program is $6,520. Other costs include an application fee of $50 and a registration fee of $100.

Financial Assistance

Payment plans and federal grants and loans are available.

New York Chiropractic College

2360 Route 89
Seneca Falls, New York 13148-0800
Phone: (315) 568-3040 / (800) 234-6922
Fax: (315) 568-3015

New York Chiropractic College (NYCC) was founded in 1919 by Dr. Frank E. Dean as Columbia Institute of Chiropractic. It is the oldest chiropractic college in the Northeast.

Accreditation

NYCC is accredited by the Commission on Accreditation of the Council on Chiropractic Education (CCE) to award the Doctor of Chiropractic (D.C.) degree. NYCC holds an Absolute Charter from the New York State Board of Regents and is regionally accredited by the Commission on Higher Education, Middle States Association of Colleges and Schools.

Program Description

The 4,990-hour Doctor of Chiropractic (D.C.) degree may be completed in ten trimesters. Course hours are divided into three areas: Center for Preclinical Studies (1,455 hours) includes anatomy, biochemistry, physiopathology, and microbiology and public health; Center for Clinical Studies (1,950 hours) includes diagnosis, diagnostic imaging, clinical laboratory, associated studies, chiropractic principles, chiropractic procedures, and ancillary therapeutic procedures; and Center for Clinical and Outpatient Services (1,585 hours) includes clinical conferences and seminars, and clinical services.

Continuing Education

NYCC offers a wide variety of seminars enabling practicing doctors of chiropractic to keep abreast of new techniques and advances in the profession. Programs leading to the diplomate status include Neurology, Nutrition, Orthopedics, Radiology, and Sports Injuries. Programs leading to certification include Electrodiagnosis Testing, Hospital Protocol, Manipulation Under Anesthesia, Rehabilitation, Meridian Therapy, and Occupational Health. License renewal/certificate programs include Applied Kinesiology, AIDS, Child Abuse, Chiropractic Adjunctive Therapy, and Chiropractic Assistant Training.

Admission Requirements

Applicants must have completed at least sixty semester hours of credit toward a baccalaureate degree from an accredited, degree-granting institution with a G.P.A. of 2.25 or higher. Specific courses in the sciences, social sciences, and humanities are required. Applicants must submit three letters of recommendation (one from a doctor of chiropractic) and interview with an admissions representative.

Tuition and Fees

Tuition is $4,380 per trimester for twenty to twenty-eight credit hours, and $185 per credit above or below this range. There is an application fee of $60; a one-time enrollment fee of $400; a general fee of $135; and a graduation fee of $162.

Housing is available for $750 double, $1,500 single, and $1,680 married per trimester. Meal plans are also available.

Financial Assistance

Federal grants, loans, and work-study; NYCC and New York State scholarships; and additional student loans including ChiroLoan and Canadian ChiroLoan.

New York Open Center

83 Spring Street
New York, New York 10012
Phone: (212) 219-2527
Fax: (212) 219-1347

The New York Open Center was founded in 1984 as a nonprofit organization and emphasized one-day or weekend workshops covering a variety of holistic practices. The center is now moving toward longer-term, in-depth programs. An assortment of topics is offered in formats ranging from one evening to one year in length.

Accreditation

The Reflexology Program prepares students to receive national certification from the American Reflexology Certification Board. The Polarity Therapy Training Program prepares students to join the American Polarity Therapy Association (APTA) as Associate Polarity Practitioners (A.P.P.).

Program Description

The one-year Aromatherapy Diploma Course is held over ten weekends and focuses on the safe and practical application of over 140 essential oils, twenty perfume absolutes, and over twenty carriers. Topics include Introductory Weekend; Chemistry; Botany; Blending, Customizing, and Perfumery; Aromatherapy Massage and Reflexology; Skin and Hair Care; Consultation and Designing Treatments; Pregnancy, Children, and First Aid; Subtle Aromatherapy and Aroma Fitness; and Psycho-Aromatherapy and the Business of Aromatherapy. The first weekend may be taken separately without registering for the year-long program.

Green Medicine: An Eight-Month Training in Herbalism offers a comprehensive overview of the medicinal and nutritional uses of Western herbs. Topics covered include A Brief History of Western Herbalism, Gaia in Action, Preparations and Dosages, Herbal Pharmacy: Making Herbal Products, the Digestive System and Liver, the Respiratory System, the Nervous System and Brain, the Endocrine System/Immune System, the Circulatory System: Blood and Lymph/Immune Systems, the Skin, Herbal Energetics, Women's Reproductive System, Men's Reproductive System, Treating Infections and Parasites with Herbs and Essential Oils, Seasonal Cleansing/Spring Tonics, Musculoskeletal System, Urinary Tract and Kidneys, Traditional Herbal Diagnosis, Materia Medica/Herbal Medicine Chest, Spring Tonics and Wild Edibles Field Trip with Pam Montgomery, and Case Taking I and II. Sessions are held on Monday evenings and Saturdays.

A 120-hour Training Program in Reflexology prepares students to receive national certification from the American Reflexology Certification Board. The curriculum includes forty-two hours of hands-on practice, twenty-eight hours of lectures and demonstrations, seventeen hours of anatomy and physiology, 30 one-hour documented sessions, two hands-on tutorial refinement sessions, and one reflexology treatment from the instructor. Instruction is divided into three sections (basic, advanced, and masters) held on Saturdays and Sundays. The thirty-hour Basic Course may be taken independently.

The 165-hour Polarity Therapy Training Program prepares students to join APTA as Associate Polarity Practitioners (A.P.P.s). Courses include Basic Polarity I and II, Basic Polarity Counseling, Polarity Reflexology, Polarity Clinic, Supervision, and Evaluation and Preparation for Practice. Courses are held Tuesday evenings or on weekends, and may be taken separately.

Tuition and Fees

Tuition for the Aromatherapy Diploma Course is $2,200 to $2,700; the introductory weekend may be taken separately for $170 to $190. Fees include all materials, workbooks, and a complete aromatherapy kit.

Tuition for the Green Medicine Course is $760 to $880.

Tuition for the Training Program in Reflexology is $1,325 to $1,375. The Basic Course taken separately is $460 plus one $50 tutorial; three private tutorials cost $50 each.

Tuition for the Polarity Therapy Training Program is $1,700 to $1,750; workbook and personal polarity sessions received are additional.

Non-members pay a $10 registration fee.

Financial Assistance

Discounts are given to members and for full payment in advance; payment plans and need-based full and partial scholarships are available.

Ohashi Institute

(*See* Multiple State Locations, page 313)

Omega Institute

260 Lake Drive
Rhinebeck, New York 12572-3212
Phone: (914) 266-4444 / (800) 944-1001

Omega Institute has been a leader in holistic learning for over twenty years, offering a blend of education and vacation. About 10,000 people come to the institute throughout the summer season. Omega's campus is located on eighty acres of hills and woodlands in the Hudson River Valley, two hours north of New York City.

Accreditation

Some programs at Omega qualify for CEUs from a variety of organizations, including the American Holistic Nurses Association (AHNA), the National Certification Board for Therapeutic Massage and Bodywork (NCBTMB), the National Board for Certified Counselors (NBCC), the National Association of Social Workers (NASW), the Certification Board for Music Therapists (CBMT), and others.

Program Description

Omega offers an extensive variety of classes and workshops in many different areas. Workshops may be taken for professional development, vacation-time enjoyment, or personal growth.

Workshops focusing on various forms of alternative medicine include Qigong for Prevention and Healing, Homeopathy, Aromatherapy, Primordial Sound Mediation, A Holistic Approach to a Healthy Immune System, Mind-Body Medicine, Past-Life Therapy Professional Training, Holistic Nursing, Holistic Somatic Methods for Bodyworkers and Therapists, Foot Reflexology, ANMA: Art of Japanese Massage, Subtle Energy Fields, Thai Massage, Ohashiatsu, Iyengar Yoga, Hatha Yoga, and others.

Among the month-long intensive trainings offered are Yoga Teacher Training, Bodywork Training, and Movement Therapy Training.

The Interdisciplinary Yoga Teacher Training Certificate Course synthesizes diverse styles and traditions of yoga. Instruction covers yoga postures and breathing techniques from traditions that include Astanga, Hatha, Iyengar, and Kripalu yoga; anatomy and kinesiology; how to teach a posture and design lesson plans; yoga philosophy; assessing individual needs; the practicalities of establishing a yoga class; and more.

The Embodiment: Interdisciplinary Bodywork Training Certificate Course is a comprehensive training program for bodyworkers, physical therapists, and others who want to give their clients a higher level of healing. Topics include how to design a session that leads to deeper engagement of the whole person; myofascial techniques; the role of awareness and intention; anatomy and physiology of fascia; take-home exercises for clients; hands-on energy healing; exercises for awakening intuition; and more.

The Movement Therapy and DansKinetics Teacher Training Certificate Program is designed for yoga teachers, bodyworkers, fitness teachers, and others who wish to explore the healing power of movement. Topics covered include the art and craft of teaching DansKinetics, a creative approach to fitness combining a cardiovascular workout with expressive movement, and organ anatomy movement exercises that strengthen the life force and integrate body, mind, and heart.

Tuition and Fees

Workshop fees vary with length and content of course.

The month-long intensive training programs cost $1,995. Cottages, dormitory housing, camping facilities (all with meals), and child care are available for an additional fee.

Financial Assistance

Partial scholarships, work-study, and a community exchange program are available; discounts are given for early registration, full-time students, and senior citizens.

Pacific Institute of Oriental Medicine

(*See* Multiple State Locations, page 313)

Polarity Wellness Network of New York

132 East 85th Street, Suite 2-1
New York, New York 10028
Phone: (212) 327-4050
Fax: (212) 327-4049

Over the past seventeen years, the International Polarity Wellness Network curriculum has been used to train hundreds of polarity practitioners worldwide.

Accreditation

The Polarity Wellness programs are accredited by the American Polarity Therapy Association (APTA).

Program Description

A 450-hour Polarity Wellness Educator Program is offered to Associate Polarity Practitioners (A.P.P.s) who wish to expand upon their learning; completion leads to certification by the International Polarity Wellness Network and fulfills eligibility requirements for status as a Registered Polarity Practitioner (R.P.P.). Requirements include Basic Craniosacral Balancing, Cranial Rhythms and Cerebrospinal Fluid, Advanced Craniosacral Balancing, Nervous System and Five Star Balancing, Energetic Nutrition, Cleansing and Bodywork, Spinal Energy Balancing, Polarity Counseling II or Body/Trance Counseling, Advanced Polarity Exercise Seminar, Professional Speaking, Practice Building and Business, Ethics and Law, clinic, supervision, electives, polarity evaluation and internship, ten receiving sessions, and fifty giving sessions. The recommended time frame for completion is twenty-one months.

The 160-hour Polarity Structural Balancing Program and the 300-hour Polarity Counseling Program are designed for bodyworkers and other health professionals who would like to incorporate aspects of polarity into established practices.

Completion of the Polarity Structural Balancing Program leads to certification through the International Polarity Wellness Network in polarity structural balancing. Requirements include Basic Craniosacral Balancing, Cranial Rhythms and Cerebrospinal Fluid, Advanced Craniosacral Balancing, Nervous System and Five Star Balancing, Spinal Energy Balancing, Anatomy Home Study, twenty receiving sessions, and thirty giving sessions. The program may be taken over one to two years.

Completion of the Polarity Counseling Program leads to certification through the International Polarity Wellness Network in polarity counseling. Requirements include Basic Polarity Counseling, Polarity Counseling II, Body/Trance Counseling, Relationship Counseling, Dream Counseling, Counseling Supervision/Study Groups/Clinic, receiving session, and giving sessions/apprenticeship. The program may be taken over two or more years.

Admission Requirements

Applicants to the Polarity Wellness Educator Program must be graduates of an A.P.P.-level program.

Tuition and Fees

Tuition for the Polarity Wellness Educator Program is $4,500, not including electives, supervision, study groups, and personal polarity sessions received.

Tuition for the Polarity Structural Balancing Program is $1,650, not including sessions received.

Tuition for the Polarity Counseling Program is $2,400.

Financial Assistance

Payment plans are available.

The Rubenfeld Center

115 Waverly Place
New York, New York 10011
Phone: (212) 254-5100
Fax: (212) 254-1174

The Rubenfeld Center offers instruction in the Rubenfeld Synergy method—a system for the dynamic integration of body, mind, and spirit that integrates elements of body/mind teachers such as F.M. Alexander and Moshe Feldenkrais, as well as the Perls' gestalt theory and Erickson's hypnotherapy. This method uses verbal expression, movement, breathing patterns, body posture, caring touch, and more to access blocked reservoirs of emotion. There are over 300 certified Rubenfeld Synergists worldwide.

Program Description

Training in the Rubenfeld Synergy method consists of three modules per year over four years, covering Rubenfeld BodyMind Exercises; Somatic Skill Building: Introduction to Use of Touch and Movement; Somatic Skill Practicum; the Theory, Technique, and Art of a Rubenfeld Synergy Session; Rubenfeld Synergy Practicum; Principles of Humanistic Psychology; Ethics, Values, and Professional Practice; Personal RSM Lessons/Sessions; written essay assignments and projects; practice and model clients; regional training; and advisor/advisee contact. Certification hinges on evaluations by faculty and staff. Training programs begin in the fall and meet three weeks per year; two days are added in the fourth year for certification. Training takes place either at the Rubenfeld Center in Greenwich Village, or in upstate New York.

Admission Requirements

Each applicant must submit an application, photos, and references, and participate in at least one workshop conducted by Ilana Rubenfeld. Applications are evaluated on the bases of professional development, personal integrity, and readiness to train for professional practice.

Tuition and Fees

There is a $50 application fee. Tuition is $3,300 for the first year, and may be raised for subsequent years; two additional days in the fourth year cost $275.

Swedish Institute School of Massage Therapy and Allied Health Sciences

226 West 26th Street, 5th Floor
New York, New York 10001
Phone: (212) 924-5900

Founded in 1916, the Swedish Institute is the oldest school of massage therapy in the United States. The school is located in the heart of midtown Manhattan, within easy walking distance of public transportation.

Accreditation

The massage curriculum at the Swedish Institute has been approved by the American Massage Therapy Association Commission on Massage

Training Accreditation/Approval (AMTA/COMTAA). The school is accredited by the Career College Association (CCA), a national accrediting agency.

Program Description

The 692-hour massage curriculum includes courses in Anatomy and Physiology, Pathology, Basic Massage (Swedish), Intermediate Massage, Medical Massage, Clinical Internship, Shiatsu, CPR and First Aid, and Business Practices.

Continuing Education

Advanced training is offered to licensed massage therapists and other health care professionals. Advanced massage classes include Aromatherapy for Massage Therapists, Alexander Technique, Chair Massage Techniques, Carpal Tunnel Massage Program, Direct Myofascial Release, Craniosacral Basics, Dr. Vodder's Manual Lymph Drainage, Ice Therapy, Hidden Energies, NLP and Ericksonian Hypnosis, Myofascial and Trigger Point Therapy, Reflexology Certification Course, Reiki, Working with a Chiropractor, and many others.

An Advanced Shiatsu and Oriental Studies Certification Program includes such courses as Acupuncture Without Needles, Advanced Hara Evaluation, Chinese Massage Therapy, Chinese Pulse Diagnosis, Iridology Simplified, Traditional Thai Massage Experience, and others.

A series of courses is offered through the International Tai Chi Institute for the continuing education of acupuncturists, Oriental medical practitioners, and massage therapists. Courses include Application of Chinese Herbs on Acupoints, Chinese Dietary Therapy, Chinese Herbal Medicine, Chinese Hydrotherapy, Tai Chi Chuan, Qigong, Taoist Meditation, Chinese Medical Treatment of Infections, and others.

Admission Requirements

Applicants must be at least 18 years of age, have a high school diploma or equivalent, be of good moral character, professional in attitude and appearance, in good physical health and capable of performing therapeutic massage, and interview with an admissions representative.

Tuition and Fees

There is a $35 application fee; tuition is $6,500; and books, uniforms, and equipment cost approximately $550.

Financial Assistance

Payment plans and federal grants and loans are available.

Teleosis School of Homeopathy

The Clocktower Building
3 Main Street
Chatham, New York 12037
Phone: (518) 392-7975
Fax: (518) 392-6456

The Teleosis School of Homeopathy will begin its educational programs in 1997 under the direction of Dr. Joel Kreisberg, a Doctor of Chiropractic (D.C.) with a degree in classical homeopathy from the Hahnemann College of Homeopathy. Dr. Kreisberg completed his advanced clinical training at a homeopathic hospital in India, and is board certified in classical homeopathy; he now serves as the president of the Council on Homeopathic Education (CHE). The school is applying for not-for-profit status.

Accreditation

The Teleosis School of Homeopathy is in the process of being accredited by the Council on Homeopathic Education (CHE). Upon completion of the practitioner program, graduates will be eligible to take examinations from the North American Society of Homeopaths, the National Board of Homeopathic Examiners, and the Council on Homeopathic Certification.

Program Description

The practitioner program is divided into two self-contained modules, each of which takes two years to complete. Ideally, the student will complete both modules in order to be a fully trained practitioner.

The 300-hour Foundation Program begins in the spring and will meet one weekend per month, ten months a year, for two years. The program will cover Homeopathic Philosophy; Materia Medica; Seventy of the Most Common Polycrests; Differentials for the Twenty Most Common Diseases Homeopathy Treats; Homeopathic Practice Methodology, including case taking, case analysis, case management, and repertory; and Personal and Practitioner Development.

The 300-hour Clinical Program begins in the fall and will meet one weekend per month, ten months a year, for two years. Topics include Long-Term Case Management; Advanced Topics in Philosophy; Materia Medica of the Smaller Remedies; Materia Medica Differentials of Extreme Pathologies; Clinical Case Management; Practice Management; and Supervision.

Continuing Education

Postgraduate clinics are open to students who have completed 300 hours of previous training, and are held in New York City and Albany. Through clinical training, students integrate their study and practice into real life situations, further develop their analysis and management skills, and consider subtler issues including problem patients, stuck cases, and practitioner burnout. The New York City postgraduate clinic meets sixty hours per year for two years; the Albany clinic, to begin in 1998, will meet fifty hours per year for two years.

Admission Requirements

The Foundation Program is open to students and professionals. Students applying for admission to the Clinical Program must have completed 300 hours of previous homeopathic training.

Tuition and Fees

There is a $50 application fee that is applied toward tuition if the student is accepted.

Tuition for the Foundation and Clinical Programs is $1,350 per program when paid in advance, $1,500 per program when paid in three installments, or $175 per month.

The New York City Postgraduate Clinic costs $1,050 per year for two years. The Albany Postgraduate Clinic costs $600 per year for two years.

Financial Assistance

A payment plan is available.

Tri-State Institute of Traditional Chinese Acupuncture

P.O. Box 890
Planetarium Station
New York, New York 10024-0890
Phone: (212) 496-7869

Main Campus and Clinic:
80 8th Avenue (4th Floor)
New York, New York 10011

Branch Clinic:
16 East 16th Street
New York, New York 10003

The Tri-State Institute of Traditional Chinese Medicine is one of the oldest acupuncture schools in the United States; it was founded in 1979 as an affiliate of the Institute of Traditional Chinese Medicine of Montreal.

Accreditation

The institute is accredited by the National Accreditation Commission for Schools and Colleges of Acupuncture and Oriental Medicine (NACSCAOM).

Program Description

The Acupuncture Therapy Institute (ATI) offers a three-year master's-level program in acupuncture designed to train acupuncture therapists to work in clinics, hospitals, medical offices, or private practice. Students must complete 1,914 hours of work at the institute, plus 290 hours of corequisites.

Year One includes Philosophical Bases, Pathways of Qi, Surface Energetics and Primal Reserves, Treatment Planning and Basic Techniques, American Acupuncture, Acupuncture Electives, Acupuncture Human Service Skills, Acupuncture Skills Review, Western Clinical Pathophysiology, Acupuncture Clinical Observation/Personal Treatment (students must receive ten acupuncture treatments), and Independent Study Project.

Year Two includes Energetic Pathogenesis and

TCM Patterns of Disharmony, Western Medical Disorders and Traditional Chinese Medical Pathology, Acupuncture Energetics, Reaction Patterns and Advanced Zang Fu Differentiation, American Acupuncture, Acupuncture Electives, Acupuncture Human Service Skills, Acupuncture Skills Review, Western Clinical Pathophysiology, Clinical Observation/Personal Treatment, Clinical Grand Rounds, and Independent Study Project.

Year Three includes Clinical Field Seminars, Acupuncture Electives, Acupuncture Skills Review, Clinical Practicum, Optional Clinical Externship, Supervision, Clinical Grand Rounds, Personal Acupuncture Treatment, Independent Study Project, and Case Presentation.

In addition to regular class work, students must complete the following outside classes: Bodywork, Anatomy and Physiology, one hundred hours of direct patient contact, and CPR certification.

Continuing Education

The Postgraduate Institute offers a 300-hour Acupuncture Certification Program for physicians, the completion of which leads to certification in New York State to practice acupuncture. Courses in the program include Philosophical Overview, the Pathways of Qi, Surface Energetics, Treatment Planning and Basic Techniques, Patterns of Disharmony, Clinical Grand Rounds, Acupuncture Skills, and Clinic. Classes are held on weekends.

The Postgraduate Institute also offers a four-module, 450-hour Program in Chinese Herbal Medicine, designed to meet or exceed the standards for eligibility for the NCCA certification examination in herbology. Courses focus on Materia Medica, Theoretical Models for Organizing Chinese Herbal Formulas, Clinical Specialties and Their Commonly Used Formulas, and Clinical Practice. Classes are held on weekends.

Admission Requirements

Applicants must have completed sixty credits at an accredited college or university, including nine credits in the biosciences and eight credits of anatomy and physiology, which must be completed before Year Three. Applicants must submit copies of professional licenses or certificates in health care (if applicable), a completed five-page essay, two letters of recommendation from health professionals, and official transcripts.

Applicants to the Acupuncture Certification Program for physicians must submit an application form along with proof of a current license in medicine, osteopathy, or dentistry.

Applicants to the Program in Chinese Herbal Medicine must be second-year students or graduates of an accredited or candidate school of acupuncture and Oriental medicine recognized by the NACSCAOM. Applicants trained outside the United States must also be Diplomates in Acupuncture of the National Commission for the Certification of Acupuncturists (NCCA).

Tuition and Fees

Tuition for the Acupuncture Therapy Institute is $3,350 per semester. Other costs include: application fee, $50; books and materials, approximately $500 to $700 for three years; and Clinical Pathophysiology fee, $100 to $200.

Tuition for the Acupuncture Certification Program for physicians is $3,975.

Tuition for the Program in Chinese Herbal Medicine is as follows: Module 1 (first year), $1,750; Modules 2 through 4 (second year), $1,950.

Financial Assistance

Payment plans and federal loans are available.

Susun S. Weed

Wise Woman Center
P.O. Box 64
Woodstock, New York 12498
Phone: (914) 246-8081

Susun S. Weed, founder of the Wise Woman Center, editor-in-chief of Ash Tree Publications, and a high priestess of Dianic Wicca, offers workshops, intensives, and apprenticeships in herbal medicine and shamanic healing, as well as correspondence courses (see page 369). Ms. Weed sits on the advisory boards of the California Institute of Integral Studies and the Rosenthal Center for Alternative

Studies at Columbia University. The Wise Woman Center was founded in 1982.

Program Description

Shamanic Apprenticeships (for women only) offer full-time, live-in learning consisting of weed walks, hands-on herbal practice, tarot readings, trances, moonlodges, and ceremonies.

Weed Wise Apprenticeships offer sixty hours of instruction, field guides and herbals, tarot reading, consultations, and more.

Three-day herbal medicine intensives and one-day workshops are offered spring through fall; courses include Green Witch Intensive, Using Herbs Simply and Safely, Herbal Medicine Chest, Chronic Problems, Magical Plants, and Menopausal Years.

Admission Requirements

Beginners and advanced students are welcome; no prior experience or education is required.

Tuition and Fees

Weed Wise Apprenticeships cost $900 to $1,000. Shamanic Apprenticeships cost $450 per week for a minimum of six weeks. Three-day intensives cost $195 to $450. One-day workshops cost $40 to $55.

Financial Assistance

Financial assistance in the form of 50 percent work/barter is available to all students; scholarships are available to women of color and Native American women.

Reese Williams, L.Ac., R.P.P.

270 Lafayette Street #805
New York, New York 10012
Phone: (212) 343-9382

Reese Williams, L.Ac., R.P.P., has offered training in polarity therapy since 1991. Mr. Williams maintains an active practice encompassing polarity, craniosacral therapy, and Oriental medicine. The teaching program, which includes guest faculty, allows students to study with experienced practitioners in small groups.

Accreditation

Both trainings are registered with the American Polarity Therapy Association (APTA). Graduates of the introductory training are eligible for Associate Polarity Practitioner (A.P.P.) certification. Students with A.P.P. certification who successfully complete the advanced training are automatically eligible for Registered Polarity Practitioner (R.P.P.) certification.

Program Description

An Introductory Training in Polarity Therapy takes the form of seven weekend seminars over seven months. Students gain an understanding of the polarity energy model, learn the basic principles and practices of polarity energy bodywork, and work with the Five Elements (ether, air, fire, water, and earth) in creating sessions that reestablish free flow of the elemental energies.

An Advanced Training in Polarity Therapy provides in-depth study and integration of polarity therapy, craniosacral therapy, and counseling in preparation for professional practice. Clinical supervision allows students to give sessions to community volunteers under the instructor's supervision. The main part of the training is structured in twelve independent modules, each four days in length, scheduled at eight-week intervals throughout the year. These modules consist of the Polarity Energy Model, Craniosacral I and II, Counseling I and II, Autonomic Nervous System, Five Element Energetics, Connective Tissue Therapy, Clinical Practice I and II, Advanced Energy Palpation, and Structural Balancing. A second part, consisting of twenty hours of polarity yoga, twenty hours of business skills, and twenty hours of energetic nutrition, is scheduled at convenient times during the year. The training may be completed in as little as twenty-four months. Students are also required to receive ten sessions from Registered Polarity Practitioners.

Continuing Education

Advanced Training Seminars are open to polarity practitioners or other body-oriented therapists who are not interested in R.P.P. certification.

Admission Requirements

For the introductory course, no specific past education is required. The Advanced Training Seminars are intended for polarity practitioners who have taken a beginning-level training and are working toward R.P.P. certification, or for other body therapy practitioners who wish to continue their professional studies.

Prospective applicants are invited to attend an open house to meet the teachers and learn more about the philosophy of the training.

Tuition and Fees

Tuition for the introductory course is $1,470, including workbook, paid in seven installments of $210 each; textbook is additional.

Tuition for the advanced course is $360 per module; Polarity Yoga, Energetic Nutrition, and Business Skills cost approximately $10 per training hour; books are approximately $175; and ten polarity sessions are additional.

NORTH CAROLINA

Body Therapy Institute

South Wind Farm
300 South Wind Road
Siler City, North Carolina 27344
Phone: (919) 663-3111 /
    (888) 500-4500 (toll-free)
Fax: (919) 663-0369

The Body Therapy Institute (BTI) was founded in Chapel Hill, North Carolina in 1983, and moved to its new home on 150 country acres in 1995.

Accreditation

BTI is licensed by the North Carolina Department of Community Colleges, Division of Proprietary School Services, which licenses only those massage schools offering a curriculum of 500 hours or more. The Massage Therapy Program is approved by the American Massage Therapy Association Commission on Massage Training Accreditation/Approval (AMTA/COMTAA) and the Florida State Board of Massage. The Polarity Therapy Certification Program meets the American Polarity Therapy Association's (APTA) requirements for certification as an Associate Polarity Practitioner (A.P.P.). The Advanced Myofascial Release Certification Program leads to the designation Certified Advanced Rolfer.

Program Description

The 625-hour Massage Therapy Certification Program is a synthesis of Eastern and Western bodywork systems. Courses include Massage Therapy (fundamentals of massage theory and practice, personal integration, deep tissue massage, polarity therapy, Oriental massage technique, and synthesis of clinical skills), Anatomy and Physiology, Somatic Psychology, Clinical Practicum, Business and Marketing Practices, Hydrotherapy and Allied Modalities, Massage Laws and Professional Ethics, Community Service Project, and HIV/AIDS Awareness. Students must also complete an American Red Cross module in First Aid/CPR, and are required to receive at least four professional bodywork sessions during the training. The daytime program is eight months in length; the evening/weekend program runs eleven months.

Community and Continuing Education

Two-day introductory massage workshops are periodically offered to the public, featuring an introduction to Swedish massage. Additionally, a thirty-hour, ten-week Introduction to Massage Therapy series is also offered to the public.

BTI offers a range of continuing education workshops and advanced training programs to the professional practitioner. Subjects include structural and energetic approaches to bodywork, movement repatterning, basic cranial work, somatic psychology, reflexology, and others.

Beginning in 1997, BTI will offer two new programs open to graduates of a 500-hour massage/bodywork program.

Advanced Myofascial Release is a 250-hour

certification program leading to the designation Certified Advanced Rolfer. Students will learn the ten-session model of structural integration proposed by Dr. Ida P. Rolf, learn advanced principles of organizing and integrating the connective tissue, and recognize and work with psychophysical shock/trauma in the body. The course is offered in a series of six 4-day sessions.

In the 155-hour Polarity Therapy Certification Program, students will learn the basic theory of polarity therapy, practice the polarity yoga exercises, learn a general balancing sequence, elemental sequences and chakra work, learn the Five Elements, and explore both orthodox and energetic models of anatomy. The course is offered in a series of three 5-day sessions.

Admission Requirements

Applicants must be at least 19 years old, have a high school diploma or equivalent, be free of communicable disease, be physically and emotionally capable of practicing massage, and interview with an admissions representative. Additionally, applicants must have received at least two massage therapy/bodywork sessions and must have taken an introductory massage class or workshop before they enroll.

Prerequisites for the Advanced Myofascial Release Program include at least one Basic Myofascial Seminar with Dr. Shea, graduation from a 500-hour massage/bodywork school or equivalent, and at least two years of professional practice.

Prerequisites for the Polarity Therapy Certification Program include graduation from a 500-hour massage/bodywork school or equivalent.

Tuition and Fees

There is a $25 application fee and a $100 registration fee. Tuition is $6,200; books cost approximately $260; a massage table costs $400 to $700; a school shirt costs $36; a First Aid/CPR course costs $35; and four professional bodywork sessions cost $30 to $60 each.

Tuition for the Introductory Massage Workshop is $95. Tuition for the ten-week Introduction to Massage Therapy Course is $195. Tuition for the Advanced Myofascial Release Course is $2,500. Tuition for the Polarity Therapy Certification Program is $1,500.

Financial Assistance

Payment plans and work-study are available.

Carolina School of Massage Therapy

103 West Weaver Street
Carrboro, North Carolina 27510
Phone: (919) 933-2212 / (919) 929-1064

The Carolina School of Massage Therapy (CSMT) is a program of the Community Wholistic Health Center, a not-for-profit membership organization that has provided educational and health care services since 1978. The Carolina School of Massage Therapy was founded in 1987.

Accreditation

CSMT's Massage Therapy Program is approved by the American Massage Therapy Association Commission on Massage Training Accreditation/Approval (AMTA/COMTAA).

Program Description

The 650-hour Massage Therapy Program includes classes in Anatomy and Physiology, Communications and Somatics, Swedish Massage/Clinic, Sports Massage/Clinic, Deep Muscle Massage/Clinic, Joint Mobilization, Polarity, Oriental Bodywork, Business Practices, Case Studies, Hydrotherapy, and Integrative Seminars.

Weekday and weekend scheduling options are available.

Community and Continuing Education

Faculty members offer additional classes outside the curriculum throughout the year that can enhance the learning experience of the student. These classes include Body Centered Therapy, Tai Chi, Experiential Anatomy, Reflexology, Polarity, Acupressure, Pregnancy Massage, and related topics.

Community education workshops are offered throughout the year. Recent topics have included

Introduction to Massage, Pregnancy Massage, and Reflexology.

Admission Requirements

Applicants must be 18 years old by the first day of class; have a high school diploma or equivalent; be emotionally and physically capable of performing the required activities; have some experience giving and receiving massage; and satisfy all requirements described in the application.

Tuition and Fees

There is a $40 application fee. Tuition is $6,320; books are approximately $300; a massage table costs $400 to $800, or a rental table costs $32 per month.

Financial Assistance

An extended payment plan and scholarships are available.

OHIO

Central Ohio School of Massage

1120 Morse Road, Suite 250
Columbus, Ohio 43229
Phone: (614) 841-1122 / (800) 466-5676
Fax: (614) 841-0387

The Central Ohio School of Massage (COSM) was founded in 1964 by Peg and Tommy Thompson, licensed massage therapists since 1953.

Accreditation

The COSM massage therapy program is approved by the American Massage Therapy Association Commission on Massage Training Accreditation/ Approval (AMTA/COMTAA). Graduates are eligible to take the Ohio State Medical Board examination for massage therapist licensure.

Program Description

The 670-hour, eighteen-month Basic Swedish Massage Course includes Anatomy, Physiology, Massage (including both theoretical and practical study of techniques, uses, limitations, and physiological effects, plus cytology, osteology, arthrology, myology, neurology, and angiology), and additional studies (including ethics, business practices, patient approach, use of heat and cold, restorative exercises, and others). Students are also required to complete a course in Basic Life Support and First Aid. Classes may be taken on a daytime or evening schedule.

Continuing Education

The 170-hour, twenty-week Myofascial Therapy Course is an advanced studies program that combines advanced Swedish massage techniques with trigger point techniques, somatic fascial releases, post-isometric muscle relaxation, and other deep tissue therapies.

Admission Requirements

Applicants to the Basic Swedish Massage Course must have a high school diploma or GED; complete and submit a Massage Preliminary Education Form to the State Medical Board of Ohio; and submit two character references, an essay, and a completed health certificate.

The Myofascial Therapy Course is open to massage therapists licensed in the State of Ohio, to other health professionals by special arrangement, and to those who have completed the first nine months of the Basic Course.

Tuition and Fees

Tuition for the Basic Swedish Massage Course is $6,300. There is an application fee of $50; books cost approximately $300; and a massage table is additional.

Tuition for the Myofascial Therapy Course is $1,750; books and supplies are approximately $300.

Financial Assistance

An interest-free payment plan is available.

Ohio Academy of Holistic Health

3033 Dayton-Xenia Road
Dayton, Ohio 45434
Phone: (513) 427-0506 / (800) 688-8211

The Ohio Academy of Holistic Health (OAH) was founded in 1987 by Patti McCormick, Ph.D., and offers a variety of educational programs in the holistic health professions. The faculty is comprised of licensed medical and mental health professionals.

Accreditation

Contact hours awarded by the academy have been approved by the American Osteopathic Association, the State of Ohio Counselor and Social Worker Board, the Ohio Nurses Association, and the Ohio Psychological Association. OAH is registered by the State Board of Proprietary Schools.

Program Description

The 209½-hour Clinical Hypnotherapy Certification Program consists of courses in Basic Hypnotherapy, Psychology for Hypnotherapists, Advanced Hypnotherapy, Hypnotherapy Preceptorship, First Aid/CPR, Medical Terminology, Anatomy and Physiology: A Holistic Model, and Therapeutic Communications.

The 177½-hour Reflexology Certification Program includes Anatomy and Physiology: A Holistic Model, Basic Reflexology, Reflexology Preceptorship, Advanced Reflexology, First Aid/CPR, Medical Terminology, and Therapeutic Communications.

The 157½-hour Holistic Health Education avocational program includes courses in First Aid/CPR; Medical Terminology; Anatomy and Physiology: A Holistic Model; Therapeutic Communications; Current Trends in Holistic Health; Holistic Health Preceptorship; six 12-hour Holistic Health Modules in Holistic Nutrition, Aromatherapy, Transformational Touch: Healing Energy Work, Nature's Path: Developing Your Herbal Medicine Chest, Energy Awareness and Healing, and Mother Earth and Compassionate Healing; and one 12-hour elective chosen from either Experiential Shamanic Workshop or Crystals: the Power Tool of Vibrational Healing.

Students must maintain a cumulative grade of 80 percent or higher.

Continuing Education

Postgraduate courses are offered in Non-Directive Imagery, Ericksonian Hypnotherapy and Neurolinguistic Programming (NLP), and Advanced Ericksonian Hypnotherapy and Neurolinguistic Programming. Other short-term programs, such as Body Reflexology, Regression Theories and Techniques, Applied Kinesiology, and Hypnoanesthesiology, are offered to specific professional groups.

Admission Requirements

Certification program applicants must be at least 21 years of age, have a high school diploma, be of good moral character, submit a goal statement, and interview with an admissions representative.

Tuition and Fees

There is a $20 application fee. Tuition for the Clinical Hypnotherapy Certification Program is $3,143. Tuition for postgraduate seminars ranges from $85 to $495, depending on length. Tuition for the Reflexology Certification Program is $2,663. Tuition for the Holistic Health Certification Program is $2,363.

Financial Assistance

Short-term OAH payment plans and extended bank payment plans are available.

Optissage, Inc.

7041 Zane Trail Road
Circleville, Ohio 43113
Phone: (614) 474-6436 / (800) 251-0007

The idea for Optissage, whose goal is "optimum performance through massage," was conceived separately by Patricia Whalen-Shaw and Len Montavon, both licensed massage therapists, a full two years before they met to form the Optissage company in 1993. Optissage is the teaching and performance of massage on animals, specifically horses, cats, and dogs. (See page 385 for information on instructional videos in equine and canine massage.)

Accreditation

Optissage is approved by the National Certification Board for Therapeutic Massage and Bodywork (NCBTMB) as a continuing education provider under category A.

Program Description

Courses are offered in equine, feline, and canine massage. Each class covers Animal Anatomy and Physiology, Massage Theory, Massage Clinical Practical, and Application.

Equine Level I is a six-day introductory massage course that emphasizes Swedish and sports massage techniques and pre- and post-event massage theory and practice. Call the school for information on bringing your horse to the clinic. The Equine Level II course includes more in-depth anatomy and physiology, massage technique applications, and injury-specific case studies.

Canine Level I is a three-day introductory course emphasizing general relaxation massage and sports massage. Participants are encouraged (but not required) to bring a canine friend. Canine Level II teaches more in-depth anatomy and massage applications.

Feline Level I is a two-day class using Swedish and sports massage techniques and exploring anatomy, physiology, and personality traits. Participants are encouraged (but not required) to bring a feline companion.

Admission Requirements

There are no minimum age or educational requirements for the Level I courses. Although not required, it is helpful if the participant is familiar with the animal's skeletal musculature and/or has studied massage therapy.

Canine or Equine Level I is a prerequisite course for Canine Level II. Equine Level I or individual therapist training and experience is a prerequisite for Equine Level II.

Tuition and Fees

There is a nonrefundable deposit of $100. Tuition for the Equine Courses ranges from $780 to $850. Tuition for the Canine Courses ranges from $100 to $299. Tuition for the Feline Level I Course is $199.

Financial Assistance

Assistance may be offered on individual case request.

The Qigong and Human Life Research Foundation Eastern Healing Arts Center, Tian Enterprises, Inc.

3601 Ingleside Road
Shaker Heights, Ohio 44122
Phone: (216) 475-4712 /
    (800) 859-4343 toll-free
Fax: (216) 752-3348

The Qigong and Human Life Research Foundation (QHLRF) is dedicated to the dissemination of information about traditional Chinese qigong. The qigong tradition taught in this system is the Inner Dan Arts and Eastern Healing Technique, introduced to the United States in 1988 by Qigong Master Tianyou Hao. In 1991, Master Hao designed the elective courses, Qigong I and II, that he teaches at the Case Western Reserve University School of Medicine. Master Hao has studied and practiced qigong for over fifty years.

Program Description

The Inner Dan Arts' Qigong System focuses on prevention (health and longevity), mind power, self-healing, and qi healing.

Intensive training options offered once a year include: Instructor Training (six days) with certification; Eastern Healing Arts (five days), which is the equivalent of Qi Healing Systems I, II, and III with certificate of completion; a guided correspondence program for instructor training that is equivalent to the six-day intensive Instructor Training; and weekend workshops in mind power and self-healing, qigong philosophy and relaxation, eastern qi healing arts, and the shao-lin stick healing techniques. Usually, two workshops are scheduled per weekend.

Weekly scheduled offerings include Beginning/ Intermediate, High, and Super Classes, Tai Chi, Qi Healing Systems I, II, and III with certification, Qigong Therapy, and Diet Class.

Tuition and Fees

Scheduled workshops in Cleveland, Ohio cost $85, plus $10 for materials. Tuition for the Instructor Correspondence Course is $1,250.

Workshops "on location" are pro-rated due to logistics. Contact QHLRF for current, pro-rated fees for other offerings.

Self-Health, Inc.
School of Medical Massage

P.O. Box 474
130 Cook Road
Lebanon, Ohio 45036
Phone: (513) 932-8712
Fax: (513) 933-9539

Self-Health, Inc., School of Medical Massage admitted its first students in 1981 and moved to its current location in 1989.

Accreditation

The Massage Program at Self-Health, Inc., is approved by the American Massage Therapy Association Commission on Massage Training Accreditation/Approval (AMTA/COMTAA).

Program Description

The 600-hour Massage Program is available in two formats: the eighteen-month program, which meets for eight hours per week, and the twelve-month honors program, which meets for twelve classroom hours per week. Some additional hours are required for the honors program and will be announced in advance.

The curriculum is divided into two tracks of study: Anatomy/Physiology and Massage. The Massage curriculum includes current psychological issues, history of massage, draping, terminology, palpatory skills, medical history taking, practice of complete therapeutic massages, business prac-

tices, and intensive review for the Ohio State Board exam. Students provide ten complete therapeutic massages with a preceptor and ten contact hours at an approved outreach site. Students must complete an Adult CPR course prior to graduation.

Admission Requirements

Applicants must have a high school diploma or equivalent; those with no science background or a grade of less than 2.25 in human sciences may be required to successfully complete a course in human anatomy/physiology prior to being considered for admission. In addition, applicants are required to submit two letters of reference, documentation of all legal name changes (such as marriage, divorce, and adoption), and a health examination form.

Tuition and Fees

Tuition is $5,300, or $5,600 for the honors program. Other costs include: application fee, $50; books and lab fees, approximately $400; massage table, $400 to $700; oils and other supplies, $50 to $100; Adult CPR certification, $25 to $35; Adjunctive Clinical Faculty, $200 to $250; and optional fourth semester cadaver study, $10.

Financial Assistance

A payment plan is available.

OKLAHOMA

Oklahoma School of Natural Healing

1660 East 71st Suite 2-O
Tulsa, Oklahoma 74136-5191
Phone: (918) 496-9401 / (800) 496-9401
Fax: (918) 496-4461

The Oklahoma School of Natural Healing was founded in 1980 by director Robert L. Groves. It is the state's oldest operating licensed school of massage therapy.

Accreditation

The Oklahoma School of Natural Healing has been licensed since 1988.

Program Description

The 250-hour Massage Technician Program meets schooling requirements for a City of Tulsa license. Courses include Anatomy and Physiology I and II, Polarity Therapy, Reflexology, Swedish Massage I and II, Business Skills, and 110 hours of Practicum.

The 650-hour Massage Therapist Program includes all of the above courses, as well as Nutrition, Myofascial Release, Hydro/Heliotherapy, Herbology, Deep Tissue Therapies, and 250 hours of Practicum.

Community and Continuing Education

The school offers a variety of community education courses and advanced training workshops.

Admission Requirements

Applicants must be over 18 years of age, have a high school diploma or GED, be of good moral character, submit a physician's statement of health, and interview with the director.

Tuition and Fees

There is a $25 application fee. The total cost of the Massage Technician Program is $1,950, including tuition, books, table, and supplies. The total cost of the Massage Therapist Program is $4,710, including tuition, books, table, and supplies.

Financial Assistance

A prepayment discount is available on professional programs; limited government assistance is available through JPTA or the Department of Vocational Rehabilitation.

Praxis College of Health Arts and Sciences

808 N.W. 88
Oklahoma City, Oklahoma 73114-2511
Phone: (405) 949-2244 / (405) 879-0224
Fax: (405) 946-7040

Praxis College was founded in 1988. In 1994, the school moved into a new 6,000-square-foot facility and purchased an existing massage center in Oklahoma City.

Accreditation

Praxis College is approved by the Associated Bodywork and Massage Professionals (ABMP) and licensed by the Oklahoma Board of Private Vocational Schools.

Program Description

The 1,100-hour Certified Massage Therapist Program includes courses in Fundamentals of Professional Practice, Pathology/Nutrition, Hydrotherapy, Human Performance, Athletic Massage, Psychotherapeutic Massage, Oriental Massage, and Energy Field Massage.

A 500-hour Associate Massage Technician Program prepares students to work in an entry-level position for a certified massage therapist, chiropractor, or physical therapist. Topics covered in this program include Basic Sports Massage, Full-Body Massage, Chair Massage, Reflexology, and Beginning Skills to Safely Practice Massage. Praxis guarantees that students who complete this program will pass the national certification exam or tuition will be refunded.

Admission Requirements

Admission requirements vary with each program; contact the admissions office for specific information.

Tuition and Fees

Tuition for the 1,100-hour program is $2,800; books and supplies are approximately $1,000. Tuition for the 500-hour program is $500, including books.

Financial Assistance

Interest-free loans, work-study, and scholarships are available.

OREGON

The American Herbal Institute

3056 Lancaster Drive N.E.
Salem, Oregon 97305
Phone: (503) 364-7242 /
(888) 437-2539 (toll-free)

The American Herbal Institute (TAHI) was founded in 1992; in 1990 and 1991, TAHI's courses were taught for the National Health Care Institute in Salem. The school has also offered a correspondence course for the past two years (see page 365).

Program Description

A course in Modern Herbal Studies may be taken for either a Certified Modern Herbalist Certificate (sixty-nine credits) or a Master's Certification (ninety credits).

Required courses for the Certified Modern Herbalist Program include Herbology I and II, Nutrition I, Anatomy/Physiology, Remedies Lab, Bowel Health, and three credits of electives.

To earn the Master's Certificate, in addition to the requirements above, students must also complete Herbology III, Nutrition II, Phytochemistry, Case Studies, Field Studies, six credits of electives, and Independent Master Studies.

Electives for both programs change from year to year and may include Reflexology, Healing with Flowers, Herbs for Men's and Women's Reproductive Health, Iridology, and Introduction to Shiatsu. Electives may be taken as individual classes independent of the certification programs.

Classes are held in the evenings at the Herb Lady store.

Admission Requirements

Classes are open to everyone.

Tuition and Fees

Tuition for the Certified Modern Herbalist Course (sixty-nine credits) is $760 (1997 estimate). Tuition for the Master's Certificate Course (ninety credits) is $990 (1997 estimate).

Ashland Massage Institute

P.O. Box 1233
Ashland, Oregon 97520
Phone: (541) 482-5134

The Ashland Massage Institute (AMI) was founded in 1988. AMI's director, Beth Hoffman, L.M.T., has studied massage and bodywork since 1979 and has been in private practice since 1983.

Accreditation

The Prelicensing Program at AMI is accredited by the Oregon State Massage Board, and the school is licensed as a private vocational school by the Oregon State Department of Education. The program exceeds the 330 class hours required for the practice of massage in Oregon; graduates are eligible to take the Oregon massage licensing exam.

Program Description

The 550-hour Massage Prelicensing Program may be completed in one or two years. Classes include Swedish Massage, Shiatsu, Hydrotherapy, Core Communication Skills, Neuromuscular Activation, Massage for Specific Conditions, Assessment Skills for the Massage Therapist, Myofascial Trigger Point Therapy, Polarity, Supervised Clinic, Business and Ethics, Introduction to Deep Tissue, Oriental Bodywork, Practical Review, Kinesiology, Anatomy and Physiology, and Pathology. Students must receive two professional massages and complete First Aid/CPR training at a local hospital or Red Cross center.

Community and Continuing Education

One- and two-day classes offered to members of the community include Introduction to Massage, Introduction to Shiatsu, Shiatsu Stretch Massage, and Timeless Face.

One- and two-day classes offered to the massage professional include Introduction to Shiatsu; Introduction to Myofascial Release; Shiatsu Stretch Massage; Mindful Touch; Timeless Face I, II, and

III; and Functional Assessment in Massage Therapy. In addition, a three-day Infant Massage Instructor Training Program prepares nurses, physical therapists, massage therapists, and other professionals to conduct the Loving Touch Parent-Infant Massage Program for parents with newborns.

Admission Requirements

Applicants must be at least 18 years of age, submit an application form, and interview with an admissions representative.

Tuition and Fees

Tuition for the Massage Prelicensing Program is $4,150. Other costs include: application fee, $30; books, approximately $245; two professional massages, $70 to $100; optional massage table, $350 to $500; and linens and oil, approximately $20. Community classes range from $55 to $160. Classes for the professional cost $55 to $295. The Infant Massage Instructor Training Program is $425.

Financial Assistance

A payment plan is available.

Cascade Institute of Massage and Body Therapies

1250 Charnelton Street
Eugene, Oregon 97401
Phone: (503) 687-8101

The Cascade Institute of Massage and Body Therapies (CIMBT) was founded in 1988 by Ruth and Tracy Wise. Ruth Wise is an R.N. with sixteen years of private practice as a massage therapist.

Accreditation

CIMBT is certified by the Oregon Massage Technicians' Licensing Board.

Program Description

The curriculum for the 565-hour Professional Training Program for Oregon State licensing includes Anatomy and Physiology, Pathology, Kinesiology, Student Clinic, Massage (including Swedish, acu-pressure energetics, deep tissue muscle sculpting, treatment of pain, and an introduction to myofascial release and trigger point therapy), Ethics, Community Outreach, Body Movement Analysis, Hydrotherapy, CPR/First Aid, and written and practical review. Students must receive at least two professional massages before starting the program, and receive at least six full-body massages during the program, three of which must be from professionals. Classes are held mornings or evenings and some Saturdays.

Continuing Education

Classes are offered to licensed massage professionals in such areas as Muscle Sculpting Bodywork; Human Cadaver Lab; Sports Massage/Onsen: Treatment of Pain; On-Site Massage; and Business Mastery.

Admission Requirements

Applicants must be at least 18 years of age; have a high school diploma or equivalent; be capable of financing their education; have received two professional massages; submit an essay, two letters of recommendation, and a letter from a doctor, naturopath, or chiropractor verifying that the applicant is in good health; and interview with an admissions representative.

Tuition and Fees

There is a $150 registration fee. Tuition is $3,985; books and supplies are approximately $250 to $400; three professional massages cost $75 to $135; and a massage table costs (average) $350.

Financial Assistance

A payment plan is available and a discount is given for early registration.

East-West College of the Healing Arts

4531 S.E. Belmont Street
Portland, Oregon 97215
Phone: (503) 231-1500 / (800) 635-9141
Fax: (503) 232-4087

East-West College of the Healing Arts (EWC) was founded in 1972 as the Midway School of Massage. In 1981 the present owner and president, David Slawson, purchased the college and integrated it into a healing arts community known as Common Ground. In 1993, under the direction of Jeff Smith, EWC purchased a 16,000-square-foot campus located in a quiet Portland neighborhood.

Accreditation

Two of EWC's massage training programs are approved by the American Massage Therapy Association Commission on Massage Training Accreditation/Approval (AMTA/COMTAA).

Program Description

The 397-hour Oregon Licensure Program is the shortest program offered by EWC. Graduates of this program are eligible to take the Oregon massage board exam. This three-term program includes instruction in massage, anatomy/physiology, kinesiology, hydrotherapy, clinical practices, and pathology.

EWC offers two AMTA-approved massage training programs. Option One, a 529-hour program, includes all the courses in the Oregon Licensure Program plus 132 hours of electives; Option Two, a 661-hour program, adds 264 hours of electives. Electives offered change from term to term but include Bodymind Therapy, Deep Tissue Massage, Externship, Hospital Massage, Neuro-Humoral (Russian) Massage, Polarity Therapy, Shiatsu, Sports Massage, and Transformational Hypnotherapy.

Independent students may enroll in individual courses without being registered in the massage training programs. Day and evening classes are available.

Continuing Education

EWC offers continuing education classes, workshops, and seminars on a regular basis that fulfill AMTA and state massage board continuing education requirements.

Admission Requirements

Applicants must be at least 18 years of age; have a high school diploma or equivalent; take the Wonderlic Basic Skills Test, a standardized test of basic math and verbal skills, administered by EWC; be approved for giving and receiving massage by a physician's statement; and have received one documented Swedish massage from a licensed massage therapist.

Tuition and Fees

Tuition for the Oregon Licensure Program is $3,732, plus a linen and oil fee of $120. Tuition for Option One is $4,973, plus a linen and oil fee of $200. Tuition for Option Two is $6,213, plus a linen and oil fee of $280. Tuition for independent students is $10.40 per hour. Other costs include: application fee, $100; books, $250 and up; massage table, $350 to $450; and professional treatments, $80 to $120.

Financial Assistance

Payment plans and limited scholarships are available.

National College of Naturopathic Medicine

11231 S.E. Market Street
Portland, Oregon 97216
Phone: (503) 255-4860
Fax: (503) 257-5929

The National College of Naturopathic Medicine was founded in 1956 and is the oldest accredited naturopathic school in North America. The college is located on a seven-acre campus seven miles from downtown Portland.

Accreditation

National College is accredited by the Council on Naturopathic Medical Education (CNME) and recognized by all state and provincial boards of naturopathic examiners, as well as by the Council of Education of the Canadian Naturopathic Association. The Homeopathic Therapeutics Certification Program is accredited by the Council on Homeopathic Education (CHE).

Program Description

The four-year, 245½-hour N.D. Program, which may also be taken in five years, prepares students for state board licensing examinations and the practice of naturopathic medicine. After passing the board licensing exam, physicians are licensed as Doctors of Naturopathic Medicine.

First-year courses include Anatomy and Lab, Physiology, Biochemistry, Medical Histology and Lab, Basic Science Clinical Correlations, Naturopathic Medical Philosophy and Therapeutics, Hydrotherapy, Palpation Lab, Psychology and Counseling, Skills of Communication, Neuroanatomy, Microbiology, Research and Statistics, Embryology, Pathology, Immunology, Psychological Assessment, and Clinic, among others.

The second-year curriculum includes Classical Chinese Medicine, Clinical/Physical Diagnosis and Lab, Clinical Case Presentations, Physical Diagnosis Lab, Laboratory Diagnosis, Pharmacology, Public Health, Physiotherapy, Clinic, Botanical Materia Medica and Pharmacognosy, Homeopathy, Nutrition, Orthopedics and Naturopathic Manipulative Therapeutics, and others.

In the third year, topics include Diagnostic Imaging, Gynecology, Obstetrics, Emergency Medicine, Minor Surgery, Office Orthopedics, Environmental Medicine, Cardiology, Pediatrics, Gastroenterology, the Doctor-Patient Relationship, Clinic, and more.

The fourth year includes Summer Clinic; Eye, Ear, Nose and, Throat; Dermatology; Endocrinology; Geriatrics; Gynecology Lab; Preventive Exercise; Stress Management; Neurology; Urology; Proctology; Oncology; Business Practice Seminar; Counseling Techniques; Medical Genetics; Jurisprudence/Medical Ethics; and Clinic.

Several elective courses are offered each term. Certificate programs in homeopathy and obstetrics consist of a series of courses that supplement the required courses in these fields. Other electives include Northwest Herbs, Chronic Viral Disease, Advanced Minor Surgery, and Natural Pharmacology.

Students may take a five-year, dual-degree program that includes both the N.D. degree and a classical Chinese medicine master's degree.

Students intending to include natural childbirth in their practices may complete five elective courses, covering the pregnancy, childbirth, postpartum, and neonatal periods, to earn a Certificate in Naturopathic Obstetrics. Certification meets the current board requirements for academic preparation in all states that require special training in this area.

A Certificate in Homeopathic Therapeutics, consisting of eight courses covering various aspects of homeopathy, is open to health care professionals (see **Admission Requirements** below). Students must also complete one hundred hours of preceptorship and a research paper; submit ten and orally present five chronic cases; submit and orally present at least ten acute cases; pass an oral exam; and submit videotapes of two first interviews of chronic cases.

Admission Requirements

Applicants to the N.D. Program must have a bachelor's degree from an accredited college, including twenty semester credits of premedical chemistry and biology, one college-level course in physics, six semester credits in the social sciences (including one course in psychology), and six semester credits of humanities. Preparatory work in anatomy and physiology is also useful. Applicants must submit two letters of recommendation and interview with an admissions representative.

Applicants to the Homeopathic Therapeutics Program must hold a degree allowing them to legally diagnose and treat disease, or requiring them to practice under the supervision of a licensed physician.

Tuition and Fees

There is a $60 application fee. Tuition for the full-time, four-year N.D. track is $13,200 per year ($10,755 per year for the five-year track); tuition for less than full-time enrollment (less than eleven credits) is $225 per credit. Summer clinic (third year only) costs $1,100; books, supplies, and diagnostic equipment are additional. Tuition for the eight 3-credit courses in the Homeopathic Therapeutics Program is $225 per credit, for a total of $5,400.

Financial Assistance

Payment plans, partial deferment, federal loans, and work-study are available.

Oregon College of Oriental Medicine

10525 S.E. Cherry Blossom Drive
Portland, Oregon 97216
Phone: (503) 253-3443
Fax: (503) 253-2701

The Oregon College of Oriental Medicine was founded in 1983 by licensed acupuncturists Eric Stephens and Satya Ambrose. OCOM is located ten miles east of downtown Portland.

Accreditation

The Master's Degree Program in acupuncture and Oriental medicine at OCOM is accredited by the National Accreditation Commission for Schools and Colleges of Acupuncture and Oriental Medicine (NACSCAOM). Graduates are eligible to take the California licensing examination for acupuncture and Oriental medicine. After passing the National Commission for the Certification of Acupuncturists (NCCA) exam, NCCA diplomates are eligible to apply to the Oregon State Board of Medical Examiners for Oregon licensing; graduates also successfully apply for licensing in many other states.

Program Description

The four-academic-year Master of Acupuncture and Oriental Medicine degree program may be completed in three calendar years.

The first year includes instruction in Traditional Chinese Medical Theory, Point and Channel Location, Medical History: East and West, Living Anatomy, Tui Na, Shiatsu, Western Medical Terminology, Qigong, Anatomy and Physiology, Chinese Herbal Medicine: The Pharmacopoeia, Case Observation and Demonstration, and more.

The second year covers such topics as TCM Pathology and Therapeutics, Point Actions and Indications, Public Health: Community Health and Chemical Dependency, Tai Chi Chuan, Advanced Qigong, Western Medical Pathology, Chinese Herbal Medicine: Formulas, Auricular Acupuncture, Topics in Clinical Research, Dynamics of Illness, and more.

The third year includes Survey of Western Physics, Clinical Internship, Seminar and Section, Herbal Patent Medicine, Jin Shin Do, Structural Diagnosis/Meridian Therapy, Research Practicum, Western Clinical Diagnosis, Diet and Nutrition, Clinical Herbal Internship, Western Pharmacology, Ethics and Practice Management, Introduction to Issues in Public Health, and Community Health Internship.

Admission Requirements

Applicants must have completed at least three years of college (ninety semester credits) at an accredited institution; OCOM recommends that students have completed four years of college. The applicant must have completed college-level courses in general biology, chemistry, and psychology; it is recommended that the applicant also have completed college-level anatomy and physiology. Applicants must submit two personal essays and two letters of recommendation, and interview with an admissions representative.

Tuition and Fees

There is a $50 application fee. Full-time tuition is $120 per credit (non-matriculated and half-time tuition is $140 per credit); clinical internship tuition is $160 per credit; the orientation fee is $50; and books and lab expenses per quarter are $75 to $200. Total estimated cost for the entire program is $26,900.

Financial Assistance

A payment plan, federal grants and loans, and work-study are available.

Western States Chiropractic College

2900 N.E. 132nd Avenue
Portland, Oregon 97230
Phone: (503) 251-5734 / (800) 641-5641
Fax: (503) 251-5723

Western States Chiropractic College (WSCC) was

founded in 1904 and is located in a residential suburb of Portland.

Accreditation

WSCC is accredited by the Northwest Association of Schools and Colleges and by the Council on Chiropractic Education (CCE).

Program Description

The 4,596-hour Doctor of Chiropractic (D.C.) degree program is typically completed in four years (twelve quarters). The curriculum is a prescribed course of study in which all core classes must be successfully completed in the proper sequence; additional non-credit elective courses may be taken for further study in an interest area.

Courses in the Division of Basic Science include Spinal Anatomy, Gross Anatomy, Cell Biology/Histology, Biochemistry, Embryology, Neuroanatomy, Physiology, Microbiology and Public Health, General Pathology, Neurophysiology, Nutrition, Clinical Microbiology and Public Health, Genetics, Clinic Research Methods, and Toxicology and Pharmacology.

The Division of Clinical Science includes courses in CPR/Emergency Care, Clinical Reasoning and Problem Solving, Physical Diagnosis, Clinical Lab, Dermatology and Infectious Disease, Patient/Practice Management, Clinical Pathology, Chiropractic Physiological Therapeutics, Clinical Nutrition, Jurisprudence and Ethics, Obstetrics, Cardiorespiratory Diagnosis and Treatment, Gastroenterology Diagnosis and Treatment, Genitourinary Survey, Narrative Report Writing, Clinical Pediatrics, Clinical Geriatrics, Clinical Psychology, Minor Surgery/Proctology, and others.

The Department of Radiology includes such courses as Radiographic Anatomy, Bone Pathology, Radiographic Technique, Soft Tissue Manipulation, Soft Tissue Interpretation, and Roentgenometrics.

Courses in the Division of Chiropractic Science include Biomechanics and Palpation, Philosophy and Principles of Chiropractic, Adjustive Technique, Soft Tissue Therapies/Rehabilitation, and Neuromusculoskeletal Diagnosis and Treatment.

The Division of Clinics covers Clinic Observation I through III and Clinic Phase I through IV-C.

The Bachelor of Science in Human Biology degree program is open only to D.C. students; consult the catalog or a WSCC representative for more information.

Continuing Education

The Division of Continuing Education and Postgraduate Studies provides education offerings through seminar, certification, and diplomate programs for D.C. graduates of all accredited chiropractic colleges. Offerings are designed to meet chiropractic relicensure credit as required by the Oregon Board of Chiropractic Examiners and by boards in neighboring states.

Admission Requirements

Applicants must have completed at least two years (sixty semester hours or ninety quarter hours) of course work at a regionally accredited junior college, college, or university with a minimum G.P.A. of 2.25 on a 4.0 scale. Specific course requirements include at least six semester hours each of biology, general chemistry, organic chemistry, and physics; and at least twenty-four semester hours of humanities and social sciences, including at least six semester hours in English composition and three semester hours in psychology.

An on-campus or phone interview may be required. Students must also complete a physical examination and college health evaluation at the Student Health Center before the end of the first year.

Tuition and Fees

There is an application fee of $50, and an enrollment fee of $30 per term. Tuition is $4,140 per term; integrated fees are $130 per term; and books and equipment are additional. Total estimated expenses for the thirty-six-month program are $51,600.

Financial Assistance

A deferred tuition payment plan, federal loans and work-study, ChiroLoan and Canadian ChiroLoan, scholarships, and veteran's benefits are available.

PENNSYLVANIA

American Academy of Environmental Medicine

(*See* Multiple State Locations, page 295)

Career Training Academy

703 Fifth Avenue
New Kensington, Pennsylvania 15068
Phone: (412) 337-1000 / (800) 660-3470

Additional Location:
ExpoMart
105 Mall Boulevard, Suite 300-W
Monroeville, Pennsylvania 15146
Phone: (412) 372-3900 / (800) 491-3470

The Career Training Academy was founded in 1986 and began offering its massage therapy programs in 1993.

Accreditation

The academy is accredited by the Accrediting Commission of Career Schools and Colleges of Technology (ACCSCT). The Therapeutic Massage Technician Program is accredited by the International Massage and Somatic Therapies Accreditation Council (IMSTAC), a division of Associated Bodywork and Massage Professionals (ABMP).

Program Description

The 300-hour, five-month Swedish Massage Practitioner Program consists of Anatomy and Physiology I and II, Aromatherapy/Homeopathic Remedies/Oils, Career Development, Kinesiology I and II, Introduction to Massage, Clinical Evaluation/Client Interaction, Therapeutic Modalities, First Aid/CPR, Practicum, and Swedish Massage I.

The 600-hour, 9½-month Therapeutic Massage Technician Program is a more advanced course in Swedish massage. The curriculum is the same as the 300-hour program, with the addition of Swedish Massage II, Body Reflexology, Sports Massage, Chiropractic Assistance/Nutrition, Basic Shiatsu, Stretching/Acuyoga, Myotherapy, and Chiropractic Assistance/Geriatric Massage.

The 300-hour, five-month Basic Shiatsu Technician Program is identical to the 300-hour Swedish Massage Practitioner Program, with the substitution of Shiatsu I for Swedish Massage I.

The 600-hour, 9½-month Advanced Shiatsu Technician Program is identical to the Basic Shiatsu Technician Program, with the addition of Shiatsu II, Body Reflexology, Sports Massage, Stretching Acuyoga, Acupressure Jin Shin I and II, Alexander Technique, and Myotherapy.

Admission Requirements

Applicants must have a high school diploma or equivalent, submit an evaluation essay and health form, and interview with a school representative.

Tuition and Fees

Tuition for the Swedish Massage Practitioner Program is $1,750; books and supplies, including table, are $715; lab fee is $65. Tuition for the Therapeutic Massage Technician Program is $3,500; books and supplies, including table, are $885; lab fee is $105. Tuition for the Basic Shiatsu Technician Program is $1,750; books and supplies, including table, are $695; lab fee is $65. Tuition for the Advanced Shiatsu Technician Program is $3,500; books and supplies, including table, are $860; lab fee is $105.

Additional fees for all programs include: application fee, $25; graduation fee, $25; insurance fee, $32; and uniforms, $216.

Financial Assistance

Federal grants and loans and veteran's benefits are available; aid is also available through Vocational Rehabilitation, Single Point of Contact, the Negro Educational Emergency Drive, the Department of Public Assistance, and the Private Industry Council.

East-West Therapeutic Massage

1701 Lancaster Avenue
Shillington, Pennsylvania 19607
Phone/Fax: (610) 775-9312

East-West Therapeutic Massage was founded in 1989 by Marilyn McGrath, B.S., who has eleven years' experience in therapeutic massage and shiatsu therapy. The school is easily accessible from Philadelphia, Allentown, and Lancaster, and prides itself on its low student-teacher ratio and highly qualified instructional staff.

Accreditation

East-West Therapeutic Massage is accredited by the International Massage and Somatic Therapies Accreditation Council (IMSTAC), a division of the Associated Bodywork and Massage Professionals (ABMP), and approved by the Pennsylvania State Department of Education.

Program Description

The 520-hour Massage Therapy/Bodywork Program consists of courses in Swedish/Therapeutic Massage, Anatomy and Physiology, Shiatsu, Reflexology, Sports Massage, Aromatherapy, Polarity Therapy, Chair Massage, Self-Development, Related Studies, Business Practice, and CPR/First Aid.

The 500-hour Shiatsu Bodywork Program consists of two levels. Level One (300 hours) includes Basic Definitions and Techniques, Classic Meridians, Diagnostic Studies, Acupressure, Anatomy and Physiology, Self-Development, Business Practice, and Related Studies. Topics covered in Level Two (200 hours) include Traditional Oriental Medicine, Seated/Side Position, Diagnostic Techniques, Extended Meridians, Macrobiotics, Advanced Techniques, and Practicum.

Students who have completed the 520-hour Massage Program may enroll in Shiatsu Level Two for a total of 720 hours.

Admission Requirements

Applicants must be at least 18 years of age (mature students under 18 may be considered); have a high school diploma or equivalent; submit three letters of reference, a physician's statement, and a written personal history; and interview with an admissions representative.

Tuition and Fees

There is a $50 application fee. Tuition for the Massage Therapy/Bodywork Program is $3,700; books are $130. Tuition for the Shiatsu Level One Program is $2,100; books are $75. Tuition for the Shiatsu Level Two Program is $1,400; books are $25.

Financial Assistance

A payment plan is available.

The Himalayan Institute of Yoga Science and Philosophy

R.R. 1, Box 400
Honesdale, Pennsylvania 18431
Phone: (800) 822-4547 / (717) 253-5551
Fax: (717) 253-9078

The Himalayan Institute was founded in 1971 as a nonprofit organization with the goal of helping people to grow physically, mentally, and spiritually. The institute's national headquarters are located on a 400-acre campus in northeastern Pennsylvania.

Other Himalayan Institute centers in the United States are located in New York, Buffalo, Pittsburgh, Glenview, Chicago, Milwaukee, Indianapolis, and Dallas/Forth Worth; in Canada, centers are located in Toronto, Calgary, and Regina. Each center has its own schedule of classes and seminars.

Program Description

The Himalayan Institute Teachers' Association (HITA) has been training, certifying, and providing continuing education for hatha yoga teachers for more than twenty years. The program provides a systematic and comprehensive study of raja yoga, the eight-limbed path. This approach to the study and practice of yoga and the development of teaching skills benefits aspiring and experienced teachers, as well as those wishing to advance in their own practice.

The requirements leading to certification include ongoing practice and study in hatha yoga, meditation training in the Himalayan Institute tradition, six home study courses (including Essential Yoga Philosophy, Asana Practice, Science of Breath, Meditation, Anatomy for Yoga, and Diet and Nutrition), two self-study projects, a ten-day intensive training (offered annually in the spring), written and practical exams, and eight weeks' teaching experience.

Community and Continuing Education

Weekend and longer seminars are also offered year-round at the national headquarters, and are designed for beginning as well as more advanced students. Among the topics and seminars offered are Meditation, Meditation Retreats, Fundamentals of Hatha Yoga (Levels 1 through 3), Subtle Body Series, Science of Breath, Specialty Yoga, Hatha Yoga Teachers' Retreats, Hatha Yoga Teachers' Training, Homeopathy for Home Use, Ayurveda and Rejuvenation, Biofeedback, Vegetarian Cooking, Herbs, Cleansing and Fasting, the Mystic's Path: Living with Power, and others.

Admission Requirements

Prerequisites include a minimum of one year's experience in intermediate-level hatha yoga, a regular personal hatha yoga practice, and membership in HITA. Certification is valid for three years. Recertification requires specified hours for personal practice, continuing education, and ongoing teaching.

Tuition and Fees

Seminars and the ten-day teachers' training intensive range from $100 to $1,000. Call to receive the Himalayan Institute's free *Quarterly Guide to Programs* or for more detailed information. Membership in the Himalayan Institute Teachers Association is $100 annually, with a $10 application fee.

Lehigh Valley Healing Arts Academy

5412 Shimmerville Road
Emmaus, Pennsylvania 18049
Phone: (610) 965-6165

The Lehigh Valley Healing Arts Academy was founded in 1987 (as the Lehigh Healing Arts Center) by director Bonita Cassel-Beckwith, who began her training in 1972 and has been teaching bodywork since 1984. The school is located in a 200-year-old farmhouse overlooking the East Penn valley.

Accreditation

The academy is currently a candidate for licensing as a private vocational school by the Pennsylvania Department of Education.

Program Description

The 500-hour Bodywork Program consists of three levels of instruction. Level I includes 150 hours in Anatomy and Physiology, Applied Anatomy, Bodywork Practice and Theory, Remedial Exercises, Business, Pathology and Medical Terminology, Reflexology, Ethics, Boundaries for Bodyworkers, One-To-One Tutorial, and Clinic. Level II (150 hours) includes Anatomy and Physiology II, Deep Tissue Sculpting, Subtle Energy Studies, Body/Mind Integration, Five Elements/Acupressure and Meridian Therapy, One-To-One Tutorial, and Level II Clinic. Level III (200 hours) features courses taught by guest lecturers as well as teachers from the school. Students in the 500-hour program are required to take CPR/AIDS Awareness, Heart-Centered Listening for Bodyworkers, and Body Usage for Bodyworkers; students then elect classes that interest them to complete as many hours as they wish. Elective courses include Carpal Tunnel Massage, Therapeutic Touch (three levels), Reiki (three levels), Reflexology, Body Psychology Through Iridology, Trager Beginning Training, Boundaries for Bodyworkers II, Introduction to Clinical Herbalism, Trager Anatomy, Trager Intermediate Level, Energy Fundamentals, and DansKinetics with Breathwork (movement for bodyworkers). Classes are held days or weekends.

Admission Requirements

Applicants must be at least 18 years of age, have a high school diploma or equivalent, submit two letters of recommendation (one from a health professional), have received at least three sessions from three different bodyworkers, submit a short essay, and submit a physician's statement of health.

Tuition and Fees

There is a $150 application fee. Tuition for Level I is $1,500; for Level II, $1,500; Level III tuition varies with the courses chosen. A massage table costs approximate $500 to $600.

Financial Assistance

Students may pay for one level at a time. Job partnership trainings may be available if licensing is approved.

Mt. Nittany School of Massage

School Facility:
P.O. Box 8
118 Boalsburg Road
Lemont, Pennsylvania 16851

Administrative Office:
106 Boalsburg Road
Lemont, Pennsylvania 16851
Phone: (814) 238-1121

The Mt. Nittany School of Massage was founded in 1995 by Anne Mascelli, a licensed massage therapist and certified Kripalu yoga teacher. The school is located in the village of Lemont, east of State College, home of Penn State University.

Accreditation

Mt. Nittany School of Massage is licensed by the Pennsylvania Department of Education. As yet there are no certification or licensing requirements in Pennsylvania. Graduates are eligible to take the national certification exam administered by the National Certification Board for Therapeutic Massage and Bodywork (NCBTMB).

Program Description

The Mt. Nittany curriculum was designed as a modular system to meet the needs of working students; each self-contained module prepares the student in specific areas of massage work. Students may choose to attend either weekend or weekday classes on a module-by-module basis, and take as long as they need to complete the training. Training may begin with either Module One or Module Two.

The 675-hour Massage Therapist Training Program consists of three modules. Module One includes 175 hours of Swedish massage, reflexology, anatomy and physiology, movement studies, communication skills, professional development, and student practice sessions. Module Two consists of 200 hours in shiatsu, polarity therapy, anatomy and physiology, qigong and tai chi, energy explorations, professional development, and student practice sessions. Module Three includes 300 hours in connective tissue massage, neuromuscular therapy, sports massage, applied technique, hydrotherapy, HIV awareness, anatomy and physiology, developing therapeutic awareness, professional development project, creative marketing, student practice sessions, current trends in health care, and healthy lifestyle practices. All graduates must take American Red Cross CPR and First Aid.

Admission Requirements

Applicants must be at least 19 years of age and have a high school diploma or equivalent. Applicants must submit a personal statement, two letters of recommendation, and a signed Agreement of Ethical Conduct, and interview with an admissions representative.

Tuition and Fees

There is a $35 application fee. Tuition for Module One is $1,600; for Module Two, $1,830; and for Module Three, $2,745. Tuition for all three modules is $5,500. Books are approximately $85; linens, oils, and optional massage table are additional.

Financial Assistance

Payment plans are available.

Myofascial Release Treatment Centers and Seminars

(*See* Multiple State Locations, page 309)

Pennsylvania Institute of Massage Therapy

93 S. West End Boulevard, Suite 102-103
Quakertown, Pennsylvania 18951
Phone: (215) 538-5339
Fax: (215) 538-8896

The Pennsylvania Institute of Massage Therapy (PIMT) was founded in 1993. The current director, Robert W. Tosh, D.C., has had a private chiropractic practice since 1985; assistant director Terry Ann Tosh is a massage therapist and trained nursing assistant.

Accreditation

PIMT is accredited by the International Massage and Somatic Therapies Accreditation Council (IMSTAC), a division of Associated Bodywork and Massage Professionals (ABMP). PIMT is licensed by the Pennsylvania State Board of Private Licensed Schools.

Program Description

The 520-hour Massage Therapy Course consists of massage theory and practical application of Swedish and deep muscle therapeutic massage. Allied modalities are covered (including reflexology, sports massage, hydrotherapy, tai chi, shiatsu, and others), as well as massage technique modifications for client conditions. The Anatomy and Physiology segment covers Medical Terminology, Cells and Tissues, Integumentary System, Skeletal System, Muscular System, Nervous System, Endocrine System, Circulatory System, Respiratory System, Digestive System and Nutrition, Urinary System, Reproductive System, Psychology, Business Practices, Deep Muscle Therapy, and a student-run clinic. Classes may be taken on a day, evening, or weekend schedule.

Continuing Education

Continuing education programs include a 110-hour Shiatsu Fundamental Program, which meets New York State requirements. Currently under development, pending licensing approval, is a Reflexognosy Program. Reflexognosy is a new technique

for realigning the structure of the body through muscle relaxation and joint movement of the foot and lower leg. In addition, Tosh Seminars presents a variety of continuing education seminars taught by other nationally recognized instructors.

Admission Requirements

Applicants must be at least 18 years of age, have a high school diploma or equivalent, and submit a physician's statement of health.

Tuition and Fees

There is a $100 enrollment fee; tuition is $3,850 for the 520-hour Massage Course. Books are $135. As of January 1998, tuition will be $4,450; books will be $150.

Tuition for the Shiatsu Program is $850; books are additional. Call for information about the Reflexognosy Program.

Pennsylvania School of Muscle Therapy

994 Old Eagle School Road, Suite 1005
Wayne, Pennsylvania 19087
Phone: (610) 687-0888
Fax: (610) 687-4726

The Pennsylvania School of Muscle Therapy (PSMT) was founded in 1982, approved by AMTA in 1986, and in 1992 became the first AMTA-approved school to be accredited by the Commission on Massage Training Accreditation/Approval (COMTAA). The school moved to its current location in 1994.

Accreditation

PSMT's Course 4—Full Curriculum Swedish Massage is accredited by AMTA/COMTAA. PSMT is one of only two schools in the world approved by IAPDMT (International Association of Pfrimmer Deep Muscle Therapists). All continuing education programs are approved by AMTA, IAPDMT, the National Certification Board of Therapeutic Massage and Bodywork (NCBTMB), and the National Athletic Trainers Association Board of Certification (NATABOC).

Program Description

Courses in the 521-hour, nine-month Course 4—Full Curriculum Swedish Massage include Theory and Practice of Massage, Sports Massage Basics, Business and Professional Ethics, Anatomy and Physiology, Pathology, Hydrotherapy, and CPR/First Aid.

Option 4C—New York State Swedish/Shiatsu Extended Massage Program combines Course 4 (above) with Advanced Anatomy and Physiology (Course 8) and Shiatsu (Course 9) in order to meet the requirements of the New York State Department of Education and to qualify students for licensing board exams in the State of New York.

Combinations of basic and advanced training are available in the form of Option 4A, which combines Full Curriculum Swedish Massage and Pfrimmer Deep Muscle Therapy (courses 4 and 2) and Option 4B, which combines Full Curriculum Swedish Massage, Pfrimmer Deep Muscle Therapy, and Advanced Techniques (courses 4, 2, and 3).

A 155-hour, beginning-level Therapeutic Massage/Tutorial is offered to cosmetologists or individuals for family use; the course consists of fifteen supervised hours and 140 hours of documented massage technique practice. This program is not AMTA/COMTAA-approved.

Classes are offered days and evenings.

Continuing Education

An eighty-hour Pfrimmer Deep Muscle Therapy Certification Program (Course 2) is offered to professionals only (applicants must have a degree in the healing arts or the equivalency of AMTA full entry requirements). Course work includes the Pfrimmer Technique; Special Applications and Conditions; History of PDMT; Review of Body Systems Relative to PDMT; Hygiene, Safety, and Posture for Therapists; Professional Ethics; and Business Ethics and Small Business Practices. Classes are held during the day for two consecutive weeks.

A forty-hour Evaluation and Correction of the Muscular System Through Advanced Techniques Program (Course 3) is offered to graduates of Course 2 and is suitable for chiropractors, physical therapists, and other advanced bodyworkers who wish to specialize in advanced corrective techniques. Course work includes Structural Evaluation, the Art of Palpation, Structural Troubleshooting, Myofascial Release, Vascular/Muscular Corrections, and Digestive/Muscular Corrections. Classes are held during the day for five full days.

Several other continuing education programs are offered periodically in such areas as aromatherapy, kinesiology, assessment of orthopedic complaints, reflexology, massage and bodywork for survivors of abuse, infant massage, basic and advanced sports massage, mother massage, bio-energetic massage, neuromuscular therapy, trigger point therapy, on-site chair massage, and others.

Admission Requirements

Applicants for the AMTA/COMTAA-approved programs must be at least 18 years of age, have a high school diploma or equivalent, interview with an admissions representative, and submit three character references and a physician certification.

There is no age or education requirement for the Therapeutic Massage/Tutorial.

Tuition and Fees

Tuition for Course 4—Full Curriculum Swedish Massage is $4,700. There is a $25 application fee and a $125 registration fee.

Tuition for Course 2—Pfrimmer Deep Muscle Therapy Certification Program is $2,500. There is an application fee of $25 and a registration fee of $100.

Tuition for Course 3—Evaluation and Correction of the Muscular System Through Advanced Techniques is $1,250. There is an application fee of $25 and a registration fee of $100.

Tuition for the Therapeutic Massage/Tutorial is $900, plus an application fee of $25 and a registration fee of $50.

Tuition for Option 4C: Course 8—Advanced Anatomy and Physiology is $900, plus an application fee of $25 and a registration fee of $50.

Tuition for Course 9—Shiatsu is $1,000, plus an application fee of $25 and a registration fee of $50.

Books, supplies, and optional massage table are additional.

Financial Assistance

Payment plans are available.

SOUTH CAROLINA

Institute for Awareness in Motion

(*See* Multiple State Locations, page 305)

Pinewood School of Massage

1000 North Pine Street, Suite 2B
Pinewood Mall
Spartanburg, South Carolina 29303
Phone: (864) 582-7558 / (864) 591-1134
Fax: (864) 582-7805

The Pinewood School of Massage was founded in 1990 to train therapists for the chiropractic clinic of Dr. H.D. Smith, with the intention of integrating massage therapy into the medical setting. The school grew as other physicians requested therapists for their offices.

Accreditation

Pinewood School of Massage received accreditation from the International Massage and Somatic Therapies Accreditation Council (IMSTAC), a division of the Association of Bodywork and Massage Professionals (ABMP), in 1996. The school is licensed under the South Carolina Commission on Higher Education. South Carolina's Massage/Bodywork Practice Act requires that a therapist receive 500 hours of training from an accredited school in order to obtain a license.

Program Description

The 500-hour, six-month Massage Therapy Program consists of three phases. The Phase I curriculum (130 hours) includes Introduction, Introduction to Other Bodywork Techniques, Introduction to Aromatherapy, Chair Sessions, Relaxation Sessions, Hydrotherapy, Anatomy and Physiology, Anatomy Homework, and review and test. Phase II (106 hours) covers Anatomy Workshop, Reflexology, Therapeutic I, Lymphatic, Prenatal, Trigger Point, Stretches, Myofascial Release I, Energy Exchange, and review and test. Phase III (98½ hours) includes Marketing, Business and Ethics, Therapeutic II, CPR, MFR II, Energy Exchange, National Exam Review, Anatomy and Physiology, Anatomy Homework, and review and test. Approximately 153½ hours will be completed as outside hours of hands-on time in workshops, chair sessions, full-body sessions, and seminars.

Admission Requirements

Applicants must be at least 18 years of age, have a high school diploma or equivalent, and submit a physician's statement.

Tuition and Fees

There is a $25 application fee $25; tuition is $4,950; and books are approximately $100.

Financial Assistance

Students interested in financing their tuition should contact the school administrator.

Sherman College of Straight Chiropractic

Mailing Address:
P.O. Box 1452
Spartanburg, South Carolina 29304
Phone: (864) 578-8770 / (800) 849-8771
Fax: (864) 599-7145

Campus Address:
2020 Springfield Road
Inman, South Carolina 29349

Founded in 1973, Sherman College of Straight Chiropractic is located on eighty acres of rolling land in Spartanburg, South Carolina. "Straight" chiropractic uses vertebral adjusting to correct subluxation, or misalignment of the vertebra; the other school of thought, "mixer" chiropractic, uses manipulation and other methods to accomplish the objective of treating symptoms and disease. The use of the term "straight chiropractic" in the Sherman College name helps to identify it with its total commitment to the teaching, research, and practice relating to vertebral subluxation.

Accreditation

The Doctor of Chiropractic degree program is accredited by the Commission on Accreditation of the Council on Chiropractic Education (CCE).

Program Description

The 4,644-hour Doctor of Chiropractic (D.C.) degree program may be completed in thirteen quarters and consists of courses that fall under the general categories of anatomy, physiology and chemistry, radiology, pathology and public health, research, diagnosis, clinic, philosophy, chiropractic technique, and business practices.

Continuing Education

Postdoctoral programs, seminars, and workshops are offered both on campus and through extension. Non-credit courses are offered in the areas of specific adjusting techniques, spinograph analysis and instrumentation, and chiropractic philosophy and communications. Continuing education workshops for license renewal are also offered.

Admission Requirements

Applicants must have completed at least sixty semester hours of undergraduate credit with a minimum 2.25 G.P.A., including specific courses in English or communication skills, psychology, biology, general and organic chemistry, and physics. In addition, applicants must submit two letters of recommendation.

Tuition and Fees

There is an application fee of $35; tuition is $3,440 per quarter; lab fees are $5 to $25 per course; books and supplies are additional.

Financial Assistance

Scholarships, federal grants, loans, and work-study are available.

TENNESSEE

Cumberland Institute for Wellness Education

500 Wilson Pike Circle, Suite 121
Brentwood, Tennessee 37027
Phone: (615) 370-9794

The Cumberland Institute for Wellness Education was established in 1989 by Judy and Daniel Seely and was sold to Chad Porter in 1991.

Accreditation

The curriculum at Cumberland Institute for Wellness Education is endorsed by the Associated Bodywork and Massage Professionals (ABMP). The institute is authorized by the Tennessee Education Commission, and the Holistic Massage Therapist Program exceeds the 500-hour education requirement for licensing in the State of Tennessee.

Program Description

The 595-hour Holistic Massage Therapist Program is a self-paced program that may be completed in as little as eleven months or as long as thirty-six months. Course offerings include Introduction to Bodywork; Touch Dynamics; Therapist-Client Interdynamics; Bodywork Ethics; Anatomy; Physiology; Kinesiology and Applied Anatomy; Nutrition Concepts; Terminology, Pathology, and Documentation; CPR; Swedish-Esalen Massage; Structural Observation and Assessment; Posture Dynamics; Lymphatic Drainage Massage; Advanced Reflexology; Neuromuscular-Somatic Release Therapy; Massage for Injury; Business-Marketing; Practitioner Internship; On-Site Massage; Acupressure Massage; Craniosacral Therapy; Touch for Health; Aromatherapy; Touch Therapy; and Body-Mind Integration. Classes are held days and evenings.

Admission Requirements

Applicants must be at least 21 years of age and have a high school diploma or equivalent.

Tuition and Fees

There is an application fee of $35; tuition is $9,625, including books. Other costs include: loan process fee, $45; equipment/supplies, $600; and ABMP insurance, $75.

Financial Assistance

Payment plans, scholarships, loans, and a prepayment discount are available.

The Massage Institute of Memphis

3445 Poplar Avenue, Suite #4
Memphis, Tennessee 38111
Phone: (901) 324-4411

The Massage Institute of Memphis was founded in 1987 by Karen E. Craig, who began her career in massage in 1976. She has produced an instructional cable TV series in Georgia and a commercial instructional massage video.

Accreditation

The Massage Institute of Memphis is authorized by the Tennessee Higher Education Commission. The 500-hour program meets Tennessee licensing requirements and enables students to take the Arkansas State Board of Massage Therapy examination as well as the national certification exam. Continuing education classes provide CEUs for the American Massage Therapy Association (AMTA), Tennessee licensing renewal, and the National Certification Board for Therapeutic Massage and Bodywork, Category B.

Program Description

The 500-hour Professional Massage Program consists of courses in Anatomy and Physiology, Massage Techniques (including basic massage theory and practice, reflexology, sports massage, and clinical practicum), and Health Services Management (including professional development, hydrotherapy, electro/heliotherapy, hygiene/practical demonstration, and AIDS/HIV education). Classes are held days and evenings.

Continuing Education

Guest lectures, seminars, workshops, and specialty classes are offered to massage practitioners and graduates.

Admission Requirements

Applicants must be at least 18 years of age, have a high school diploma or equivalent, be of good moral character and in good health, interview with an admissions representative, and submit two letters of reference and a recent photo.

Tuition and Fees

There is a $20 application fee. Tuition is $4,300; individual courses are $10 per hour. Books are $200; supplies are approximately $80; a massage table costs approximately $400; and a hydrotherapy field trip costs $100.

Financial Assistance

A payment plan and Tennessee and Arkansas Vocational Rehabilitation are available.

Middle Tennessee Institute of Therapeutic Massage

394 West Main Street, Suite A15
P.O. Box 1200
Hendersonville, Tennessee 37077-1200
Phone: (615) 826-9500
E-mail: mtinst@nc5.infi.net

The Middle Tennessee Institute of Therapeutic Massage (MTITM) began its first class in 1996 with forty-three students.

Accreditation

MTITM is approved by the Associated Bodyworkers and Massage Professionals (ABMP) and will be seeking accreditation from the American Massage Therapy Association Commission on Massage Training Accreditation/Approval (AMTA/COMTAA) upon eligibility in 1998. Massage therapists must have at least 500 hours of education from an approved school in order to be licensed in the state of Tennessee.

Program Description

The Certified Massage Therapist Program includes over 500 hours of instruction. The curriculum includes Introduction to Massage, Touch Concepts, Client/Therapist Relations, Introduction to Pharmacology, Introduction to Reflexology, Shiatsu, Mind/Body Awareness Education, Anatomy and Physiology, Kinesiology, Nutrition, CPR/First Aid, Swedish Esalen Massage, Russian Therapeutic Massage, Sports Massage, Lymphatic Drainage Massage, Business and Marketing, Aromatherapy, and Intern Clinic. Classes are held days, evenings, and weekends.

Continuing and Community Education

Continuing education workshops offered to practicing massage therapists and enrolled students include Introduction to Clinical Massage I: Therapeutic Strategies for the Low Back, Clinical Massage II: Therapeutic Strategies for the Neck, and Clinical Massage III: TMJ and Carpal Tunnel.

Workshops open to the public include Relaxation Massage for Couples, the Magic of Healing: Mind/Body Education, and Relaxation Massage for Everyone.

Admission Requirements

Applicants must be at least 21 years of age, have a high school diploma or equivalent, and interview with an admissions representative.

Tuition and Fees

There is a $15 application fee; tuition is $5,600, including books; and a massage table costs $350 to $500. Fees for workshops range from $75 to $250.

Financial Assistance

A payment plan is available.

Reiki Plus Institute

130 Ridge Road
Celina, Tennessee 38551
Phone: (615) 243-3712
Fax: (615) 243-4657

The Reiki Plus Institute was founded in 1987 by director David G. Jarrell, who in 1981 became the twenty-fourth Reiki Master in the world.

Accreditation

The institute is accredited by the National Certification Board for Therapeutic Massage and Bodywork (NCBTMB) as a continuing education provider.

Program Description

The institute offers training in a variety of holistic and spiritual healing techniques, and offers two certifications in holistic practice. Basic Practitioner Training Seminars include Reiki Plus First Degree (twenty hours), which teaches techniques to use with the self and with clients to promote healing, relaxation, and the reduction of stress. Students give and receive group treatment. In Reiki Plus Second Degree (fifteen hours), students receive the attunement to the Second Degree Level of Reiki Energy, learn how Second Degree is combined with mystical teachings, and activate, direct, and apply Second Degree energy to self and clients.

The Reiki Plus Practitioner's Program includes seven individual seminars: Applied Esoteric Psychology and Anatomy (twenty-five hours); Advanced Reiki Plus Second Degree (fifteen hours); Physio-Spiritual Etheric Body, which teaches how to unite the physical and etheric bodies in order to allow spiritual harmony to flow through them (twenty hours); The Healer's Role as a Counselor (twenty hours); Exploring Partnerships With Self and Others (twenty hours); Intuitive Evaluation of Clients' Consciousness (twenty hours); and Spiritual Discernment (twenty hours). Students who have completed this program are awarded the certificate Reiki Plus Practitioner.

An Advanced Practitioner's Program and Advanced Reiki Plus Practitioner Certification are also available.

Continuing Education

Continuing education classes include Astro-Physiology and Psychology, Astro-Physiology and Healing Techniques, Reiki Plus Third Degree Practitioner, Spinal Attunement Technique, and others.

Tuition and Fees

Tuition is charged separately for each seminar and ranges from $200 to $300.

Financial Assistance

Discounts of $25 to $50 per seminar are offered for early registration.

Tennessee Institute of Healing Arts

5779 Brainerd Road
Chattanooga, Tennessee 37411
Phone: (423) 892-9882 / (800) 735-1910
Fax: (423) 892-5006
E-mail: tiha@aol.com

The Tennessee Institute of Healing Arts (TIHA) was founded in 1989 by massage therapist Alan Jordan as an outgrowth of the Chattanooga Massage Therapy Center. Since that time, the growth of the school has required three moves to larger locations; the school moved to its current 6,000-square-foot facility in 1994.

Accreditation

TIHA is nationally accredited by the Accrediting Commission of Career Schools and Colleges of Technology (ACCSCT). Graduates are eligible for licensure in Tennessee. TIHA is a Florida Board of Massage-approved school, and graduates are eligible to take the Florida State Licensure Exam.

Program Description

The twelve-month (or eighteen-month part-time), 1,000-hour Professional Massage Therapist Training Program consists of a Core Massage Therapy Program that includes Swedish Massage, Deep Tissue Massage, Neuromuscular Therapy, Russian Massage Technique, Clinical Sports Massage, and Relational Bodywork; Secondary Modalities, consisting of Oriental Therapies, Reflexology, Polarity Therapy, Massage During Pregnancy, On-Site Massage, Hydrotherapy, Geriatric and Illness Care Massage, and Mastectomy/Breast Reconstruction Massage; Anatomy and Physiology, which includes Lecture, Lab, and Clinical Pathology; Support Classes, including Professional Ethics, Communication Skills, Marketing and Business, Nutrition, CPR and First Aid, Self-Care Through Movement, Statutes/Rules and History of Massage, and AIDS/HIV Education; and Practicum, consisting of Documented Massage Practice, Student Clinic, Research Project, and Documented Professional Massage. Classes meet during the day (full-time) or evenings and weekends (part-time); student clinic is held on Saturdays.

Upon graduation, students will receive a diploma in massage and neuromuscular therapy from TIHA and certification in neuromuscular therapy from the International Academy of Neuromuscular Therapy in St. Petersburg, Florida.

Admission Requirements

Applicants must be at least 18 years of age, in good health, and must have a high school diploma or equivalent. In addition, applicants must submit two personal references and interview with an admissions representative.

Tuition and Fees

Tuition is $6,500. Other costs include: application fee, $100; books, approximately $350; supplies, approximately $100; massage table, $450 to $850; liability insurance, $35; three professional massages, approximately $135; and lab fee, $25.

Financial Assistance

Payment plans are available.

TEXAS

Academy of Oriental Medicine

2700 West Anderson Lane, Suite 304
Austin, Texas 78757
Phone: (512) 454-1188
Fax: (512) 444-4131

The Academy of Oriental Medicine was founded in 1992 by Annie and Stuart Watts. Stuart, a licensed acupuncturist and Doctor of Oriental Medicine (N.M.) has been in clinical practice since 1972, has taught acupuncture for more than eighteen years, and was founder and past director of Southwest Acupuncture College and founder of the International Institute of Traditional Medicine, both in Santa Fe. The academy moved to its present facility in 1995.

Accreditation

The Oriental Medicine Program at the academy is a candidate for accreditation with the National Accreditation Commission for Schools and Colleges of Acupuncture and Oriental Medicine (NACSCAOM). Graduates meet the qualifications established by the Texas State Board of Medical Examiners necessary to apply for a Texas Acupuncture License. Graduates are also approved by the New Mexico Acupuncture Board; the New Mexico license conveys the title of Doctor of Oriental Medicine.

The Oriental Bodywork Program is approved by the American Oriental Bodywork Therapy Association (AOBTA). In Texas, all Oriental bodyworkers must be registered Swedish massage therapists to practice; laws differ from state to state, so prospective students are encouraged to check their own state requirements.

Program Description

The 2,880-hour Oriental Medicine Program (1,032 hours clinic), is designed to be completed in three years, though some students may take up to six years to complete the program. First-year courses include Philosophy of TCM, Acupuncture Points, Clinical Observations and Theater, Oriental Bodywork, Business Management, Biomedical Survey, Medical Terminology, Internal Martial Art, Survey Microbiology and Infectious Disease, Survey Histology, Public Health, and Pathophysiology. Second-year courses include Internal Oriental Medicine, Oriental Practical and Theory, Chinese Herbal Pharmacy, Clinical Practicum and Theater, Oriental Bodywork, Herbal Classic Texts, Western Pharmacology, Internal Martial Art, Physical Assessment, Western Medical Diagnostic Techniques, and Special Guests Seminars. Third-year courses include Chinese Herbal Formulations, Clinical Practicum and Theater, Business Management and Ethics, Nutrition, Ethical and Legal Issues, Psychology, CPR, Internal Medicine—Western, Internal Martial Art, Herbal Advanced Syndrome Differentiation, Herbal Clinical Practicum, Special Guests Seminars, Nutrition, Surgery and Urology—Western, Internal Medicine—Herbal, NCCA Preparation, Psychiatric Diseases—Western, and Obstetrics—Western.

In the one-year, 588-hour program in Oriental bodywork, students may specialize or major in either Jin Shin Do, shiatsu, or tui na. The curriculum includes 180 hours of the Oriental bodywork major and seventy hours of a combination of other Oriental bodywork practices, plus Clinical Practicum, Oriental Medical Theory, Anatomy and Physiology, Business and Ethics, CPR, Oriental Nutrition, Qigong, and Safety and Sanitation.

Admission Requirements

Applicants to the Oriental Medicine Program must have completed at least sixty semester credits of college-level, general education course work from an accredited college with a minimum G.P.A. of 2.0, and at least six semester credits in anatomy and physiology; have a high degree of competency in the English language; interview with the admissions director; submit two letters of reference, preferably from health professionals; submit a handwritten statement; and show a keen desire to study Oriental medicine and become a healer of high ethical standards.

There are no age or educational requirements for admission to the Oriental Bodywork Program.

Tuition and Fees

A catalog costs $5. Tuition for the entire Oriental Medicine Program is $18,813. Other costs include: application fee, $75; intern's annual insurance, required in second and third year of study, approximately $400; books, approximately $250 per trimester; and clinic supplies, approximately $250 per year.

Tuition for the Oriental Bodywork Program is approximately $4,420 to $5,255, depending on the number of credits per trimester. Other costs include: registration fee, $55; student insurance, $400; books and supplies are additional.

Financial Assistance

Limited work-study is available, as well as aid from the Texas Rehabilitation Commission.

American College of Acupuncture and Oriental Medicine

9100 Park West Drive
Houston, Texas 77063
Phone: (713) 780-9777
Fax: (713) 781-5781
E-mail: 102657.1730@compuserve.com

The American College of Acupuncture and Oriental Medicine was founded in 1992 as the American Academy of Acupuncture and Traditional Chinese Medicine. The college has steadily grown into its new 16,500-square-foot facility, and assumed its current name in May 1996.

Accreditation

The college's Professional Diploma Program is accredited by the National Accreditation Commission for Schools and Colleges of Acupuncture and Oriental Medicine (NACSCAOM).

Program Description

The three-year Professional Diploma Program in acupuncture and traditional Chinese medicine may also be completed in up to six years of part-time study.

The first-year curriculum includes such courses as History and Philosophy of TCM, Physiology of TCM, Herbology, Human Anatomy and Physiology, Histology and Pathology, Microbiology, Etiology and Pathogenesis of TCM, Diagnosis Theory of TCM, Anatomical Acupuncture Points, Auricular Acupuncture, Tai Chi and Qigong, Hygiene and Public Health, Western Medical Terminology, CPR, First Aid and CNT (Clean Needle Techniques), and others.

The second-year curriculum includes Differentiation of Syndromes, Anatomical Acupuncture, Herbology, Herbal Prescription, Histology and Pathology, Clinic Observation, Usage of Acupoints, Techniques of Acupuncture, Office and Clinical Management, Scalp Acupuncture, Acupressure and Tui Na, Health Psychology, Ethics and Patient Communication, and others.

The third-year curriculum includes Treatment of Common Diseases, Pharmacology, Clinical Internship, Herbal Clinical Studies, Advanced Acupuncture Techniques, Diagnostic Methods of Western Medicine, and others.

Elective courses include Chinese Medical Terminology, Nutrition and Dietetics, Chinese Medicine and Modern Immunology, Review Class, and Basic Chinese.

Admission Requirements

Applicants must have completed at least sixty semester hours of general academic college-level courses, interview with an admissions representative, and submit two letters of recommendation.

Tuition and Fees

There is a $50 application fee; tuition is $145 per credit full-time and $150 per credit part-time. Books and materials cost approximately $300 per semester; graduation fee is $200.

Financial Assistance

A payment plan is available.

Asten Center of Natural Therapeutics

(See Multiple State Locations, page 297)

Austin School of Massage Therapy

2600 West Stassney Lane
Austin, Texas 78745
Phone: (512) 462-3005
Fax: (512) 462-3265

The Austin School of Massage Therapy was founded in 1985, and has grown to be the largest in Texas, with classes held in twelve cities. The school will graduate some 750 students in 1996.

Accreditation

The Austin School of Massage Therapy is accredited by the International Massage and Somatic Therapies Accreditation Council (IMSTAC), a division of Associated Bodywork and Massage Professionals (ABMP). The 300-hour program meets the requirements of the Texas Department of Health for registration eligibility in the state of Texas.

Program Description

The 300-hour Level One Training includes 250 hours of instruction in Massage Technique (topics include Swedish massage, stretching, awareness of energetics, sports massage, trigger points, on-site massage, and others), Anatomy and Physiology, Hydrotherapy, Health and Hygiene, Business Practices and Professional Ethics, Practical Applications, and a fifty-hour internship.

Continuing Education

Continuing education workshops are offered in such areas as myofascial release, trigger point therapy, reflexology, rhythmic massage, energetic techniques, and neuromuscular therapy. Internships and teacher training are also available.

Admission Requirements

Applicants must be at least 18 years old and have a high school diploma or equivalent. A student may be ineligible for state registration if he or she has been convicted of an offense involving prostitution or sexual offenses within the past five years.

Tuition and Fees

A $100 deposit is due with the application. Tuition is $2,575, including all books, hand-outs, use of a massage table during class, and a polo shirt.

Financial Assistance

Payment plans, limited scholarships, and limited work-study are available.

Hands-On Therapy School of Massage

Primary Site:
625 Gatewood Drive
Garland, Texas 75043
Phone: (214) 240-9288
E-mail: hotschool@aol.com

Intern Clinic:
2009 North Galloway
Mesquite, Texas 75149
Phone: (214) 285-6133

Hands-On Therapy was founded in 1990. Owner/director Carolyn Scott has been practicing bodywork since 1980 and is currently the president of the Texas Chapter of the American Massage Therapy Association (AMTA).

Accreditation

The Hands-On Therapy massage curriculum is approved by AMTA and recognized by the Texas Department of Health.

Program Description

The 300-hour Basic Program consists of Swedish Massage, Anatomy and Physiology, Health and Hygiene, Hydrotherapy, Business Practices and Professional Ethics, and a fifty-hour internship.

The 200-hour Advanced Program provides the additional requirements for national certification as well as AMTA membership. Courses include Deep Tissue Massage, Trigger Point, Sports Massage, Chair Massage, Reflexology, and Shiatsu.

Classes are held days, evenings, and weekends, on a slow or fast track.

Continuing Education

A variety of workshops are offered to the massage professional. These include Aromatherapy, Manual Lymph Drainage, Spinal Touch, Trager, Zen Shiatsu, State Board Test Review, Shiatsu II, Orthobionomy, and any of the advanced program courses.

Admission Requirements

Applicants must be physically, mentally, emotionally, and financially capable of completing the course, be free of criminal convictions, interview with an admissions representative, and tour the school prior to admission.

Tuition and Fees

Tuition for the Basic Program is $2,250; books are $174, and supplies are $50. Tuition for the Advanced Program is $1,600; books are $90. Workshops are individually priced.

Financial Assistance

Early registration discounts, interest-free financing, and long-term financing are available.

The Institute of Natural Healing Sciences, Inc.

4100 Felps Drive, Suite E
Colleyville, Texas 76034
Phone: (817) 498-0716 / (800) 448-4954
Fax: (817) 281-1414

The Institute of Natural Healing Sciences (INHS) was founded in 1985 by Charlotte Small, and moved to its present site in 1988.

Accreditation

The INHS curriculum is approved by the American Massage Therapy Association (AMTA), and INHS is registered with the Texas Department of Health.

Program Description

The 300-hour Basic Course includes classes in Anatomy, Physiology, Joint Mobilization, Health and Hygiene, Business Practices and Ethics, Hydrotherapy, Traditional Swedish Massage Techniques, and a fifty-hour internship.

Continuing Education

A 290-hour Advanced Course is offered to students who have completed the Basic Course requirements and have graduated from a program approved by AMTA or the Associated Bodywork and Massage Professionals (ABMP). Classes include Reflexology, Sports Massage, Shiatsu and On-Site Chair Massage, Polarity Therapy, Craniosacral Balancing, Myofascial Release, and Clinical Applications of Massage Therapy.

Admission Requirements

Prospective students must be at least 18 years of age; have a high school diploma or equivalent; submit a physician's written verification that the applicant is physically capable of participating in this course of study; interview with an instructor or director; provide two letters of character reference; and be free of any criminal convictions within the past five years.

Tuition and Fees

There is a $50 application fee. Tuition for the Basic Course is $2,150. Other costs include: books and supplies, $183; linens and oil, approximately $95; AMTA student membership, Department of Health Registration, and ABMP membership and liability insurance, $421. Tuition for the Advanced Course is $2,150; books are $145.

Financial Assistance

A payment plan is available.

The Lauterstein-Conway Massage School

213 South Lamar, Suite 101
Austin, Texas 78704
Phone: (512) 474-1852 / (800) 474-0852
Fax: (512) 474-1883

The Lauterstein-Conway Massage School (TLC) was founded in 1989, though its core curriculum was developed in 1982 while David Lauterstein taught deep massage and anatomy at the Chicago School of Massage. Lauterstein and John Conway later co-evolved the curriculum at the Texas School of Massage Studies.

Accreditation

TLC's two-semester, 550-hour program is accredited by the American Massage Therapy Association Commission on Massage Training Accreditation/Approval (AMTA/COMTAA). The school is registered with and regulated by the State of Texas Department of Health.

Program Description

TLC offers 750 hours of education divided into three semesters.

Semester One consists of the 300 hours required by the Texas Department of Health and is the first semester of the AMTA/COMTAA accredited program. Courses include Swedish Massage, Human Anatomy, Human Physiology, Hydrotherapy, Human Health and Hygiene, Business Practices and Ethics, and a fifty-hour internship.

Semester Two is the second semester of the AMTA/COMTAA accredited program. Courses include Advanced Anatomy and Physiology, Sports Massage, Structural Bodywork, Deep Massage, Zen Shiatsu, Integrative Bodywork, Movement Skills, and Professionalism, Ethics, and Business Practice. Semester Two students must have current certification in CPR/First Aid.

Semester Three is a 200-hour program for practicing therapists who want to learn advanced methods of working with clients. Courses include Craniosacral Work, Advanced Structural Bodywork, Clinical Applications in Bodywork, Psychology of Bodywork, Zero Balancing, and Advanced Integrative Bodywork.

Students may choose between day, evening, or primarily weekend classes.

Admission Requirements

Applicants must be at least 18 years of age, have a high school diploma or equivalent, be of sound mind and body, submit a physician's letter, and interview with an admissions representative.

There is no prerequisite training for Semester One. Semester Two requires at least 250 hours of massage therapy training or registration in Texas as a massage therapist. Semester Three requires at least 500 hours of training in massage therapy.

Tuition and Fees

Tuition for Semester One is $2,300 (includes $100 application fee); for Semester Two, $2,300; and for Semester Three, $1,850. Books are approximately $117 for Semester One, $83 for Semester Two, and $48 for Semester Three. Linens and oils are approximately $55 per semester; a massage table is approximately $400 to $600; and CPR/First Aid certification is approximately $35.

Financial Assistance

Payment plans, early registration discounts, and partial scholarships are available.

National Iridology Research Association

(*See* Multiple State Locations, page 311)

Parker College of Chiropractic

2500 Walnut Hill Lane
Dallas, Texas 75229-5668
Phone: (214) 438-6932 /
   (800) GET-MY-DC (admissions)
Fax: (214) 352-8425

Parker College of Chiropractic was founded in 1978. The college is named for Dr. James William Parker, who established eighteen chiropractic clinics in Texas and founded the Parker Chiropractic Resource Foundation, which has held nearly 350 four-day postgraduate seminars (the Parker School for Professional Success) attended by over 200,000 chiropractors.

Accreditation

Parker College of Chiropractic is accredited by the Southern Association of Schools and Colleges and by the Council on Chiropractic Education (CCE).

Program Description

The 4,852½-hour Doctor of Chiropractic (D.C.) degree program may be completed in nine trimesters of full-time study.

Trimesters I through III include Assembly, Seminars for Success, Systemic Anatomy, Embryology, Histology, Cell Biology, Introduction to Chiropractic, Chiropractic Philosophy, Ethics, Gross Anatomy, Physiology, Biochemistry, Palpation, Spinal Biomechanics, Normal Radiographic Anatomy, Fundamentals of Diagnostic Imaging, Research and Statistics, Neuroscience, Microbiology, Diversified Technique, and Extra-Spinal Biomechanics.

Trimesters IV through VI include Assembly, Physiology, Pathology, Public Health, Neuroscience, Thompson Technique, Clinical Orthopedics, Physical Diagnosis, Radiographic Exam Technique, Pharmacology/Toxicology, Visceral Diagnosis, Lab Diagnosis, Clinical Neurology, Bone Pathology, Gonstead Technique, Upper Cervical Technique, Student Clinic, Building a Student Clinic Practice, Emergency Care, Physiological Therapeutics, Chiropractic Theories, EENT, Differential Diagnosis, and Bone Pathology.

Courses in trimesters VII through IX include Assembly, Seminars for Success, Chiropractic Theories, Clinical Nutrition, Physiological Therapeutics, Clinical Psychology, Sacro-Occipital Technique, Soft Tissue Pathology, OB/GYN, Dermatology, Internship Lecture and Practicum, Risk Management/Malpractice, Chiropractic Philosophy, Geriatrics/Pediatrics, Flexion/Distraction, Activator, Applied Kinesiology, Rehabilitation Procedures, Chiropractic Economics, Jurisprudence, and Communications.

A Bachelor of Science degree in anatomy may be earned simultaneously with the D.C. degree; consult the catalog or a college representative for additional information.

The Chiropractic Assistant Program is an ongoing two-year course of study leading to licensure in Florida; contact the college for additional information. Other C.A. courses are presented in relevant areas of interest.

Continuing Education

Postgraduate education programs are offered in chiropractic orthopedics, clinical neurology, chiropractic roentgenology, the evaluation of sports injuries and their management, chiropractic principles and technique, clinical diagnosis, practice management, special license renewal symposia, physiological therapeutics in chiropractic, meridian therapy/acupuncture, clinical nutrition, and chiropractic assistant.

Postgraduate courses leading to diplomate status include Diplomate American Board of Chiropractic Orthopedists (DABCO); Diplomate American Chiropractic Academy of Neurology (DACAN); and Diplomate American Chiropractic Board of Nutrition (DACBN). Each requires 300 to 360 hours or approximately three years to complete. The college also offers a one-hundred-hour Certification in Sports Injuries.

Admission Requirements

Applicants must have completed at least sixty semester hours (two academic years) of college-level credit at an accredited institution with an overall G.P.A. of at least 2.25 on a 4.0 scale and a grade of C or better in each science course. Specific course requirements include at least six semester hours each in biological science, general or inorganic chemistry, organic chemistry, physics, and English or communicative skills; at least three semester hours of psychology; at least fifteen semester hours of humanities or social sciences; and from four to twelve semester hours of electives. It is highly recommended that a student take anatomy and physiology prior to attendance. Texas licensure laws require additional hours of prerequisite science courses beyond those listed above; see the catalog for details.

Applicants must also be physically capable of performing manipulative procedures and submit three letters of recommendation (one preferably from a Doctor of Chiropractic).

Tuition and Fees

There is a $35 application fee. Tuition and fees are $4,602 per trimester; books and supplies are approximately $618 per trimester; and there is a graduation fee of $130.

Financial Assistance

Federal grants, loans, and work-study; state grants; scholarships; ChiroLoan; Bureau of Indian Affairs; and veterans' benefits are available.

Phoenix School of Holistic Health

Phone: (713) 974-5976
Fax: (713) 974-3563

Phoenix Southwest
6610 Harwin, Suite 256
Houston, Texas 77036

Phoenix North
2611 FM 1960 West, Suite H100
Houston, Texas 77068

The Phoenix School of Holistic Health was founded in 1986 by director William Barry, L.Ac., R.M.T., M.T.I. Phoenix has advanced the field of massage therapy by its creation of Massage Body Mechanics, one of the main types of body protection methods useful in keeping stress out of the shoulders and back, and Holistic Massage, a formal method to determine massage parameters and give the most suitable massage for the client's constitution.

Accreditation

The 300-hour Certification Program in Massage is a state-approved program leading to registration as a massage therapist in Texas.

Program Description

The 300-hour Certification Program in Massage integrates the two principal areas of circulatory massage and allied sciences. Circulatory massage consists of 125 hours of training in Swedish massage, Swedish remedial gymnastics, holistic massage, massage body mechanics, and state board examination classes. Allied sciences consists of Anatomy and Physiology (seventy-five hours), Hydrotherapy (twenty hours), Business Practices and Ethics (fifteen hours), Health and Hygiene (fifteen hours), and Clinic Internship (fifty hours). Classes are held on a day, evening, and weekend schedule.

Continuing Education

Advanced courses in acupressure, shiatsu, aromatherapy, sports massage, bodywork, and structural balancing are offered throughout the year.

Admission Requirements

Applicants must have a high school diploma or equivalent or successfully pass a standardized test of basic math and verbal skills; demonstrate a willingness to be of service to the community; display an ability to work well in a group setting; and interview with an admissions representative.

Tuition and Fees

Tuition is $2,550, including books, handouts, and oils; purchase of a massage table is not required.

Financial Assistance

Payment plans, veterans' benefits, Texas Rehabilitation Commission funding, and limited work-study are available.

Texas Chiropractic College

5912 Spencer Highway
Pasadena, Texas 77505-1699
Phone: (713) 487-1170 / (800) GO-TO-TEX
Fax: (713) 487-2009

Texas Chiropractic College was founded in San Antonio in 1908 by Dr. J.N. Stone, a pioneer in the field of chiropractic. In 1965, the college relocated to Pasadena.

Accreditation

Texas Chiropractic College is accredited by the Commission on Accreditation of the Council on Chiropractic Education (CCE), and by the Commission on Colleges of the Southern Association of Colleges and Schools as a Level V postsecondary institution. The college is also recognized by the Federation of Chiropractic Licensing Boards. Licensure requirements vary by state; students should contact the Board of Chiropractic Examiners in the state in which they intend to practice for current requirements.

Program Description

The ten-trimester, 4,605-hour Doctor of Chiropractic (D.C.) degree program may be completed in five years (attending Fall and Spring trimesters) or as little as three-and-one-third years by also attending Summer trimesters.

First-year (trimesters 1 through 3) classes include Histology, Gross Human Anatomy, Chiropractic Principles, Human Biochemistry, Palpation, Research Methodology, Spinal Anatomy, Physiology, Clinic Clerkship, Human Embryology, General Microbiology, Spinal Biomechanics, Human Neuroanatomy, Adjusting Procedures, Abnormal Psychology, and Pathology.

Second-year (trimesters 4 through 6) courses include Pathology, Physiology, Clinic Clerkship, Chiropractic Principles, Adjusting Procedures, Public Health and Hygiene, Appendicular Biomechanics, Toxicology/Pharmacology, X-Ray Physics, Physical Exam and Diagnosis, Introduction to Radiology, Nutrition, Obstetrics and Gynecology, Pediatric and Geriatric Diagnosis, X-Ray Positioning, Clinical Neurology, Clinical Case Applications, Orthopedics, Skeletal Imaging, and Internal Diagnosis.

Third-year (trimesters 7 through 9) classes include Spinal Imaging, Clinical Lab Diagnosis, Orthopedics, Student Clinic, Dermatology, Internal Diagnosis, Adjusting Procedures, Physical Medicine and Rehab, Case Management, Emergency Procedures, Ethics and Jurisprudence, Insurance and Office Procedures, and Clinic.

The tenth trimester consists of Clinic and Preceptorship.

Students may also complete a Bachelor of Science degree in human biology. See the catalog for specific information.

Continuing Education

A range of continuing education opportunities is offered to the Doctor of Chiropractic, from extensive diplomate-level classes of 300 hours to twelve-hour weekend seminars. Programs are offered that make the doctor eligible for examination leading to diplomate status in neurology (DACAN) or orthopedics (DABCO). Certification programs are also offered in the following areas: Certified Chiropractic Sports Physician (CCSP), clinical nutrition, clinical pharmacology, and manipulation under anesthesia (MUA).

Admission Requirements

Applicants must have completed at least two years (sixty semester hours or ninety quarter hours) of prechiropractic college work at a regionally accredited college or university, with a minimum G.P.A. of 2.5 on a 4.0 scale for all college work; all prerequisite science courses must carry a grade of C or better. Applicants must have completed, or must complete by the term of enrollment, the following courses: six semester hours of biological science with lab; six semester hours of inorganic chemistry; six semester hours of organic chemistry; six semester hours of physics; six semester hours of English or communication skills; three semester hours of psychology; and fifteen semester hours of social sciences/humanities electives. Course work in computer skills and statistics is strongly recommended.

Applicants must also submit an essay and two personal references, one of which must be from a Doctor of Chiropractic; interview with an admissions representative; and have the physical strength and bodily coordination to perform chiropractic manipulative techniques, the manual dexterity to perform safely and effectively in the laboratories and in diagnosis, and sufficient auditory sense and speaking ability to conduct health history interviews and clinical examinations. Physically disabled students who cannot meet the physical qualifications will be subject to a review/evaluation for admission eligibility.

Tuition and Fees

There is a $50 application fee; tuition is $4,100 per trimester. Other costs include: basic and lab fees,

$300 per trimester; graduation fee, $75; and books and equipment, approximate total for the entire program, $3,950.

Financial Assistance

Federal grants, loans, and work-study; scholarships; state grants; ChiroLoan; other loan sources; veterans' benefits; and aid from state rehabilitation agencies are available.

Texas Institute of Traditional Chinese Medicine

4005 Manchaca Road, Suite 200
Austin, Texas 78704
Phone: (512) 444-8082 / (512) 346-3336
Fax: (512) 444-6345
E-mail: 104106,1367@compuserve.com
Internet: http://www.ccsi.com/~texastcm

The Texas Institute of Traditional Chinese Medicine held its first class in January 1990, and is the oldest school of acupuncture and Oriental medicine in Texas. A sister-school relationship is maintained with the Heilongjiang College of Traditional Chinese Medicine in Harbin, People's Republic of China.

Accreditation

The Oriental Medicine Program has been admitted to candidacy status by the National Accreditation Commission for Schools and Colleges of Acupuncture and Oriental Medicine (NACSCAOM). The institute is approved by the Texas State Board of Acupuncture Examiners, and graduates are eligible to test for state licensure.

Program Description

The three-year, 2,400-hour Oriental Medicine Program runs forty-six weeks per year. The first-year curriculum includes such classes as Fundamental Theories of TCM; Chinese Terminology and Phonetics; Point Location; Diagnosis and Differentiation; Five Element Theory and Application; Qigong; Anatomy, Physiology, and Histology; CPR; Bio-

medical Concepts and Terminology; Special Acupuncture Techniques; TCM Herbology; Meridian Theory; and Clinical Observation and Evaluation.

Year Two consists of Meridian Acupoint Energetics and Application; TCM Prescriptionology; Internal Medicine (Acupuncture); Biomedical Diagnosis: Lab Test; Clinical Internship; Scalp and Ear Acupuncture; Food, Diet, and Vitamins; Biomedical Pathology and Bacteriology; and more.

In Year Three, the curriculum includes Classics: Shang Han Lun; Patent Herbs and Herbal Prescription Preparation; Tui Na; Directed Research: Acupuncture; Fire Needle and Moxibustion on Needle; Biomedical Pharmacology; Internal Medicine: Herbology; TCM Gynecology; Practice Management and Ethics; Counseling and Communications; Licensure Requirements and Examination Preparation; Hygiene, Public Health, and Referral Modalities; Clinical Internship; and more.

Classes are held Monday through Thursday nights and during the day on Saturday. Most students hold full-time jobs.

Admission Requirements

Applicants must have completed at least sixty hours of accredited college-level course work; some basic science and biomedical courses are recommended. Applicants must also interview with an admissions representative and submit a letter explaining why they wish to attend.

Tuition and Fees

There is a $50 application fee and a $50 registration fee per semester. Tuition is $1,800 per semester for the first year and $105 per semester credit in subsequent years. Other costs include: herb use fee, $60; clinic use fee (third to sixth semesters), $75 per semester; liability insurance (third through sixth semesters), approximately $200 per semester; books and supplies, approximately, $150 per semester; and time payment fee, $25 to $50. Total costs are approximately $2,250 per semester in the first year, and $2,600 per semester thereafter.

Financial Assistance

Payment plans are available.

The Winters School, Inc.

4625 Southwest Freeway, Suite 142
Houston, Texas 77027
Phone: (713) 626-2200
Fax: (713) 626-2230

The Winters School was founded in 1984 by owner and president Nancy Winters. Ms. Winters has served on the Advisory Council on Massage Therapy for the Texas Department of Health and was included in the 1996 *International Who's Who of Entrepreneurs.*

Accreditation

The Winters School is a Texas State registered massage school; the curriculum fulfills state requirements for registration as a massage therapist.

Program Description

The 300-hour Massage Therapy Program includes Human Anatomy, Human Physiology, Hydrotherapy, Human Health and Hygiene, Business Practices/Ethics, Swedish Massage Therapy, and Internship. Classes are held days and evenings, three to four times per week for four to eight months.

Admission Requirements

Applicants must submit a completed application form and verification that the applicant has received at least one professional bodywork session from a registered massage therapist.

Tuition and Fees

There is a $200 application fee; the balance of tuition is $2,200. Books and supplies cost approximately $300, three bodywork sessions cost $150, and a recommended massage table costs $350 to $800; massage table rentals are available for $5 per day.

Financial Assistance

Payment plans are available.

UTAH

Myotherapy College of Utah

3350 South 2300 East
Salt Lake City, Utah 84109
Phone: (801) 484-7624 / (800) 432-5968
E-mail: myo@xmission.com

Myotherapy College of Utah was founded by Jim and Shirley Foster in 1987. It is housed in an 8,000-square-foot facility in the midst of the Rocky Mountains, on the eastern edge of Salt Lake City.

Accreditation

Myotherapy College of Utah is accredited by the Accrediting Commission of Career Schools and Colleges of Technology (ACCSCT) and is certified by the International Myomassethics Federation (IMF). The 780-hour Basic Core Course fulfills Utah's requirement for 600 hours of instruction and prepares students for the Utah State Massage Technician Licensing Exam.

Program Description

The 780-hour Basic Core Course in massage therapy consists of Swedish Massage, including theory, lab, clinical practice, and specialized massage; Anatomy, including anatomy and physiology, functional anatomy, and common pathology; General Education, consisting of study skills, practice building and Utah law, and psychology for the massage therapist; Bodywork, including therapeutic principles, survey of bodywork modalities, acutherapy, polarity, introduction to shiatsu, and Touch for Health I; and electives that include Shiatsu II, Touch for Health II, Basic Sports Massage, Business Practices, and others.

Continuing Education

Advanced classes are available.

Admission Requirements

Applicants to the Basic Core Course must have a

high school diploma or equivalent, interview with the admissions director, and submit a written personal statement. Applicants to advanced courses must have a license to perform massage or similar qualifications in a health care field; applicants who have not graduated from the Basic Core Course must pass an extensive anatomy exam and practical hands-on evaluation before taking any advanced classes.

Tuition and Fees

There is a $25 application fee and a $100 registration fee. Tuition is $140 per quarter credit, or $5,460 total for the thirty-nine-credit Basic Core Course. Books cost $540 to $650; an optional massage table and supplies are additional.

Financial Assistance

A payment plan and financial aid are available to those who qualify.

The School of Natural Healing

P.O. Box 412
Springville, Utah 84663
Phone: (800) 372-8255

The School of Natural Healing was founded in 1953 by John R. Christopher, N.D. While the school's emphasis is on correspondence study (see page 369), residence study in the Wasatch Mountains is available to complement the correspondence programs in herbology.

Program Description

One-, three-, and six-day residence programs include one hour per day of classroom instruction with a master herbalist; one hour per day of herbal preparation and natural therapy workshop; one half-hour per day of nutritional instruction; and the use of facilities that include a therapy room, preparations lab, herbarium, and research library.

In order to receive the Master of Herbology degree, students must, in addition to completing the correspondence course, attend a six-day certification seminar. These seminars are held at least

once per year and run Monday through Friday; an examination is administered on Saturday.

Tuition and Fees

Tuition for the one-day course is $300, including one correspondence course. Tuition for the three-day course is $650, including one correspondence course. Tuition for the six-day course is $1,200, including one correspondence course. Lodging and meals are available for $50 per person per day.

Tuition for the Master of Herbology certification seminar is $395; meals and lodging are $375 for the week.

Utah College of Massage Therapy

25 South 300 East
Salt Lake City, Utah 84111
Phone: (801) 521-3330 / (800) 617-3302
Fax: (801) 521-3339

The Utah College of Massage Therapy (UCMT) was founded by Norman Cohn in 1986; its certification program became the first of its kind in Utah. In 1996, the school moved into its 25,000-square-foot facility in downtown Salt Lake City.

Accreditation

The Utah College of Massage Therapy is accredited by the American Massage Therapy Association Commission on Massage Training Accreditation/Approval (AMTA/COMTAA). UCMT is also accredited by the Accrediting Council for Continuing Education and Training (ACCET), and thus eligible to offer student financial aid.

Program Description

The 780-hour, six-month daytime or 712-hour, one-year evening Massage Therapy Programs both include Massage Therapy I and II; Anatomy, Physiology, and Kinesiology; Professional Development; CPR/First Aid; AIDS Awareness; Feldenkrais Movement/Bodywork; Infant Massage; Acupressure; Touch for Health I and II; Hydrotherapy/Cryotherapy; On-Site Massage; Shiatsu; Sports

Massage I and II; Sports Injury Massage; Proprio Deep-Tissue Bodywork; Trigger Point Therapy; Facilitated Stretching; Injury Massage; Craniosacral Bodywork; and Student Clinic Internship. The daytime program also includes Reflexology, Hydrotherapy, and Russian Sports Massage.

Enrichment classes are available. Topics include tai chi, yoga, qigong, educational kinesiology, hydrotherapy, reflexology, and sports massage.

An eighteen-hour, hands-on Introduction to Massage Therapy course is offered several times per year. It is not required for enrollment, but is designed to serve as an introduction to both the field of massage therapy and UCMT.

Admission Requirements

Prospective students must have a high school diploma or equivalent or pass an ability to benefit test.

Tuition and Fees

Tuition for the daytime program is $5,600, for the evening program, $5,200. Other costs include: registration fee, $100; books/manuals, $320; uniform, $27; massage table, $451; linens, $25; and lab fee, $90. Tuition for the Introduction to Massage Therapy Course is $84 per person or $150 per couple.

Financial Assistance

Federal grants and loans are available.

VERMONT

Sage Mountain Herbal Retreat Center

P.O. Box 420
East Barre, Vermont 05649

The Sage Mountain Retreat Center was cofounded in 1989 by Rosemary Gladstar, author of the book *Herbal Healing for Women* and founder of the California School of Herbal Studies.

Program Description

A variety of programs in herbal education are offered in Vermont, around the world, and by correspondence (see page 368).

The Spirit and Essence of Herbs: An Herbal Apprentice Program is a two-week intensive apprenticeship program limited to thirty students. Topics include identification of wild edible and medicinal plants; wild food cooking; herbal preparations, such as infusions, decoctions, solar and lunar infusions, salves, oils, and tinctures; materia medica: herbal therapeutics; field trips; plant walks; and more. This program is also offered one weekend per month over seven months.

Beyond Herbology 101, a five-day program in advanced herbal studies, features well-known teachers and focuses each year on a different aspect of herbalism.

Admission Requirements

There are no minimum age or educational requirements.

Tuition and Fees

Tuition for the Spirit and Essence of Herbs Herbal Apprentice Program is $1,200 for the two-week intensive program, and $1,050 for the seven-month program. Tuition for both programs includes the *Science and Art of Herbalism* correspondence course, all materials and handouts, vegetarian meals, camping, and/or dormitory-style lodging.

The cost of Beyond Herbology 101 is $450, including vegetarian meals, camping, and/or dormitory-style lodging.

Financial Assistance

A few work-study scholarships are available for each program.

Vermont College of Norwich University

Adult Degree Program
Montpelier, Vermont 05602
Phone: (802) 828-8500 / (800) 336-6794
Fax: (802) 828-8508

Vermont College is part of Norwich University, founded in 1819. While the main campus is in Montpelier, the college also has an adult learning center in Brattleboro.

Accreditation

Norwich University is accredited by the New England Association of Schools and Colleges, which permits Vermont College to provide fully accredited programs of study.

Program Description

The Adult Degree Program allows students to earn a Bachelor of Arts degree primarily by studying at home. Each semester, students choose a topic or subject area to study in depth for six months, and work with a faculty mentor to develop a detailed study plan involving reading and writing as well as other forms of creative expression, field work, or educational experiences. Students should expect to commit twenty hours per week to the program and to attend a seven-day residency in Montpelier at the beginning and end of every semester.

Self-directed study is available in the area of holistic studies. Students in the Holistic Studies Cycle have designed study projects that include An Exploration of Holistic Health Practices, Transpersonal Psychology, Substance Abuse Counseling and Movement Therapy, Herbology, Shamanic Healing, and Body/Mind Healing with a Focus on Visualization Techniques. Some of the faculty who work with students in the Holistic Studies Cycle include a naturopathic physician and a practicing psychotherapist interested in non-Western healing traditions.

Requirements of the degree include study in the humanities, fine arts, social sciences, math, and science. Transferred credits may be used toward these requirements. Fifty percent of ADP graduates go on to graduate school; some use the ADP bachelor's degree as preparation for continued education in acupuncture, homeopathy, movement therapy, and other holistic therapies.

Admission Requirements

Applicants must submit official high school or college transcripts, a personal essay, and three letters of recommendation, and interview with an admissions representative.

Tuition and Fees

There is a $35 application fee; tuition is $3,695 per semester, including residency room and board.

Financial Assistance

Federal grants and loans, state grants, loans, scholarships, and specialized grants are available.

The Vermont School of Professional Massage

14 Merchant Street
Barre, Vermont 05641
Phone: (802) 479-2340 / (800) 287-8816

The Vermont School of Professional Massage was founded in 1989 by Faeterri Silver, who has been licensed for the practice of massage since 1981.

Accreditation

The Vermont School of Professional Massage is recognized by the State of Vermont, and graduates are eligible to take the National Certification Board for Therapeutic Massage and Bodywork (NCBTMB) exam.

Program Description

The 600-hour Massage Therapy Program may be taken either full-time days (nine months) or part-time evenings (twenty-one months). The curriculum includes Human Anatomy and Physiology, Massage Theory and Practice (including exposure to Trager, shiatsu, manual lymph drainage, muscle energy technique, strain/counterstrain, chair, sports, pregnancy, infant, geriatric, and light touch, which includes reiki, polarity, and direction of energy), Massage Practicum Clinic, Medical Terminology, Office Procedures and Business Practices, and Adjuncts (covering the areas of assessment, pathology, kinesiology, CPR/First Aid, hydrotherapy, business, and ethics).

Continuing Education

A one-hundred-hour summer intensive for health professionals is offered every other summer in even years. Other workshops and seminars are offered periodically, covering specific techniques and regions of the body.

Admission Requirements

Potential applicants are evaluated on desire and ability; a personal interview is encouraged.

Tuition and Fees

Tuition is $3,600, including instruction, books, and practicum materials.

Financial Assistance

Payment plans and Vermont Students' Assistance Corporation (VSAC) grants are available.

VIRGINIA

Eastern Institute of Hypnotherapy

P.O. Box 249
Goshen, Virginia 24439-0249
Phone: (540) 997-0325 / (800) 296-MIND
Fax: (540) 997-0324

The Eastern Institute of Hypnotherapy was founded in 1989. Allen S. Chips, D.C.H., the primary instructor for both hypnotherapy training programs, pioneered the Chips and Associates Hypnotherapy Centers and has conducted over 7,000 hours in clinical private practice.

Accreditation

EIH is the only hypnotherapy school to receive the endorsement of the Association for Research and Enlightenment in Virginia Beach, Virginia.

Program Description

The one-hundred-hour Hypnotherapy Certification Program consists of forty in-class hours of instruction covering History, Misconceptions, Susceptibility, Rapport, Suggestibility Tests, Induction Methods, Mind/Brain Testing, Post-Hypnotic Suggestion, Ericksonian Methods, NLP Therapy, Weight Loss, Introduction to Regression, Case Histories, Research Studies, Hypnosis Phenomena, Self-Hypnosis, Deepening Trance, Dangers, Signs of Hypnosis, Suggestive Therapy, Smoking Cessation, "Past Life" Therapy, and others.

The 125-hour Certified Master Hypnotherapist Program consists of forty-five hours of in-class instruction, documentation of ten experiential sessions, and a research assignment. The course includes Strategic Therapy, the Multisession Format, Client-Centered Therapy, Unconscious Triggers, Finding the Engram, Goal Management, NLP for Reframing Negative Feeling States, Timeline Induction and Regression Methods, Advanced Study in Transformational Models, Phobia, Fear and Anxiety Models, Soul Retrieval, Hypnotherapy for Briefest Trauma Recovery, Alternate Realities and Guidance, and more.

Admission Requirements

Registration, a deposit, and a goal statement are required. The Certified Master Hypnotherapist Program is open to the certified or professional hypnotherapist who is licensed or certified as a helping professional and is familiar with regressive trance-state therapy.

Tuition and Fees

Tuition for the Hypnotherapy and Certified Master Hypnotherapist Courses is $950, including all materials.

Financial Assistance

Payment plans, early registration discounts, and group discounts are available.

Equissage

P.O. Box 447
Round Hill, Virginia 22141
Phone: (540) 338-1917 / (800) 843-0224

The Equissage company was founded in 1989 by two certified massage therapists, for the purpose of offering massage therapy services to the equine athlete. The company initially marketed its services to East Coast racetracks. After gaining national media exposure, the company produced a full-length instructional video and in 1991, introduced the nation's first training program in equine sports massage therapy. There are more than 800 graduates worldwide.

Accreditation

Currently there are no state regulations governing the certification of equine sports massage therapists.

Program Description

The sixty-hour Certification Program consists of classroom study and individualized practical applications, and is limited to seven students. Topics include history of the use of massage on animals, introduction to sports massage for humans, demonstration of Equissage on equine subjects, equine muscle anatomy and physiology, stress point therapy, hands-on application, and business and marketing plans.

Admission Requirements

A love of animals is the most important qualification for success. A background in massage therapy is preferable but not mandatory.

Tuition and Fees

Tuition is $795.

Fuller School of Massage Therapy

3500 Virginia Beach Boulevard, #100
Virginia Beach, Virginia 23452
Phone: (757) 340-7132

The Fuller School of Massage Therapy was founded in 1983. The school building includes one large classroom and three massage therapy rooms, with seven additional therapy rooms available for classes and treatments.

Accreditation

The Fuller School of Massage Therapy is accredited by the Virginia Board of Education as a proprietary school. Graduates of the Certification Program are eligible to take the national certification exam administered by the National Certification Board for Therapeutic Massage and Bodywork (NCBTMB).

Program Description

The 250-hour Basic Program in massage therapy includes courses in Anatomy and Physiology, Reflexology, Hydrotherapy and Aromatherapy, Medical Massage and Deep Tissue Techniques, Oriental Massage, Myotherapy and Neuromuscular Therapy, Sports Massage, On-Site Massage, Business Management and Professional Ethics, and CPR/First Aid. Students also schedule a minimum of ten hours of individual practices; a minimum of ten hours of video viewing; and a minimum of twenty-five intern massages, for which they will be compensated at the time of certification.

During or after the Basic Program, students may continue with the Certification Program; student hours can total over 800. Students may take one or all of the courses, which may include Advanced Anatomy and Physiology, Mind/Body Integrative Therapy, Marketing/Business Practices and Professional Ethics, Hydrotherapy, Advanced Sports Massage, Polarity, Aromatherapy, Injury Assessment and Therapy, Oriental Massage, Medicinal Herbs and Nutrition Healing, and Integration of Clinical Skills.

Admission Requirements

Applicants must be over 18 years of age, have a high school diploma, interview with an admissions representative, and have received at least one professional massage.

Tuition and Fees

There is a $50 enrollment fee; an optional massage table costs approximately $400.

Tuition for the Basic Program $1,650, and books are $70. Tuition for the Certification Program is $6 per credit hour; books are additional.

Financial Assistance

Payment plans, veterans' benefits, and Vocational Rehabilitation are available.

Harold J. Reilly School of Massotherapy

215 67th Street at Atlantic Avenue
P.O. Box 595
Virginia Beach, Virginia 23451-0595
Phone: (757) 437-7202
Fax: (757) 422-4631

The Harold J. Reilly School of Massotherapy was founded by Dr. James Windsor and Dr. Harold Reilly in 1987. The school is a department of the Association for Research and Enlightenment (A.R.E.), a nonprofit organization founded in 1931 and dedicated to helping people better their lives through the Edgar Cayce readings.

Accreditation

The Harold J. Reilly School of Massotherapy is a member of the Virginia Association of Private Career Schools and is licensed by the Commonwealth of Virginia Department of Education. The school is accredited by the American Massage Therapy Association Commission on Massage Training Accreditation/ Approval (AMTA/COMTAA).

Program Description

The unique curriculum, with a basis in Swedish massage, focuses on personal transformation and emphasizes a balanced lifestyle as recommended in the Edgar Cayce readings. The program is designed to train individuals not only as massage therapists, but as healers desiring to integrate mind, body, and spirit.

The 600-hour Massage Program may be completed in six months of full-time study (twenty-five to thirty hours per week), or may be taken on a part-time basis. The 500-hour Certificate Program requires sixteen months of part-time evening study.

Classes offered include Beginning Massotherapy: Fundamentals of Cayce/Reilly Massage, Intermediate Massage, Sports Massage, Clinical Massage, Swedish, Integrative Massage, Clinical Experience/Practicum, Applied Kinesiology, Chair Massage, Geriatric Massage, Pregnancy and Massage, Foot Reflexology, Jin Shin Do Body-Mind Acupressure, Therapeutic Touch, Anatomy and Physiology I and II, Body/Mind Integration, Hydrotherapy, Professional Business Development and Ethics, Cayce Home Remedies, and Dreams and Meditation. In addition, specialized workshops are offered throughout the year in a variety of disciplines including Beginners Massage Workshops, Advanced Cayce/Reilly, Manual Lymph Drainage, First Aid/CPR, and others.

Admission Requirements

Applicants must have a high school diploma or equivalent; be able to speak and understand English; submit a physician's statement of health and two letters of reference from professional persons; and interview with an admissions representative.

Tuition and Fees

Tuition and fees for the 600-hour Massage Program are $4,500. Tuition for the 500-hour Certificate Program is $7.50 per hour. There is a $35 application fee; books and supplies cost $300 to $375; two professional massages cost $60 to $90; CPR/First Aid training costs $36; and a recommended massage table costs $300 to $600.

Financial Assistance

Payment plans, scholarships, and Canadian student loans and partial scholarships are available.

National Center for Homeopathy

801 North Fairfax Street
Suite 306
Alexandria, Virginia 22314
Phone: (703) 548-7790
Fax: (703) 548-7792

The National Center for Homeopathy, a nonprofit organization, is the largest homeopathic organization in the United States. The center offers seminars and training programs for both the consumer and the licensed health care professional, and also promotes health through homeopathy via a number of other professional services (see page 351).

The center's summer instruction program is an outgrowth of the Postgraduate School for Physicians in Homeopathy, established in 1922. Since that time, courses have been held almost every year. Courses are held at Marymount University in Arlington, Virginia, but NCH is not affiliated with Marymount University.

Accreditation

The National Center for Homeopathy's beginning-level postgraduate courses are accredited by the Council on Homeopathic Education (CHE).

Program Description

Courses for consumers include Homeopathy 101—Foundations in Homeopathy, a two-day seminar providing a solid foundation in homeopathy; Homeopathy 102—Basic Acute Homeopathy, a five-day course providing practical instruction in the use of homeopathy for cuts, burns, sprains, dental problems, and more; Homeopathy 103—Intermediate Acute Homeopathy, a five-day course exploring more advanced acute remedies; Homeopathy 104—Understanding Chronic Prescribing, a four-day course exploring the treatment of chronic disease; and Study Group Workshop, a two-day seminar offering practical instruction in starting a study group, attracting members, sponsoring speakers, teaching the use of materia medica, and more.

Courses for health care providers include Homeopathic Prescribing I for Professionals, a five-day course concentrating on the treatment of the most common acute problems seen in a general practice, including first aid, otitis media, gastroenteritis, backaches, and more; and Homeopathic Prescribing II for Professionals, a five-day course covering treatment of pneumonia, hepatitis, kidney diseases, and other acute and chronic conditions.

Courses open to both consumers and health care professionals include Introduction to Veterinary Homeopathy, a two-day introduction to the use of homeopathy for both acute and chronic diseases in animals; Intermediate Veterinary Homeopathy, a two-day seminar; Topics in Advanced Homeopathy, a five-day course covering materia medica of forty rare remedies; Advanced Veterinary Homeopathy, a two-day seminar focusing on case analyses, remedy selection, and evaluation; and Philosophy of Homeopathic Medicine, a two-day seminar that offers a comprehensive examination of the roots and philosophy of homeopathy. Admission to successive course levels requires appropriate prerequisites.

A certificate of attendance will be furnished upon completion of each course; no degrees or diplomas are given.

Admission Requirements

It is an NCH educational ethic that it will freely share homeopathic knowledge with all persons and will not deny it to anyone because of his or her professional background.

In order to be eligible for professional courses, health care professionals need a current health care license from a state licensing board; allied health care professionals need a letter from their physician-employer; full-time students enrolled in a course of study that leads to eligibility to be licensed as a health care provider must present proof of enrollment; foreign health care providers must submit copies of valid licenses to practice medicine in their country.

Tuition and Fees

The NCH membership fee is $40. Courses range from $165 to $190 for the two-day seminars and $300 to $445 for the five-day courses. Tuition for professionals is $495 per course, or $940 for both Prescribing courses. The Study Group Workshop is $100. Required books must be purchased separately. Room and board is available in college-style dormitories (single occupancy) for $110 to $275 per course.

Financial Assistance

Tuition discounts are available to spouses/domestic partners of registrants (50 percent), full-time students enrolled in a course leading to eligibility to be licensed as a health care provider (50 percent), other full-time students (15 percent), and senior citizens age 62 and up (10 percent). Discounts do not apply to room and board. A limited number of tuition grants and loans are available; members of an NCH affiliated study group may compete in a scholarship essay contest.

The Polarity Center

309 Williamsburg Road
Sterling, Virginia 20164
Phone: (703) 471-4014

The Polarity Center was founded in 1980 by Bhagwant Khalsa, a polarity therapist, shamanic healer, and former vice-president of the Board of Directors for the American Polarity Therapy Association.

Accreditation

Training at the Polarity Center is accredited by the American Polarity Therapy Association (APTA).

Program Description

The A.P.P. (Associate Polarity Practitioner) Program is a 155-hour, first-level program that leads to A.P.P. certification in accordance with APTA standards. The principles of polarity therapy are introduced through classes in Nutrition and Cleansing Techniques, Polarity Theory, Bodywork, Polarity Yoga, Communication Skills, and Energetic Anatomy.

The R.P.P. (Registered Polarity Practitioner) Program is a 495-hour, twenty-month program focusing on developing skills necessary for becoming a professional practitioner. Students gain an understanding of the Five Elements and learn to integrate body, mind, and spirit in healing work. Training includes supervision and feedback on craniosacral, nutritional counseling, polarity yoga, and counseling skills, and extensive work with the nervous systems, structural balancing, and sound. Upon completion of the program, students may apply to APTA for R.P.P. status. R.P.P. certification requires fifty hours of anatomy and physiology, which is provided in the training.

Ongoing classes are offered in shamanic healing. These include Shamanic Art: Mask and Shield Building; Basic and Advanced Shamanic Journeying; Nature Rituals; Rites of Passage; Medicine Wheel Teachings; Sacred Songs and Shamanic Dancing; and Soul Retrieval Training.

Admission Requirements

The most important requirement is the applicant's sincerity and commitment to polarity therapy. Students applying for the A.P.P. Program must complete an application and interview with the director. Students applying for the R.P.P. Program must have completed an A.P.P. program or equivalent, complete an application, and interview with the director.

Tuition and Fees

Tuition for the A.P.P. Program is $1,500, including APTA membership; books are additional. Tuition for the R.P.P. Program is $3,270, including retreat; books are approximately $80.

Financial Assistance

Payment plans are available; a 10 percent discount is given for full payment upon registration for the A.P.P. Program only.

Richmond Academy of Massage

2004 Bremo Road, Suite 102
Richmond, Virginia 23226
Phone: (804) 282-5003

The Richmond Academy of Massage was founded in 1989.

Accreditation

The Richmond Academy of Massage is affiliated with the Associated Bodywork and Massage Professionals (ABMP) and has been issued a certificate to operate by the Virginia State Board of Education.

Program Description

The 500-hour Professional Training for Certification in Massage Therapy Program covers such topics as anatomy, physiology, Swedish and therapeutic massage, sports massage, geriatric massage, shiatsu, trigger point therapy, on-site corporate massage, and First Aid/CPR. The program, coupled with an estimated 600 hours of out-of-class work, leads to certification as a massage therapist. Classes meet two evenings per week and on twelve Saturdays for a full year.

Admission Requirements

There is no minimum age or educational requirement. Applicants must submit three personal references.

Tuition and Fees

There is a $50 application fee. Tuition is $3,600; a massage table costs $60 to $600, and books and supplies are additional.

Financial Assistance

A payment plan is available.

Satchidananda Ashram—Yogaville

Buckingham, Virginia 23921
Phone: (800) 858-YOGA / (804) 969-3121

Sri Swami Satchidananda (Sri Gurudev) founded Integral Yoga International in 1966. Integral yoga teaches that peace is within each one of us, and that to realize that peace, we need a healthy and easeful body and a clear mind in order to live a useful life.

Program Description

Satchidananda Ashram—Yogaville offers a number of courses, workshops, and retreats addressing such topics as meditation; raja yoga; transcending fear, anger, and depression; and more, along with several teacher training programs.

The month-long Hatha Yoga Teacher Training teaches students to become instructors of Integral Hatha Yoga Beginners I while refining their own personal practices of asana, pranayama, and meditation. Also included are classes in Yogic Diet, Anatomy and Physiology, and Yoga Philosophy.

The three-week Advanced Teacher Training offers instruction in teaching Beginners II and Intermediate-Level Integral Hatha Yoga classes, as well as pranayama classes.

In the one-week Prenatal Teacher Training, students study the asanas that are used specifically for pregnancy. Included are diet and nutrition, yogic breathing, and visualizations for labor and delivery.

Tuition and Fees

Tuition for the Hatha Yoga Teacher Training Course

is $1,600; for the Advanced Teacher Training Course, $975; and for the Prenatal Teacher Training Course, $475. Tuition for all programs includes dormitory accommodations, meals, and books.

Virginia School of Massage

2008 Morton Drive
Charlottesville, Virginia 22903
Phone: (804) 293-4031

The Virginia School of Massage was founded in 1989 by Jerry Toporovsky, a massage therapist who also founded the Baltimore School of Massage.

Accreditation

The school was awarded a certificate to operate by the State Board of Education, and is certified by the National Certification Board for Therapeutic Massage and Bodywork (NCBTMB) as a Category A continuing education provider.

Program Description

There are two options for enrolling in the Massage Therapy Training Program: students may enroll in the Basic Course only and then, if interested in continuing, enroll in the 500-hour program at the intermediate level; or, students may enroll directly into the 500-hour program.

The twenty-week Basic Course meets one day per week. It serves as an introduction to massage and provides a foundation for further training; it also functions as the first term of the 500-hour program. The curriculum includes training in Swedish massage, seated techniques, proper body mechanics, an introduction to polarity therapy, and anatomy and physiology. Students must practice three hours per week.

The 500-hour Massage Therapy Training Program consists of Basic, Intermediate, and Advanced Courses and related weekends and workshops. The Basic Course is described above. The twenty-week, second-term Intermediate Massage Course meets one day per week and explores deep tissue work, energy concepts, underlying muscle groups, body type analysis, an overview of bodywork modalities, and mind/body relationships; in addition, students must practice three hours per week. The twenty-week, third-term Advanced Massage Course meets twice a week and covers myofascial release bodywork, advanced training in energy work, advanced sensitivity training, in-depth anatomy and physiology, advanced training in body mechanics, business practices, communication skills, and more; students must practice a total of forty hours. Intermediate and Advanced students also participate in a total of seven 1-day workshops in bodywork modalities that may include shiatsu, reflexology, therapeutic touch, sports massage, and craniosacral therapy.

Admission Requirements

Applicants must be at least 18 years of age, have a high school diploma or equivalent, and be physically able to perform the massage manipulations taught in the program.

Tuition and Fees

There is a $50 application fee for the Basic Course; tuition is $650; books and lab fee are $40.

There is a $100 application fee for the Massage Therapy Training Program. Tuition is $4,150; books and lab fee are $135; linens and oil for supervised practice sessions are additional.

Financial Assistance

Payment plans, a limited number of partial scholarships, and private loans are available.

WASHINGTON

Alexandar School of Natural Therapeutics

4032 Pacific Avenue
Tacoma, Washington 98408
Phone: (206) 473-1142
Fax: (206) 473-3807

The Alexandar School of Natural Therapeutics was founded in 1980 by Aliesha Alexandar, L.M.P., who served for six years as president of the Washington State Massage Therapy Association Board.

Accreditation

The 600-hour Massage Therapy Program exceeds the State of Washington professional licensing requirement.

Program Description

The 600-hour Massage Therapy Program may be completed in either a six-month or ten-month format. Classes include Swedish Massage I and II, Anatomy and Physiology, Basic Muscle Anatomy and Kinesiology, Advanced Muscle Anatomy and Kinesiology and Remedial Exercise, Medical Massage and Treatments, Living Kinesiology, Body Psychology, Student Clinic/Treatments, Shiatsu Massage, On-Site Massage, Sports Massage I and II, Aromatherapy and Herbal Facial and Body Treatments, Hydrotherapy, Nutrition, and Practice Management/Business Practice.

Admission Requirements

Applicants must be at least 18 years old, have a high school diploma or equivalent, and be in good health.

Tuition and Fees

Tuition is $5,800, including a $100 application fee. Books, supplies, AIDS training, CPR, First Aid, and student liability insurance total approximately $400 more; a massage table costs $300 to $700.

Financial Assistance

Payment plans, veterans' benefits, Dept. of Vocational Rehabilitation, Employment Security, and Labor and Industries retraining programs are available.

Bastyr University

14500 Juanita Drive Northeast
Bothell, Washington 98011
Phone: (425) 823-1300
Fax: (425) 823-6222
Internet: www.bastyr.edu
E-mail: admiss@bastyr.edu

Bastyr University was founded in 1978 as the John Bastyr College of Naturopathic Medicine. In 1994, the university received an $840,000 grant from the National Institutes of Health Office of Alternative Medicine to establish a Center for Alternative Medicine Research in HIV/AIDS. In 1996, the university moved from its Seattle location to nearly fifty acres of woods and fields on the northeast shore of Lake Washington. The 186,000-square-foot complex includes a whole foods, vegetarian cafeteria and expanded classroom, research, and laboratory facilities.

Accreditation

Bastyr University is accredited by the Commission on Colleges of the Northwest Association of Schools and Colleges. The Naturopathic Medicine Program is accredited by the Council on Naturopathic Medical Education (CNME). The master's degree programs in acupuncture and Oriental medicine are accredited by the National Accreditation Commission for Schools and Colleges of Acupuncture and Oriental Medicine. The Didactic Program in Dietetics is approved by the American Dietetic Association Council on Education.

Program Description

The four-year, 327-credit Doctor of Naturopathic Medicine Program prepares students to take the Naturopathic Physicians Licensing Exam (NPLEX). Results of this exam are used in all states that license naturopathic physicians. The program consists of two years of pre-clinical curriculum, two years of clinical naturopathic medicine curriculum, fifteen credits of electives, and 1,122 hours (fifty-one credits) of clinical experience. Topics covered in the pre-clinical curriculum include Human Anatomy, Physiology, Biochemistry, Histology, Living Anatomy, Embryology, Human Pathology, Immunology, Infectious Diseases, Genetic Counseling, Research Methods and Design, Physical and Clinical Lab Diagnosis, Pharmacology, Fundamentals of Traditional Chinese Medicine, Naturopathic Philosophy, Hydrotherapy, Massage, Botanical Medicine, Fundamentals of Ayurvedic Medicine, Basic Foods/Diet Assessment, Homeopathy, and more. The clinical naturopathic medicine curriculum covers such areas as Addictions and Disorders, Botanical Medicine, Gynecology, Psychological Assessment, Pediatrics, Cardiology, Minor Surgery, Geriatrics, Sports Medicine, Endocrinology, Diagnostic Imaging, Oncology, and more. Clinical experience includes Preceptorships, Clinic Assistant Shifts, Patient Care Clinic Shifts, and Physical Medicine Shifts.

A two-year, forty-six-credit Homeopathic Medicine Certificate Program is offered to licensed practitioners with basic training in homeopathic medicine. The program is offered in three-day weekend and week-long summer intensives to accommodate the working clinician. Courses include Philosophy and History, Practice Methodology, Materia Medica, Ethics, Homeopathic Dispensary and Pharmacology, Clinical, Research, Independent Research Project, and Final Project.

The Master of Science degree in acupuncture and Oriental medicine (MSAOM) is a four-year program offering training in acupuncture, Oriental medicine, Chinese herbal medicine, and the health sciences. The curriculum includes Organic Chemistry; Biochemistry; Anatomy and Physiology; Western Clinical Science and Disease Processes; Acupuncture Techniques, Diagnosis, Pathology, and Therapeutics; and Chinese Herbal Materia Medica and Therapeutics. Clinical training is integrated with course work beginning with the second year.

The Master of Science degree in acupuncture (MSA) is a three-year program in acupuncture, Oriental medicine, and the health sciences. Requirements are the same as those of the MSAOM, with the omission of requirements in Chinese herbal medicine and language.

A one-year Certificate in Chinese Herbal Medicine is offered to acupuncturists, N.D.s, currently enrolled N.D. students, MSA students, or individuals with equivalent background. The course work includes clinical training. Other postgraduate programs currently being developed include a Certificate Program in Five Element Theory and Practice and a Certificate Program in Japanese Acupuncture.

The Master of Science degree in nutrition balances a "whole foods" approach with an understanding of human behavior, human biochemistry, and nutrient metabolism, and emphasizes patient education and motivation. Course work includes nutritional assessment, diet therapy, disease processes, the psychology of addiction, and principles of whole foods. Graduates work as nutrition counselors, clinical nutritionists, and as consultants to the food and fitness industries.

The Didactic Program in Dietetics and Dietetic Internship Program are designed to fulfill the American Dietetics Association's academic requirements for Registered Dietitians and to provide performance requirements for entry-level dietitians through supervised practice.

Bastyr offers an undergraduate Bachelor of Science degree in natural health sciences with majors in either nutrition or Oriental medicine to advanced undergraduates who wish to complete their B.S. degree. The programs prepare students for advanced studies and, in the case of the nutrition major, for work as nutrition educators in association with other health care practitioners.

Community and Continuing Education

Health care professionals can participate in Bastyr University's continuing professional education programs through home study, seminars, workshops, and intensives. Current programs for professionals include home study courses in Herbal Medicine: An Introduction (two contact hours) and Phytotherapy: Herbal Medicine Meets Clinical Science (Part I, 1½ contact hours, Part II, two contact hours). Other offerings include a series of Japanese Acupuncture Workshops and a conference in Clinical Applications of Natural Medicine.

Bastyr offers a Distance Learning Program for those who are unable to attend as full-time students, but who are interested in learning more about natural health and nutrition. Written assignments, a toll-free telephone number, and voice-mail boxes for each instructor foster greater understanding of course material. Courses take ten to sixteen weeks to complete, and include a term project and proctored final exam. No degrees are available through this program, but students may receive a Certificate of Completion, and some courses may be applied toward degree programs. Courses include Nutrition I and II, Nutrition and Herbs, Nutrition in the Natural Products Industry, Introduction to Nutrition in Natural Medicine, Diet

and Behavior, and Fundamental Principles of Traditional Chinese Medicine. Additional courses are under development.

Admission Requirements

All applicants must submit official transcripts and letters of recommendation, and to interview with an admissions representative.

Applicants to the Doctor of Naturopathic Medicine Program must have completed a bachelor's degree or at least 135 quarter credits (ninety semester credits) and significant life experience. The minimum G.P.A. requirement is 2.5. Prerequisite courses include college-level algebra or precalculus; statistics; general chemistry with labs; organic chemistry with labs; general biology or a combination of courses to include cell and molecular biology, genetics, botany, and taxonomy with labs; physics; psychology; English; and humanities. Required science courses must have been taken within seven years of matriculation. Scores on standardized tests (GRE or MCAT) are not required. Students entering the program who have graduated from an accredited professional school or program (including M.D., D.O., D.C., and others) and who are legally qualified to practice may apply for advanced standing.

Applicants to the Master of Science programs in acupuncture or acupuncture and Oriental medicine must have completed a bachelor's degree with an overall minimum G.P.A. of 2.25. Prerequisite courses include college-level algebra or precalculus, general chemistry, general biology with lab, and general psychology.

The Certificate in Chinese Herbal Medicine Program is open to currently enrolled students of acupuncture and Oriental or naturopathic medicine, acupuncturists, N.D.s, and other health care professionals. Current students or graduates of Bastyr University need only submit the application form and a brief statement regarding their interest in Chinese herbal medicine. All others must submit a current résumé, two letters of recommendation, and transcripts.

Applicants to the Master of Science in nutrition program must have completed a bachelor's degree with an overall G.P.A. of 2.25. Prerequisite courses include college-level algebra or precalculus, general chemistry, general biology with lab, general and developmental psychology, anatomy and physiology, organic chemistry with lab, nutrition, foods, microbiology, biochemistry, and basic statistics.

Students transferring into the Bachelor of Science in natural health sciences programs with majors in nutrition or Oriental medicine must have completed ninety quarter credits (sixty semester credits) with an overall G.P.A. of 2.25. Prerequisites include at least fifty-four general education quarter-credits, including English and public speaking, college-level algebra or precalculus, general chemistry, general biology with lab, and general psychology.

Applicants to the Homeopathic Medicine Certificate Program must submit two letters of recommendation, transcripts, verification of professional licensure and at least 250 hours' study in homeopathy, a written case presentation, and an admissions interview. The program is open to M.D.s, N.D.s, L.P.N.s, D.O.s, D.C.s, and P.A.s.

Tuition and Fees

The catalog costs $5; there is a $60 application fee for the degree and certificate programs and a $25 fee for non-matriculated and/or non-degree programs.

Tuition for clinic credits is $185 per credit hour and for other credits, $162 per credit hour. Total first-year costs, including tuition, fees, books, and supplies, are as follows: four-year N.D., $14,270; five-year N.D., $9,765; MSAOM, $13,235; MSA, $12,170; MSN, $6,915; BSNHS-OM, $12,790; and BSNHS-Nutrition, $8,340. Tuition for the Homeopathic Medicine Certificate Program is $175 per credit.

Costs for the Distance Learning Program are as follows: registration fee, $25; tuition, $162 per credit; materials, approximately $50 per course; and shipping and handling, $15 U.S. and $60 international.

Financial Assistance

Federal loans, federal and Washington State work-study programs, federal Pell Grants, and limited scholarships are available.

Brenneke School of Massage

160 Roy Street
Seattle, Washington 98109
Phone: (206) 282-1233
Fax: (206) 282-9183

The Brenneke School of Massage was founded in 1974.

Accreditation

Brenneke is accredited by the Accrediting Council for Continuing Education and Training (ACCET). The Professional Licensing Program is accredited by the American Massage Therapy Association Commission on Massage Training Accreditation/Approval (AMTA/COMTAA) and approved by the Washington State Massage Board.

Program Description

The 650-hour, twelve-month Professional Licensing Program includes Swedish Massage, Anatomy and Physiology, Professional Development, Business, Advanced Massage Techniques, Kinesiology, Pathology, Event Sports Massage, Introduction to Myofascial Technique or Trigger Point Therapy, AIDS Education, Student Clinical Hydrotherapy, Student/Teacher Clinic, and Treatment Case Studies. Electives include Therapeutic Touch; Connective Tissue Massage; Polarity; Manual Lymph Drainage; Reiki; Lomi Lomi; Shiatsu; Foot Reflexology; Introduction to Herbology; Cadaver Anatomy; Introduction to Body, Mind, and Spirit; and more.

As of January 1998, Brenneke will be offering both a 650-hour and a 1,000-hour Professional Licensing Program. The 1,000-hour program will have a January starting date; please call for additional information.

Continuing Education

Brenneke offers graduate education in clinical sports massage, connective tissue massage, lymphatic massage, and myofascial release technique. These courses are in module format and may be taken individually or in the full series for a graduate certificate.

Nationally-known massage therapists present specialty workshops at Brenneke throughout the year. Brenneke also offers continuing education workshops on a monthly basis for the licensed massage practitioner; these may include Shiatsu, Foot Reflexology, Herbology, Lomi Lomi, Infant Massage, Running Injuries, Advanced Sports Massage, Reiki, Introduction to Craniosacral Therapy, and many others.

Massage Therapy for the Novice is a two-day introductory course in Swedish massage that is open to the public, and is also a prerequisite for the Professional Licensing Program.

Admission Requirements

Applicants must be at least 18 years of age by the beginning of class, be physically and emotionally capable of performing and receiving massage, have a high school diploma or equivalent, interview with the director of admissions, and successfully complete the introductory class.

Tuition and Fees

The Massage Therapy for the Novice course costs $100, which is applicable toward tuition if the student enrolls in the Licensing Program.

Tuition for the Professional Licensing Program is $6,350. Other costs include: application fee, $100; massage table, approximately $250 to $500; and one professional massage per term, $30 to $50. Several elective classes require a copayment—Cadaver Anatomy, $170, and Reiki, $50.

The graduate continuing education series costs $450 to $550; this varies with hours and number of modules. Monthly continuing education classes cost $40 each.

Financial Assistance

Federal grants and loans are available to those who qualify.

Brian Utting School of Massage

900 Thomas Street
Seattle, Washington 98109
Phone: (206) 292-8055/ (800) 842-8731
Fax: (206) 292-0113

The Brian Utting School of Massage was founded in 1982 by Brian Utting, who has practiced massage in chiropractic and pain clinics for several years.

Accreditation

The Professional Massage Licensing Program is accredited by the American Massage Therapy Association Commission on Massage Training Accreditation/Approval (AMTA/COMTAA), and certified by the Washington State Department of Health and Division of Professional Licensing, the Washington State Board of Massage, and the Oregon Board of Massage Technicians. The school is approved by the National Certification Board for Therapeutic Massage and Bodywork (NCBTMB) as a continuing education provider.

Program Description

The 900-hour Licensing Program includes theoretical grounding in Anatomy and Physiology, Kinesiology, Pathology, and Pathophysiology; Theoretical Applications, including body mechanics and movement analysis, cadaver anatomy at Bastyr University, First Aid, CPR, AIDS/HIV training, hydrotherapy theory and applications, indications and contraindications, palpation skills, and muscle palpation; Professional Preparation, including business and marketing skills, communication skills, internship program, professional ethics, and student clinic; and Bodywork Techniques that include Swedish massage, deep tissue massage, circulatory massage, art and technique of deep touching, deep muscle therapy, clinical massage, injury evaluation and treatment, connective tissue massage, neuromuscular technique, foot reflexology, pregnancy massage, and sports massage. Classes may be taken on a day or evening schedule.

Optional student support classes include Introduction to Anatomy for Massage Students, Conditioning for Massage Students, and Learning Skills Tutorial.

Continuing Education

Continuing education courses are typically offered in areas such as manual lymph drainage, craniosacral, on-site (chair) massage, injury assessment and treatment, Ben Benjamin: Survivors of Abuse, shiatsu, and Trager.

Admission Requirements

Applicants must have a high school diploma or equivalent, have no criminal convictions, submit a certificate of health, and be able to give and receive massage. Applicants must also participate in an introductory one-day workshop and interview with one or more admissions committee members. A prior class in anatomy is recommended.

Tuition and Fees

Tuition is $6,500, including a $100 registration fee and a $100 enrollment fee; books, massage table, and supplies cost approximately $1,200.

Financial Assistance

Payment plans, personal loans, veterans' benefits, and aid from the Washington State Department of Labor and Industries are available.

The Center for Yoga of Seattle

2261 N.E. 65th Street
Seattle, Washington 98115-7066
Phone: (206) 526-9642 / (800) 964-2669

The Center for Yoga of Seattle was founded by Richard Schachtel, who has taught yoga for over twenty years and is personally certified by B.K.S. Iyengar to teach his method; Schachtel has traveled to India eight times to study with the Iyengars. The Center for Yoga of Seattle offers up to forty classes a week at four studios.

Program Description

The Center for Yoga of Seattle offers a two-year, four-course program in Yoga Teacher Training as well as two 6-day intensives (Level I and II).

The four-course program, suitable for Northwest residents, meets one Saturday per month and is equivalent to taking both the Level I and Level II

six-day intensives with the addition of 50 percent more class time overall. Topics covered include understanding and teaching the Iyengar yoga standing poses, shoulderstand cycle, sitting forward bend cycle, classical sun salutations, backarches, headstand, jumping sun salutations, standing and seated twisting poses, and others; beginning pranayama techniques; relaxation techniques; setting up yoga classes; and more. In the six-day intensives, students meet for approximately five-and-a-half hours each day.

Students receive a certificate of completion at the end of each program that may be helpful in obtaining employment. However, this is not a Certified Iyengar Yoga Teacher certificate, which requires assessment, a written exam, and a history of teaching Iyengar yoga for several years. The six-day intensives may be taken as preparation for Iyengar certification.

Tuition and Fees

Tuition for each of the courses in the four-course program is $250 for early registrants and $300 for those enrolling within thirty days of the course. Tuition for each six-day intensive is $450 for early registrants and $495 for those enrolling within thirty days of the course. For those registering for both Level I and Level II intensives, tuition is $800 for early registrants and $890 within thirty days of the start of the course.

Inexpensive lodging is often available with a local yoga student for $125 per week.

Financial Assistance

A payment plan is available.

Institute for Therapeutic Learning

9322 21st Avenue N.W.
Seattle, Washington 98117
Phone: (206) 783-1838

The Institute for Therapeutic Learning was founded in 1988 by Jack Elias, a licensed clinical hypnotherapist and certified NLP practitioner. Elias is the author of *Finding True Magic*.

Accreditation

Completion of the 150-hour program will enable students to qualify for certification and membership as clinical hypnotherapists in state and national hypnosis associations. At this time, 150 hours is the generally recognized minimum level of training.

Program Description

The 150-hour Transpersonal Clinical Hypnotherapist Program consists of six 25-hour phases: Full Spectrum Hypnosis Training; Transpersonal Regression Therapy; Transpersonal Therapy; Transpersonal Hypnotherapy Applications; Comprehensive Work with Inner Archetypes, Couples, and Groups; and Releasing Unwanted Influences: Future Progression. Upon completion of each of the second through sixth phases, students must conduct a one-hour hypnotherapy session. Training is offered in both a weekend format and a 150-hour summer intensive.

The 150-hour program may also be taken through correspondence, either for certification or for personal growth without certification.

After the live training, students may take an additional 150 hours of independent study (with tapes), and receive certification in recognition of 300 hours of training.

Admission Requirements

A high school diploma or equivalent are prerequisites for enrolling.

Continuing Education

Continuing education, mentorship classes, and supervision are available.

Tuition and Fees

Tuition for the Transpersonal Clinical Hypnotherapy Program ranges from $1,500 prepaid to $1,800; books are approximately $104. Tuition for the same program by correspondence ranges from $1,500 to $1,590, depending on payment schedule; books cost $211. Tuition for the noncertification correspondence program is $600 to $750 (this is for training manuals and tapes only; omits tutorials and submission of homework).

Financial Assistance

The institute is on the approved training list of the Division of Vocational Rehabilitation.

International Foundation for Homeopathy (IFH)

P.O. Box 7
Edmonds, Washington 98020
Phone: (206) 776-4147
Fax: (206) 776-1499

The International Foundation for Homeopathy's five instructors include two full-time practicing homeopaths with N.D. degrees, Judyth Reicheberg-Ullman and Robert Ullman; Ellen Goldman, N.D., Chair of the Homeopathy Department at Bastyr University; Karl Robinson, M.D., with twenty years' experience in the practice of homeopathy; and Durr Elmore, D.C., N.D., a practicing homeopath and editor of *Simillimum: The Journal of The Homeopathic Academy of Naturopathic Physicians.*

Accreditation

IFH's intermediate-level postgraduate course is accredited by the Council on Homeopathic Education (CHE).

Program Description

The IFH Professional Course consists of two 120-hour segments, Level I and Level II. Graduates will understand homeopathic philosophy, take and analyze cases, find the rubrics of the case in the repertory, learn materia medica and identify the group of remedies that best fit the case, find the simillimum, and have the essential skills for success in homeopathic practice. Classes meet Thursday through Sunday (twenty-four classroom hours per session), once a month for five months for each level.

Admission Requirements

Admission is open to licensed medical practitioners and four-year and two-year college graduates who have completed courses in anatomy and physiology.

Tuition and Fees

Tuition is $1,995.

Financial Assistance

Payment plans are available.

Northwest Institute of Acupuncture and Oriental Medicine

1307 North 45th Street
Seattle, Washington 98103
Phone: (206) 633-2419
Fax: (206) 633-5578

The Northwest Institute was founded in 1981 as a nonprofit educational organization. The institute and teaching clinic are located in the Wallingford area of Seattle on a hill above Lake Union.

Accreditation

The institute's Master of Acupuncture Degree Program is accredited by NACSCAOM, and the institute is approved by the Washington State Department of Licensing. The combined Acupuncture/ Herbal Program is approved by the Acupuncture Examining Committee in California, making graduates of this program eligible to take the California acupuncture examination.

Program Description

The 2,285-hour Master of Acupuncture Program may be completed in as little as three years, but must be completed within five years. Courses include Fundamental Principles of Traditional Chinese Medicine, Meridians and Points, Anatomy and Physiology, Cell Biochemistry, Acupressure, Qi Techniques, Traditional Diagnostic Skills, Zang-Fu Pathology, Clinic Observation, Differential Diagnosis, Acupuncture Techniques, Western Disease Process, Microbiology, Physical Assessment, Chinese Nutrition, Counseling Skills and Ethics, Acupuncture Therapeutics, Western Clinical Science, Introduction to Chinese Herbology, Clinic Assistant, Medical Referral, Neuromusculoskeletal Therapeutics, Pharmacology, Research Design, Clinical Problem Solving, Western Nutrition, Chinese Medical History, Practice Management, Survey of American Medicine, Palpatory Skills, and others.

Continuing Education

The Herbal Studies Concentration is open to second-year students in the Acupuncture Program or to certified acupuncturists. This program is required for students seeking a license in acupuncture in California. Courses include Chinese Nutrition, Introduction to Chinese Herbology, Materia Medica, Chinese Herbal Formulas, Herbal Internal Medicine, Herbal Classics, Herbal Clinic Internship, and others.

A nine-weekend program in toyo hari acupuncture is presented over a ten-month time frame. Toyo hari is a refined system of Japanese five phase meridian therapy derived from the medical classics *Su Wen, Ling Shu,* and *Nan Jing.* All participants receive NIAOM continuing education certificates each weekend; those who complete the entire program will receive an official Toyo Hari Medical Association Certificate.

The Northwest Institute is developing a number of other certificate programs. Some of these include Japanese Acupuncture, Oriental Bodywork, Auriculotherapy, Pediatric Acupuncture, and Energy Field Medicine. Each program has its own entrance requirements and specific curriculum.

Admission Requirements

Applicants for the Master of Acupuncture Program must have completed three years (ninety semester credits) of accredited college or university study (bachelor's degree recommended), including one course in both general biology and general psychology. Applicants must also submit an essay and two letters of recommendation, and complete a personal interview.

Applicants for continuing education in acupressure, traditional Chinese medicine, Western academic courses, and clinical training will undergo specific evaluation of their educational background in order to ascertain whether it is sufficient for the requested area of continuing education.

Tuition and Fees

There is a $50 application fee. Tuition is $122 per academic credit for six or more credits per quarter, $132 per academic credit for less than six credits per quarter, and $8 per hour for standard clinical training. The total tuition for the three-year Master of Acupuncture Program is $22,660; books and supplies are approximately $1,000 over the three years.

Tuition for the Toyo Hari Acupuncture Training Program is $1,850 for professionals, $1,700 for alumni, and $1,550 for students; the rate per weekend is $180 for professionals, $165 for alumni, and $150 for students. Continuing education seminars and workshops cost $75 to $330.

Financial Assistance

Federal loans are available.

Seattle Massage School

7120 Woodlawn Avenue N.E.
Seattle, Washington 98115
Phone: (206) 527-0807
Fax: (206) 527-1957

The Seattle Massage School was founded in 1974. The school has campuses in Seattle, Tacoma, and Everett, and students have access to the Bastyr University library.

Accreditation

The Seattle Massage School's curriculum is approved by the American Massage Therapy Association Commission on Massage Training Accreditation/Approval (AMTA/COMTAA). The school is nationally accredited by the Accrediting Council for Continuing Education and Training (ACCET), licensed by the Washington State Workforce Training and Education Coordinating Board, and approved by the Washington State Board of Massage.

Program Description

Massage instruction is offered in a 745-hour Basic Program and a 901-hour Comprehensive Program.

The Basic Program is offered in the evenings only and does not include supervised hands-on Student Clinic. The Comprehensive Program is offered mornings or evenings and includes the Student Clinic; students may take the Hospital Internship Program during Term Four in place of Student Clinic if accepted into the program.

The programs are taught in four 11-week terms and may be completed within twelve months. The curriculum for both programs includes Anatomy and Physiology, Kinesiology, Massage Theory, Massage Practice, Student Development, Communication and Learning Skills Workshop, First Aid/CPR, Seated Massage, Professional Development, AIDS Education for Massage Professionals, Pregnancy Massage Workshop, Hydrotherapy Workshop, Sports Massage Workshop, Massage for Chronic Pain Workshop, Business Skills Workshop, and Student Project.

Continuing Education

Continuing education hours are available for Term Three and Four students who choose to participate in the Teaching Assistant Program. Continuing education events are offered to licensed massage practitioners throughout the year in a variety of massage techniques and advanced massage treatments.

Admission Requirements

Applicants must be at least 18 years of age upon graduation from the Seattle Massage School and have a high school diploma or equivalent. Applicants must complete an admission interview, a registration packet, and financial agreements. Previous experience in massage is not required, but may be helpful.

Tuition and Fees

There is a $100 registration fee. Tuition for the Basic Program is $7,064; for the Comprehensive Program, $8,331. Books are approximately $150, supplies are approximately $300, and a massage table and accessories are approximately $700.

Financial Assistance

Payment plans and federal financial aid are available to those who qualify.

Soma Institute

730 Klink Road
Buckley, Washington 98321
Phone: (360) 829-1025
Fax: (360) 829-2805

The Soma techniques were developed and the institute founded in 1978 by Bill M. Williams, Ph.D., and Ellen Gregory Williams, Ph.D. Soma neuromuscular integration, or Soma bodywork, is a ten-lesson process of body therapy that structurally rebalances the body and reconditions the nervous system.

Accreditation

In order to practice Soma neuromuscular integration in the State of Washington, one must hold a Washington massage license or other license that allows external touch.

Program Description

The Soma Institute offers a twofold training program. Students who hold a state license or are from states that do not require a license may take the Soma Neuromuscular Integration Training (Soma Training) alone. Those who do not hold a license in either massage or physical therapy take both the Foundation Training, designed to prepare the student to take the Washington State Board of Massage licensing exam, and the Soma Training.

The Foundation Training consists of 200 hours of classroom instruction that, when combined with Soma Training, meets the 500-hour requirement for Washington State licensing. Courses include Anatomy and Physiology, Contraindications, Pathophysiology, Kinesiology, Basic Technique of Massage, and Psychology for the Bodyworker.

The 368-hour Soma Training consists of Principles of Soma Neuromuscular Integration (including myofascial anatomy and physiology, skeletal anatomy, and structural integration), Soma Neuromuscular Integration Training (which includes two demonstrations of each of the ten session series and hands-on practice), Social and Psychological Integration, Clinical Application of Soma Principles, Structural and Anatomical Assessment, Student Development, Client Development and Practice, and Somassage Technique.

Admission Requirements

Applicants must have a high school diploma or equivalent, be examples of health, and interview with an admissions representative. Admission to Soma Training is based, in part, on assessment of the student's commitment to succeed as a Soma practitioner as demonstrated by a college degree, state licensing, self-employment, or other criteria. Applicants must have received the ten sessions of Soma bodywork or, in some cases, another form of structural integration.

Tuition and Fees

Tuition for the Soma Training is $7,350; for the Foundation Training, $1,650. Books, supplies, massage table, linens, and First Aid/CPR/AIDS training are additional. Student liability insurance is furnished by the school.

Financial Assistance

A payment plan is available, and a discount is given for full payment before classes begin.

Spectrum Center School of Massage

Mailing Address:
1001 North Russell Road
Snohomish, Washington 98290
Phone: (206) 334-5409 / (800) 801-9451

School Address:
12506 18th Street N.E., Suite 1
Lake Stevens, Washington 98258-9728

The Spectrum Center School of Massage was founded in 1981. Owner/director Barbara Collins is a licensed massage practitioner with a background in education, Swedish massage, and deep tissue therapies.

Accreditation

The Spectrum Center is accredited by the Washington State Board of Massage.

Program Description

The ten-month, 520-hour Professional Massage Training Course is composed of two 5-month semesters. The curriculum includes Anatomy, Physiology, and Pathology; Business Practices; Clinical Treatments; Deep Tissue/Advanced Techniques; Human Behavior; Hydrotherapy; Indications and Contraindications; Kinesiology; Lymphatic Drainage; Massage Theory and Practice; Medical Terminology; On-Site; Polarity; Sports Massage; Study Skills; AIDS Training; Pregnancy Massage; Foot Reflexology; and Student Clinic. Classes are held days and evenings.

Admission Requirements

Applicants must be at least 18 years of age, have a high school diploma or equivalent, and interview with an admissions representative.

Tuition and Fees

Tuition is $4,200. There is a $150 registration fee, supplies and insurance are $200, books cost approximately $250, and a massage table costs $200 to $650.

Financial Assistance

Payment plans are available.

Sri Chinmoy Institute of Ayurvedic Sciences

Ayurvedic and Naturopathic Medical Clinic
2115 112th Avenue N.E.
Bellevue, Washington 98004
Phone: (206) 453-8022
Fax: (206) 451-2670
E-mail: ayurveda@ayush.com
Internet: http://www.ayush.com

In 1995, the American School of Ayurvedic Science, founded in 1992 by Dr. Virender Sodhi, moved to a larger location and changed its name to the Sri Chinmoy Institute of Ayurvedic Sciences. Dr. Sodhi completed his medical training in northern India, obtained his N.D. degree from Bastyr University, and is currently a faculty member of the Southwest College of Naturopathic Medicine in Arizona.

Program Description

The Sri Chinmoy Institute plans to become the first Ayurvedic university in the country to offer a four-year degree program combining Ayurvedic and naturopathic medicine. At this time, three classes, each eleven hours in length, are offered.

Introduction to Ayurveda 1 is an introductory course in Ayurvedic principles. Topics covered include natural body rhythms, body types (doshas), using food as medicine, and stress reduction using meditation, breathing exercises, and yoga.

Ayurvedic Nutrition 1 offers instruction in the Ayurvedic model of nutrition. Food properties such as energy, action on body type, and pharmacology are discussed, as are food combining and Ayurvedic principles of cooking.

Ayurvedic Massage 1 explains the basic principles of Ayurvedic massage, including the exchange of energy between participants, essential oils and herbs, and instruction in performing massage.

Classes meet two evenings per week for two-and-a-half weeks.

Admission Requirements

Applicants must be high school graduates.

Tuition and Fees

Tuition is $110 per class.

Tri-City School of Massage

26 East Third Avenue
Kennewick, Washington 99336
Phone: (509) 586-6434

The Tri-City School of Massage was founded in 1968 around the kitchen table of Ruth Williams, who had been an American Massage Therapy Association (AMTA) member since 1947 and served as AMTA's national president, historian, and national education director.

Accreditation

The Tri-City School of Massage curriculum has been approved by the AMTA Commission on Massage Training Accreditation/Approval (COMTAA) and the Washington State Board of Massage; graduates are eligible to take the state board exams.

Program Description

The 850-hour Massage Therapy Program consists of 576 classroom hours and 274 independent study hours. Courses include Anatomy and Physiology, Health and Hygiene, Pathology, Hydrotherapy, AIDS Awareness, Massage Theory (Swedish), Applied Anatomy and Kinesiology, Business and Professional Ethics, Medical Gymnastics, Body Mechanics, Massage-Related Techniques (such as connective tissue, positional release, reflexology, sports massage, acupressure, magnetic therapy, massage in pregnancy, baby massage, iridology, and on-site massage), Thesis, and Clinical Application (150 massages). Classes are held in the evenings, with daytime study halls.

Admission Requirements

Students must have a high school diploma or equivalent, should be financially and mentally stable, and in good physical health. There is no age requirement.

Tuition and Fees

There is a $100 registration fee; tuition is $4,200. Other costs include: massage table, $450 to $600; linens and bolsters, $160 to $210; uniform, $35; massage oil, $30; optional field trip, $25 to $35; optional AMTA student membership and Washington chapter fee, $178; and optional flash cards, $20.

The Wellness Institute

(*See* Multiple State Locations, page 321)

Yoga Centers

2255 140th Avenue N.E., Suites E & F
Bellevue, Washington 98005
Phone: (206) 746-7476
Internet: http://www.yogacenters.com/yoga

Yoga Centers was founded in 1992 by Aadil Palkhivala, who has studied with B.K.S. Iyengar for over thirty years and was one of Iyengar's first students to receive the Advanced Certificate. The name Yoga Centers means yoga "centers" you in your body/life/mind. Yoga Centers offers the advanced kedric wall-rope system, pelvic swings, abundant props, two studios, and a retail store.

Program Description

The seven-day Beginning Teacher Training is for beginning teachers or serious students interested in the basics of props, adjustments, therapeutic application of poses, and daily asana practice. It includes over forty hours of teacher training, plus over ten hours of regular classes.

The Intermediate/Advanced Teacher Training is held over nine days (sixty hours plus over ten hours of regular classes) and offers a deeper understanding of the use of props, adjustment, and therapeutic applications of poses, as well as pranayama, yoga philosophy, and meditation.

Admission Requirements

At least one year of practice is suggested prior to enrollment in Beginning Teacher Training. Permission is required for the November Intermediate/Advanced Class only.

Tuition and Fees

The Beginning Teacher Training Course costs $495 to $595, depending on the registration date. The Intermediate/Advanced Teacher Training Course costs $645 to $745, depending on the registration date.

Financial Assistance

Payment plans and early registration discounts are available.

Yoga Northwest

P.O. Box 4231
Bellingham, Washington 98227
Phone: (360) 647-0712

Program Description

A Teacher Training Program with Felicity Green is offered each August at Yoga Northwest, and has a different focus each year. The training prepares students for Iyengar yoga certification assessments that are held annually in several major cities throughout the United States. In 1996, the nine-day, $475 training focused on preparing for Junior Intermediate Certification and included asana, pranayama, yoga philosophy, and peer teaching. Contact Yoga Northwest for information on current programs.

WEST VIRGINIA

Mountain State School of Massage

Mailing Address:
P.O. Box 4487
Charleston, West Virginia 25364
Phone: (304) 926-8822

Facility:
3407 River Lane
Malden, West Virginia 25306

Mountain State School of Massage was founded in 1995. Director Robert Rogers graduated from the Florida School of Massage in 1986 and has advanced training in sports massage and polarity therapies.

Accreditation

The Mountain State School of Massage program is approved by the West Virginia Department of Education. Graduates are eligible to take the national certification exam administered by the National Certification Board for Therapeutic Massage and Bodywork (NCBTMB).

Program Description

The 750-hour Therapeutic Massage Program includes instruction, supervised practice, and directed independent study. The curriculum consists of Massage Therapy (including the techniques of Swedish massage, reflexology, chair massage, neuromuscular therapy, sports massage, polarity, shiatsu and the five element theory, and connective tissue massage); Massage Practicum; Hydrotherapy; Human Anatomy, Physiology and Kinesiology; Awareness and Communication Skills; Massage Law and Business Practices; CPR, First Aid, and Communicable Diseases; and directed independent study. Classes are held during the day.

A home study program currently in development will consist of self-paced learning as well as required hands-on training at the school.

Continuing Education

Continuing education workshops are offered throughout the year. These have included Present-Centered Awareness Therapy, Connective Tissue and Awareness, and Light Touch Therapy.

Admission Requirements

Applicants must be at least 19 years of age (this requirement may be waived through personal interview), have a high school diploma or equivalent, and submit a biographical essay. An interview may be required.

Tuition and Fees

There is a $50 application fee. Tuition is $5,600; books are approximately $300; an optional massage table is $400 to $600; and liability insurance is $150 to $200. Supplies are additional.

WISCONSIN

Blue Sky Educational Foundation

Professional School of Massage and
    Therapeutic Bodywork
220 Oak Street
Grafton, Wisconsin 53024
Phone: (414) 376-1011
Fax: (414) 692-6387

The Blue Sky Professional School of Massage was founded in 1985 by Blair and Karen Lewis. Blair is a physician's assistant specializing in preventative medicine and the holistic treatment of chronic disease. Karen is a certified massage therapy instructor and has more than eighteen years of massage therapy experience. Blair and Karen have trained and taught in many styles of therapeutic bodywork, including polarity, craniosacral therapy, neuromuscular therapy, and Ayurvedic massage.

Accreditation

The Professional School of Massage is recognized by the International Myomassethics Federation (IMF). Graduates are eligible to take examinations with IMF and the American Massage Therapy Association (AMTA), as well as the national certification exam administered by the National Certification Board for Therapeutic Massage and Bodywork. The City of Milwaukee has approved the curriculum.

Program Description

The 800-hour Professional Massage Curriculum consists of three trimesters of study. First-trimester courses include Learning Strategies, Experiential Anatomy and Physiology: The Return of Joy, Muscles and Bones, World of Natural Medicine, Juicing for Health, Introduction to Massage: Full Body Relaxation Techniques, Reflexology/Foot Massage, Facial Massage, Polarity, Clinical Preceptorship, Hatha for Health Professionals, and Healthy Cooking, Healthy Life. Courses in the second trimester include Clinical Anatomy and Physiology, Muscles and Bones, Therapeutic Techniques, Neuromuscular Therapy: Paul St. John Method, Advanced Massage Techniques for the Low Back, Ayurvedic Facial Massage, Lymphatic Massage, Sports Massage, Tai Chi Chuan, and Movement Therapy. Third-trimester courses include Allied Health Sciences Review, Clinical Pathology in the Massage Practice, Medical Terminology and Writing Progress Notes, Therapeutic Techniques and Specialty Areas, Introduction to the Business World, Professional Field Placement, Community Service, and On-Site Clinical Experience. Students must also choose two electives from Meditation, Reiki, Sports Massage, Seated Therapeutic Massage, Neuromuscular Therapy, Whole Body Herbal Massage, Touch for Health, and others. Other graduation requirements include CPR and First Aid certification, human anatomy coloring book, 200 clinical hours, a written report, twenty-five massages on teaching staff, an oral classroom presentation, homework, and exams. Classes are held days and evenings; weekend seminars are required for all students.

Community and Continuing Education

Many courses are open to the general public. The Please Touch Program meets once a week for ten weeks, and offers an introduction to massage for the public or for potential students.

Nationally recognized continuing education seminars are periodically offered on such topics as myofascial release, sports massage, NMT, Ayurvedic massage, advanced massage, polarity, and on-site chair massage.

Admission Requirements

Applicants must be at least 18 years of age, have a high school diploma or equivalent, be emotionally stable and physically able to perform techniques taught in the program, have received two professional massages, submit two letters of recommendation (preferably one from a health professional) and a health professional's statement, and interview with an admissions representative.

Tuition and Fees

There is an application/interview fee of $35; tuition is $5,200. Supplies cost $500, including books, charts, lab fees, and materials; an optional massage table costs $350 to $700; and IMF and/or AMTA membership, exams, and license cost $100 to $300. The Please Touch Program costs $250, or $400 for household couples.

Financial Assistance

A payment plan is available.

Lakeside School of Natural Therapeutics, Inc.

1726 North 1st Street
Milwaukee, Wisconsin 53212
Phone: (414) 372-4345
Fax: (414) 372-5350
E-mail: lakeschool@aol.com

Lakeside School of Natural Therapeutics, a non-profit organization, was established in 1985. The 3,000-square-foot school is located downtown in Milwaukee's historic Brewers Hill area.

Accreditation

The Massage Therapy Training Program at Lakeside School is approved by the American Massage Therapy Association Commission on Massage Training Accreditation/Approval (AMTA/COMTAA) and by the Wisconsin State Educational Approval Board. There is no state licensing for massage therapists in Wisconsin; the 600-hour program at Lakeside School meets or exceeds any city licensing requirement in the State of Wisconsin.

Program Description

The 600-hour Massage Therapy Training Program consists of Anatomy, Physiology, and Pathology; Kinesiology; Theory and Practice of Massage (with an emphasis on Swedish massage, but also including an introduction to reflexology, sports massage, trigger point therapy, shiatsu, connective tissue manipulation, and energy work); Range of Motion, Stretching, and Joint Mobilization; CPR; First Aid; Hydro- and Heliotherapy; HIV Awareness; Business and Professional Practice Issues; and Body Mechanics and Clinician Self-Care. Classes are held days and evenings/weekends.

Admission Requirements

Applicants must be at least 18 years of age, have a high school diploma or equivalent, be physically capable of providing massage, have experienced at least one professional massage, be capable of effective interpersonal communication, and interview with an admissions representative.

Tuition and Fees

There is a $30 application fee. Tuition is $4,700; books are $150 to $250, and uniforms, supplies, and massage table are additional.

Financial Assistance

Payment plans are available.

Midwest Center for the Study of Oriental Medicine

Racine Main Campus:
6226 Bankers Road, Suite 5
Racine, Wisconsin 53403
Phone: (414) 554-2010
Fax: (414) 554-7475

Chicago Campus:
4334 North Hazel, Suite 206
Chicago, Illinois 60613
Phone: (312) 975-1295

Originally founded in Chicago in 1979, the Midwest Center's main campus moved to Racine in 1991. The Midwest Center continues to offer a limited number of classes in Chicago (any student taking classes in Chicago must complete more than 50 percent of their education in Racine). The school is affiliated with the Guangzhou University of Traditional Chinese Medicine.

Accreditation

The acupuncture program is accredited by the National Accreditation Commission for Schools and Colleges of Acupuncture and Oriental Medicine (NACSCAOM). Graduates of this program are qualified to take the examination given by the National Commission for the Certification of Acupuncturists (NCCA) and individual state examinations, and are eligible to apply for a Wisconsin State acupuncture license. The program meets the core curriculum requirements of both the Council of Colleges of Acupuncture and Oriental Medicine (CCAOM) and the American Oriental Bodywork Therapy Association (AOBTA).

Program Description

The 2,028-hour Acupuncture Therapist Certification Program may be completed in three academic years. Courses include Foundation of Oriental Medicine, Chinese Medical Pathology, Point Location, Anatomy, Physiology, Neurology, Oriental Massage Therapy, Oriental Philosophy, Needle Technique, Accessory Techniques, Chinese Differential Diagnosis, Eight Principle Treatment Strategy, Pathology, Acupuncture Treatment Strategy, Practice Management/Medical Issues, Physical Examination, Chinese Medicine Clinic Review, and Bio-Medicine Clinic Review. Guided research projects are required in Chinese medical history, holistic medical systems, and pathology research sources; a major academic, clinical, or research paper is also required, as are 660 hours of clinical internship. Internships are available at hospitals in China.

Admission Requirements

Applicants must have an associate's degree or sixty postsecondary semester credit hours with a minimum G.P.A. of 2.0 from an accredited school, two letters of recommendation, and an interview with an admissions representative.

Tuition and Fees

There is a $30 application fee; tuition is $7,595 per year or $22,785 total. Mandatory fees, including malpractice insurance, are $1,363; books and supplies (approximate for the entire program) are $650.

Financial Assistance

Payment plans are available. Financial aid is available for those who qualify at the main campus in Racine. Students waiting for financial aid approval must pay tuition.

Wisconsin Institute of Chinese Herbology

6921 Mariner Drive
Racine, Wisconsin 53406
Phone: (414) 886-5858

The Wisconsin Institute of Chinese Herbology was founded in 1990 by Arthur D. Shattuck, a national board certified acupuncturist, Chinese herbalist, and noted author and lecturer in the areas of Chinese medicine and Chinese herbology. The institute shares a building with the Wisconsin Institute of Natural Wellness (see below).

Accreditation

All courses offered by the institute are approved by the National Commission for the Certification of Acupuncturists (NCCA) to provide continuing education units for acupuncturists and Chinese herbologists. The institute is licensed by the Educational Approval Board (EAB) of the State of Wisconsin.

Program Description

An eight-month Chinese Herbology Course meets one evening per week and offers a comprehensive program in the science and art of Chinese herbology. The course combines lectures, practicums, related reading assignments, fieldwork, three original papers, and successful completion of thirty case studies for over 450 hours of participation. Topics covered include anatomy, physiology, Chinese diagnostic techniques, Chinese herbal botany, and chemistry. Each student will develop a collection of raw herbs, many harvested from the institute's own herbal gardens.

Community and Continuing Education

Several one-day and weekend seminars are offered in topics related to Chinese herbology.

Tuition and Fees

Tuition is $2,400; books cost $150, and fees are $75.

Financial Assistance

A discount is given for payment in full by the first class; a payment plan is available.

Wisconsin Institute of Natural Wellness

6921 Mariner Drive
Racine, Wisconsin 53406
Phone: (414) 886-5858

The Wisconsin Institute of Natural Wellness was founded in 1995 by Anne M. Frontier, a certified massage therapist with training in shiatsu, reiki, and Swedish massage, and Arthur D. Shattuck, a national board certified acupuncturist, Chinese herbalist, and noted author and lecturer in the areas of Chinese medicine and Chinese herbology. The institute shares a building with the Wisconsin Institute of Chinese Herbology (see page 280).

Accreditation

The institute is a candidate for accreditation with the American Massage Therapy Association Commission on Massage Training Accreditation/Approval (AMTA/COMTAA), and is approved by the Educational Approval Board of the State of Wisconsin. Graduates are qualified to take the national AMTA exam or International Myomassethics Federation (IMF) certification, and will be qualified to take the forthcoming National Commission for the Certification of Acupuncturists Diplomate of Chinese Bodywork national board certification.

Program Description

The 650-hour Professional Massage Therapy Certification Program combines the treatment principles of Chinese medicine with Western massage modalities. The curriculum includes Hands-On Therapy: Massage Theory and Techniques; Massage Anatomy: Bones and Muscles; Meditation and Personal Growth: A Self-Exploration; Anatomy and Physiology: East Meets West; Clinical Experience; Tai Chi; Independent Study; CPR Training; and weekend intensives in the areas of Shiatsu, Reiki, Jin Shin Do, Tui Na, Business and Marketing, Feng Shui, SoMove (a movement therapy that incorporates the work of Thomas Hanna, Alexander, and Feldenkrais), and Medical Intake, Assessment, and Record Keeping. Students may choose evening classes or same-day afternoon and evening classes.

Continuing Education

Many weekend intensives are offered in additional Chinese medical modalities such as feng shui, Chinese herbology, and tui na.

Admission Requirements

Applicants must have a high school diploma or equivalent; be physically able to perform the required work; be free of communicable disease as documented by a physician; have had two documented full body massages; submit two character references, an essay, and two photos; visit the institute; and interview with an admissions representative.

Tuition and Fees

Tuition for the Professional Massage Therapy Program is $4,400, including a $300 deposit; books and materials cost approximately $200, and a massage table costs $300 to $600.

Financial Assistance

A payment plan is available.

CANADA

Tuition at Canadian schools is in Canadian dollars unless otherwise noted. Please note that GST stands for Goods and Services Tax.

ALBERTA

Massage Therapy Training Institute

Mount Royal College
Continuing Education and Extension
4825 Richard Road S.W.
Calgary, Alberta T3E 6K6
Canada
Phone: (403) 240-6867 (office/information) / (403) 240-3833 (registration)

Mount Royal offered its first massage course in 1982. In 1991, the one-hundred-hour course was developed into a 500-hour, part-time program, and in 1993, the program was extended to 700 hours and a full-time option was added.

Accreditation

Each province has its own licensing requirements; students are encouraged to investigate the requirements of the province in which they intend to practice prior to enrolling.

Program Description

The 700-hour Massage Therapy Certificate Program consists of ten core courses and two clinical practicums, and may be taken over ten months (full-time) or on a part-time basis over as long as six years. Core courses include Introduction to Therapeutic Massage, Basic Anatomy and Physiology, Advanced Studies of Joints and Soft Tissues, Pathology, Advanced Massage Techniques I and II, Interpersonal Communication Skills, the Professional Role of the Massage Therapist, Marketing and Career Development, CPR and Standard First Aid, and Clinical Practicum I and II.

Admission Requirements

Applicants must have an Alberta high school diploma or equivalent or be a mature student age 23 or older. A Grade 12 biology credit would be beneficial, but is not required. Applicants to the full-time program must submit an application form and interview with an admissions representative.

Tuition and Fees

Tuition is charged on a per-course basis and ranges from $85 to $585 per course; the total cost of ten courses and two clinical practicums is $3,960. Books and supplies are approximately $650.

Financial Assistance

Full-time students are eligible to apply for Alberta student loans. Part-time students may be eligible to receive bursaries of up to $600 per semester.

BRITISH COLUMBIA

Coastal Mountain College of Healing Arts

(formerly the Wild Rose College of Natural Healing)

1745 West 4th Avenue
Vancouver, British Columbia V6J 1M2
Canada
Phone: (604) 734-4596
Fax: (604) 734-4597

Coastal Mountain College was founded in 1989 as Wild Rose College of Natural Healing by Terry Willard, Ph.D., a Canadian herbal specialist and natural healing practitioner. The associated Wild Rose College of Natural Healing in Alberta offers a correspondence study program (see page 370).

Accreditation

Coastal Mountain College is a registered Private Postsecondary Education Institution in British Columbia.

Program Description

The three-year Holistic Counseling Diploma and Certificate Program includes such courses as Counseling Skills; Counseling Theory and History; Ethics for the Counselor; Nutrition; Holistic and Alternative Counseling; Personal and Group Processes; Herbs for the Holistic Counselor; Holistic Counseling: Theory/Practice; Traditional Chinese Medicine; Gestalt; Business of Counseling; Existential Counseling; Dreamwork; Human Development; Spiritual Development; Sex, Gender, and Relationship; and others.

The three-year Clinical Herbalist Diploma Program offers instruction in Herbology, Pharmacy, Biochemistry, Botany, Nutrition, Ecology, Materia Medica, Pharmacognosy, Anatomy, Counseling, History Taking, Energetics, TCM/Ayurvedic Diagnosis, Iridology, Research Skills, Business Skills, and others, along with field work and projects. A further one-hundred-hour practicum is to be completed outside the college at additional cost.

The eight-month Practical Herbalist Certificate Program is designed for those who wish to go into the business of manufacturing, growing, and/or selling herbs. Course work in the Herb Growing and Harvesting Curriculum includes Herbology, Business Skills, Biology, Ecology, Botany, Pharmacy, Pharmacognosy, Permaculture, and Farming Placement. Courses in the Retail and Manufacturing Curriculum include Herbology, Business Skills, Biology, Ecology, Botany, Pharmacy, Physiology, Materia Medica, Pharmacognosy, Retail Skills, and Industry Experience.

Admission Requirements

Citizens of the United States, Greenland, and St. Pierre-Miquelon may apply for Student Authorizations at any port of entry. All other foreign students require visas and/or passports.

Tuition and Fees

A catalog costs $7 ($10 U.S.). Total tuition for the Holistic Counseling Program is $21,303. Total tuition for the Clinical Herbalist Diploma Program is $23,510. Total tuition for the Herb Growing and Harvesting Curriculum of the Practical Herbalist Certificate Program is $6,525; total tuition for the Retail and Manufacturing Curriculum is $9,135.

Dr. Vodder School—North America

(*See* Multiple State Locations, page 323)

Dominion Herbal College

7527 Kingsway
Burnaby, British Columbia V3N 3C1
Canada
Phone: (604) 521-5822
Fax: (604) 526-1561
E-mail: herbal@uniserve.com

Dominion Herbal College was founded by Dr. Herbert Nowell, a naturopathic physician, in 1926.

Program Description

The college offers both classroom and home study herbalism programs and a classroom aromatherapy program. A four-year Clinical Phytotherapy Tutorial Diploma Course consists of correspondence study and an annual week-long seminar in Vancouver (see page 365).

The three-year Clinical Herbal Therapist Diploma Program consists of four-day weekends in class once a month, fifteen to twenty hours of home study each week, and 500 practical clinical hours. Those who complete the course are eligible for membership in the Canadian Herbalists' Association of British Columbia, and the Canadian Herbal Practitioner Association, as well as herbal associations in other jurisdictions.

Apprenticeship Programs with Ryan Drum, Ph.D., C.H., M.H. (Waldron Island, Washington) or David O'Reilly, C.H. (Oliver, British Columbia) are designed for the seriously committed student. In the Washington apprenticeship, the student learns to grow, harvest, dry, and process herbs and seaweed; in the British Columbia apprenticeship, cultivating, wildcrafting, and the preparation of dried medicinal herbs will be balanced with organic agriculture. Dominion Herbal College certification will be granted upon completion.

The Clinical Aromatherapy: The Nuvelt Method Diploma Course consists of eighty hours in class (over four months) and sixteen hours of clinic practice; classroom and clinic hours take place on Saturdays only. The curriculum includes Principles of Natural Therapeutics, Physio-Medicalism, Materia Medica, Practical Procedures, Full-Body Manual Lymphatic Draining, and Clinic Practicum.

Admission Requirements

Applicants who have not taken high school-level chemistry, anatomy and physiology, and pathology may enroll in a prerequisite package program available through correspondence.

Tuition and Fees

Tuition for the Clinical Herbal Therapist Course is $18,500 plus GST (Goods and Services Tax); there is a $50 registration fee, and books and equipment are additional.

Tuition for the Clinical Aromatherapy Course is $2,500 plus GST; there is a $50 registration fee, and books, essential oils, and equipment are additional.

Costs for the prerequisite correspondence courses are as follows: Anatomy and Physiology, $350 plus GST (all materials included); Chemistry, $225 plus GST (books additional); and Pathology, $225 plus GST (books additional).

Contact the college for dates and costs of the Apprenticeship Programs.

Financial Assistance

Payment plans are available.

Vancouver Homeopathic Academy

P.O. Box 34095
Station D
Vancouver, British Columbia V6J 4M1
Canada
Phone: (604) 708-9387

Program Description

Two options are available for training in classical homeopathy: a one-year Foundation Course and a three-year Homeopathy Program; the Foundation Course is the first year of the three-year program, but may be taken independently.

Year One—Foundation Course will not train students to be homeopathic practitioners, but will provide a sound systematic understanding of homeopathic philosophy and principles. Students will learn how to apply homeopathy effectively as a means of self-help in simple first aid and everyday acute situations. This course also provides a basis for further study. A Certificate of Attendance will be given at the end of the first year.

Year Two provides a deepening of first-year concepts. Live cases will be taken and discussed with students. Topics include remedy reaction, second prescription, different forms of case analysis, potency and repetition, case management, miasms and nosodes, obstacles to cure, case taking, hierarchy of symptoms, and pathology.

Year Three covers different aspects of case taking and analysis, different views of miasms, long-term and difficult case management, repertory work and interpretation of symptoms, family groupings of remedies, therapeutics, and practical issues in practice. Those who meet the requirements will receive a Diploma of Classical Homeopathy (D.C.H.) at the end of the third year.

Courses are held in Vancouver on eleven weekends.

Admission Requirements

Applicants for the first year must be at least 21 years of age, have a high school diploma, be fluent in written and spoken English, and have a strong desire to study homeopathy.

Students entering the second year must have taken or must take concurrently a college-level course in anatomy and physiology. Students entering the third year must have taken a First Aid and CPR course.

Tuition and Fees

Tuition for Year One is $1,900; for Year Two, $2,025; and for Year Three, $2,075. GST and books are additional.

Financial Assistance

Payment plans are available.

Yasodhara Ashram

Box 9
Kootenay Bay, British Columbia V0B 1X0
Canada
Phone: (604) 227-9224 / (604) 227-9225 /
   (800) 661-8711
Fax: (604) 227-9494
E-mail: yashram@worldtel.com

The Yasodhara Ashram was founded in 1963 by Swami Sivananda Radha, one of the foremost authorities on Kundalini yoga and Eastern yoga psychology. Swami Radha has written several books on yoga and spiritual life and has established a number of Radha Houses that offer workshops and ongoing classes.

Accreditation

Yasodhara Ashram is accredited by the Private Postsecondary Education Commission of British Columbia.

Program Description

The ashram offers a wide range of options for training, upgrading, or certification in Kundalini yoga, dreams, the Hidden Language of Hatha Yoga, and hatha. The Yoga Development Course is a prerequisite for all subsequent teacher training. Classes include the week-long Hatha Training for Teachers: Bridging to the Reflective Path, and the eighteen-day Hidden Language of Hatha Yoga Teacher Certification.

The Yoga Development Course (YDC) is an intensive three-month program in all aspects of yoga and self-development. The courses in this program are dedicated to the investigation of mind and consciousness through Kundalini yoga, prayer dance, hatha yoga, mantra yoga, satsang, dream work, and growth workshops.

A variety of other courses are offered throughout the year, including a week-long immersion in the Kundalini system, Karma yoga work opportunities, mantra, music and consciousness, and a program for teens.

Continuing Education

Annual refresher courses are offered to those who have completed certification programs.

Tuition and Fees

Tuition for the Yoga Development Course is $6,000; for the Hatha Training for Teachers, $610, and for the Hidden Language of Hatha Yoga, $1,700. These costs include three meals per day and shared accommodations; private rooms are available at additional cost. A children's program of activities, including swimming, crafts, hiking, music, and yoga, costs $20 per day.

Financial Assistance

Limited scholarships are available.

ONTARIO

Canadian Academy of Homeopathy

(*See* Multiple State Locations, page 322)

Canadian College of Massage and Hydrotherapy

(*See* Multiple State Locations, page 322)

The Canadian College of Naturopathic Medicine

60 Berl Avenue
Etobicoke, Ontario M8Y 3C7
Canada
Phone: (416) 251-5261
Fax: (416) 251-5883

The Canadian College of Naturopathic Medicine (CCNM), founded in 1978 as the Ontario College of Naturopathic Medicine, is the only recognized college of naturopathic medicine in Canada. The college is located about ten minutes north of Lake Ontario.

Accreditation

CCNM is a candidate for accreditation with the Council on Naturopathic Medical Education (CNME). The college is recognized by the five Canadian provinces that license naturopathic physicians (Alberta, British Columbia, Manitoba, Ontario, and Saskatchewan); in the United States, Arizona considers graduates of the college for licensure. Students who plan to practice in the United States should contact their states' naturopathic licensing boards for more information.

Program Description

CCNM offers a four-year, full-time professional program in naturopathic medicine leading to the Doctor of Naturopathic Medicine (N.D.) diploma. The two major areas of study are basic medical sciences and clinical and naturopathic disciplines.

First-year courses include Anatomy and Embryology; Histology; Physiology; Biochemistry; Naturopathic Medical History, Philosophy, and Principles; Introduction to Psychology; Soft Tissue Manipulation; Stress Management; Community and Environmental Health; Homeopathy; Immunology; Introduction to Pathology; Nutritional Biochemistry; Counseling; Hydrotherapy; and Introduction to Traditional Chinese Medicine.

Second-year courses include Pathology, Differential Diagnosis, Laboratory Diagnosis, Homeopathic Medicine, Acupuncture and Traditional Chinese Medicine, Clinical Nutrition, Botanical Medicine, Radiology, Microbiology, Pharmacology, Naturopathic Manipulation, and Clinic.

Third-year courses include Orthopedics, Therapy by Physical Agents, Acupuncture and Traditional Chinese Medicine, Homeopathic Medicine, Botanical Medicine and Pharmacognosy, Counseling Skills, Clinical Nutrition, Naturopathic Manipulation, Gynecology, Naturopathic Assessment, Diagnostic Imaging, Counseling, Obstetrics, Pediatrics, and Clinic.

Fourth-year courses include Case Studies in Naturopathic Medicine, Skills of Communication, Practice Management, Jurisprudence/Ethics, Minor Surgery, and Clinic.

Admission Requirements

Prerequisites for admission to the program include three years of full-time university studies at an accredited institution (a Bachelor of Science degree is recommended); required courses include one year of general biology, one year of general chemistry, and one semester of organic chemistry, all completed with a grade of C or better. Additional requirements include official transcripts, two letters of reference, a personal statement, an interview with the admissions team, and a copy of a birth certificate.

Graduates from other professional programs who are legally qualified to practice (D.C., D.O., M.D., D.D.S., and others) may apply for advanced standing. Potential applicants may attend orienta-

tion evenings and/or the Student for a Day program.

Tuition and Fees

Tuition for the regular full-time program is $9,450 per year. Tuition for the Advanced Standing Program is $6,332 for the first year and $9,450 for the second and third year. Other costs include: application fee, $100; transcript evaluation fee, $25; student card, $25; Naturopathic Students' Association, $25; and graduation fee, $50.

Financial Assistance

Ontario Student Assistance Plan (OSAP), federal loans, child care bursaries, scholarships and bursaries to second-, third-, and fourth-year students, and a payment plan are available.

Canadian Memorial Chiropractic College

1900 Bayview Avenue
Toronto, Ontario M4G 3E6
Canada
Phone: (416) 482-2340
Fax: (416) 482-9745

The Canadian Memorial Chiropractic College (CMCC) was founded in 1945 and is Canada's largest chiropractic college. Approximately 80 percent of the chiropractors in Canada are graduates of CMCC.

Accreditation

CMCC is accredited by the Council on Chiropractic Education (CCE—Can.), Inc. Through a reciprocal agreement with CCE (U.S.A.) and the Austral-Asian Council on Chiropractic and Osteopathic Education (ACCOE), graduates of CMCC are eligible to apply for licensure in countries under their jurisdiction, which includes most countries around the world.

Program Description

The 4,500-hour Undergraduate Professional Program consists of three 9-month periods and one 12-month period over four years. The curriculum is distributed among five divisions: Biological Sciences (Anatomy; Physiology and Biochemistry; Pathology and Microbiology), Chiropractic Sciences (Applied Chiropractic Studies; Chiropractic Principles and Practice), Clinical Sciences (Clinical Diagnosis; Radiology), Clinical Education (Herbert K. Lee Walk-In Clinic), and Research (Applied Research and Biometrics; Investigative Projects).

Community and Continuing Education

A two-year Postgraduate Residency Program is offered in three areas of special study: clinical sciences, radiology, and sports sciences. Upon completion, students are eligible to take examinations leading to certification as a Fellow of the College of Chiropractic Sciences (Canada), Fellow of the College of Chiropractic Radiology (Canada), or Fellow of the College of Sports Sciences (Canada).

Both on- and off-campus programs are offered for continuing education credit for licensure. These weekend programs include current basic and clinical research, technique updates, philosophy, principles, and practice management issues.

In addition, Extension Education Programs are offered to field practitioners, chiropractic support staff, and the general public.

Admission Requirements

Applicants to the Undergraduate Professional Program must have completed at least three years of study (ninety credit hours) in any discipline at a Canadian university or its equivalent; it is strongly recommended that applicants have completed courses in organic chemistry, biology, psychology, humanities, and/or social sciences. Applicants must also interview with an admissions team and submit two essays, three references, and an autobiographical sketch.

Tuition and Fees

Tuition is $10,735 ($13,360 foreign) per year. Other costs include: laboratory and library fee, $340 per year; student activity fee, $100 per year; Student Canadian Chiropractic Association fee, $20 per year; books, approximately $950 per year; spinal column model, approximately $150; and diagnostic equipment, approximately $450.

Financial Assistance

Canada Student Loan Program, provincial student loans, and private scholarships are available.

Canadian School of Natural Nutrition

10720 Yonge Street, Suite 220
Richmond Hill, Ontario L4C 3C9
Canada
Phone: (905) 737-0284; Correspondence
Course Division: (905) 852-9660 /
    (800) 328-0743
Fax: (905) 737-7830

The Canadian School of Natural Nutrition (CSNN) was founded by Danielle Miscampbell, R.N.C. It is the first organization in Canada to offer a classroom program in natural nutrition that qualifies the student for the professional designation R.N.C. (Registered Nutritional Consultant). Classes are held at Richmond Hill, Toronto, Scarborough, and Mississauga. A correspondence program is offered that leads to the same designation (see page 381).

Accreditation

The Diploma in Natural Nutrition is approved by the Nutritional Consultants Organization of Canada (NCOC). Graduates of CSNN with a cumulative average of 80 percent or higher will be asked to submit an application to NCOC without any further exams. Upon acceptance by the NCOC, graduates are given the R.N.C. designation.

Program Description

The Diploma Course in Natural Nutrition includes 200 hours of classroom instruction and 200 hours of independent study, including ten case studies. The program may be completed in one year of daytime classes or two years of evening classes. Courses include Fundamentals of Nutrition, Anatomy and Physiology, Symptomatology, Pediatric Nutrition, Preventive Nutrition, Optimal Nutrition, Introduction to Herbal Therapies, Chemistry and Biochemistry, Eco-Nutrition, Psychology and Nutrition, Kinesiology and Allergies, Alternative Diets, Clinical

Research, R.N.C. Practice, and Symptomatology Review.

Admission Requirements

Interest, enthusiasm, and dedication are the only prerequisites for this course. However, if a student has previous related education, the director will review the relevant transcripts and decide on course exemptions if applicable; maximum course exemption is 25 percent of the program.

Tuition and Fees

Tuition is $3,500 plus GST (Goods and Services Tax); books are additional.

Financial Assistance

Flexible payment plans of one, two, or four installments within the study period are available.

East West Centre

90 Barton Avenue
Toronto, Ontario M6G 1P6
Canada
Phone: (416) 530-1571

The East West Centre was founded in 1988 by Malca Narrol and Ron Rosenthal; Malca is now the sole director of the centre.

Program Description

The centre offers the Nova Healing Arts Program, Levels One through Three, a macrobiotic and natural health care leadership training program, in a series of eight weekend seminars dealing with Oriental diagnosis, the body/mind, and ancient healing arts theory. Level One includes Healing the Whole Person, Healthy Choices for a Healthy Life, Oriental Diagnosis and Body Reading, Shiatsu Massage Part 1, a Specialty Cooking Weekend, the Macrobiotic Way to Health and Healing, Tools for Change: Using the Energy of Life, and Healing in the Kitchen. Levels Two and Three address such topics as Energetic Medicine, Shiatsu Plus, Shamanic Visions, Macrobiotic Treatment of Dis-

ease, Counseling Practicum, Cooking and Meal Planning for Specific Needs, Diagnosis and Recommendation Practicum, and others.

Other workshops and seminars include a six-class series on the Basics of Healthy Cooking, evening lectures on such topics as macrobiotic cooking, feng shui, and Oriental diagnosis, and community dinners made with organic ingredients.

Admission Requirements

There are no age or educational requirements.

Tuition and Fees

Tuition for the Nova Healing Arts Program Level One is $1,650. Levels Two and Three are under development; contact the school for tuition information. Workshops and seminars run from $15 to $39 per class, or $165 to $195 for the five- or six-class series.

Financial Assistance

Payments are spread over several months.

Homeopathic College of Canada

3255 Yonge Street
Toronto, Ontario M4N 2L5
Canada
Phone: (416) 481-8816 /
　(888) DRHOMEO (toll-free)
Fax: (416) 481-4444
E-mail: homeocol@inforamp.net

The Homeopathic College of Canada (HCC) was founded in 1995; in 1996, HCC and Humber College (one of Canada's largest community colleges, founded in 1966) formed a partnership to develop a full-time homeopathy program.

Accreditation

HCC is accredited by the Manitoba Homeopathic Association, the Ontario Homeopathic Association, and the Pacific Homeopathic Association of British Columbia. Canadian college and university credits are given for some courses.

Graduates of the 3,045-hour Homeopathic Doctorate Program receive the diploma Doctorate in Homeopathic Medicine (DHMS) and are eligible to take either the OHA or PHABC Board Qualifying Examination in order to register as a Homeopathic Doctor. Graduates should ascertain whether the title Homeopathic Doctor (H.D.) is permitted by the government in the jurisdiction of their practice.

Program Description

The 3,045-hour Homeopathic Doctorate Program is a three-year, full-time program that includes an intensive clinical internship, a research project on environmental health, and a thesis on homeopathy. The curriculum includes Anatomy and Physiology, Biochemistry, Botany, Clinical Externship, Community Health, Complementary Modalities, Differential Diagnosis, Emergency Medicine, Environmental Medicine, Ethics and Law, Homeopathy, Homeopathic Therapeutics, Lab Analysis, Nutrition, Pathology, Pharmacology, Physical Examination, Practice Management, Psychology, Stress Management, and Toxicology.

The Homeopathic Doctorate Program for physicians and health care practitioners is open to doctors and consists of 702 hours of homeopathic instruction, plus 506 hours of clinical internship. The classroom course may be completed in two academic years or twenty months. Courses include Botany, Clinical Externship, Complementary Modalities, Environmental Medicine, Ethics and Law, Homeopathy, Homeopathic Therapeutics, Lab Analysis, Nutrition, Pharmacology, Practice Management, Psychology, and Stress Management.

Classes are held evenings and weekends at the Humber College North Campus, 205 Humber College Boulevard, Etobicoke, Ontario. The teaching clinic runs throughout the year on weekdays at both the Etobicoke and Toronto locations. Under special circumstances, students may apply for a partial load.

A fourteen-week Homeopathic Technologist Program consists of 280 hours of theory and eighty hours of practice, and serves to familiarize the student with complementary methods and natural remedies in a clinical setting. The curriculum includes Homeopathy, Traditional Medicine, Nutrition, Business Management, Pharmacology/Toxicology, and Practicum.

The First Aid/Acute Correspondence Certificate is a home study course open to pharmacists, pharmacist's assistants, and others. The program consists of twenty-four lessons to be completed within twelve months, and is not intended to produce homeopathic practitioners. The course includes Introduction and History, Principles, Symptomatology, Repertories, Case Taking, Classical and Contemporary Materia Medica, Homeopathic First Aid for Children, Allergic Reactions, Sprains and Fractures, Preparing for Surgery and Dental Operations, Spinal Injuries, Homeopathy for Pets, and more. It is the student's responsibility to find HCC-approved proctors to supervise examinations.

Admission Requirements

All applicants must submit a résumé, a handwritten letter, and two letters of reference.

Applicants to the Homeopathic Doctorate Program must have an Ontario secondary school diploma including Ontario academic credits in English, math, biology, and chemistry, BC Dogwood Diploma or equivalent, plus two years of study at the college/university level. Those who do not meet these requirements may apply as a special applicant; contact the registrar for further information.

Applicants to the Homeopathic Doctorate Program for physicians and health care practitioners must hold an N.D., M.D., D.C., D.O., D.D.S., D.V.M., or Ph.D. degree.

Tuition and Fees

Tuition for the Homeopathic Doctorate Program is $6,900 per year on the two-payment plan, or $6,550 per year if paid in full. Tuition for the Homeopathic Doctorate Program for health care practitioners is $7,400. Tuiton for the Homeopathic Technologist Program is $1,650. Tuition for the First Aid/Acute Correspondence Certificate Program is $950; books are additional. Tuition costs do not include 7 percent GST.

Other costs include: application fee, $50; student card, $15 per year; Ontario Homeopathic Association membership, $25 per year; graduation fee, $35; Homeopathic Board Examination, $200; and malpractice insurance, $100.

Financial Assistance

Payment plans and a prepayment discount are available.

Kikkawa College

3 Riverview Gardens
Toronto, Ontario M6S 4E4
Canada
Phone: (416) 762-4857
Fax: (416) 762-5733

Founded in 1981, Kikkawa College was the first school in Ontario to offer a 2,200-hour curriculum, and the first to adopt the orthopedic approach to determine the nature of soft tissue dysfunction.

Accreditation

Kikkawa College operates under the auspices of the Private Vocational Schools Division of Ontario's Ministry of Education and Training. Its Massage Therapy Program is recognized by the College of Massage Therapists of Ontario, and graduates are eligible to take licensing exams throughout Canada and the United States.

Program Description

The 2,200-hour Massage Therapy Program may be completed in either two years or eighteen months. The three major areas of study are Massage Theory and Technique (covering Swedish massage, hydrotherapy, remedial exercises, and treatments), Applied Medical Sciences (including anatomy, physiology, pathology, and clinical science), and Human Sciences and Practice Management (which covers issues related to professionalism, ethics, regulations, therapeutic relationship skills, and practice management systems through practical experiences in the classroom). Community outreach is an integral part of the program, and students gain experience at Sunnybrook Hospital and Variety Village, an athletic facility for the disabled. Students also provide massage therapy treatments at the on-campus teaching clinic.

A seventy-six-hour Pre-Admission Course is open to all applicants to the Massage Therapy Program, but is especially helpful for those who have been out of school for several years, have a limited science background, or have had limited success with science courses in the past. The course covers Basic Study Skills, Levels of Organization in Nature, The Cell: The Basic Unit of Life, Homeostasis: Equilibrium and Steady States, and the Body in Motion, and concludes with a personal assessment and evaluation.

A twelve-hour Introduction to Massage Course is also available.

Admission Requirements

Applicants must have an Ontario Grade 12 diploma or its equivalent with a minimum overall grade average of 65 percent; science credits at Grade 11, 12, or OAC are also required. Applicants who do not have the necessary science credits are encouraged to enroll in the Pre-Admission Course. Applicants who intend to apply as mature students (a mature student is one who is 19 years of age or older and does not meet the minimum admission requirements) may be required to take a qualifying exam and/or interview with an admissions representative.

Tuition and Fees

There is a $50 application fee and a $100 registration fee. Tuition is $6,700 per academic year; books, materials, and supplies are approximately $1,000 per academic year. The Pre-Admission Course costs $350 plus $24.50 GST (Goods and Services Tax).

Financial Assistance

A payment plan and Kikkawa College Bursary are available.

Reaching Your Potential

4261—A14 Highway 7, Suite 246
Unionville, Ontario L3R 9W6
Canada
Phone: (905) 474-1848
Fax: (905) 415-1362
E-mail: harrisw@internetfront.com

Reaching Your Potential was founded in 1996, though founder Sherry Smith, R.N., R.P.P., R.C.S.T., has been the Toronto organizer for another polarity organization since 1990 and has been involved with holistic healing since 1979. Ms. Smith is the current president of the Ontario Polarity Therapy Association.

Accreditation

Trainings are accredited by the American Polarity Therapy Association (APTA).

Program Description

Introduction to Polarity Therapy is a one-weekend workshop designed for those who are interested in polarity therapy either as a potential career or on a recreational level. It is a prerequisite for those who plan to continue with the Level 1 Training. Topics include Basic Polarity Theory; the General Session; Balancing the Five Elements and Seven Chakras; Basic Polarity Exercise; Food, Energy, and Polarity; and Attitude, Energy, and Polarity.

The Level 1 Polarity Therapy Certification Training consists of 125 classroom hours; graduates are qualified to apply for Associate Polarity Practitioner (A.P.P.) registration with APTA. Topics include General, Functional, and Structural Contacts (fifty hours); Theory (thirty hours); Assessments (five hours); Polarity Exercise (five hours); Diet (five hours); Attitude (five hours); Managing Your Practice (five hours); and Clinical Feedback (twenty hours). For registration as an A.P.P., five personal polarity sessions are required.

The Level 2 Polarity Therapy Certification Training consists of 360 classroom hours; graduates are qualified to apply for Registered Polarity Practitioner (R.P.P.) registration with APTA. Topics include General, Functional, and Structural Contacts (one hundred hours); Theory (seventy hours); Assessments (twenty hours); Polarity Exercise (twenty hours); Diet (twenty hours); Attitude (forty-five hours); Managing Your Practice (thirty-five hours); and Clinical Feedback (fifty hours). For registration as an R.P.P., ten personal polarity sessions are required.

Admission Requirements

Introduction to Polarity Therapy is the prerequisite for Level 1. Level 1 is the prerequisite for Level 2.

Tuition and Fees

Tuition for the Introduction to Polarity Therapy course is $200.

Tuition for the Level 1 Training is $1,300; this includes the Introduction to Polarity Therapy workshop. Books cost $150, and personal polarity sessions are additional. Tuition for the Level 2 Training is $3,600; books and personal polarity sessions are additional.

Financial Assistance

Extended payment plans are available.

Shiatsu Academy of Tokyo

320 Danforth Avenue, Suite 206
Toronto, Ontario M4K 1N8
Canada
Phone: (416) 466-8780
Fax: (416) 466-8719

The Shiatsu Academy of Tokyo was founded in 1990 by Kensen Saito.

Accreditation

The Shiatsu Academy of Tokyo operates under the governing auspices of the Private Vocational Schools Division of the Ontario Ministry of Colleges and Universities.

Program Description

The two-year Professional Shiatsu Practitioner Course leads to a Basic Shiatsu Practitioner Diploma. Courses include Shiatsu Theory, Shiatsu Technique, Shiatsu Practice, Anatomy, Stress Management Clinic, Physiology, Pathology, Professional Ethics, and Business Practice. Classes are held Tuesday through Thursday evenings. Students are required to practice shiatsu at the school clinic after the second semester.

Continuing Education

Postgraduate courses may be offered in sports shiatsu in the future.

Admission Requirements

Applicants must have completed high school or may qualify as mature students.

Tuition and Fees

Tuition is $3,900; books, uniforms, and other expenses are approximately $440.

Shiatsu School of Canada

547 College Street
Toronto, Ontario M6G 1A9
Canada
Phone: (416) 323-1818 / (800) 263-1703
    (toll-free in the U.S. and Canada)
Fax: (416) 323-1681
E-mail: shiatsu@istar.ca

The Shiatsu School of Canada was founded in 1986 by Kaz and Yasuko Kamiya and is, at present, the only school outside of Japan teaching shiatsu to the 2,200-hour standard. The school teaches both the Namikoshi Thumb and Masunaga Meridian styles of shiatsu.

Accreditation

The Shiatsu School of Canada is registered and approved as a private vocational school under the Private Vocational Schools Act.

Program Description

The one-hundred-hour Shiatsu Certificate Program consists of Level I, an introduction to basic techniques and theories of shiatsu and basic concepts of Oriental medical theory such as yin-yang, qi, and meridians; and Level II, in which students learn additional techniques and stretches, meridian diagnosis, practical shiatsu diagnosis, and individual treatment.

The 2,200-hour Career Training Program may be completed in one-and-a-half years of full-time study or two-and-a-half years of part-time study. The curriculum includes Shiatsu Practice, Shiatsu Treatment, Shiatsu Theory, Eastern Medical Theory, Student Clinic, Human Anatomy, Human Physiology, Human Pathology and Symptomatology, Auxiliary Modalities, Communication Skills, Public Health, Self-Care, Ethics and Jurisprudence, Nutrition, and Business.

Graduates of a diploma program in shiatsu therapy may apply for admission to the fourteen-month Postgraduate Certificate Program in acupuncture, held one evening per week and one weekend per month. Both Chinese and Japanese acupuncture techniques are taught, in classes that include Point Location and Indication, Meridian Theory, Advanced Diagnosis, Differential Diagnosis, Needling and Other Techniques, Clinical Practicum, and Japanese Acupuncture and Moxibustion Theory and Practice.

Chiropractors, doctors, massage therapists, and other qualified professionals can take the Prerequisite Acupuncture Program, which includes a seventy-five-hour Eastern Medical Theory course and thirty hours of shiatsu in addition to the regular acupuncture courses. This course of study is seventeen months long.

Free information sessions and shiatsu demonstrations are held at least once per month.

Admission Requirements

The one-hundred-hour Certificate Program is open to any interested student.

Those applying for admission to the 2,200-hour Career Training Program should be at least 18 years of age, physically and mentally sound, and have completed Grade 12 or be a mature student (at least 19 years of age and out of school for at least one year). Applicants must submit two letters of personal reference, a physician's letter, two photos, and an essay, and interview with an admissions representative.

Those applying for admission to the Acupuncture Therapy Program must have a diploma in shiatsu therapy (2,200 hours since 1986; 800 or 1,600 hours prior to 1986), be a Japanese licensed shiatsu therapist, or have equivalent training. Applicants must submit two letters of personal reference, a physician's letter, two photos, and an essay, and interview with an admissions representative.

Tuition and Fees

Tuition for Level I of the Certificate Program is $600; Level II is $300.

Tuition for the Career Training Program is $10,500 plus GST (Goods and Services Tax); this includes a $100 registration fee. Other costs include: application fee, $10; books, approximately $700; and shiatsu kit, approximately $160; clinic pants are additional.

Tuition for the Postgraduate Certificate Program in acupuncture is $3,500 plus GST; tuition for the Prerequisite Acupuncture Program is $4,500 plus GST. Books cost approximately $200 and clinic materials, $120; other materials and uniform are additional.

Financial Assistance

Payment plans, a discount for early payment, a bring-a-friend discount, and the Ontario Student Assistance Program are available.

Sutherland-Chan School and Teaching Clinic

330 Dupont Street, 4th Floor
Toronto, Ontario M5R 1V9
Canada
Phone: (416) 924-1107

Grace Chan and Christine Sutherland founded the Sutherland-Chan School and Teaching Clinic in 1978 in an effort to bring massage therapy into the mainstream. Graduates have consistently earned the highest marks on the Board exams of all the massage therapy schools in Ontario.

Accreditation

The massage therapy curriculum at Sutherland-Chan is approved by the American Massage Therapy Association Commission on Massage Training Accreditation/Approval (AMTA/COMTAA). The school is accredited by the College of Massage Therapists of Ontario, the Ministry of Education and Training, and the Association of Physiotherapists and Massage Practitioners of British Columbia. Graduates are eligible to take licensing exams in both Canada and the United States.

Program Description

The two-year Massage Therapy Diploma Program

consists of courses in Anatomy, Business, Clinical Assessment, Clinical Practicum, Clinical Theory, Hydrotherapy, Massage Techniques (including contraindications, draping, assessment using palpation, basic and advanced massage skills, joint play, trigger point therapy, lymph drainage, and sports techniques), Massage Treatments (including history taking, recognition of symptoms, application of massage and hydrotherapy techniques, self-care, evaluation of client progress, and clinical records), Pathology, Physiology, Remedial Exercise, and Therapeutic Relationships. In Terms Three and Four, students participate in outreach programs in settings that include hospitals, senior citizens' residences, sports injury clinics, and rehabilitation centers. Classes are generally held during the day, with the exception of some classes and/or clinics on evenings or Saturdays.

A sixteen-hour Introduction to Massage course offers nonprofessionals instruction in performing a full-body massage, and meets the admission requirement for an introductory-level course (see below). A twenty-four-hour Pre-Admission Science Course, designed for the diploma applicant with a weak science background, focuses on basic biochemistry, cell structure and function, and an overview of body systems.

Admission Requirements

Applicants must have a high school diploma or equivalent; have taken OAC biology, Standard First Aid, and CPR; and have completed the Introduction to Massage or other sixteen-hour, basic massage course. Applicants must also submit an employment résumé for the previous five years, two letters of reference, and a letter from a medical doctor indicating good health and freedom from communicable diseases.

Tuition and Fees

Tuition for the Introduction to Massage course is $200. Tuition for the Pre-Admission Science Course is $400.

Tuition for the Massage Therapy Diploma Program is $14,500. There is a $50 application fee and a $100 registration fee; books, supplies, and uniform cost approximately $2,100.

Financial Assistance

Payment plans, Ontario and Canada student loans, and limited scholarships are available.

QUEBEC

Feldenkrais Institute of Somatic Education

P.O. Box 363, Station Delorimier
Montreal, Quebec H2H 2N7
Canada
Phone/Fax: (514) 529-5966

The Feldenkrais Institute of Somatic Education was founded in 1991 by Yvan Joly, M.A., Feldenkrais trainer, and registered psychologist. The next four-year program will begin in early 1998. Instruction is in English and French.

Accreditation

The four-year training program is accredited by the Feldenkrais Guild.

Program Description

The four-year, 160-day training program leads to a diploma that allows participants to apply for the status of Guild Certified Feldenkrais Practitioner. The theory behind the Feldenkrais method, anatomy and physiology, neuropsychology, cybernetics, physics, biomechanics, helping relationships and interviewing, and theories and practices of learning and communication will be presented. Halfway through the program, participants will be allowed to teach Awareness Through Movement classes; students may teach hands-on Functional Integration upon completion of the program.

Tuition and Fees

There is a $50 application fee; tuition is $3,500 per year.

Financial Assistance

Tuition may be paid in two installments per year.

Health Training Group

(*See* Multiple State Locations, page 324)

Le Centre Psycho-Corporel

675, Marguerite Bourgeoys
Quebec, Quebec G1S 3V8
Canada
Phone: (418) 687-1165 / (800) 473-5215
Fax: (418) 687-1166
E-mail: opsante@mlink.net

Le Centre Psycho-Corporel was founded in 1980. All instruction, as well as the catalog, is in French.

Program Description

Le Centre Psycho-Corporel offers two levels of instruction: a 432-hour (minimum) Massage Program and a 1,000-hour (minimum) Massotherapy Program. Required courses for both programs include Introduction to Massage (Californian, shiatsu, and Swedish); Anatomy, Physiology, and Pathology; Professional Aspects; and Professional Intervention. Electives include Manual Lymph Drainage, Trager, Sports Massage, Reflexology, Shiatsu, Qigong, Relaxation, Hygiene, and more.

Admission Requirements

Applicants must be at least 18 years of age, have a high school diploma or equivalent, submit a résumé and recent photograph, and have taken a twelve-hour introductory course in massage.

Tuition and Fees

Tuition for the 432-hour program is $4,295; tuition for the 1,000-hour program depends on the courses chosen. There is a $75 application fee.

Financial Assistance

Financial assistance is available through the Bank of Montreal.

Sinvananda Ashram Yoga Camp

(*See* Multiple State Locations, page 325)

MULTIPLE STATE LOCATIONS

The programs listed in this section either have branches in different locations, or they are seminar-type programs that travel to different states or provinces in any given year. These programs are broken down into United States and Canadian listings, and are listed alphabetically.

UNITED STATES

American Academy of Environmental Medicine

10 East Randolph Street
New Hope, Pennsylvania 18938
Phone: (215) 862-4544
Fax: (215) 862-4583

The American Academy of Environmental Medicine (AAEM) is a professional organization founded in 1965 as the Society for Clinical Ecology (see page 348 for membership information). The academy is interested in expanding the knowledge of interactions between individuals and their environment as reflected in their total health. Members may attend seminars and courses at reduced rates.

Accreditation

AAEM is accredited by the Accreditation Council for Continuing Medical Education (ACCME) as a sponsor of continuing medical education for physicians.

Program Description

AAEM's Basic Instructional Courses are held at various locations; the 1996 courses were held in Dearborn, Michigan.

Part I: Environmental Medicine in Everyday Practice explores specific causes of many common chronic and recurrent diseases.

Part II: Diagnostic Testing and Immunotherapy in Environmental Medicine teaches the most effective diagnostic and immunotherapy modalities for handing allergy problems found in all practices.

Part III: Chemical Toxicity and Sensitivity: Mechanisms, Patient Diagnosis, and Treatment provides an understanding of how environmental chemicals contribute to common diseases and how to evaluate and effectively treat these diseases.

Part IV: Nutrition as It Relates to Environmental Medicine shows the powerful role that nutrition can play in causing and treating diseases.

Part V: Indoor Air Quality Assessment and Remediation for Practicing Physicians explores ways to assess and remediate indoor air quality problems, stressing evaluation and treatment of the home environment.

Courses I through IV are required for provisional members to attain full membership. Each course meets for two-and-a-half days; two courses are scheduled over a three-day period so that all four required courses may be completed within a one-year span (i.e., two courses in April 1996 and two in April 1997).

Admission Requirements

Courses are geared toward physicians (M.D. and D.O.); allied health professionals such as nurses, technicians, physicians' assistants, registered dietitians, and others, must be accompanied by their M.D. or D.O. sponsor unless the sponsoring physician has previously attended a primary/basic course by AAEM or is a practicing member of AAEM.

Tuition and Fees

Tuition ranges from $225 to $375 per session, depending on membership and professional status.

American Academy of Medical Acupuncture

5820 Wilshire Boulevard, Suite 500
Los Angeles, California 90036
Phone: (213) 937-5514
Fax: (213) 937-0959
E-mail: KCKD71F@prodigy.com

The American Academy of Medical Acupuncture (AAMA) was founded in 1987 by a group of physicians who were graduates of the Medical Acupuncture for Physicians training programs sponsored by UCLA School of Medicine. AAMA serves as both a professional (see page 345) and certifying (see page 336) organization. The symposium and review classes are held at locations throughout the country.

Accreditation

AAMA has created a proficiency examination for physicians who have incorporated acupuncture into their medical practice; the Board of Directors awards a Certificate of Proficiency in Medical Acupuncture to those who successfully pass this exam. The exam is the first step toward establishing a formal recognized board certification program.

Both the Symposium and the Examination Review Course have been approved for continuing medical education (CME) credits.

Program Description

An annual four-day Medical Acupuncture Symposium addresses the use of acupuncture in the practice of contemporary medicine for physicians (M.D.s or D.O.s) with little or no acupuncture knowledge, as well as for those with years of experience. Workshops typically cover such topics as an introduction to acupuncture, energetics and manual medicine, applications of medical acupuncture in the management of disease, research, and more.

A two-day Examination Review Course has been developed by John Reed, M.D., who has taught the clinical portion of the introductory program at the symposium for several years. This course requires some advance home study work and two full days on-site prior to the exam.

Admission Requirements

The Symposium is designed for physicians (M.D.s and D.O.s) interested in or already practicing acupuncture; only M.D.s and D.O.s may attend. The Review Course is for physicians already proficient in medical acupuncture.

Tuition and Fees

Registration for the Medical Acupuncture Symposium costs approximately $175 to $675, depending on AAMA membership status and date of registration; discounts are given for early registration. Registration for the Examination Review Course is $375; the examination costs $500.

American Yoga Association

513 South Orange Avenue
Sarasota, Florida 34236
Phone: (813) 953-5859 / (800) 226-5859

The Easy Does It Trainer Program was created by the American Yoga Association's founder, Alice Christensen, for use with people with physical limitations due to age, convalescence, injury, or substance abuse recovery.

Program Description

The American Yoga Association's Easy Does It Program consists of specially adapted classical yoga exercises, breathing techniques, and guided relaxation. The Easy Does It Trainer Program is geared toward geriatric health practitioners, nurses, physical therapists, nursing home staff, and others who care for the elderly or those with physical limitations. The association offers on-site programs at various colleges or continuing education programs throughout the country. The curriculum may be adapted to cover several weeks or days, and a certificate is awarded upon completion.

Instruction includes goals and objectives of the Easy Does It Program; the physical, mental, and emotional benefits; how to teach five to eight seated and standing exercises; how to practice and teach two breathing techniques; how to teach relaxation; how to apply the techniques to those recovering from substance abuse or injury; and how to motivate clients to continue with the program.

Tuition and Fees

Fees vary with the length of the course.

Asten Center of Natural Therapeutics

797 Grove Road, Suite 101
Richardson, Texas 75081-2761
Phone: (214) 669-3246

121 West Legion
P.O. Box C
Whitehall, Montana 59759-1503
Phone: (406) 287-5670
Fax: (406) 287-7900

The Asten Center of Natural Therapeutics was founded by Paige Asten in Dallas, Texas in 1983; in 1990, an additional facility was opened in Whitehall, Montana. The Montana school is located in a valley surrounded by mountain ranges; the Texas school is located near Dallas/Fort Worth in an office complex served by DART (Dallas Area Rapid Transit).

Accreditation

The Asten Center is licensed by the Montana Department of Commerce and recognized by the Texas Department of Health. The 550-hour Massage Therapy Program (offered in Texas) is approved by the American Massage Therapy Association Commission on Massage Training Accreditation/Approval (AMTA/COMTAA), and is also approved by the State of Iowa.

Program Description

In Montana, the 605½-hour Massage Therapy Program is divided into two sections: Basic Massage Therapy (286 hours) and Specialized Massage Therapy (319½ hours). Courses in the Basic Section include Anatomy, Physiology, Swedish Massage, Hydrotherapy/Cryotherapy, Health/Hygiene, Business Practices and Ethics, Range of Motion, How to Study, and Externship. Classes in the Specialized Section include Anatomy and Physiology, Reflexology, Trigger Point Therapy, Sports Massage, Special Problems, and Clinical Application.

In Texas, the 550-hour Massage Therapy Program is also divided into Basic and Specialized Sections. The Basic Section consists of 300 hours of instruction and is the minimum required by the Texas Department of Health, Rules, and Regulations for registration. When combined with the Specialized Section (250 hours), this program is approved by AMTA/COMTAA. The Basic Section includes instruction in Anatomy and Physiology, Health and Hygiene, Hydrotherapy, Swedish Massage, Business Practices and Ethics, and Internship. The Specialized Section adds instruction in Sports Massage, Trigger Point Therapy, Reflexology, Focus Classes, and Clinical Application Classes that include treatment for sprained ankle, carpal tunnel syndrome, whiplash, TMJ dysfunction, sciatic pain, tennis elbow, spinal deviations, and other dysfunctions.

Admission Requirements

Applicants must be at least 18 years of age, be free of contagious disease, and interview with an admissions representative. Students in Texas must also sign a medical release form and either take AMTA student membership or obtain other malpractice insurance within the first two months of enrollment.

Tuition and Fees

In Montana, the total course fee is $5,080, including tuition, massage table and travel bag, face cradle, books, AMTA student membership, massage lotion, and CPR training; linens are additional.

In Texas, tuition for the Basic Massage Therapy Section is $2,480. Tuition for the Specialized Massage Therapy Section is $2,359. Other costs include: books, $122 for the Basic Section and $36 for the Specialized Section; AMTA student membership, $188; First Aid/CPR classes, $35; linens, lotion, and clothing, $150; and an optional portable massage table, $249.

Financial Assistance

Payment plans, student loans, and aid from the Texas Rehabilitation Commission and the Texas Commission for the Blind are available. Students in Texas who register for both sections consecutively receive a $495 reduction in tuition.

BioSomatics

P.O. Box 206
Grand Junction, Colorado 81502
Phone: (970) 245-8903

Educational director Carol Welch has been devoted to developmental movement since 1979 and is one of only thirty-eight individuals trained by Thomas Hanna. BioSomatics blends her own distinctive approach to Somatic Movement reeducation, which combines principles from Hanna Somatics with the worlds of dance and yoga.

Seminars are held across the United States and Canada in such cities as Seattle, Denver, Albuquerque, Tucson, Des Moines, Maui, Vancouver, and Regina (Saskatchewan). For information on instructional videos, see page 379.

Program Description

There are six seminars offered in BioSomatics Movement Education in the tradition of Thomas Hanna.

The Posture and Movement Seminar runs two-and-a-half days and is a primer in somatic education. Topics include use of the pandicular response (the primary hands-on method of clinical education) for the reeducation of habitual flexion and extension patterns, how habitual postural patterns are the underpinning of many physical problems, movement to avoid or reverse stuck posturing, and relanguaging problems in sensory terms. This seminar must be taken before any of the subsequent seminars.

The three-day Landau Seminar covers clinical somatic education to address habituation of the Landau reflex, movements for senile posture, how to build somatic education into your practice, and more.

The three-day Trauma Reflex Seminar covers clinical somatic education to address habituation of the startle and trauma reflexes, explorations in verbal and mental imagery, movements in the reeducation of the relationship of the ankle, knee, and hip to the torso, and more.

The three-day Startle Reflex Seminar teaches releasing deeper effects of the startle reflex, movements for joints, developmental stages of movement, roller work to self-adjust tension, and more.

The three-day Renegotiating and Transforming Trauma Seminar teaches neurological coordination/tension patterns, control over evolutive scoliosis through sustained position traction, renegotiating birth trauma, and more.

The two-day Pure Movement Seminar covers the use of movement to create healthy spines, moving the body to adjust the emotions, increasing sensitivity for feeling the movements of the spine, tissues, and bones, and more.

A certificate of completion will be awarded after attending all seminars twice and passing an evaluation of hands-on skills. Two years of practice and application, six case history studies, and ten private somatic sessions are required before taking the certification evaluation. The certificate of completion entitles the practitioner to be known as a Resource for BioSomatic Education.

Admission Requirements

The certification/evaluation program is intended for practitioners in orthodox or complementary medicine, therapy, or education. A knowledge of anatomy and physiology is recommended, as is experience in some form of body-oriented therapy and/or psychotherapy or movement education. Applicants must answer a brief questionnaire and submit a résumé and a letter of recommendation.

Tuition and Fees

Tuition for the Posture and Movement Seminar is $275; for the Landau Seminar, $350; for the Trauma Reflex Seminar, $350; for the Startle Reflex Seminar, $350; for the Renegotiating and Transforming Trauma Seminar, $350; and for the Pure Movement Seminar, $250.

Financial Assistance

A discount is given for early registration.

Day-Break Geriatric Massage Project

P.O. Box 1629
14600 Drake Road
Guerneville, California 95446
Phone: (707) 869-0632
Fax: (707) 869-1686
E-mail: dwmiesler@aol.com

The Day-Break Geriatric Massage Project was founded in 1991. Along with massage instructor training, the organization offers books, videos, client evaluation kits, workshops, and a quarterly newsletter.

Program Description

Level 1: The seventeen-hour workshop covers an introduction to aging; client assessment and contraindications; modification of standard massage techniques; practical hands-on work; and how to establish a geriatric massage practice. Workshops are offered throughout the country.

Level 2: The correspondence course covers an overview on aging; *The ABCs of Geriatric Massage* video; finding and dealing with community support groups; age-related health problems; contraindications; client assessment and development of a treatment plan; two weekly half-hour treatment sessions for four consecutive weeks; establishing and promoting your business; and community relations.

Level 3 consists of the seventeen-hour workshop plus the correspondence course or the symposium.

Level 4: The annual symposium exposes therapists to various methods and philosophies. Topics covered in the past include ice massage, lymphatic and visceral massage, and advanced geriatric massage. The symposium is held in Guerneville, California.

The Geriatric Massage Instructor Training Program consists of the seventeen-contact-hour workshop, fifty-two study hours through correspondence, forty to forty-eight study hours at the annual symposium, and 120 contact hours of instructor learning modules. Practitioners are certified in geriatric massage after completion of the seventeen-hour workshop.

The instructor learning modules require two 8-session studies on elderly clients with a major problem (such as Parkinson's or stroke), exams, participation in workshops as an observer, assistant, and copresenter, and participation at a four-day hands-on seminar in California.

Admission Requirements

Applicants must be an insured member of ABMT, AMTA, IMA, or NANMT and should be a mature massage therapist with a minimum of one hundred hours of formal massage training, including Swedish massage. In addition, applicants should have worked with seniors in either a family or health care setting, should have some teaching experience or talent for teaching, must have easy access to a computer and fax machine, and should have an e-mail address.

Tuition and Fees

Costs are as follows: membership, $35; workshop, $200; correspondence course, $265; symposium (approximate), $765; instructor enrollment fee, $400; and four-day instructor seminar, $400.

DoveStar Institute

New Hampshire Location:
50 Whitehall Road
Hooksett, New Hampshire 03106-2104
Phone: (603) 669-9497 / (603) 669-5104
Fax: (603) 625-1919

Massachusetts Location:
120 Court Street
Plymouth, Massachusetts 02360
Phone: (508) 830-0068
Fax: (508) 830-0288

In 1973, Kamala Renner started the Yoga Retreat Center and Massage School in Hooksett, New Hampshire. In 1978, the center became known as the EarthStar Holistic Center and DoveStar Institute, and was licensed as a holistic therapy trade school in 1981. Training is held in Hooksett, New Hampshire; Plymouth, Massachusetts; and Hilton Head Island, South Carolina.

Accreditation

DoveStar Institute is licensed by the New Hampshire Postsecondary Education Agency and the Commonwealth of Massachusetts Department of Education, and the curriculum is designed to meet New Hampshire state licensing requirements. The curriculum is approved by the Associated Bodyworkers and Massage Practitioners (ABMP), the Transformational Hypnotherapists' Association (THA), and the American Council of Hypnotist Examiners (ACHE).

Program Description

The 240-hour Reiki-Alchemia Core Energy Work Program integrates the healing techniques of alchemia, which utilizes transformational and transmutational life force energy qualities, with the Usui method of reiki, which activates universal life force energy with the Usui master keys. Required courses include Vibrational Healing, Alchemia Bodywork, Reiki First Degree, Etheric Release, Hypnotherapy, Alchemia Breathwork, RENEW, and Four Forces, plus a four-day intensive and five electives.

Kriya massage incorporates the universal four forces (centripetal, centrifugal, gravity, and electromagnetic) into classical massage techniques. The Kriya Massage Program for New Hampshire licensure is a 750-hour program. Required courses include Kriya Massage, Kriya Reflex Massage, Kriya Joint Massage, Kriya Sports Massage, Client Analysis Alchemia Bodywork, Client Pathology, Sports Hydrotherapy, Spa Hydrotherapy, Detox Hydrotherapy, Health Services Management, Business and Marketing, State Rules and Regulations, Adult CPR, and Anatomy and Physiology, plus the choice of one course each in the areas of Oriental, energy work, somato-emotional release, and anatomy and movement, plus seven electives. Six supervised kriya bodywork practicums and clinical are also required.

The Kriya Massage Program for national certification is a 500-hour program that includes Kriya Massage, Kriya Reflex Massage, Kriya Joint Massage, Alchemia Bodywork, Health Services Management, and Anatomy and Physiology, plus the choice of one course each in the areas of Oriental,

energy work, and somato-emotional release, plus seven electives. Six supervised kriya bodywork practicums and clinical are also required.

The 750-hour Oriental Bodywork Program for New Hampshire licensure includes Kriya Massage, Kriya Reflex Massage, Shiatsu Stretching, Shiatsu Points, Acupressure, Acupressure Massage, Reiki First and Second Degree, Qigong, RENEW, Four Forces, Alchemia Yoga, Client Pathology, Sports Hydrotherapy, Spa Hydrotherapy, Detox Hydrotherapy, Health Services Management, Business and Marketing, State Rules and Regulations, Adult CPR, and Anatomy and Physiology, plus six supervised Oriental bodywork practicums, five electives, clinical, and two hours of sessions with a certified instructor.

The 750-hour Kriya Equine Bodywork Program includes required courses in Kriya Massage, Kriya Joint Massage, Kriya Sports Massage, Strain/Counterstrain, Acupressure, Alchemia Bodywork, Reiki First and Second Degree, Trigger Points and Myofascial, Neuromuscular, Alchemia Breathwork, Sports Hydrotherapy, Equine Rapport, Equine Strain/Counterstrain, Equine Joints and Trigger Points, Equine Acupressure, Equine Pathology, Equine Hydrotherapy, Equine Performance Massage, Equine Performance Kinesiology, Equine Clinical Kinesiology, Equine Musculoskeletal, Skeletal, Muscle, Circulatory, and Nervous System, and Anatomy and Physiology, plus six electives and clinical application.

The goal of alchemical synergy is to connect with the "inner master" or "inner adult" and reclaim responsibility for oneself. The 500-hour Alchemical Synergy Core Holistic Counseling Program includes required courses in Hypnotherapy (1 through 6), Four Forces, Inner Alignment, Inner Commitment, Inner Harmony, Inner Power, and Four Forces Counseling, plus eight electives, five supervised hypnotherapy practicums, assisting with Hypnotherapy Courses 1 through 6, and receiving forty-four hours of hypnotherapy sessions.

The 2,000-hour Professional Holistic Practitioner Program involves extensive training in holistic health care. Requirements include at least 500 hours of training in each of the Bodywork, Synergy, and Reiki-Alchemia Programs; clinical practice in each of these areas; a personal journal of fifty sessions received; and a thesis.

The 250-hour Intermediate Kriya Massage Program is to be completed in conjunction with a Kriya Core Program. It includes Kriya Massage, Kriya Joint Massage, Kriya Reflex Massage, Kriya Sports Massage, Client Analysis, Alchemia Bodywork, Health Services Management, and Anatomy and Physiology, plus the choice of one class each from the areas of energy work and somato-emotional release, plus clinical.

The eighty-hour Jin Shin Acupressure Program may be completed in conjunction with either the Oriental or Kriya Bodywork Programs. Required classes include Acupressure 1 through 3, clinical, and acupressure work-ups on two people.

Alchemical Hypnotherapy Certifications are offered in either 200- or 350-hour programs, and are to be completed with the Alchemical Synergy Core Program. The 200-hour Hypnotherapy Program includes Hypnotherapy 1 through 6, four electives, and three practicums. The 350-hour Alchemical Hypnotherapy Program includes Hypnotherapy 1 through 6, six electives, three supervised practicums, assisting at Hypnotherapy courses 1 through 6, and receiving twenty-two hours of hypnotherapy sessions.

Other intermediate certifications include Therapeutic Massage, with courses in Alchemia Bodywork, Etheric Release, Craniosacral Bodywork, Cellulomes, Trigger Points and Myofascial, Neuromuscular Massage, and RENEW; Sports Massage, with courses in Strain/Counterstrain, Massage for Athletes, Shiatsu Stretching, Shiatsu Points, Cellulomes, Muscle Energy Techniques, Neuromuscular Massage, and Sports Pathology; and RENEW (Releasing Energy with Neuroemotional Work) Practitioner, which includes courses such as Acupressure, Hypnotherapy, RENEW, and Applied Kinesiology. The Therapeutic and Sports Massage Programs must be taken in conjunction with a Kriya Core Program; RENEW Practitioner may be completed in conjunction with any core program.

The Reiki Master Teacher Program consists of Reiki First, Second, and Third Degree Therapist required courses, as well as forty hours of supervising healing circles, assisting in Reiki First, Second, and Third Degree classes, attending Master Teacher classes, and receiving Reiki Master Teacher Attunement. Completion requires a minimum of one year of study with a Reiki Master Teacher.

Alchemia yoga is a form of physical movement that incorporates the holistic approach to physical fitness. The 523-hour Alchemia Yoga Teacher Program consists of required courses in Alchemia Yoga, Strain/Counterstrain, Acupressure, Alchemia Bodywork, Reiki First Degree, Alchemy and Physiology, Hypnotherapy, Alchemia Breathwork, RENEW, Four Forces, Kinesiology Theory, and Anatomy and Physiology, as well as assisting at alchemia yoga classes and practice teaching.

A DoveStar Teacher Certification Program is offered that emphasizes holistic health. Students must monitor a variety of classes, attend teacher training classes, complete certification in a field of choice, assist at two-day seminars, supervise practicums, and attend a week-long teacher training intensive.

Admission Requirements

Applicants must interview with an admissions representative.

Tuition and Fees

Tuition for the Reiki-Alchemia Program is $2,525, plus a $125 enrollment fee.

Tuition for the Kriya Massage Program for New Hampshire licensure is approximately $5,800. There is a $125 enrollment fee; books are approximately $300, supplies are $150, and a massage table is additional.

Tuition for the Kriya Massage Program for national certification is approximately $3,945. There is a $125 enrollment fee; books are approximately $250, supplies are $100, and a massage table is additional.

Tuition for the Oriental Bodywork Program for New Hampshire licensure is approximately $6,045. There is a $125 enrollment fee; books are approximately $300, and supplies are $150.

Tuition for the Kriya Equine Bodywork Program is approximately $6,655. There is a $125 enrollment fee; books are approximately $200, and supplies are $150.

Tuition for the Alchemical Synergy Program is $3,675; there is a $125 enrollment fee, and books are $100.

Tuition for the Professional Holistic Practitioner Program varies with courses; there is a $125 enrollment fee.

Tuition for the Intermediate Kriya Massage Program is $2,235; for the Jin Shin Acupressure Program, $780; for the Hypnotherapy Program, $2,135; and for the Alchemical Hypnotherapy Program, $2,455.

Tuition for the Reiki Master Teacher Program is $1,705, plus a $125 enrollment fee. Tuition for the Alchemia Yoga Teacher Program is $4,095, plus a $125 enrollment fee. The cost of the DoveStar Teacher Certification Program varies depending on the classes selected and the area of certification; contact DoveStar for more information.

Financial Assistance

Work-study is available.

East West Academy of Healing Arts/Qigong Institute

450 Sutter, Suite 2104
San Francisco, California 94108
Phone: (415) 788-2227

The East West Academy of Healing Arts was founded in 1973 by Dr. Effie Poy Yew Chow, an acupuncturist and psychiatric nurse. Dr. Chow uses the Chow Integrated Healing System, in which modern Western practices are blended with ancient Eastern healing arts. Seminars are held in San Francisco, Spokane, Toronto, Vancouver, Anchorage, Honolulu, and other locations in the United States and Canada. The Qigong Institute, a nonprofit organization, is a subsidiary of the East West Academy of Healing Arts (see page 356).

Program Description

Three-day weekend seminars in Qigong Miracle Healing include an introductory lecture and demonstration, Basic Skills I, and Basic Skills II. In the seminar series, Dr. Chow teaches basic qigong principles and demonstrates qigong healing. Participants learn qigong "scanning" and healing techniques and everyday applications.

Tuition and Fees

The introduction and demonstration cost $20; Basic Skills I costs $135; Basic Skills II costs $135; and the Friday, Saturday, and Sunday workshops combined cost $225.

Feldenkrais Resources

830 Bancroft Way, Suite 112
Berkeley, California 94710
Phone: (510) 540-7600 / (800) 765-1907
Fax: (510) 540-7683

Mailing Address:
P.O. Box 2067
Berkeley, California 94702

Feldenkrais Resources was founded in 1983; it is the leading school for the postgraduate training of Feldenkrais practitioners, and also the publisher of Dr. Feldenkrais' audio- and videotape programs, and books and audiotapes of leading Feldenkrais practitioners (see page 377).

Accreditation

The East Coast Feldenkrais Professional Training Program is fully accredited by the Feldenkrais Guild and recognized by all international Feldenkrais teacher organizations throughout Europe, Australia, Israel, and South America. Upon completion of the second year of training, qualified students will be authorized to teach Awareness Through Movement to the public. At the end of the fourth year, students become practitioners of both Awareness Through Movement and Functional Integration, and will be eligible for full membership in the Feldenkrais Guild. The program is held in Montclair, New Jersey.

One-day Feldenkrais Method Workshops for prospective training program participants and the general public are held in New York, New Jersey, Delaware, and the Washington, D.C./Baltimore area.

Program Description

The East Coast Feldenkrais Professional Training Program meets forty days per year over three-and-a-half years in a weekend-based format. The program offers extensive practical experience and in-depth training in both Awareness Through Movement and Functional Integration, as well as a thorough exploration of the theory underlying the Feldenkrais method through lectures, discussions, study groups, and readings.

Admission Requirements

There are no prerequisites.

Tuition and Fees

Tuition is $3,600 per year, plus a $50 application fee. The one-day workshops cost $50 with pre-registration and $60 at the door as space permits.

Financial Assistance

Payment plans are available, as well as a limited number of work-scholarships and tuition reduction plans for students traveling from Canada.

Health Enrichment Center

1820 North Lapeer Road
Lapeer, Michigan 48446-7771
Phone: (810) 667-9453

Indiana Location:
6801 Lake Plaza Drive, Suite A102
Indianapolis, Indiana 46220-4052
Phone: (317) 841-1414

Health Enrichment Center (HEC) was founded in 1985 and is owned and operated by Sandy Fritz. Decentralized facilities for the Therapeutic Massage Program are offered regionally throughout Michigan, with additional classroom and office facilities in Indianapolis.

Accreditation

The Health Enrichment Center is accredited by the Accrediting Commission of Career Schools and Colleges of Technology (ACCSCT). The Therapeutic Massage Program is approved by the American Massage Therapy Association Commission on Massage Training Accreditation/Approval (AMTA/COMTAA). All programs are registered with the Associated Bodywork and Massage Professionals (ABMP). HEC has program approval in Washington, Oregon, Texas, Ohio, and Ontario, Canada. In Michigan and Indiana, licensing and regulation of massage is controlled by local governments.

Program Description

The 1,000-hour Therapeutic Massage Program consists of 500 classroom hours and 500 directed-study hours. Topics covered in the classroom include Anatomy and Physiology, Nutrition, Biology of Health and Wellness, Muscle Stress Reduction Techniques, Applied Kinesiology, Movement Re-education, Proprioceptive Integration, Therapeutic Massage Techniques, Sports Massage, Clinical Experience Lab, and Ethics and Business Practices. Directed-study hours require a massage log, written essay exams, research paper, presentation, procedure manual, required projects, and anatomy coloring book. Classes are held days or evenings. This program may also be completed in an equivalent workshop format, a pay-as-you-go program of individual workshops.

The 240-hour Clinical Approaches Program is opened to graduates of any 500-hour massage therapy program from a state-licensed school. The program focuses on the application of therapeutic massage in more complex situations. Students attend classes for eleven weekends.

A 256-hour Subtle Energy Therapies Program is open to students who have taken body energy and polarity. The core curriculum consists of Advanced Craniosacral; Anatomy and Physiology of Energy; Essence, Aromatherapy, and Homeopathy; One Brain; Power of Word Intention; Somato Positional Release; Supervised Practice Time; Triune Polarity Energy; Under the Code; Movement and Yoga; and review and testing.

Continuing Education

Graduates are eligible to take the 1,300-hour Massage Practitioner, 2,000-hour Advanced Practitioner, and 5,000-hour Master Bodywork Therapist Advanced Diploma Programs. These programs are continuations of the Therapeutic Massage Program. See the catalog for details.

Individual workshops ranging from four hours to six days are offered in various fields of bodywork, including Magnets and Healing, Hyperventilation Syndrome, Hypnosis for Self-Help, Homeopathy, and many others.

Admission Requirements

Applicants must be at least 18 years of age, have a high school diploma or equivalent, be physically capable of performing massage, be of good moral character, and be conversant in the English language.

Tuition and Fees

There is a $25 application fee in Michigan and a $100 registration fee in Indiana.

Tuition for the Therapeutic Massage Program is $3,600; books are approximately $325. The cost of this program in the equivalent workshop format is as follows: tuition, $4,000 to $4,500; orientation and conference fee, $100; books, approximately $300; and testing fees, $500.

Tuition for the Clinical Approaches Program is $2,400; books are approximately $350.

Tuition for the Subtle Energy Therapies Program is $2,400; books are approximately $250.

Tuition for the Massage Practitioner Program is $1,750 to $1,975.

Tuition for the Advanced Practitioner Program varies depending on choices.

Tuition for the Master Bodywork Therapist Program is $2,000.

Financial Assistance

Limited scholarships and a payment plan are available.

Hellerwork International

406 Berry Street
Mount Shasta, California 96067
Phone: (916) 926-2500 / (800) 392-3900
Fax: (916) 926-6839
E-mail: Hellerwork@aol.com
Internet: http://www.hellerwork.com

Hellerwork, created by Joseph Heller in 1979, is a discipline that includes bodywork, movement, and dialogue as a step in developing consciousness. Like Rolfing, the massage component of Hellerwork focuses on the connective tissue, or fascia, and attempts to correct body misalignment by releasing tension in the fascia. Today there are over 225 certified Hellerwork practitioners in twenty-nine states and seven foreign countries. Training is offered by practitioners located throughout the United States (including Hawaii), as well as Europe, Japan, and New Zealand.

Program Description

The Hellerwork Practitioner Training is a 1,250-hour certification program. The curriculum is the same for every training although the format may vary. The curriculum includes Human Evolution and Gravity, Introduction to Body Systems, Applied Human Anatomy and Physiology, Myofascial Anatomy, Principles and Techniques of Structural Bodywork, Gross Anatomy Lab, Structural and Functional Assessment, Deep Tissue Bodywork Practicum, Body Awareness and Movement Lab, Psycho-Somatic Movement Analysis, Hellerwork Movement and Practicum, Communicating Movement Lessons, Ergonomics, Introduction to Psychological Inquiry, Fundamentals of Dialogue, Intra/Interpersonal Communications, Client Development, Business Standards/Ethics, and Marketing Your Practice.

Special training is offered for the health care professional.

Admission Requirements

Applicants must be at least 21 years of age, have a high school diploma or equivalent, have received the Hellerwork series, interview with the director of the chosen training, and complete any educational prerequisites required for the chosen training.

Tuition and Fees

Tuition is approximately $12,995, but varies with location.

Financial Assistance

A payment plan is available.

Institute for Awareness in Motion

P.O. Box 50624
Columbia, South Carolina 29250
Phone/Fax: (803) 799-6258

The Institute for Awareness in Motion began offering advanced trainings to Feldenkrais practitioners in 1989.

Program Description

A four-year Feldenkrais Practitioner Training Program will begin in 1997 and be held in Dahlonega, Georgia. Future trainings may be offered beginning in 1998 or 1999. After two years, students are given provisional recognition of the ability to teach Awareness Through Movement; upon completion of the program, practitioners are qualified to practice Functional Integration. Four-week training sessions will meet twice per year for four years.

Admission Requirements

Applicants should have the desire to learn and to teach the Feldenkrais Method.

Tuition and Fees

There is a $50 application fee; tuition is $3,500 per year.

Integrative Yoga Therapy

2975 Pacific Heights Drive
Aptos, California 95003
Phone: (408) 688-9642

Integrative Yoga Therapy (IYT) blends timeless yoga techniques with the concepts of mind-body health. The program was founded by Lesley Grant, a somatic therapist who developed one of the country's first yoga and meditation-based self-healing programs in a medical setting. The two-week residential program is offered in a variety of locations including Colorado, California, Arizona, British Columbia, and Massachusetts.

Program Description

The Integrative Yoga Therapy Training Program consists of a two-week residential program followed by a four-month internship and home study course. In the residential program, students work in small groups with a personal mentor who will continue to guide them during the internship phase. The internship includes teaching the eight-week IYT yoga program, completing eight individual sessions, studying the IYT manual, and completing the accompanying workbook.

The main areas of study are the Art and Science of Yoga, Understanding the Mind-Body Connection, and Awakening the Spirit of Yoga. Students become certified teachers of the IYT Yoga and Stress Management Program, learn a methodology for one-on-one yoga therapy sessions, gain an understanding of the traditional psychology of yoga, explore the field of mind-body health, study key yoga postures in depth and understand how the asanas work with the mind and emotions, learn guided imagery techniques and a variety of deep relaxation techniques, learn the relationship between yoga and Ayurveda, and more.

Tuition and Fees

Tuition and fees vary with location and accommodations, ranging from $985 to $1,955. This includes tuition, accommodations, vegetarian meals, training manual, workbook, and personal supervision for the four-month internship/home study.

International Alliance of Health Care Educators

11211 Prosperity Farms Road, Suite D-325
Palm Beach Gardens, Florida 33410
Phone: (561) 622-4334 (administration) /
   (800) 233-5880 (registration)
Fax: (561) 622-4771

The International Alliance of Health Care Educators (IAHE) is a coalition of health care educators dedicated to the advancement of progressive therapeutic modalities. The alliance shares the staff expertise and established resources of The Upledger Institute, an educational, clinical, and research center founded in 1985 by John E. Upledger, D.O.,

O.M.M., who developed craniosacral therapy nearly twenty-five years ago. The IAHE also sells educational tapes and related products (see page 377).

Accreditation

Practitioners use workshops to fulfill continuing education requirements for a variety of different professions. Students are advised to consult their professional state board prior to registration.

Program Description

The IAHE offers continuing education workshops throughout the United States, Canada, Europe, the Far East, and the Caribbean to health care providers such as massage therapists, osteopathic physicians, chiropractors, M.D.s, nurses, and others. Three-, four-, and five-day workshops are offered through the IAHE in Florida in such areas as Upledger Craniosacral Therapy, SomatoEmotional Release, visceral manipulation, St. John Method of neuromuscular therapy, Zero Balancing, process acupressure, mechanical link, Aston therapeutics, spinal release, developmental manual therapy, Holoenergetics, trauma release therapy, energy integration, fascial mobilization, and lymph drainage therapy.

Craniosacral therapy certification is offered at two levels.

Certification in Craniosacral Therapy Techniques is offered after completion of the four-day Craniosacral Therapy I and II courses and successful testing. In these courses, students explore the anatomy and physiology of the craniosacral system, develop light-touch palpation skills and fascial release techniques, learn to evaluate and treat cranial-base dysfunction, and more.

Craniosacral Therapy Diplomate Certification is offered after completion of Craniosacral Therapy I and II, SomatoEmotional Release I and II (each four days in length), the five-day Advanced I Craniosacral Therapy course, and successful testing. In the SomatoEmotional Release classes, students learn to integrate hands-on techniques with verbal dialoguing, help the patient identify and expel negative emotional experiences, participate in class exercises designed to strengthen the relationship between the conscious and unconscious mind, and more. The Advanced I Craniosacral Therapy course is an in-depth experience for the serious practitioner, in which students observe and participate in therapy sessions.

Admission Requirements

In most cases, workshop admission requires participants to hold a current health care license or certificate, or to be enrolled in an educational program granting licensure or certification.

Tuition and Fees

Tuition varies by course and ranges from $350 to $1,500.

Financial Assistance

A discount is given to full-time students.

International Institute of Reflexology

5650 First Avenue North
P.O. Box 12642
St. Petersburg, Florida 33733
Phone: (813) 343-4811
Fax: (813) 381-2807

Foot reflexology was originally developed by the late Eunice Ingham, whose nephew is president of the International Institute of Reflexology (IIR). The institute serves as both a professional organization and an educational institution, as it offers a worldwide referral service, educational seminars, certification programs, and advanced training.

Accreditation

The program at IIR is approved for fourteen continuing education credits by the Florida Board of Massage, Florida and California Nurses boards, and the National Certification Board for Therapeutic Massage and Bodywork (NCBTMB).

Program Description

Two-day seminars are offered throughout the United States and Canada to both professionals and laypersons. Seminars include lecture and practical, film graphics, and charts.

A certification exam may be taken by those who have attended at least two full two-day seminars and have completed one year of practice after the first seminar. The exam includes both written and practical components.

Admission Requirements

There are no age or educational requirements.

Tuition and Fees

Two-day seminars cost $250, or $80 for former students. The certification exam costs $160.

International Veterinary Acupuncture Society

268 West 3rd Street, Suite 2
P.O. Box 2074
Nederland, Colorado 80466-2074
Phone: (303) 258-3767
Fax: (303) 258-0767
E-mail: ivasjagg@msn.com

The International Veterinary Acupuncture Society was founded in 1974 as a nonprofit educational organization. Class locations may vary. The 1997–1998 course will be held in Tampa, Florida.

Accreditation

The veterinary acupuncture course qualifies for fifty hours of continuing education credits for 1996 and fifty hours for 1997.

Program Description

A 110-hour series of four seminars in basic veterinary acupuncture is offered to licensed graduate veterinarians. The course covers small and large animal acupuncture equally, as well as TCM and scientific aspects of acupuncture. Session One provides a basic understanding of TCM principles, their relationship to Western medicine, and the fundamentals of needling technique. Session Two provides a working knowledge of TCM diagnostic approaches and small animal and equine acupuncture. Session Three integrates the diagnostic and treatment regimens, and Session Four enables attendees to incorporate the basic knowledge of acupuncture into clinical practice.

Topics covered include the Meridian Pathways, Fundamental Substances, Zang-Fu Organs, Causes of Disease, Special Action Points, Acupuncture Points and Meridians, the Circadian Clock, the Five Phases (Elements), the Eight Principles, Zang-Fu Pathology, Bi Syndrome, TCM, Points and Clinical Applications, Empirical Point Use and TCM Applications, Small Animal and Large Animal Western Acupuncture, Neurophysiology, Applied Neurology, Incorporating Acupuncture into Your Practice, Legal Aspects, Dealing with Failures, Electro-Acupuncture, History of Acupuncture, and practical laboratories.

Upon completion of the course, graduates are eligible to take the IVAS certification exam. Requirements for certification include being a licensed veterinarian in good standing; attendance at all four seminars; payment of the examination fee and passing scores on written and practical exams; submission and approval of the required case report; and forty hours spent with a certified member with approved case load or at IVAS-approved regional clinical workshops.

Admission Requirements

The course is open only to licensed graduate veterinarians.

Tuition and Fees

Tuition is $2,400 for all four sessions, including course notes and a one-year membership in IVAS.

Jin Shin Jyutsu, Inc.

8719 East San Alberto
Scottsdale, Arizona 85258
Phone: (602) 998-9331
Fax: (602) 998-9335

Jin Shin Jyutsu physio-philosophy is an ancient art of harmonizing the body's life energy. The art was revived in the early 1900s by Master Jiro Murai in Japan and given to Mary Burmeister, who brought it to the United States in the 1950s. Jin Shin Jyutsu does not involve massage or manipulation; it is a gentle art in which the fingertips are placed (over clothing) on safety energy locks to harmonize and restore the energy flow. It can be applied as self-help or by a trained practitioner. Seminars are held throughout the world.

Accreditation

The full Basic Seminar and the Now Know Myself Seminar are approved for continuing education credits by the California Board of Registered Nursing and the National Certification Board for Therapeutic Massage and Bodywork (NCBTMB). The Instructor Training in Self-Help Seminar is approved for continuing education units by the California Board of Registered Nursing.

Program Description

Each five-day Basic Seminar consists of two parts: Part I introduces the dynamic qualities of the twenty-six safety energy locks, the trinity flows, the concepts of depths within the body, and the physio-philosophy of Jin Shin Jyutsu, through lecture and hands-on application. Part II introduces the twelve organ flows, listening to pulses, the special body flows, and how these contribute to harmonizing body, mind, and spirit. Once a student has completed three full basic seminars, a certificate is issued signifying attainment of minimum practitioner-level training.

The five-day Now Know Myself Seminar further examines the wealth of information in Parts I and II. Participants experience "hands-on" daily as both practitioners and receivers.

The three-day Jin Shin Jyutsu Instructor Training in Self-Help (IT IS) is designed for those who wish to share self-help in a class setting or with friends. IT IS teaches how to present Jin Shin Jyutsu self-help confidently and in a clear and simple way.

Admission Requirements

For the Basic Seminars, Part I is a prerequisite for Part II. Applicants to the Now Know Myself Seminar must have completed the Basic Seminar three times. Applicants to the IT IS Seminar must have completed the Basic Seminar three times and have a basic knowledge of Mary Burmeister's self-help books.

Tuition and Fees

Tuition for Part I is $350 for new students and $180 for review students. Tuition for Part II is $250 for new students and $120 for review students. The Now Know Myself Seminar is $600. The Instructor Training in Self-Help Seminar is $275 for new students and $150 for review students.

Maui School of Yoga Therapy

Gary and Mirka Kraftsow
1030 East Kuiaha Road
Haiku, Hawaii 96798
Phone: (808) 572-1414
Internet: http://www.viniyoga.com

Gary Kraftsow began his Viniyoga studies with T.K.V. Desikachar in India twenty-two years ago. He has been an educator and therapist since 1976, conducts yoga seminars throughout the United States and Europe, and was the first American certified to train teachers in the Viniyoga lineage. Viniyoga is defined as the appropriate application of asana, pranayama, sound, visualization, meditation, and relaxation respecting individual needs. Workshops are held on Maui and in various locations throughout the mainland United States and Europe.

Program Description

There are fourteen units of study covered in seven sessions. Topics include Principles of Breath and Movement, The Science of Sequence, Principles of Adaptation, Observation: Reading the Body, Human Energy System, Pranayama, Bandhas and Mudras, Sound and Chanting, Meditation, Developing Personal Ritual, Teaching Methodology, Introduction to Yoga Therapy, Musculoskeletal Yoga Therapy, Common Pathologies, and Emotional Health. Private sessions and a retreat are also important parts of the program. The number of private sessions depends on the student's current level of proficiency and understanding. Some training work may also be done via fax, phone, and correspondence.

Admission Requirements

Please contact the school for admission requirements and opportunities to begin Viniyoga studies prior to starting the formal training program.

Tuition and Fees

Each seven-day training intensive on Maui costs $390. Costs for just the weekend classes are $120. Weekday classes cost $160. Additional costs (for private sessions, retreats, and so on) will vary according to the student's level of proficiency and understanding.

The Michael Scholes School for Aromatic Studies

117 North Robertson Boulevard
Los Angeles, California 90048
Phone: (310) 276-1191 / (800) 677-2368
Fax: (310) 276-1156
E-mail: mhscholes.aol.com

The Michael Scholes School for Aromatic Studies (formerly Aromatherapy Seminars) was founded in 1989 as a resource for essential oil education for both personal and professional use. Courses are held throughout the United States and Canada. Home study courses are described on page 361. Books, videos, blending kits, and other products are also available; see page 360.

Program Description

A one-year Aromatherapy Diploma Course (held in Los Angeles, New York, and Calgary, Alberta) consists of ten weekends or sixty evening classes. The course focuses on the practical applications of over one hundred essential oils, forty perfume absolutes, and over twenty-five carriers, presented through live lectures and demonstrations, video review, essential oil comparison, slide presentations, and practical blending. Topics include History, Distillation, Safety and Toxicology, Chemistry, Botany, Blending, the Aromatic Consultation, Designing Treatments, Basic Anatomy and Physiology, Massage Demonstration, Reflexology, Case Study Review, Hands-On Treatment, Anatomy of Skin and Hair, Child Care and First Aid, Ritual Use, Subtle Energy, the Chakra System, Fragrance and the Mind, Business of Aromatherapy, and more. Classes may also be taken individually.

A five-day Certification Program (offered in Miami, Vancouver, New York, Los Angeles, and Atlanta) offers instruction in the Botanical Families Approach, the Chemistry of Essential Oil Constituents, Hippocratic Temperaments, Blending, Aromatherapy and Massage, Subtle Aromatherapy, Aromatherapy and Skin and Hair Care, Aromatherapy for Pregnancy and Child-Care Workshop, AromaFitness Workshop, Psycho-Aromatherapy, the Business of Aromatherapy, and Hands-On Application.

Other specialty courses, educational tours, and residential programs are offered.

Admission Requirements

Those wishing to enroll in the five-day Certification Program must have taken one of the home study courses or attended a live class and completed all course requirements.

Tuition and Fees

Tuition for the one-year Diploma Course is $2,300 to $2,700. Tuition for the five-day Certification Program is $575.

Financial Assistance

A payment plan and work-study are available.

Myofascial Release Treatment Centers and Seminars

Routes 30 and 252
Suite 1, 10 South Leopard Road
Paoli, Pennsylvania 19301-1569
Phone: (800) FASCIAL

Physical therapist John F. Barnes originated the myofascial release approach and teaches all of the Myofascial Release I and II, Cervical-Thoracic, and Myofascial Unwinding Seminars. Seminars are held throughout the country.

Accreditation

Myofascial Release Seminars are approved for continuing education credits by many organizations, including the California Board of Registered Nursing, the National Certification Board for Therapeutic Massage and Bodywork (NCBTMB), several state boards of massage therapy, physical therapy associations, occupational therapy boards, and others.

Program Description

Myofascial Release I is a twenty-hour, hands-on introductory course that includes instruction in Anatomy of Fascia and Related Structures, Whole-Body Inter-Relationships, Development of Palpation Skills, Myofascial Release Techniques, and Craniosacral Therapy. This is a prerequisite for more advanced seminars.

The twenty-hour Cervical-Thoracic Myofascial/Osseous Integration Seminar covers specific myofascial release, joint mobilization, and muscle energy techniques for the thoracic-lumbar region, sternum, rib cage, thoracic spine, and other areas.

The twenty-hour Fascial-Pelvis Myofascial/Osseous Integration Seminar covers specific myofascial release, joint mobilization, and muscle energy techniques for the erector spinae, pelvic floor, lumbar area, sacroiliac joints, lower extremities, and other areas.

The twenty-hour Myofascial Unwinding Seminar teaches an effective movement facilitation technique utilized to decrease pain, increase range of motion, eliminate subconscious holding or bracing patterns, and more.

In the twenty-hour Myofascial Release II Seminar, students learn advanced myofascial release techniques and cranial procedures.

Twelve-hour introductory workshops include a Myofascial Mobilization Workshop that introduces myofascial release for upper and lower extremities, cervical, thoracic, and lumbar areas; and Pediatric Myofascial Release, in which myofascial release is presented for the evaluation and treatment of head injuries, cerebral palsy, birth trauma, scoliosis, pain, headaches, and more.

Admission Requirements

Applicants must be licensed to touch, i.e., as a physical therapist, physical therapy assistant, occupational therapist, occupational therapy assistant, massage therapist, athletic trainer, or speech and language therapist.

Tuition and Fees

Tuition for the Myofascial Release I, Fascial Pelvis Myofascial/Osseous Integration, Cervical Thoracic Myofascial/Osseous Integration, Myofascial Unwinding, and Myofascial Release II Seminars is $650 per seminar, $595 if registered two weeks prior to seminar date, or $325 for full-time undergraduate students and assistants.

Tuition for the Myofascial Mobilization Workshop and Pediatric Myofascial Release Workshop is $400 per seminar, $350 if registered two weeks prior to seminar date, or $225 for full-time undergraduate students and assistants.

Fees include workbook and materials.

National Institute of Classical Homeopathy

46 Suffield Street
Agawam, Massachusetts 01001
Phone: (860) 651-5213
Fax: (860) 651-7814
E-mail: thakkars@aol.com

The National Institute of Classical Homeopathy was founded in 1995. Director Sadhna Thakkar worked with Dr. Rajan Sankaran, author of the books *Spirit of Homeopathy* and *Substance of Homeopathy,* for four years. Classes are held on weekends in Los Angeles and Toronto.

Program Description

The institute offers two levels of instruction. Level I, based on *Spirit of Homeopathy,* covers principles of homeopathy, case-receiving, management, and the basis of potency selection, and includes extensive use of repertories and materia medica. Level II, based on *Substance of Homeopathy,* includes the concepts of kingdoms, the theory and application of miasms, and the creative use of repertories and new provings.

Admission Requirements

Level I is open to students familiar with the basics of homeopathy; some basic sciences are required. Level II is open to practitioners only.

Tuition and Fees

Registration is $75; tuition for Level I is $1,300, and for Level II, $1,650.

Financial Assistance

Payment plans and a 10 percent prepayment discount are available.

National Iridology Research Association

27676-B Tomball Parkway
Tomball, Texas 77375
Phone: (281) 255-4044
E-mail: MDJones@iridology.com

The National Iridology Research Association was founded in 1982 and strives to raise the levels of iridology education and practice in the United States. See page 352 for membership information.

Program Description

NIRA offers a Certification Program in Iridology that includes: Introduction to Applied Iridology, which covers the history and development of iridology and discussion of models—European, Applied Iridology, American, and Emotional (a minimum of three hours of classroom work; this portion can be extended at the instructor's discretion); Pre-Certification Course in Applied Iridology, which includes eye anatomy and physiology, topography and mapping of the iris, constitutional types and subtypes, pigmentation, corneal arcus, pupil tonus, iris structure, iris photography, and research (fourteen hours with a NIRA-certified instructor); Certification Intensive, which emphasizes case studies, combinations of signs, exceptions to rules, collarette study, specific constitutions and syndromes, emotional iridology models, and introduction to sclera/conjunctiva signs (twenty hours with a NIRA-cer-

tified instructor); and Certification Testing, in which the student must complete a typed slide case analysis at home and pass a written exam. Certified iridologists are given a certificate and listed in the *Iridology Review*. It will take approximately four months to complete the Pre-Certification and Certification Courses and to take Parts 1 and 2 of the Certification Test.

Continuing Education

Every two years, each certified iridologist must complete two NIRA-approved continuing education classes.

Admission Requirements

A course in anatomy and physiology from an accredited source must be completed at any time during the certification process.

Tuition and Fees

Classes are approximately $100 per day, with discounts given to early applicants and NIRA members (fees may vary among instructors). A class workbook is provided with the Pre-Certification and Certification Courses. Section I of the examination, Slide Analysis, costs $50. Section II, the Certification Exam, costs $75.

New England School of Homeopathy

356 Middle Street
Amherst, Massachusetts 01002
Phone: (860) 253-5040 / (800) NESH-440
Fax: (860) 253-5041

The New England School of Homeopathy (NESH) was founded in 1987 by Dr. Paul Herscu, D.C., N.D., D.H.A.N.P. Its purpose is to translate homeopathic philosophy into the successful and predictable practice of medicine. Most courses are held in the Northeast.

Program Description

NESH has provided training in classical homeopathy for over 1,500 students in the United States and abroad. Courses are designed to educate the beginner and to enhance and broaden the practicing homeopath's knowledge so that consistent, favorable results are delivered. For a current course schedule, contact NESH at the above address.

Admission Requirements

The NESH student body includes a wide range of health care practitioners, from medical, osteopathic, and naturopathic doctors to nurses, acupuncturists, chiropractors, psychologists, and non-doctor professional homeopaths. NESH also welcomes interested lay people at every level, from beginners to experienced practitioners. Applicants must submit a completed application form.

Tuition and Fees

Tuition ranges from $500 to $2,000, depending on the length of the course.

Financial Assistance

A payment plan is available.

New Hampshire Institute for Therapeutic Arts

153 Lowell Road
Hudson, New Hampshire 03051
Phone: (603) 882-3022

Maine Location:
39 Main Street
Bridgton, Maine 04009
Phone: (207) 647-3794

The New Hampshire Institute for Therapeutic Arts (NHITA) was founded in 1983. The institute in Hudson, New Hampshire shares space and clinical facilities with the Merrimack Valley Integral Health Center. The Bridgton, Maine facility also serves as a clinic for massage therapy and natural therapeutics.

Accreditation

The Massage Therapy Program at NHITA is approved by the American Massage Therapy Association Commission on Massage Training Accreditation/Approval (AMTA/COMTAA), and meets licensing requirements for the states of Maine and New Hampshire.

Program Description

The nine-month, 750-hour Massage Therapy Program includes courses in Embryology; First Aid, CPR, and Emergency Procedures; Anatomy and Physiology; Swedish Massage; Ethics and Professionalism; Reflexology; Reflex and Pressure Point Therapies; Public Health and Hygiene; Pathology; Hydrotherapy; Neuromuscular Technique; Human Sexuality; Nutrition; Neurology; Circulatory Massage; Lymphatic Drainage Massage; Eastern Techniques; Sports Massage; and Polarity, as well as a research report, research presentation, health service management, and massage practicum.

Community and Continuing Education

Continuing education, enrichment, and self-care programs are offered at both locations. Typical offerings include Yoga for You, Therapeutic Touch, the Four Temperaments and Birth Order, Seated Massage, Introduction to Homeopathy, Neurolinguistic Programming, Craniosacral Technique, Iridology, Circulatory Massage, Home Health Hydrotherapy, Wilderness First Aid, and Somatic Integration.

Admission Requirements

Applicants must be at least 18 years of age, have a high school diploma or equivalent, and interview with an admissions representative.

Tuition and Fees

There is a $35 application fee. Tuition is $4,825; books are approximately $300; a massage table is approximately $500; and oils and linens are approximately $125.

Tuition for continuing education and self-care classes varies from $10 to $225.

Financial Assistance

A payment plan is available.

Ohashi Institute

12 West 27th Street
New York, New York 10001
Phone: (800) 810-4190
Fax: (212) 447-5819

The Ohashi Institute was founded in 1974 by Ohashi, a young Japanese healer who sought to bridge (his name means "big bridge") the gap between Eastern and Western philosophies of healing. He created a program of bodywork, Ohashiatsu, that incorporates Eastern healing philosophy, natural movement, and touch techniques to balance body, mind, and spirit. The institute has branches in Baltimore, Chicago, Italy, and the Netherlands.

Program Description

The 300-hour Ohashiatsu program consists of nine required courses: Beginning Ohashiatsu I and II, Anatomy I and II for Ohashiatsu, Oriental Diagnosis, Intermediate Ohashiatsu I and II, and Advanced Ohashiatsu I and II. In addition, students are required to attend a minimum of ten practice classes and receive five private sessions from three or more certified Ohashiatsu instructors or consultants.

Continuing Education

Postgraduate education is offered through the Instructor Training Program or the Consultant Program.

Instructor Training takes twelve to eighteen months to complete and prepares the instructor to teach Beginning I and II levels. The course includes conducting practice classes, assisting certified Ohashiatsu instructors during four courses, and confirming teaching techniques through tutorials.

The Consultant Program allows graduates to continue their education and to use the Ohashiatsu trade name in developing their clientele. This entails continuing education, annual training, and tutorials.

Admission Requirements

Applicants need only have an open mind and a willingness to learn; there is no minimum age or educational requirement.

Tuition and Fees

Students proceed at their own pace and pay for each course individually.

The Beginning I course costs $455. Ohashi's Beginning I course taught by Ohashi costs $515. The Beginning II course costs $495. The Intermediate I course costs $595. The Intermediate II course costs $685. The Advanced I course costs $825. The Advanced II course costs $940. The Oriental Diagnosis course costs $395. The Anatomy I and II courses cost $340.

Additional expenses include: three tutorials, $65 each; Advanced II tutorial, $150; private sessions, $65; certificate of completion, $30; and required texts.

Financial Assistance

A work-study program is available. A $30 discount is offered for early registration.

Pacific College of Oriental Medicine

7445 Mission Valley Road, Suite 105
San Diego, California 92108-4408
Phone: (619) 574-6909
Fax: (619) 574-6641

Pacific Institute of Oriental Medicine
915 Broadway, Third Floor
New York, New York 10010
Phone: (212) 982-3456

The Pacific College of Oriental Medicine, Inc. (a California proprietary corporation) operates under the name of Pacific College of Oriental Medicine in San Diego and as Pacific Institute of Oriental Medicine in New York.

Accreditation

The Master of Traditional Oriental Medicine degree is accredited by the National Accreditation Commission for Schools and Colleges of Acupuncture and Oriental Medicine (NACSCAOM). Pacific College is approved by the California Acupuncture Committee, a division of the state medical board, and graduates of the Master of Traditional Oriental Medicine degree program are eligible to take the state of California Acupuncture Licensing Examination and the national certification exam given by the National Commission for the Certification of Acupuncturists (NCCA).

Pacific Institute's Diploma of Acupuncture and Diploma of Traditional Oriental Medicine Programs are accredited by NACSCAOM. Graduates of these programs are eligible to take the national certification exam given by NCCA and/or any acupuncture licensing exam required by New York. Currently, the state of New York uses the NCCA exam to determine licensing eligibility.

Program Description

The 2,807-hour Master's Program (California) or the Diploma of Traditional Chinese Medicine (New York) may be completed in a three-year accelerated track, or in four years or longer. Four years is the normal, full-time course of study. Course requirements include Oriental Medicine, Acupuncture Points, Herbology, Anatomy, Tui Na, Tai Chi Chuan, Clinical Techniques, Introduction to Orthopedic and Neurological Evaluation, Biophysics, CPR, Needle Techniques, Ethics/Philosophy, Pathophysiology, Biochemistry, Clinical Herbs, Clinical Science, Pharmacology, Biology, Diagnosis/Evaluation, Physical Exam, Eastern Nutrition, Western Nutrition, Qigong, and others.

Students in the 2,198-hour Diploma of Acupuncture Program (New York) may complete it in less than three years, depending on student ability and class availability. Courses include many of those required in the four-year programs.

Pacific College offers several programs of instruction in massage.

The Massage Technician Program consists of 112 hours of instruction leading to a certificate and eligibility for San Diego city licensing in massage. Instruction includes practical skills and tui na, an Oriental body therapy. An accelerated program may be completed in three weeks. Classes include Circulatory Massage, Public Safety and Hygiene,

Business Management and Ethics, Anatomy, and Tui Na Hand Techniques.

The 555-hour Massage Therapist Certificate Program emphasizes Oriental medical theory, advanced tui na, and shiatsu. The program generally takes three trimesters to complete. Courses include those listed under the Massage Technician Program as well as Oriental Medicine, Acupuncture Points, East-West Deep Tissue, Tui Na Structural Techniques, CPR/First Aid, Jin Shin, Qigong, Thai Massage, Shiatsu Massage, electives, and supervised massage practice.

The 1,115-hour Holistic Health Practitioner Program offers comprehensive training in practical massage skills, along with a deeper understanding of Oriental medical theory. Students study tui na and shiatsu, acupuncture point location and functions, movement therapies, and nutrition. The program generally takes five to six trimesters to complete, and graduates may apply to the city of San Diego for licensing as a holistic health practitioner. In San Diego, such practitioners may own and operate their own massage establishment, whereas massage technicians and massage therapists must work in a clinic or spa owned and operated by a holistic health practitioner, acupuncturist, chiropractor, or other health professional, or do out-call massage (massage in the client's home). Classes include those listed under the Massage Therapist Certificate Program as well as Tai Chi Chuan, Clinical Tui Na, Seitai Shiatsu, Alexander Technique, Clinical Counseling, Pediatric Tui Na, Sports Tui Na, Eastern Nutrition, Western Nutrition, and supervised massage practice.

Students may also take a combination of courses that lead to certificates in tui na or Chinese health and exercise, or an Oriental Body Therapist Certificate that meets the curriculum standards established by the American Oriental Bodywork Therapy Association (AOBTA).

Admission Requirements

For the Master of Traditional Oriental Medicine Degree Program (California), the Diploma of Traditional Oriental Medicine (New York), and the Diploma of Acupuncture (New York), applicants must have completed at least sixty semester units (two years) at the baccalaureate level or the equivalent. Applicants for the New York programs must have completed, within these sixty units, nine units in the biosciences. Applicants must also complete a personal essay, interview with the admissions committee, and be able to communicate in English.

Tuition and Fees

There is a $50 application fee and a $10 registration fee for all courses.

In California, tuition for the Master of Traditional Oriental Medicine Program is $26,320 plus fees, CPR, and supplies (estimated at $2,142). Tuition for the Holistic Health Practitioner Program is $7,260 plus fees, supplies (estimated at $350), CPR, and First Aid. Tuition for the Massage Therapist Program is $3,800 plus fees, supplies (estimated at $175), CPR, and First Aid. Tuition for the Massage Technician Program is $600, plus fees and supplies (estimated at $100).

In New York, tuition for the Diploma of Acupuncture Program is $21,646 plus fees, CPR, and supplies (estimated at $1,681). Tuition for the Diploma of Traditional Oriental Medicine Program is $28,162 plus fees, CPR, and supplies (estimated at $2,142).

Financial Assistance

Federal grants and loans are available to eligible acupuncture/traditional Oriental medicine students who are enrolled on at least a half-time basis.

Phoenix Rising Yoga Therapy

P.O. Box 819
402 Park Street, 2nd Floor
Housatonic, Massachusetts 01236
Phone: (413) 274-3515 / (800) 288-9642
Fax: (413) 274-6166
E-mail: PRYToff@aol.com
Internet: www.pryt.com

Phoenix Rising Yoga Therapy was founded in 1986 by Michael Lee, who holds a master's degree in holistic education and has directed programs at the Kripalu Center for Yoga and Health. The school currently has training locations in Lenox, Massachusetts; La Jolla and Watsonville, California; Columbia, Maryland; Tampa, Florida; and Canada, and has offered programs in Canada, Pennsylvania, Oregon, Georgia, Arizona, the state of Washington, and Washington, D.C.

Accreditation

Phoenix Rising Yoga Therapy is an approved provider with the NBCC (National Board of Certified Counselors). CEU credits are available for some nursing associations.

Program Description

Professional Certification Training Courses are offered at three levels.

Level 1 consists of thirty-two hours of instruction focusing on the principles and practice of Phoenix Rising Yoga Therapy. Students learn techniques for assisting clients in yoga therapy postures, precautions, physical benefits, counter postures, how to guide clients in a body scan to determine areas of tension, and general outlines for yoga therapy sessions.

Level 2 (thirty-two hours) focuses on therapeutic dialogue techniques, including listening, following, questioning, and responding techniques, as well as how to use the yoga therapy session as part of a transformational life process.

Level 3 takes the form of an internship/practicum. It requires twenty practice sessions, attendance at a three-day workshop focusing on refinement of skills, a presentation of the student's work, selected readings, exchange sessions with peers, and attendance at practice days in the student's area. Work is spread over six months (242 hours).

Admission Requirements

Level 1 is open to those who have been practicing any traditional style of yoga regularly for at least three months, or who have been engaged in another body-oriented discipline. Level 1 is a prerequisite for Level 2, and Level 2 is a prerequisite for Level 3.

Tuition and Fees

Level 1 costs $495; Level 2 costs $525; Levels 1 and 2 may be taken consecutively over nine days for $995; and Level 3 costs $1,895.

Financial Assistance

Payment plans are available.

Polarity Realization Institute

126 High Street
Ipswich, Massachusetts 01938-1248
Phone: (508) 356-0980 (Massachusetts) /
    (207) 828-8622 (Maine)

The Polarity Realization Institute, founded in 1980, supports and promotes higher levels of self-healing and self-realization through honoring the life force with love, respect, and integrity. Weekend and evening programs are currently offered in both Ipswich, Massachusetts and Portland, Maine.

Accreditation

Programs at the Polarity Realization Institute are accredited by the International Massage and Somatic Therapies Accreditation Council (IMSTAC), a division of the Associated Bodywork and Massage Professionals (ABMP), and by the American Polarity Therapy Association (APTA). All massage trainings of 600 hours or more enable students to meet the eligibility requirements of the national certification exam administered by the National Certification Board for Therapeutic Massage and Bodywork (NCBTMB). The 880-hour Holistic Massage and Bodywork Program meets the New Hampshire licensing exam eligibility requirements. The institute is licensed by the Commonwealth of Massachusetts Department of Education and by the State of Maine Department of Education.

Program Description

The 650-hour Polarity Realization Certification Program is divided into two levels: a 160-hour Level 1 training and an additional 490-hour Level 2 training. The levels may be taken together or individu-

ally, and may be completed in eighteen months or longer. Classes may be attended at either location.

Level 1 prepares students to receive the Associate Polarity Practitioner (A.P.P.) level of recognition from APTA. Students are guided toward an understanding of healing energies and polarity principles and assisted with personal healing and professional needs, with an emphasis on reaching higher levels of clarity, harmony, and inner peace. Additional requirements include thirty documented student practice sessions, five sessions received from professional polarity practitioners, and five additional outside study hours.

Level 2 prepares students to receive Registered Polarity Practitioner (R.P.P.) registration from APTA. There are nine components to this training: Polarity Systems Work (176 hours); Polarity Yoga and Nutrition (forty-eight hours); Anatomy and Physiology (forty-eight hours); Business Skills (thirty-two hours); Raising Your Sublime Energies (fifteen hours); Lifestyle Commitment; Outside Work (one hundred sessions given, ten sessions received, and First Aid/CPR); Internship (forty hours); and Clinical Supervision (twenty-four hours).

Holistic Massage and Bodywork Programs are offered in lengths of 180, 600, 750, and 880 hours. The 180-hour Therapeutic Massage Program requires Module 1—Therapeutic Massage and Basic Anatomy and Physiology. The 600-hour Holistic Massage and Bodywork Program requires Modules 1, 2A or 2B, 190 hours in Module 3, and Modules 4 and 5. The 750-hour Holistic Massage and Bodywork Program requires Modules 1, 2A, 342 hours in Module 3, and Modules 4 and 5. The 880-hour Holistic Massage and Bodywork Program requires Modules 1, 2A, 438 hours in Module 3, and Modules 4 and 5.

Module 1—Therapeutic Massage consists of 180 hours: ninety-six hours of therapeutic massage, forty-eight hours of anatomy and physiology, thirty documented sessions (thirty hours), and six professional sessions received (six hours). Module 1 may be taken without continuing with other modules.

Module 2A—Polarity Realization Associate Certification consists of 160 hours: polarity realization therapy theory and bodywork (120 hours), thirty documented sessions given (thirty hours), five professional sessions received (five hours), and additional outside study (five hours).

Module 2B—Intermediate Therapeutic Massage consists of 160 hours: massage theory and bodywork (120 hours), thirty documented sessions given (thirty hours), five professional sessions received (five hours), and additional outside study (five hours).

Module 3 consists of 190 to 460 hours in advanced bodywork and massage electives that include Clinics, Hydrotherapy, Business Skills, and other topics.

Module 4 consists of fifty-six hours in Advanced Anatomy and Physiology.

Module 5 consists of twenty-four hours in Advanced Integration and Evaluation.

Admission Requirements

Polarity Level 1 is open to all who wish to learn more about polarity therapy. Level 1 is a prerequisite for Level 2. Massage Module 1 is open to all who wish to learn about therapeutic massage. A phone interview is required.

Tuition and Fees

Tuition for Polarity Level 1 is $1,425. There is a $50 registration fee; five required sessions cost $200 to $300; books and supplies cost $80; and a massage table costs $300 to $600. Tuition for Level 2 is $3,957. There is a $50 registration fee, which is waived for students going directly from Level 1 to Level 2; ten required sessions cost $400 to $600; books and supplies cost $80; and a First Aid/CPR class costs $60.

Tuition for the 180-hour Massage Program is $1,710; for the 600-hour program, $5,087; for the 750-hour program, $6,622; and for the 880-hour program, $7,591. Additional costs include books and supplies, $110 to $160; and a massage table, $350 to $550; outside sessions are additional. Modules and classes may be taken individually.

Financial Assistance

Interest-free payment plans are available.

The School for Body-Mind Centering

189 Pondview Drive
Amherst, Massachusetts 01002-3230
Phone: (413) 256-8615
Fax: (413) 256-8239

Body-Mind Centering is a system of movement reeducation and hands-on repatterning developed by Bonnie Bainbridge Cohen. It is an experiential study based on the embodiment and application of anatomical, physiological, psychological, and developmental principles, utilizing movement, touch, voice, and awareness. Certification classes are taught in Amherst, Massachusetts; Berkeley, California; and Amsterdam, Holland.

Program Description

Certification programs in Body-Mind Centering last for four terms. The Massachusetts term is seven weeks each summer; the California and Amsterdam terms are divided into three 2-week modules. Material covered includes the relationship of the body systems to movement and touch, developmental movement, and perceptions. Classes are taught by Bonnie Bainbridge Cohen and certified teachers of Body-Mind Centering.

In order to be certified as a practitioner of Body-Mind Centering, students must complete all the courses in the four-term certification program; additional studies outside the school (before or after beginning the program) in anatomy, physiology, kinesiology, counseling, movement, bodywork, nutrition, mind practices, and music, voice, and/or visual arts; eight private sessions and eight supervised sessions with a certified practitioner or teacher; one hundred hours of community service; and a final project and presentation.

Admission Requirements

The certification program is designed for those with some experience in the fields of movement, dance, bodywork, body-related psychotherapy, or other body-mind disciplines.

Tuition and Fees

Tuition is $3,700 per term; books, supplies, and individual sessions are additional.

Financial Assistance

A discount is given for early registration.

School for Self-Healing

1718 Taraval Street
San Francisco, California 94116
Phone: (415) 665-9574
Fax: (415) 665-1318

The School for Self-Healing, founded in 1984, offers training not only in San Francisco, but in other U.S. cities and in England, Brazil, Hungary, and Israel. Founder Meir Schneider, Ph.D., L.M.T., is the author of *Self-Healing: My Life and Vision* and co-author of *The Handbook of Self-Healing: Your Personal Program for Better Health and Increased Vitality*; he and Carol Gallup have written a column, "Self-Healing," for *Massage* magazine since March 1996. Though blind at birth, Schneider used his unique self-healing method to restore his vision.

Accreditation

The School for Self-Healing is licensed by the State of California and is approved to offer continuing education credits to nurses. A Massage Practitioner Certificate is awarded upon successful completion of Segment B; this satisfies the requirements for a license in San Francisco. Prospective students are advised to consult local authorities, as massage licensing requirements vary from county to county.

Program Description

The Meir Schneider Self-Healing Method combines massage, movement, and other tools into powerful therapies that can strengthen vulnerable organ systems and reverse degenerative conditions.

The Self-Healing Practitioner/Educator Training consists of Level One (Segments A and B), Level Two, and an apprenticeship. Segment A (Supporting Breathing, Circulation, Digestion, and the Spine and Joints) consists of eighty hours in eight consecutive days of beginning massage and movement. Segment B (Supporting Muscles, the Nervous System, and the Visual System) consists of eighty-four hours in eight-and-a-half consecutive days of intermediate massage and movement and beginning vision improvement exercises. In Level Two: Professional Training (one hundred hours), students perform about forty hands-on sessions with clients and participate in evaluating many more; topics include advanced client evaluation and assessment, client-related pathology, exercise selection and invention, advanced discussion of self-healing principles, beginning client education, and more. In the apprenticeship, students spend 500 hours working directly under the supervision of Meir Schneider or another instructor, and self-healing principles and techniques are integrated into full practice.

Admission Requirements

Segment A applicants must have a high school diploma or equivalent and be able, in the opinion of the instructor, to complete the course work with the accommodations that the school is able to offer.

Tuition and Fees

Tuition for Segment A is $1,200, plus $150 for books and materials; tuition for Segment B is $1,100, plus $49 for books and materials; tuition for Level Two is $1,900; and tuition for the apprenticeship is $1,900. There is a $100 registration fee for all courses; the total cost of the program is $6,699.

Financial Assistance

Payment plans are available; some discounts apply.

Stens Corporation

6451 Oakwood Drive
Oakland, California 94611-1350
Phone: (510) 339-9053 / (800) 257-8367
Fax: (510) 339-2222
E-mail: STENSCO@aol.com

The Stens Corporation offers professional biofeedback training at locations throughout the country, and is a national leader in sales of biofeedback equipment.

Accreditation

The Professional Biofeedback Certificate Program is accredited by the Biofeedback Certification Institute of America (BCIA). The program provides most of the hours required to take BCIA's national examination, with the exception of the required thirty hours of clinical supervision and ninety hours of direct treatment with patients. Stens Corporation can help with finding an appropriate supervisor for clinical supervision. Direct treatment can be done with clients in your own office or in another therapist's office; supervision is not required.

Program Description

The Professional Biofeedback Certificate Program consists of two parts.

Part One: Didactic Education and Clinical Biofeedback Training is a four-day, thirty-six-hour program held Saturday through Tuesday. The program covers Introduction to Biofeedback and Clinical Applications (Fight/Flight Response, Selye's General Adaptation Syndrome, Behavioral Medicine, Progressive Relaxation, Diaphragmatic Breathing, and more), Instrumentation (Environmental Noise, Terms and Concepts, EMG, EEG, GSR and TEMP, Respiration, Panel Controls, and more), and Hands-On Training (including EMG Lab, TEMP Lab, GSR Lab, Computer Experience, Patient Demonstration, and Role-Playing).

Part Two: Clinical Applications and Case Conference is a five-day, forty-four-hour program held Wednesday through Sunday. The program covers Stress-Related Disorders and Procedures: Clinical History and Evaluation (Structure of the Autonomic Nervous System, Treatment Planning, Migraine Headaches, Asthma, Dental Disorders, Anxiety, EMG Scanning, Current Research, and more), Business and Financial Issues (Forms and Records, Insurance Reimbursement, Referral Sources, and more), and Adjunctive Techniques (including Learning Theory, Visualization, Placebo, Nutrition, Medications, Autogenic Training, Guided Imagery, and Hypnosis).

The Stens Corporation also offers a series of three-day BCIA Exam Review Courses, as well as a computer software program, Self-Assessment in Biofeedback, that is based on the BCIA test blueprint.

Community and Continuing Education

The first two days of Surface EMG for Chronic Pain Management (a four-day seminar) and Clinical Applications of EEG Biofeedback (a four-day seminar) are combined with the last two days of Part II in the same location.

Admission Requirements

There are no minimum age or educational requirements.

Tuition and Fees

Part One of the Professional Biofeedback Certificate Program costs $795; Part Two costs $995. The three-day BCIA Exam Review Course costs $495. The Surface EMG for Chronic Pain Management Seminar costs $795. The Clinical Applications of EEG Biofeedback Seminar costs $795.

3HO International Kundalini Yoga Teachers Association

Route 2 Box 4 Shady Lane
Espanola, New Mexico 87532
Phone: (505) 753-0423
Fax: (505) 753-5982
E-mail: ikyta@nnm.cc.nm.us

The 3HO International Kundalini Yoga Teachers Association, founded in 1969 by Yogi Bhajan, Ph.D., Master of Kundalini yoga, offers Kundalini Yoga Teacher Training in several cities worldwide under the auspices of Kundalini Research Institute (KRI), and as summer intensives in New Mexico under the direct supervision of Yogi Bhajan. In the past, the training has been held in Toronto, Ottawa, Vancouver, Boston, New York, Portland, Seattle, Phoenix, Los Angeles, Anchorage, Washington, D.C., and Espanola, New Mexico. In 1997, the training will be held in at least thirty other U.S. cities; call for an updated list.

Program Description

The five-month, 110-hour, Level 1 Kundalini Yoga

Teacher Training Certification Program covers the Eight Limbs of Yoga and the Patanjali Sutras; the History and Philosophy of Kundalini Yoga, the Eighty-One Facets of the Mind, and the Ten Bodies; Kundalini Yoga Kriyas, Pranayama, Mantras, and Meditations; 3HO Lifestyle Techniques, including Sadhana for the Aquarian Age and the Science of Hydrotherapy; and practicums in class presentation and curriculum development. Instruction is divided into three units: the Conceptual Foundation of Kundalini Yoga and the Basics of Practice; Intermediate Practices and the Deeper Mastery of Personal Vitality and Breath; and Advanced Techniques and Mastering Your Word. Students may participate as either a full-time certification student or as a full- or part-time workshop student without certification. Classes are held as weekend intensives and on weeknights. Students may learn about the program by attending one of the regularly scheduled classes.

The association is currently developing Level 2 and Level 3 Certification Programs.

Admission Requirements

Applicants must be at least 17 years of age and have a high school diploma.

Tuition and Fees

Tuition (estimated) is $1,300 paid in full, $425 per unit, or $250 per weekend intensive or series of five weeknight practicums.

Financial Assistance

A discount is given for prepayment.

The Trager Institute

21 Locust
Mill Valley, California 94941-2806
Phone: (415) 388-2688
Fax: (415) 388-2710
E-mail: tragerd@trager.com

The Trager approach is a system of movement education created and developed by Milton Trager, M.D. The approach uses gentle movements to help release deep-seated physical and mental patterns and facilitate deep relaxation, increased physical mobility, and mental clarity. The positive results are reinforced by Mentastics, simple movements that the client can do on his or her own. Trainings are held throughout the country.

Accreditation

The Trager Institute is approved by the National Certification Board for Therapeutic Massage and Bodywork (NCBTMB), and by the California Board of Registered Nursing as a continuing education provider; the institute is also approved by the Florida Department of Professional Regulation to provide continuing education credits for Florida state massage therapists. In the State of California, the Trager Certification Program is approved by the Council for Private Postsecondary and Vocational Education.

Program Description

The Trager Institute's Professional Certification Program takes a minimum of six months to complete. The program consists of a six-day Beginning Training, a five-day Intermediate Training, and a six-day Anatomy and Physiology Training, with a period of fieldwork and evaluations after the Beginning and Intermediate Trainings. The fieldwork consists of giving at least sixty Trager sessions without charge and receiving at least twenty sessions, as well as completing at least five tutorials (private lessons).

Exemption from the anatomy and physiology training is given to those with medical or paramedical licensure, or those who are graduates from 500-hour (or more) massage certification programs.

Expansion of certification requirements is planned for 1997.

Continuing Education

A certified Trager practitioner is required to take at least one 3-day practitioner training per year for the first three years; after that time, one training is required every three years. In addition, one tutorial is required for each year of practice, along with receiving four sessions from certified practitioners.

Admission Requirements

Membership in the Trager Institute is a prerequisite for beginning the program. Applicants must receive at least two sessions from a certified Trager practitioner, or receive one session and attend either an introductory workshop or six hours of Mentastics classes.

Tuition and Fees

Student membership fees are $85 per year. Tuition for the Beginning Training is $600; for the Intermediate Training, $500; and for Trager anatomy and physiology, $600. One-day introductory workshops range from $45 to $75. Public Mentastics classes range from $5 to $8 per hour. Sessions with certified practitioners range from $35 to $75. Tutorials range from $25 to $45 per hour and usually last two hours. The total certification program is approximately 270 hours and costs approximately $2,500 plus membership dues.

The Wellness Institute

3716 274th Avenue S.E.
Issaquah, Washington 98027
Phone: (206) 391-9716 / (800) 326-4418

The Wellness Institute was founded by Diane Zimberoff, M.A., in 1985. Six-day Certification Seminars are offered in various locations throughout the country, including Chicago, New York, Houston, Savannah, Syracuse, Detroit, Boston, Seattle, Denver, Atlanta, and Honolulu, and around the world from Kuwait to Taiwan. Seminars are taught by various institute trainers.

Accreditation

The six-day Certification in Hypnotherapy is approved for continuing education units for M.S.W.s, Ph.D.s, M.F.C.C.s, and others by many national associations and state licensing boards.

Program Description

The Wellness Institute offers a six-day Certification in Hypnotherapy. Training combines traditional hypnosis, Ericksonian techniques, and NLP with Gestalt and Transactional Analysis into a therapeutic approach called Hypno-Behavioral Therapy that addresses mind, body, and spirit. Topics include Introduction to Hypnosis, How to Induce and Deepen Hypnotic Trance, Self-Hypnosis, Treating the Dysfunctional Family with Hypnotherapy, the Mind/Body Connection, Sexual Abuse, Multiple Personality, NLP and Ericksonian Techniques, Hypnosis with Children, Eating Disorders, Birth Trauma, and others.

Continuing Education

Advanced training is available.

Admission Requirements

Certification is open to Ph.D. and master's-level therapists or the equivalent in practice.

Tuition and Fees

Tuition is $895.

Financial Assistance

A discount is given for early registration.

Wyrick Institute for European Manual Lymph Drainage

P.O. Box 99745
San Diego, California 92169
Phone: (619) 273-9764

Wyrick Institute was founded in 1984 by Dana Wyrick, who has been practicing manual lymph drainage since 1982. Basic classes are held in San Diego and elsewhere in the United States; advanced classes are held in San Diego.

Program Description

The institute offers Basic and Advanced Courses in manual lymph drainage.

In the five-day Basic Body Course, students receive an introduction to manual lymph drainage theory, learn the five basic movements, and use these movements in routines effective on all parts of the body. Students receive a certificate of completion.

In the five-day Advanced Body Course, students perfect the basic techniques and learn therapeutic movements for the head, abdomen, and joints. An examination is given and a diploma awarded.

Admission Requirements

Applicants must have a health license or local minimal massage license.

Tuition and Fees

Tuition is $500 to $600 per course.

CANADA

Canadian Academy of Homeopathy

3044 Bloor Street West, Suite 203
Toronto, Ontario M8X 1C4
Canada
Phone: (416) 503-4003
Fax: (416) 503-2799

The Canadian Academy of Homeopathy was founded in 1986 by a group of naturopathic physicians to provide high-quality educational programs in homeopathy, and to promote the practice of homeopathic medicine throughout Canada and the world. Classes are held in Toronto and Montreal.

Accreditation

The postgraduate, advanced-level courses at the Canadian Academy of Homeopathy are accredited by the Council on Homeopathic Education (CHE).

Program Description

The Homeopathic Program is offered in four successive parts that total 728 hours of instruction. Part I (seventy hours) consists of Introduction to Homeopathy, Homeopathic First Aid, and Principles and Practice of Acute Prescribing. Part II is an Introduction to Chronic Prescribing (154 hours). Part III: Advanced Chronic Prescribing (504 hours) is the most comprehensive segment of the program, covering such topics as History, Philosophy, the Basis of Medicine, Homeopathy: The Science of Therapeutics, Practice (including case taking, case analysis, repertorization, the prescription, the follow-up visit, the second prescription, difficult cases, homeopathy and prophylaxis, diet regimen and supportive measures during homeopathic treatment, and the use of the computer in homeopathy), Materia Medica, Study of the Repertory, Clinics, and 152 hours of practice. Part IV consists of forty-eight hours of continuing education over two years.

Classes meet seven hours a day during a four-day session, six times per year. Students may either audit the class to improve their skills or study to become a Fellow of the Canadian Academy of Homeopathy (FCAH). All classes are audio- and videotaped and are available for sale.

Admission Requirements

Part I is open to primary contact health care professionals trained in pathology and diagnosis (N.D., M.D., D.O., D.C., D.D.S., nurse practitioners, physician's assistants, midwives, D.V.M., pharmacists, nurses, and psychologists), or to students enrolled in such a program.

Tuition and Fees

Tuition is $440 per four-day class; clinical training is arranged on an individual basis with the instructor. Classes on audio- or videotapes are an additional $85 each.

Canadian College of Massage and Hydrotherapy

49 Lorne Street
P.O. Box 1270
Jackson's Point, Ontario L0E 1L0
Canada
Phone: (905) 722-3162 / (905) 722-6557
Fax: (905) 7223106

The Canadian College of Massage and Hydrotherapy (CCMH) was founded in 1946, as requested by the Department of Veterans' Affairs and the Canadian Veterans' Institute, in order to create opportunities for World War II veterans to train as massage therapists and aid in the rehabilitation of other veterans. The school has locations in both Canada and the United States, with the main school and clinic in Jackson's Point and Sutton, Ontario; other locations include the American School campus in Boca Raton, Florida; a Toronto teaching clinic; and a sports clinic in Denver, Colorado.

Accreditation

The curriculum at CCMH is approved by the American Massage Therapy Association Commission on Massage Training Accreditation/Approval (AMTA/COMTAA). In Canada, CCMH is accredited by the National Accreditation Commission.

Program Description

The college offers massage therapy programs of 2,200 hours in Jackson's Point (full-time), Toronto (full- and part-time), and Boca Raton, Florida (full-time), as well as a 700-hour, full-time program in Boca Raton.

Towards the 2,200 hour program, preparatory courses in Anatomy, Physiology, and Massage Theory are held at the Jackson's Point facility during the weekends in July and November (prior to September and January enrollment). The 2,200-hour, two-year curriculum includes Terminology, Osteology, Myology, Splanchnology (the study of organs), Pathology, Neurology, Ir (the study of the therapeutic use of light), Massage Theory, Self-Care, Assessments, Principles of Treatments, Sports Outreach, Institutional Care, Neurophysiology, Kinesiology, Remedial Exercises, Nutrition, Public Health, Hydrotherapy, First Aid, CPR, and more.

The 700-hour program includes Anatomy/Histology, Physiology/Pathology, Massage Theory and Practice, Dietetics and Nutrition, Hydrotherapy Theory and Practice, Introduction to Allied Modalities, HIV/AIDS, Remedial Exercise, Self-Care and Communication, Business Management, Hygiene and Public Management, First Aid and CPR, and State of Florida Rules and Regulations.

Continuing Education

Additional programs offered in Toronto include Shiatsu Introduction, Shiatsu Advanced Course, Reflexology, Aromatherapy Introduction, Nutritional Science, Herbology Introduction, Iridology, and Acupuncture. Additional massage therapy-related instruction is available in the form of optional courses in Deep Tissue, Joint Play, Connective Tissue, Sports Medicine, Lymphatic Technique, Reflexology, Homeopathic Medicine and Acupuncture, and Shiatsu.

Admission Requirements

Applicants must have completed Grade 12 or equivalent, including Grade 12 or 13 biology, chemistry, or anatomy credit. Applicants must also have received at least three professional massages.

Tuition and Fees

Tuition for the 2,200-hour program is $12,950, including linens and incidental clinic supplies; First Aid/CPR, clinical shirts, and exam copies are additional. Tuition for the 700-hour program is $4,100 in United States funds.

Financial Assistance

Payment plans and student loans are available.

Dr. Vodder School—North America

P.O. Box 5701
Victoria, British Columbia V8R 6S8
Canada
Phone/Fax: (250) 598-9862
E-mail: drvodderna@tnet.net

The Dr. Vodder School—North America was founded in 1994, although the Dr. Vodder method of manual lymph drainage was started by Emil and Estrid Vodder in France in the 1930s and has been taught in North America since the 1970s; the current director, Robert Harris, has been teaching the technique since 1987. The postgraduate training in manual lymph drainage is the most comprehensive program of its kind in North America.

Accreditation

The Dr. Vodder School—North America is approved by the National Certification Board for Therapeutic Massage and Bodywork (NCBTMB) as a continuing education provider. Courses may be eligible for continuing education credit from various local and national licensing bodies.

Program Description

Manual Lymph Drainage and Combined Decongestive Therapy Training is offered in four consecutive parts (Basic and Therapy I, II, and III), each of which lasts five days, for a total of 160 hours of classroom education. The first two courses are offered independently at various locations throughout North America.

The forty-hour Basic Program covers anatomy and physiology of the lymph vessel system, connective tissue, effects of MLD, contraindications, and MLD treatment of the full body, including all basic strokes. The forty-hour Therapy I covers special techniques for the joints, the head, and deep abdominal work, introducing the student to therapeutic applications; advanced theory and current research is discussed. Therapy II and III, taught consecutively for eighty classroom hours, cover various pathologies with an emphasis on lymphedema treatment in the context of combined decongestive therapy; bandaging and specific MLD treatments are taught. Students who successfully complete the oral, written, and practical exams at the end of the course may describe themselves as Vodder-Certified MLD Therapists.

Continuing Education

An annual twenty-five-hour Review Course is available to therapists to update and review their skills. Certified therapists must attend a review at least every two years to maintain their certification.

Admission Requirements

Enrollment is open to licensed or certified health care practitioners, including massage therapists who have completed a minimum of 500 hours at a massage therapy school, or who have successfully completed the national certification exam.

Tuition and Fees

Tuition is approximately $550 per five-day course.

Health Training Group

3789 Hampton Avenue
Montreal, Quebec H4A 2K7
Canada
Phone: (514) 485-7853 / (514) 485-6373
   (Eastern Canada) /
   (604) 858-8963 (Western Canada) /
   (206) 527-0807 (Seattle) /
   (808) 322-0048 (Hawaii)
Fax: (514) 486-9252

The Health Training Group, founded in 1986 by Howard Kiewe and Gayle Lang, offers training in Eastern and Western Canada, Seattle, Hawaii, Finland, and Sweden. Director Howard Kiewe has taught polarity therapy and other holistic methods internationally for over twelve years, and has published original research on polarity therapy's electrical characteristics.

Accreditation

Both the Associate Polarity Practitioner (A.P.P.) and Registered Polarity Practitioner (R.P.P.) training Programs are accredited by the American Polarity Therapy Association (APTA).

Program Description

The 245-hour Level I A.P.P. Training consists of classroom work (119 hours) offering an in-depth study of all aspects of polarity, guided independent study in polarity theory (twenty-five hours), clinical practice and integration (one hundred hours), and testing (one hour). Classes are held over three days (weekends). Students who wish to become registered with APTA must also have five private sessions with an R.P.P.

The 740-hour Level II R.P.P. Training consists of classroom work (379 hours), guided independent study (sixty hours), clinical practice and integration (300 hours), and testing (one hour). The classroom schedule consists of eighteen weekend seminars. Students who wish to become registered with APTA must also have ten private sessions with an R.P.P. (in addition to the five required for A.P.P.).

Admission Requirements

Because the A.P.P. guided independent study begins with work that develops the necessary knowledge base, there are no other prerequisites. Completion of a Level I A.P.P. Program is a prerequisite for the Level II R.P.P. Program.

Tuition and Fees

Tuition for the Level I Training is $1,250, including books; private R.P.P. sessions are additional. Tuition for the Level II Training is $3,400, including books; private R.P.P. sessions are additional.

Financial Assistance

A payment plan and prepayment discount are available.

Sinvananda Ashram Yoga Camp

673 Eighth Avenue
Val Morin, Quebec J0T 2R0
Canada
Phone: (819) 322-3226 / (800) 263-YOGA
Internet: isyvc-hq@nordnet.intlaurentidesq.ca

In 1968, Swami Vishnu-devananda developed the first Yoga Teacher's Training Course in the West. Since then, more than 7,500 teachers have been trained in accordance with his program. Teacher's Training Courses are taught in Quebec, California, New York, Europe, the Bahamas, and India.

Program Description

Four-week Yoga Teacher's Training Courses are taught by senior disciples personally trained by Swami Vishnu-devananda. The full daily schedule reflects the ancient yogic Gurukula system of training, in which the student's daily life itself was his or her yoga practice. The curriculum includes Asanas (to increase flexibility, strength, and concentration and receive training in teaching techniques); Pranayama (daily practice of breathing exercises); Meditation; Mantras and Japa Yoga (science of the spiritual power of sound vibrations); Vedanta and Philosophy (study of the wisdom of India's sages); Bhagavad Gita (study of the classical paths of yoga); Chanting; Karma Yoga (the yoga of selfless service); Yogic Diet (the principles behind vegetarianism); and Kriyas (purification techniques). No meat, fish, eggs, alcohol, tobacco, or non-prescription drugs are allowed, and participation in all classes is mandatory.

Admission Requirements

A basic knowledge of yoga postures is helpful but not essential.

Tuition and Fees

Teacher's Training Courses in Canada and the United States cost $1,350 (U.S.) for tent or shared rooms, and $1,700 to $1,845 (U.S.) for dormitory lodging; books are additional.

APPENDICES

Accrediting Agencies and Councils on Education

Before you commit yourself (as well as your time and money) to a particular program, it is a good idea to learn as much as you can about the program. Naturally, you should send for a catalog from the school, but an agency that accredits schools in your chosen field of study can provide you with additional information. This section lists the names and addresses of a number of agencies that accredit, approve, or recommend schools or programs within schools. You may want to contact these agencies about a particular program you have in mind.

GENERAL

Accrediting Commission of Career Schools and Colleges of Technology (ACCSCT)

2101 Wilson Boulevard, Suite 302
Arlington, Virginia 22201
Phone: (703) 247-4212
Fax: (703) 247-4533

ACCSCT is an accrediting agency for private colleges and schools offering occupational, trade, and technical education. In order to become accredited, institutions must be open to the public, have been in operation for at least two years, have graduated at least one class of students from its longest program, and conduct a self-assessment that evaluates how well the school meets accreditation standards. Schools must submit documentation of compliance with standards in the areas of admission policies, advertising and promotion, enrollment agreement, faculty, financial stability, instructional materials, placement, student complaints, student progress, student recruitment, and tuition and refund policies. The commission conducts on-site reviews to verify information in the self-assessment.

Accrediting Council for Continuing Education and Training (ACCET)

1560 Wilson Boulevard, Suite 900
Arlington, Virginia 22209
Phone: (703) 525-3000
Fax: (703) 525-3339

The Accrediting Council for Continuing Education and Training (ACCET) is a voluntary group of educational organizations affiliated for the purpose of improving continuing education and training. Through its support of an independent accrediting commission, ACCET promulgates and sustains the standards for accreditation, along with policies and procedures that measure and ensure educational standards of quality. ACCET is recognized for this purpose by the U.S. Secretary of Education and, accordingly, is listed by the U.S. Department of Education as a nationally recognized accrediting agency.

In order to become accredited by ACCET, schools must have been in operation for at least two years, must document financial and administrative capability, and must document their educational mission within prescribed guidelines. School representatives must attend a pre-accreditation workshop and document compliance with standards, after which the council conducts an on-site review.

ACUPUNCTURE AND ORIENTAL MEDICINE

National Accreditation Commission for Schools and Colleges of Acupuncture and Oriental Medicine (NACSCAOM)

1010 Wayne Avenue, Suite 1270
Silver Spring, Maryland 20910
Phone: (301) 608-9680
Fax: (301) 608-9576
E-mail: 73352.2467@compuserve.com

NACSCAOM was established in June 1982 by the Council of Colleges of Acupuncture and Oriental Medicine (CCAOM) as a means of fostering excellence in acupuncture and Oriental medicine education. The commission acts independently to evaluate professional master's degree and master's-level certificate and diploma programs in acupuncture and Oriental medicine, with a concentration in both acupuncture and herbal therapies. The commission establishes accreditation criteria, arranges site visits, evaluates programs, and publicly designates those that meet the criteria. The commission is the sole agency recognized by the U.S. Department of Education and the Commission on Recognition of Postsecondary Accreditation to accredit professional programs in this field.

To be eligible for accreditation, a program must comply with fourteen essential requirements that provide minimum guidelines for assessment of broad areas of institutional structure. These include purpose, legal organization, governance, administration, records, admissions, evaluation, program of study, faculty, student services and activities, library and learning resources, physical facilities and equipment, financial resources, and publications and advertising.

To meet the requirements of NACSCAOM, a professional program in acupuncture must be a resident program of at least three academic years in length; must demonstrate attainment of professional competence; must have both adequate clinical and biomedical clinical sciences components; and must include the minimum core curriculum as outlined in the *Accreditation Handbook.*

A professional program in Oriental medicine must be a resident program of at least four academic years in length; must demonstrate attainment of professional competence; must have both adequate clinical and biomedical clinical sciences components; and must include the minimum core curriculum as outlined in the *Accreditation Handbook.*

As of May 1996, twenty-one programs had achieved NACSCAOM accreditation, and twelve had achieved candidacy status.

BIOFEEDBACK

Biofeedback Certification Institute of America (BCIA)

10200 West 44th Avenue, Suite 304
Wheat Ridge, Colorado 80033
Phone: (303) 420-2902

The Biofeedback Certification Institute of America (BCIA) was established in 1981 to create and maintain standards for biofeedback practitioners, and to certify those who meet these standards. The BCIA Didactic Education Accreditation Program was established in 1990 to recognize quality providers of didactic education in biofeedback training.

The didactic hours required for educational programs to be eligible for BCIA accreditation include: Introduction to Biofeedback (three hours); Preparing for Clinical Intervention (six hours); Neuromuscular Intervention: General (six hours); Neuromuscular Intervention: Specific (three hours); Central Nervous System Interventions: General (two hours); Autonomic Nervous System Interventions: General (seven hours); Autonomic Nervous System Interventions: Specific (eight hours); Biofeedback and Distress (four hours); Instrumentation (eleven hours); Adjunctive Techniques and Cognitive Interventions (seven hours); and Professional Conduct (three hours).

Educational institutions, private training programs, state chapters, clinics, and individuals may all be accredited through this program.

CHIROPRACTIC

The Council on Chiropractic Education (CCE)

7975 North Hayden Road
Suite A210
Scottsdale, Arizona 85258
Phone: (602) 443-8877
Fax: (602) 483-7333

The Council on Chiropractic Education (CCE) was incorporated in 1971 as an independent national chiropractic college accrediting organization. It is sponsored and funded by the American Chiropractic Association (ACA), the International Chiropractors' Association (ICA), and the accredited colleges; it is also sponsored by the Federation of Chiropractic Licensing Board (FCLB).

The criteria for accreditation utilized by CCE cover the areas of organizational structure, missions and goals, policies and procedures, program objectives, inputs/resources, outcomes, evaluation, planning, and effectiveness. Criteria for the curriculum include a minimum of 4,200 fifty-minute hours that must address at least twenty-five required subject areas.

There are currently sixteen CCE-accredited institutions in the United States, and four in Canada, England, and Australia that hold accredited status under reciprocal agreements.

HERBOLOGY

American Herbalists Guild (AHG)

P.O. Box 1683
Soquel, California 95073
Phone/Fax: (408) 464-2441

There is currently no agency that accredits, approves, or regulates schools of herbology. However, the Education Committee of the American Herbalists Guild (AHG) is presently occupied with a number of projects mandated by the governing council. These include the development of educational guidelines for professional herbalists as a means of providing general direction to students to further their study of herbal medicines; the development of guidelines for clinical training; development of a mentorship program, in which a newer member would be teamed up with an experienced herbalist through the first one or two years of professional membership; and the establishment of a council of schools that is intended to be a forum for the discussion and development of appropriate methods of ensuring that adequate standards are adhered to in the training of clinicians of herbal medicine.

The AHG recommendations for training in the Western biomedical model include a total of 640 hours in Western sciences (including anatomy, physiology, pathology, botany, toxicology, and related disciplines), 730 hours in the herbal and therapeutic areas (including materia medica, therapeutics applications, ethnobotany, herbal pharmacy, formulating and prescribing, and dispensing skills), ninety hours in the area of therapeutic orientation (covering Western constitutional and clinical approaches, history and philosophy of Western medicine, and ethics in clinical practice), ninety hours in additional modalities (such as psychology and counseling, nutrition and diet therapy, and CPR and First Aid), and 400 hours of clinical practicum. Other recommended topics include political and legislative issues, developing teaching skills, relaxation and stress management, and growing herbs.

The AHG Directory of Herbal Education is available for $7.95.

HOMEOPATHY

Council on Homeopathic Education (CHE)

801 North Fairfax Street, Suite 306
Alexandria, Virginia 22314

Joel Kreisberg, President
Council on Homeopathic Education
3 Main Street
Chatham, New York 12037
Phone: (518) 392-7975
Fax: (518) 392-6456
E-mail: teleosis@igc.apc.org

The Council on Homeopathic Education was founded in 1982 as an independent agency with the goals of establishing, insuring, and improving the quality of homeopathic education in the United States; acting as a resource center regarding the content of lectures, seminars, and academic programs dealing with homeopathy; and setting up standards for and evaluating such presentations or institutions. Participating organizations include the International Foundation of Homeopathy, the American Institute of Homeopathy, the Homeopathic Academy of Naturopathic Physicians, and the National Center for Homeopathy. The council is currently completing the process of federal recognition.

Educational programs are evaluated at two levels: graduate and postgraduate programs. These include introductory, beginning, intermediate, advanced, and episodic programs. Council approval is required for continuing education credit by the American Board of Homeotherapeutics.

Organizations or institutions applying for approval must have been in operation for a minimum of two years; less-established programs and episodic seminars may be granted endorsement status only. A minimum number of hours of instruction are required in each course category level.

Currently, five programs have been endorsed by CHE: the National Center for Homeopathy, the International Foundation for Homeopathy, the Canadian Academy of Homeopathy, the Hahnemann College of Homeopathy, and the National College of Naturopathic Medicine's Homeopathic Therapeutics Certification Programs.

Ontario Homeopathic Association (OHA)

P.O. Box 852
Station "P"
Toronto, Ontario M5S 2Z2
Canada
Phone: (416) 488-9685

According to the Ontario Homeopathic Association, homeopathy is currently unregulated in Canada and anyone can claim to be a homeopath or homeopathic doctor. But in 1859, homeopathy was regulated in Ontario; a homeopathic doctor required three years of training, including medical sciences, plus a clinical externship. The OHA considers standards similar to these to be the minimum that should be implemented in Canada now, and accredits professional educational programs accordingly.

HYPNOTHERAPY

International Medical and Dental Hypnotherapy Association

4110 Edgeland, Suite 800
Royal Oak, Michigan 48073-2285
Phone: (810) 549-5594
Fax: (810) 549-5421

While the International Medical and Dental Hypnotherapy Association does not accredit hypnotherapy programs, it does provide a list of approved schools throughout the United States, Canada, Australia, Brazil, and the West Indies. The main function of the organization is to certify hypnotherapists through an examination process and continued education, and to maintain a directory of certified hypnotherapists (see page 340).

MASSAGE THERAPY AND BODYWORK

American Massage Therapy Association (AMTA)

Commission on Massage Training
Accreditation/Approval (COMTAA)
820 Davis Street, Suite 100
Evanston, Illinois 60201-4444
Phone: (847) 864-0123
Fax: (847) 864-1178

AMTA/COMTAA serves as the primary accrediting agency for schools and programs in the field of massage therapy. Currently, sixty-five schools have met the requirements for accreditation or approval.

The accreditation process consists of three components: the self-study, in which the institution or program initiates a process of self-evaluation through a series of specific questions; an on-site visit, in which the accrediting agency sends a team of educational, administrative, and financial experts to the school to verify the self-study; and the final evaluation and decision by an independent accrediting commission.

Prior to applying for accreditation, four requirements must be met: the program must be at least 500 hours in length; the program must have graduated at least two classes; the program must have operated for a minimum of two years; and the program must meet applicable state laws regarding the operation of postsecondary vocational programs.

The 500 hours of instruction must be in-class, teacher-supervised instruction and must consist of one hundred hours of anatomy and physiology, 300 hours of massage theory, technique, and practice (200 hours of which must focus on gliding strokes, kneading, direct pressure, deep friction, joint mobilization, superficial warming techniques, percussion, compression, vibration, jostling, shaking, and rocking; and one hundred hours of which must include contraindications, benefits, business, history, ethics, and legalities of massage), and one hundred hours of additional courses designed to meet the schools' specific program objectives, including First Aid and CPR.

In addition to the core curriculum requirements, COMTAA also has standards for an institution's purposes and goals, organization, curriculum development, clinic, externship/field experience, licensing, methods and materials, classroom conduct, facilities, equipment, learning resources, educational personnel, admission requirements, recruitment and placement, student evaluation and completion, program evaluation, management, financial practices, tuition policies, and insurance.

Schools and programs in this book are listed as either "approved" or "accredited" by AMTA/COMTAA. The difference between an "approved" and an "accredited" program is that the approved schools have not had an actual on-site visit to follow-up on the self-study report sent in by the schools. In 1988, AMTA decided to place a moratorium on the approval process because it was not legally defensible and did not prevent the possibility of approving schools that failed to provide a quality education in an ethical manner. AMTA/COMTAA is requesting that those programs currently operating under "approved" status follow through and become fully accredited. Approved schools have until the year 2000 to become accredited; after that time, the list of schools will consist only of those that have completed the accreditation process.

An updated listing of approved and accredited programs is available at the above address.

American Oriental Bodywork Therapy Association (AOBTA)

Glendale Executive Campus
Suite 510
1000 White Horse Road
Voorhees, New Jersey 08043
Phone: (609) 782-1616
Fax: (609) 782-1653

While AOBTA is not an accrediting agency, fifteen schools of Oriental bodywork are members of the AOBTA Council of Schools and Programs (COSP). In order to be accepted for membership, schools and programs must successfully meet certain criteria that include offering a program of at least 500 hours of study. Contact AOBTA for additional information.

Associated Bodywork and Massage Professionals (ABMP)

International Massage and Somatic
   Therapies Accreditation Council (IMSTAC)
28677 Buffalo Park Road
Evergreen, Colorado 80439-7347
Phone: (303) 674-8478 / (800) 458-2267
Fax: (303) 674-0859

In 1995, ABMP announced the inception of its accreditation program for schools of massage, bodywork, and somatic therapies. ABMP's International Massage and Somatic Therapies Accreditation Council (IMSTAC) established standards based on faculty, curriculum, operations, and career development, and oversees the accreditation process. In order to be considered for accreditation, schools must offer a program of at least 500 hours, must have been in existence for at least two years, and must have graduated at least one class. Currently, fourteen schools have met IMSTAC accreditation standards; contact ABMP/IMSTAC at the above address for an updated list.

In addition, ABMP reviews curricula of schools offering a minimum of one hundred hours of training; graduates of curriculum-reviewed schools are eligible for ABMP membership. This is by no means a guarantee of training or employment, nor does it constitute accreditation or approval; it simply indicates that the educational program meets or exceeds general membership standards.

The Feldenkrais Guild

P.O. Box 489
Albany, Oregon 97321-0143
Phone: (541) 926-0981 / (800) 775-2118
Fax: (541) 926-0572
E-mail: feldngld@peak.org

The Feldenkrais Guild is the professional organization of Guild Certified Feldenkrais Practitioners/ Teachers and also maintains standards of practice, certification, training accreditation, and professional conduct. Accredited trainings offer a minimum of 800 class hours over a minimum of three years; most trainings meet over four years. See page 353 for additional information.

International Myomassethics Federation, Inc. (IMF)

Nancy E. Chubbs, Secretary
15251 Purdy Street
Westminster, California 92683
Phone: (800) 433-4463

The International Myomassethics Federation (IMF), founded in 1971, is primarily a professional membership organization (see page 354), but also offers curriculum approval to schools of myomassology and related fields throughout the country. Contact IMF for additional information.

NATUROPATHY

Council on Naturopathic Medical Education (CNME)

c/o Robert B. Lofft, Executive Director
P.O. Box 11426
Eugene, Oregon 97440-3626
Phone: (541) 484 6028

The Council on Naturopathic Medical Education, founded in 1978, is recognized by the U.S. Secretary of Education as the national accrediting agency for educational programs leading to the Doctor of Naturopathy or Doctor of Naturopathic Medicine (N.D.) degrees. Accreditation or candidacy is a requirement for American colleges to participate in federal student loan programs.

CNME considers for accreditation only four-year, in-residence, doctoral-level programs that prepare students to become licensed naturopathic physicians in the eleven states and four Canadian provinces that recognize the profession. Accredited programs must consist of at least 4,200 clock hours, including 1,200 clinic hours under the supervision of licensed physicians. The council does not accept accreditation applications from correspondence schools and does not provide information about them.

Currently, two schools are accredited (Bastyr University and National College of Naturopathic Medicine) and two are candidates for accreditation (Southwest College of Naturopathic Medicine and the Canadian College of Naturopathic Medicine).

POLARITY THERAPY

American Polarity Therapy Association (APTA)

2888 Bluff Street, #149
Boulder, Colorado 80301
Phone: (303) 545-2080
Fax: (303) 545-2161

The American Polarity Therapy Association accredits schools and training centers that develop course descriptions based on the APTA *Standards for Practice,* which defines competencies required for practitioners to be certified by APTA at two levels: an entry level (155 hours of training) called Associate Polarity Practitioner (A.P.P.), and an advanced level (615 hours of training) called Registered Polarity Practitioner (R.P.P.). Currently, twenty-seven schools offer A.P.P. training and twelve offer R.P.P. training; contact APTA for an updated list.

As a nonprofit organization, APTA's primary mission is to advance the profession of polarity therapy. See page 356 for membership information.

YOGA

American Yoga Association

513 South Orange Avenue
Sarasota, Florida 34236
Phone: (813) 953-5859 / (800) 226-5859

Currently there is no national certification of yoga instructors, nor any national agencies accrediting or approving schools of yoga. Some organizations may certify teachers after a week of instruction; others, after three or more years of study and practice. The American Yoga Association recommends that prospective students ask the following questions: Does the teacher practice yoga exercise, breathing, and meditation daily? Does the teacher study regularly with a teacher of his or her own? Is the teacher a vegetarian? Does he or she smoke or use drugs? Is he or she nutritionally aware? Yoga should influence the teacher's entire lifestyle. Is the teacher knowledgeable in anatomy and physiology; in the effects of the exercises, breathing, and meditation; and in varying exercises for each person's capabilities?

For additional information, contact the American Yoga Association.

Licensing and Certification

One of the most important things you should consider before committing to a program is whether or not it is sufficient to allow you to practice in the location you want. In some places, licensing requirements for alternative practitioners are determined at the state level; in others, the individual county or city determines the level of education needed for a license. This section gives a general description of the types of laws and licensing requirements that are currently in place for a number of fields of alternative medicine. Students are strongly urged to contact the appropriate boards or licensing agencies in the state in which they intend to practice before putting down a deposit on any educational program.

ACUPUNCTURE AND ORIENTAL MEDICINE

American Academy of Medical Acupuncture (AAMA)

5820 Wilshire Boulevard, Suite 500
Los Angeles, California 90036
Phone: (213) 937-5514
Fax: (213) 937-0959
E-mail: KCKD71F@prodigy.com

The American Academy of Medical Acupuncture (AAMA) was founded in 1987 by a group of physicians who were graduates of the Medical Acupuncture for Physicians training programs sponsored by UCLA School of Medicine. AAMA serves as an educational, certifying, and professional (see page 345) organization.

AAMA has created a proficiency examination for physicians who have incorporated acupuncture into their medical practice; the Board of Directors awards a Certificate of Proficiency in Medical Acupuncture to individuals who successfully pass this exam. The exam is the first step toward establishing a formal, recognized, board certification program. The examination is held at various locations throughout the United States, and the examination fee is $500. An optional Review Course is given on the two days prior to the exam; see page 296.

National Commission for the Certification of Acupuncturists (NCCA)

P.O. Box 97075
Washington, D.C. 20090-7075
Phone: (202) 232-1404
Fax: (202) 462-6157

At the present time, acupuncture licensure is available in thirty-three states and the District of Columbia. Since its inception in 1984, NCCA has certified more than 4,700 acupuncturists and 200 practitioners of Chinese herbology. NCCA is itself certified by the National Commission for Certifying Agencies.

NCCA has established four separate certification programs: Diplomate in Acupuncture and Chinese Herbology, Diplomate in Acupuncture, Diplomate of Chinese Herbology, and Diplomate of Oriental Bodywork Therapy. Earning the designation demonstrates to patients and employers that the recipient has met national professional standards of skill and knowledge necessary for a safe and competent practice. Certification is also critical in those states that license or certify acupuncturists according to eligibility or examination requirements, as NCCA certification is part of those requirements.

In order to meet NCCA certification requirements in acupuncture and Chinese herbology, practitioners must be 18 years of age or older; qualify to take the examination through either completed formal schooling in acupuncture and Chinese herbology, being third- or fourth-year students in acupuncture and Chinese herbology (students must complete their education in order to be certified), completed apprenticeship in acupuncture and Chinese herbology, professional practice of acupuncture and Chinese herbology, or a combination of training and experience; subscribe to a national code of ethics; pass all portions of the NCCA acupuncture and Chinese herbology examination; successfully complete the Clean Needle Technique Course offered by the Council of Colleges of Acupuncture and Oriental Medicine; and be of good moral character.

Exams are administered twice a year, in San Francisco in the spring and in Ryebrook, New York in the fall. Certification fees are $695 for the acupuncture exam ($395 application fee and $300 examination fee), $545 for the Chinese herbology exam ($395 application fee and $150 exam fee), and $945 for both exams ($495 application fee and $450 exam fee).

AROMATHERAPY

National Association for Holistic Aromatherapy (NAHA)

P.O. Box 17622
Boulder, Colorado 80308-7622
Phone: (415) 731-4634
Fax: (415) 564-6799

The National Association for Holistic Aromatherapy (NAHA) is a nonprofit educational organization that is currently working with the Canadian Federation of Aromatherapists to establish cross-national standards of aromatherapy practice. NAHA intends to offer certification to those who complete the Aromatherapy Certification Program, which includes

home study, courses with a variety of teachers, and individual hands-on research and practice by the student. For information on NAHA membership, see page 347.

BIOFEEDBACK

Biofeedback Certification Institute of America (BCIA)

10200 West 44th Avenue, Suite 304
Wheat Ridge, Colorado 80033
Phone: (303) 420-2902

Biofeedback practitioners are not required by law to be certified. The Biofeedback Certification Institute of America (BCIA) was established in 1981 to create and maintain standards for practitioners who use biofeedback, and to certify those who meet these standards.

The certification process involves a review of credentials, written and practical examinations, and recertification. All applicants for certification must hold a bachelor's degree or higher in an approved health care field from an accredited institution and have at least 200 hours of training that includes sixty hours of didactic education in biofeedback, including a course in human anatomy or physiology and a counseling course and practicum; personal experience with biofeedback; and 140 hours of supervised clinical biofeedback training.

Candidates must obtain their didactic biofeedback education from either a regionally accredited academic institution or a BCIA-accredited training program in the eleven Blueprint Areas, which are: Introduction to Biofeedback; Preparing for Clinical Intervention; Neuromuscular Intervention: General; Neuromuscular Intervention: Specific; Central Nervous System Interventions: General; Autonomic Nervous System Interventions: General; Autonomic Nervous System Interventions: Specific; Biofeedback and Distress; Instrumentation; Adjunctive

Techniques and Cognitive Interventions; and Professional Conduct.

Candidates should be prepared to document that they are licensed in a BCIA-approved health care field or are supervised by an individual who meets BCIA's qualifications for supervisors.

Certification is granted for four years. Recertification requires continuing formal education and/or the retaking and passing of the written exam.

Examinations are offered twice each year. Fees are $25 for the application packet and $375 for certification.

CHIROPRACTIC

Chiropractic is the least "alternative" of the therapies included in this book. All fifty states, plus the District of Columbia, the United States Virgin Islands, and Puerto Rico, license chiropractors as health care providers; all fifty states and the District of Columbia authorize chiropractic services as part of their Workers' Compensation Programs, and most states include chiropractic in commercial health-and-accident policies. Chiropractic treatment is authorized under Medicare, Medicaid, and the Vocational Rehabilitation Program, and is included as a medical deduction under the Internal Revenue Code.

In general, to obtain a Doctor of Chiropractic (D.C.) degree, students must complete at least two years (some states require four years) of preprofessional college-level work, and four years of residential instruction at a chiropractic college. For a graduate to be eligible for licensure, the college must be accredited by the Council on Chiropractic Education (CCE) and/or approved by the state board. (For information on CCE accreditation, see page 331.) National board exams and some state assessment are also required. Qualifying examinations cover the areas of basic science, clinical science, clinical competency, practical skills, and jurisprudence.

For additional information regarding licensure, contact:

Federation of Chiropractic Licensing Boards

901 54th Avenue, Suite 101
Greeley, Colorado 80634
Phone: (970) 356-3500
Fax: (970) 356-3599

HOMEOPATHY

American Board of Homeotherapeutics

801 North Fairfax Street, Suite 306
Alexandria, Virginia 22314
Phone: (703) 548-7790

The American Board of Homeotherapeutics is a medical specialty board in homeopathic medicine. Candidates who successfully pass the written and oral examinations are awarded the Diplomate in Homeotherapeutics (D.Ht.), signifying the attainment of the requisite knowledge and experience necessary to engage in homeopathic medical practice. Only M.D.s and D.O.s may apply for the examination.

In order to be eligible for the examination, applicants must meet the following prerequisites: be eligible for American Institute of Homeopathy membership (currently licensed medical or osteopathic physicians in the United States); hold an M.D. or D.O. degree and be licensed to practice medicine in the state or province in which they reside; have practiced homeopathy for a minimum of three years; have accumulated at least 150 hours of approved homeopathic education credits and provide documentation of such; function under unquestionable moral and ethical standards, to which two members of ABHt have attested; present ten chronic treated cases, each of which must have been treated for at least one year; and apply to the office of the National Center for Homeopathy, which serves as the central office of the American Board of Homeotherapeutics, at least two months prior to the examination.

Council for Homeopathic Certification (CHC)

1709 North Seabright Avenue
Santa Cruz, California 95062
Phone: (408) 421-0565

The Council for Homeopathic Certification (CHC) was created to provide recognition for homeopathic practitioners who have attained a high level of competence, and to assist the public in choosing appropriately qualified homeopaths from all professional backgrounds. The council's board is comprised of homeopaths from major health care professions as well as professional homeopaths, and cooperates with existing homeopathic educational and professional organizations to promote excellence in classical homeopathic practice.

In order to be eligible to take the certification exam, candidates must have a total of 500 hours of training in homeopathy from an established teaching institution, or a total of 500 hours from a formal institution and external seminars. For those who have taught themselves homeopathy or learned under the personal guidance of another practitioner, CHC has devised a point system so that practitioners may qualify for the exam in different ways. Candidates should have at least one year of practical experience in practicing homeopathy and must submit five cases with follow-up interviews over a six-month period.

The six-and-a-half hour certification exam consists of a written exam covering both classical homeopathy and human sciences, and an oral exam given at a separate time (at present, conducted over the phone) that focuses on the candidate's clinical knowledge, case management, and other aspects of the candidate's professional practice. Exams are held in various locations throughout the country. The application fee of $300 consists of a $250 exam fee and a non-refundable $50 application fee. Successful candidates will receive a certificate stating that they are Certified in Classical Homeopathy and may use the designation "C.C.H."

Homeopathic Academy of Naturopathic Physicians (HANP)

Susan Wolfer, Executive Director
P.O. Box 12488
Portland, Oregon 97212
Phone: (503) 795-0579
Fax: (503) 795-7320
E-mail: hanp@igc@apc.org
Internet: www.healthy.net/hanp

Naturopathic physicians may take the HANP Board Certification Examination (HBCE) in order to become board certified in homeopathy. In order to be eligible for board certification, physicians must be a graduate of an HANP-approved naturopathic college; be licensed to practice naturopathic medicine; have completed 250 hours of specialty training in homeopathy; submit five cured chronic cases; pass the written and oral examinations; be in practice for at least one year prior to certification; and present two letters of recommendation.

National Board of Homeopathic Examiners (NBHE)

President: Dr. Marcia C. Sasso, D.C.,
      D.N.B.H.E.
5663 N.W. 29th Street
Margate, Florida 33063
Phone: (305) 974-3456

The National Board of Homeopathic Examiners was incorporated in 1987 to create standardized interprofessional testing for the certification of homeopathic practitioners.

The board administers a comprehensive exam every six months that tests basic proficiency in homeopathic philosophy, materia medica, case taking, miasms, preparations and potencies, repertorization, Einsteinian quantum physics, Arndt Schultz law, all of Hahnemann's Aphorisms in the Organon, and the keynotes, essences, and indications for remedy prescription. The examination consists of closed- and open-book exams, plus a practical/oral examination in which the examinee is required to take a case history and make recommendations. Upon successful completion of all three parts, a candidate is granted status with the NBHE.

Eligibility for taking the exam for diplomate status requires that candidates have previously earned a Ph.D., D.C., M.D., D.O., A.P., N.D., O.M.D., or equivalent level degree and have received training in homeopathy at a board certified institution. Certificate status is available to non-doctorate candidates. Annual renewal requirements include continuing education, service requirements, and an annual renewal fee.

The board is currently working with the U.S. Department of Education in an effort to become a nationally recognized examining board.

National Center for Homeopathy

801 North Fairfax Street, Suite 306
Alexandria, Virginia 22314
Phone: (703) 548-7790

In the United States, the treatment of one individual by another with homeopathic remedies may be construed as the practice of medicine. Since homeopathic remedies are classified as drugs by the FDA (although most are available over-the-counter), one must usually be a licensed health care provider in order to practice homeopathy, according to the National Center for Homeopathy.

All states license M.D.s (medical doctors) and D.O.s (doctors of osteopathy); several license N.D.s (naturopathic physicians) to diagnose and treat illness. Outside of these, other health care practitioners may or may not be allowed to use homeopathic remedies, depending on the laws of their state.

In the United States, Bastyr University in Seattle, Washington and National College of Naturopathic Medicine in Portland, Oregon offer four-year programs leading to the N.D. degree. Graduates from these programs are eligible to obtain licenses in certain states (see Naturopathy, page 342) and to incorporate homeopathy into their practice.

Those who already possess a degree in health care may complete one of several advanced training courses in homeopathy and may legally practice homeopathy in accordance with the laws of the individual state.

Homeopathy is currently unregulated in Canada, meaning that anybody can claim to be a homeopath or homeopathic doctor, according to the Ontario Homeopathic Association (OHA).

North American Society of Homeopaths (NASH)

10700 Old County Road 15, #350
Plymouth, Minnesota 55441
Phone: (612) 595-0459

The North American Society of Homeopaths (NASH) is an organization of professional practitioners dedicated to developing and maintaining high standards of homeopathic practice. It is a professional membership organization (see page 351 for membership information) that also certifies and maintains a register of qualified homeopaths. To become a registered member (R.S.Hom. (NA)), practitioners must submit a curriculum vitae, ten cases, and two professional references.

HYPNOTHERAPY

International Medical and Dental Hypnotherapy Association

4110 Edgeland, Suite 800
Royal Oak, Michigan 48073-2285
Phone: (810) 549-5594
Fax: (810) 549-5421

The purpose of the International Medical and Dental Hypnotherapy Association is to provide the public with excellently trained certified hypnotherapists who work in harmony with health care professionals to assist those undergoing medical procedures or challenges. Hypnotherapy helps reduce stress and pain for patients, thereby promoting healing.

The association certifies hypnotherapists and provides referrals. To become certified, a hypnotherapist must have completed 120 hours of basic and advanced training from an approved school of hypnotherapy; pass oral and written certification exams; use hypnotherapy as a professional, full- or part-time; and agree to complete thirty CEUs annually for renewal of membership. Certified member dues are $135 for new members and $65 for renewal.

MASSAGE THERAPY AND BODYWORK

Currently, nineteen states offer a credential in the form of licensing, certification, or registration to practicing massage therapists. Many of these use the national certification exam administered by the National Certification Board for Therapeutic Massage and Bodywork (NCBTMB) as their licensing exam (see below). Whether or not a given state administers massage practice laws, local or county laws may still apply. In states that govern massage, the potential practitioner should contact the Board of Massage (generally a function of the Department of Health) for requirements. The American Massage Therapy Association (AMTA) chapter in any state will also be able to provide up-to-date information on massage laws; it might also be useful to contact a massage therapist currently practicing in the desired locality.

American Massage Therapy Association (AMTA)

Commission on Massage Training
   Accreditation/Approval (COMTAA)
820 Davis Street, Suite 100
Evanston, Illinois 60201-4444
Phone: (847) 864-0123
Fax: (847) 864-1178

In addition to serving as the primary accrediting agency for schools and programs in the field of massage therapy (see page 333), the American Massage Therapy Association administers an Event Sports Massage Certification Exam. The exam is open to all active AMTA members in good standing. For additional information, contact the AMTA education programming manager.

International Myomassethics Federation, Inc. (IMF)

Nancy E. Chubbs, Secretary
15251 Purdy Street
Westminster, California 92683
Phone: (800) 433-4463

The International Myomassethics Federation, Inc., (IMF) offers certification testing in basic and therapeutic myomassology, infant massage, sports massage, reflexology, and basic and therapeutic instructor. Contact IMF for additional information.

National Certification Board for Therapeutic Massage and Bodywork (NCBTMB)

8201 Greensboro Drive, Suite 300
McLean, Virginia 22102
Phone: (703) 610-9015 / (800) 296-0664

NCBTMB is an independent, private, nonprofit organization that fosters high standards of ethical and professional practice through a recognized credentialing program that assures the competency of practitioners of therapeutic massage and bodywork.

Candidates may demonstrate eligibility to take the national certification examination either through specific hours of education/training or through the portfolio review process. In the first method, candidates must have completed 500 clock hours of formal training at an established school of massage and/or bodywork (after May 1, 1997, these hours must have been completed at a state-licensed training institute or the school must show exemption from licensing status), with at least one hundred hours in anatomy and physiology; at least 200 clock hours in massage and/or bodywork theory and practice, including at least two clock hours of ethics; and the remainder of clock hours in related education. Candidates must show successful completion of their entire program (i.e., if a program is 700 hours in length, candidates must have successfully completed all 700 hours).

Candidates whose education does not meet the above requirements may be eligible through the portfolio review process. Course work requirements are 200 hours of formal education and training in massage therapy and/or bodywork, including at least two hours of ethics; one hundred hours of anatomy and physiology; and 200 hours of adjunct/related education and/or professional experience.

The national certification examination application fee is $165; portfolio review candidates must submit an additional $25 review fee. Once a candidate is determined to be eligible to take the exam, the candidate will be sent a list of testing center locations. Exams are administered on a computerized testing system. The exam covers human anatomy, physiology, and kinesiology (30 percent), clinical pathology and recognition of various conditions (15 percent), massage/bodywork theory, assessment, and practice (40 percent), adjunct techniques and methods (5 percent), and business practices and professionalism (10 percent).

NATUROPATHY

Several states and provinces have laws that specifically register or license Doctors of Naturopathy (N.D.s) to diagnose and treat illness— these are Alaska, Arizona, Connecticut, Hawaii, Maine, Montana, New Hampshire, Oregon, Utah, Vermont, Washington, Alberta, British Columbia, Manitoba, Ontario, and Saskatchewan. In the District of Columbia, naturopathic physicians must register in order to practice. Other states that are currently considering legislation to license naturopaths include California, Colorado, Idaho, Massachusetts, Minnesota, Nebraska, North Carolina, Pennsylvania, Texas, and Vermont. The state of Florida recognizes naturopaths licensed in other states.

Every state or province has its own licensing board and its own requirements for licensure, though each requires a minimum of 4,000 hours of training in specific areas. Nearly all the states and provinces that license naturopathic physicians use the Naturopathic Physicians Licensing Examinations developed by the NPLEX board (below). Many states have reciprocal licensing agreements with other states that license naturopathic physicians.

National Board of Naturopathic Examiners

1377 K Street N.W., Suite 852
Washington, D.C. 20005
Phone: (202) 682-7352
Fax: (208) 448-2657

The National Board of Naturopathic Examiners administers the NPLEX exam used by many states in the licensing of naturopathic physicians. Contact the board for additional information.

NUTRITION

Macrobiotic Educators Association (MEA)

Kushi Institute
P.O. Box 7
Becket, Massachusetts 01223
Phone: (413) 623-5741
Fax: (413) 623-8827

The Macrobiotic Educators Association was created to establish and maintain qualifications for teachers of the Kushi approach to the macrobiotic way of life. The Kushi Institute welcomes all experienced and knowledgeable macrobiotic educators to join the MEA by participating in the MEA Membership Program, a five-day residential intensive that is held twice yearly at the Kushi Institute. The program currently assesses membership qualifications in two fields of macrobiotic education—macrobiotic health care and macrobiotic cooking instructors—and includes a written exam, an oral presentation on either macrobiotic health care or macrobiotic cooking, a media-style interview, an original written composition, and demonstration of personal education sessions or cooking classes. Teachers may apply for one or both programs.

Requirements for admission into the five-day intensive are: previous certification by the Kushi Institute or prior Kushi Institute Review Board status; at least five years' macrobiotic teaching experience; or completion of the three levels of the former Kushi Institute Leadership Program or the current Dynamics of Macrobiotics Program (or their equivalent), and letters of recommendation from two macrobiotic teachers.

MEA members are included in a special referral directory, receive a 30 percent discount at most Kushi Institute U.S.A. programs, are recommended to media representatives requesting macrobiotic contacts, and are invited to attend an annual three-day MEA Continuing Education Conference for Teacher Development with Michio and Aveline Kushi.

Nutritional Consultants Organization of Canada (NCOC)

1201 Division Street
Kingston, Ontario K7K 6X4
Canada
Phone: (800) 406-2703
Fax: (613) 544-9256

The Nutritional Consultants Organization of Canada (NCOC) was founded in 1983 as a voluntary, independent, nonprofit organization that provides standards of practice for nutritional consultants. The organization awards the designation Registered Nutritional Consultant (RNC) to those applicants who have been approved by the Board of Examiners. The educational requirements may be met by a bachelor's degree in holistic nutrition or equivalent, including study at the Canadian School of Natural Nutrition (see page 287). Applicants who have professional experience may also earn the designation by passing an examination with a grade of 80 percent or better. Effective in September 1997, proficiency must be demonstrated at the postsecondary level in clinical nutrition research, geriatric nutrition, digestion, therapeutic and clinical nutrition, biology, lipid metabolism, life cycle, sports nutrition and pathology, anatomy, chemistry, biochemistry, vitamins, minerals, allergies, preventive nutrition, environmental pollution, and several other areas. The examination fee is $187. To receive the designation, applicants must also be active members of NCOC. The one-time registration fee of $294 covers the application fee and a one-year membership; an annual fee of $107 is required to maintain the registration. (Prices include GST.)

REFLEXOLOGY

There is no national licensure for reflexologists, though practitioners may choose to become certified by the American Reflexology Certification Board.

American Reflexology Certification Board (ARCB)

P.O. Box 620607
Littleton, Colorado 80162
Phone: (303) 933-6921
Fax: (303) 904-0460

ARCB is a nonprofit corporation whose primary goal is to certify the competency of reflexologists meeting certain basic standards. ARCB is an independent organization and its certification process does not interfere with or negate the certification programs offered by individual schools.

In order to take the certification exam, applicants must be 18 years of age or older; have a high school diploma or equivalent; have completed a hands-on reflexology course beyond the introductory level (it is recommended that one hundred hours of testing prerequisite include thirty hours of reflexology instruction covering theory, history, and hands-on work; twenty-five hours of anatomy and physiology related to reflexology and the study of the lower leg and foot; five hours of business practice involving ethics and local/state laws; and ten hours of additional work in any of the above); and submit thirty documentations (copies of thirty different client records on ARCB forms; these must note areas of stress and tenderness, and the applicant must have seen each client at least three times). The last two requirements must equal a total of one hundred hours.

The examination has three parts: a written component that tests theoretical knowledge, a practical component that tests technique and pressure, and supporting documentation from client files. The total testing fee is $225 (including a $100 non-refundable processing fee). Exams are conducted nationally on an ongoing basis.

Professional Associations and Membership Organizations

Another source of information about a particular school or field of study is a professional organization within that field. This section lists just a fraction of the hundreds of organizations that cater to the needs of practicing professionals, but that may also be open to students of the profession or interested individuals. These organizations usually offer a newsletter and/or magazine to their members, as well as discounts, referrals, and information about the field.

ALTERNATIVE MEDICINE— GENERAL

Office of Alternative Medicine (OAM) Clearinghouse

National Institutes of Health
P.O. Box 8218
Silver Spring, Maryland 20907-8218
Phone: (888) 644-6226
Fax: (301) 495-4957

The Office of Alternative Medicine was created by congressional mandate in 1992 to facilitate the evaluation of alternative medical treatment modalities. The OAM sponsors research, provides technical support for preliminary studies of alternative medical practices, sponsors grant-writing and clinical research workshops, sponsors conferences, and serves as a public information clearinghouse. Materials currently available at no cost include a General Information Package, a Research Information Package, a Cancer Information Package, and an AIDS Information Package. The quarterly OAM newsletter, *Complementary and Alternative Medicine at the NIH,* is available at no charge; it covers legislative developments and conferences and includes a calendar of complementary and alternative medicine events. The OAM Internet home page, to be launched in 1997, will also include this information.

ACUPUNCTURE AND ORIENTAL MEDICINE

American Academy of Medical Acupuncture (AAMA)

5820 Wilshire Boulevard, Suite 500
Los Angeles, California 90036
Phone: (213) 937-5514
Fax: (213) 937-0959
E-mail: KCKD71F@prodigy.com

The American Academy of Medical Acupuncture (AAMA) was founded in 1987 by a group of physicians who were graduates of the Medical Acupuncture for Physicians Training Programs sponsored by the UCLA School of Medicine. Their goal is to promote the integration of traditional and modern forms of acupuncture with Western medical training. AAMA creates and endorses courses in medical acupuncture (see page 296); conducts an annual symposium; publishes a scientific journal, *Medical Acupuncture*; provides information about news in the field; and serves as a resource for practitioners. AAMA has also developed a proficiency exam that leads to a Certificate of Proficiency in Medical Acupuncture (see page 336).

Membership is limited to physicians (M.D., D.O., or equivalent) and full-time fellows, residents, and medical students with an interest in acupuncture. Annual dues range from $50 for students to $285 for a full membership.

American Association of Acupuncture and Oriental Medicine (AAAOM)

433 Front Street
Catasauqua, Pennsylvania 18032
Phone: (610) 266-1433
Fax: (610) 264-2768

AAAOM was incorporated in 1983, and is the oldest and largest professional organization of its kind in the United States. The organization has become the nation's strongest advocate for national recognition of the Oriental medicine profession. Its goals are to have acupuncturists licensed in every state as independent health care providers; to have acupuncturists as covered providers under all insurance policies and Medicare; and to promote research, educate the public, and set high standards for the education of acupuncture practitioners.

Membership benefits include a subscription to *The American Acupuncturist* newsletter, referral services, update bulletins covering association news and legislative reports, member discounts on seminars and supplies, and more. The association also maintains a library of articles and treatments for particular diseases.

Annual dues are $30 for students currently enrolled in a school of acupuncture, and $175 for joint or allied health professionals ($60 for a first-year practitioner, $90 for a second-year practitioner).

APPLIED KINESIOLOGY

International College of Applied Kinesiology—U.S.A.

6405 Metcalf Avenue, Suite 503
Shawnee Mission, Kansas 66202
Phone: (913) 384-5336
Fax: (913) 384-5112

The International College of Applied Kinesiology, founded in 1975, is a professional association that promotes the science of kinesiology through research programs, training seminars, and a semiannual conference.

Membership is open to licensed physicians, including chiropractors, dentists, and M.D.s; other health care professionals; and students enrolled in programs leading to such licensing. Annual dues are $400 for professionals and $25 for students. Membership benefits include quarterly and semi-annual newsletters, annual publications, annual meetings, patient referrals, and more.

Introductory courses offered by the International College of Applied Kinesiology are part of the Essentials of Applied Kinesiology—The One-Hundred-Hour Certified Course, which is divided into eight individual sessions. These two-day sessions are offered throughout the United States and the world. Other courses that have been offered beyond the Essentials courses include Common Sense in Nutrition from Pediatrics to Geriatrics, Hands-On Pain Relief, the Definitive Disc Seminar, Relieving Fatigue, Chiropractic and Pain Control, and others. Fees for courses vary, depending on the instructor. Interested physicians should contact ICAK for a course schedule.

AROMATHERAPY

National Association for Holistic Aromatherapy (NAHA)

P.O. Box 17622
Boulder, Colorado 80308-7622
Phone: (415) 731-4634
Fax: (415) 564-6799

The National Association for Holistic Aromatherapy is a nonprofit educational aromatherapy organization founded in 1988 and run entirely by volunteer members. NAHA is in the process of creating an outline of standards for an Aromatherapy Certification Program; NAHA intends to offer certification to those who complete this program, which includes home study, courses with a variety of teachers, and individual hands-on research and practice by the student.

Membership benefits include a subscription to *Scentsitivity Quarterly,* a newsletter featuring essential oil research, case studies, product reviews, information on aromatherapy education, and more; listings of reliable aromatherapy sources, schools, practitioners, and books; and a conference and trade show. Those at all levels of aromatherapy are invited to join. Membership fees are $35 for Friends of Aromatherapy and $50 for professional or business members.

AYURVEDA

The Ayurvedic Institute

P.O. Box 23445
Albuquerque, New Mexico 87192-1445
Phone: (505) 291-9698

The Ayurvedic Institute is a nonprofit educational corporation. In addition to its on-site and correspondence courses (see pages 196 and 362), the institute publishes a quarterly journal, *Ayurveda Today,* and offers Ayurvedic and Western herbs, audio- and videotapes, and other Ayurvedic products. Members receive the quarterly journal and a 10 percent discount on products purchased. Regular membership is $25 in the United States and $35 outside the United States.

BIOFEEDBACK

The Association for Applied Psychophysiology and Biofeedback (AAPB)

10200 West 44th Avenue, Suite 304
Wheat Ridge, Colorado 80033-2840
Phone: (303) 422-8436 / (800) 477-8892
Fax: (303) 422-8894

Founded in 1969, the Association for Applied Psychophysiology and Biofeedback is the foremost international association for the study of biofeedback and applied psychophysiology, with over 1,900 active members and forty-four state chapters. The organization encourages scientific research, seeks to integrate biofeedback with other self-regulatory methods, promotes high standards of professional practice, and disseminates information to the public.

Membership is open to both professionals and students. Benefits include reduced registration fees for the annual meeting and workshops; a subscription to the quarterly journal, *Biofeedback and Self-Regulation,* and the quarterly newsmagazine *Biofeedback*; discounts on AAPB publications; and a membership directory. Optional membership sections include the Brainwave Section, Non-Licensed Practitioners Section, SESNA Section (for providers of surface EMG), Education Section, and Technology Developers Section. Dues are $30 for students, $85 for regular or associate individual, and $275 for associate corporate; section memberships range from $5 to $150.

CHIROPRACTIC

American Chiropractic Association

1701 Clarendon Boulevard
Arlington, Virginia 22209
Phone: (703) 276-8800
Fax: (703) 243-2593

The American Chiropractic Association is chiropractic's largest organization, with over 22,000 members. The association monitors legislation, enhances the image of chiropractic through public relations, and advocates the highest ethical standards for its members.

Membership benefits include access to legislative and legal resource libraries, ACA Visa or MasterCard Gold Card, automobile rental discounts, free or discounted IRC on-line information services, discounted hotel rates, product sales discounts, subscriptions to the monthly newsletter, *ACA Today* and the *Journal of the American Chiropractic Association,* and much more. (Partial *JACA* subscription is available for student members.) Membership dues range from $30 for students to $600 for general membership.

International Chiropractors Association (ICA)

1110 North Glebe Road, Suite 1000
Arlington, Virginia 22201
Phone: (703) 528-5000

The International Chiropractors Association provides financial assistance to currently enrolled chiropractic students through its King Koil ICA Scholarship and the Auxiliary of ICA Scholarship.

Applications are available through student chapters of ICA (SICA). ICA also provides information on chiropractic education, including undergraduate requirements, college admission, and Council on Chiropractic Education (CCE) accredited schools.

ENVIRONMENTAL MEDICINE

American Academy of Environmental Medicine (AAEM)

10 East Randolph Street
New Hope, Pennsylvania
Phone: (215) 862-4544
Fax: (215) 862-4583

The American Academy of Environmental Medicine, founded in 1965 as the Society for Clinical Ecology, is an international association of physicians and other professionals interested in the interactions between individuals and their environment as reflected in their total health. In addition to their educational programs for physicians and other health professionals (see page 295), AAEM also has a book sales center, a list of recommended references and resources, and more.

Membership is open to practicing physicians, non-physician professionals, students of approved medical or osteopathic schools, and interested organizations; at least two letters of recommendation are required. Benefits include a subscription to the *Journal of Nutritional and Environmental Medicine* and the quarterly newsletter, *The Environmental Physician.* A directory of all members is distributed annually and a program syllabus from the annual seminar is available for purchase. Membership dues range from $25 for students to $275 for an M.D. or D.O. provisional member. Candidates are evaluated for full membership after completion of Instructional Courses Part I through IV (see page 295).

National Foundation for the Chemically Hypersensitive

1158 North Huron Road
Linwood, Michigan 48634
Phone: (517) 697-3989

The National Foundation for the Chemically Hypersensitive is a nonprofit volunteer organization dedicated to research, education, dissemination of information, patient-to-doctor referrals, patient-to-attorney referrals, Social Security, Disability, and Workers Compensation information, networking, housing assistance, and compilation of case histories and studies. Dues are $20 (includes newsletter) for general membership, $45 for doctors who treat the chemically injured, and $175 for corporations, government agencies, and attorneys.

HERBOLOGY AND FLOWER ESSENCE THERAPY

American Herb Association

P.O. Box 1673
Nevada City, California 95959

The American Herb Association is an educational and research organization dedicated to increasing the public's knowledge about herbs, and increasing the use of herbs and herbal products.

Members receive *The AHA Quarterly,* a twenty-page newsletter that reports on the latest scientific studies, herb books, international herb news, legal and environmental issues, and more. Annual membership is $20 ($24 for Canadian/Mexican members and $28 for foreign members). AHA also has an *Herb Education Directory* ($3.50), *Herb Products Directory* ($4), and *Recommended Herb Book List* ($2.50).

American Herbalists Guild

P.O. Box 1683
Soquel, California 95073
Phone/Fax: (408) 464-2441

The American Herbalists Guild, founded in 1989, is the only professional, peer-review organization in the United States for herbalists specializing in the medicinal uses of plants. AHG offers educational guidelines for herbalists and students (see page 331); serves as an information referral center; represents herbalists to the FDA, Congress, and other regulatory agencies; and promotes further research, education, and study of herbal medicine.

Members receive the quarterly newsletter, *The Herbalist,* discounts on herb publications and databases, an optional referral listing in the membership directory, and a discount on the annual symposium. Membership is offered at three levels: Student, $35; Associate, $50; and Professional, $85. AHG also provides a membership directory (free for members; $2 for non-members), a *Directory of Herbal Education* ($7.95), a recommended reading list ($2), and other materials.

Flower Essence Society

P.O. Box 459
Nevada City, California 95959
Phone: (916) 265-9163 / (800) 548-0075
Fax: (916) 265-6467
E-mail: fes@nccn.net

The Flower Essence Society is a nonprofit, international network of flower essence practitioners, researchers, educators, and others dedicated to the advancement of flower essence therapy. Membership benefits include a 10 percent discount on books, photographs, and educational programs, and the members' newsletter. Membership dues start at $20.

Herb Research Foundation

1007 Pearl Street, Suite 200
Boulder, Colorado 80302-9953
Phone: (303) 449-2265
Fax: (303) 449-7849

The Herb Research Foundation was founded in 1983 as a center for herbal research and education. The foundation gathers scientific, historical, and cultural information on herbs and educates members, the media, manufacturers, legislators, professionals, and regulatory officials from the FDA, USDA, and FTC regarding herb safety and benefits.

Members receive *HerbalGram,* an eighty-page, full-color journal with feature stories, regulatory updates, research summaries, events calendar, and more; answers to questions about uses of herbs (which suppliers of herbs may not legally answer); and copies of literature on file for a minimal cost. Annual membership starts at $35.

United Plant Savers

P.O. Box 420
East Barre, Vermont 05649

United Plant Savers is a new, nonprofit organization dedicated to saving endangered and threatened medicinal plants. The organization provides resources for obtaining plants and seeds for replanting, supports conservation efforts through horticultural practices, develops programs for school systems to replant endangered or threatened plant species in their native environment, and makes information available to herbalists and interested groups and individuals on threatened or endangered medicinal plants. Sliding membership fees range from $35 to $100.

HOMEOPATHY

Homeopathic Academy of Naturopathic Physicians (HANP)

P.O. Box 12488
Portland, Oregon 97212
Phone: (503) 795-0579
Fax: (503) 795-7320

HANP is a specialty society within the profession of naturopathic medicine, and is affiliated with the American Association of Naturopathic Physicians. The organization offers board certification in classical homeopathy to qualified naturopathic physicians, encourages the development and improvement of homeopathic curricula at naturopathic colleges, and publishes the quarterly professional journal, *Simillimum,* which includes one hundred pages of cases, materia medica, news, philosophy, and discussion of practical applications of homeopathic concepts.

General membership ($45) is open to everyone with an interest in homeopathy.

International Foundation for Homeopathy (IFH)

P.O. Box 7
Edmonds, Washington 98020
Phone: (206) 776-4147
Fax: (206) 776-1499

IFH is a nonprofit educational foundation dedicated to the growth of classical homeopathy. In addition to training homeopaths (see page 271), the foundation provides homeopathic information and referral and publishes the bimonthly magazine, *Resonance,* as well as an annual professional case conference and book of cases cured with homeopathy. Basic membership is $40; a sample magazine is $2.

National Center for Homeopathy

801 North Fairfax Street
Suite 306
Alexandria, Virginia 22314
Phone: (703) 548-7790
Fax: (703) 548-7792

The National Center for Homeopathy is a nonprofit membership organization and the largest homeopathic organization in the United States. In addition to offering seminars and training programs in homeopathy for consumers and health care professionals (see page 261), the center provides information and literature to the public, the media, the government, and the health care industry, and publishes the monthly magazine, *Homeopathy Today.* The center also compiles the annual *Directory of Practitioners and Resources* and coordinates over 170 affiliated study groups across North America.

Annual membership is $40 ($55 outside the United States and Canada), and includes the directory, the magazine, and discounts on NCH books, products, and its annual conference.

North American Society of Homeopaths (NASH)

10700 Old County Road 15, #350
Plymouth, Minnesota 55441
Phone: (612) 595-0459

The North American Society of Homeopaths (NASH) is an organization of professional practitioners dedicated to developing and maintaining high standards of homeopathic practice. The organization certifies and maintains a register of practitioners (see page 340), supports the development of training programs in classical homeopathy, supports research, and promotes public awareness of homeopathy.

Associate membership is open to everyone. Membership benefits include a copy of the annual journal, *The American Homeopath,* and a quarterly newsletter. Dues are $45 for students, $65 for supporting, and $100 or more for Special Friend of NASH.

Ontario Homeopathic Association (OHA)

P.O. Box 852
Station "P"
Toronto, Ontario M5S 2Z2
Canada
Phone: (416) 488-9685

The objectives of the Ontario Homeopathic Association are to promote the science, art, and philosophy of homeopathy; to encourage professional and educational activities among members of the association; to encourage the standardization of educational requirements for homeopathic practitioners; and to encourage continuing research and trials in homeopathy. Graduates of accredited homeopathic schools who meet OHA guidelines are invited to apply for professional membership. Benefits include a referral service, computer services to repertorize cases, notification of lectures and seminars, continuing education, discounts on homeopathic books, liability insurance, and *Health and Homeopathy,* the journal of the International Academy of Homeopathy. Professional membership dues are $275 per year.

Other health practitioners, students, and interested individuals are also welcome to join OHA at reduced rates ($25 to $150). Benefits for these members include *Health and Homeopathy,* book discounts, and notification of lectures and seminars.

HYPNOTHERAPY

International Medical and Dental Hypnotherapy Association

4110 Edgeland, Suite 800
Royal Oak, Michigan 48073-2285
Phone: (810) 549-5594
Fax: (810) 549-5421

The International Medical and Dental Hypnotherapy Association (IMDHA) certifies hypnotherapists (see page 340) and provides referrals to certified hypnotherapists. It also makes available a list of IMDHA-approved schools in the United States, Canada, Australia, Brazil, and the West Indies, and publishes a bimonthly newsletter, *Subconsciously Speaking.* Certified member dues are $135 for new members and $65 for renewal.

National Association of Transpersonal Hypnotherapists

Eastern Institute of Hypnotherapy
P.O. Box 249
Goshen, Virginia 24439
Phone: (540) 997-0325 / (800) 296-MIND

The National Association of Transpersonal Hypnotherapists (NATH) sponsors an annual conference, sells a variety of books appropriate for self-help or continuing education, and publishes a tri-annual newsletter, *The Bridge,* that includes articles on existing and new transpersonal methodology, book reviews, continuing education opportunities, legislative changes, and more. Annual dues are $24 for associate membership, $36 for certified adjunct membership, and $48 for certified membership.

IRIDOLOGY

National Iridology Research Association

27676-B Tomball Parkway
Tomball, Texas 77375
Phone: (281) 255-4044
E-mail: MDJones@iridology.com

NIRA, founded in 1982, is dedicated to raising the levels of iridology education and practice in Ameri-

ca. The association sponsors certification seminars (see page 311) and distributes home-study videos (see page 376), audiocassettes, slide kits, charts, and more.

Members receive a newsletter; *Iridology Review,* a quarterly publication covering research, news, events, and more. Membership starts at $45 per year ($25 for students).

MASSAGE THERAPY AND BODYWORK

American Massage Therapy Association (AMTA)

820 Davis Street, Suite 100
Evanston, Illinois 60201-4444
Phone: (847) 864-0123
Fax: (847) 864-1178

AMTA is the oldest and largest national organization representing the massage therapy profession. Founded in 1943, it has over 25,000 members and chapters in all fifty states. AMTA strives to advance the practice of professional massage therapy through the sponsorship of national certification, school accreditation, continuing education, professional publications, legislative efforts, and public relations. In 1990, AMTA created a nonprofit foundation to fund massage therapy-related scholarships, research, and community outreach.

Membership benefits include professional liability insurance, a products discount, continuing education, the *Massage Therapy Journal,* a *Hands On* newsletter, an annual convention and conferences, and more. Dues are $169 for associate membership and $235 for professional active membership; state chapter dues are up to $30 additional.

AMTA provides up-to-date information on accredited and approved schools and programs (see page 333), addresses of state boards administering massage practice laws, and a list of chapter chairs to contact for further information.

American Oriental Bodywork Therapy Association (AOBTA)

Glendale Executive Campus
Suite 510
1000 White Horse Road
Voorhees, New Jersey 08043
Phone: (609) 782-1616
Fax: (609) 782-1653

Founded in 1990, the American Oriental Bodywork Therapy Association (AOBTA) is a not-for-profit professional membership association of Oriental bodywork practitioners. Currently, the organization serves well over 1,000 members throughout the United States and abroad.

Membership benefits include protection and representation of the interests, rights, and professional standards of Oriental bodywork therapy; high quality educational opportunities; the *Pulse* quarterly newsletter and an anticipated biannual *Journal of Oriental Bodywork Therapy* (members receive an advertising discount); optional liability, group health, and disability coverage; membership directory; and more.

Membership is offered at three levels: Student ($30 dues plus $10 application fee); Associate (eligible after 150 hours of instruction; $75 dues plus $30 application fee); and Certified Practitioner (eligible after 500 hours of instruction; $100 dues and $30 application fee).

Associated Bodywork and Massage Professionals (ABMP)

28677 Buffalo Park Road
Evergreen, Colorado 80439-7347
Phone: (303) 674-8478
Fax: (303) 674-0859

ABMP is dedicated to promoting ethical practices and legitimate standards of training, protecting the rights of practitioners, and educating the public as to the benefits of massage, bodywork, and somatic therapies.

Member benefits include professional liability insurance, an international referral service, *Massage and Bodywork* magazine, a members-only newsletter, regulatory interaction, *The Successful Business Handbook, ABMP's Yellow Pages, The Touch Training Directory,* discounted group insurance, rental cars, lodging, and much more.

Several levels of membership and dues apply to students and professionals: student memberships begin as low as $50 per year (with limited benefits) while dues for certified professionals are $229 (with complete benefits).

The Feldenkrais Guild

P.O. Box 489
Albany, Oregon 97321-0143
Phone: (541) 926-0981 / (800) 775-2118
Fax: (541) 926-0572
E-mail: feldngld@peak.org

The Feldenkrais Guild is the professional organization of Guild Certified Feldenkrais Practitioners/Teachers. The guild maintains standards of practice, certification, training, accreditation, a code of professional conduct, and a grievance process; provides information regarding legislative and licensing issues; publishes a directory, journals, and newsletters; maintains the North American Amherst Training Video Library; promotes Feldenkrais through public relations activities; and maintains a central office for the sale of books, tapes, and more.

Membership is open to graduates and trainees of accredited training programs. Benefits include a listing in the international directory and on the Internet; an annual issue of the *Feldenkrais Journal;* a quarterly newsletter; discounts on books, tapes, and brochures; group insurance information; and more. Annual dues are $60 for students, and $300 for practitioners.

International Massage Association

3000 Connecticut Avenue N.W., Suite 308
Washington, D.C. 20008
Phone: (202) 387-6555
Fax: (202) 332-0531

The International Massage Association (IMA) was founded in 1994; membership exceeded 9,000 within its first thirty months. Its goals are to take massage into the mainstream through the unity of massage practitioners; to educate those who have never tried massage; to assist in the success of its member practitioners; and to provide insurance to members. IMA assists massage practitioners with setting up a credit card merchant account, advertising, financial advice, marketing videos, an Internet referral service, and insurance. Membership is $99, and $49.50 for students.

International Myomassethics Federation, Inc. (IMF)

Nancy E. Chubbs, Secretary
15251 Purdy Street
Westminster, California 92683
Phone: (800) 433-4463

The International Myomassethics Federation, Inc., (IMF) was founded in 1971 to serve the myomassology/bodywork community. "Myomassethics" is a three-part term: "myo" refers to muscle, "mass" refers to massage, and "ethics" is a tribute to the high personal and professional standards members hold for themselves.

IMF is an organization of health-service myomassologists who individually practice various forms of therapeutic touch. IMF's purposes are to improve the image and quality of massage services, to provide resources enabling massage professionals to increase their knowledge and skills, and to educate the public about the benefits and variety of healthy touch alternatives.

Membership benefits include an annual educational convention; continuing education programs and resource information; certification testing in basic and therapeutic myomassology, infant massage, sports massage, reflexology, and basic and therapeutic instructor; affiliation with state organizations; and *The Intra Myomassethics Forum,* a quarterly publication. For membership categories and dues, contact IMF.

NATUROPATHY

American Naturopathic Association

1377 K Street N.W., Suite 852
Washington, D.C. 20005
Phone: (202) 682-7352
Fax: (208) 448-2657

Founded in 1896, the American Naturopathic Association promotes the practice and education of naturopathy. Membership is open to students, laypeople, and physicians. Contact the association for additional information.

NUTRITION

American Natural Hygiene Society, Inc. (ANHS)

P.O. Box 30630
Tampa, Florida 33630
Phone: (813) 855-6607

The American Natural Hygiene Society (ANHS), founded in 1948, is the oldest natural health organization in the United States. ANHS advocates a total-health approach that emphasizes all aspects of healthful living.

Members receive *Health Science* magazine, discounts on seminars and conferences, a quarterly book and tape catalog, and discounts on all books, pamphlets, and video- and audiotapes. Membership dues are $25 in the United States and Canada, and $45 elsewhere.

The American Vegan Society

56 Dinshah Lane
P.O. Box H
Malaga, New Jersey 08328-0908
Phone: (609) 694-2887

The American Vegan Society is a nonprofit educational membership organization teaching a compassionate way of living that includes veganism— living on the products of the plant kingdom—and excludes the use of animal products such as leather, wool, fur, silk, and animal oils.

Members receive the quarterly publication *Ahimsa,* which contains articles, recipes, and a listing of available books, videos, charts, audiocassettes, and more pertaining to veganism. Membership is open to vegans, vegetarians, and non-vegetarians. Dues start at $18 per year.

Canadian Natural Health Association (CNHA)

(formerly Canadian Natural Hygiene Society)

439 Wellington Street West #5
Toronto, Ontario M5V 1E7
Canada
Phone: (416) 977-CNHA /
    (416) 322-4225 (24 hours)
Fax: (416) 977-1536

The Canadian Natural Health Association was founded in 1960 as a nonprofit, educational, charitable organization dedicated to teaching healthful living in accordance with natural hygiene principles. Natural hygiene is a way of life that recognizes the needs of the body for pure, raw, vegan foods; proper sleep; exercise; fresh air; water; and sunlight. Emphasis is placed on the superiority of raw fruits and vegetables, nuts, and seeds; the

harmful effects of too much protein, drugs, food additives, pesticides, meat, and immunization; fasting as a means of regaining and maintaining vigorous health; and the importance of fresh air, sunshine, exercise, rest and sleep, and emotional poise.

Members receive a monthly newsletter, *Living Naturally*; a directory of practitioners offering discounts to CNHA members; discounts on books, charts, videos, and audiotapes; and reduced admission to CNHA-sponsored lectures. Membership dues are $20 for seniors and students, $35 for individuals, and $40 for families.

North American Vegetarian Society

P.O. Box 72
Dolgeville, New York 13329
Phone: (518) 568-7970
Fax: (518) 568-7979
E-mail: navs@telenet.net

The North American Vegetarian Society, founded in 1974, is a nonprofit educational organization dedicated to promoting vegetarianism and to providing support to new and long-time vegetarians.

Membership benefits include four issues of the NAVS newsmagazine, *Vegetarian Voice,* which features in-depth articles, recipes, reports on activism, book reviews, and local vegetarian group listings; discounted conference registration; and books and merchandise. Dues are $20 for U.S. and $23 for Canadian or foreign individuals; $26 for U.S. and $29 for Canadian or foreign families.

One Peaceful World (OPW)

Box 10, 308 Leland Road
Becket, Massachusetts 01223
Phone: (413) 623-2322
Fax: (413) 623-8827
E-mail: opw@macrobiotics.org

Toronto Office:
Phone: (416) 488-4960
Fax: (416) 488-3610

One Peaceful World is an international macrobiotic information network and membership society founded by Michio and Aveline Kushi. There are national OPW offices in over twenty-six countries. Membership benefits include a subscription to the *One Peaceful World* newsletter, featuring articles by Michio and Aveline Kushi, scientific-medical updates, recipes, menus, and news about macrobiotic activities around the world; a free book and discounts on selected books from One Peaceful World Press and other publishers of macrobiotic books and study materials; the latest information regarding macrobiotic, environmental, and holistic activities throughout the world; and the opportunity to take part in tours, seminars, and special programs. Annual dues are $30 for individuals (one free book), $50 for families (two free books), and $100 for supporting members (three free books).

The Vegetarian Resource Group

Vegetarian Journal
P.O. Box 1463
Baltimore, Maryland 21203
Phone: (410) 366-VEGE
E-mail: thevrg@aol.com

The Vegetarian Resource Group is a nonprofit organization working with businesses and individuals to bring about healthy changes in the school, workplace, and community. Physicians and registered dietitians aid in the development of nutrition-related publications and answer questions about the vegetarian diet. The group also develops and sells books, software, and other resource materials; gives presentations at annual meetings of nutrition-related organizations; provides information to the media; sponsors gatherings and one-day conferences; and aids in the creation of local vegetarian groups.

Members receive *Vegetarian Journal,* a thirty-six-page, bimonthly publication covering such topics as vegetarian meal planning, nutrition, natural food product reviews, and more. Membership dues are $20 per year ($10 additional in Canada and Mexico, $20 additional in other foreign countries).

POLARITY THERAPY

American Polarity Therapy Association (APTA)

2888 Bluff Street, #149
Boulder, Colorado 80301
Phone: (303) 545-2080
Fax: (303) 545-2161

The American Polarity Therapy Association (APTA) is a nonprofit organization dedicated to the advancement of the profession of polarity therapy. In addition to accrediting educational programs (see page 335), APTA provides services that include practitioner certification, educational conferences, the quarterly newsletter *ENERGY,* a mail-order bookstore containing all polarity titles and related works, and referrals to trainings and practitioners. Membership is open to all. Annual membership dues are $125 for R.P.P.s (Registered Polarity Practitioners), $85 for A.P.P.s (Associate Polarity Practitioners), $60 General, $40 for students, and $125 Institutional.

QIGONG

Qigong Institute/East West Academy of Healing Arts

450 Sutter Street, Suite 2104
San Francisco, California 94108
Phone: (415) 788-2227
Fax: (415) 788-2242

The Qigong Institute is a subsidiary of the East West Academy of Healing Arts (see page 302). The Qigong Institute seeks to promote qigong for health and healing through education, research, and clinical work. Membership benefits include the *Qigong Newsletter,* free admission to designated monthly professional lectures on qigong, a discount on videos and publications, and international conferences.

Membership dues start at $8 for the newsletter only, $25 for student membership (includes admission to designated lectures), and $40 for general membership (includes admission to designated lectures).

The International Council of Reflexologists was established in 1990 to meet the needs of the profession by providing an international forum for the exchange of ideas, promoting international conferences, and supporting the development of local, regional, and national associations.

Annual membership is $40 and benefits include the *ICR Newsletter,* discounts on conference fees, and printed research studies.

REFLEXOLOGY

International Council of Reflexologists (ICR)

P.O. Box 621963
Littleton, Colorado 80162
Fax: (303) 904-0460

Self-Study Resources

This chapter provides a listing, arranged alphabetically by specialty, of periodicals, videos, correspondence courses, and other materials that offer basic instruction, serve as handy reference sources, offer a unique perspective, provide ongoing education, or otherwise serve to familiarize you with a field of study.

Although it may be tempting, especially in a field as unregulated as alternative medicine, to forgo the expensive, time-consuming, and inconvenient classroom education in favor of an easier home-study course, you should think about how you want to apply your knowledge. Correspondence courses can be valuable for learning how to treat yourself or your family with nutrients, but if you are preparing for a career in alternative medicine, you should consider classroom training.

ALTERNATIVE MEDICINE— GENERAL

CORRESPONDENCE STUDY

School of Natural Medicine

P.O. Box 7369
Boulder, Colorado 80306-7369
Phone: (303) 443-4882
Fax: (303) 443-8276
E-mail: snatmed@aol.com

The School of Natural Medicine (SNM) offers natural physician training through on-site seminars and a three-week August Summer School, in conjunction with home study courses; the cost is $2,600 for the full package.

SNM home study courses are offered separately in Iridology and the Foundation of Natural Medicine (fourteen lessons); Herbal Medicine (twelve lessons); and Naturopathy (twelve lessons). Courses are $500 each, or all three for $1,200 (these courses are also included in the full package above).

SNM also offers a clinic, an herbal pharmacy, and a publications department with books, videos, and audiotapes.

PERIODICALS

Alternative Medicine Digest

Box K
Milton, Washington 98354
Phone: (800) 990-9499
Fax: (206) 922-9858

Alternative Medicine Digest is published bimonthly by Future Medicine Publishing. It serves as a digest of journals, research, conferences, and newsletters in alternative medicine and includes feature articles, columns, and departments such as Prescribing—For Yourself, the Holistic Physician, Natural Pharmacy, the Politics of Medicine, and Alternative Medicine Reviews. Subscriptions are $18 for six issues or $30 for twelve issues; back issues are available for $4 each.

Dr. Andrew Weil's Self Healing

Subscription Department
P.O. Box 788
Mt. Morris, Illinois 61054
Phone: (800) 523-3296

Dr. Andrew Weil is known for his holistic approach to healing, as seen in his best-selling books *Natur-*

al Health, Natural Medicine, and *Spontaneous Healing.* Dr. Weil publishes a monthly, eight-page newsletter that includes feature articles, tips on healthy living, self-healing recipes, health in the news, and Q&A. Subscriptions are $29 for twelve issues.

New Age Journal

42 Pleasant Street
Watertown, Massachusetts 02172
Phone: (617) 926-0200

New Age Journal is published bimonthly with additional special issues published each fall and winter. It covers a broad range of body/mind and alternative health care practices. It includes features and special reports, plus such departments as Tools for Living, Food, Natural Health Adviser, Mind/Body, and Arts and Media. It is widely available at newsstands or by subscription for $24 per year.

ACUPRESSURE

CATALOG

Hands-On Health Care

Acupressure Institute
1533 Shattuck Avenue
Berkeley, California 94709
Phone: (510) 845-1059 /
   (800) 442-2232 (outside California)

In addition to their educational programs in acupressure (see page 66), the Acupressure Institute offers the *Hands-On Health Care* catalog of products, which includes healing books, instructional videos, charts, acupressure point flash cards, audiotapes, massage aids, workbooks and charts for equine and canine acupressure, and more.

CORRESPONDENCE STUDY

The G-Jo Institute

P.O. Box 848060
Hollywood, Florida 33084
Phone: (954) 791-1562
Internet: http://www.funtimes.com/
   healthexpo/g-jo.html

The G-Jo Institute, founded in 1976, offers a correspondence program, the Master of G-Jo Acupressure Home Study Certification Program. The course includes a Basic G-Jo training manual, video, audiocassette, Advanced G-Jo manual, Master of G-Jo Acupressure Certification Test, wall chart, eye improvement program, and Inner Organ Balancing and "Tune-Up" program for $149, plus $5 for shipping and handling.

ACUPUNCTURE AND ORIENTAL MEDICINE

CORRESPONDENCE STUDY

Bastyr University

14500 Juanita Drive Northeast
Bothell, Washington 98011
Phone: (425) 823-1300
Fax: (425) 823-6222
Internet: www.bastyr.edu
E-mail: admiss@bastyr.edu

Bastyr University (see page 265 for a full description) offers a Distance Learning Program for those who are unable to attend as full-time students, but who are interested in learning more about natural health and nutrition. Written assignments, a toll-free telephone number, and voice-mail boxes for each instructor foster greater understanding of course material. Courses take ten to sixteen weeks to complete, and include a term project and proctored final exam. No degrees are available through this program, but students may receive a Certificate of Completion, and some courses may be applied toward degree programs. Courses include Nutrition I and II, Nutrition and Herbs, Nutrition in the Natural Products Industry, Introduction to Nutrition in Natural Medicine, Diet and Behavior, and Fundamental Principles of Traditional Chinese Medicine. Additional courses are under development.

Tuition is $162 per credit. There is a $25 registration fee, and materials are approximately $50 per course. Shipping is $15 U.S., $60 international.

PERIODICALS

The American Acupuncturist

Joining the American Association of Acupuncture and Oriental Medicine entitles the member to receive their newsletter, *The American Acupuncturist.* See page 346 for membership information.

AROMATHERAPY

CATALOGS

The Michael Scholes School for Aromatic Studies

117 North Robertson Boulevard
Los Angeles, California 90048
Phone: (310) 276-1191 / (800) 677-2368
Fax: (310) 276-1156
E-mail: mhscholes@aol.com

The Michael Scholes School for Aromatic Studies offers a comprehensive line of books, essential oils, and other aromatherapy supplies, as well as three books: *The Most Commonly Asked Questions on Aromatherapy* and *A Pocket Guide to Aromatherapy* by Michael Scholes, and *A Pocket Guide to Aromatherapy and Pet Care* by Joan Clark. Send for a free catalog.

True Essence Aromatherapy Ltd.

2203 Westmount Road N.W.
Calgary, Alberta T2N 3N5
Canada
Phone: (403) 283-8783 / (800) 563-8938

True Essence Aromatherapy Ltd. offers books, essential oils, and other aromatherapy supplies.

CORRESPONDENCE STUDY

The Atlantic Institute of Aromatherapy

16018 Saddlestring Drive
Tampa, Florida 33612
Phone/Fax: (813) 265-2222
E-mail: syllah@aol.com

The Atlantic Institute of Aromatherapy offers a number of aromatherapy courses (see page 131), as well as correspondence study.

The Aromatherapy Practitioner Correspondence Course is a home study course useful for health care providers (such as massage therapists, nurses, and others) as well as the beginning student or lay person. The course is designed to be taken over a period of six to twelve months.

Part One—Basic covers such topics as the history of aromatics; production processes, quality, and purity of essential oils; effect of essential oils on human physiology; treatment methods and applications; safety data and toxicity studies; and a detailed study of fifty-five essential oils. The course includes samples of essential oils, blending materials, reference charts, and monographs on fifty-five oils with scientific references. The cost is $475, with two recommended texts.

Advanced Studies includes a study of the essence in its natural environment; the main botanical families of aromatic plants; essential oil chemistry and constituent properties; research on essential oil properties, with references; and research on olfaction. Separate Graduate Studies specialize in medical/nursing applications, perfumery, and skin/body care treatments. Advanced and Graduate Studies are under revision; costs to be announced.

Jeanne Rose Aromatherapy

219 Carl Street
San Francisco, California 94117-3804
Phone: (415) 564-6785
Fax: (415) 564-6799

Jeanne Rose Aromatherapy offers correspondence courses in both aromatherapy and herbal studies (see page 367 for the Herbal Studies Course); the two courses may be combined for $675.

The Aromatherapy Studies Course ($350) offers instruction in the uses of over 200 essential oils; distillation; making hydrosols; the therapeutic use of essential oils by application, inhalation, and ingestion; the treatment of a variety of physical and mental conditions; making body care treatments; and formulating blends. It is strongly recommended that students take the Herbal Studies Course either prior to or during the Aromatherapy Studies Course.

The Michael Scholes School for Aromatic Studies

117 North Robertson Boulevard
Los Angeles, California 90048
Phone: (310) 276-1191 / (800) 677-2368
Fax: (310) 276-1156
E-mail: mhscholes@aol.com

The Michael Scholes School for Aromatic Studies offers two home study courses designed to complement one another.

Beyond Scents, a twenty-hour course, consists of four 90-minute audiocassettes, one 95-minute video, a home study workbook, twenty-three essential oil samples, and additional supplies. The cost is $250.

The Aromatherapy Series, a thirty-five-hour course, consists of five 90-minute audiocassettes, fifty-five essential oil samples, a home study work-

book, ten carrier oil samples, and several blending bottles, vials, and pipettes. The cost is $275.

Students may register for both courses for $450. Either course meets the prerequisite for attending the five-day Certification Course, described on page 309).

Pacific Institute of Aromatherapy

P.O. Box 6723
San Rafael, California 94903
Phone: (415) 479-9121
Fax: (415) 479-0119

The Pacific Institute of Aromatherapy offers a six-part correspondence course in aromatherapy. The course covers Essential Oils (including production methods, basics of distillation, purity and adulteration, and synthetic vs. natural), Structure and Energy (research on the effects of essential oils on the body), Treatment of Disease (medical applications of essential oils and aromatic hydrosols), Cosmetology (including typical applications of essential oils in skin care, clays, hydrosols in skin care, and natural facial mask compositions), Psychology of Fragrance (effects of fragrance materials), and Toxicology (the safe use of essential oils). The course costs $320, including essential oil sample, and should be completed within twelve to fourteen weeks.

True Essence Aromatherapy Ltd.

2203 Westmount Road N.W.
Calgary, Alberta T2N 3N5
Canada
Phone: (403) 283-8783 / (800) 563-8938

True Essence Aromatherapy offers two home study courses designed to complement one another. These courses were developed by the Michael Scholes School for Aromatic Studies (see above).

Beyond Scents, a twenty-hour course, consists of four 90-minute audiocassettes, one ninety-five-minute video, a home study workbook, and twenty-two essential oil samples. The cost is $325.

The Aromatherapy Series, a thirty-five-hour

course, consists of five 90-minute audiocassettes, fifty-five essential oil samples, a home study workbook, ten carrier oil samples, and several blending bottles, vials, and pipettes. The cost is $375.

Both courses meet the prerequisite for attending the five-day Certification Course (see page 309).

PERIODICALS

Scentsitivity Quarterly

Joining the National Association for Holistic Aromatherapy entitles the member to receive their newsletter, *Scentsitivity Quarterly*. (See page 347 for membership information.)

AYURVEDA

CATALOG

American Institute of Vedic Studies

1701 Santa Fe River Road
Santa Fe, New Mexico 87501
Phone: (505) 983-9385
Fax: (505) 982-5807

The American Institute of Vedic Studies offers a selection of books, tapes, and correspondence courses (below) in Ayurveda, tantra, yoga, Vedic astrology, Vedas, and Hinduism.

CORRESPONDENCE STUDY

American Institute of Vedic Studies

P.O. Box 8357
Santa Fe, New Mexico 87504-8357
Phone: (505) 983-9385
Fax: (505) 982-5807
E-mail: vedicinst@aol.com

The American Institute of Vedic Studies was founded in 1988 by David Frawley (Vamadwa Shasmi), a Vedic teacher and professional herbalist.

The institute's comprehensive correspondence course is designed for both health care professionals and serious students; no medical background is required. The course, which takes about 250 hours to complete, offers instruction in such topics as History of Ayurveda; Sankhya and Yoga Philosophy; the Three Gunas and Five Elements; Ayurvedic Anatomy and Physiology; Constitutional Analysis; Mental Nature; the Disease Process; Diagnostic Methods of Pulse, Tongue, Abdomen, Questioning, and Observation; Ayurvedic Psychology; the Six Tastes; Ayurvedic Herbalism; Ayurvedic Therapeutic Measures; Subtle Healing Modalities of Aromas, Color, Gems, and Mantras; Yoga Psychology Therapies; Ayurvedic Counseling; Herbal Treatment of the Channel Systems; Ayurvedic Massage; and others. Course fee is $300; books are additional.

Ayurveda Holistic Center

82A Bayville Avenue
Bayville, New York 11709
Phone/Fax: (516) 628-8200

The Ayurveda Holistic Center offers a one-year certification program in Ayurveda, both on-site and through correspondence. (See page 207 for program description.) The center also sells a variety of herbal products and books, as well as educational consultation services.

The Ayurvedic Institute

P.O. Box 23445
Albuquerque, New Mexico 87192-1445
Phone: (505) 291-9698

The Ayurvedic Institute offers a correspondence course, Lessons and Lectures on Ayurveda, in addition to its on-site courses (see page 196). The correspondence course consists of twelve lessons: History and Philosophy; the Three Doshas; the Human Constitution; Doshas, Dhatus, and Malas; Pathology; Diagnosis; Therapeutic Theory; Therapeutics of Indigestion; Food; Medicinals; Lifestyle and Routine; and Rejuvenation and Virilization. Study materials include a two-tape lecture series by Dr. Robert E. Svoboda, a tape of pronunciation of Sanskrit terms, and three written examinations. Students are allowed one year to complete the course. The cost of the course is $270; a required text is $10.

Institute for Wholistic Education

33719 116th Street
Twin Lakes, Wisconsin 53181
Phone: (414) 877-9396
Fax: (414) 889-8591

The Institute for Wholistic Education offers a four-part Ayurvedic home study course covering the fundamental principles of Ayurveda. This first-year program covers such topics as Basic Foundations and Principles of Ayurveda; Anatomy and Physiology from an Ayurvedic Perspective; Ayurvedic Etiology, Symptomatology, and Therapeutics; Ayurvedic Nutrition; Ayurvedic Herbology; Stress Management; and Health, Longevity, and the Disease Process. The cost is $250, including books.

A second-year program is offered to those who have completed the first-year program, and includes such topics as the Disease of Lightness and Nourishing Therapy, the Disease of Heaviness and Lightening Therapy, the Disease of Dryness and Oleation Therapy, the Multiple Attribute Diseases, and others. The cost is $250, including books.

Other courses include Hidden Science Behind Hatha Yoga ($250), Psycho-Bio-Cosmosis ($350), and Spiritual Path of Knowledge ($195).

The institute also sells a wide variety of books, body care products, bulk herbs and spices, herbal formulas, essential oils, and more.

PERIODICALS

Ayurveda Today

Joining The Ayurvedic Institute entitles the member to receive their quarterly journal, *Ayurveda Today*. See page 347 for membership information.

BIOFEEDBACK

PERIODICALS

Biofeedback/Biofeedback and Self-Regulation

Joining the Association for Applied Psychophysiology and Biofeedback entitles the member to receive their quarterly journal, *Biofeedback and Self-Regulation* and the quarterly newsmagazine, *Biofeedback*. See page 347 for membership information.

CHIROPRACTIC

CATALOG

American Chiropractic Association

1701 Clarendon Boulevard
Arlington, Virginia 22209
Phone: (800) 368-3083

The ACA has a catalog of software packages, audiotapes, videotapes, slides, and books for the practitioner or student. For professionals, the catalog includes chiropractic billing and nutrition software, chiropractic exercise videos, new patient orientation slides, and more.

PERIODICALS

ACA Today/Journal of the American Chiropractic Association

Joining the American Chiropractic Association entitles the member to receive their monthly newsletter, *ACA Today,* and the *Journal of the American Chiropractic Association* (student members receive a partial subscription to *JACA*). See page 348 for membership information.

ENVIRONMENTAL MEDICINE

PERIODICALS

Journal of Nutritional and Environmental Medicine/ Environmental Physician

Joining the American Academy of Environmental Medicine entitles the member to receive the *Journal of Nutritional and Environmental Medicine* and the quarterly newsletter, *Environmental Physician.* See page 348 for membership information.

Our Toxic Times

Chemical Injury Information Network (CIIN)
P.O. Box 301
White Sulphur Springs, Montana 59645
Phone: (406) 547-2255

The Chemical Injury Information Network, a non-profit organization, publishes a monthly newsletter, *Our Toxic Times,* for those suffering from chemically-related health problems. Topics recently covered include carpet testing, Gulf War Syndrome, chemical hazards, state news, and workplace air quality. There is no set subscription rate; an annual donation, in any amount, is required to maintain membership.

FLOWER ESSENCE THERAPY

CATALOG

Flower Essence Society

P.O. Box 459
Nevada City, California 95959
Phone: (916) 265-9163 / (800) 548-0075
Fax: (916) 265-6467
E-mail: fes@nccn.net

In addition to their weekend classes and week-long intensive (see page 83), the Flower Essence Society offers a catalog of books, audiocassettes, flower essences, herbal flower oils, aroma lamps, and more. Shipping is additional. FES member and practitioner discounts are available. See page 349 for membership information.

GUIDED IMAGERY

CORRESPONDENCE STUDY

Academy for Guided Imagery

P.O. Box 2070
Mill Valley, California 94942
Phone: (415) 389-9324 / (800) 726-2070
Fax: (415) 389-9342

Martin Rossman, M.D., and David E. Bresler, Ph.D., founded the Academy for Guided Imagery in 1989 to provide instruction for counseling professionals in the imagery process. See page 64 for their 150-hour Certification Program.

Interactive Guided Imagery is available as an accredited, self-paced study program that includes three video and/or nine audio instructional tapes, two experiential audiotapes, a companion notebook with lecture outlines, and a 491-page manual of current articles, research, scripts, and patient handouts. This twelve-hour program teaches fundamental skills to help clients work successfully with imagery. The cost is $195.

The academy also offers a variety of other audiocassettes, videos, and books.

HERBOLOGY

CORRESPONDENCE STUDY

The American Herbal Institute

3056 Lancaster Drive N.E.
Salem, Oregon 97305
Phone: (503) 364-7242

The American Herbal Institute offers classroom instruction in herbal studies (see page 229) as well as a Modern Herbal Studies Correspondence Course. This course consists of six sections: Herbology I and II, Nutrition, Anatomy and Physiology, Herbal Remedies Lab (twenty-three projects/lessons), and How to Practice Medicine Without a License (legal issues involved in the practice of herbal medicine). The $475 tuition includes all books, videos, and instructional materials.

The Australasian College of Herbal Studies

P.O. Box 57
Lake Oswego, Oregon 97034
Phone: (503) 635-6652 / (800) 48-STUDY
Fax: (503) 697-0615
E-mail: australasiancollege@herbed.com
Internet: http://www.herbed.com

Founded in New Zealand in 1978 and in the United States in 1991, the Australasian College of Herbal Studies offers eleven correspondence certificate courses covering various aspects of herbal medicine, as well as other fields of alternative medicine. Courses include Diploma in Herbal Studies ($745); Certificate in Herbal Studies: Herbal Medicine for the Home Herbalist ($373); Certificate in Nutrition, Body Care, and Herbalism ($325); the Basics of Herbalism ($163); Certificate in Natural Therapies ($651); Certificate in Flower Essences ($349); Certificate in Iridology ($349); Certificate in Homeopathy ($349); Certificate in Aromatherapy ($455); Certificate in Homeobotanical Therapy ($505); and Diploma in Homeobotanical Therapy ($1,040). Prices listed are for the continental United States; prices are higher elsewhere. Sample courses are available for $25 to $30. Payment plans are available.

Dominion Herbal College

7527 Kingsway
Burnaby, British Columbia V3N 3C1
Canada
Phone: (604) 521-5822
Fax: (604) 526-1561
E-mail: herbal@uniserve.com

Dominion Herbal College was founded by Dr. Herbert Nowell, a naturopathic physician, in 1926. The college offers classroom programs in aromatherapy and clinical herbal therapist (see page 283), as well as several home study courses covering various aspects of herbal medicine.

The four-year Clinical Phytotherapy (herbal medicine) Tutorial Diploma Course includes approximately twenty to thirty hours of home study per week, annual summer seminars, a minimum of 500 hours of clinical training under the supervision of a qualified practitioner, and a clinical exam at the end of the fourth year. Students must have completed high school-level chemistry and biology courses or high school chemistry and the Chartered Herbalist Program (below). The curriculum covers Herbal Materia Medica, History and Practice of Herbal Medicine, Pathology, Anatomy and Physiology, Nutrition and Dietetics, Pharmacology, Differential Assessment, Pharmacy, Laboratory Medical Science, Psychiatry, Ethics and Medical

Jurisprudence, and more. The cost is $375 per quarter (plus GST for Canadian students); books, exams, seminars, equipment, and clinical training are additional.

The Chartered Herbalist Diploma Program consists of sixty lessons in three parts, and may be completed in six to twelve months. Topics include Anatomy and Physiology, History of Herbalism, Herbal Remedies and Their Preparation, Selected Herbal Formulas for Various Ailments, Properties and Conditions for Use of Over 200 Herbs, Environmental Pollution, Tonics for Babies and Small Children, Animal Health Care, and more. The cost is $900 plus $63 GST (Goods and Services Tax); students outside Canada do not pay GST, but must pay $100 for postage.

Upon successful completion of the Chartered Herbalist Program, students are eligible to apply to the Master Herbalist Program, which includes research and a thesis on an aspect of herbalism; the cost is $400 plus GST.

The ten-month Phytomedicine for Pharmacists Course was designed specifically for pharmacists and covers the phytochemistry and phytodynamics of today's most commonly used botanicals, herbal therapeutics, nutritional herbs, and how to counsel patients with herbs that can be used safely over-the-counter. There is a required practicum. Tuition is $2,000 plus GST and a $100 registration fee; books and seminar are additional.

A specially structured home study course in clinical phytotherapy is offered to health care professionals at the physician's level who are interested in developing a working knowledge of botanical medicine. Tuition is $400 per quarter for sixteen quarters, plus GST; books, seminars, and clinical training are additional.

Payment plans are available.

East West School of Herbalism

Box 712
Santa Cruz, California 95061
Phone: (800) 717-5010

The East West School of Herbalism was founded by Michael Tierra, C.A., N.D., who maintains an herb and acupuncture clinic in Santa Cruz, has created a line of herbal products, teaches, and writes about the uses of herbs. The school is approved by the California Board of Registered Nursing to offer continuing education credit for 400 contact hours.

Introduction to East West Herbalism is designed for the beginning herbal student; it includes seven lessons in the basic principles of herbal home health care, including remedies for particular conditions, herbal therapeutics, the use of food and herbs in health and healing, and the foundations of planetary herbal theory. The course costs $100. There are no tests in this introductory course.

A home study course in herbal medicine includes twelve lessons presented with Michael Tierra's book *The Way of Herbs*. Topics include the History of Herbology, A Balanced Diet: The Key to Health, Herbs as Special Foods, Ayurveda Tridosha Theory, Chinese Theory: Yin and Yang, the Chinese Theory of Five Elements, Chinese Differential Diagnosis, the Nature of Medicinal Herbs, Herbal Formulary, Herbal Remedies, and Herbal Therapeutics. The course costs $185.

The Professional Herbalist Course includes the twelve lessons covered in the herbal medicine course above, followed by an additional twenty-four courses covering Materia Medica, Advanced Oriental Diagnosis, the Six Stages of Disease, Empty-Full Analysis and Water, Blood and Chi Diseases, the Four Radicals and Symptom-Sign Diagnosis, Specific Diseases and Their Treatments, and the Art of Simpling. The course costs $520, or each of the three 12-lesson sections may be purchased individually for $185.

A week-long seminar is offered each year in the mountains near Santa Cruz (see page 80).

Herbal Healer Academy

HC32, 97-B
Mt. View, Arkansas 72560
Phone: (501) 269-4177
Fax: (501) 269-5424

The Herbal Healer Academy was founded in 1988 by Dr. Marijah McCain, a board certified and licensed naturopathic doctor, master herbalist, and homeopath. The academy sells a wide variety of bulk herbs, herbal formulas, aromatic oils, vitamins, flower remedies, water purifiers, and more, and offers several certificate courses through correspondence.

The 101—Herbology Course includes twenty-two lessons in herbal preparation and usage, natural medicine healing techniques, and herbal projects. Students learn to make salves, tinctures, cough medicines, herbal baths, and more. Each lesson costs $18, plus $3.50 for postage.

The 102—Reflexology Course covers the study and practice of the use of foot reflex points to stimulate natural healing. The cost is $75, plus $6 for shipping.

Course 103—Acupressure is an introductory course teaching the basic principles of acupressure. Texts and exams are included in the course fee of $100, plus $6 for shipping.

Course 104—Flower Remedy Practitioner's Course is designed to provide an expanded approach to flower remedies, and includes the complete forty-bottle flower essence practitioner's kit. Previous healer experience is helpful. The cost is $375, plus $6 for postage.

Course 105—Hypnotherapy Practitioner's Course offers home study in hypnotherapy by Master Hypnotist Peter Draper. The course consists of three modules (four lessons each). The cost is $695 complete or $250 per module; books are additional.

Course 106—Vibrational Medicine Techniques features hands-on healing, polarity, and energy work. Books, case studies, and tests are included in the course fee of $225, plus $7 for shipping.

Course 107—Entities: Healing Work in the Unseen Realms offers an in-depth look at the other realms that influence the human condition. Students learn to recognize negative energies and help clear them to restore client health and well-being. Prerequisite: Course 106. The cost is $150, plus $6 for shipping.

Institute of Chinese Herbology

c/o Acupressure Institute
1533 Shattuck Avenue
Berkeley, California 94709

Phone: (510) 845-1059 /
(800) 442-2232 (outside California)

The Institute of Chinese Herbology offers herbalist home study courses through the Acupressure Institute (see page 66).

The Comprehensive Herbalist Training Course consists of three sections. Section One includes Introduction to Chinese Medicine (covering such topics as theory of disease, hot and cold, excess and deficiency, chi, yin and yang, introduction to diagnosis, and others) and Introduction to Chinese Herbs (covering categories of herbs, herbs and formulas that regulate chi, legal aspects of practicing herbology, preparation of formulas, and more). Section Two includes the Art of Diagnosis (reading the tongue, pulse, and face), Key Concepts of Chinese Herbology (root and branch, six stages of cold, four phases of heat, and more), and Therapeutic Principles of Chinese Herbology (such as clearing heat and fire, dryness, yin deficiency and deficiency fire, dispersing wind and damp, and others). Section Three covers Herbal Therapies for Organ Dysfunctions (covering the classification of disharmonies of the lungs, spleen, liver, heart, kidney, and gynecological), Clinical Case Studies, and Where Do I Go From Here? (a discussion of career opportunities and requirements). Tuition for Section One is $290; for Section Two, $495; and for Section Three, $395. Prepayment discounts are available.

An Advanced Herbalist Certification Program is open to those who have completed the Comprehensive Herbalist Training Course. Students must submit thirty written case studies and pass a written take-home exam. Tuition is $495.

Jeanne Rose Aromatherapy

219 Carl Street
San Francisco, California 94117-3804
Phone: (415) 564-6785
Fax: (415) 564-6799

Jeanne Rose Aromatherapy offers correspondence courses in both herbal studies and aromatherapy (see page 361 for the Aromatherapy Course description); the courses may be combined for $675.

The three-volume, thirty-six-lesson Herbal Studies Course ($475) includes Seasonal Herbal (twelve lessons covering Folklore and Symbolism, Herbs and Diet, Internal Care, External Care, Gardening, Aromatherapy and Color Therapy, Astrology, and more); Medicinal Herbal/Therapeutics (twelve lessons covering herbal remedies for each of the organ systems); and Herbal Practice (twelve lessons covering Herbs in History, Materia Medica, Ancient Herbalism, Moonlore, Herbal Foods, Ritual, and more).

The New Mexico Herb Center

120 Aliso S.E.
Albuquerque, New Mexico 87108
Phone: (505) 265-0795
Fax: (505) 232-3522

The New Mexico Herb Center offers both classroom and correspondence instruction in herbology.

A six-module correspondence course on video covers portions of the material offered in the Foundations of Herbalism residential program (see page 202). Topics include Anatomy and Physiology of Women's Health; Herbal Protocols for Endometriosis, PMS, Pregnancy, Menopause, and Gynecological Health; Herbal Pediatrics; Anatomy and Physiology of the Immune System; Herbal Protocols for Strengthening the Immune System; and Introduction to Herbal Preparation. Tuition is $500.

After completing the above program, students may register for advanced modules that include taped lectures and corresponding assignments. Modules cover Anatomy and Physiology of the Digestive System; Anatomy and Physiology of the Respiratory System; Anatomy and Physiology of the Nervous System; and Anatomy and Physiology of the Cardiovascular System. Tuition for each module is $125.

Sage Mountain Herbal Retreat Center

P.O. Box 420
East Barre, Vermont 05649

Rosemary Gladstar is the founder of the California School of Herbal Studies and co-founder of Sage Mountain Herbs; she teaches workshops in Vermont and around the world (see page 257), and offers a correspondence course, the Science and Art of Herbology.

The ten-lesson course covers such topics as Wild Plant Identification, Herbal Preparation, Medicinal Terminology, Herbal First Aid, Herbal Therapeutics, Hay Fever and Allergies, Traditions of Herbalism, Herbs for Children, Herbal Stimulants, Kitchen Medicine, Herbs for Women's Health, Herbs for Winter Health, Herbs for Men's Health, Herb Gardening, Treatment of Infections and Infestations, Preventive Health Care, Sources of Nutrition in Herbs, Guide for Skin Care and Hydrotherapy, Legal Herbalism, Understanding Flower Essences, Aromatherapy for the Herbalist, the Immune System, and more.

The entire program costs $350; Lesson One may be purchased for $20 to sample the course, and the payment may be applied to the remainder of the tuition.

School of Herbal Medicine

P.O. Box 168
Suquamish, Washington 98392
Phone: (360) 697-1287

Founded in the United States in 1981, the School of Herbal Medicine's correspondence course is an outgrowth of an accredited program that has been in operation in England for over one hundred years. The course offered here is the "Americanized" version (with changes to some of the British terms and substitution of herbs with those more common in North America) of the curriculum taught in England.

The curriculum includes the Philosophy and Practice of Herbal Medicine; Basic Anatomy and Physiology; a Study of Pathology (based on orthodox medical science); a Basic Understanding of Diagnosis; and a Detailed Study of Native Remedies, including cultivation and preparation. Optional seminars with noted herbal practitioners will be held periodically.

The course is designed to be completed in one

year (four quarters), but students may proceed at their own pace. An optional final exam may be taken. Successful students will receive a Certificate of Proficiency (which does not constitute a license to practice herbal medicine professionally). The cost of the course is $125 per quarter ($500 total); the anatomy and physiology textbook and postage are additional.

The School of Natural Healing

P.O. Box 412
Springville, Utah 84663
Phone: (800) 372-8255
Fax: (801) 489-8341

The School of Natural Healing, founded by John R. Christopher, N.D., in 1953, offers some residence programs (see page 256) as well as three correspondence courses in herbology.

The Vitalist Program enables the student to understand the basic principles of natural healing. Topics covered include Health 100: Be Your Own Doctor; Philosophy 200: Vitalistic Principles of Health; Nutrition 300: Vital Nourishment and Cleansing; and Sciences 400: Studying Nature for Vitality. Tuition is $345.

The ten-course Herbalist Program is designed to train students in the use of herbs growing in their area. The course begins with the Vitalist Program described above and continues with Herbology 500: Featuring the Christopher Method; Identification 600: Recognizing the Herbs Under Your Feet; Stewardship 700: Growing and Harvesting Medicine; Therapeutics 800: Herbal Formulations and Therapy; Pharmacy 900: Advanced Technique for Preparations; and Seminar 1000: Dr. Christopher's Herbalist Seminar (over sixteen hours of lecture on video). Tuition is $845.

The seventeen-course Master Herbalist Program enables students to become effective teachers of the natural healing arts. After completing courses 100 through 1000 described above, students continue with History 1100: The Evolution of Natural Healing; Professorial 1200: Teaching the Art of Natural Healing; Research 1300: Advancing the Art of Natural Healing; Physiology 1400: Dynamics of the Human Body; Botany 1500: Taxonomy and Description of Herbs; Pharmacognosy 1600: Constituents of Materia Medica; and Jurisprudence 1700: Applications for Master Herbalists. Tuition is $1,285. After completing the correspondence study, students must attend a six-day certification seminar at the school's health retreat in the Wasatch Mountains in order to take the examination and receive the degree of Master of Herbology (M.H.). Tuition for the seminar is an additional $395; meals and lodging are available for $375 for the week.

Tuition for correspondence programs includes all required books and materials. Courses may be taken individually for $100 each. Student loan programs are available.

Susun S. Weed

Wise Woman Center
P.O. Box 64
Woodstock, New York 12498
Phone: (914) 246-8081

Susun S. Weed, green witch and author of the *Wise Woman Herbals*, offers three correspondence courses in addition to her resident programs (see page 220).

Green Witch focuses on personal and spiritual development; in this course, students learn to create rituals, prepare an herbal first aid kit, and develop wise woman ways of living and healing.

Spirit and Practice of the Wise Woman Tradition focuses on the Three Traditions of Healing (Wise Woman, Heroic, and Scientific) and the Six Steps of Healing as you learn to help others.

Green Allies explores herbal medicine through direct experiences with plants, plant spirits, and plant medicines.

Each course is $350 and includes a booklet of twenty-six projects and experiments, video- and audiotapes, your choice of six or seven books from the course book list, and special books for each course, such as field guides. Payment may be made in four installments.

Wild Rose College of Natural Healing

#400, 1228 Kensington Road, N.W.
Calgary, Alberta
Canada T2N 4P9
Phone: (403) 270-0936 / (888) WLD-ROSE
Fax: (403) 283-0799

The Wild Rose College of Natural Healing, founded in 1975, offers two correspondence programs: Master Herbalist (for U.S. students) and Wholistic Therapist (for U.S. and Canadian students). Correspondence courses may be taken individually or as part of a program; prices range from $95 to $450. Some evening and weekend classes are offered in Calgary and in the Edmonton area.

The 560-credit Master Herbalist Program may be completed in nine months to two years. Mandatory courses include Human Biology, Physiology, Herbology, Pharmacognosy, Iridology, Counseling Options, and a thesis. Students are also required to complete forty credits in hands-on therapies such as reflexology, acupressure, Touch for Health, or massage. Cost of the mandatory courses is $1,470; a 20 percent discount is given if the full package is purchased at once.

The 925-credit Wholistic Therapist Diploma Program is the minimum training required by the Canadian Association of Herbal Practitioners for alternative practice in Canada. Mandatory courses include Human Biology, Physiology, Herbology, Pharmacognosy, Nutrition, Vitamins and Minerals, Iridology, Counseling Options, and a thesis. Students are also required to complete one hundred general interest credits and 105 credits in hands-on therapies such as reflexology, acupressure, Touch for Health, or massage. Cost of the mandatory courses is $1,860; a 20 percent discount is given if the full package is purchased at once.

Wild Rose offers a Building Health Holistically Correspondence Course that fulfills the requirement for one hundred general interest credits. This eighteen-lesson course teaches the science of building health and stimulating the natural healing process through nutritional and herbal therapies. The cost of this course is $175.

Wilderness Leadership International

24414 University #34
Loma Linda, California 92354
Phone: (909) 796-8501

Wilderness Leadership International offers several correspondence courses of interest to the beginning herbalist. Wild Plants to Eat covers the identification, edible parts, habitat, preparation, and nutritive value of over one hundred edible wild plants found in North America. The cost is $50 plus $16.90 for books.

Natural Remedies covers hydrotherapy, massage, uses of charcoal, diseases and their home remedies, medicinal herbs, and more. The cost is $50 plus $15.45 for books.

In Introduction to Herbal Usage, students learn about the uses of common herbs, herbal formulas, herbs for health problems, herbal aid for emergencies, nutritional value/toxicity, herbal preparations, and cleansing. The cost is $50 plus $6.95 for books.

Herbs For Health covers single herbs and their uses, herbal combinations, herbal remedies for more than one hundred ailments, gathering and preserving of herbs, first aid with herbs, and more. The cost is $65 plus $19.90 for books.

Dining on the Wilds is a six-hour set of videos with two reference manuals covering the identification, habitat, season, edible parts, preparation, herbal usage, and nutritive value of 280 wild edible plants. The cost is $149.95 plus $6 for shipping.

PERIODICALS

The AHA Quarterly

Joining the American Herb Association entitles the member to receive The AHA Quarterly, a twenty-page newsletter that reports on the latest scientific studies, herb books, international herb news, legal and environmental issues, herbs in the movies, and more. See page 349 for membership information.

HerbalGram

Joining the Herb Research Foundation entitles the

member to receive *HerbalGram,* an eighty-page, full-color journal containing feature stories, research summaries, regulatory updates, book reviews, an events calendar, and more. See page 350 for membership information.

The Herbalist

Joining the American Herbalists Guild entitles the member to receive the AHG quarterly newsletter, *The Herbalist.* See page 349 for membership information.

Herbs for Health

Interweave Press, Inc.
201 East Fourth Street
Loveland, Colorado 80537-5655
Phone: (970) 669-7672 /
   (888) 844-3727 (subscriptions)

Herbs for Health, published bimonthly, includes articles, Q&A, book reviews, newsbreaks in herb research, a calendar of events, and more. It is available at newsstands or by subscription for $24 in the U.S. and $31 in Canada per year.

SOFTWARE

GlobalHerb

Dominion Herbal College
7527 Kingsway
Burnaby, British Columbia V3N 3C1
Canada
Phone: (604) 521-5822
Fax: (604) 526-1561

Dominion Herbal College distributes GlobalHerb, natural medicine computer software for Windows or Mac that contains information on over 1,200 supplements, 1,000 supplement actions, 6,000 herb names, 15,000 chemical and organic constituents, 5,700 treatable conditions, and more than 90,000 footnotes from 149 books and journals. The database includes foreign and alternate names, chemical constituents of each supplement, recommended

dosages and warnings, color photos, and regular upgrades. This database is useful to retailers, pharmacists, alternative health practitioners, manufacturers, and herbal consumers. The cost is $699 for Mac, $699 for Win Editor, and $599 for Windows.

VIDEOS

Gifts From the Healing Earth

Ellen Evert Hopman
P.O. Box 219
Amherst, Massachusetts 01004
Phone: (413) 323-4494
E-mail: saille333@aol.com

Ellen Evert Hopman, master herbalist, author, lay homeopath, and psychotherapist, teaches on-site classes in herbal healing (see page 171) and has also produced a video, *Gifts From the Healing Earth.* In it, she demonstrates the preparation of an herbal salve, birch beer, heart wine, lavender wine, dandelion salad, arabic gum powder, vegetable tonic, a comfrey poultice, and a cedar smudgestick. The cost is $29.95 plus $3 for postage.

Goldenseal Media

3014 North 400 West
West Lafayette, Indiana 47906-5231
Phone/Fax: (317) 497-9381

Goldenseal Media offers a carefully selected group of videos about herbs, wild foods, and natural medicines. Videos start at $19.95 plus shipping. Goldenseal Media also offers the *Directory of Herbal Education,* a listing of herb courses around the nation. Owner Laura Clavio also performs storytelling and lectures with herbal themes.

Herbal Preparations and Natural Therapies

Morningstar Publications
44 Rim Road
Boulder, Colorado 80302
Phone: (303) 444-6072 / (800) 435-1670

Debra Nuzzi St. Claire, an herbalist for over twenty-five years, demonstrates how to create and use a home herbal medicine chest in the Morningstar video, *Herbal Preparations and Natural Therapies.* The four-hour video offers instruction in making salves, tinctures, extracts, liniments, lozenges, oxymels, powders, skin care products, and much more; covers wildcrafting, preservation, and storage techniques; and includes a therapy section that teaches how to use herbal poultices, castor oil packs, plasters, steams, and other herbal therapies. Included with the video are a 140-page illustrated laboratory reference/resource manual and a 140-page *Pocket Herbal Reference Guide.* The cost is $149, including shipping.

HOMEOPATHY

CATALOG

Homeopathic Educational Services

2124 Kittredge Street
Berkeley, California 94704
Phone: (510) 649-0294
 (inquires and catalogs) /
 (800) 359-9051 (orders only)
Fax: (510) 649-1955
E-mail: mail@homeopathic.com
Internet: http://www.homeopathic.com

Homeopathic Educational Services (HES) provides health professionals and the general public with homeopathic information, education, and products. Their thirty-two-page catalog contains an exhaustive collection of books, remedies, cassette tapes, external applications, software, videos, veterinary homeopathy products, and introductory-, intermediate-, and advanced-level courses on tape. See page 374 for homeopathic correspondence study courses.

CORRESPONDENCE STUDY

The American Academy of Clinical Homeopathy

612 Upland Trail
Conyers, Georgia 30207
Phone: (770) 922-2644 / (800) 448-7256
Fax: (770) 388-7768

The American Academy of Clinical Homeopathy offers a two-part correspondence course in clinical homeopathy. The course was developed by Luc Chaltin, president of Newton Laboratories (a producer of homeopathic remedies) and a practicing homeopathic physician for over thirty years.

 Part I: Theory covers such topics as the Theory of Homeopathy, the Hahnemanian Concepts, the Origin and Evolution of Diseases, Homeopathic Constitutional Typology, the Miasms and Their Influence on Health, the Typology of Dr. Henri Bernard, and more. The cost is $300 plus $5 for shipping.

 Part II: Practice offers instruction in the Diagnosing and Homeopathic Treatment of Acute and Chronic Diseases, Clinical Materia Medica, Clinical Repertory Listing the Remedies Used with Chronic Diseases, and more. The cost is $300 plus $5 for shipping.

 An introductory section serves as a primer and prerequisite to the correspondence course and explains the principles of homeopathic diagnosing and prescribing; the registration fee and introductory section cost $10 plus $5 for shipping.

Ashwins Publications

P.O. Box 1686
Ojai, California 93024
Phone: (805) 646-6622
E-mail: ashwins@aol.com

Designed for parents, health professionals, and others interested in receiving a practical introduction to homeopathy, the home study course, Homeopathic Medicine in the Home, offers instruction in Women's Health, Homeopathy for Children and

Newborns, Immunizations, Psychological Homeopathy, Homeopathy Principles and Philosophy, Homeopathic Materia Medica—Remedy Pictures, Homeopathy for Accidents and Injuries, Homeopathic Pet Care, and more. The twelve lessons, consisting of reading and written assignments, each require about seven hours' work; the average course completion time is six months. The complete course fee of $355 includes three required texts. This course is commended by the Council on Homeopathic Education.

The British Institute of Homeopathy

520 Washington Boulevard, Suite 423
Marina Del Rey, California 90292
Phone: (310) 335-1205
Fax: (310) 827-5766

The British Institute, founded in London in 1987, offers home study courses in homeopathy, human sciences, nutrition and herbology, and homeopathic pharmacy.

The Diploma Course in Homeopathy consists of twenty-nine lessons, covering History of Homeopathy, Sources of Remedies, Homeopathic Pharmacy, Homeopathic Materia Medica, Constitutional Prescribing, Combination Remedies, Case Histories, Computerized Homeopathy, and more. The cost is $1,500.

A Postgraduate Course is available to graduates of the Diploma Course or those with at least 300 classroom hours and experience in homeopathy; it takes one to two years to complete. Topics include Advanced Homeopathic Pharmacy, Current Research in Homeopathy, New Remedies, Advanced Bach Remedies, Establishment and Management of a Homeopathic Practice, Setting Up a Research Program, and more. The cost is $1,950.

The Human Sciences Program consists of fourteen lessons divided into two modules: Anatomy and Physiology, and Pathology and the Nature of Disease. The cost is $375 per module.

The Nutrition and Herbology Program covers Herbal Medicine, Common Medicinal Herbs, Nutritional Therapy, Vitamins—Sources, Minerals, Trace Elements, Amino Acids, Protein, Phytochemicals, Enzymes, and more. The cost is $400.

Programs may be combined. Books are available at additional cost.

A course in homeopathic pharmacy is designed to meet the needs of registered pharmacists and leads to a Diploma in Homeopathic Pharmacy (D.H.Ph.). Pharmacy assistants nominated by pharmacists may take the course and earn a Diploma of the Institute of Homeopathy (D.I.Hom.). The home study program consists of written lessons supplemented by audio- and videotapes and practical training in the pharmacy. The 300-hour Diploma Course in Homeopathic Pharmacy combines the one-hundred-hour Basic Course with the 200-hour Advanced Course. The curriculum in the Diploma Course includes Sources and Preparation of Homeopathic Medicines, Formulations, Remedies, Tinctures, Homeopathic Prescriptions, Dispensing, Potencies, Biochemic Remedies, Homeopathic First Aid, Computerized Homeopathy in the Pharmacy, and much more. The Basic Homeopathic Pharmacy Course costs $650, the Advanced Homeopathic Pharmacy Course costs $1,110, and the Diploma in Homeopathic Pharmacy Course costs $1,650. Graduates may enter the Postgraduate Diploma Program (above).

Payment plans are available.

Hahnemann Academy of North America (HANA)

P.O. Box 3024
Pagosa Springs, Colorado 81147
Phone: (970) 264-2460 / (970) 264-6413

The Hahnemann Academy of North America offers a Homeopathic Study Course that includes 500 hours of taped seminars and 5,000 pages of written materials. This is a home study program, not a correspondence course. The thirty-two-tape sets and four books cost $2,500.

HANA also offers a seventy-hour Lotus Medicine Program, which includes studies in medical alchemy, spagyrics, Egyptian medicine, and medical astrology. The six-tape sets cost $450.

Portions of either program may be purchased separately.

The School of Homeopathy

Homeopathic Educational Services
Store and Delivery Address:
2036 Blake Street
Berkeley, California 94704

Mailing Address:
2124 Kittredge Street
Berkeley, California 94704
Phone: (510) 649-0294
Fax: (510) 649-1955

The School of Homeopathy, established in the United Kingdom in 1981, has developed an international correspondence study course in two parts: an extensive Foundation Course in homeopathy ($1,495) and an Advanced Course ($1,895 if taken as continuation of Foundation Course, $2,095 for direct enrollment) offering deeper study to those who may wish to become practitioners. Each part is based upon over eighty hours of tapes of "live" lectures given at the school, supported by study notes and cross-references to related chapters from recommended texts (texts are additional). Each course requires over 1,000 hours of study and may be completed in as little as one year. Students may pay in advance and receive both courses for $2,890.

Additional courses are also offered, including Anatomy and Physiology ($350) and Pathology and Disease ($450).

See page 372 for a catalog of homeopathic products.

PERIODICALS

Health and Homeopathy

Joining the Ontario Homeopathic Association entitles the member to receive *Health and Homeopathy,* a publication of the International Academy of Homeopathy that includes articles on homeopathy and holistic medicine, environmental health, and more. See page 351 for membership information. Subscriptions are available without OHA membership for $15 per year; write *Health and Homeopathy,* The

International Academy of Homeopathy, 3255 Yonge St., Toronto, Ontario, Canada M4N 2L5.

Homeopathy Today

Joining the National Center for Homeopathy entitles the member to receive *Homeopathy Today,* a monthly magazine full of practical information on learning about and using homeopathy, plus the latest information on events, news, and seminars nationwide. See page 351 for membership information.

The New England Journal of Homeopathy

The New England School of Homeopathy
115 Elm Street, Suite 210
Enfield, Connecticut 06082
Phone: (800) NESH-440
Fax: (203) 253-5041

The New England School of Homeopathy publishes the *New England Journal of Homeopathy,* a quarterly journal that includes cases, materia medica, book reviews, and more. A one-year subscription costs $40.

Resonance

Joining the International Foundation for Homeopathy entitles the member to receive the bimonthly magazine, *Resonance,* which covers all aspects of homeopathy. See page 350 for membership information.

Simillimum

Joining the Homeopathic Academy of Naturopathic Physicians (general membership is open to everyone with an interest in homeopathy) entitles the member to receive the quarterly professional journal, *Simillimum,* which includes one hundred pages of cases, materia medica, news, philosophy, and discussion of practical applications of homeopathic concepts. See page 350 for membership information.

HYPNOTHERAPY

CATALOG AND PERIODICAL

The Bridge

National Association of Transpersonal
 Hypnotherapists
Eastern Institute of Hypnotherapy
P.O. Box 249
Goshen, Virginia 24439
Phone: (540) 997-0325 / (800) 296-MIND

Joining the National Association of Transpersonal Hypnotherapists entitles the member to receive the triannual newsletter, *The Bridge,* which includes articles on existing and new transpersonal methodology, book reviews, continuing education opportunities, legislative changes, and more. See page 352 for membership information. The Resource Department sells a variety of books appropriate for self-help or continuing education.

INDEPENDENT AND CORRESPONDENCE STUDY

American Institute of Hypnotherapy

16842 Von Karman Avenue, Suite 475
Irvine, California 92714
Phone: (714) 261-6400 /
 (800) 634-9766 (California) /
 (800) 872-9996 (outside California)
E-mail: aih@hypnosis.com

AIH offers bachelor's degrees in clinical hypnotherapy through independent study programs. Credit may be earned in three ways: assigned directed independent study courses; approved seminars and tutorials; and approved special research projects. There is no residency requirement.

Students enrolling with approximately sixty semester units of undergraduate work may complete a Bachelor of Clinical Hypnotherapy degree (120 units of credit). Required directed independent study courses include Personal and Professional Ethics, Self-Hypnosis, Effective Self-Presentation: Communication Skills for the Hypnotherapist, Personality Theories, Super Learning, Family Therapy, Communication: The Essence of Relationships, Basic Principles of Hypnosis and Behavior Modification: Parts I and II, Hypnosis and the Law, and Clinical Hypnotherapy Training. The remainder of the program may be completed through electives.

A hands-on training course in clinical hypnotherapy is offered in Irvine, San Diego, Santa Clara, Culver City, West Covina, and other locations throughout the country.

Bachelor's degree applicants must have completed at least sixty semester units of undergraduate credit.

There is a $25 application fee and a $75 registration fee. Tuition for the bachelor's degree is $1,000 per module (maximum three modules); books and postage are additional. A payment plan is available.

Hypnosis Motivation Institute

18607 Ventura Boulevard, Suite 310
Tarzana, California 91356
Phone: (818) 758-2746 / (800) 600-0464 /
(800) 682-4464 (student information)

The Hypnosis Motivation Institute offers over one hundred hours of hypnotherapy instruction on a nine-volume video series, Foundations In Hypnotherapy. Topics include many of those covered in the resident program (see page 86), such as Hypnotic Modalities, NLP, Ericksonian Hypnosis, Kappasinian Hypnosis, Hypnotic Regression, Dream Therapy, Hypno-Diagnostic Tools, Hypnodrama, Advanced Child Hypnosis, Medical Hypnosis, Fears and Phobias, Defense Mechanisms, Emotional and Physical Sexuality, Systems Theory, Adult Children of Dysfunctional Families, Sexual Dysfunction, Low Blood Sugar, Eating Disorders, Substance Abuse, Crisis Intervention, Counseling and Interviewing, Habit Control, Law and Ethics, Advertising and Promotion, First Consultation, Mental Bank Seminar, and others. In addition, tutors are available for one hour per volume for questions and the sharing of practical experiences. Those who complete the program are eligible for Master Hypnotist Certification with the Hypnotists' Union.

The Foundations in Hypnotherapy Program is open to applicants at least 18 years of age. The cost of the entire program is $4,455; each of the nine volumes may be purchased separately in any order for $495 per volume.

The Institute for Therapeutic Learning

9322 21st Avenue N.W.
Seattle, Washington 98117
Phone: (206) 783-1838

The Institute for Therapeutic Learning offers a 150-hour, classroom-based Transpersonal Clinical Hypnotherapist Certification Program that may also be taken by correspondence, either for certification or for personal growth (see page 270).

Wesland Institute, Inc.

3367 North Country Club Road
Tucson, Arizona 85716
Phone: (602) 881-1530

Wesland Institute, Inc. offers a one-hundred-hour, classroom-based Hypnotherapy Certification Program that is also available as a home study program on videotape for $1,200 (a $100 damage deposit is required). Included with the videotapes are classroom handouts and a blank audiotape for student questions. Topics covered are the same as those in the classroom-based program (see page 63).

IRIDOLOGY

CORRESPONDENCE STUDY

National Iridology Research Association

27676-B Tomball Parkway
Tomball, Texas 77375
Phone: (281) 255-4044
E-mail: MDJones@iridology.com

NIRA offers certification seminars throughout the country (see page 311), membership in its association (see page 352), home study programs, and a variety of videos, charts, and other products.

PERIODICALS

Iridology Review

Joining the National Iridology Research Association entitles the member to receive *Iridology Review,* a quarterly publication covering research, news, events, and more. See page 352 for membership information.

MASSAGE AND BODYWORK

CATALOGS

The Feldenkrais Guild

P.O. Box 489
Albany, Oregon 97321
Phone: (800) 775-2118 / (541) 926-0981
Fax: (541) 926-0572
E-mail: feldngld@peak.org

The Feldenkrais Guild, the professional organization of Guild Certified Feldenkrais Practitioners and Teachers, has a catalog of materials that includes books, articles, a directory of practitioners and teachers, merchandise, and audio- and videotapes. Of particular interest is *The Feldenkrais Method: Awareness Through Movement,* in which Stephen Rosenholtz, Ph.D., discusses posture, breathing, and using the imagination to increase smooth functioning and effective movement in two series of eight lessons ($39.95 for each of four videotapes or $125 for the complete set); *Workstation Workout,* a set of two videos demonstrating various movement methods (including Feldenkrais) designed for use in the workspace ($49 per set); and *Excerpts from Workstation Workout,* which features two 15-minute sections from the original *Workstation Workout* ($19.95). A twelve-minute video that gives an overview of the Feldenkrais method and its founder, Moshe Feldenkrais, is available for $20. Shipping and handling are additional.

Feldenkrais Resources

830 Bancroft Way, Suite 112
Berkeley, California 94710
Phone: (800) 765-1907 / (510) 540-7600
Fax: (510) 540-7683

The Feldenkrais Resources catalog offers a broad selection of audio- and videotapes, books, and more. Instructional tapes include the *San Francisco Evening Class, Awareness Through Movement Basic Series, Relaxercise,* and *The Work of Dr. Moshe Feldenkrais.* Audiotapes cost $30 to $70 and videotapes cost $25 to $90. For information on their professional training programs, see page 302.

International Alliance
of Health Care Educators

11211 Prosperity Farms Road, Suite D325
Palm Beach Gardens, Florida 33410-3487
Phone: (800) 311-9204, ext. 9288

In addition to their classes and workshops (see page 305), the International Alliance of Health Care Educators offers a line of instructional videos, charts, audiotapes, posters, and slides dealing with Upledger Craniosacral Therapy, zero balancing, Aston Therapeutics, process acupressure, spinal release, the St. John method of neuromuscular therapy, and lymph drainage therapy, among other modalities. Individual videos cost $60 to $75; packaged series of four, six, and ten videos are available for $200 to $450. Send for a catalog.

Jin Shin Jyutsu, Inc.

8719 East San Alberto
Scottsdale, Arizona 85258
Phone: (602) 998-9331
Fax: (602) 998-9335

In addition to seminars offered throughout the world (see page 307), Jin Shin Jyutsu, Inc., sells a number of self-help books, charts, and more.

CORRESPONDENCE STUDY

Bev Johnson

12239 East Prince of Peace Drive
Eagle River, Arkansas 99577

Bev Johnson has been a massage practitioner since 1979 and is approved by the National Certification Board for Therapeutic Massage and Bodywork (NCBTMB) as a continuing education provider (Category A). Home study courses currently offered that meet recertification requirements include Professional Ethics and Alternative Healing Techniques (a video course); tuition for these three-credit courses is $30 per course. Courses likely to become available in 1997 include Intuitive Massage and Bodywork, Chinese Medicine and Acupressure (video course), and Holistic Therapy.

PERIODICALS

Feldenkrais Journal

Joining the Feldenkrais Guild entitles the member to receive the annual *Feldenkrais Journal* and the quarterly newsletter. See page 353 for membership information.

Massage and Bodywork Magazine

Joining the Associated Bodywork and Massage Professionals entitles the member to receive *Massage and Bodywork Magazine,* a quarterly publication covering techniques, business practices, upcoming events, and industry news. See page 353 for membership information.

Massage Magazine

1315 West Mallon
Spokane, Washington 99201-2038
Phone: (800) 533-4263

Massage is one of the leading publications in the field and can often be found in bookstores. The magazine features articles on technique, business and related modalities, profiles of therapists, book and video reviews, a directory of resources, and more. The cost is $22 for one year (six issues).

Massage Therapy Journal

Joining the American Massage Therapy Association entitles the member to receive *Massage Therapy Journal,* a quarterly magazine that features articles on such subjects as technique, massage for special populations, research, and more, along with book reviews, events, and more. See page 352 for membership information.

VIDEOS

The Dr. Vodder Method of Manual Lymph Drainage and the Treatment of Lymphedema

Dr. Vodder School—North America
P.O. Box 5701
Victoria, British Columbia V8R 6S8
Canada
Phone/Fax: (250) 598-9862
E-mail: drvodderna@tnet.net

In addition to classroom instruction (see page 323), Dr. Vodder School—North America offers an instructional videotape, *The Dr. Vodder Method of Manual Lymph Drainage and the Treatment of Lymphedema.* The nineteen-minute video reviews the basic course material covering effects and indications of MLD and the anatomy of the lymph system; lymphedema is discussed, and a synopsis of the treatment and bandaging of an edema patient is shown. The cost is $25 U.S., $30 Canadian (includes GST, postage, and handling).

Massage and Meditation

Phillips School of Massage
101 Broad Street
P.O. Box 1999
Nevada City, California 95959
Phone/Fax: (916) 265-4645

Judy Phillips, founder of the Phillips School of Massage, has produced a video, *Massage and Meditation,* that offers instruction in massage techniques; the body-mind connection and how massage influences the body, emotions, memories, and thoughts; and relaxation through a guided visualization. The cost is $29.95 plus $3 for postage and handling.

Meridian Shiatsu!

Shiatsu School of Canada
547 College Street
Toronto, Ontario
Canada M6G 1A9
Phone: (416) 323-1818 / (800) 263-1703
Fax: (416) 323-1681

The Shiatsu School of Canada offers a seventy-five-minute video, *Meridian Shiatsu!,* by director and founder Kaz Kamiya. In it, Kamiya-sensei demonstrates a full-body, free-form meridian shiatsu treatment, with each position explained and supported with detailed charts. A study guide is included. The cost is $40 plus GST (Goods and Services Tax) and $4 for shipping.

Reflexes 101/Spine and Joints 102

BioSomatics
P.O. Box 206
Grand Junction, Colorado 81502
Phone: (800) 321-6032
Fax: (970) 241-5653

In addition to the seminars offered throughout the United States and Canada (see page 298), BioSomatics offers two instructional videos. *Reflexes 101* (seventy-six minutes) covers an overview of sensory motor amnesia, how it can be overcome by movement reeducation, and the three pathological processes by which it occurs. *Spine and Joints 102* (forty minutes) is based on movement patterns for the well-being of the spine, the long muscles of the back, and the small muscles joining the vertebrae. Each video is $39.95 plus $4 shipping.

RxUB CORPS

P.O. Box 14198
Columbus, Ohio 43214
Phone: (614) 329-1245

RxUB CORPS offers a limited number of continuing education seminars as well as a series of instructional video correspondence courses. Courses currently available include *Hot Herbal Body-wraps/Lipolysis Massage* ($75 plus $9.97 shipping, includes wrap oil, wrap tea, thermometer, shower caps, and wrap sheets); *Mud Bath/Thalassotherapy* ($55 plus $8.32 shipping, includes natural mud, thalassotherapy gel, and wrap sheets); *Paraffin Bath* ($50 plus $7.25 shipping, includes paraffin cloths, wrap sheets, and paraffin applicator); and *Pore Manipulation and Exfoliation* ($80 plus $9.47 shipping). Ohio sales tax is additional. Equipment and materials are also available. Other courses currently being developed include Stretching, Post (Cesarean) Partum Low Back Pain, Posture Analysis, Manual Muscle Testing, Soft Tissue Injuries, and others; call or write for details.

Shiatsu Massage School of California

2309 Main Street
Santa Monica, California 90405
Phone: (310) 396-4877 / (310) 396-2130
Fax: (310) 396-4502

In addition to classroom instruction (see page 109), the Shiatsu Massage School of California (SMSC) offers shiatsu/amma therapy instruction on video. *Level I: Long Form* shows amma meridian massage (one hour; $35); *Level I (Short Form)* addresses acupressure therapy (thirty minutes; $20); *Level II: Intermediate Level* covers shiatsu/amma massage therapy (one hour; $35). Textbooks are available, including *DoAnn's Long Form and Short Form* ($27.50) and *DoAnn's Do-In* ($25.50). A discount is given on multiple titles; postage is $1.50 per video.

NUTRITION

CATALOG

Kushi Institute

P.O. Box 7
Becket, Massachusetts 01223-0007
Phone: (413) 623-5741
Fax: (413) 623-8827
E-mail: kushi@macrobiotics.org

In addition to their programs and seminars in macrobiotics and natural health (see page 172), the Kushi Institute has a catalog of books, videotapes, audiotapes, kitchenware, cookware, and hard-to-find macrobiotic staples such as sea vegetables, dried foods, beverages, and more. A Macrobiotic Starter Kit features two books (*The Macrobiotic Way* and *The Macrobiotic Cancer Prevention Cookbook*), a macrobiotic cooking video, and a selection of macrobiotic staple foods for $99 plus shipping.

CORRESPONDENCE STUDY

American Academy of Nutrition

College of Nutrition
Phone: (800) 637-8325 (toll-free)

In California:
3408 Sausalito
Corona Del Mar, California 92625-1638
Phone: (714) 760-5081
Fax: (714) 640-2390
E-mail: aancal@aol.com

In Tennessee:
1200 Kenesaw
Knoxville, Tennessee 37919-7736
Phone: (423) 637-8329
Fax: (423) 524-1692
E-mail: aantn@aol.com

The American Academy of Nutrition is accredited by the Accrediting Commission of the Distance Education and Training Council. Courses at the academy have been approved for continuing education credits by organizations such as the American College of Sports Medicine, the American Dietetic Association, and others, and are approved as independent study offerings for registered nurses in all fifty states.

The Comprehensive Nutrition Program is a non-degree program designed for health and nutrition professionals or those who wish to help family and friends on an informal basis. The program includes six courses: Understanding Nutrition I and II, Environmental Challenges and Solutions, Vegetarian Nutrition, Anatomy and Physiology, and Nutritional Counseling Skills. Tuition is $1,485, including all books, materials, and shipping charges. Students are allowed fifteen months to complete the program.

To earn an Associate of Science degree in applied nutrition, students must complete sixty credit hours of study. Courses include Understanding Nutrition I and II, Vegetarian Nutrition, English: Reading Enhancement, Anatomy and Physiology, Environmental Challenges and Solutions, Human Biology, General Chemistry, Eating Disorders and Weight Management, Organic Chemistry and Biochemistry, Nutrition Counseling Skills, Business Mathematics, Clinical Nutrition, and both general and nutrition electives chosen from Direct Marketing, Psychology, Managing a Small Business, Public Speaking, Child Development, Sports Nutrition, Community Nutrition, Healthy Aging, Women's Special Health Concerns, Medicinal Herbs and Other Alternative Therapies, and Pregnancy, Pediatric, and Adolescent Nutrition. Tuition is $1,285 per segment; each segment consists of five courses. Total tuition for four segments is $5,140, including all books, materials, and shipping charges. Students are allowed fifteen months to complete each of the four segments.

Any course may also be taken individually for $290 per course, including study guide; books and videos are purchased separately. Students are allowed four months to complete each course.

The academy participates in the American

Council on Education program for the transfer of college credits. Students wishing to transfer credits to another college or university must take a proctored exam upon completion of each course. There is a $20 fee for each exam.

Applicants must have a high school diploma or equivalent.

Bastyr University

14500 Juanita Drive Northeast
Bothell, Washington 98011
Phone: (425) 823-1300
Fax: (425) 823-6222
Internet: www.bastyr.edu
E-mail: admiss@bastyr.edu

Bastyr University offers a Distance Learning Program for those who are unable to attend as full-time students, but who are interested in learning more about natural health and nutrition. Written assignments, a toll-free telephone number, and voice-mail boxes for each instructor foster greater understanding of course material. Courses take ten to sixteen weeks to complete, and include a term project and proctored final exam. No degrees are available through this program, but students may receive a Certificate of Completion, and some courses may be applied toward degree programs. Courses include Nutrition I and II, Nutrition and Herbs, Nutrition in the Natural Products Industry, Introduction to Nutrition in Natural Medicine, Diet and Behavior, and Fundamental Principles of Traditional Chinese Medicine. Additional courses are under development.

Tuition is $162 per credit. There is a $25 registration fee, and materials are approximately $50 per course. Shipping is $15 U.S., $60 international.

Canadian School of Natural Nutrition

10720 Yonge Street, Suite 220
Richmond Hill, Ontario L4C 3C9
Canada

Phone: (905) 737-0284
Fax: (905) 737-7830
Correspondence Course Division
(905) 852-9660 / (800) 328-0743

The four-module correspondence course in natural nutrition qualifies graduates for the same R.N.C. designation as the classroom program and consists of the same curriculum (see page 287 for course description). The correspondence program takes approximately 500 study hours to complete; a final exam is required. Tuition is $1,700 (plus GST), including books; there is an extra charge for foreign students. Tuition may be paid in four installments of $435 (plus GST), due prior to receipt of each of the four modules.

The National Institute of Nutritional Education, Inc.

1010 South Joliet
Suite 107
Aurora, Colorado 80012
Phone: (303) 340-2054 / (800) 530-8079
Fax: (303) 367-2577
E-mail: nited@aol.com
Internet: http://www.nines.com

The National Institute of Nutrition Education (NINE), Inc., is a student-driven distance education institution that offers courses and a certificate in the nutrition sciences. Graduates receive the designation C.N. (Certified Nutritionist).

NINE is an accredited member of the Distance Education and Training Council (DETC). The accrediting commission of DETC is a recognized member of the Commission on Recognition of Postsecondary Accreditation and is listed by the U.S. Department of Education as a nationally recognized accrediting agency. The institute is approved and regulated by the Colorado Department of Higher Education, Division of Private Occupational Schools.

Each course in the six-course Certified Nutritionist Program consists of twelve to eighteen modules. Students take quizzes at the end of every module, and a proctored exam (to be arranged by the student) at the end of every class. The classes are Health and Wellness Survey; Anatomy and Physiology; Normal Nutrition; Contemporary Clinical Nutrition; Professional Aspects of Counseling; and Practice Management, Ethics, Legal Aspects, and Case Studies.

In order to graduate, the student must have completed the six required courses (or received waiver or transfer credit for courses not completed), maintained a cumulative G.P.A. of 2.0 or higher on course examinations, and satisfied all financial obligations to the institute. In addition, to receive the C.N. designation, the student must commit to the Certified Nutritionists' Professional Code of Ethics. The program takes about twenty-four to thirty months to complete.

The institute promotes professional continuing education programs for C.N.s who wish to keep their certification current. For more information on this program, contact the Continuing Education Department at the institute.

Applicants must have at least one of the following: a four-year college degree in a field other than health care sciences; two or more years of college in the field of health care sciences and two or more years of work experience in a related field; or documented seminars, workshops, and certification programs equivalent to 120 hours in a science-related industry or professional education/training program and three or more years of work experience in a related field. Applicants must submit an enrollment agreement, a résumé, a goals statement, two letters of recommendation, and official transcripts of previous college study.

Fees are $466.50 per course; this covers tuition, textbooks, study guides, examinations, and certification. There is a one-time registration fee of $150.

Payment plans are available, as well as group rates for organizations wishing to train several employees.

Vegedine

3835 Route 414
Burdett, New York 14818
Phone: (607) 546-7171
Fax: (607) 546-4091

The Association of Vegetarian Dietitians and Nutrition Educators (VEGEDINE) offers a correspondence course in basic nutrition for vegetarians/vegans under the instruction of George Eisman, R.D. Mr. Eisman has been a Registered Dietitian since 1978, has taught nutrition at the college level since 1980, and is the author of *The Most Noble Diet.*

The correspondence course covers the basic elements of human nutrition, vegetarian (vegan) sources of nutrients, vegetarian food analysis, and the chronic disease risk implication of dietary change toward vegetarianism. The eighteen study units cover Carbohydrates, Fiber, Fats, Protein Quality and Quantity, Digestion and Absorption, Weight Control, Fat-Soluble Vitamins, Major Minerals, Trace Minerals, Vegetarian Foods, Diet-Related Chronic Disease, Life Cycle and Vegetarianism, and Risks and Benefits of Vegetarian Diets. The course fee is $118, payable as a $10 application/processing fee and three installments of $36 each.

This course is also available in book form for those who prefer to teach themselves; the cost is $18.95 plus $2 for shipping.

PERIODICALS

Ahimsa

Joining The American Vegan Society entitles the member to receive the quarterly publication *Ahimsa,* which features articles, recipes, and a listing of available books, videos, charts, audiocassettes, and other items relating to veganism. See page 355 for membership information.

Balance Macrobiotic Magazine

60 Martin Street
King City, Ontario L7B 1J3
Canada
Phone: (905) 833-7425
Fax: (905) 833-7426
E-mail: balance@cycor.ca
Internet: http://www.turq.com/balance

Balance Macrobiotic Magazine is produced by One Peaceful World Canada, part of an international organization offering books, macrobiotic cooking classes, and more (see page 355). *Balance* is a quarterly publication that includes articles and recipes and is available by subscription for $10 per year in Canada and the U.S. and $15 per year elsewhere.

Gateways

Los Angeles East West Center
for Macrobiotic Studies
11215 Hannum Avenue
Culver City, California 90230
Phone: (310) 398-2228

In addition to their macrobiotic classes (see page 94), the East West Center plans to publish *Gateways* three times per year. Features will include Kitchen Alchemy: The Art of Healthy Cooking, Question and Answer Forum, Personal Testimonials, Book Reviews and Poetry, Shopping and Restaurant Guide, Healthy Traveling Tips, and more. The cost is $20 for three issues.

Health Science

Joining the American Natural Hygiene Society entitles the member to receive *Health Science,* a bimonthly magazine that features articles, recipes, Q&A, a professional referral list, and more. See page 354 for membership information.

Living Naturally

Joining the Canadian Natural Health Association entitles the member to receive *Living Naturally,* a bimonthly newsletter that features articles, a calendar of events, raw foods recipes, and more. See page 355 for membership information.

Triangle Macrobiotics Association, Inc.

P.O. Box 2755
Durham, North Carolina 27715
Phone: (919) 383-4265 (editor)

Triangle Macrobiotics Association (TMA) distributes a newsletter five times a year that includes a calendar of North Carolina events, recipes, resources, and more. Membership dues are $10 for students, $15 for individuals, and $20 for couples. The *TMA Cookbook* of members' recipes is available for $5 plus $1.25 for postage.

Vegetarian Journal

Joining the Vegetarian Resource Group entitles the member to receive *Vegetarian Journal,* a bimonthly, thirty-six-page magazine that features articles on such subjects as vegetarian meal planning, nutrition, recipes, natural food product reviews, and more. See page 356 for membership information.

Vegetarian Times

4 High Ridge Park
Stamford, Connecticut 06905
Phone: (800) 829-3340 (subscriptions)

Vegetarian Times, published monthly, includes features and departments such as In the Kitchen, Monthly Fare, Close to Home, and Mind/Body. It is widely available at newsstands or by subscription for $19.97 for eight months.

Veggie Life

Box 412
Mt. Morris, Illinois 61054-8163

Published bimonthly by EGW Publishing (Concord, California), *Veggie Life* includes features and departments that cover Cooking, Growing, and Feeling Good. It is widely available at newsstands or by subscription for $21 per year.

QIGONG

PERIODICALS

Qigong Institute Newsletter

Joining the Qigong Institute entitles the member to receive the *Qigong Institute Newsletter,* as well as discounts on a variety of books and reprinted articles, videotapes of meetings, conference proceedings, and other publications. See page 356 for membership information.

VIDEOS

The Qigong and Human Life Research Foundation

Eastern Healing Arts Center,
    Tian Enterprises, Inc.
3601 Ingleside Road
Shaker Heights, Ohio 44122
Phone: (216) 475-4712 /
    (800) 859-4343 (toll-free)
Fax: (216) 752-3348

The Qigong and Human Life Research Foundation offers classroom training (see page 226), workshops, correspondence courses, and courses on video. A series of six videos consists of the basic contents of the elective courses, Qigong I and II, at Case Western Reserve University School of Medicine. They are *Introduction to Qigong*; *The Principles of the Three Basic Techniques: Standing, Breathing, Meditation*; *Three Basic Theories: Qi, Channels, Yin-Yang Balance*; *Self-Healing Technique: Balance Standing and Finished Forms* (includes audiotape); and *Qigong Relaxation: Breathing and Concentration Techniques* (includes audiotape).

Other videos available include *Acupressure Self-Massage: Forty Forms* (includes audiotape);

Special Shao-Lin Sticks (includes one set of sticks); and *Tai-Chi Qigong 17* (includes audiotape). Contact Tian Enterprises, Inc., for a current price list on all videos.

REFLEXOLOGY

PERIODICALS

ICR Newsletter

Joining the International Council of Reflexologists entitles the member to receive the quarterly *ICR Newsletter*. See page 357 for membership information.

REIKI

CATALOG

Vision Publications

The Center for Reiki Training
29209 Northwestern Highway #592
Southfield, Michigan 48034
Phone: (810) 948-8112 / (800) 332-8112
Fax: (810) 948-9534
E-mail: center@reiki.org
Internet: http//www.reiki.org

In addition to their Reiki Teacher Certification Program (see page 178), the Center for Reiki Training offers a variety of reiki-related audiotapes and books, reiki tables, music for relaxation and healing, clothing and jewelry, healing tools, and more. Shipping, handling, and tax are additional.

VETERINARY MASSAGE

VIDEOS

Optissage, Inc.

7041 Zane Trail Road
Circleville, Ohio 43113
Phone: (614) 474-6436 / (800) 251-0007

Optissage, creator of clinics in equine, canine, and feline massage (see page 225), also offers instructional videos in equine and canine massage for $39.95 each plus shipping. Both videos cover theory and massage technique adaptations and show massage demonstrations.

YOGA

CATALOG

The Himalayan Publishers

R.R. 1, Box 405
Honesdale, Pennsylvania 18431
Phone: (800) 822-4547
Fax: (717) 253-9078

The Himalayan Publishers offer a variety of books as well as audio- and videotapes on yoga, meditation, purposeful living, and health and well-being. Shipping is additional.

PERIODICAL

Yoga Journal

P.O. Box 468018
Escondido, California 92046-9018
Phone: (800) 334-8152 (subscriptions)

Yoga Journal is a bimonthly publication of the California Yoga Teachers Association, a nonprofit California educational corporation. Departments include Food, Practice, Well-Being, Asana, World of Yoga, Self-Care for Beginners, Profile, and others. *Yoga Journal* is widely available at newsstands or by subscription for $19.97 in the U.S. and $26.37 in Canada.

VIDEOS

Nada Productions

2216 N.W. 8th Terrace
Ft. Lauderdale, Florida 33311
Phone/Fax: (954) 563-4946

Nada Productions sells a wide variety of books, audiotapes, and videos in basic and advanced yoga. The *Yoga At Home* video series offers beginning and two levels of intermediate instruction in yoga, each with soothing flute and tanpura background music. The *Beginning Class* costs $19.95; the *Intermediate Class I,* $24.95; and the *Intermediate Class II,* $24.95. These classes are also available on audiotape for $9.95. Shipping is $3 for the first item and twenty-five cents for each additional item up to $7.)

Conventional Medical Schools Offering Courses in Alternative Medicine

As alternative (or "complementary") medicine becomes more accepted, some conventional medical schools in the United States are now beginning to include courses in alternative medicine in their programs. Most schools offer only one or two courses, but the University of Arizona's Program in Integrative Medicine is a two-year program for practicing physicians; it is described on page 60. This section lists some of the schools that offer complementary medicine courses. Contact the schools for more information.

Albert Einstein College of Medicine

"Complementary Medicine"
Ellen Tattleman, M.D.
3544 Jerome Avenue, 3rd Floor
Bronx, New York 10467
Phone: (718) 933-2400
Fax: (718) 515-5418

Boston University School of Medicine

"Public Health Perspectives on Alternative
  Health Care"
Allan R. Meyers, Ph.D.
School of Public Health
80 East Concord Street
Room A302
Boston, Massachusetts 02118
Phone: (617) 638-5042
Fax: (617) 638-5374

Case Western Reserve University School of Medicine

"Chinese Qigong I and II"
Tianyou Hao
Electronics Design Center
10900 Euclid Avenue
Cleveland, Ohio 44106-7200
Phone: (216) 368-2955
Fax: (216) 368-8738

Columbia University College of Physicians and Surgeons

"Survey in Alternative/Complementary
  Medicine"
Woodson Merrell, M.D.
44 East 67th Street, Suite 1B
New York, New York 10021
Phone: (212) 535-1012
Fax: (212) 535-1172

"Tai Chi for Patients and Practitioners"

Leila Kozak, M.S.
Rosenthal Center
Columbia University College
   of Physicians and Surgeons
630 West 168th Street
New York, New York 10032
Phone: (212) 305-1468
Fax: (212) 305-1495

Cornell Medical College

"Complementary Medicine"

Raymond Chang, M.D.
Department of Medicine, Box 412
Memorial Sloan-Kettering Cancer Center
1276 York Avenue
New York, New York 10021
Phone: (212) 639-8137

Eastern Virginia Medical School

"Complementary and Alternative Medicine"

Jeff Levin, Ph.D., M.P.H.
Department of Family and Community
   Medicine
721 Fairfax Avenue
Norfolk, Virginia 23507
Phone: (757) 446-7462
Fax: (757) 446-5196

Emory University School of Medicine

"Complementary Medical Practice"

Linda R. Gooding, Ph.D.
Department of Microbiology and Immunology
3107 Rollins Research Center
Atlanta, Georgia 30322
Phone: (404) 727-5948
Fax: (404) 727-0293

Georgetown University School of Medicine

"The Program of Mind-Body Studies"

James S. Gordon, M.D.
Center for Mind-Body Medicine
5225 Connecticut Avenue N.W., Suite 414
Washington, D.C. 20015
Phone: (202) 966-7338
Fax: (202) 966-2589

Harvard Medical School

"Alternative Medicine: Implications for
Clinical Practice and Research"

David M. Eisenberg, M.D./Debi Arcarese
Center for Alternative Medicine Research
Beth Israel Hospital
330 Brookline Avenue
Boston, Massachusetts 02215
Phone: (617) 667-3995
Fax: (617) 677-7070

"Medical Hypnosis and Behavioral Therapy"

Owen Surmen, M.D.
Massachusetts General Hospital
ACC 878
15 Parkman Street
Boston, Massachusetts 02114
Phone: (617) 728-2991
Fax: (617) 728-7641

Howard University College of Medicine

"Alternative Medicine, Preventive Medicine, and
Decision Making"

Adnan H. Eldadah, M.D., Dr.Ph.H.
520 West Street, N.W.
Washington, D.C. 20059
Phone: (202) 337-5855

Indiana School of Medicine

"Complementary Medicine, Developing
New Health Paradigms"
Vimal Petel
635 Barnhill Drive
MS 128
Indianapolis, Indiana 46202
Phone: (317) 274-4662
Fax: (317) 278-2018

Jefferson Medical College
of Thomas Jefferson University

"Seminar in Alternative/Complementary
Medicine;" "Mindfulness Meditation Based
Stress Management;" "Spiritual Seminar"
Steve Rosenzweig, M.D.
Emergency Medicine
1020 Sansom Street
Philadelphia, Pennsylvania 19107
Phone: (215) 955-6844
Fax: (215) 923-6255

Johns Hopkins School of Medicine

"The Philosophy and Practice of Healing"
Gail Geller, Sc.D. and Robert M. Duggan
Department of Pediatrics
Johns Hopkins Medical Institution
550 North Broadway, Suite 511
Baltimore, Maryland 21205-2004
Phone: (410) 955-7894
Fax: (410) 955-0241

Medical College of Pennsylvania

"Folk and Popular Health Care Alternatives I;"
"Folk and Popular Health Care Alternatives II"
Bonnie O'Connor, Ph.D.
Community and Preventive Medicine
3300 Henry Avenue
Philadelphia, Pennsylvania 19129
Phone: (215) 842-8540
Fax: (215) 843-2448

Mount Sinai School of Medicine/
City University of New York
Medical School

"Survey Course in Complementary and
Alternative Medicine"
Patricia A. Muesham, M.D.
Phone: (212) 946-5700
Fax: (212) 861-1165
E-mail: pm2@doc.mssm.edu

"The Power of Subtle Body: Innovative Qigong;"
"Mind-Body Techniques and Healing;"
"Hypnotherapy;" "Introduction to Biofeedback
Techniques and Medical Practice;"
"Preparation for Certification in Biofeedback;"
"Science of Yoga"
Joyce Shriver, Ph.D.
Office of Student Affairs
Mount Sinai School of Medicine
1 Gustave L. Levy Place
New York, New York 10029
Phone: (212) 241-7273
Fax: (212) 369-6013

"Culture, Health, and Illness"
George Brandon, Ph.D.
CUNY Medical School
Sociomedical Sciences
135th Street at Convent Avenue
Room Y206G
New York, New York 10031
Phone: (212) 650-5417
Fax: (212) 650-7387

New York Medical College

"Alternative Therapies with Special Focus on Acupuncture and Homeopathy"
Ravinder Mamtani, M.D.
Department of Community and Preventive Medicine
New York Medical College
Munger Pavilion
Valhalla, New York 10595
Phone: (914) 993-4378
Fax: (914) 993-4576

Ohio State University College of Medicine

"Maharishi Ayur-Veda"
Ohio State University
Department of Pathology
SL Hall, Room M-407
320 West 10th Avenue
Columbus, Ohio 43210
Phone: (614) 293-3976
Fax: (614) 293-5984

Penn State College of Medicine

"Folk and Alternative Health Systems"
David J. Hufford, Ph.D.
Department of Humanities
Penn State College of Medicine
P.O. Box 850
Hershey, Pennsylvania 17033-0850
Phone: (717) 531-8037
Fax: (717) 531-3894

St. Louis University School of Medicine

"Alternative Medicine"
George A. Ulett, M.D., Ph.D.
Department of Family and Community Health
6484 Clayton Avenue
St. Louis, Missouri 63139
Phone: (314) 645-0860
Fax: (314) 645-0973

Southern Illinois University School of Medicine

"Chinese Acupuncture"
Terrill Mast, Ph.D.
801-3 Rutledge
Southern Illinois University
School of Medicine
P.O. Box 19230
Springfield, Illinois 62794-1217
Phone: (217) 782-5770
Fax: (217) 785-2024

Stanford University School of Medicine

"Alternative Medicine: A Scientific View"
Wallace Sampson, M.D.
Division of Medical Oncology
Santa Clara Valley Medical Center
751 South Bescom Avenue
San Jose, California 95126
Phone: (408) 885-4146
Fax: (408) 885-4148

SUNY at Buffalo School of Medicine

"Alternative/Complementary Healing Modalities"
Sharon Ziegler, M.D.
Deaconess Center
Department of Family Medicine
1001 Humboldt Parkway
Buffalo, New York 14208
Phone: (716) 887-8227
Fax: (716) 887-8124

Tufts University School of Medicine

"Survey Course in Alternative Medicine"
Glenn Rothfield, M.D.
Spectrum Medical Arts, Suite 303
Arlington, Massachusetts 02174
Phone: (617) 641-1901
Fax: (617) 641-3963

Uniformed Services University of the Health Sciences

"Complementary and
Alternative Medicine Series"
Eron G. Manusov
Uniformed Services University
  of the Health Sciences
4301 Jones Bridge Road
Bethesda, Maryland 20814-4799
Phone: (301) 295-3632
Fax: (301) 295-3100
E-mail: Manusov@USUHSB.USUHS.MIL

University of California, Los Angeles School of Medicine

"Psychoneuroimmunology"
Fawzy Fawzy, M.D.
Department of Psychiatry and Biobehavioral
  Science
760 Westwood Plaza
C8-861NP1
Los Angeles, California 90024
Phone: (310) 826-0248
Fax: (310) 826-0323

"Medical Acupuncture for Physicians"
Joseph Helms, M.D.
2620 Milvia Street
Berkeley, California 94704
Phone: (510) 841-7800
Fax: (510) 841-3240

"Introduction to Complementary Medicine"
David Diehl, M.D.
Department of Medicine
Olive View Drive, 2B-182
Sylmar, California 91342
Phone: (818) 364-3205
Fax: (818) 364-4573

"Integrative East West Medicine"
Ka Kit Hui, M.D.
200 UCLA Medical Plaza
Suite 420
Los Angeles, California 90095
Phone: (310) 206-1895
Fax: (310) 794-1896

University of California, San Francisco School of Medicine

"The Healer's Art"
Rachel Naomi Remen, M.D.
Commonweal
P.O. Box 316
Bolinas, California 94924
Phone: (415) 868-2642
Fax: (415) 868-2230

"Introduction to Homeopathic Medicine"
Michael Carlston, M.D.
987 Airway Court, Suite 14
Santa Rosa, California 95403
Phone: (707) 545-1554
Fax: (707) 545-1595

"Complementary Medicine Overview"
Delia Pratt, M.D.
Community Hospital at Sonoma County
3124 Chanota Road
Santa Rosa, California 95403
Phone: (707) 545-5228
Fax: (707) 575-1513

"Complementary Ways of Healing"
Ellen Hughes, M.D.
University of California School of Medicine
400 Parnassus Avenue, A-405
San Francisco, California 94143-0320
Phone: (415) 476-3185
Fax: (415) 502-4189

University of Cincinnati School of Medicine

"Alternative Approaches to Medical Treatment"
Lois Grimenstein, L.P.N.
Department of Family Medicine
141 Health Professionals Building
Eden and Bethesda Avenues
Cincinnati, Ohio 45267-0582
Phone: (513) 558-4066
Fax: (513) 558-3440

University of Louisville School of Medicine

"Alternative and Paranormal Health Claims"
Thomas Wheeler, Ph.D.
319 Abraham Flexner Way
Room 515, Building A
Louisville, Kentucky 40292
Phone: (502) 852-6287
Fax: (502) 852-6222

"Behavioral Medicine;" "Alternative Medicine"
Leah Dickstein, M.D.
Department of Psychiatry and
    Behavioral Sciences
Abell Administration Center, Room 202
Louisville, Kentucky 40292
Phone: (502) 852-6185
Fax: (502) 852-8937

University of Maryland School of Medicine

"Introduction to Complementary
(Alternative) Medicine"
Brian Berman, M.D.
Division of Complementary Medicine
Kernan Hospital Mansion
2200 Kernan Drive
Baltimore, Maryland 21207-6697
Phone: (410) 448-6672
Fax: (410) 448-6674

University of Miami School of Medicine

"Art and Science of Acupuncture"
Janet Konefal, Ph.D.
P.O. Box 016960 (D79)
Miami, Florida 33101
Phone: (303) 243-4751
Fax: (303) 243-3646
E-mail: jkonefal@med.miami.edu

University of New Mexico

"Alternative Medicine Course"
Martin Kantrowitz, M.D.
Lee Stephenson
Office of Continuing Medical Education
Box 517
Albuquerque, New Mexico 87131
Phone: (505) 277-6611
Fax: (505) 277-7087
E-mail: lstephen@medusa.unm.edu

University of North Carolina, Chapel Hill School of Medicine

"Principles and Practices of Alternative Complementary Medicine"
Susan Gaylord, Ph.D.
Phone: (919) 966-5945
Fax: (919) 962-0467

University of Virginia School of Medicine

"Healing Options: Complementary Medicine for Physicians of the Future"
Pali Delavitt, M.A.
Phone: (804) 977-6246
Fax: (804) 977-4256

University of Washington School of Medicine

"Alternative Approaches to Healing"
James Whorton, Ph.D.
Department of Medical History and Ethics
Box 357120
Seattle, Washington 98196
Phone: (206) 616-1817
Fax: (206) 616-7515
E-mail: jwhorton@u.washington.edu

Wayne State School of Medicine

"Introduction to Alternative/Complementary Medicine"
Marilyn Laken, Ph.D.
Department of OB/GYN
Hutzell Hospital
4707 St. Antoine
Detroit, Michigan 48201
Phone: (313) 577-1147
Fax: (313) 577-2045

Yale School of Medicine

"Alternative Medicine in Historical Perspectives"
Maria Trumpler, Ph.D.
History of Medicine
P.O. Box 208015
New Haven, Connecticut 06520-8015
Phone: (203) 785-4338
Fax: (203) 737-4130

"The Mind and Medicine"
Howard P. Kahn, Ph.D.
436 Orange Street
New Haven, Connecticut 06511
Phone/Fax: (203) 624-9411
E-mail: hpkahn@aol.com

Bibliography

ALTERNATIVE HEALTH CARE—GENERAL

Aihara, Cornellia and Herman Aihara with Carl Ferré. *Natural Healing from Head to Toe.* Garden City Park, NY: Avery Publishing Group, 1994. ISBN 0-89529-496-6.

This is a self-help guide to over 200 common disorders and a macrobiotic view of their treatment using whole foods and medicinal preparations. The book also contains an explanation of the healing concepts of macrobiotics and over 200 recipes.

The Burton Goldberg Group. *Alternative Medicine: The Definitive Guide.* Fife, WA: Future Medicine Publishing, 1994. ISBN 0-9636334-3-0.

This book explains alternative therapies from acupuncture to yoga, with descriptions of typical treatment sessions, conditions benefitted, and where to find a practitioner, plus alternative treatment options for scores of specific health conditions.

Grossman, Richard. *The Other Medicines.* Garden City, NY: Doubleday, 1985. ISBN 0-385-15835-1.

This book presents the history, philosophy, and first-person experiences of homeopathy, Chinese medicine, and other schools of alternative health care, plus a natural first aid section that explores acupressure, meditation, and everyday plants as remedies.

Kastner, Mark and Hugh Burroughs. *Alternative Healing: A Complete A–Z Guide to Over 160 Different Alternative Therapies.* La Mesa, CA: Halcyon Publishing, 1993. ISBN 0-9635997-1-2.

This is a concise encyclopedia of alternative health care modalities that covers both the common (acupuncture, herbal medicine, and naturopathic medicine) and the not-so-common (Hoffman quadrinity process, radix, and urine therapy).

Murray, Michael and Joseph Pizzorno. *Encyclopedia of Natural Medicine.* Rocklin, CA: Prima Publishing, 1991. ISBN 1-55958-091-7.

This provides an explanation of the basic principles of health and an extensive discussion of nutritional, botanical, lifestyle, and other treatments for over seventy problems, from acne to varicose veins.

Stein, Diane. *The Natural Remedy Book for Women.* Freedom, CA: The Crossing Press, 1992. ISBN 0-89594-525-8.

This is a woman's guide to the use of naturopathy, herbs, homeopathy, amino acids, acupressure, aromatherapy, flower essences, and other natural methods in the treatment of both general ailments and those specific to women.

Tenney, Deanne. *Introduction to Natural Health.* Provo, UT: Woodland Books, 1992. ISBN 0-913923-82-6.

This is a primer in traditional remedies including herbology, aromatherpay, reflexology, chiropractic, and others, along with the basics of nutrition and a table of twenty common herbs, that serves as an introduction to natural health.

Bibliography

Tenney, Louise. *The Encyclopedia of Natural Remedies.* Pleasant Grove, UT: Woodland Publishing, 1995. ISBN 0-913923-98-2.

This is a comprehensive guide that covers prevention, health maintenance, cleansing diets, children and health, nutritional supplements, and more, plus causes, herbal formulas, and nutritional therapy for over one hundred ailments.

Weil, Andrew. *Natural Health, Natural Medicine: A Comprehensive Manual for Wellness and Self-Care.* Boston: Houghton Mifflin, 1995. ISBN 0-395-73099-6.

This is a general guide to preventive health care using basic natural treatments. The book includes home remedies, such as nutritional supplements, herbs, dietary changes, exercise, and stress reduction, for common disorders.

ACUPRESSURE

Bauer, Cathryn. *Acupressure for Women.* Freedom, CA: The Crossing Press, 1987. ISBN 0-89594-232-1.

The homework that the author, an acupressure practitioner, gave to clients became the basis for this book. Bauer simply and clearly explains the Five Elements Theory, and line drawings illustrate the various acupressure points. Nutrition and biological influences are also discussed.

AROMATHERAPY

Keville, Kathi and Mindy Green. *Aromatherapy: A Complete Guide to the Healing Art.* Freedom, CA: The Crossing Press, 1995. ISBN 0-89594-692-0.

This is a thorough guide to aromatherapy from its history and theories to therapeutic uses, instructions for creating skin care products, techniques for home distillation and blending, and a materia medica listing uses of common essential oils.

Wilson, Roberta. *Aromatherapy for Vibrant Health and Beauty.* Garden City Park, NY: Avery Publishing Group, 1995. ISBN 0-89529-627-6.

This book provides an introduction to thirty-six essential oils that includes folklore and herbal heritage, medicinal uses, beauty benefits, emotional effects, primary actions, and cautions where appropriate. The author lists common conditions that can be treated with aromatherapy, plus ways of using aromatherapy, from air fresheners to steam inhalations.

AYURVEDA

Frawley, David and Vasant Lad. *The Yoga of Herbs: An Ayurvedic Guide to Herbal Medicine.* Twin Lakes, WI: Lotus Press, 1986. ISBN 0-941524-24-8.

This book discusses the basics of Ayurvedic medicine and provides an explanation of herbal energetics and management of individual doshas. Detailed explanations of the uses of eighty-eight therapeutic herbs are given, plus how to prepare herbs according to Ayurvedic principles.

Lad, Vasant. *Ayurveda: The Science of Self-Healing.* Wilmot, WI: Lotus Press, 1984. ISBN 0-914955-00-4.

This book provides a simple, practical explanation of the principles and practical applications of Ayurveda. Topics covered include the five elements, the human constitution, disease process, attributes, diagnosis, lifestyle, medicinals, and more.

Miller, Light and Bryan Miller. *Ayurveda and Aromatherapy: The Earth Essential Guide to Ancient Wisdom and Modern Healing.* Twin Lakes, WI: Lotus Books, 1995. ISBN 0-914955-20-9.

This book discusses the basics of Ayurveda and the use of aromatherapy for the correction of dosha imbalance. Applications of essential oils include Ayurvedic blending, personal care, cooking, health enhancement, Indian massage, and more.

Morningstar, Amadea with Urmila Desai. *The Ayurvedic Cookbook: A Personalized Guide to Good Nutrition and Health.* Wilmot, WI: Lotus Press, 1990. ISBN 0-914955-06-3.

This book provides over 250 recipes specifically designed to balance each Ayurvedic constitution, but created with the Western diner in mind. General background on Ayurveda and the attributes and nutritional needs of each constitution are included.

Svoboda, Robert E. Prakruti. *Your Ayurvedic Constitution.* Twin Lakes, WI: Lotus Press, 1989. ISBN 0-945669-00-3.

This is an in-depth yet very readable look at the characteristics of the three doshas and eight possible constitutional types, with recommendations for each regarding food, nutrition, routine, balance, disease, and rejuvenation.

CHIROPRACTIC

Joseph, Vincent T. and Terry Cox-Joseph. *Adjustments: The Making of a Chiropractor.* Norfolk, VA: Hampton Roads Publishing, 1993. ISBN 1-878901-54-0.

This is a first-person account of the experiences of a chiropractor in training and in practice.

Rondberg, Terry A. *Chiropractic First: The Fastest Growing Healthcare Choices . . . Before Drugs or Surgery.* The Chiropractic Journal, 1996. ISBN 0-9647168-2-8.

This is a very readable, easy-to-understand introduction to the history, philosophy, and practice of chiropractic.

ENVIRONMENTAL ILLNESS

Bower, John. *The Healthy House: How to Buy One, How to Build One, How to Cure a "Sick" One.* New York: Carol Publishing Group, 1993. ISBN 0-8184-0550-3.

This book tells you everything you need to know to create a healthy home: choosing the least toxic location, heating, ventilation, plumbing, flooring, and much more. The health problems associated with various building materials are also discussed.

Lawson, Lynn. *Staying Well in a Toxic World: Understanding Environmental Illness, Multiple Chemical Sensitivities, Chemical Injuries, and Sick Building Syndrome.* Chicago: Noble Press, 1993. ISBN 1-879360-33-0.

This is a must-have book for anyone suspecting chemical sensitivity. It describes problems associated with carpeting, pesticides, food additives, and other common chemicals, and what to do about them. Forward by Theron G. Randolph, M.D.

Rogers, Sherry A. *Tired or Toxic? A Blueprint for Health.* Syracuse, NY: Prestige Publishing, 1990. ISBN 0-9618821-2-3.

This provides a clear yet in-depth explanation of the mechanisms behind the symptoms of environmental illness and mineral deficiencies. Suggestions on detoxifying the home, diet, person, and mind are given.

GUIDED IMAGERY

Naparstek, Belleruth. *Staying Well with Guided Imagery.* New York: Warner Books, 1994. ISBN 0-446-51821-2.

Written by a psychotherapist who also produces an audiotape series, this introduction to guided imagery explains what it is, how it works, and how to use it for personal growth. The book includes twenty scripts to aid the immune response and cardiovascular system and for common complaints such as headaches, allergies, and more.

HERBOLOGY

Castleman, Michael. *The Healing Herbs: The Ultimate Guide to the Curative Power of Nature's Medicines.* Emmaus, PA: Rodale Press, 1991. ISBN 0-87857-934-6.

This book delineates the history, healing powers, dosages, and contraindications for one hundred healing herbs. It also includes a history of herbal healing and tips on storing, preparing, and obtaining herbs.

Green, James. *The Male Herbal: Health Care for Men and Boys.* Freedom, CA: The Crossing Press, 1991. ISBN 0-89594-458-8.

This is a guide to the use of herbs for men's general health care as well as for specific male problems.

Hoffman, David. *The Information Sourcebook of Herbal Medicine.* Freedom, CA: The Crossing Press, 1994. ISBN 0-89594-671-8.

This book lists thousands of information sources for the serious herbalist or researcher. It includes the reproduction of dozens of MEDLINE abstracts and instruction on subscribing to and accessing various online databases.

Murray, Michael T. *The Healing Power of Herbs / 2nd edition.* Rocklin, CA: Prima Publishing, 1995. ISBN 1-5595-8700-8.

This is an intelligent reader's guide to thirty-seven herbs that includes a general description, terminology, chemical composition, history and folk use, pharmacology, clinical applications, dosage, and toxicity for each, followed by recommended herbs for specific health conditions.

Nuzzi, Debra. *Pocket Herbal Reference Guide.* Freedom, CA: The Crossing Press, 1992. ISBN 0-89594-568-1.

This is a pocket-sized, quick reference guide covering therapeutic uses of over 140 medicinal plants and natural formulas for over one hundred common health problems, plus a how-to section on poultices, packs, steams, and more.

Tenney, Louise. *Today's Herbal Health / 3rd edition.* Pleasant Grove, UT: Woodland Books, 1992. ISBN 091392383-4.

This is a comprehensive guide to both single herbs and their combinations. For each herb, a description is given of the parts used, how it acts in the body, the vitamins and minerals it contains, and ailments for which it is commonly used.

Tierra, Lesley. *The Herbs of Life: Health and Healing Using Western and Chinese Techniques.* Freedom, CA: The Crossing Press, 1992. ISBN 0-89594-498-7.

This is a comprehensive book for the beginning or intermediate student of herbology. The author clearly explains the concepts of heating and cooling energies of both herbs and illnesses, discusses the properties and indications of Western and Chinese herbs in turn, and provides step-by-step instructions in making poultices, plasters, tinctures, and more.

Tyler, Varro E. *The Honest Herbal: A Sensible Guide to the Use of Herbs and Related Remedies. Third Edition.* New York: Pharmaceutical Products Press, 1993. ISBN 1-56024-287-6.

A recognized authority on the uses of herbs, Tyler takes an honest look at the efficacy of herbs, with findings and recommendations that may surprise the traditional herbalist. Many references to scientific research studies are given.

HOMEOPATHY

Hammond, Christopher. *The Complete Family Guide to Homeopathy: An Illustrated Encyclopedia of Safe and Effective Remedies.* New York: Penguin Studio, 1995. ISBN 0-670-86157-X.

This book provides an introduction to homeopathy filled with color photos and easy-to-use tables covering common ailments, with profiles of more than eighty homeopathic remedies.

Jonas, Wayne B. and Jennifer Jacobs. *Healing with Homeopathy: The Complete Guide.* New York: Warner Books, 1996. ISBN 0-446-51869-7.

This is a comprehensive yet readable guide to homeopathy that covers its origins, cycles, theory, and research, plus a guide to home treatment with chapters on injuries and first aid, babies, children's illnesses, women's health, and other common problems.

Weiner, Michael and Kathleen Goss. *The Complete Book of Homeopathy.* Garden City Park, NY: Avery Publishing Group, 1989. ISBN 0-89529-412-5.

This is a comprehensive book covering the principles and history of homeopathy, the use of homeopathy in first aid and minor illnesses, homeopathic remedies, case studies, and questions and answers about homeopathic treatment.

HYPNOSIS

Wallace, Benjamin. *Applied Hypnosis: An Overview.* Chicago: Nelson-Hall, 1979. ISBN 0-88229-415-6.

Though this book is somewhat dated, the basics covered here—hypnotizability, hypnotherapy, hypnotic anesthesia and analgesia, habit control, stage hypnosis, and more—are still relevant and offer a useful introduction to the field.

Wolberg, Lewis. *Hypnosis: Is It For You?* New York: Dembner Books, 1982. ISBN 0-934878-15-3.

This book is a good introduction to hypnosis that covers, in a clear, readable manner, the effectiveness of hypnosis, who can be hypnotized and the depth of trances, the induction process, how hypnosis works, pain control, relieving symptoms, answers to common questions, and more.

Yates, John M. and Elizabeth S. Wallace. *The Complete Book of Self-Hypnosis.* Chicago: Nelson-Hall, 1984. ISBN 0-8304-1033-3.

This book is a primer in the use of self-hypnosis for the control of weight, pain, addictions, and more. It includes steps to self-hypnosis and hypnotic techniques.

IRIDOLOGY

Jensen, Bernard and Donald V. Bodeen. *Visions of Health: Understanding Iridology.* Garden City Park, NY: Avery Publishing Group, 1992. ISBN 0-89529-433-8.

This is a detailed look at the art and science of iridology by one of America's pioneering iridologists. It includes dozens of color photos, illustrations, and charts.

MASSAGE AND BODYWORK

Claire, Thomas. *Bodywork: What Type of Massage to Get—and How to Make the Most of It.* New York: William Morrow, 1995. ISBN 0-688-12581-6.

This book explains in detail the practices and philosophies of various styles of massage including Swedish, myofascial release, shiatsu, reflexology, reiki, therapeutic touch, craniosacral therapy, polarity therapy, and more, plus a glossary and resources.

Goodman, Saul. *The Book of Shiatsu.* Garden City Park, NY: Avery Publishing Group, 1990. ISBN 0-89529-454-0.

This book provides an in-depth look at shiatsu, from how shiatsu works to step-by-step instructions for whole-body shiatsu, including acupressure points for specific symptoms and diagnostic techniques.

NUTRITION

Balch, James F. and Phyllis A. Balch. *Prescription for Nutritional Healing, Second Edition.* Garden City Park, NY: Avery Publishing Group, 1997. ISBN 0-89529-727-2.

This is a handy guide that lists important nutrients, including vitamins, minerals, enzymes, herbs, and amino acids, for use in the treatment of ailments from abscesses to yeast infections.

Buist, Robert. *Food Chemical Sensitivity: What It Is and How to Cope with It.* Garden City Park, NY: Avery Publishing Group, 1986. ISBN 0-89529-399-4.

This book discusses how the consumption of food additives can contribute to asthma, hyperactivity, skin disorders, migraines, and other ailments, and explains how to identify and eliminate contaminants in our diet.

Dunne, Lavon J. *Nutrition Almanac: Third Edition.* New York: McGraw-Hill, 1990. ISBN 0-07-034912-6.

This book contains an in-depth look at the absorption and storage, dosages and toxicity, beneficial effects, deficiency effects, and human and animal tests conducted on vitamins, minerals, and other nutrients. Includes beneficial nutrients for dozens of ailments, a table of food composition, and a section on herbs.

Haas, Elson M. *Staying Healthy with Nutrition: The Complete Guide to Diet and Nutritional Medicine.* Berkeley, CA: Celestial Arts, 1992. ISBN 0-89087-481-6.

This is a comprehensive guide to diet and nutrition featuring a detailed analysis of the various types of nutrients, an evaluation of foods and diets (including vegetarianism, macrobiotics, fasting, and more), how to build a healthy diet, and special diets and supplement programs for specific needs.

Heidenry, Carolyn. *An Introduction to Macrobiotics: A Beginner's Guide to the Natural Way of Health.* Garden City Park, NY: Avery Publishing Group, 1992. ISBN 0-89529-464-8.

This book discusses the basic principles and practical application of the macrobiotic diet: disease as imbalance, nature's designs, recommended foods and foods to avoid, yin and yang, and more.

Jensen, Bernard. *Foods That Heal.* Garden City Park, NY: Avery Publishing Group, 1993. ISBN 0-89529-563-6.

This book presents a history of use, therapeutic benefits, and nutrient information for dozens of fruits and vegetables, plus over one hundred natural foods recipes.

Lieberman, Shari and Nancy Bruning. *The Real Vitamin and Mineral Book, Second Edition.* Garden City Park, NY: Avery Publishing Group, 1997. ISBN 0-89529-769-8.

This is a guide to nutritional supplements: the RDAs, ODAs (Optimum Daily Allowance), adverse effects, and how to design your own supplement program. Includes abstracts of scientific studies on vitamins, minerals, and other nutrients.

Null, Gary. *The Complete Guide to Sensible Eating.* New York: Four Walls Eight Windows, 1990. ISBN 0-941423-37-9.

More a complete guide to sensible living, this book offers an introduction to various nutrients, detoxification, food allergies, vegetarianism, weight management, and a rotation diet, plus the basics of herbs, exercise, environmental medicine, candida, selecting a health practitioner, and much more.

Null, Gary. *No More Allergies: Identifying and Eliminating Allergies and Sensitivity Reactions to Everything in Your Environment.* New York: Villard Books, 1992.

This book discusses how environmental toxins and food allergies can affect physical and mental functioning. It covers allergies and the immune system, chemical poisoning, childhood allergies, indoor pollutants, and much more.

Null, Gary. *Nutrition and the Mind.* New York: Four Walls Eight Windows, 1995. ISBN 1-56858-021-5.

This book provides an introduction to orthomolecular psychiatry (vitamin therapy) in the treatment of dozens of disorders, including alcoholism, anxiety, depression, insomnia, obsessive-compulsive behavior, schizophrenia, hypoglycemia, attention deficit disorders, and many others, plus summaries of scientific articles.

Ohsawa, George. *Essential Ohsawa: From Food to Health, Happiness to Freedom*. Garden City Park, NY: Avery Publishing Group, 1994. ISBN 0-89529-616-0.

The father of macrobiotics discusses the principles of macrobiotics and the philosophy that governed his productive life; includes photos and anecdotes from those who knew him best.

Sharon, Michael. *Complete Nutrition: How To Live In Total Health*. Garden City Park, NY: Avery Publishing Group, 1994. ISBN 1-85375-076-X.

This is a comprehensive guide to nutrition covering macronutrients, vitamins and enzymes, minerals and trace elements, special health foods, supplementation, food allergies, herbs, vegetarianism, fasting, exercise, and more.

Sultenfuss, Sherry Wilson and Thomas J. Sultenfuss. *A Woman's Guide to Vitamins and Minerals*. Chicago: Contemporary Books, 1995. ISBN 0-8092-3509-9.

This is a very readable review of the scientific literature on vitamins, minerals, and herbs for the healthy, non-pregnant woman. Each vitamin and mineral is discussed individually, with a synopsis of notable studies, food sources, recommendations, antagonists, toxicity, and a suggested dosage.

Ulene, Art. *The NutriBase Nutrition Facts Desk Reference*. Garden City Park, NY: Avery Publishing Group, 1995. ISBN 0-89529-623-3.

This book provides nutritional information for over 40,000 foods that includes calories, protein, carbohydrates, fat, saturated fat, sodium, cholesterol, fiber, vitamins, and minerals, plus information for fast food items by restaurant.

Werbach, Melvyn. *Healing Through Nutrition: A Natural Approach to Treating 50 Common Illnesses with Diet and Nutrients*. New York: HarperCollins Publishers, 1993. ISBN 0-06-270033-2.

This is a guide to dietary factors, healing diets, and nutritional healing plans using supplementary vitamins, minerals, and other nutrients to treat fifty conditions including heart disease, learning disabilities, ulcers, premenstrual syndrome, infertility, fatigue, and many more.

POLARITY THERAPY

Siegel, Alan. *Polarity Therapy: The Power That Heals*. San Leandro, CA: Prism Press, 1987. ISBN 0-907061-85-0.

This book provides an introduction to basic energy theory and the five elements, with numerous illustrated life-energy balancing techniques.

REFLEXOLOGY

Carter, Mildred and Tammy Weber. *Healing Yourself with Foot Reflexology*. Englewood Cliffs, NJ: Prentice Hall, 1997. ISBN 0-13-244120-9.

This is a step-by-step guide to improving your life and that of others with reflexology. This book explains how reflexology works, complete with benefits, charts, and techniques.

Douglas, Inge. *The Complete Illustrated Guide to Reflexology*. Rockport, MA: Element, 1996. ISBN 1-85230-919-5.

This book clearly explains the basics of reflexology, and is illustrated with numerous color photos. It covers reflexology and relaxation, understanding energy, foot anatomy, mapping of foot reflexes, techniques, case studies, and detailed treatment sequences.

Wills, Pauline. *The Reflexology Manual*. Rochester, VT: Healing Arts Press, 1995. ISBN: 0-89281-547-7.

This book covers the history of reflexology, pressure point and massage techniques, and step-by-step directions on giving treatments. It also contains many clear color photographs, accompanied by arrows showing the direction of massage, making techniques easy to understand and perform.

REIKI

Horan, Paula. *Empowerment Through Reiki: The Path to Personal and Global Transformation*. Wilmot, WI: Lotus Light, 1992. ISBN 0-941524-84-1.

An experienced reiki master describes how reiki energy works, how it can be used, and the effects that may be achieved.

Stein, Diane. *Essential Reiki: A Complete Guide to an Ancient Healing Art*. Freedom, CA: The Crossing Press, 1995. ISBN 0-89594-736-6.

This book provides an explanation of the ancient system of "laying on of hands" that includes the first, second, and third degree. Covers the basic principles of reiki, the reiki symbols, distance healing, opening the Kundalini, passing attunements, teaching reiki, and more.

TRADITIONAL CHINESE MEDICINE

Beinfield, Harriet and Efrem Korngold. *Between Heaven and Earth: A Guide to Chinese Medicine*. New York: Ballantine Books, 1991. ISBN 0-345-35943-7.

Required reading at several schools of TCM, this book is a comprehensive guide for the serious student. Topics include eastern and Western philosophy, yin and yang, diagnosis, the five-phase theory and archetypes, acupuncture, Chinese herbs, and culinary alchemy.

McNamara, Sheila. *Traditional Chinese Medicine*. New York: BasicBooks, 1996. ISBN 0-465-00629-9.

This book provides an introduction to the history, philosophy, and principles of TCM, with an A-to-Z guide to conditions and their remedies. Addresses the use of herbs, acupuncture, qigong, and diet.

Porkert, Manfred and Christian Ullman. *Chinese Medicine*. New York: William Morrow, 1988. ISBN 0-688-02917-5.

This book explains the fundamentals of traditional Chinese medicine in detail, with comparisons to Western medicine. Concepts of diagnosis and therapeutic techniques are covered.

Svoboda, Robert and Arnie Lade. *Tao and Dharma: Chinese Medicine and Ayurveda*. Twin Lakes, WI: Lotus Press, 1995. ISBN 0-914955-21-7.

This book provides an introduction to and comparison of the theories and practices of traditional Chinese medicine and Ayurveda.

VETERINARY CARE

Macleod, George. *Cats: Homeopathic Remedies*. Santa Rosa, CA: Atrium Publishers Group, 1990. ISBN 0-85207-190-6.

Written for cat lovers interested in an alternative approach to the treatment of illnesses, this book uses only the common remedies. For each disorder, the author describes clinical signs and a number of suggested homeopathic treatments.

Macleod, George. *Dogs: Homoeopathic Remedies*. Santa Rosa, CA: Atrium Publishers Group, 1992. ISBN 0-85207-218-X.

This book is written in the same style and format as *Cats,* above. It is useful to any dog owner who wants to try homeopathic remedies for specific disorders.

Stein, Diane. *The Natural Remedy Book for Dogs and Cats.* Freedom, CA: The Crossing Press, 1994. ISBN 0-89594-686-6.

This is a guide to the use of naturopathy, vitamins and minerals, herbs, homeopathy, acupuncture and acupressure, flower essences, and gemstones for the treatment of common disorders in dogs and cats.

YOGA

Christensen, Alice. *The American Yoga Association Wellness Book.* New York: Kensington Books, 1996. ISBN 1-57566-025-3.

This is a step-by-step guide for the beginner or seasoned practitioner. It includes basic daily routines, individualized programs for the treatment of specific disorders, and advanced techniques.

Mishra, Rammurti S. *Fundamentals of Yoga: A Handbook of Theory, Practice, and Application.* New York: Harmony Books, 1987. ISBN 0-517-56422-X.

This book explains the science of yoga for the serious beginner. It includes lessons on using yoga to control mental and physical states, and illustrations of yoga postures.

Notes

INTRODUCTION

1. Deanne Tenney. *Introduction to Natural Health* (Provo, UT: Woodland Books, 1992), 5.

2. Karen Baar. "The Real Options in Healthcare," *Natural Health,* November/December 1994, 95.

3. Dana Ullman. "Renegade Remedies?" *Utne Reader,* November/December 1993, 42.

AROMATHERAPY

1. The Burton Goldberg Group. *Alternative Medicine: The Definitive Guide* (Fife, WA: Future Medicine Publishing, 1994), 55.

2. *Ibid.,* 57.

3. Kathi Kevilee and Mindy Green. *Aromatherapy: A Complete Guide to the Healing Art* (Freedom, CA: The Crossing Press, 1995), 15.

4. Roberta Wilson. *Aromatherapy For Vibrant Health and Beauty* (Garden City Park, NY: Avery Publishing Group, 1995), 3.

5. Robert Tisserand. *Aromatherapy: To Heal and Tend the Body* (Twin Lakes, WI: Lotus Press, 1988), 163.

AYURVEDA

1. Vasant Lad. *Ayurveda: The Science of Self-Healing* (Twin Lakes, WI: Lotus Press, 1984), 18.

2. The Burton Goldberg Group. *Alternative Medicine: The Definitive Guide* (Fife, WA: Future Medicine Publishing, 1994), 68.

3. *Ibid.,* 70.

4. David Frawley and Vasant Lad. *The Yoga of Herbs: An Ayurvedic Guide to Herbal Medicine* (Twin Lakes, WI: Lotus Press, 1986), 15.

BIOFEEDBACK

1. Mark Kastner and Hugh Burroughs. *Alternative Healing: The Complete A–Z Guide to Over 160 Different Alternative Therapies* (La Mesa, CA: Halcyon Publishing, 1993), 37.

2. Rossi, Ernest Lawrence. *The Psychobiology of Mind-Body Healing: New Concepts of Therapeutic Hypnosis* (New York: W.W. Norton, 1986), 109–110.

CHIROPRACTIC

1. Nathaniel Altman. *Everybody's Guide to Chiropractic Health Care* (Los Angeles: Jeremy P. Tarcher, 1990), 10–11.

2. *Ibid.,* 16–19.

3. Council on Chiropractic Education. *Biennial Report: February 1994–January 1996* (Scottsdale, AZ: Council on Chiropractic Education, 1996), 23.

ENVIRONMENTAL MEDICINE

1. The Burton Goldberg Group. *Alternative Medicine: The Definitive Guide* (Fife, WA: Future Medicine Publishing, 1994), 206.

2. *Ibid.,* 206–207.

3. Sherry Rogers. *Tired or Toxic? A Blueprint for Health* (Syracuse, NY: Prestige Publishing, 1990), 21.

4. The Burton Goldberg Group. *Alternative Medicine,* 207–208.

5. John Bower. *The Healthy House: How to Buy One, How to Build One, How to Cure a "Sick" One* (New York: Carol Publishing Group, 1993), 16.

GUIDED IMAGERY

1. Naparstek, Belleruth. *Staying Well with Guided Imagery* (New York: Warner Books, 1994), 18, 22, 26.

2. The Burton Goldberg Group. *Alternative Medicine: The Definitive Guide* (Fife, WA: Future Medicine Publishing, 1994), 248–249.

HERBAL MEDICINE

1. Michael T. Murray. *The Healing Power of Herbs, 2nd edition* (Rocklin, CA: Prima Publishing, 1995), 1.

2. *Ibid.*

3. Jeanne Rattenbury. "The Other Health Care Reform," *Chicago,* January 1995, 62.

4. Murray. *The Healing Power of Herbs,* 97–100.

5. David Hoffman. *The Information Sourcebook of Herbal Medicine* (Freedom, CA: The Crossing Press, 1994), 7.

6. Alan Gathright. "More Patients are Looking Beyond Western Medicine to Herbal Treatments," *Knight-Ridder/Tribune News Service,* September 2, 1994, 0902K6214.

7. Michael Castleman. "Legalize It!" *Mother Jones,* November–December 1994, 43.

8. Caren Goldman and Deborah France. "Days in Lives: Natural Health 1994 Career Guide," *Natural Health,* May–June 1994, 92.

9. Michael Tierra. "East West Master Course in Herbology" (Santa Cruz, CA: East West School of Herbalism), 9.

HOMEOPATHY

1. Christopher Hammond. *The Complete Family Guide to Homeopathy: An Illustrated Encyclopedia*

of Safe and Effective Remedies (New York: Penguin Studio, 1995), 19.

2. The Burton Goldberg Group. Alternative Medicine: The Definitive Guide (Fife, WA: Future Medicine Publishing, 1994), 272.

3. Ibid.

HYPNOTHERAPY

1. The Burton Goldberg Group. Alternative Medicine: The Definitive Guide (Fife, WA: Future Medicine Publishing, 1994), 306.

2. John M. Yates and Elizabeth S. Wallace. The Complete Book of Self-Hypnosis (Chicago: Nelson-Hall, 1984), 1.

3. Lewis R. Wolberg. Hypnosis: Is It For You? (New York: Dembner Books, 1982), 22.

4. Yates and Wallace. The Complete Book of Self-Hynposis, 30.

5. Ibid., 4–6.

IRIDOLOGY

1. Mark Kastner and Hugh Burroughs. Alternative Healing: The Complete A–Z Guide to Over 160 Different Alternative Therapies (La Mesa, CA: Halcyon Publishing, 1993), 130.

2. Dr. Bernard Jensen and Dr. Donald V. Boden. Visions of Health: Understanding Iridology (Garden City Park, NY: Avery Publishing Group, 1992), 74–83.

3. Ibid.

MASSAGE THERAPY AND BODYWORK

1. Mary Crews and Rick Rosen/American Massage Therapy Association. "A Guide to Massage Therapy in America," 1995, 9.

2. Gayle MacDonald. "A Review of Nursing Research: Massage for Cancer Patients," Massage Therapy Journal, Summer 1995, 54, citing Ferrell-Torry A.T. and Glick O.J., "The Use of Therapeutic Massage as a Nursing Intervention to Modify Anxiety and the Perception of Cancer Pain," Cancer Nursing, 1993, 16:93–101.

3. Jessica Cohen. "The Healing Touch," The Natural Way, February–March 1995, 61.

4. "Alternative Medicine: Expanding Medical Horizons: A Report to the National Institutes of Health on Alternative Medical Systems and Practices in the United States," prepared under the auspices of the Workshop on Alternative Medicine, Chantilly, VA, September 14–16, 1992, 14, citing The New England Journal of Medicine, January 28, 1993.

5. Ibid., 125.

6. Ibid., 128.

7. Rosemary Feitis. Ida Rolf Talks About Rolfing and Physical Reality (New York: Harper and Row, 1978), 31.

8. "Alternative Medicine," 132.

9. Ibid., 126.

10. Robert K. King and Gene B. Arbetter. "The Boom in Body Work," Conscious Choice, 1995, 38.

NATUROPATHY

1. *National College of Naturopathic Medicine Catalog 1995–1997* (Portland, OR: National College of Naturopathic Medicine, 1995), 1–2.

NUTRITION

1. Elson M. Haas. *Staying Healthy with Nutrition: The Complete Guide to Diet and Nutritional Medicine* (Berkeley, CA: Celestial Arts, 1992), 775.

2. *Ibid.,* 361.

3. George Ohsawa. *Essential Ohsawa: From Food to Health, Happiness to Freedom* (Garden City Park, NY: Avery Publishing Group, 1994), 18–26.

4. Lavon J. Dunne. *Nutrition Almanac: Third Edition* (New York: McGraw Hill, 1990), 78, 192.

5. *Ibid.,* 117.

6. *Ibid.,* 82, 80.

POLARITY THERAPY

1. Dr. Randolph Stone. *Polarity Therapy Vol II*, 207, quoted in *Polarity Therapy* (brochure), (Boulder, CO: American Polarity Therapy Association).

2. Alan Siegel. *Polarity Therapy: The Power That Heals* (San Leandro, CA: Prism Press, 1987), 5.

3. Thomas Claire. *Bodywork: What Type of Massage to Get—and How to Make the Most of It* (New York: William Morrow, 1995), 329.

REFLEXOLOGY

1. The Burton Goldberg Group. *Alternative Medicine: The Definitive Guide* (Fife, WA: Future Medicine Publishing, 1994), 109.

2. Thomas Claire. *Bodywork: What Type of Massage to Get—and How to Make the Most of It* (New York: William Morrow, 1995), 222.

3. The Burton Goldberg Group. *Alternative Medicine,* 109.

4. *Ibid.*

TRADITIONAL CHINESE MEDICINE

1. The Burton Goldberg Group. *Alternative Medicine: The Definitive Guide* (Fife, WA: Future Medicine Publishing, 1994), 450.

2. Sheila McNamara. *Traditional Chinese Medicine* (New York: BasicBooks, 1996), xiii.

3. *Ibid.,* 28.

4. Manfred Porkett with Christian Ullman. *Chinese Medicine* (New York: William Morrow, 1982), 69.

5. McNamara. *Traditional Chinese Medicine,* 99.

6. Mark Kastner and Hugh Burroughs. *Alternative Healing: The Complete A–Z Guide to Over 160 Different Alternative Therapies* (La Mesa, CA: Halcyon Publishing, 1993), 108.

7. The Burton Goldberg Group. *Alternative Medicine,* 37–38.

8. *Ibid.,* 38.

9. *Ibid.,* 44.

Veterinary Massage

1. Mary Schreiber. "Healing Hands," *Practical Horseman,* July 1993, 55.

2. International Association of Equine Sports Massage Therapists. "Analysis/Tabulation of 1995 National ESMT Survey," *Stable Talk*, Summer 1995.

Yoga

1. Clint Willis. "Fitness," *Lear's,* November 1993, 40.

2. *Ibid.*

3. The Burton Goldberg Group. *Alternative Medicine: The Definitive Guide* (Fife, Washington: Future Medicine Publishing, 1994), 474.

4. *Ibid.,* 471.

The Practitioner Survey

1. *The Alternative Medicine Yellow Pages: A Comprehensive Guide to the New World of Health* (Fife, WA: Future Medicine Publishing, 1994).

Index

Index

Index

Index

Index

Index